# THE
# ENGINEER
# OF
# HUMAN
# SOULS

# THE ENGINEER OF HUMAN SOULS

*Josef Skvorecky*

WASHINGTON SQUARE PRESS
PUBLISHED BY POCKET BOOKS NEW YORK

A Washington Square Press Publication of
POCKET BOOKS, a division of Simon & Schuster, Inc.
1230 Avenue of the Americas, New York, N.Y. 10020

English translation copyright © 1984 by Paul Wilson

This book was originally published in Canada (in Czech) as
*Príběh inženýra lidských duší* (in two volumes) by Sixty-Eight Publishers
Corporation, Toronto, Canada, in 1977.
Copyright © 1977 by Josef Skvorecky

Cover artwork copyright © 1985 by Fred Marcellino

Library of Congress Catalog Card Number: 83-48888

ISBN: 0-671-55682-7

First Washington Square Press printing November, 1985

10 9 8 7 6 5 4 3 2 1

WASHINGTON SQUARE PRESS, WSP and colophon are
registered trademarks of Simon & Schuster, Inc.

Printed in the U.S.A.

ACKNOWLEDGEMENTS

The expression "the engineer of human souls" is held, by many political indoctrinators, to be Stalin's definition of the writer: as an engineer constructs a machine, so must a writer construct the mind of the New Man.

With grateful acknowledgements to the Canada Council for their support during the writing of this novel; and to the Canada Council, the Ministry of Multiculturalism, and the Toronto Arts Council, whose continued support helped to make possible its translation and publication in English.

The author is grateful to the writers whose works are quoted from in this novel, and to the following writers for the use of excerpts from their works:

Albert Camus, *Carnets 1942-1951,* copyright © Albert Camus 1963, translated by Philip Thody. Published by Hamish Hamilton.

Vladimir Holan, *The Collected Works of Vladimir Holan,* volume VII, copyright © Vladimir Holan 1970. Published by Odeon Publishers.

Josef Kainar, Flamengo: *Kure v Lodinkach,* Supraphone Records, Prague 1972, No. 1 13 1287. Translated by Paul Wilson.

H.P. Lovecraft, *At the Mountains of Madness,* copyright © 1939, 1943 by August Derleth and Donald Wandrei, © 1964 by August Derleth. Published by Arkham House. Paperback edition published by Ballantine.

Ezra Pound, *The Cantos,* copyright © 1934, 1937, 1940, 1948 © 1956 by Ezra Pound. Published by New Directions Publishing Corporation (US), and Faber and Faber (UK).

Colin Wilson, *The Outsider,* copyright © Colin Wilson 1956. Published by Victor Gollancz (UK), and Houghton Mifflin (US).

TO SANTNEROVA

Truth lies in the nuances.

ANATOLE FRANCE

What thou Lovest well remains,
                    the rest is dross
What thou lov'st well shall not be reft from thee
What thou lov'st well is thy true heritage .

EZRA POUND

Listen Tor, here's the real problem: whatever happens, I shall always defend you against the guns of the firing squad. You, on the other hand, must consent in my execution.

ALBERT CAMUS

On days when sadness came, I surrendered to laughter;
Having surrendered, I became gloomy.

VIKTOR DYK

To Generalize is to be an Idiot. To Particularize is the Alone Distinction of Merit. General Knowledges are those Knowledges that Idiots possess.

WILLIAM BLAKE

Come now let us consider the generations of Man,
Compound of dust and clay, strengthless,
Tentative, passing away as leaves in autumn
Pass, shadows, wingless, forlorn,
Phantoms deathbound, a dream.

ARISTOPHANES

# Contents

# The
# Engineer
# of
# Human
# Souls

# CHAPTER ONE

The skies they were ashen and sober;
    The leaves they were crispèd and sere –
    The leaves they were withering and sere;
It was night in the lonesome October....
                    EDGAR ALLAN POE, "Ulalume"


The whole range of thought and feeling, yet all in organic
relation to a ridiculous little waltz tune.
                    ALDOUS HUXLEY


# Poe

O utside the window, which is high, narrow and gothic, the cold
    Canadian wind blends two whitenesses: snowflakes sifting down
from lowering clouds and snowdust lifted and whirled by the wind from the
land stretching southwards to Lake Ontario. The snow swirls through a
white wasteland broken only by a few bare, blackened trees.

Edenvale College stands in a wilderness. In a few years the nearby
town of Mississauga is expected to swell and envelop the campus with more
variety and colour, but for the time being the college stands in a wilderness,
two and a half miles from the nearest housing development. The houses
there are no longer all alike: people have learned something since George F.
Babbitt's time. Perhaps it was literature that taught them. Now there are at
least four different kinds of bungalow spaced at irregular intervals so that
the housing development looks like a Swiss village in one of those highly
stylized paintings. It is pretty to look at.

But I see it only in my mind's eye, as I look out on the white, cold,

3

windy Canadian landscape. Often, as my thoughts flow, I conjure up again the many wonderful things I have seen in this country of cities with no past. Like the Toronto skyline with its black and white skyscrapers, some plated with golden mirrors, thrusting their peaks into the haze, glowing like burnished chessboards against the evening twilight above the flat Ontario landscape, and beyond them a sun as large as Jupiter and as red as an aniline ruby sinking into the green dusk. God knows why it's so green, but it is. The Toronto skyline is more beautiful to me than the familiar silhouette of Prague Castle. There is beauty everywhere on earth, but there is greater beauty in those places where one feels that sense of ease which comes from no longer having to put off one's dreams until some improbable future – a future inexorably shrinking away; where the fear which has pervaded one's life suddenly vanishes because there is nothing to be afraid of. Gone are the fears I shared with my fellows, for although the Party exists here, it has no power as yet. And my personal fears are gone too, for no professional literary critics in Canada will confine me in arbitrary scales of greatness. My novels, published here in Czech by Mrs. Santner's shoestring operation, are widely read by my fellow Czechs but hardly ever reviewed, because there is no one to review them. There are those two or three grateful laymen who lavish praises on them in the émigré press, their flatteries sandwiched between harvest home announcements and ads for Bohemian tripe soup; they are literate, but they do not understand literature. Then there is Professor Koupelna in Saskatchewan. Every once in a while Passer's mail-order firm in Chicago sends him one of my books as a free gift along with his order of homemade jelly and Prague ham. The book arouses a savage and instinctive outrage in the good professor which he mistakes for the spirit of criticism and he fires off a broadside to the journal of the Czechoslovak Society for Arts and Sciences in America. Fortunately, his attack is launched from such a pinnacle of erudition that most Society members find it repellent. And his erudition has so many gaps in it that even those who are not repelled remain unconvinced.

I feel wonderful. I feel utterly and dangerously wonderful in this wilderness land.

Dianne O'Donnell, the Irish girl from Burnham Lake Settlement, with the stunning red hair and the sweet, creamy complexion, is rattling off an oral paper behind me on *The Narrative of Arthur Gordon Pym* by Edgar Allan Poe. She is in a hurry to get it over with, while I'm hoping she will spin it out to save me from having to talk too long myself. I know the book she has copied her material from, and at least it's not Coles Notes. As a matter of fact, it's a rather worthy book by Professor Quinn, and she has reproduced his argument faithfully, omitting nothing. Right now, although I didn't ask her to (but it is in Quinn), she is comparing *Pym* to *Moby Dick*.

"The introductory sentences are practically the same: 'My name is Arthur Gordon Pym' and 'Call me Ishmael.' Both talk about the town of Nantucket. Some of the characters in both novels concern themselves with hidden meanings: Pym and Peters try to decipher the hieroglyphics carved into the rocks on the islands of Ts ..." – she stumbles over the word with its Slavonic cluster of consonants – "... Tsalal. The crew of the *Pequod* puzzle over the golden doubloon Ahab has nailed to the mast. Pym and Augustus, at the beginning of the story, almost perish on the sea. Ishmael visits a whalers' chapel and studies the memorial plaque bearing the names of sailors lost at sea...."

I peer into the white vortexes outside the window and, in the warmth of the room, I know how inhumanly icy they are. The howling wind is barely audible inside and I can hear again in my mind the sounds of the Russian poetry I once read to my students. Poe, I'm afraid, bores them. The horror films on television are far more horrifying. So I try to enliven him as best I can, which was one reason I recited the Russian version to them. The other reason was that I had again succumbed to my foolish but probably irrepressible desire to explain the inexplicable. And I had succumbed because Irene Svensson, with her graceful and supercilious face, had stood up to declare "The Raven" a worthless, sentimental piece of tripe. It was an act of revenge, for she had noticed how my voice broke (I can't help it, I'm sentimental) whenever I read the lines:

Tell this his soul with sorrow laden if, within the distant Aidenn,
It shall clasp a sainted maiden whom the angels name Lenore ...

and she thought it would be a clever way to get back at me in front of the others for having tortured her, last term, in the privacy of my office, where I had donned my professorial mask and browbeaten her like a drill sergeant. But I hadn't reported her plagiarism to the Dean. I cannot bring myself to be genuinely nasty to anyone called Irene. It is one of my ancient inhibitions. Irene Svensson therefore produced a new paper and she thought, this time, she had put one over on me. But luck was against her. Having first underestimated my scholarship, she now failed to reckon with Murphy's Law. She bought a ready-written essay from a shady operation calling itself Term Papers Inc. Two years before, they had sold the same paper to a pretty Chinese student from Trinidad by the name of Priscilla Wong Sim, who had turned to Term Papers Inc. at my indirect suggestion – to pass her with a clear conscience I had to have at least one essay from her in which every second word was not misspelled and there were no such oriental mysteries as "This novel is a novel. It is a great work, for it is written in the form of a book."

Irene ended up in my office again. This time she confessed in tears and it was a delight to see that proud, sophisticated face with its smug mouth dissolve gently into the face of an uncertain little girl from Oshawa, Ontario. But where, I wondered, was her feminine instinct? Didn't this Swedish girl smelling of deodorant and lavender realize that I could never ever have brought myself to report her to the Dean?

It was not, of course, her lack of instinct; it was her inability to understand my kind of experience. She had no way of knowing, even if her name had not been Irene, that life had long since immunized me against the temptation to inform on anyone, regardless of what authority demanded it. My reluctance is as impregnable as the Iron Curtain. I lived too long in a country where even the most pristine truth, once reported to the authorities, becomes a lie.

I commanded Irene Svensson to write her essay in my presence. She took her Parker Silver Ballpoint and one of those lined notepads students use and for the next two hours she fabricated a paper on "The Function of Colour in Hawthorne's *The Scarlet Letter*." She was perspiring so heavily I could detect the faint aroma of a girls' gymnasium through the lavender, and as she gnawed on the end of her Parker the indelible ink stained her mouth. For the next two weeks she came to lectures with lips like the dead Ligeia's.

And so, in the face of her revenge, I had succumbed to the preposterous desire to square the circle, to demonstrate that something written well, as Hemingway once said, can have many meanings: I brought Yesenin-Volpin's Russian adaptation of "The Raven" along to one of my lectures on Poe.

The swirling white whirlwind outside the window is now creating a hissing filigree of sound on the glass, and I can hear the sound of Poe in Russian:

> *Kak-to noch'yu v chas terrora,*
> *Ya chital vpervye Mora....*

The hard Russian *r*'s rolled through the drowsy lecture room. It was winter then too, with a gale blowing outside, a week before the Christmas holidays. "Cheap, mechanical inner rhymes," Irene had said, her mouth curling into a shorthand of disdain. "The contemporary critics didn't call him a jingle man for nothing." Clearly she had prepared for her revenge. "In reality his monotonous poetry is only a weak, watered-down version of English romantic poetry and has scarcely anything at all to contribute to modern sen ..." – she hesitated – "... sensibility." She had destroyed the effect. No one in the class appeared to have noticed but she knew I had and she flushed with anger.

> *I v somneni i v pechali*
> *ya sheptal: "To drug edvali,*
> *Vsekh druzey davno uslali....*

Tears rose to my eyes. I wanted to strike back at Irene but I could not. I had to stop reading for a moment until my Pavlovian reaction to poetry, conditioned by my own experiences – national and international, fascist and communist – had subsided. Irene had the advantage because, as far as she was concerned, my hesitation was further evidence of my ridiculous sentimentality. My eyes slipped over the Cyrillic script:

> *O Prorok, ne prosto ptitsa!*
> *Est'li nyne zagranitsa,*
> *Gde svodobny ob iskusstve*
> *ne opasen razgovor?*
> *Esli est', to dobegu li*
> *ya v tot kray, ne vstretiv puli?*
> *V Niderlandakh li, v Peru li*
> *ya reshil by staryy spor –*
> *Romantizma s realizmom*
> *do sikh por ne konchen spor!*
> *Karknul Voron:* Nevermore!

Dianne chirrups on. Soon she'll be over and done with it. "There has never existed a writer who concentrated more on utterly personal experience. He was the first and greatest artist of abnormal psychology. He displayed a tendency to immerse himself in problems, the solution to which assumed an almost brilliant perspicacity without demanding any actual experience of life whatsoever." She has switched her unacknowledged sources and is now parroting Krutch. I look into the flurrying snow and a well-fed raven (or simply a black bird) stalks circumspectly through a corridor of white vortexes, and the phantom ship of Captain Guy looms up out of the white fog.

> *"Nikagda!" – skazala ptitsa....*
> *Za moryami zagranitsa....*
> *Tut vlomilis' dva soldata,*
> *sonnyy dvornik i mayor....*

Irene sat down, pleased with her ambiguous victory – the mechanical internal rhymes of a drunken jingle man – and I angrily fought back the tears. Her revenge for my exposing her twice and humiliating her thrice (her lips were still a shade of aquamarine) was achieved.

> *Pered nimi ya ne sharknul,*
> *odnomu v litso lish' kharknul,*
> *No zato kak prosto garknul*
> *chernyy voron:* Nevermore!
> *I vazhu, vazhu ya tachku,*
> *Povtoryaya:* Nevermore ...
> *Ne podnyat'sya ...* Nevermore!

I had to pretend to blow my nose, long and hard. The disrespectful eyes of the young of this young and innocent country looked at me with curiosity. I read them my own English translation of the Russian.

> Once at night in time of terror
> I first was reading Thomas More....
>
> Racked with doubt and sorrow
> Whispered: "It could hardly be a friend
> All my friends have been imprisoned....
>
> O Prophet, plainly no mere bird
> Is there no foreign country
> Where to argue freely about art
> Portends no peril sore?
> Shall I ever reach that region
> If such be, and not be shot?
> In Peru or Netherlands
> I'd settle that old contentious score
> Of the realist and romantic
> Still disputing as before
> Croaked the raven: "Nevermore!"....
>
> "Never, never!" quoth the bird....
> That foreign land's beyond the sea....
> Whereupon in burst two soldiers
> A drowsy porter and a major....

I did not click my heels before them
merely spat into a face,
But the Raven, sombre Raven
simply croaked out: "Nevermore!"
Now I push a wheelbarrow
keep repeating: "Nevermore ..."
There's no rising.... Nevermore.

The translation murdered everything, the rumbling Russian *r*'s, Poe's "O", the saddest of all vowels, far, far sadder in Russian than in the language of the Stratford genius, that court lickspittle, but I could still hear the Russian verses rumbling in my ears, interpreting E.A.P. with immeasurably greater understanding than the literary critics possess, despite a long century and a great ocean between them, displaying a knowledge of life that Poe, through some secret twist of fate and despite what Krutch said, did have – a knowledge that Joseph Wood Krutch does not possess.

*Ya boyus' drugoy puchiny*
*v tsarstve, gryaznom s davnikh por....*
*Karknul Voron:* Nevermore!

For I have feared since time of yore
Yet another such abyss
in realms corrupted heretofore....
Croaked the Raven: "Nevermore!"

"If Pym's pilgrimage is not interpreted as a voyage of Mind, then it is nothing more than one of the many quite ordinary accounts of sea adventures." And Dianne stops as though someone had cut her off. I turn around. She stares at me with her green Irish eyes, somewhat sheepish, not on my account but because she is ashamed for having put on such a display of intellectuality in front of her classmates. Premature cynicism is not a characteristic of young Canadians. She has finished reciting her plagiarized paper, and there is only one unpleasantness left to endure: my questions – assuming, of course, that I'm curious about anything.

I look around. Ted Higgins, who plays tight end for the Varsity Blues, is crouched down behind Davidson's edition of Poe, eating his lunch. Irene Svensson (and this too is a part of her revenge, this ostentatious lack of interest) is provocatively painting her nails with something that looks like stovepipe silvering. Vicky Heatherington, who plays trombone in the school jazz band, is flirting with a shaggy fellow called William Wilson Bellissimmo, his hair as bristly as his Americanized triple-double-consonanted surname. They are struggling over something in Vicky's right hand and Bellissimmo has his arm round her shoulders. Her trombone-enlarged breasts swell under a T-shirt sporting the garish picture of a man. Once, when I asked her who it was, she told me it was a self-portrait of Van Cock. Behind these dallying lovers the sad eyes of Veronika Prst peer at me and through me. She is a moody girl from the Vinohrady district of Prague. On her way back from a tour of Cuba she defected to Canada, and in her first week in class she fought bitterly with Larry Hakim, who had once gone to Cuba to help with the sugar-cane harvest.

"Do you really believe that?" I ask Dianne. "I mean, that *Pym* is either a pilgrimage of the soul or else just an ordinary thriller?"

Dianne stiffens. She can't admit she has no opinion of her own, so she responds with an obstinate "yes," and my unfettered thoughts carry me back to the wooden cabin on the wooden schooner of Captain Guy, to a distant time of primal terror, a time when each night before falling asleep I sailed with Jules Verne over a blue-black sea, through a cleft in the giant glaciers, the alabaster gateway of the southern passage, towards a lukewarm sun glowing low over the horizon, while before the ship stretched a tranquil, gently rippled sea, and in the distance, land, and immensely far away, wild purple mountains. Why and how they came to be purple I did not yet know. Arctic swallows swooped through the air, I saw Poe in a hovel in Baltimore scratching away with a goose-feather pen in a cold winter room, just like me in that bed, in that wooden cabin, held captive by the impenetrable curtain hung around the protectorate of Böhmen und Mähren, completely cut off from all avenues to the beautiful Antarctic, Poe a captive of poverty, dreaming on paper of the Wilkes expedition that had left Jeremiah Reynolds behind and sighing Reynolds' name on his deathbed – why? Because he might have lived Reynolds' life? In the beautiful and ghastly freedom of the purple mountains of madness? But Reynolds' life was not his: Poe's life ebbed away in a grim prison of poverty, in the airless stench of a New England hovel. A pilgrimage of the soul? A pilgrimage *in* the soul. A magnificent boyhood adventure. Only the rich, the successful, the important, the powerful ever cease to be boys and girls.

Those tears. Perhaps they were a disgrace – Anglo-Saxons are, it is popularly believed, unsentimental. Anglo-Saxons with names like Bellissimmo, Hakim, Svensson. But now Irene is silent. Perhaps she at least had appreciated the exotic, guttural rumbling of *Kak-to noch'yu v chas terrora, ya chital vpervye Mora*. Her grey, northern eyes observed me unprotestingly, thoughtfully. To my surprise, for I had given her a C minus in the freshman course, she enrolled this year in my sophomore course, which was partly intended to reiterate in depth (that, at least, was the theory) the same material covered in the freshman course. Poe, therefore, is on the course again, and this year Irene's papers are excellent. Perhaps she has hired a teaching assistant to help her, or perhaps she has actually begun to study. Generally she keeps silent, observing me.... *Kak-to noch'yu v chas terrora....* Once at night in time of terror.... We have always been surrounded by terror and by the beauty that is an inseparable part of it.

•

*Karlsbad*
*The 7 March 1942*

*Dear Dan,*
*I adres you with these few lines to let you know I am well and hope you are enjoying the same blesing at present. Im here at the Karlsbad spa for a week and doing fine, on a special deal for workers laid on by Rinehard Hydrick. In the old days only the rich came here but now its for workers to. We get 4 meals a day, breakfast is bread with artaficial honey or marmalade and for dinner we get meat 3 x a week and then tea and a roll in the afternoon and a tart on sundays and for supper they give us as much as the noon meal. Its all laid on for workers by the Reich Protecter Rinehard Hydrick. Herr Schilink picked me to go because Dr. Selich told him I got shadows on my lungs so they sent me off on this Rinehard Hydrick thing so I wouldn't come down with TB. I am doing fine. Are you still working on Mesershmits? After this Rinehard Hydrick thing is over I wont be coming back to the plant because I volanteerd to work in the Reich they need skilled bakers and besides the pays better where they work nights. I will write to you, hope things are fine with you too. Pity they cant enclude you on this Rinehard Hydrick thing but its only for workers but maybe now your working in a factory they could let you in on it. Its nice here. To conclude my leter please exsept my warmest wishes and dont bother writing, in 6 days I leave for the Reich and I'll send my adres from there and then you can write me. To conclude my letter please exsept my warmest wishes and fondest memries.*
*Your freind,*
*Lojza*

•

I really should start something up with Irene Svensson. She betrays all the signs of expecting it. True, she's young enough to be my daughter, but then here I am with the aura of a man who has lived in police dictatorships and who was in an anti-Nazi resistance group during the war. When I mention this to girls from Chignecto Bay or Yellowhead Pass, I cleverly refer to it as a "guerrilla group"; they are more familiar with that expression and it has heroic connotations for them. Moreover, this interesting man, myself, was a writer, which everybody knows is a dangerous profession in a police state. His best friend was executed (I have made Comrade Hubert Stein my best friend, although there was never any love lost between us; still, that he was executed is the pure truth, or rather the filthy truth, and a little imaginative embellishment can do no harm). Finally, this man was driven out of his own country by Soviet tanks and now, in his forty-eighth year, is physically well-preserved with naturally wavy hair shot through with strands of silvery grey that sparkle, thanks to modern aerosol cosmetics, with an interesting dull shine.

So I shouldn't hesitate with Irene Svensson. The popular notion is that modern girls are willing, though I cannot say from personal experience, for my needs in that regard are well attended to by Margitka, at least for the time being.

And yet, who can say? I really ought to start something. Those beautiful, faded eyes from Kiruna are constantly watching me. Her grandfather, she said, used to own iron mines in Kiruna, a city of the midnight sun. How beautifully that sun would have reflected in those irises of steel, and in her yellow hair, always so carefully and expensively groomed at Vidal Sassoon's, so distant from the weeping-willow look of the uniform majority. She never raises her head. When I ask her a question, her answer suggests that she has actually read the book I assigned and may even have prepared for the lecture by looking into some secondary sources. Her mouth still curls disdainfully but she no longer makes light of E.A.P. Once, not long ago, she even volunteered the remark that Poe was a magnificent visual artist. "By which I don't mean," she went on, "his romantic insights." To illustrate she cited Poe's description of the explosion of the *Jane Guy* on Tsalal Island. I praised her and began to wonder whether she might not have a literary, almost writerly sensitivity. Perhaps, I thought, she really is doing her own papers this year for I could not recall a single analysis of the scene in any of those secondary sources – though I must admit I'm not particularly well versed in that literature myself. Then, as I was driving home through the grey, black, and white Edenvale wilderness towards the shimmering towers of downtown Toronto, I suddenly remembered having praised that very scene in last year's freshman course. Whatever this denied Irene in the way of original thinking, it certainly made her no less interesting.

Only it's not so simple any more. Once it was easy to set me on fire, and when I burned, I burned with delight. Now it's no longer possible. And Margitka looks after my well-being very nicely.

●

But during the war it was simple. I had been thrown out of the welding section in the Messerschmitt factory for feigning incompetence and transferred to the machining section. There stood two drill-presses and at one of them was a lanky girl in a threadbare sweater and crumpled skirt, a tall, bony girl with a pretty, pale face and a kerchief, the kind that old women wore, tied under the chin. She had cotton stockings on, and a pair of ski socks that had been washed a thousand times rolled down over a pair of men's highland brogues. She looked at me, her black eyes glowed, and I went up in flames on the spot like Jan Hus.

"Your job is to drill the counter-sinks," Vachousek the foreman explained. "See if you can do it without buggering it up. But they got to be done exactly to gauge, to within half a millimetre. The norm is one cross-bracket every ten minutes and then you take it over there to Svestka and Hetflajs for the next stage. Nadia here will show you how."

He nodded at the lanky girl. She grinned a wide toothy grin, like Poe's Berenice. She had beautiful, healthy teeth and a smile from ear to ear. Later, when I learned more about the poverty and misery she endured at home, I couldn't understand how she made it through the war with such healthy teeth. Years later I learned from a brochure in Dr. Zizala's waiting room in Etobicoke that there is less tooth decay among the hungry nations because they can't afford sugar. The Jirouseks couldn't either. They used saccharin.

"Mmmmm!" Nadia would sigh blissfully and swallow the entire jam tart in one bite. Occasionally, despite the war, my mother would bake jam tarts. Her brother was the manager of Count Czernin's estate and he not only saw to it that we didn't starve, he made sure we didn't even go wanting. "Mmmmm! That's delicious!" she said. "Got another one?"

So I gave her all four of my tarts and watched as she downed them like a virtuoso. I felt good because she liked them. When we kissed afterwards, her mouth tasted of jam, not of bread as it usually did. But then she pushed me away and said, "Leave me be!"

"But Nadia!"

"Franta will know what I've been about."

"So what?"

"I love him."

"Don't you love me too?"

"Sure, but you aren't about to marry me."

That silenced me. I had certainly never given a thought to marrying her. I wasn't working-class like Nadia. The idea that a man had to have a career before getting married was still firmly rooted in my mind. That meant university and the Nazis had closed all the universities down. Moreover, Nadia was older than I was, and her Franta was a weaver, who unlike me had been successfully retrained as a welder. She and I would neck in the ferroflux room in a kind of glassed-in cubicle. Vlada Nosek would lock us in there whenever he went to goof off in the can. On his way back he would rattle the key in the lock for an unnaturally long time, we would quickly stop kissing, and Nadia would blush. But she would always go back again with me.

"Now just grab ahold of it like this," she explained that day when I first met her, placing a bony hand with broken fingernails and inflamed scratches on the duralumin cross-bracket. "But whatever you do, don't pull down too hard on the drill. When you reckon it's countersunk enough, you take a measure of the hole with this here." And she demonstrated how to use the gauge, an iron, cone-shaped affair with a handle that slid neatly into the conical counter-sink. "It has to fit perfect, so it's better to drill the holes just a bit too small," she said. "Then you can always just finish it up with a little touch. If you make it too deep, they have to throw it out and we'll catch it from the foreman."

I looked at the duralumin cross-bracket and admired how dextrously she worked on it.

"What's it for, anyway?" I wasn't really interested, but I felt like chatting.

"It goes on the aeroplanes, the Messerschmitts. There's four screws go into them counter-sinks to hold the drum."

"The drum?"

"That holds the bullets," she said. "For the machine-gun."


"The Messerschmitt Bf 109-F," lectured Benda, "couldn't match the fire power of the Spitfires so they had to mount two Mauser MG 151/20 millimetre cannons, one under each wing. They couldn't get them to fit inside the wing, so they designed the Ruestsatz RL underwing cannon gondola inside a metal fairing that looks like an upside-down bathtub."

"I know," I said. "They screw them on in the final stage of assembly."

"Inside the fairing there's a drum mag for the ammo. It's screwed onto that duralumin mounting bracket."

It was obvious even to me, with my complete lack of technical talent, why there was all this fuss over precision. Benda, who knew everything about aircraft by heart, confirmed it. "It's as clear as day. If you countersink the holes too deep, then when they screw on the ammo mag it'll stretch the metal thin and as soon as you start shooting...."

"The mag might fall off," said Prema.

"Right," said Benda. "That's why they use those gauges."

Prema, who was interested in planes only as potential objects of sabotage, closed his eyes and said dreamily, "Can't you just see it, gentlemen? The Hun has a Spitfire in his cross-hairs, he presses the trigger – *ratatatat* – both his ammo drums go ripping off and he's up shit creek."

We were sitting under a dim lightbulb in the tobacco warehouse, dreaming of heroic exploits. And that was when I got my stupid idea.

It was all because Nadia had said to me, her eyes glowing like coals with something other than love, "If I only knew who done that, I'd do anything for him! Anything. I mean it, Danny. He's a real hero."

Nadia and her reverence for heroes robbed me of the last traces of my common sense.

Taking advantage of the fact that Franta was in hospital with appendicitis, I had tempted her out on a date. My parents had gone to Count Czernin's estate on Saturday to replenish their larder and so on Sunday after church I waited until I heard the clumping of Nadia's heavy boots on the staircase. I opened the door. For a young girl – she was just past nineteen – she seemed to find walking up the stairs rather difficult, but I attributed that to her permanent hunger. She wore a Sunday kerchief on her head and her pale cheeks were flushed a vivid red. Perhaps it was the brogues she was wearing as well – she was quite out of breath. I led her into the living room and straightaway offered her one of my mother's tarts.

"What about your parents?" I asked when she told me how she had given her Uncle Venhoda the slip after church; but she had to be back in half an hour at the very outside, she said, otherwise he would get to wondering where she was. She explored our room with hungry eyes – the bronze chandelier with its crystal tear-drops, and other wonders – and her little nostrils quivered beautifully.

"Want some more?" I asked. She nodded. I went to look in the kitchen and Nadia followed me without invitation. Mother had left Sunday dinner for me on the kitchen range – broiled horsemeat sauerbraten. Nadia trembled. I switched on the stove. "It'll be ready in a minute," I said. "Are your parents still alive?"

"My dad is," she said, "but he's in a concentration camp." She looked around, then sat down on the squat, square stool by the stove. Class instinct, I say today when I recall it – that stool was the traditional throne of Czech serving girls – but that didn't occur to me then. Under her black, threadbare Sunday skirt, I caught a glimpse of pale blue bloomers. She didn't appear to be ashamed of them. She took off her kerchief, turned to the mock sauerbraten – at the same time showing me her pretty profile – and her nostrils quivered again.

"What did they take him away for?"

"On account of he was a member of the Sokol gymnastic society. He was leader of the group in my village – Cerna Hora."

"What did" – I quickly corrected the ominous past tense – "what does your dad do?" But Nadia paid no attention to such nuances of grammar. The prospect of the possible – and probable – death of her father did not evoke tears and fear in her but a direct and uncomplicated hatred.

"He was on the throstle at Mautner's," she said. "He taught gymnastics in Cerna Hora and made a speech on President Masaryk's birthday. That was long before they banned the Sokol. It was almost three years ago."

"Have you had any … word from him?"

"Not in ages. Poor old man might even be dead by now, for all I know. Listen, Danny…."

"Yes?"

"It's probably a sin – but, you know, I could kill a German easy. Couldn't you?"

"Well … sure," I said uncertainly, because I had grave doubts about it. Yet in the end I killed my German and Nadia didn't – but who could have known that then? The mock sauerbraten smelled wonderful. It was almost eleven. I dished her out the whole serving – a generous one, since in my mother's opinion I hadn't yet achieved my full growth – and I watched enchanted while the bony girl worried over the stewed horsemeat like a starving cat.

"Mmmmm, that's delicious!" she exclaimed, praising the meal as she had the tarts and as she would, many times in the future, the strudels, poppy-seed muffins, buns and homemade horsemeat loaf I would give her. It crossed my mind that the way to her heart might lead through her stomach. But I didn't really believe that. Nadia wasn't like that. As soon as she had finished eating I took her in my arms and she let me kiss her, returning my kisses with kisses as ravenous as her gargantuan appetite. Her mouth smelled of marinated horsemeat. And it was then that she confessed her boundless admiration for the unknown hero who two months earlier had blown up the gasoline warehouse in Kostelec.

●

*June 10, 1943*
*Prague*

*My dear Dan,*
*Do you recall those wonderful lines: "Then I saw the Congo creeping through the black, Cutting through the jungle with a golden track"? I don't know why those lines keep echoing in my mind, whether I'm trying to sleep or clinging to the fire engine as we rush to put out a fire.*

*Perhaps it's because I must cling to something beautiful as well – in my mind. I've discovered a new poet here; his name is Erich Kästner. Our Einsatzführer, Ernst Hübel, lent me a collection of his poems called* Eine kleine lyrische Hausapotheke. *What magnificence! For example:*

Ein Mathematiker hat behauptet
dass es allmählich an der Zeit sei,
eine stabile Kiste zu bauen,
die tausend Meter lang, hoch und breit sei.

In diesem einen Kubikkilometer
hätten, schrieb er im wichtigsten Satz,
sämtliche heute lebenden Menschen
(das sind zirka zwei Milliarden) Platz!

Man könnte also die ganze Menschheit
in eine Kiste steigen heissen
und diese, vielleicht in den Kordilleren,
in einen der tiefsten Abgründe schmeissen.

Kreischend zögen die Geier Kreise.
Die riesigen Städte stünden leer.
Die Menschheit läg in den Kordilleren.
Das wüsste dann aber keiner mehr.

*What do you think of that?*
*I'm able to write so openly because a friend of mine is going to Hradec on a pass and he'll mail this letter to you. Erich Kästner, you see, lives in Switzerland. He had to leave Germany almost as soon as the Hitlerites took over. Our Einsatzführer, however, isn't one of them. We got to know each other after he came across my copy of Eliot during a barracks inspection. "Because I do not hope to turn again, Because I do not hope, Because I do not hope to turn...." I often repeat those lines to myself. Hübel's father is a grammar-school teacher and does belong to the Hitlerites, but only to avoid trouble because of something he did before the takeover. Isn't it absurd, Danny? When I walk through the streets in the Home Guard uniform I look like an SS man. And Ernst looks even more like one – he's blond with blue eyes, a bit like Heydrich. And as we walk side by side, we whisper Kästner's poetry to each other, taking turns with the lines. Me: "Da*

lägen wir dann, fast unbemerkbar," *and he:* "als würfelformiges Paket." *Then me:* "Und Gras könnte über die Menschheit wachsen." *And our Einsatzführer:* "Und Sand würde daraufgeweht."

*Life is beautiful, Dan, but if it weren't for poetry –* "*In the room the women come and go, talking of Michelangelo.*"

*Look after yourself, dearest Dan! We must survive the war. And then....*

        *Sincerely,*
        *Jan*

●

Next term, our department is moving to a new building. It is already finished. It has windows of copper glass that admit the sun's light but not its heat, and conversely, from the outside it is impossible to see in, so that one might strip naked before a whole meadowful of co-eds eating their noontime french fries with ketchup on the sun-drenched grass, and present a full frontal nude to the light, if not to the warmth, of the sun. The architect also accommodated the wishes of the more radical students: instead of furniture, some of the lecture rooms will have bumps of various shapes on the floor, all covered with wall-to-wall carpeting. I, as professor, will sit on one of these bumps, and on and among the others, like Gulliver among the breasts of the Brobdingnagian women, will sit my students. It is supposed to help them relax, increase their attention span and, in the long run, improve their results. Altogether, a great deal of experimentation goes on in our college. Not long ago Rocky McBeth made a final application to the Dean to purchase some old Royal Canadian Air Force parachutes. He wanted to hang them from the classroom ceilings to cover the windows and create something like a tent, with soft lighting and a feeling of womblike security and intimacy. The aim was to help nervous students let themselves go and concentrate more fully on the arts and sciences we lecture them about.

Moving to a new building has its problems, however. Rocky, who looks like Dürer's self-portrait and therefore like Jesus Christ, is up in arms. He feels exasperated, slighted. Why should he, of all people, have been assigned an office without windows, only air conditioning and fluorescent lighting, when he alone among his colleagues really needs windows? They all know he has a parachute set up experimentally in his office, and that in order to study the psychological effect of the parachute he absolutely must have natural daylight, not fluorescent tubes.

A staff-room dispute begins – quiet at first, but rapidly developing into a wild wrangle. The principal remarks in dry Oxford accents that anyone finding the new college building not to his taste is perfectly free to resign. Freddy Cohen, our chairman, flushes as red as a McIntosh apple and calls it an unfair remark. The atmosphere turns icy and I steal a glance at my watch. I don't care whether I have a window or not. I try to be in my office as little as possible because I have never liked offices.

My colleagues are caught up in the argument and they put up a hard struggle. They are awfully nice people, and despite my accent and occasional odd turns of phrase they have accepted me as one of their own. But the dispute over the windows has aroused their political passions. They battle on intensely, gravely, delivering themselves of magnificent sentences, full of sophisticated Anglo-Saxon irony. I am overwhelmed by an absurd feeling of tenderness. It seems to me that I love them, these dear Americans, so sincerely angered by the principal's attempts to deny Rocky his human rights.

Rocky is the only Canadian in our English department – a wide-eyed lad from the Maritimes and a specialist in seventeenth-century British literature. Recently, however, he discovered the prehistoric world of dadaism, fauvism and surrealism, and entered it wholeheartedly. Those old European "isms" aroused his creativity. Early last Monday morning I arrived at the college to find a mammoth puppet sewn together from plastic garbage bags, and obviously stuffed with garbage, leaning up against the main building. It reached to the third floor and its silver hub-cap eyes stared blankly across the Edenvale wilderness towards Lake Ontario in the distance. He must have worked on it all weekend. I had no idea how he could have sewn that ten-metre bubble-man together, and propped it upright against the façade. But there the magnificent super-doll sat until the next day, when it disappeared on the principal's orders. What it represented I do not know. Nothing.

The meeting adjourns in disagreement. Rocky, his black beard proudly thrust forward, vanishes into his tent; I disappear into my office, reappear at once in my fur coat, clutching my briefcase, and flee down the back stairs because I have no desire to talk to anyone about the problem of windows or no windows, or any other problem for that matter. The day is darkening into an Ontario evening, illuminated below by snow and above by the sky aglow with light from the golden skyscrapers on Front Street. I want to drive towards them quickly, undisturbed. I must be growing old. I try to drown myself in thought, and my thoughts are mostly memories.

By now the college is empty. The students have left by the last bus or driven off in their battered cars. I walk down the long, empty, heated corridor to the exit.

Suddenly I hear music coming from somewhere. Jazz. Or rather what we used to call jazz when we played it in Kostelec. I mean swing. *When I was a little girl way back then, I wore a red red ribbon* – it sounds odd here, the Czech voice of Evina Fitzpilarova echoing down the antiseptic college corridor, its walls a collage of posters advertising courses in speed-reading, announcing lectures on the true face of the counter-revolution in Chile, demanding greater rights for women, offering cheap typing and the chance to believe in Hare Krishna. The music is coming from the half-open doorway of the student common room, which is connected to the closed-circuit campus station, Radio Edenvale. I enter. It is a huge, empty room, the tables littered with the remnants of food bought from the automatic food dispensers ranked along the opposite wall, their bright electric eyes burning into the gloom. Mechanically they offer to the gaping emptiness their donuts, rubber tarts, trigonometrical synthetic chicken sandwiches, coffee, extra-strong coffee, tea and ersatz bouillon in a can – Canadian futurism. The electric eyes glow into the white dusk beyond the wide windows and from the loudspeaker comes Evina's voice.... *the ribbon's gone, my hair gets in my eyes, and life's just no fun any more* – I stand there, staring, listening. The music ends, and another voice issues from the loudspeaker, a girl's voice, speaking English with a hint of an accent that is characteristic of Veronika Prst, who is talking to no one.

"So here I am looking out of the window," the voice says, "and, well, we are having some real Canadian winter with the snow flurrying and we will not be able to see the stars again tonight, I mean the moon. There is supposed to be a full moon tonight. Everyone has gone home, haven't they? So I'm going to play you some rock and roll, something you've never heard before, you poor dears. 'The Long Black Limousine.' Do you know about that black limousine? The Czech secret police murdered a girl and blamed it on the West Germans. On West German spies. Everyone knew who really did it, but they all had to keep their mouths shut. So here it is. 'The Long Black Limousine.' Played by the Flamingo group and sung by Marie Rotterova."

Veronika falls silent, Rotterova comes up:

> An angel came and sang to me
> A sad song in my dreams;
> It wasn't rain that washed away
> The touch of angel wings.

I find myself wondering if Veronika's interpretation of the lyrics is not just wishful thinking on her part – whether Rotterova and the young men in the Flamingo group were not in fact subtly propagating the police version of the affair, not because they believed it but so that they might be allowed to play music by Simon and Garfunkel or whoever it was they were trying to imitate. But in the empty common room of Edenvale College, in the middle of this wilderness that slopes down to Lake Ontario, the song has an eerie ring of terror about it. Tears well into my eyes, as they do when I read "The Raven." I can see her in my mind, that Dubcekian orphan, that sad Czech girl, alone inside the broadcasting studio on the sixth floor of the college, sending her rock-and-roll message into the empty cafeteria to fall at best on the uncomprehending ears of the Italian cleaning ladies.

So I, at least, stand and listen. The only one here who understands:

> So little time is left to me
> Then why, oh why should I
> Be she whom fate has chosen now
> To mount the scaffold and die?

"That's Czechoslovak?" I hear behind me. I turn around, startled. It's Irene Svensson, in an elegant coat with an inner lining of sealskin, bought no doubt in an expensive Yorkville boutique. She has materialized like a spirit.

"No, it's Czech," I say, and add, irritated because after almost two years of instruction from me even the most dull-witted Canadian girl should know it: "There is no such thing as the Czechoslovak language."

"Really?" she says as though hearing it for the first time, and she turns to listen to the music. "She's got a terrific voice," she says coolly. Her blonde hair falling casually across her baby sealskin collar sparkles in the light from the Coke machine.

> I love my life of tears and woe
> Love everything I've been
> Then why do visions haunt me
> Of a long, black limousine?

"What's it about?" asks Irene. I explain briefly about the murdered girl, and give her Veronika's interpretation.

"Why did they kill her?"

"I don't know."

"But they must have had a reason."

"They certainly must have."

"And you don't know what it was?"

"No."

"But why? A young girl...."

"Have you ever read James Bond?"

She flashes her luxuriously faded eyes at me.

"No. Should I read him, Professor?"

"Not for literary reasons. But he is a part of our, if you like, our culture. And a symptomatic one at that."

A group of cleaning women enter the common room. We cross the room to the glass doors and pass through them into the night. The blizzard is over. Behind us I can still hear Veronika's small and lonely voice: "It is almost six. And still snowing cotton wool outside. How about something for Christmas? It's almost here. Here it is. *Purpura.*" From a fellow by the name of Jirzhi Suchy."

It is snowing cotton wool. We walk beside the college building towards the parking lot.

"Okay," Irene says. "I'll buy him to take on the trip. Which one do you suggest, Professor?"

"Bond? Any one you like. Each book is a perfect *pars pro toto.*"

"Isn't that Latin?"

"It means if you've read one, you've read them all."

The snow crunches under Irene's boots of soft, grey leather that look more like gloves made specially to fit round her slender calves. Snowflakes come to rest on her hair like northern fireflies.

"I'm glad I caught you before I left, sir," she is saying to me. "I wanted to apologize. I can't come to classes next week."

"Anything serious?"

"I'm flying to Hawaii with Mother. She's going on doctor's orders, but she's afraid to fly alone and Father doesn't have the time to go with her. I'll only be away a few days. It never takes her that long to get used to it."

"I envy you. I hope you get a nice tan."

"Too much sun doesn't suit me," she replies, stopping beside a small, fiery red Porsche. She turns her faded eyes on me. I see the windows of the common room reflected in them.

"Were you ever in Kiruna?" I ask.

"When I was a kid. My grandfather lived there."

"I know. I was there too."

"Really? When was that?" She asks with genuine interest.

"It'll be almost — ten years now. Perhaps you were even there at the same time. Ten years ago you must have still been a little girl."

"Perhaps...," says Irene. The faded eyes search me, uncertain of something.

I say, "The sun there must have suited you. The northern sun."

"Did you like it in Kiruna?"

"Very much. If I had a choice, I'd live there. Or in San Francisco."

"So what are you doing in Toronto?"

"I have a job in Toronto."

The idea has probably never occurred to Irene before.

"I see," she says. And then, "Can I give you a lift?"

"My car's over there."

For a while there is silence between us. Her eyes still search me. Then, with what seems to me a touch of irony, she says, "That's too bad."

Everything seems to be happening according to some formula. Irene slips gracefully into her earth-clinging car with God-knows-what horsepower, her sealskin coat falls open, the sky overcast with luminous smog illuminates her nylon knees and young thighs. An absurd thought crosses my mind: Irene does not have pale blue bloomers. The small car roars to life and leaps out of the parking lot like a tiger. A slim hand in a driver's glove gestures carelessly from the window, a northern queen's farewell. I shall probably start something with her after all.

•

*10 Oct., 1943*

*Halloo there, Daniel,*

*Here I am in Prague at the School of Graphic Arts. I got admitted with pull, natch, and if you were to guess that old man Balas managed it, you'd be right. He was always touting me as a child prodigy – draw, Vrata! – and all I ever did was cover the blackboard with pictures of life in Kostelec. Balas always got so carried away by them he never noticed how I'd always manage to sneak a female nude or two into those Brueghelesque knots of bodies. And I was only twelve years old at the time. It's worse now I'm turning eighteen. He got me in here partly to give me a boost and partly to rob the Reich of one more pair of hands, because I hear Balas is reading some awfully strange books, all dog-eared and well-fingered, and hanging about with oddball types who have nothing to do with art.*

*Have I told you how it all came about? It happened in three phases, as Balas would say, a dialectical triad of events (but I don't expect you to know bugger-all about that, you're just a dumb sax-player from Kostelec). The first event was Mr. Dasek coming in for lye, which we keep way up on the shelves about three metres off the floor. So I get the ladder – a kind of step-ladder affair with a little platform on top to stand on – and I climb up and reach for the lye but even on my tiptoes I can only just touch the box with my fingertips. So I kind of coax it over to the edge of the shelf, the idea being to tip it over and then catch it.*

But as soon as it tipped so did the step-ladder and so, according to the nexus of causality, did I. And I forgot to mention that Mr. Helebrant had soda pop of various hues lying on their sides on the shelves with their necks protruding and the box of lye, picking up speed as it neared the ground according to the third law of motion (or is it the second?), clipped the tops off about twenty bottles and a many-coloured shower poured down upon me. I was already lying on the ground since I am heavier than a case of lye. It was like having twenty drunks piss on you at once, each of them after taking a different miracle drug that makes you pass rainbow water.

Now that, for your edification, was the thesis. All old Helebrant did was dock the damage from my wages. Otherwise, he wasn't too upset.

Next the Helebrants' girl Janka tried to put the wind up me (as my father would say) by calling me an old fogey because I don't smoke. So I stole one of my brother's weeds, went into the stockroom, sat down on a barrel, and tried to learn how to smoke the damn thing. Suddenly in comes Mr. Helebrant, lets out a huge roar, snatches the butt from my lips and grinds it out between his thumb and index finger, thus burning himself. Turns out the barrel was full of gasoline. This time Mr. Helebrant said any more clumsy irresponsibility from me and he'd chuck me out of the chemists' apprentice course and turn me over to the tender mercies of the Labour Office, which would in all likelihood pack me off to the Reich.

That was the antithesis.

Unfortunately there was more of both – clumsiness and irresponsibility – because he caught me before I managed to have my way (clumsiness), not with one of the barterable brides of Kostelec but with his very own daughter Janka (irresponsibility). Even though I got practically nowhere with her, he chucked me out of the course, and that, my dear boy, was the synthesis.

Fortunately, Professor Balas appeared like an angel out of Prague for the weekend (now he's sporting a beard squared off at the bottom that reminds me of those pudding-bowl haircuts my mother used to give me) and he said he'd get me into the School of Graphic Arts where his word carries a lot of weight, which it does, and here I hope to stay safe and sound till the war's over. I guess you won't be going to the Reich either, since you're so active in the Reich's armament industry in Kostelec, so we'll meet after the war in Prague. At six o'clock in the evening at The Chalice.

Yours,
Vrata

*P.S. Give a kiss to Janka Helebrantova for me when she delivers this sealed epistle to you. I have now managed to have my way with her. When she was here in Prague on an excursion to see* The Bartered Bride.

•

I knew the unknown hero. I eventually discovered his identity, but only after it was all over, and by chance rather than design. It was quite the affair. The warehouse blew up just as I was coming back with Irena from the woods where I had taken her picture in various poses that she considered seductive – quite rightly, at least as far as I was concerned. I still have the photographs with me today, in Toronto. They show a pretty, small-town girl in a floral-pattern dress. She had bandy legs, but I didn't mind. I later explained this to myself with the aid of Bacon, Lord Verulam as quoted by E.A.P. when he wrote: "There is no exquisite beauty without some *strangeness* in the proportion." Of course Poe had in mind Ligeia's eyes; whether he would have extended his dictum to include bandy legs, I cannot say. But I thought Verulam's statement was valid and later, in my many writings, where Irena is always present though not omnipresent, I made her legs straight and beautiful. As we walked through the deep woods, pausing frequently for snapshots, I tried to persuade her to let me take her picture without her clothes on, and naturally she declined. All that I ever managed in that line – and it wasn't until later at the Jericho pool – was photographing her in a bathing-suit, and she didn't even have on the two-piece variety. On the other hand she did have a lovely gap between her thighs right below her little pussy, and in looking through the viewfinder of my Voigtländer I focused through that space directly on the face of Zdenek, who was sitting behind her on a towel. It was my first lesson in artistic symbolism.

We strolled back to town along the river. I had my Voigtländer optimistically loaded with fresh film because I thought her father, the alderman, might not be home and I might persuade her to change her mind, and as we walked in the shade cast by the woods on the other side of the river below the brewery, suddenly we heard the explosion, a long, rumbling *brrrrrrroooom!* We both whirled around in time to see an enormous mass of flame and smoke billowing out of the Velcl warehouse. "Oh God!" Irena shouted. The pornographer in me quickly made room for the war photographer. In a few leaps and bounds – which was precisely how I did it – I hurried as close as I dared to the fire and immortalized it on film. The smoke was rolling out, darker, thicker and more threatening, when suddenly something began crackling like popcorn and a large, flaming projectile shot out of the black smoke straight towards me. I leaped to one side and a burning barrel crashed to earth and exploded a little way behind me. Once again

I jumped aside, landing this time on the steep riverbank. My feet skittered out from under me and, in my freshly washed trousers and Bombay shirt, I slid swiftly and smoothly into the water. But though I was entirely immersed in the frigid water my photo-journalistic reflexes were still active and I had the presence of mind to hold the camera over my head. At that moment (which would be of political advantage to me later on) I felt, absurdly, like the son of King Kong on a sinking island, holding Fay Wray aloft in his paw. Fortunately, the river was shallow and I was soon scrambling back up the bank where, covered in mud, I completed my work as *ad hoc* photo-journalist.

When I looked around, I saw the alderman dragging Irena along the riverbank and calling out to me, "Mr. Smiricky, please go home at once, right this minute!" At first I couldn't understand why he was being so insistent, then I noticed two grey DKWs full of German soldiers racing along the road from the station to the warehouse, which in the meantime had become a giant sparkler. I understood his worry at once and, like an American commando in the Pacific, I jumped back into the river, waded across to the other side where, hidden by the woods, I loped past the brewery into the town and home. On the way, I snapped a few more pictures.

Luckily, no one was at home. I changed my clothes and locked myself in the bathroom that Father used as a darkroom. The photographs of the fire were ready in an hour; I completely forgot about the other film, the one I had taken of Irena, which was in a bakelite cassette in my pocket. I didn't think of it again until I was surveying the work in which I had captured a catastrophe unprecedented in the history of Kostelec, but by then the developer was already back in the bottle so I put Irena aside until next time. I was burning with impatience to show my pictures to Prema.

Prema Skocdopole was the leader of an underground organization with which I was loosely associated, as one might say today. So far the group had done nothing heroic, except for occasionally cutting telephone wires in the woods at night, wires we hoped connected the military headquarters in town with Berlin. We were wrong about that. All we ever managed to do was sever connections between the Alois Jirasek country restaurant and chalet at Cerna Hora and the Kostelec post office.

I hurried over to the Skocdopoles'. Small groups of people were already gathering in the streets, talking excitedly. I made it to the tobacco warehouse in record time, ran up to the second floor where the Skocdopoles' flat was and rang the bell. There was no answer. I rang again, and a third time. Then I walked down the corridor and around the corner to where Prema had a small room of his own with a separate entrance. I tapped on the door.

"Who's there?" said Prema's voice on the other side of the door.

"It's me, Danny."

"Come on in, quick!"

The door opened, I slipped inside the room and stared. Prema was wearing a shirt, and his left arm, from the elbow to the shoulder, looked like a piece of fried bacon. The flesh was fiery red and swollen and there were strips of burnt cloth embedded in it.

"My God," I said, "were you there too?"

"I was the one who blew it up, for God's sake!" Prema grimaced. "It hurts."

The sweat was pouring from his forehead, his face was ashen. "Christ," I said, "have you got something to put on it?"

"I put some Nivea on it, but it burns like the devil. And anyway, there's none left."

"I think my mother's got some. I'll go get it."

"Nivea won't...." he paused for a moment and the perspiration poured down his face, "... be worth a goddam. Haven't you got any oil at home?"

"What kind?"

"You know, vegetable oil or something for sunburn."

"I don't think we do."

Both of us were silent. Prema sat down on the bed and rested his arm on the bedside table. "Christ on a crutch! It hit me before I had a chance to get clear. It was just a drop or a spoonful, but look at the bloody mess it made."

I looked at it. It was an ugly wound. "What about the others?"

"I did it by myself. The place was practically unguarded. There's just one old Austrian geezer looking after it and he's always asleep on the job – oh fuck! Fuck!"

"Look," I said, "I'm going for Dr. Labsky. He writes me out certificates of non-competence when I miss the odd shift. He did it for Benda too, remember? When he shot himself full of pichuric acid to make it look like he had jaundice and Labsky wrote down that he had gallstones?"

Prema moaned. I'd never heard anyone really moan before, but that's what it must have been. He simply uttered a strange sound.

"Labsky's okay, I know, but this is a matter of life and death. I just hope he doesn't turn chickenshit."

We both looked at the crisp flesh on his shoulder.

"We've got to do something about it."

"I suppose we do."

Prema grimaced again and roared out another obscenity. That decided me.

"I'm going for Labsky. Meanwhile, take a look at this."

I left him the pictures so that he could at least have some satisfaction from what he had done – to the Germans, at any rate.

I knew Dr. Labsky's waiting-room would be full as usual. It had not yet become the custom to make appointments and doctors had no receptionists. You simply came into the waiting-room, counted the number of people already there, and made certain that no one who arrived after you tried to get in before you, something that frequently happened. And because during the war almost everyone tried malingering, I knew that there would be at least fifteen people in the waiting-room.

It was only when I reached the street that the full impact of Prema's exploit hit me, and inspired by the magnitude of the deed I decided on a stratagem that also required a certain degree of heroism. A very insignificant degree, to be sure – a tiny amount of bloodshed – but blood all the same, blood shed for the motherland. When I put it that way to myself, it sounded foolish, though strictly speaking it was true. But if Prema could blow up a fuel dump, I was certainly not going to shy away from a little bit of pain. I took my penknife and a clean handkerchief out of my pocket and closed my eyes. I imagined that gigantic sparkler, the blazing barrels bursting like popcorn, falling golden into the dark green shadow of the woods and hissing in the shallow river – and I sliced the ball of my thumb right down to the bone. I hissed with the pain, a stream of blood spurted out and catching it in my handkerchief, I held it to my nose and smeared the fresh blood all over my face. Thus camouflaged, I rushed into Dr. Labsky's waiting-room.

As I had expected, the room was full, but my bloodied face made an impression on the patients. Through the handkerchief I mumbled something about a motorcycle accident and an old fellow stood up and began pounding on the door of the doctor's office with the urgency of someone dealing with a life-and-death situation.

"What is it?" came Dr. Labsky's voice from the other side of the door. He sounded distinctly annoyed.

"Doctor, there's an accident out here. Young fellow's all cut up."

The old man had exaggerated my injuries somewhat, but I could hear the doctor say, "Just a moment." A moment later the door opened a crack and Dr. Labsky stuck his head out. He was almost six feet tall, handsome, still young, about thirty-five years old. "I'm dizzy," I mumbled through the handkerchief. "Must be the loss of blood."

"Come in," said the doctor peevishly, while his eyes assessed my proximity to death. "And don't bleed all over my carpet."

My handkerchief hadn't deceived him and I had the strong impression that my heroic mission had come at an inappropriate moment.

Marie Dreslerova was standing beside the examining table doing up her blouse. She was blushing like a peony. I tried to apologize. "Excuse be," I said through my handkerchief.

She lifted her nose haughtily – no doubt her own cynical assessment of the real degree of danger I was in. "So what have you been up to this time, Danny boy?" she said disparagingly, hissing her *s*'s like a snake. She glanced at the handsome doctor.

"All right, Miss Dreslerova," he said, saccharin-sweet. "Now you just take three of those pills every day, and drink lots of water and – ah – let's have a look at you in a week."

Despite the jam we were in, an angry jealousy swept through me. Let's have a look at you in a week. How precise that was. On the examining table. Marie walked proudly out of the office on the most beautiful pair of legs in Kostelec, and I turned to the doctor.


He came to the Skocdopoles' a quarter of an hour after me and asked Prema the same questions I had. When he was satisfied that it had been a solo operation, he took his instruments out of the obstetrical bag and started cleaning the wound. Prema ran the gamut of grimaces and obscenities. Finally the doctor filled out a form we both knew well – the certificate of non-competence – and then he thought for a while.

"I can only give you three days off, otherwise you'd have to go for an official check-up and that would mean a lot of people would have to be let in on it."

"I know what you mean," Prema said. "Three days is enough."

"You don't say," retorted Dr. Labsky. "You'll get a fever, but there's nothing to be done about it. You'll just have to stick it out."

"Don't worry, Dr. Labsky."

The doctor gave him a long, hard look. "I'm not worried," he said. "They don't take doctors as hostages. They need doctors. But did you give any thought to what you were doing, my friend?"

Something like a frown crossed Prema's face. "Sure," he said, but it didn't sound convincing.

"How many do you think they'll take, eh?"

Prema was silent.

"Fifteen? Twenty? Fifty?"

Prema still said nothing.

"And how many of those won't come back?"

In the end they took forty-eight hostages, among them my own father. He came back, but ten didn't. And thus I was introduced to the relativity of human actions.

"But it's war!" Prema insisted. "And if everybody was yellow – well, somebody's got to do something."

Dr. Labsky measured him once more with his steady look. "You probably think you're a hero, don't you?"

"No, I don't," said Prema quickly, "but it's war. We've got to show the Germans...."

"If you were really a hero, you'd turn yourself in. That way you'd save the lives of all the innocent people who are going to suffer for this."

Dr. Labsky stood up. "But it's better you don't. They'd make you tell them who patched you up because it's obviously a professional job. So put on a new bandage every three hours. I'll come by tomorrow. Goodbye."

He snapped his obstetrical bag shut, bent down so that he wouldn't bump his head on the lintel, and was gone.

We were silent. We both felt miserable. "God damn it," said Prema after a while. "You know I never thought of that. Do you think he's right?"

"Sure. They wouldn't believe you'd bandaged yourself like that."

"That's not what I meant," said Prema exasperatedly. "I mean, do you think it was a stupid thing I did? That it wasn't worth it? I never even thought a lot of people might get it in the neck on account of me."

"But you said yourself, it's war."

"Sure, but they'll round up innocent people. Maybe they'll even shoot some of them."

"They may be innocent, but they're chicken. Chickens don't win wars."

Saying that made me feel heroic. I had no idea how soon I would regret not having remained one of those who were chicken. Prema thought hard. He was no longer sweating. The cooling ointments were beginning to work, but his pale, sunken Mongolian cheeks were burning, perhaps with an incipient fever.

"I could go underground," he said, "and then write the Gestapo a letter of confession."

"Then they'd just keep on arresting people till they caught you. Remember when Heydrich was knocked off? They threatened to shoot every third person till the assassins were caught."

"That's a fact," said Prema and added, somewhat abruptly, "I could shoot myself and then write the letter – I mean the other way around."

"You've got nothing to shoot yourself with."

"Sure I do."

He had never told me that. I was envious. My father had had a pistol before the war, but when the Germans came he hid it somewhere, so I was weaponless. Later, during the uprising of May 1945, he couldn't find it; he spent the whole revolution looking for it in vain.

"Don't be crazy," I said. "They'd still use what you did as an excuse to settle scores with people they're out to get anyway. And if you do give yourself up, there'll be one less person around who isn't chicken."

Thus I used sophistry to help Prema resolve the eternal dilemma of human heroism. Or at least I gave a boost to his instinct for survival. Even heroes have that. I didn't go home until it was dark, and in spite of the expected reprisals, the slaughter of innocents, I was warmed by the sensation that I had taken part in an effective conspiracy, one that had all the earmarks of adventure and perhaps even of heroism – if it was not just a youthful indiscretion.

I rang the bell and my mother opened the door. She was in tears.

The reprisals had already begun.

They had begun at home.

●

In front of me, a river of blood; flowing towards me, a river of gold. During those long, brief decades that divide me from the moment when through the gap between Irene's thighs I saw the sharply focused face of my rival Zdenek Pivonka, I have grown used to the fact that almost everything can mean many things, but that the primal, the real meaning, the concrete reality, is ultimately the best. The most beautiful. The most valid. I am driving a red Duster along the Queen Elizabeth Way. It's dark and it's rush hour. The river of blood, the rear lights of the column of cars in front of me; the river of gold, the dazzling headlights of the cars creeping out of Toronto to the towns spread out along the lakeshore: Etobicoke, Mississauga, Clarkson, Oakville and on to Hamilton, St. Catharines and Niagara-on-the-Lake. It has stopped snowing, and the thousands of artificial lights on the earth illuminate the low clouds over the flat Ontario landscape, and the clouds sparkle like stardust. In front of me, the tall skyscrapers of downtown Toronto rise unevenly into the glittering evening, fingers of black and white, vertical golden towers. The red signal lights on top of the CN Tower blink at me, warning Jumbos homing in on the airport not to skewer themselves on its needle tip. A beautiful, safe, Canadian, pre-Christmas winter night. There is nothing like it in Europe, in my part of Europe. Before me lies a night in which nothing can harm me. Day follows night, and the worst that can happen to me, apart from a heart attack (the delayed effect of many nights back home), is that Irene Svensson will get over her compromising mood and in a fit of pure malice read up something on Poe that I'm not familiar with (but she'd be better off waiting till we take Joyce) and try to make a fool of me in front of Bellissimmo and Ted Higgins – assuming of course that they would understand what was happening, which is hardly likely. That is the worst situation I can imagine.

I feel splendid, and once again it seems to me that life is good, that in fact I've always had a good life because I have survived everything with impunity and now live in a country where, if I drive carefully, I won't even get a ticket.

My mind wanders. In my thoughts I see my father coming back home less than a month after the Gestapo picked him up, his leg stinking like Gorgonzola. Dad was a war hero too; they said that about everyone who was badly wounded in the First World War, and Dad got his wound at Zborov. But he seldom boasted about it, because he was heroically wounded on the wrong side of the front by a bullet that had probably come from the machine-gun of a Czech legionnaire. He occasionally tried to improve on his story by maintaining that he was wounded while trying to desert to the enemy but no one believed him, least of all me. Dad was thoroughly Czech. He always did his duty conscientiously while thinking the opposite of what he was expected to think. But he did his duty. He didn't try to desert to the other side. Not him. On an order from his Austrian lieutenant he cautiously went over the top, but because caution is of little avail in war he fell back almost as soon as he stepped out of the trench, his leg shattered by a bullet. The battle had been raging for several days and there was neither the time nor the means to move all the wounded out behind the lines. So Father, his leg mutilated, lay in the cellar of a bombed-out château, suffering from pain and thirst. The orderly all but ignored the wounded and instead spent his days digging through the rubble towards the wine-cellar while the shrapnel whistled and whined overhead. At last he made it through, disappeared into the dark and re-emerged with his arms full of dusty, moss-covered bottles. The wounded and dying began to wail and the orderly handed out the bottles left and right like St. Nicholas. He was a wise man and he knew that his vial of iodine and tiny box of aspirins would help them far less than alcohol, which heals all pain. "And wouldn't you know it!" my father always said when telling the story, "I bunged the neck off my bottle, tilted her back and, Danny, out flowed a syrup as black and thick as molasses! Couldn't drink it, couldn't eat it. That wine must have been a good three hundred years old and it was bad right down to the bottom."

So, moaning and complaining of thirst all night long, he edged nearer and nearer to death. The orderly kept running outside, and next morning he came in quite beside himself saying the chaplain had come to administer the last rites. I don't know how much their spirits were raised by that news, since several had already passed away in the night. It probably didn't make much difference to my father, as he was not religiously inclined. He went in more for physical fitness, hiking and gymnastics. The piece of cloth hanging over the bombed-out entrance was flung back and a little priest fresh from the seminary walked in, white as death but comely as a doll. The poor fellow had probably never seen so many dead bodies in one place, and as he peered around, my father moaned, "Karel!"

The priest was his brother, my Uncle Karel. He had wanted to be a chemical engineer, but he had an affair with a girl called Josephine and her parents married her off to a tax clerk, and less than a year later she died of fever during childbirth. My uncle resolved to remain faithful to her beyond the grave and entered a seminary.

In that château, beneath the flying shrapnel, my uncle did something that did not entirely square with his responsibilities as an army chaplain. True, he did administer the last rites to several of the wounded who had not yet died, and he humbly suffered one of them to berate him as a cleric and obscurantist – the fellow was a member of the Society of Free Thinkers and became so overwrought that he fell into a coma and didn't last till sundown. Immediately after that my uncle deserted. He bribed a local farmer, loaded Father onto a haywagon, and then he and the farmer transported Father back from the front. There my uncle got a *bumashka*, or special pass, for in those days chaplains in the Austrian army had the same standing as a *politruk* today, and he managed to squeeze Father and himself into a hospital train going to Lvov. In Lvov he reserved a compartment in an express train to Vienna, and in Vienna he put Father in an officers' hospital. This done, he obediently returned to the front.

By now my father's leg was in such a state that they wanted to amputate it. In the end they didn't, and fifty years later my father died during an operation on his shin-bone, which by that time had completely deteriorated. When I came to the hospital with Father's funeral clothes the doctor said that had they amputated it at the time, he would have been saved much suffering and might have lived many more years. Apart from the leg, he'd been in wonderful condition. Physically, perhaps – but I'm not so sure. In Vienna he had protested, "A Sokol without a leg? A hiker without a leg?" So my uncle, before he returned to the front, had once again applied his chaplain's leverage and the esteemed and overworked Professor Lebensold was persuaded to undertake an experiment to save the leg.

We live in a world of absurd circumstances, accidental, perhaps the unfathomable caprices of a cruelly jesting God. The festering appendage was saved – and went on festering for another fifty years, still attached to my father. Father suffered. He no longer trained, but if he couldn't train himself he drove others all the harder. Among his protégés was Irena, which meant that despite my hatred for physical exercise I joined Sokol, the patriotic gymnastic society. Before I was able to do anything about Irena, however, the Germans banned Sokol.

I am in bliss. At the Jarvis Street exit, the three-lane column of cars separates smoothly into two, one of them continuing along the Gardiner Expressway, the second, with me in it, no less smoothly descending the curving ramp and passing through the green light. My eye is caught by an immaculately luminescent billboard for "Breggfast" with a freckled turnip-faced brat stuffing himself with eggs done sunny side up. On an impulse I decide to consummate my feeling of well-being with supper at the Benes Inn, where they cook the best sauerbraten north of the United States border. So I turn onto Richmond and from there onto University Avenue. A few blocks later I stop for a red light, and a group of young Chinese girls in knitted woollen caps, obviously medical students, cross the street in front of me. They have faces like oriental dolls. The green light comes on. A black medical student hurries across after the Chinese and, dazzled by the headlights, she blinks the huge whites of her eyes at me. I feel as though I'm in Paradise. I am in Paradise. Nothing can unsettle me. I don't remember ever experiencing such an evening back home. I think of Father, who also loved sauerbraten, and poor Nadia, how she would stuff herself. Had they amputated his leg, God knows how Father might have ended up. With one leg missing, Neuthaler, the judge, might simply have considered him the banal victim of an everyday car accident and Father might have gone straight to Belsen. But our absurd God sometimes plays beneficial tricks on us.

The Benes Inn glows more alluringly than the other shops in the colourful pre-Christmas night along Eglinton Avenue. Large blue letters on beige glass are lit evenly from inside so that in the entrance one is bathed in a blue-beige light. Someone is just hurrying out. I step aside and behold! the round, Slavonic face of Milena Cabicarova, whom we lovingly but somewhat unjustly call Dotty. And she starts right in: "Hi, Danny! Where have you been hiding out all this time? What's the matter, too lazy to give me a buzz? I'll be real angry if you don't drop over to see me, really I will. 'Fraid I have to rush now and anyway, you got a date inside, right? So long, and no excuses, okay?"

She sidles past me in a pair of silver horrors from one of the schlock-shops on Yonge Street. The soles are about a foot thick and the boots are plastered with silly little golden words like LOVE, DEAR, HEART, DOVE, but now, as I look closely, I see they are not so silly, for hidden away among those relics of romantic poetry, in quite small letters, is the word FUCK, and nearby, in even smaller letters, is the word OFF, and the whole glittering creation reaches to just above Dotty's knees, followed by a foot of attractive nylon-covered thigh and above that the briefest of minis made from a material the colour and texture of pink tinfoil. Visions of Christmas sugar-plums fill my mind, and I fail to notice what Dotty has on from her waist up because she's past me now and all that has caught my eye is a huge golden screw dangling from a chain around her neck. I turn to watch her go. Her overcoat, made of artificial leather patches and long enough to reach the ground, is flying out behind her, a wide-brimmed turquoise hat balances precariously on her head and from beneath it glossy chestnut hair, the envy of many a woman, falls straight to her shoulders. But Dotty has dyed the fringes of her hair violet, and it looks as though a poorly fastened purple halo has slipped down around her neck. The final effect of all this is to make her look like a scatterbrained hooker. But Dotty is not that at all. During the day she labours industriously as a teller (or a "telleress," as she says) in the Royal Bank of Canada on the corner of Bloor and Yonge, soberly dressed in the costume of her profession. It is only in the evening that she compensates extravagantly for what Communism denied her in the past. The fact that Dotty managed to leave Czechoslovakia legally shows how unjustified her nickname really is. In the summer of 1968, when hippies and marijuanos from all over the world were flocking to Prague, she roped in a chump from Saskatchewan and thus liberated herself from the dictatorship of the proletariat. She stayed with him until they got to Toronto, where his money ran out. But it was far enough for Dotty. She remained his wife long enough to get landed immigrant status and then liberated herself from the chump as well. She had never got beyond public school in Czechoslovakia, so renouncing her citizenship cost her no more than a few hundred dollars. The instant she became legally a Canadian she flew back to Prague and she went straight to Wenceslas Square dressed in creations that came partly from the Salvation Army store, partly from Honest Ed's proletarian bargain emporium, and partly from Buffalo's black shops, so that all her old cronies could see and admire her. The high point of this demonstration of freedom in a police state came, by her account, when some poor cop on the beat stopped her and said, in what was probably one of the few complete sentences he knew, "What do you think this is, comrade, a fancy dress ball?" That was as far as he got, for Dotty's fluent English froze any remaining words on his tongue.

Sometimes I think Dotty emigrated chiefly for those homecomings. Yet she always comes back to Canada, refreshed and in high spirits, to begin again the great hunt, armed with her lasso which, please God, will one day settle around a Croesus. I wish her success with all my heart, for Dotty is my dearest friend in the Czech community here, even though her aggressive sex appeal leaves me unmoved. But neither she nor I mind and, anyway, I rather suspect that beneath her flamboyant exterior Dotty is really just an old-fashioned Czech housewife. And I, because I am no Croesus, can never be anything more than her friend.

In fact it appears that her lasso may be about to settle around a gentleman by the name of Brian Zawynatch, who made his way up through the rag trade and now supports himself entirely (and very handsomely) on income from stocks and real estate. I'm almost inclined to pray to our seldom charitable Lord that Mr. Zawynatch become ensnared for good in Dotty's noose.

●

Father told us about it when he came back from the Gestapo jail with his leg smelling like Gorgonzola. The leg required two hours of treatment daily: cleaning, rinsing, disinfecting, powdering, bandaging. Naturally that was impossible in prison, so when they brought him to trial the judge sniffed the air and demanded menacingly to know what the stench was. Then he turned to the guard and snapped, "Are you not taking care to see that prisoners wash according to regulations?" The Hradec prison where they had taken my father was not a concentration camp, but discipline was tough and that included strict hygiene.

"I am, Herr Gerichtsrat!" replied the guard, clicking his heels together. Then he turned to my father and roared, "Why do you smell?"

The unkindly directness of the question evoked in my father a reaction that was a throwback to the days of the Austro-Hungarian empire. He thrust his chest forward and barked out energetically, "*Ich melde gehorsamst,* I do not smell."

"Don't try to tell me you don't when you do. You can fart in your cell if you want, but not before the court."

"I respectfully declare that I did not fart," declared my father, still standing at attention. He had very quickly assumed the role of Svejk, that most classic of all Czech military heroes.

"Then why do you smell?"

"It's my leg that smells."

The judge misunderstood. "Then you ought to wash your feet! There is a bucket, soap and a towel in every cell, is there not?"

"I respectfully declare that there is," said my father, now playing the role to the hilt, even though – as he never failed to point out when telling the story – he was almost pissing himself with fright. "I respectfully declare that it is not my *feet* that smell, but my *leg!*"

This hygienic anomaly seemed to arouse the judge's interest. He leaned forward over the bench. "Am I to understand that your *leg* rather than your *feet* smell – and only one leg, at that?"

"I respectfully declare that that is correct."

"Which leg is it?"

"I respectfully declare that it's the left one. *Ein Beinschuss aus dem Ersten Weltkrieg.*"

This made the judge sit up. "You fought in the First World War?"

"*Jawohl!*" said Father.

"In which army?"

"*In der k. und k. Österreichischen Armee in Galizien.*"

"What regiment?"

In strict military terminology, and with model brevity and lucidity, my father named the regiment, the company, the platoon, the location of the battle and the day he was wounded. The judge sat there looking somewhat puzzled. Then he leafed through some files.

"What was the name?"

"Smiritzki!"

The judge started, peered closely at Father and then said, "Hearing adjourned."

So they let Father go. *Frontkameradschaft* had overcome both national and racial barriers. The judge was an Austrian. He invited Father to his office, and to make his truce with the good soldier complete they got drunk together on juniper brandy. They parted next morning with tears in their eyes, singing an old army song from the time of Field Marshal Windischgrätz. It had turned out that the young lieutenant whom Father, terrified but obedient, had followed out of the trench, only to be hurled back at once wounded but a hero, was none other than this judge, whose name was Neuthaler. So Father didn't get home from prison until two days after they released him, and he arrived with his leg stinking like Gorgonzola and alcohol on his breath.

●

Dotty vanishes like a comet into the waiting taxi and at last I enter the comfortable warmth of the Benes Inn. Inside, in the traditional American-style semi-darkness, the subdued voices of Pilarova and Matuska are coming over the PA system singing "Go No Farther." If Mr. Benes knew it was a Russian song he would cut it out of the tape. At this hour the place is not yet full. At some tables there are Canadians eating sauerbraten, with a steaming mountain of dumplings almost untouched on a hot dish in front of them. At other tables the Czechs sit over their sauerbraten, the hot dish empty, hillocks of dumplings emerging from a sea of sour-cream sauce on their plates.

I make my way to a group of four men sitting at a corner table. I recognize Mr. Pohorsky, Milan, and Frank who represents the extreme right and, although it's something of an anachronism these days, is probably the most decent person in the émigré community. I don't know the fourth person, who introduces himself as Magister Maslo. He has nervous, shifty eyes, as though he were suffering from a chronic fever. My arrival has interrupted something Mr. Pohorsky was saying, but as soon as I sit down he picks up where he left off. I listen intently, for one always learns something from Mr. Pohorsky.

"Ten grand!" says Mr. Pohorsky. "Ten grand, boys. It should be a snap to raise that. I've got it all figured out. Take the new arrivals alone and without even going outside Canada there's almost fifteen thousand of them. If each of them coughs up a paltry seventy-five cents, that makes eleven thousand two hundred and fifty smackers! If they give half a buck apiece, it comes to seven thousand five hundred. I know it's not enough, but don't forget there's about thirty thousand post-February and prewar emigrants here too!"

Magister Maslo notes these facts down on a paper napkin. Perhaps he wants to check on them. He needn't bother. I know that Mr. Pohorsky has everything worked out correctly. "If every one of the post-February and the prewar bunch comes across with only a *quarter*, it's another seven and a half, making a total of fifteen grand. And I only need ten!"

"What's this for?" I query.

"Radio," replies Frank.

"Ethnic radio?"

"Ethnic be damned. American radio!"

"You mean commercials?"

"Not commercials," cries Mr. Pohorsky, almost insulted. "Quality programs. D'you know how much an hour of time costs on a first-class station, the kind that the whole American network will pick up?"

"I have no idea."

"A measly two thousand bucks! That's five hours for ten grand, and if I split them into five-minute spots I get sixty programs. And I tell you boys, give me five minutes a day over two months on an American network, and I'll move America!" Mr. Pohorsky's eyes are burning with Demosthenian fire. "Two months, and American public opinion will force those clowns in the White House to break off diplomatic relations with the Czechoslovak Republic!"

"Are you going to narrate the thing yourself, Mr. Pohorsky?" I ask. His English is not the best. But he has that worked out too.

"I'm going to write it, and we'll hire somebody to read it. Voskovec, for instance."

"They won't let him do it for nothing. He's in the actors' union."

"Then we'll pay him," decides Mr. Pohorsky. "Look, boys. My figures are based on the assumption that the new emigrants will come up with seventy-five cents each. But in fact most of them will give a whole buck, and if only half of those fifteen thousand do that...." Magister Maslo makes some rapid calculations on his napkin and Mr. Pohorsky is swept up in mathematical visions where everything works according to plan. The rotund Mr. Benes comes up to the table, declares with gentle reproach that he hasn't seen me here for a long time (I was here two days ago) and inquires whether I wouldn't like a little something before supper. I decide on a Rusty Nail, not that it tastes any better than the conventional Manhattans or Bloody Marys, but there is within me still something of my old attachment for surrealism. And I ask Milan about his women.

•

My acquaintance with Milan began with a potentially dangerous mix-up, and it is by no means certain that it will not end that way. After seven years in the West one loses that very useful habit of mind which President Gottwald called "alertness and vigilance in the defense of socialism" – a phrase that became embedded in the nation's subconsciousness. Late one afternoon, I returned home from the college to find a message in Czech on my telephone answering-machine. The man who left the message had clearly been taken aback by the technology. And I should have caught the hesitation in the voice, the utter absence of any Canadianisms in the Czech, and even the slight hint of an Eastern Bohemian dialect. But being neither alert nor vigilant any more, I failed to notice the tell-tale signs until much later when, already in trouble, I made the answering-machine repeat its message over and over again: "Ah ... this is Novak. I ... I'd be very grateful if I could speak with you. I'm ... here for a few days and I'm staying at the Hilton Hotel. Would you please be kind enough to ... to call me ... goodbye."

He didn't leave his room number, and the name – so common in Czech that there used to be a special club of Novaks in Prague – naturally meant nothing to me. Thoughtlessly, I classified the caller as one of Mrs. Santner's many émigré readers who sometimes invite me to their hotels for a drink when they come to Toronto on business. I am always on for a free drink, so I dialed the Hilton and asked the receptionist to find Mr. Novak for me. It took some time. At last he said, "Room 3316, sir."

The phone on the thirty-third floor rang but no one answered. The receptionist broke in – "I'm sorry, there's no reply, sir" – and instead of thanking him, hanging up and trying again at hourly intervals (it would have been worth it, for one drink almost always leads to another and my readers insist on paying), I left my name and number with the receptionist and went down to the basement of our pile of bricks (as Dotty would say) at 100 Wellesley Street, for a swim in the pool.

When I got back the telephone was ringing.

"Hello?"

"Oh – this is Novak."

"How do you do?"

I waited to see what Novak had on his mind. And he was clearly waiting for me to speak first. I still hadn't twigged to anything. After a long pause he said awkwardly, "You – called me? There was a message with my key...."

"Yes, I got a message from you."

"You did?"

"Yes, I did. From Mr. Novak, the Hilton Hotel."

"But – I'm afraid I didn't call you...." And then he added quickly, with a ludicrous over-politeness typical of Prague (but I still twigged to nothing), "Of course I know you, Mr. Smiricky. I've read all your books, even those you've published in exile. They pass round from hand to hand back home. People type them out – "

Suddenly I understood what had happened, and the realization was as unexpected as that explosion, so many years ago, at the Velcl warehouse. And I felt that the consequences might be analogous if not as drastic – but then we're not at war. I felt sick. Novak's flattery was ominous. "Wait!" I almost shouted. "Are you from Prague?"

"Yes. I'm here on a Cedok Tour."

Too late, but firmly none the less, I tried to close the barn door. Ideas chased themselves round my head with cybernetic swiftness, but none was of any use. All I could muster was: "So you didn't call me, then?"

"Oh, no! I would never have taken the liberty, only I found your message here. Along with my key...."

Novak's voice fell off abruptly as he came to the same conclusion that I had. "Just a minute, Mr. Smiricky – I believe there's been a mistake. There's another Novak on the tour with us and he's from Prague, too, I think. I don't know him, but I could feel him out, discreetly, of course."

"That – that would be very kind of you, indeed," I said lamely. Barrels of gasoline, from a time long since past but not entirely vanished in my country across the Atlantic, burst into flames. "Thank you."

"Don't mention it." Now Novak began to talk briskly and obligingly and my forgotten alertness and vigilance quickened into new life. He spoke fawningly, with an unconvincing admiration for the heroes of the pen. "I was most pleased, sir, to be able to speak with you. And – one thing I beg of you," and here he paused briefly, his voice so laden with unctuous sentiment that I broke out in a sweat, "please do keep up the good work. There's a terrible need for that kind of thing back home!"

I hung up. My hands were trembling. I had been flung back into ancient times, into one of the constant dilemmas of life in a People's Democracy.

Was the secret agent Novak No. 1 (the one who left me the message) or Novak No. 2 (who had got my reply by mistake)? I never gave a thought to why No. 1, if he were an agent, was supposed to be spying on me, for I concluded long ago that the agents of the State Security Police are in fact indulging in their own peculiar version of art for art's sake. Moreover, it is a strongly formalistic art, fashioned according to certain old models, and based on years of habit so that they go on indulging in it even when there is no longer any reason to do so. In short, the secret police arrange for informers to spy on me because that is what secret police are supposed to do. They collect information because they feel they must – and you never know when some tid-bit of information may be useful to the authorities, may provide an excuse to prosecute someone, anyone. Formula art.

Arming myself with a double – or perhaps it was a triple – frigid Scot (as Dotty would say), I sat down in my armchair, my hands now shaking so violently that I slopped whisky over my shirt. In the past two years about seven of those creatures have visited me, and their technique has always followed a clear pattern. The telephone rings. A voice says, "Good morning (or good afternoon). This is So-and-so calling. I'm a pensioner, sir, in Toronto visiting my daughter. Would you mind very much, sir, if I paid you a visit? I won't take up much of your valuable time. I have a message from Mr. Vaculik."

Vaculik is a writer particularly unloved by the Czech police, but on this last point the pattern varies; sometimes the message is from Vaclav Havel; occasionally it's from Jiri Suchy, once in a blue moon it's from Bohumil Hrabal, who is as closely watched as his trains. It is never from Pavel Kohout. This omission is a clue in itself because even the police know that Kohout, of all people, would hardly have something to say to me. He appears, thinly disguised – as the professors of literature would say – as the buffoon in too many of my dime novels. Not because I hate him; as a matter of fact I'm rather fond of him. But given his enthusiastically socialist past, he's a sitting duck for satire – and I'm a sucker for such things; I would rather murder my own mother than resist the temptation to put him in a book. So because I already know, or think I know, what's coming, I say, "All right, come on over."

The pensioner comes over, takes a look around, and I pour him a whisky. "And what does Mr. Vaculik have on his mind?" I ask. Of course I know what the message is already.

The pensioner takes a quick swallow to fire his courage and says, "Vaculik sends his greetings."

"My thanks to him. And what does he want of me?"

"Well...." The pensioner hesitates, and this means either that he is struggling to say what he has been instructed to say (that Vaculik, for example, is offering to send me manuscripts from Prague through a secret channel, or that he is asking me for financial assistance through Tuzex), or simply that he doesn't know what he should say. In the latter case he's kosher. He takes another quick swallow, often emptying his glass because he's used to drinking slivovice. "Well," he says awkwardly, "that was all, actually. He just sends his greetings."

"Do you know Mr. Vaculik personally?"

"As a matter of fact – no. I just happened to bump into him by accident...." And now follows one of three variations: at a soccer match, in the Pinkas beer hall, or at the sauna. (Why the sauna, I can't say. Suppressed writers, it seems, frequent saunas. Perhaps the hidden microphones are so full of moisture the tapes are incomprehensible.) Then my guest continues, "... and it came out in the course of the conversation that I was going to visit my daughter in Toronto, and so Mr. Vaculik (Havel, Suchy, Hrabal – but Hrabal is never in the sauna; for him it's always the Pinkas beer hall; they are well informed) asked me to convey his greetings to you."

"My thanks to him." I pour out the rest of the whisky. Whether it's the whisky – which he is not used to drinking, especially straight – or the long-suppressed desire to rail against conditions back home, or, of course, an attempt at *captatio benevolentiae,* whatever it is, the pensioner's tongue is loosened and he spends the next half-hour heaping frenzied abuse on the regime. To hear him, the uninformed layman might imagine that Czechoslovakia was ruled by a gang of devils incarnate – Prime Minister Strougal with a long red tongue, chief ideologue Bilak with a tail in his trousers, Husak reeking of sulfur – and that people live in a hell akin to that described by Father Arnall in *A Portrait of the Artist as a Young Man.* What the pensioner appears to suffer most acutely from is the lack of intellectual – and chiefly literary – freedom. After half an hour, either his suppressed longing to heap abuse has been satisfied or he has concluded that he will not gain my confidence and, whiskied up, he totters off into the cheerful Toronto night.

Are these people telling the truth? Did they really try to shed unwanted fat in a sauna with the taut and muscular Vaculik? Or do they merely visit me so that they can brag to their drinking cronies back in Prague about their illicit visit with a banned writer? Or have they purchased their trip to Canada with a promise which they fulfill merely *pro forma,* in this rather slapdash way?

I don't know. I would give a lot to find out. The uncertainty nags me.

But this time, I thought – slumped in my armchair that day and staring blankly over the glittering sea of downtown Toronto – this time perhaps there's more at stake than just one old pensioner getting bawled out in the cream-tiled headquarters of the State Security Police in Prague. This could be a far more dangerous situation – and I will have one of those two Novaks on my conscience. If Novak No. 2 is the informer, then Novak No. 1 is in trouble. If Novak No. 1 is the informer, and Novak No. 2 keeps his promise to feel him out, then Novak No. 2 is in a jam. My only hope lies in the possibility that neither one is a secret agent. Or in a more likely possibility – that they both are.

At that point the telephone rang. I answered it.

"Good evening. This is Novak. I called you once before, but you had some kind of tape-recorder or something...."

So Novak No. 2 hadn't had time to feel out Novak No. 1 yet. I quickly arranged to meet him at a bar called The Jolly Miller near the Hilton. He claimed he would recognize me. He didn't address me as "sir." Was he a secret agent? Or wasn't he?

I waited nervously in The Jolly Miller for about twenty minutes. The interior was almost dark, as in most North American bars. I had sat down at a corner table – and when my eyes got used to the gloom, I received a shock that took me right back to Prague. Directly opposite me, at a row of tables, sat about fifteen young men, all with long hair, all casually dressed, all drinking beer and staring intently straight at me. It was like being in the middle of an absurd play by Havel. My hands began to shake again and I sat there like a hypnotized rabbit, the focal point of fifteen indefinable, frozen stares. Then something behind me cracked, the half-familiar sound of a hard fist meeting a hard chin. I swung round and absurdity became American realism. On a small platform in the corner, behind me and a little above my head, was a television set. They were killing time watching serial violence.

Greatly relieved, I amused myself for the next twenty minutes by staring at the staring young men, several of whom turned out to be girls wearing the same patchwork denim uniform. Then an unmistakable figure with short hair appeared – Mr. Novak, carrying under his arm a paper bag with the word SUPRAPHONE, the Czechoslovak gramophone company, emblazoned across it. He wasn't alone. Another closely cropped man was with him and I wondered for a moment if in the interim the two Novaks had come to an agreement. But the second man introduced himself as Milan Fikejz.

They sat down, I ordered drinks and we were silent for a while. The stone-faced youths were still intently watching the Mafia sharpshooters above our heads trying in vain to gun down Kojak from a range of five paces. Then Novak took the Supraphone bag from his lap and handed it to me.

"I've brought you a sort of souvenir," he said. "I hope you like it."

"Oh, my goodness, thank you!" and from the bag I drew a new record of songs by Jiri Suchy, one that Novak had evidently had to stand in line to buy (if he wasn't working for the police). "Thank you so much, this is wonderful!" I cried, not mentioning that I had three copies at home already. I still have good friends in Prague who remember my loyalty to the Semafor Theatre and my fondness for a certain chanteuse there who sings very little.

"I should explain," said Novak. "This is to make up for a record of yours that I lost a long time ago – I mean that you lost because of me."

A record of mine, lost because of him? I peered at him; he had the face of a fifty-year-old rank-and-file subject of socialism. It betrayed nothing.

"You probably don't recollect," he said, and something in his voice reminded me of my native North East Bohemia. "We only met once. And I borrowed the record from Haryk who borrowed it from you – 'I've Got a Guy.' I played it at the rink and Ceeh tore into the booth and took it away from me and – "

•

It had been one of the minor horrors – an insignificant little horror, really – among the many horrors of our life.

"The shit has hit!" said Haryk by way of welcome when I got back from the factory at seven in the evening, still in a daze from an especially long session with Nadia in the ferroflux room and with my lips rather swollen (I had even touched her breasts but it was more like running my finger over her ribs). "That clot Novak played 'I've Got a Guy' at the rink and Ceeh noticed."

I snapped out of my daze at once.

"What did you lend it to him for, you clot? I lent it to *you!*"

"How was I to know he was such a clot? He said he didn't have a clue there were any vocals on it and so he went for a skate. He says as soon as he heard the vocals come on he tore back to the booth but Ceeh got there ahead of him and confiscated it."

"Cripes! What d'you think he'll do?"

The question evoked a host of unpleasant possibilities. Herr Ceeh's name had been Mr. Czech before the Nazi occupation – a typical Czech rat. An American song at a public skating rink – Lord above, that was all we needed!

"Whatever he does," said Haryk, "it won't be decent. We'd better start figuring out what we're going to do about it."

There was nothing original about the solution we came up with: we decided to bribe him. Not, of course, in almost worthless Reich currency but in alcohol, hard alcohol if possible.

There was nothing original about our source either. We went to see Lim.

He peeked through a slot in his door and when he saw it was us he opened up. He had a peculiar kind of cottage industry set up in the kitchen. Marie Dreslerova was working for him too, and when she saw me she put on her most inaccessible expression. Lenecek the barber sat beside her with another fellow from the fifth form whom I knew only by sight. Each of them had a brush and a bowl of ready-mixed water-colours and they were briskly colouring in some ink sketches. I took a closer look at what they were doing. It was a drawing of Prague Castle, Hradcany, and it looked like something Rosta might have done. They worked smoothly: Lenecek painted the roofs a deep red, the fifth-former did the trees green and Marie, with a few dextrous strokes of the brush, filled in the sky a gentle azure blue, leaving two white spaces for clouds. They were mass-producing originals.

"What's the deal?" asked Lim.

We explained what the deal was, and Lim left to see what he could do while we talked to the speed-painters. It turned out that Lim was speculating in patriotism. In addition to these three, he had hired a network of sales representatives who persuaded potential buyers that when the Americans started bombing Prague, it would probably be the end of the historic skyline, and this hand-painted quasi-original would become a priceless memento. Later I learned that Lim had sold about seven thousand of them at a hundred crowns each and Marie had made enough to spend a month in Prague, although her parents wouldn't let her go.

Lim was back in an hour. Two bottles of counterfeit French cognac had been enough to put things right and Ceeh had returned the record to him. But out of malice, or perhaps for ideological reasons, which is almost the same thing, he returned it broken in seven pieces.

It was getting late. The cottage industrialists were getting ready to leave, and we followed them. Outside the house I said goodbye to Haryk and the others and joined Marie, who had set off alone in the opposite direction. She was wearing her famous blue winter coat with the white fur-fringed hood that made a V for Victory when it hung down her back and she had on felt boots and ribbed knee socks. A powdery snow was falling now, and in the faint blue light of the blacked-out street lamp Marie's golden hair looked like platinum and the snowflakes on it were like diamonds.

But before I could ask her for a date she began first, sweetly, and with an expert's knowledge of what I was about to say. "Look, before you make your pitch – I hear you've got a new girl, a factory girl."

"Who told you that? It's a lot of crap."

"I hear Vlada Nosek locks you and her up together in a workshop."

The bastard! And I had thought he was discreet. I couldn't very well cover it up, so I employed the usual argument, one that she had no doubt heard at least a dozen times already: "Well, a fellow's got to have a girl, and you keep turning me down."

"But a factory girl!"

"Factory girls are the only kind there are in a factory. Anyhow, that's not important. The important thing about girls is whether they're good-looking or not."

"That's what *you* think," said Marie. "It's not that she's a factory girl. But I hear she has a fiancé."

"What if she does? You've got Kocandrle too."

"Yes, but *her* fiancé is a man of violence. I hear workers are like that. So just watch your step, Danny boy."

This confounded me. "What do you mean by that?"

"I just mean you should be careful, that's all. Hi, Franta!"

Kocandrle had obviously been waiting for her. He emerged from the swirling snow and stared at me with an unpleasant lack of goodwill.

"Scram!" he commanded.

"Oh, come on Franta!" said Marie.

"Put your shirt back on," I said. "I'm not going to eat her."

He knew that too. He knew I wouldn't even get close.

"If I were you, I'd get a move on so I wouldn't catch cold," he said.

"Hey, relax!" I countered weakly. "So long, Marie."

"Bye bye, Danny," she said sweetly. She obviously felt sorry for me.

I walked home through the snow filled with helpless anger, and with anxiety over what Marie had said. At home, when I took off my coat, I reached into my coat pocket for the fragments of the record. I took them into my room and arranged them on the bed. There were exactly seven pieces, impossible to put back together again, and I felt like crying. Why "I've Got a Guy"? Why the honeyed tones of Chick Webb's saxophones? Never again would they play me to sleep. For the first time in my life perhaps – because of this record broken in the malice of his black soul by Ceeh, a party member who had been bribed by two bottles of denatured cognac – I was touched by the irrevocable perishability of some things. All the elements in this little incident were to recur many times in our lives: the destruction of beauty, the ideological malice of the Black Hundreds, and high-proof bribery. Three of the fundamental experiences of our lives.

And the man responsible for setting that fiasco in motion was now sitting in a beer parlour on Queen Street in Toronto, saying, "... and then you had to get Lim to help you bribe him with cognac. A little later they sent me off to the Reich for conscription labour, so you probably don't remember me...."

I had the very clear sensation of a divine presence, and God was a practical joker. That Novak remembered the incident was hardly surprising: in the intervening years I had become famous, which meant the destruction of that record must have surfaced afresh in his memory every time he came across my name in print. It resurfaced in mine only occasionally, when I thought of Kostelec, and there was so much to remember about Kostelec. Still, I had the distinct sensation of a divine intervention, malicious and jocular. It was a surrealistic feeling – that is, a feeling of Truth. I was moved.

"Mr. Novak," I said, "I hate to have to say this, but perhaps this time, for a change, it's me that's got you into hot water." And I told him about the potential trouble caused by my answering-machine.

He paled, trying not to let his consternation show. But I have experienced such efforts at self-control myself, and a terrible regret, a helpless grief, filled me.

"Wait," he said unsteadily. "Which one could it be?"

"It's the bald-headed one," said Fikejz, joining the conversation, "the one who's always carrying on about how he trains groups of girl gymnasts for the Spartakiada. The one who bought *Playboy* yesterday."

The purchase of *Playboy* could have helped to explain the man's obsession with women's gymnastics. But this made Novak even more nervous. A group trainer in a mass athletic movement ... on the other hand, a full-time undercover cop would hardly have to pretend that much commitment. "Oh, him," he said, swallowing. "Just a moment – didn't he have to call someone in Toronto, some cousin or other who has a son working for the Voice of America? He told Matatko about it."

"Could be a red herring. Does Matatko know him?"

"That's just it, he doesn't. Never met him before this trip."

"Oh, Jesus."

Earl Hines was playing at the Colonial Tavern. I suggested that we go and listen to him, hoping that the sight of a living legend might help the former swing fan recover his equanimity and forget, for a while at least, the Eastern European problem imported to Canada by the Czechoslovak Travel Agency.

It didn't help. I poured into him – it's odd, we never started to use the familiar term for "you"; but we were both almost fifty, quite different from when Ceeh had traumatized us, perhaps for life – I poured into him countless sodas lightly dashed with whisky, and although he was enthusiastic about Hines' powerhouse, he was somewhere else in thought. I knew where. In the pleasant Bohemian countryside preoccupied by darkness.

Perhaps Milan Fikejz had his thoughts fixed there as well – he said nothing about Hines at all but remained silent, sipping his whisky spritzer. Around midnight, when we were getting ready to leave, he suddenly said, "Jarda" – meaning Novak – "I'm staying here."

He did not mean that he had no intention of leaving the Colonial Tavern. The same night he got his suitcase from the hotel and I took it home with me. Next day he came for the suitcase, bringing with him the news that they hadn't been able to determine if the second Novak was an informer or not. Once again that terrible sorrow descended on me, the despair of helplessness. I took Milan to Manpower and Immigration and helped him squeeze a work permit out of them for one year. And for a long time after I was awakened at night by the thought of the man who had brought a replacement for a long-forgotten record across an ocean of water and time, and whom I could not help.

•

"What's this fellow like, your fiancé?" I asked Nadia inquisitively. He was still in hospital recovering from his appendectomy; apparently there had been complications, but he was clearly going to survive. Nadia and I were sitting on a crate near the drills and she was eating a slice of my bread with pork-dripping (Mother always gave me two because she thought, or hoped, that I was still growing). We had a fifteen-minute break. They had recently increased the working day to thirteen and a half hours, and they gave us two fifteen-minute breaks, one at nine and the other at five, with another half an hour for lunch. That gave me an hour a day to talk with Nadia – as long as the fellow who wanted to marry her remained in hospital. It was impossible to walk her home. In the first place, she lived up in Cerna Hora; it was only four kilometres away, but the rise from Kostelec was four hundred metres, so with the extended working hours that meant I would have made it back home sometime around midnight (allowing time for kissing in the woods), and I had to get up at five (and Nadia at four). In the second place it was only a theoretical possibility anyway, because every day after work Nadia dutifully joined a bunch of highlanders from Cerna Hora for the trek home. In winter especially, when the wind howled and drove the snow like needles into your face, they would trudge together straight up the steep hill, the men taking turns leading the way as though in a bicycle race. They all knew that Nadia was engaged, and some, instead of sitting off by themselves during their lunch break, were beginning to come round to the drills and give us disapproving looks. But Nadia was young and thoughtless, perhaps she liked me and almost certainly she was glad to get my food. But since Marie Dreslerova's warning, all this had begun to make me feel uneasy, as though violence was hanging in the air. Which was why I asked her, "What's this fellow like, the one who wants to marry you?"

"He's kind-hearted and he's a hard worker," she said, her wide mouth smeared with dripping.

"Is he strong?"

"I should say so! He can lift me up in one hand!"

That in itself did not necessarily mean much. Despite the regular influx of provender from the Czernin estate, she seemed to be getting thinner every day.

"Does he get angry easily?"

"Depends. Sometimes."

"What's he like when he gets angry?"

"Oh, he shouts and stuff like that."

"And – has he ever beaten you up?"

"No. He's never been that mad at me yet. But sometimes he's beat up fellows in the pub when they got his back up."

This was not encouraging. I chewed on my bread while visions of impending violence whirled in my mind.

"But supposing he ever did get angry with you?"

"Oh, he's kind to me."

"But just supposing. Supposing someone told him about me, for instance...."

She thought. Perhaps the idea had never crossed her mind. She looked at me with those burning eyes, covered her greasy mouth with her grimy hand and began to laugh so hard that little drops of dripping sputtered out between her fingers.

"Oh, he'd really give it to me!"

"Would he give you a thrashing?"

She was still giggling into her hand. Her saintly simplicity was beginning to annoy me. The burning eyes peered out merrily at me from between the fingers and she said precisely what I had feared. "He'd give *you* a thrashing first."

The factory siren announcing the end of the break forcefully underlined her conviction.

•

*January 17, 1944*
*Terezin*

*Danny!*
*The constable, the one who comes in here to work, promised me he'd send you this note. I have a great favour to ask you. Could you possibly go to see Dolf – I don't want to write to him because they're probably keeping an eye on him – and tell him that if I don't come back, the miniature portrait of my mother is not at your home but at my girlfriend W.'s place? I forgot to tell him myself, but he should be informed so he won't expect your father to give it to him and then think he's holding on to it. My friend W. will certainly give it to him if I don't come back.*

*Things are very bad here and people are constantly being sent off in transports. They take them to Poland somewhere, and no one ever comes back. I feel terribly sad and desperate. Why did all this have to happen? I think a lot about the past and I've just recalled how we used to play together in the sand in the courtyard when we were kids and how your dad shouted at us from the third-floor window and it made me laugh even though there was nothing really to laugh about. But we were only children. I don't really expect to come back, Danny, so why shouldn't I tell you that I regret not having got really close with anyone while I was still free, not even with Bert, because I'm going to die and I'll never know what it's like. Sometimes I think that I'll lose my mind and that it would really be for the best. But that won't happen. Nothing I really wish for ever happens. And if it does, it never lasts long.*

*I have to finish. The constable will soon be here.*

*Danny, pray for me to return – even if I'm not a Christian. After all, you used to be so religious. You were even an acolyte.*
*Your friend,*
*Becky*

●

"But why? Why should they go after you?"

Magister Maslo looks at me, his eyes brimming with chronic fever. "You don't believe me either?"

"No – that is, of course I believe you, I know they do things like that, but what reason did they have for singling you out?"

"I write articles. I'm dangerous to them. I have an influence on the young."

"Oh, I see. I'm afraid I haven't read anything you've – "

"I write for *Scouting in Exile*," he interrupts. "People like Peroutka or Tigrid aren't so much a threat. Their audience is the middle and older generation and the Bolsheviks have already given up on them. But I influence the young."

His hands are trembling as though he is afflicted with Parkinson's disease. He raises his glass of Pilsen. Some of it dribbles onto his nondescript necktie. "You see? My nerves are completely shot. Just try to put yourself in my place, sir. On the Queen Elizabeth Way at midnight, eighty-five miles an hour and all of a sudden they start forcing you over into the ditch."

"They train them for it specially," puts in Frank. "In Israel."

"Where?"

"In Israel," repeats Frank. "They don't have superhighways in the Soviet Union. So for jobs like that, the Jew centres in Moscow use Israel."

"That's odd – and they say Moscow sides with the Arabs."

"The Arabs are Jews too. Sadat's just admitted it publicly. He says he's a Semite too. The Moscow Jews have divvied things up fifty-fifty with the Washington Jews. The Moscow Jews run the show in the East and the Washington Jews run things in the West. Of course, all the time they pretend to be the bitterest of enemies. But the fact remains, world Jewry is out to rule the world."

How refreshing it is to hear an ideology that brings all the tormented contradictions of the world together in such a grand dialectical unity. But Magister Maslo disagrees.

"I'm afraid I have to argue with you on that," he tells Frank. "The Jews are advocates of democracy. That's why they persecute them in the Soviet Union."

"On the surface," states Frank. "But what about Kaganovitch? What about Beria?"

"The important thing from our point of view is whether or not the Jews support our cause," says Mr. Pohorsky. "And they do. In Los Angeles I met a fellow called George Koenig – a factory owner, really rolling in it. Right now I'm bound to silence because we haven't got all the details worked out yet. But I can tell you this much: I will soon have some good news!"

And, bound to silence, he says no more. We return to the subject of Magister Maslo's midnight adventure on the highway.

"A black limousine, a Cadillac," says the old scout. "It pulls up beside me at eighty-five and starts forcing me over to the right-hand shoulder, right where there's a steep drop down to the lake."

I quickly try to remember a cliff along the Queen Elizabeth Way, and I can't think of one. But then no one ever tried to force me down it either.

"So I accelerate to ninety," Magister Maslo continues. I imagine the 1956 Chevrolet that he bought from an out-of-work Ph.D. for ninety dollars. "The Caddy speeds up too. I slow down, so do they. If I hadn't had my wits about me ... but it must have been divine Providence. I'd never have thought of it myself." He pours the dregs of his beer down his sinewy throat. "So I slow down, so does the Caddy, and then at just the right moment I step on the gas, shoot out and pass them on the left and then *I* start forcing *them* towards the cliff. They panic, hit the brakes, and go into a skid.... Before they could straighten out, I caught up with a column of cars doing ninety and stayed with them all the way to Toronto. They didn't dare try anything then." Once more he raises the trembling glass, but he has already drunk or spilled it all. "The bill, please," he honks at a black waitress. She calls Mr. Benes and Magister Maslo pays. "Excuse me, gentlemen, I have to go to bed. My nerves are all ... you know...."

We remain silent until Magister Maslo passes through the blue-beige fluorescence and is swallowed up by the Toronto night, teeming with Czech agents.

"His nerves really are shot," I say.

"Is it any wonder," says Frank darkly, "with Zionist hit-men out to get him?"

"He's also got ten years in the uranium mines behind him," adds Pohorsky. "I knew him. They gave him a rough time. He's a homo, and those Commie butchers are extremely moral."

●

"I'd do anything for a man like that, Danny, anything! And he should have shot that Kraut while he was at it, the one who was guarding the place."

"They'll shoot him themselves," I said. Nadia looked suddenly concerned.

"You mean you think they'll execute him for it?"

"You bet. He must have fallen asleep or something. Imagine, letting them blow up a fuel dump in broad daylight!"

Nadia's bloodthirstiness did not extend to execution. "See what I mean?" she said, without really noticing the illogicality of it. "He should've shot him. He would've been better off."

"Who?"

"The guard."

"You feel sorry for him?"

"Oh come on, Danny!" she protested unconvincingly. She looked round the kitchen. "Have you got any Melta?"

I jumped up obligingly, put the kettle that Mother used for making coffee on the stove, and from a recess in the cupboard took a hidden supply of prewar Meinel – real coffee. Nadia got up from the stool, walked over to the cupboard and looked at the cups.

"They're beautiful!" she said. "We've got nice ones too, from Granny, but nothing like these."

I took a cup from the tea service and showed Nadia a wonder of the ceramicist's art. When you held the cup against the light, you could see the portrait of a beautiful geisha girl at the bottom, like a photograph. It was not a drawing; the effect was created by alternating layers of white porcelain of different thicknesses. Nadia reacted with unexpected curiosity. "Who is it?" she asked.

God knows why I replied as I did. "It's Rebecca Silbernaglova."

"Who's she?"

"Just a girl. We've hidden this for her family while the war's on."

She turned her burning eyes towards me and became very serious. Then she peered inside the cup once more. "She's pretty. But she looks Japanese."

"Well, she's a Jew. And Jews are really an oriental race too."

"Is she your girl?"

I was young and frustrated and nothing bad had ever happened to me. I was flattered that this lanky beauty from Cerna Hora should associate me erotically with a Tokyo prostitute.

"Well, yes. I mean she was. They took her off to Terezin."

Again she turned her eyes, fiery as death, on me. How little I knew.

"Danny, they'll kill her there. Like my dad."

I could think of nothing to say.

"But you've got to avenge her!"

Terrible, burning black eyes.

"I'm going to avenge my father too. I don't know how yet. The fellows in our village have this organization but they won't let girls into it. So I got to think up something myself."

"But how do you know he's dead?"

"I just know it, Danny, I feel it. Besides, it's been ages since we last heard from him. He's dead. I dream about him nights."

I sighed. Briefly, I thought of persuading Prema to let her join us. But Prema would not have wanted her either; he had a basic aversion to girls, in or out of conspiratorial activities. Then too, Nadia would probably discover that it was Prema who had blown up the gasoline dump and she would have her hero. In her own words, she'd have done anything for him. So I rejected the idea and merely said, "We'll think of something."

Nadia gazed into the cup again. The coffee had begun to boil. I took the pot off the stove and drowned the imaginary portrait of Rebecca in the aroma of prewar times.

•

The doorman stops me in the lobby. "You have a visitor, sir."

I look around. Beneath an assemblage of toy cars and old dolls by a Mr. Skopicak (the grandees of the Lincoln-Bellevue Development Corporation give him a rent-free apartment for one such work of art a month), a girl in a fashionable overcoat, with a small crocodile in the shape of a handbag, rises from the plush armchair.

"Mr. Smiricky?" she asks in Czech.

"Yes?"

"My name is Svobodova. I called you from Ottawa, if you remember?"

"Ah, so you're the one," I say, confronting yet another dilemma. Perhaps she is telling the truth, but I'm inclined to think not. Even so, after those seven old age pensioners they have at least come up with a more interesting variation on the theme. "Please come up."

In the apartment she takes off her coat, revealing an expensive silk blouse and tight leather pants. Unfortunately her thighs are too spindly for them. I automatically pour her a Scotch on the rocks, straight up, though the Mata Hari has requested lots of water. For myself, following the time-honoured practices of experienced prostitutes, I pour a "golden spritzer," a highly diluted version of whisky and soda.

"Are you here on a Cedok Tour?" I ask, knowing she had mentioned something about a student exchange over the phone. The trick works. Mata Hari has forgotten about her student exchange.

"Oh no, I couldn't possibly have flown all the way to Toronto to see you if I were. No, I've come to visit my fiancé. In Ottawa."

I keep trying her. "I thought he was an American. Cheers!"

I swallow some watered-down whisky, covering the glass with my hand, and the girl takes a healthy swig of her Scotch. It is pleasing to see that, in a Prague full of Miss Universes, the State Police are utterly incapable of recruiting anyone more alluring than this weedy creature. She is as flat as a plate, her face marred by cream-covered pustules. Who is she supposed to seduce? Me? A man once branded a pornographer by the Party itself – and, who knows, perhaps by the government, as well, as if there were any difference?

"He *is* an American," she says, beating a confused retreat, "but he lives in Ottawa. He's representing an American firm there."

"Ah." I grin raffishly, as befits my role. "So it's a real romance, then! Where did you land him?"

"In Paris. He made me swear I'd join him in New – that is, in Ottawa. That was all very well. But!"

She falls silent. I resolutely take a drink of my amber-coloured water and the conditioned reflex works – only the ice remains in her glass.

"But what?"

She assumes a self-demeaning expression. She is clearly about to admit to a romantic crack-up to give herself room to manoeuvre and, eventually, an excuse to stay a few more days in Toronto.

"They turned out to be a lot of fancy words. When I got to Ottawa, I discovered he was already married."

"Well, you certainly fell for it, my girl!" I suddenly realize that her story is following the pattern of my fictions. All my protagonists are losers in one way or another. Draining her glass again, she confirms my suspicions.

"You know how it is. I'm a woman – and not even Gloria Steinem can liberate us from the slavery that is in us, in that supple and gentle organization of tissue and chemistry...."

She has even learned to quote from my novels. They have prepared her thoroughly, though she ought not to have forgotten that student exchange.

"Goodness gracious me," I say. "I should be bursting with pride." I rise, gather up the empty glasses, and go into the kitchen.

"Indeed you should," she says, rising as well. "I could only have your book for a day" – she's with me in the kitchen now – "and I gobbled it up in a single sitting. I even had time to copy some passages out."

Turning my back to her, I manage to pour another large Scotch over some tiny ice cubes, and an amber-coloured soda water for myself.

"I'm also supposed to pass on greetings to you from Lester."

Now this is an original variation. I am beginning to feel genuinely flattered. Perhaps they have handed my case over to older, more experienced investigators.

"You know him?"

"Yes, I do. That is, I know him through Janda." Janda is a pop music critic who belongs, approximately, to her generation. There is a careful verisimilitude about everything. "I told him I was coming here."

"So here's to Lester!" I raise my glass enthusiastically.

"You have no idea how many admirers you have in Prague. Male *and* female." Yes, she's been well instructed, if not quite so well chosen. She empties a third of her glass at once. Fortunately, they forgot to give her basic training in alcohol consumption.

"Really? And what about Suzi Kajetanova? You know, what I regret most is that she never writes me. When we said goodbye in Prague, she swore – ah, but promises were made to be broken. Or perhaps she's afraid...."

We return to the living room and sit down. I take the armchair, she sits on the chesterfield.

"That's more likely," she says. "If – you want," and I notice with gratification that she is beginning to hiccup, "I'll pass on the word to her."

"What?"

"That she should write to you."

"You know her?"

"Yes. Well, only superficially."

"If she's afraid, she won't trust you."

The remark takes her aback. "She'll trust me."

"Here's to Suzi! Long may she sing!"

She almost sucks her glass dry.

"Ah," she sighs. "I can hardly believe I'm actually sitting here with you...."

"And yet here you sit!" I rise and go into the kitchen, wondering whether I can risk bringing the bottle back with me. I decide to chance it. She doesn't even ask for ice.

"D-don't you want to send any other messages?"

"Who to?"

"Like Stein, or Barvirek. I kn-know them all."

I encourage her to name-drop. As I expected, our acquaintances are curiously similar.

"Who else do you know? I mean, of my friends?"

She even begins to count them on her fingers: "There's Doctor Rus, Mr. Stejskal from Odeon Publishers...."

I make up a name. "Do you know Plnoves?"

"Of course I do."

"My goodness, you seem to know everyone."

"I certainly do."

"You must be a very popular girl."

"I certainly am!"

Her eyes are beginning to cross. Just one more small Scotch and there'll be two of me.

"But tell me, how is it they let you come here in the first place? It can't have been that easy."

"I – I'll tell you. But top secret, okay? I have a good friend who's m-manager of the bank and he gave me a promissory note to buy hard currency. That's more important than a passport, a prossimory note."

"He must be a very good friend indeed."

"Very good."

"Do you know him?"

The question startles her slightly, but she maintains control. "N-naturally, you old silly."

"So here's to the bank manager."

"Here's to him!"

Just to be certain, I make up three nonexistent entities in the next round: Mrs. Ramesova, Snow White and the Café Komplex. She knows them all, and claims to be just like *that* with the crowd at the Komplex.

I'm a little disappointed. The agents entrusted with the liquidation of Magister Maslo were more professional about it. Or were they? Letting an amateur in a 1956 Chevrolet get the better of them? But what, in fact, is Miss Svobodova's mission?

First, I repeat the question. "Tell me, how *did* they let you out? It can't be easy nowadays."

"But I've told you already."

"Oh, of course. I must be a little groggy. It was a student exchange, wasn't it?"

I open another bottle.

"No! My fiancé!"

"But you couldn't possibly have given that as a reason for going to Canada, that you were chasing after a guy."

"No, of course not. I told them I was going to a ci-congress."

"What cicongress?"

"Don't make fun of me. Not a cicongress, a congress!" she hiccups. "The World Federation of Circus Artists."

"You're a circus artist?"

"Of course not. My uncle is in charge of personnel there. He wrote me in as a jug-juggler."

"It's in Ottawa, is it – this congress?"

"Yes, Ottawa."

"There's no congress there at all," I say toughly.

"All right, so there isn't."

"Well, is there or isn't there?"

"I don't know! And I couldn't care less!"

"Now I understand. Your uncle, the personnel man, made this whole congress up just so you could go to Canada on a study trip to meet your married American fiancé."

"That's it." She gets up but by this time she is having difficulty with her equilibrium. "Where is your little girl's room?"

I show her to it.

I hear the sound of laughing waters behind the door.

•

I wait – disappointed and pleased. Unmasking her was so unexpectedly easy that I am still plagued by the old dilemma. Am I wronging a genuine, though ridiculous, admirer of my concoctions who by some surrealistic trick has evaded the clutches of that pataphysical regime on the other side of the Curtain and, risking everything, has spent her hard-won currency allowance to come and declare her literary love for me?

I reject that idea. The circle of common acquaintance is too wide. Also she has come here for too many reasons at once. The worm of doubt, however, is indestructible. Am I doing her an injustice? Am I not succumbing to the paranoia of the ex-prisoner's spirit, since I associate with so many ex-political prisoners here? And with dyed-in-the-wool anti-Communists? And even with that representative of Czech fascism, Frank Obnova?

But it's all too Dada. I remember suddenly an eighth pensioner who came to visit me with a message. His was a new variation: a message from my father. When I told the pensioner – all the while feeling embarrassed for him – that the only way he could have visited my father was with a candle on All Souls' Day, he was so alarmed that he almost knocked over his whisky. He turned red and began stuttering and spluttering a new version. The message, he said, was really from my mother but he hadn't wanted to say so for fear I might think the worse of her, since she was a widow and he, the pensioner, a widower. I reassured him that I would be only too happy if my mother, as a widow, had a lover like him, but that unfortunately that would be impossible since my mother had never been a widow; it was my father who was the widower and he never remarried. He took a few moments to sort out that conundrum, then jumped up as though he had seen Frankenstein's monster and fled, leaving behind a beaver cap he had bought in Canada.

And yet I had had second thoughts even about him. Could he have been so poorly briefed? Perhaps the security officer who did it was drunk and mixed me up with someone else. Or perhaps the pensioner suffered from geriatric amnesia. Are such enormous confusions really possible? Might it not be, after all, that he had simply wanted to impress his friends?

The worm of doubt is a terrible animal.


During Mata Hari's absence I replenish the reservoir, unnecessarily, for that intimate relationship between interrogator and interrogatee, so often remarked upon in prison memoirs, is by now fully established. Only the roles have been reversed.

"Why do you do it?"

"Because. Why shouldn't I do it?"

"Are you doing it for the world revolution?"

"What?"

"You have a nice blouse."

"Don't I? It c-cost seventy dollars."

"It suits you. The pants too."

"Come on over here and sit down. Beside me. You're being so dis-distant."

"Forget it," I say. "It's my time of the month."

It is a crude joke. Not even Philip Marlowe would have dared use it. And anyway, Marlowe was a moral detective, while I am a counter-revolutionary libertine.

But Mata Hari laughs. "Aren't you the fil-filthy one! Just like they write about you."

"What is it you're supposed to find out?"

"Everything."

"What, for example? Mistresses?"

"Yes, mistresses too."

"I can have mistresses if I please. I'm not married."

"I mean married mi ..." – she tries to pronounce the word without trip-ping over it but she can't – "mi-mistresses."

"My-my love, wouldn't you like a cup of coffee?"

"That would be terrif-if...."

"Terrific."

I get up and go to the kitchen. I plug in the percolator and phone for a taxi. It arrives before the coffee is ready. She protests. She wants to stay the night with me.

"My-my love," I say, "if you were Geraldine...."

Her informer's instinct rouses itself for a last feeble effort: "Who is Ge-geraldine?"

"A grandmother I know," I say truthfully, for scarcely had they released her from prison when Geraldine rapidly began to make up for her five-year famine, made bitter by attempts at lesbian love that were constitu-tionally alien to her. Her daughter must have inherited her appetite, because she became a mother at fifteen. Geraldine is thirty-eight. By the time she's fifty she may well be a great-grandmother.

I help my visitor into her coat, take her down in the elevator and put her in the taxi.

"Ho-hotel Windsor Arms," she says to the driver.

The night, full of agents, swallows up my helpless, incompetent Prague Mata Hari, the dialectical opposite of the once wide-eyed and cheerful

Geraldine, who of course was working for the French. If only they would send a new Geraldine to seek me out ... for Geraldine I would fabricate something for them ... something credible....

I go back up to my apartment and drink the black coffee from the percolator, coffee as black as Geraldine's unforgettable eyes, as black as the blazing, feverish eyes of that girl even farther in the past.

•

*The 27 February 1944*
*Oberscharau*

*Dear Dan,*

*I adres you with these few lines to let you know I am well and hope you are enjoying the same blesing at present. I'm sending you greetings from the Reich. I'm working at my trade here. The boss is strict but theres food enough and considering theres a war on its good. I'm working nites, but thats how it is in a bakery as you know. I'm sending greetings from Oberscharau which is near Berlin, the ARS goes off almost every nite but we don't go into the shelters, there has to be bread and pastry even if it started raining pitchforks. They've only bomed Oberscharau twice, mostly they fly on to Berlin. Its terible the inocent people losing there lives. Akerman the boss says the Reich has a secret vengence wepon to pay the Pluto Crats back for killing inocent women and children, he says its a death ray and no one can escape from it and after the war there is going to be a new Europe. I sleep days and afternoons I often go to the movies, they are showing some real good films, I realy enjoy Pandoor Trenk also the sinking of the Titanik and Om Kruger are great also Jud Sis the way they hung him in the cage, I havnt seen nothing like it yet and Romance in Miner was okay too, also Ich fertrowe dere mine frow with the Czech star A. Mandlova and Ruman, both of them are realy good only now she calls herself Lilaladina. I like Heidmar Hataier best she is the prettiest and Ilse Verner is pretty too. My health isnt what it used to be since I dont get much sleep now and I'm spiting blood but the doctor says its a bronkial catar. My adres is A. Muton bei Akerman Bakerei Hans-Jost Str. 5 Oberscharau bei Berlin. To conclude my letter please exsept my warmest wishes and fondest memries.*

*Your freind*
*Lojza*

•

"What'll we do?" asked Nadia. In the cupboard I had discovered one of Mother's specialities, poppyseed cakes, and Nadia was now stuffing herself with sweet poppyseed and drinking from the Silbernagls' cup.

She drank until at last she saw the Japanese girl on the bottom again.

"She's real pretty." She held the cup against the white slope of Cerna Hora outside the window. A snow-laden cloud shrouded the tourist restaurant and the village at the top of the hill. On the slope, on the Port Arthur Restaurant at its foot, on the brewery and on the river, a thick snow was falling.

Nadia turned her incandescent eyes on me. "What are we going to do?"

"I don't know yet. It's got to be well thought out first."

"But what?"

And that was when the foolish idea flashed through my mind. Dazzled by the black light from those smouldering eyes, I failed to perceive just how foolish it was. Prema's heroic act was still fresh in our minds, and the way that lanky girl with her beautiful mouth, staring into the teacup, felt about it was enough to cloud my reason completely.

"I won't tell you yet," I replied. "Like I say, it has to be well thought out."

"And when're you going to tell me?"

"Maybe tomorrow."

"Honest to God?"

"Honest to God."

Nadia sighed, took a last look at Rebecca and stood up. "I'll help you with the dishes. Thanks. It was really delicious!"

She put on Mother's apron — she could wind it around herself twice — rolled up the sleeves of her shabby sweater, put everything in the sink and started in to work. I picked up a dishtowel. A sensation of immense bliss drove out the white cold of a wartime Sunday afternoon. It was a sensation that I never experienced again.

# CHAPTER TWO

The rain when it falls doesn't vex me,
Let me stumble and fall into graves;
The mists make me blind, it can't trouble my mind
For I'm just walking on, walking on.

I swim in the water with serpents
And the salt it gets into my hair,
I'm walking through Hell, Eldorado as well
And all seven seas have I fared.

Oh, sometimes a hummingbird's beauty
And sometimes a journey through flames;
Yes, I've died and been reincarnated
And from diamonds I've fashioned my dreams.

JOSEF KAINAR

Art is sickness and stupidity is another name for health.

COLIN WILSON

●

# Hawthorne

Is she an actress too?" asked Wendy.

"Who?"

"The wife of that actor, the one you said you knew."

Is this Wendy's idea of a joke? My educated colleague Mrs. Webster –
an Englishwoman Webster brought back with him from the British
Museum instead of the long-sought confirmation of a controversial dating
of one of Elizabeth I's court masques – told a similar anecdote about
Wendy. She told it with amazement, because although she was well aware
of the theory, it was her first practical encounter with the fact that there are
associative differences in the primary meaning of words. Mrs. Webster had
just delivered a forty-minute exposition of black humour in Evelyn
Waugh's *The Loved One,* when Wendy McFarlane, that remarkable Scottish girl from Horseman's Saddle in Northern Ontario, put up her hand and
said, "Mrs. Webster, I don't understand. As far as I can remember, there are
no blacks in *The Loved One* at all."

At first, Mrs. Webster thought Wendy was trying to be funny. Wendy's freckled face looks as though she is constantly making fun of things. But it was just that the term meant one thing at Cambridge University and another in Horseman's Saddle. And Wendy's question to me is not a joke either. Her experience comes chiefly from television, mine from the European *teatrum mundi*. And her question today has to do with Costa Gavras' film *The Confession,* which a handful of the students have been to see, about the Stalinist show trials of the early fifties in my country. Two years before all my students had seen Costa Gavras' film on Greece, because the reviews called it the best film ever made about post-war fascism. Fascism holds an attraction for these innocents; Communism does not, hence the drop in attendance. Fascism was one of the great disgraces of their world whereas Communism, they feel, has nothing to do with them. Moreover Greece, because of the digested history they have been exposed to, is far more familiar to them than a republic whose name sounds as strange in their ears as Ruritania. And so the cheerful Wendy asked me, "Is she an actress too?"

I had told them that I knew the wife of one of the men who was executed after the trial, and Wendy had understood it in terms of show business, which was how I discovered that Costa Gavras' *Confession* was just another movie for them. In their brief lives they had seen hundreds like it. Barnaby Jones punches people's teeth out, Kojak gives the third degree, Cannon beats heads against the wall.

I despaired for those legions of students who are taught American Literature by someone from Harvard who, lecturing on the function of colour in *The Scarlet Letter,* deals only with the function of colour in *The Scarlet Letter.* I suppose for them, for all of them, it will always be just a movie. Until the fall of the Western world.

I am standing once more by the gothic window, thinking of such things instead of the symmetrical structure of *The Scarlet Letter,* on which Higgins the tight end is just reading a paper. Caught unawares by a recent philippic I delivered against plagiarism (it had to do with the paper Dianne O'Donnell copied from Quinn), Higgins interlards every sentence with a self-protective "as David Levin writes." (Looking over his shoulder, I see these qualifications were added later, in a different ink.) The main characters in the novel, as David Levin writes, symbolize The Public Sinner – Hester; the Secret Sinner – Arthur; and the Unpardonable Sinner – Chillingworth.

The tight end can scarcely carry the ball past the word "unpardonable." His voice fades and I assume he is finished. I turn around. Wendy's arm is waving in the air again. I nod, and she asks, irrelevantly, "Sir, I've heard that in Europe they used punishments just like that until quite recently. At the beginning of the century in Germany, under fascism, when someone married a Jewess, he had to wear a big JL sewn to his coat, standing for Jew Lover, just like Hester had to wear the scarlet A for Adultress."

Ah Wendy! Blessed ignorance! That unforgivable sin of trans-Atlantic civilization!

●

*July 5th, 1945*
*Kostelec*

*My Dear Dan,*
*I very much regretted not finding you at home. I was only in Prague for a day and had to return the same evening because of my deadline. The journey wasn't a complete waste, however. I found a copy of J. Fric's* Artificial Flowers *in a secondhand bookshop, something I've long wanted to have. I knew only fragments of it from some of Nezval's notes. And it is beautiful poetry: full of social commitment and at the same time modern, a little like Wolker, but very original. And not as dry as S.K. Neumann.*

> *The siren wails and great life*
> *Cannot dwell upon those miners' fate*
> *Because perhaps two billion souls*
> *Make love and hate.*

*I read the collection going back on the train, and this made up, in part at least, for the disappointment of not having had an opportunity to talk to you.*

*But above all it calmed me down after what I went through that afternoon – the real reason for my visit to Prague. As you know I edit the youth union magazine in Kostelec,* Voice of Czechoslovak Youth. *Because of this, or more precisely because of certain of my articles, they summoned me to the central office in Prague. I had no idea that I'd be "on the carpet." The first article was an editorial on Winston Churchill. I consider it an act of extreme ingratitude that he was not re-elected this year. Why, he was perhaps the only, and most certainly the most forceful, opponent of any form of compromise with Hitler. He saved England and thus he saved us too, and if you think it through to the end, he saved the Soviet Union as well – at least I cannot imagine how the Soviets could have defended themselves had England made a separate peace with Hitler, leaving the Germans in effect with a protected rear in Europe. So I wrote an article that was, I admit, rather* sentimental, called "Goodbye, Mr. Churchill." You may even have read it. And believe it or not, they told me at the central office that the article was reactionary! That Churchill was an imperialist and that his insistence on pursuing the war with Hitler had nothing whatsoever to do with humanitarian aims such as, for example, aiding the occupied nations, but purely and simply with defending the interests of the British Empire and British capitalists.

I was utterly flabbergasted. You must understand, I'm not so naive as to think that Churchill's only concern was the fate of the occupied nations. Certainly he also had the fate of the Empire at heart, and perhaps even of the capitalists too. But purely and simply? The comrade at the central office repeated it over and over again, all the time wearing an expression which said he knew absolutely everything and I absolutely nothing.

Do you know what it reminded me of, Dan? Once during the war, before they sent me to the Reich, I was walking past the sweetshop where the Kostelec branch of the Hitlerjugend had a display window. They had stuck up a poster with questions and answers on it, like a scholastic exercise. It was in German and it went: "THE IDEOLOGICAL LEADER'S QUESTION: Who is Winston Churchill? — THE HITLER YOUTH'S REPLY: Winston Churchill is the world's greatest warmonger who, in the interests of international capitalism, reaction and the Jewish plutocracy, is calling for the pursuit of a war against the New Europe and, in his hatred of National Socialism, has even entered into a pact with Bolshevism."

I feel somehow uneasy, Dan. You talked about something like that during the war, but I didn't give you much credence. I read Blok —

> a cig in his teeth, his cap cocked to one side,
> the penitentiary peering at us from his eyes.

Dan, this person, this comrade — and he called me "comrade" too, though I pointed out that I am a member of neither the Communist nor the Social Democratic Party — this person-comrade had neither a cig in his teeth, nor a cap on his head, and from his eyes peered....

I don't know, Dan. I feel almost furtive writing this to you. Then he bawled me out for an article on Rosta's paintings. Did you read it? It was basically a review of Rosta's portrait of Marie Dreslerova, which I genuinely like and believe to be beautiful in the true and full sense of the word. (You, a well-known lover of women, will not agree with me, but I think the picture is more beautiful than Marie in corpore.) But the true source of poetry, I was told by this comrade-person, is not, as I wrote, Beauty, but Class Hatred, Class War. And he recommended *that I read Wolker: "at the very bottom, poor man, I see hatred." But that is only a single poem, a single aspect of Jiri Wolker — and even here what makes it a poem is the fact that it is beautiful, not the fact that it speaks of hatred.*

*Dan, I feel rather uneasy. Perhaps my nerves have not yet recovered; after all, the war was over only yesterday. But perhaps — I hope, Dan, that you were not right!*

*Yours sincerely,*
*Jan*

●

They are sweating over a test. I'm a sadist with a soft heart. The test was unannounced, but it's on a theme that I did, after all, take up with them only last week, and there is a wealth of information about it in Coles Notes — "The Function of Colour in *The Scarlet Letter*." Of course half of them were not at the lecture. Wendy, for example. Instead of writing, she's drawing something again. I shall no doubt learn some rather piquant things about Hawthorne's notorious little colours. Irene Svensson is writing with a strict, almost erudite expression on her face. She hasn't missed a single class since the beginning of term. Vicky is chewing her pen the way the girls in the sixth form of the Kostelec grammar school used to during Mr. Bivoj's math tests. I don't know why Wendy's funny, dappled face, freckle upon freckle, attracts me. Her papers are always far more like collages than written work. On the title page of the last one, for example, she had pasted a portrait of Marilyn Monroe by Andy Warhol, reverently leaving the next page blank. I thought perhaps she had done this to separate Warhol's work from the essay by Wendy the apprentice, unworthy of such proximity. But on the following page there was merely a quotation from *The Philosophy of Composition:* "The death, then, of a beautiful woman is, unquestionably, the most poetical toppic in the world...." I corrected the spelling and turned the page. The next leaf contained a single word: LIGEIA. But it was executed in very special lettering. Wendy must have pored over the works of Arcimboldo in the library and then combined the inspiration gleaned there with the fantasy of a *Penthouse* cartoonist. "L" was a seated female nude in profile. "I" was a female frontal nude with a ginger mons (probably a self-portrait) and a melon on her head. "A" was a man and a woman, both naked, facing and propping each other up, while the man's erect organ.... I turned the page, curious to see whether Wendy's essay would be equally spicy. But the text was still not forthcoming. The Arcimboldian title was followed by a bald professorial restatement of the assignment, copied from my list of essay topics: "Choose one of Poe's stories and demonstrate how Poe applied his own theoretical postulates to the structure of stories." Again that was all. Once more I turned the page, somewhat impatiently. There was only a large Roman numeral one. I turned again. A quotation, this time my paraphrase of one of Poe's principles: "The very first sentence should contain in essence the atmosphere, the emotional content of the story and its final effect. Professor Daniel Smiricky." Beneath it was a pen drawing, with the superscription "Ligeia," of a woman's face with eyes like saucers, round but empty. The inspiration was clearly Little Orphan Annie, but in strict accordance with my formula it was obviously meant to represent the final effect of the story, for at the end of Wendy's book (it could scarcely be called a paper) I discovered a woman's face very like the first one, this time entitled "Lady Rowena," with eyes just as round and, in one of them, the portrait of Ligeia from the beginning of the volume, miniaturized by Xerox. Here Wendy was confronted with a problem: in Poe's story Ligeia does not become two persons, she merely transmigrates, but Wendy's aesthetic feeling compelled her to put something into the second eye as well. She could certainly have drawn a realistic pupil, but that would not have been interesting enough for her surrealist soul, so she put a photograph of a penguin in the eye instead. This was a case of *faute de mieux,* for later, in the office, she explained to me that it was to have been a raven but she couldn't get a photograph of a raven in time for the deadline so she used what she had at hand. In a way, this confirmed the validity of the inscription that graced the absolutely final page: FINIS CORONAT OPUS!

Between this proclamation of joy and the quotation from me on page 7 there were forty-two pages forming a series of sequences. Each was introduced by a page with a Roman numeral from II to XII, followed by a picture: an old castle (Lady Rowena's seat), a woman's face with a disgustingly distorted mouth ("some strangeness in the proportion"), a girl playing a lute that looked like an electric bass guitar, and from the lutanist's mouth a balloon bearing in exquisite but microscopic calligraphy the first stanza of "The Conqueror Worm," and so on. Each picture was followed by a page containing an excerpt from one of Poe's theoretical essays and then a page bearing a quotation from "Ligeia" to illustrate the theoretical principle. At the end of each quote there was a beautifully pointed star and at the bottom of the page, beneath a decorative line, instead of a reference to the page and edition there was a commentary on the quotation, for example: "It is clear that this introductory sentence perfectly embodies Poe's notions of tonal colouring." Or: "The macabre aesthetics expressed in the famous statement 'the death, then, of a beautiful woman is, unquestionably, the most poetical toppic in the world' could find no more pregnant object than this dreamlike portrait of Ligeia who achieved what Poe's own spouse could not." Are these intelligent commentaries Wendy's own? I experienced a strange sense of disappointment, as though the intervention of Wendy's own ideas somehow disrupted the grand unity of collage and quotation. So with my strict colleague Webster and his holy war against plagiarism in mind (I am normally too lazy for this), I spent a whole day in the library. It was a fruitful day, and in the end it satisfied my yen for a homogeneity of style, for the footnotes were quotations as well, this time unacknowledged. Even that annoyed me, for it disturbed Wendy's otherwise conscientious editorial work – but Wendy was more conscientious than I gave her credit for being. Two days later she was waiting for me outside the lecture room, and with the same expression as the girls from Kostelec used to apologize to Mr. Bivoj when "indisposition" prevented them from coming to write his tests, she gave me a page that she had "neglected to include in her paper." It was inscribed (again, after Arcimboldo, the capital "P" was a very buxom woman standing at attention in profile) POSTSCRIPT and contained a complete list of the critical sources that I had spent an entire day tracing down with only partial success.

So I could not even reproach her for plagiarism. I spent another full afternoon over the paper, while an inner struggle went on between the well-paid professor and the former fellow-traveller of surrealism. The fellow-traveller won. I awarded the paper, as thick as a small dissertation, a B on the grounds that the penguin in Lady Rowena's eye was inappropriate. Wendy was disappointed; she had expected a better mark for so much effort. I was afraid therefore that she would elect a more conventional form for her next effort. Her paper on Hawthorne was, however, not written, but created on sheets of various colours and every page carried in the upper right-hand corner a large decorative scarlet letter, cut out of silk, and sewn on with an ornamental stitch. Taken all together, these letters formed the legend: ADULTERY: VOLUNTARY SEXUAL INTERCOURSE OF A MARRIED PERSON WITH SOMEONE OTHER THAN HIS OR HER LAWFUL SPOUSE. From this, one can deduce the length of the paper.

It was also the only text the work contained. I gave her an A minus.

And while Ted Higgins is saying that, as Lelland Schubert has written, the strict symmetry of The Scarlet Letter is created by three scenes under the gallows, which begin, end and divide the novel in half, and between which, once again in strict symmetry, are three pairs of chapters in units of two and three set against each other in the mirror of a central chapter, all of which, as Lelland Schubert writes, is framed by texts that are only very loosely associated with the novel but which provide a balancing symmetry: "The Customs House" scene and the Conclusion; while Ted Higgins is telling us how Lelland Schubert writes all this, my eye falls on something that Nathaniel Hawthorne has actually written: "'Goodwives,' said a hard featured dame of fifty, 'I'll tell ye a piece of my mind. It would be greatly for the public behoof, if we women, being of mature age and church-members in good repute, should have the handling of such malefactresses as this Hester Prynne' ... 'This woman has brought shame upon us all, and ought to die. Is there no law for it?' ... cried another female, the ugliest as well as the most pitiless of these self-constituted judges."

I raise my eyes, gazing beyond the window into the white wilderness that ends in the thick black line of Lake Ontario which in winter divides the cold land from the forlorn grey sky, and my vision shifts from the outer to the inner eye and I see a long procession of the ugliest and most pitiless women, all of whom have put in one or more appearances in my own life, in roles similar to those of the women in Hawthorne's fiction. They too cried out for punishments, "harsh but just" as the phrase ran in my own country if not in Salem. Women young and old, one-legged and hunchbacked, obese and gaunt, women with horsey faces or horsey legs, and women superficially self-assured but scarred somewhere within by a freak of biochemistry or a quality of ruthlessness which, for all we know, may well be a handicap – an organic inferiority of the spirit. "She stopped me in Red Square in Moscow," I was told once, long ago, by Jana Honzlova, a singer, "and she said, 'Comrade Honzlova, get back to your hotel this very instant and change your clothes! You're supposed to be representing Czechoslovakia and here you are walking around like a floozie!' That was a reference to my skirt, which I had made myself because I had no money for a store-bought one, let alone a seamstress. I'd buttoned two huge pockets to the skirt, big enough for Marx and his *Kapital* so I wouldn't have to drag my handbag around Moscow. And she said it in Russian, like the First Secretary of the Pygmy Communist Party, because Boris was with me – he was handsome, fair-haired, Russian, and a count on top of it all. 'Do you understand, *Comrade* Honzlova?' It was all out of pure, comradely envy," said Honzlova venomously ... and from that buried stratum of memory my mind leaped forward again to Edenvale College and *The Blithedale Romance:* "... unless there be real affection in his heart, a man cannot, – such is the bad taste to which the world has brought itself, – cannot more effectually show his contempt for a brother-mortal ... than by addressing him as 'friend.' Especially does the misapplication of this phrase bring out that latent hostility which is sure to animate peculiar sects, and those who, with however generous a purpose, have sequestered themselves from the crowd." "Comrade!" cried Honzlova. "You could have made three comrades out of her and they'd have all been slobs. Even if she'd had her clothes done at Rosenbaum's, she'd still have looked like a bloated snowman!" Honzlova was bristling with indignation, although it had all happened two years before, possessed by a healthy instinctive feminine anger which,

Hawthorne would say, guides the great and warm heart intuitively to the truth about a world that is forever falsified by prettied-up words. "The bitch! If she ever tries that with me again, I'll stab her with this penknife!" From her pocket (where not only Marx with his *Kapital,* but a living Comrade Brezhnev would have fit as well) Honzlova pulled out a pocketknife. In its handle was a bathing-beauty in a suit that slowly descended, obviously a gift from a colleague back from a tour of the West for which Honzlova had not been politically approved. She waved it before my eyes. I was delighted, for I knew this Comrade Satrapova. She had once written an anonymous letter to the secretariat of the Writers' Union accusing me of sleeping with the wife of a certain Comrade Kozak, who I didn't even know existed (it later came out that Satrapova had mistaken me for someone in the Party apparatus whose wife Comrade Kozak was sleeping with). She had inadvertently written the letter on the back of a State Song and Dance Troupe letterhead on which she had roughed out a resolution condemning a play by Vratislav Blazej called *Where is the Official?* At first the resolution had been rejected by the troupe's Revolutionary Trade Union cell because the play was given a positive though not unqualified review in the Party newspaper *Rude Pravo,* but Satrapova kept the resolution for another day (it was written in general terms, and was therefore universally applicable). In the meantime the play was filmed, whereupon *Rude Pravo* attacked it for Titoism and the troupe's Revolutionary Trade Union passed a sharper version of Satrapova's original resolution. It was easy to discover who had actually written the resolution simply by asking Honzlova. The furious young woman grasped my arm and said, "Listen. D'you know Cincibus, the sound-technician? When he joined the troupe he was so green he nearly drove himself crazy at his first concert because he discovered that the mike wasn't picking up The Satrap's voice. I tell you, he tried everything to get the mike to pick up her croaking. He almost stuffed it right through the bitch's buckteeth and down her throat, but it still wouldn't register anything. He could hear the three of us, but not The Satrap. So he said, 'Jana, either my hearing is shot or it's the greatest acoustical mystery since the dawn of time. This is a brand new Shure and not only does it not pick up her voice, it doesn't pick up a thing! Your quartet sounds like a trio! What the hell's going on, Jana?' D'you understand?" That was Honzlova asking me. "I don't," I said. "Maybe she has a voice like a nightingale, so she only emits tones that other nightingales can hear and it looks like they're just opening and closing their beaks?" "You've got it!" she said. "That wallowing hippopotamus has a voice that we call in the trade a cadre supersopranino!" "What's that?" I asked, and she explained it to me, as she once had to Cincibus. The microphone did not pick up Comrade Satrapova's voice because during a live stage production her voice never emerged from her throat, for the simple reason that Comrade Satrapova could not sing a note. Yet she was chairwoman of the Party Organization in the Song and Dance Troupe and a permanent employee of the Ministry of the Interior with special qualifications for chaperoning journeys to the alien West. "And what about the trio? How can you get away with sounding like a trio when your songs are arranged for a quartet?"

"Danny, you're just a hick sax-player from the sticks without an ounce of political savvy in your bones," said Honzlova. "Isn't it obvious? Fedor Krsiak, the arranger, writes them as trios. It's a public secret that Comrade Satrapova has a voice like a dog-whistle."

Honzlova, that remarkable person whose own oral folklore was far more pungent than the folk songs she sang for a living. I thought of her and of Hawthorne; the sun came out over the flat Ontario landscape and the land sparkled like a Christmas window at Eaton's. No, people don't change and no regimes are ever entirely new. It's just that some are more powerful than others, God help us! Doesn't Hawthorne say, "Cannot you conceive that a man may wish well to the world, and struggle for its good, on some other plan than precisely that which you have laid down?" Hawthorne puts that question to a radical comrade, for whom, as for Hollingworth, "mankind ... is but another yoke of oxen, stubborn, stupid and sluggish," that must be pricked with a goad. "But are we his oxen? And what right has he to be the driver?" Yet Hawthorne was not a scientific socialist, and this quotation – which I use in the class to demonstrate to barely interested young men and women the nature of Lenin's conception of the Party as the vanguard of the working classes – would only make a Marxist-Leninist laugh. Scientific ideology is not a *contradictio in adjecto,* he would say, if he were capable of honesty. It is a method of scientifically exploiting false consciousness.

●

*May 10, 1946*
*Kostelec*

*Danny:*
*He's born, he weighs 2.2 kilos and he's going to be called David! You can't imagine how happy I am, or can you? You know everything about me, even how I felt when I finally got home and Leo was missing and I was wretched with grief and fear that they'd killed him. But that's all over now, for both of us, for all of us! Now David* IS *and you* MUST *come to the christening. Of course I'm just joking – naturally we're going to have a bris. Wanda will be there as well, and also one very distant cousin of mine who besides me is the only one left of our family, and knowing you, you'll certainly find her interesting. She's*

*nineteen, and she's just been accepted at drama school. But why am I*
*trying so hard to convince you to come? Of course you will come!*
*Because of David, so you'll be here when they perform the bris-ening.*
                            *Yours,*
                            *Becky*

•

It was becoming steadily clearer that the hearing was heading for catastrophe. Milan, in a much dry-cleaned off-the-rack suit from The National
Clothing Enterprise in Prostejov, entered the witness stand, placed his large
flat hand on the never-opened Bible, and as soon as he had completed his
first English sentence – "so help my God" – making a mistake in even so
simple a formula – I stopped hoping. And nothing in the hearing gave me
reason to start hoping again.          .

The intention of Milan's lawyer in this Canadian mini-monster trial
was to demonstrate, first, that in Czechoslovakia Milan had suffered
harassment and discrimination for his political and religious opinions and,
secondly, that if he was deported back to Czechoslovakia he would once
more face persecution, and even be in danger of losing his freedom or his
life. From the Canadian side, this was the first and last time the word "freedom" came up. Milan, on the other hand, repeated it like a mantra. The
court, it appeared, was indifferent. I listened uneasily while the man ear-
marked for deportation attempted to present himself as a victim of what
sounded like the Persecution of the Christians, and gloomily I studied the
faces of the three presiding judges. His Honour Mr. Justice Przitelczuk
seemed to offer a ray of hope. Mr. Melieux – I didn't know what to think
about him. Mrs. Braithwaite looked like one of Hawthorne's shrieking
women, and the tiny flame of optimism set alight by the gaggle of consonants in the Justice's name was stifled whenever my eye caught the large
mole on her nose. The crown attorney was scarcely thirty years old, silent
and nondescript, the only remarkable thing about him being the huge signet
ring he wore.

Milan tried as best he could. From quasi-sentences that rang like an
unfamiliar idiom, his life story could be roughly pieced together as follows:
His father was a small entrepreneur who after the Communist takeover in
February 1948 had been allowed to stay on as manager of his now nationalized business because he had joined the Communist Party. Milan had
wanted to become an electronics engineer after matriculating, but since the
university had already filled its quota of places he had to take electrical
engineering instead, and couldn't begin studying electronics until a year
later. Despite his laborious struggle to make the facts clear in a foreign

language, Milan came nowhere near looking like a Christian about to be flung to the lions. I stared at Mr. Justice Przitelczuk and thought of the defeated Bandera units fleeing from the Ukraine, then at Mr. Melieux and thought of the visit of the long-nosed general to Quebec. Milan stated that after getting his diploma he was offered an engineering position in Brno which he refused; instead, he managed to stay in Prague by finding work as head of the maintenance crew in the Hotel Flora, a job not commensurate with his university qualifications. It occurred to me that since Brno is no farther from Prague than Toronto is from Buffalo, he should at least have pointed out that the two cities were not connected by a superhighway.

The only bright spot was the witness for the defence, Mr. Newton from Ontario Place. In his confidence-inspiring business suit, he made Milan out to be the bearer of all the most venerable old-Canadian virtues. But these were not important; the essential thing was to demonstrate persecution – not that the defendant was diligent, industrious, optimistic and willing to succeed.

That was the kind of game it was. Only the potential deportee attempted to use the word "freedom" as a trump. Between those panelled walls, the word sounded old-fashioned, like something that had outlived its time. The world has moved on. The issue is no longer freedom, that absolutist ideal of eighteenth-century madmen, but the extent to which freedom may permissibly be limited. It is only beyond those limits that persecution begins. The word "persecution" has a much more modern ring to it.

And Milan obstinately clung to his defence: freedom, freedom, freedom. It fell like a seed on soil exhausted by too many harvests. I sit here now over the remnants of Mrs. Benes' dumplings and look at him, pale and not at all the optimist Mr. Newton described him to be, because he won't have a verdict for another two weeks. And I wonder whether the Quebecker Melieux and the Monarchist Braithwaite will consider freedom sufficient cause. Will they understand what it is all about? Perhaps Przitelczuk will. I think of Irene Svensson, who has become – in my course at least – a real crammer. She understood. I had asked everyone in the class to be prepared, at the next lecture, to discuss the relevance of *The Scarlet Letter* to our times. Conditioned by my own obsessions, I did not expect that Bellissimmo would find relevant the sexual prudery that still reigns – so he says – in Canada today; that Ted Higgins would find relevant the form of the novel, which, as Lelland Schubert has said, is symmetrical, or that Wendy McFarlane would admit to finding nothing relevant in the novel because she was not entirely certain what relevant meant and she had lost her dictionary. Irene Svensson, her hair a shining wave, and wearing a dark green dress with amber buttons, an orchid among the thorns of her denimed classmates, opened her book with a hand on which an amber bracelet burned with a clear flame and in an accent that was almost Oxford declared, "Page 119 in Norton's Critical Edition." And she read, "She assumed a freedom of speculation, then common enough on the other side of the Atlantic, but which our forefathers, had they known of it, would have held to be a deadlier crime than that stigmatized by the scarlet letter." She closed the book and said in the tones of a young scholar, "The editor, in a footnote, says that Hester is here displaying the characteristic qualities of a feminist heroine. But I think that this passage has a far wider validity, and that it is relevant to the present and the world in which we live. There are some countries where intellectual nonconformity is still considered a crime worse than ordinary lawlessness, not to mention sexual immorality."

She had understood. I hoped that Mr. Justice Przitelczuk would understand too, and overrule his colleagues on the bench.

•

"Have you figured something out yet?" Nadia demanded on Monday during the morning break.

"I'm working on it. It's – rather a complicated business...."

"Tell me!"

"Not till I've got it all worked out in detail, Nadia. I'll have to make a sketch."

Nadia's eyes burned in the shadow of the glossy, greased steel drill. All over the huge factory hall, people were eating their lunches, men in blue coveralls and women in everything from sweat-suits to the thick grey skirt and patched sweater that Nadia wore. A cadaverous winter morning light fell upon the assembly through windows in the roof that were painted over in blue. Nadia licked the pork dripping from her grease-stained fingers.

"First I'll have to get something turned on the lathe before...."

"Before what?"

"Before I'll be able to do it."

"You? And what about me? You gave your word I could be in on it too!"

"I don't know, Nadia. It's risky."

"Things like that is always risky."

"That's just what I'm saying."

"I'm not afraid."

"But I am!"

"So don't do it, then!" There was lightning in her eyes. Was it contempt? She was suddenly different.

"I mean I'm afraid to drag you into it."

"But it's the other way around," she said. "It's me dragging you into it. All you got to do is think it up. That's what you're a man for, isn't it?"

"Right. It's a man's business." Then I found myself echoing Prema. "It seems irresponsible to me to drag our women into it."

"Am I your woman? I got a fiancé, and you aren't him."

"That's what I mean. How about asking Franta first?"

"He wouldn't let me."

"And I should let you, is that it?"

"You got nothing to say about it one way or the other!"

The siren went, signalling the end of the break. Svestka and Hetflajs jumped up in unison behind us and began pounding the duralumin with their pneumatic hammers. The two of us remained sitting down.

"But Nadia, I'm only ...," I began, but I was interrupted by the domineering voice of Oberkontrolleur Otto Uippelt, the chief inspector for quality control. "*Na, meine Herrschaften?*"

Gently, he pointed out that we had not reacted as promptly to the siren as Svestka and Hetflajs. Nadia tried to set things right but she banged her head against the drill handle and sat back down again with her legs akimbo in their coarse woollen stockings and working boots, like someone in a Chaplin film. I jumped up too, but hit nothing, turned to the Oberkontrolleur and before I could stop myself blurted out a word that we used in the band: "Sorry!" I said, in English.

I realized at once what I'd done, but it was too late. Uippelt's eyebrows shot upwards and his pince-nez fell off – one gag on the heels of another. He glared at me with pale blue eyes. He had a close-cropped brush-cut, and a little Führer moustache that twitched in the middle of his round face. Ridiculously, the idea came to me that he looked like Babbitt. I was then reading the book, in the original.

"*Was ... haben ... Sie ... gesagt?*" Herr Uippelt asked slowly. He sounded more surprised than menacing.

Mesmerized by those little pale blue eyes, I put my other foot in it. "I'm sor – *verzeihen Sie, Herr Obermeister!*"

"*War ... das ... Englisch?*"

"*Ja, bitte. Ich ... ich....*"

"*Kommen Sie mit mir,*" he snapped and turned around. On the back of his dark grey cotton frock was the impression of a swastika that some revolutionary had chalked on the seat of his chair. I forced myself to make a nonchalant face at Nadia, but my legs felt weak. Nadia did not return my look. Her expression was one of quite ordinary terror. I thought how stupid it would be to drag this village girl into an escapade worthy of Prema. Nadia, of course, was not behaving according to the gangsters' etiquette I had learned from Prema's dog-eared copy of *The Life of Legs Diamond* and so didn't even know what a poker face was. If her fear for herself was anything like my own....

I plodded along behind the plump neck of Herr Uippelt. It occurred to me, irrelevantly, that the plumpness was caused mostly by muscle and by hairstyle, for there was hardly any fat on Uippelt. And all the time I had the distinct feeling that my sphincter muscles were about to give up. The icy panic of a mouse caught in the trap – though nothing had even happened yet. And here I was about to commit sabotage!

He led me into his glassed-in office and sat down on a desk strewn with blueprints. He made me stand.

Without even being aware of it I stood at strict attention. He stared at me like a blue-eyed suckling pig, but it wasn't his usual *geheime Staatspolizei* squint.

"'Sorry' ...," he said ponderingly. "*Warum haben Sie diesen Englischen Ausdruck benützt?*"

"I'm – I'm learning English," I replied in German. "I said it without thinking."

"*Warum lernen Sie Englisch?*"

Oh God! Why, indeed, did a citizen of the Protektorat learn English with the Reich waging a victorious war against the English-speaking world? Why not learn Italian? Or, if you like – given the way the Italians were conducting the war – why not learn Japanese?

"I – we used to take it in school. I haven't been able to forget it...."

"*Warum wollen Sie's nicht vergessen?*"

He had me cornered.

"I ... I...."

"*Na?*"

Once more the words flew involuntarily out of my mouth. The source of this next evident untruth was my teacher at the time, Mr. Katz, now probably dead. "Once you know something, no one can take it away from you."

Uippelt raised his eyebrows, set his pince-nez on his nose, and I lost my courage. Against my will, I began babbling like a quisling. "I mean – after the war we will – I mean Germany will occupy England – and then we will need to know English – *vielleicht*...."

The little blue eyes blinked and Herr Obermeister leaned towards me over the blueprints. I expected an explosion in elegant, baroque German, but Uippelt merely said in a soft, confidential voice, "Bullshit."

I thought I'd misheard. Mechanically, I searched my mind for a German word that might have a similar sound. The Obermeister went on in

English, "Don't kid me, son. You don't believe we're going to win this war."

It was scarcely possible for a whole German sentence to sound like an English one. Particularly when I had the impression that it was Wallace Beery talking.

"You" – I swallowed – "you speak English?"

"Sure I do," said Mr. Babbitt. "Ever hear of the Bund?"

"Su ..." I hesitated, but then went manfully on in English. "Sure I have."

"I was one of them," he said, and sombrely took off his pince-nez. "I've come home to the Reich. *Ich hab heim ins Reich gekehrt.*"

Did he sigh? What was he thinking? Now he gave an unmistakably genuine sigh.

"*Na gut.* Next time watch your tongue. *Sie können gehen.*"

"*Jawohl. Danke schön.*"

I almost clicked my heels together, but the Oberkontrolleur now appeared so entirely Anglo-Saxon that I overcame the urge and quickly left the glassed-in office. When I reached the large cutting machines I turned around. Herr Uippelt was still sitting motionless in his cage, staring into space. The similarity was truly striking: George F. Babbitt.

I walked around the machines and saw Nadia. She was working with unusual diligence, perhaps because Hetflajs was standing over her, worried he wouldn't get his ration of schnapps if they didn't meet the quota. My fear had vanished. I felt extraordinarily elated.

Nadia slapped the finished cross-bracket into Hetflajs' hand, Hetflajs trotted over to his machine and Nadia started working on another one. I began working as well, in a dilly-dallying sort of way. Nadia turned to me and hissed, "For the Lord's sake, Danny, what happened?"

"Hang on, Nadia," I said. "Herr Oberkontrolleur is an American."

•

Before the three judges retired to consider their case, the signet-ringed crown attorney made a final speech. It was brief, but unfortunately cogent. "Mr. Fikejz," he said, "has attempted to demonstrate that if he is deported to Czechoslovakia, charges will be laid against him and he will be imprisoned, which is sufficient grounds to show persecution on the basis of which you may, Your Honours, grant him the status of political refugee. Of course when Mr. Fikejz left Czechoslovakia, he knew that by doing so he would be breaking a law valid in that country. We, of course, may have our own opinions concerning such laws but this does nothing to alter the fact that these laws do apply in Mr. Fikejz's country, and he violated them in the full knowledge that in doing so he was committing a punishable offence. If, therefore, he is deported to Czechoslovakia and taken into custody there, it will not be persecution but merely prosecution."

The words were delivered like a bad pun. We wilted.

And so here we are again in the Benes Inn, Milan sitting over his bowl of unfinished dumplings. Dotty is caressing him with her expressionistically coloured fingers, and Mr. Benes is asking if we wouldn't like a little something sweet for our sweet-tooths. And the Vietnam draft-dodger Larry Hakim had quoted Hawthorne back at Irene Svensson in retaliation: "Of all varieties of mock-life, we have surely blundered into the very emptiest mockery, in our effort to establish the one true system." Hakim had claimed that this applied to America.

Perhaps there is something in Hawthorne's statement that does indeed apply to America. But Hakim's interpretation doesn't interest me much – I have been hardened by the Middle European climate. Can the relevance that Irene found in Hawthorne interest His Honour, Mr. Justice Melieux? Why should it?

●

*12 March, 1949*

*Ahoj Danielles,*
*Just imagine, I'm a reactionary! Of course the ideological faith-healers prognosticate recovery, and to make the prognosis come true, here I am – recovering in the brown coal mines of Kladno – a command performance, so to speak. All because of that stupid idea to write a play! Me – an artist, a realist and a soon-to-be graduate of the School of Graphic Arts! You should have stopped me, brother. But what do you know about it? For you, culture begins and ends with what comes out of a saxophone and maybe, at the most, a peeyes doo tayatra with a pretty girl in it who takes all her clothes off.*

*My peeyes was a sort of parable, the sort Venerable Father Meloun used to tell us, you remember, like the one about the Prodigal Son and the whore, the one Christ stuck up for when she was about to get stoned because I guess he liked her, and similar stories from life. I chose the one about Noah's ark – how they're building the ark and some people work on it while the rest spend all their time talking about it, checking everybody else's credentials and bumping one another off. You know what I mean. Or maybe you don't because you're not in the Party. I know you think I'm an asshole for joining the Party and not seeing right away that everything is, well, let's say a teeny bit different from what we expected, but I thought everything would be exactly as* described. So today, as a result, party members are astonished and non-party members wonder at it all. But unlike you, you cautious son-of-a-bitch, I have always been reckless and enthusiastic. Why, even during the Depression I felt sorry for the workers standing around unemployed while I walked past them on my way to Soucek's for tripe. Sometimes you went with me, but it was like you never saw them, because you always were an introverted swine. So right after the coup I joined the Party, and to this day I think it was the right thing to do, except that then I thought the Party was Greta Garbo and today I see that she has a few blemishes on her kisser. But it's only the soul-searching buggers like yourself who fall out of love again the moment a wart appears on their sweetie-pie's nose.

Now about those cosmetic faults:

The theatrical program was like dropping a moon – with two halves to it. The first was written by the actor Stovicek. It was called *Xenia Latrinovna Stolichnaya* and it was about a certain Comrade in Charge of Auxiliary Services in Public Rest Rooms or, as we would have called her in the days of the first bourgeois republic, a lavatory attendant. This particular comrade comes up with a proposal to improve the service so that better and even, perhaps, more joyful use may be made of the productive capacity of Public Rest Rooms, or what was referred to in the first bourgeois republic by the needlessly alien term "toilet" (popularly called "shithouse," from the German *Der Scheiss*). According to her proposal, all workers desirous of availing themselves of these public rest rooms for purposes of executing the Big Rest would first pay and then arrange themselves in an orderly line in front of the cubicles. When there were precisely as many workers as there were cubicles – and only then – Comrade Stolichnaya would press a button, thus setting in motion a mechanism to open all the cubicle doors at once. The workers would then enter, drop their drawers or lift their skirts as the case might be, sit down and shit (a contracted form of the colloquial paradigm "he she it"). Meanwhile, Comrade Stolichnaya would line up the next shift and take their money. When the line-up was full, she would press another button that set the flushing mechanism in motion, pause the regulation ten seconds for wiping and another ten seconds for the pulling up of drawers and the letting down of skirts, and then by pressing a third button set in motion a mechanism that opened all the doors at once. The comrades who had finished relieving themselves would exit to the left, while from the right would enter those comrades who had yet to relieve themselves, and Comrade Stolichnaya would begin lining up a third shift. For comrades who had shat themselves, either because their allotted time inside was too short *or because their wait in line was too long, Comrade Stolichnaya would have ready a clean change of underwear which she would rent out for a one-hundred-crown deposit upon presentation of a citizen's identification card.*

*As you can see, a constructive satire, so to speak.*

*Just before the première the Ministry of Culture came up with a new one: the theatre was ordered to perform the program the night before opening night in front of a group of "workers' cultural advisors."*

*When the comrade workers' cultural advisors saw the play about Comrade Xenia Latrinovna, it provoked a very pungent discussion in the rest rooms and beverage rooms during the intermission. After the intermission, they watched my socialistical-realistical parable about the toiling workers and the talking workers all building an ark for the purpose of setting off for the Promised Land.*

*As I peered into the auditorium from behind the proscenium, I began to feel like availing myself of the rest rooms. A straight case of nerves. In the final scene the toiling workers revolt against the talking workers and then they break into song (to a foxtrot rhythm):*

> *Please allow us to make a suggestion*
> *and present you a new counter-plan:*
> *that aristocrats, even the new ones,*
> *should have to lend a hand!*

*At this point one of the cultural advisors rose to his feet. He must have been very heavily working class, because during intermission in the beverage room he had smoked a pipe that reminded me of our comrade President. Anyway, he shouted out in my native dialect, "This has gone far enough!"*

*And indeed, that was as far as it went. The song froze on the lips of the comrades playing the toiling workers, while the workers' advisor clambered the steps to the stage and bellowed even louder, "This is beginning to look like a matter for the comrades from the Interior to look into."*

*I felt proud that my play had made such an impact but even so, when the comrade's intervention was over, I resorted to the rest rooms after all.*

*Then I resorted to the beverage room.*

*Fortunately I came to, not in a house of correction, but at home. Jana was applying an ice-pack to my forehead and appealing to my reason, saying I should stick to painting pictures of the First of May and tractors grazing in the meadows, and not write plays, not even constructively critical ones.*

*Now I'm deep in a field-study of our working class – and I mean deep: deep down in the mines. A book has fallen into my hands, published through the good offices of the Socialist Academy. It's called* The Life of Comrades Marx and Engels, *wherein I read that Comrade Engels had a girlfriend who worked in the factory which he ran to finance Comrade Marx's studies. So I intend my next play to be a love story about Comrade Engels and his girlfriend the factory girl. I would like to make him more human for our working class, because he seems to me somehow too marble-like.*

*Jana says that if I do it, it will be the end of everything.*

*So I don't know.*

*I suppose it's time to go with my comrades-of-the-mine to the beverage room, except that they tell political jokes and anecdotes there, and I know what I should do. Of course, I have to confess, shameful though that be, that I don't do it.*

*So I don't know what to do.*

*Advise me, Cole Man Haw Kins!*

*Except I know you'll piss on me. You take me for a fool because, in spite of it all, I believe.*

*Maybe I'm not as clever as you but you'll see that in the end I'm right, which is what you, the clever one, will see that you are not.*

*With this prophecy I take my leave of you, but not at all for ever,*

> *Yours,*
> *Vrata, playwright*

•

"The young lady will certainly have some," Mr. Benes says coaxingly to Dotty Cabicarova. "Ladies like sweet things, after all."

"And gentlemen prefer blondes!" shouts Mr. Zawynatch, throwing his arms around Dotty's plump shoulders. She is wearing a T-shirt that would have got her locked up in Prague. The front depicts a naked man, his back to the public, lying on top of a woman. He is covering most of her body but the parts of her that protrude are likewise unmistakably naked. When Dotty turns around, a naked woman is revealed on the back of the T-shirt, her back to the public. She is lying on top of a man, and the parts of him that stick out are likewise naked. Dotty has thus transformed herself into a walking advertisement for intercourse, and it has worked. The lasso has settled around its mark and our Dotty is getting married. We're celebrating the engagement, and Mr. Zawynatch orders strudel and Brazilian coffee with Cointreau for the whole table.

Mr. Benes, his head still cocked to one side, scurries off to the kitchen, past electrically back-lit painted windows glowing with a frieze of Czech geographical-historical mythology: the sacred hill Rip, Prague Castle, Karlstejn and The Last Stop of J.A. Comenius on his Journey into Exile. Mr. Benes' younger son also bustles to and fro in the atmospheric dusk, while the elder son mixes drinks at the bar and from the wall behind him a permanently installed portrait of T.G. Masaryk, founding father of the Czechoslovak Republic, presides over the restaurant in the company of more ephemeral queens and first ministers – Elizabeth II and Pierre Elliott Trudeau (Mr. Benes has brought with him to Canada the incurable Czech propensity for framed heads of state). His daughter-in-law, clad in a national costume, is dispensing beer and drinks, alternating coquettish smiles at the customers with strict glances as she keeps an eye on the work of three small Chinese bus-boys and one svelte black waitress. In the kitchen – invisible to the guests – Mrs. Benes is cooking her sauerbraten and putting apples in the strudel. The restaurant is alive with busyness and exotic food. It occurs to me that Lewis' *Work of Art* is embodied here. The relentless ascent of Mr. Benes is an exact manifestation of the American rags-to-riches story which experts claim is a myth. Perhaps it is because Mr. Benes is an immigrant and is ignorant of American legends that he has made it reality.

"They say you're a writer," says Mr. Zawynatch, interrupting my reverie.

I allow that I am.

"How'd you like to get one of your books published? It can be arranged."

Not wishing to embarrass Mr. Zawynatch, I don't tell him that Mrs. Santner has been publishing my work in Czech for three years now.

"I'd have nothing against it," I say. "Do you know a Canadian publisher?"

"I don't mean here, I mean in Prague."

"That's probably out of the question. I'm banned in Prague."

Mr. Zawynatch shakes his hands to indicate dissent and bares his teeth, a beautiful set of pearly dentures from the best dentist money can buy.

"No, no, it's not like that at all."

"What's not like that?"

"It's all just a kind of game."

"A game?"

Mr. Zawynatch lowers his voice. "Look. You know President Husak?"

I nod.

"No, you don't. He's my best friend. It's a secret, of course. We were sent down together. He got sentenced to life, I got death."

"How is it you're still alive?"

"Well, it was like this," says Mr. Zawynatch, running his fingers through his hair so that his seven massive rings leave furrows behind them. He straightens out his emerald bow-tie with its purple polka dots, that hovers like a butterfly over his vaulted chest encased within a pea-green shirt with sky-blue stripes. The shirt blooms between the wide lapels of a dinner jacket which is made of essentially pink material but, by some miracle of textile technology, glitters with a green phosphorescence. Mr. Zawynatch's cuff-links are gold, the size of a discus for juveniles, each one embossed with the bust of a buxom woman, Medusa perhaps. His small legs are thrust beneath the table, concealing canary-yellow socks and shoes that must have been purchased at an op-art exhibition or a chess tournament. They feature checks that are black and almost gold.

I am delighted to see how well matched the engaged couple are.

"When they pronounced the sentence, I knew I had nothing to lose, so I took advantage of my right to a final statement. I spoke for two whole hours. When I finished, the chairman of the tribunal was so bowled over that he commuted my sentence to two years. Gus – Gustav Husak, you know – and me got sent to the same prison, but I escaped after six months."

He looks at me to see how I'm taking this. I whistle soundlessly in admiration. Mr. Zawynatch laughs.

"So as I say, sir, I know Gus. I know him very well. Last time I was in Prague we met, secretly of course, and I have all this straight from him. He's playing a kind of game with Moscow. It won't be any problem to publish your novel."

"But my name is on the index of banned writers."

"You can publish it under another name."

I try to explain to him that the nature of my work makes that impossible.

"If I give the word to Gus, Gus will arrange it," he says with a wave of his hand. "Everything's agreed. They just present it that way to the masses, you know. Everything's completely all right. Absolutely okay."

This claim rouses Magister Maslo from his lethargy. So far he's only been pecking apathetically at his strudel. "What do you mean, 'Everything's all right'?"

"Just what I said. An agreement between America, Russia and China. Everything else is just for show."

"An agreement about what?" shouts Magister Maslo.

"An agreement, that's all."

"What agreement? What about Israel? The Middle East? What about Portugal?"

"The Jews are behind it," says Frank darkly.

"It's all arranged with the Jews, too," asserts Mr. Zawynatch. "The Jews have an agreement with the Arabs. Over the oil."

Dotty says nothing. She's stuffing herself with strudel, which she can afford to do now since she's almost wearing a wedding dress. What will it be like? Sky-blue with bright green flowers?

"But they're at war! The terrorists – "

"You mustn't be misled by appearances."

"How else should I look at it?"

"See here," said Mr. Zawynatch, placing a reassuring hand with its seven rings on Magister Maslo's nervous arm. "On the face of it, everyone's at each others' throats. But in fact nothing is happening. Everything is all right."

His idyllic world view has a distinctly tranquillizing effect on me. Not on Magister Maslo, however.

"But they're trying to kill me! Last night they fired a shot through my window!" And he points to a tiny wound on his face that has an odd resemblance to a shaving nick. "A piece of broken glass did that."

"Just relax, Mr. Maslo," says Mr. Zawynatch, smiling the smile of someone in the know. "That kind of thing, of course, is necessary. Minor incidents, assassinations, local wars, you know – small change. Otherwise the agreement couldn't be covered up. The masses have to believe that the big powers are struggling for control of the world. But *de facto* it's a rigged game. Everything is quite in order."

We are silent, overwhelmed by such a simple truth.

"But – where's the sense in it all?" sighs an appalled Magister Maslo after a pause.

"Jewish world government." Frank's voice sounds like the echo of a bad conscience.

"No, it's not that," says Mr. Zawynatch. "It's obvious."

"*What* is obvious?" Maslo explodes, almost in tears.

"Everything," says Mr. Zawynatch. He exudes the quiet certainty of a man who owns real estate and has access to private information unavailable to the masses. "Naturally governments cannot reveal this. The agreements are strictly secret. But everything is in order. Nothing is about to happen. You may rest assured of that."

And he begins to eat his strudel. A slab of freshly baked apple drops onto his striped shirt.

"Brian! Watch out! You've dribbled something on yourself again," cries Dotty. "You'll never learn to eat properly, you pig!" But she says it lovingly.

Mr. Zawynatch takes a silk handkerchief with a red maple leaf on a turquoise background out of his breast pocket and energetically wipes his shirt. The smell of sandalwood wafts round us.

●

The men's washroom was crowded as usual but nobody was sitting on the toilets. I peered through the thick clouds of smoke from home-grown tobacco and glimpsed Ponykl in the far corner. I made my way towards him but Kos caught me by the sleeve.

"Smiricky, c'mere!"

Even in the near-darkness he was easily recognizable by his spattered coveralls. His job was to spray the underside of the wings on the Messerschmitts blue, and then to stencil the German cross on. In the paint department you were supposed to wear a mask that looked like a dog muzzle over your nose, but Kos claimed you couldn't breathe with it on and he worked without one. By now his complexion had a bluish hue, and he coughed and hawked and spat blue phlegm into the urinal.

"You're a student, ain't you? Ain't you, now?" he said. "Look. We was having this argument about how big the moon is. I say it's as big as a prewar five-crown piece. Malina here says it's as big as one of them round loaves of bread."

"When it's full," said Malina, a gardener who worked in the welding section.

"Of course when it's full, stupid," said Kos. "When it's just a sliver of a thing, then it's like the sliver of a five-crowner."

"It's relative," I said. "It all depends on how far away you look at the coin or the loaf of bread. If you were to put a five-crown piece or a loaf of bread as far away from us as the moon is, you'd see bugger all."

"That shows how much you know, you fucking dodo," said Malina.

"In fact the moon is as big as a quarter of the earth."

"Don't give us that, you heifer!"

"I'm not. If you want to know how big the moon is, you have to measure it against the size of the visible sky. That means you have to draw an imaginary line across the sky and measure how much of the line the full moon covers."

They eyed me suspiciously. I looked around for Ponykl. He was just stubbing out an almost invisible butt and getting ready to leave.

"If, like you say, the moon was as big as a quarter of the earth, then it'd have to cover a quarter of the sky," declared Kos.

"Then it'd have to be four times as close as it is, maybe more," I said. "I don't know."

"You don't know fuck all anyway. It's as big as a five-crowner, and that's the end of it."

"The hell it is! If it was that small, you couldn't fucking see it, you dingo!" said Malina, coming very close to understanding the notion of relativity.

"Inspector!" called someone from the doorway. I leaped to the nearest toilet bowl, beating Kos to it, let my trousers down and sat on the filthy seat while an annoyed Kos had to push towards the door with the others who hadn't got a place. In a few seconds the room had emptied, except for the row now sitting on the bowls. Lenecek, the barber, who had on a pair of overalls, was still standing by the bowl nearest the door. His zipper had got stuck and he was struggling with it to no apparent avail. When Eisler appeared in the doorway Lenecek, instead of continuing his convincing battle with the zipper, sat down on the toilet in his overalls.

Eisler was familiar with such dodges. Modelling himself after the great Sturmbannführers, he stood over Lenecek rocking back and forth in boots that were polished to less than Sturmbannführer standards, and said with heavy Prussian irony, "*Na Lenecek, was ist das?* Are we shitting into our drawers?"

"I have the runs, sir."

"And what advantage is there in shitting into one's trousers?"

Lenecek could not come up with a logical response.

"Get up and come with me to the Betriebsleiter."

Eisler rocked back and forth once more but his stretched and shapeless boots refused to squeak, so he began strutting with a martial step along the row of toilets to see whether all the trousers were down.

He stopped at the cubicle next to me, where Ponykl was sitting. Unlike the rest of us, who had dropped our trousers around our ankles so that our winter knees gleamed out at the guard, Ponykl had pulled his trousers up over his knees and this caught Eisler's attention. He approached the bowl and leaned over. Ponykl's shirt-tail was hanging out over the bowl at the back and again there was nothing to be seen. So Eisler reached down, lifted the shirt and almost thrust his nose straight into the toilet. At that very moment Ponykl shat with a pyrotechnical flourish. Eisler jumped as though hit directly by mustard-gas.

"*Sie sind aber ein Schwein, Ponykl!*"

"I've got a bad case, sir."

Eisler stepped back and roared, "You – a bad case? I'll give you a bad case! You come here to talk anti-Reich talk!"

He gave our whole row an evil look.

"*Sie haben zehn Sekunden!* Anyone who doesn't commence shitting in ten seconds is coming with me to the Betriebsleiter!"

With a swift jerk of his arm he unveiled a Swiss wrist-watch and began counting out loud: "*Eins – zwei – drei –* "

There was a loud explosion of gases mixed with liquid matter being forced out under great pressure. Both the guard and I looked around. The already condemned Lenecek had taken advantage of the altercation with Ponykl to free the zipper and he was now sitting on the bowl with bare knees showing. Eisler rushed over to him.

"Wait, Lenecek! That doesn't count!" he roared. "It's not going to do you a bit of good. You're coming with me even if you're still shitting like a cow!" He stood over Lenecek until he had wiped himself with the first page of *Der Neue Tag* with its list of names of those fallen for Führer and Country, and ignoring the rest of us he escorted the barber off to the Betriebsleiter.

We all got up.

"Olda," I said to Ponykl. "I need something from you."

"What?"

"Can you turn me out a couple of these on the lathe?" I said, pulling out a sketch I had made the evening before. Ponykl looked it over.

"Can do," he said. "You wouldn't happen to have a cig, would you?"

Without replying I took out a packet I'd been carrying around just in case. Ponykl modestly took only one and we left the washroom which was already beginning to fill up with another shift.

●

It is snowing thickly, as befits the last day of lectures before the Christmas recess. At the bus-stop I see the familiar sealskin coat, stylized hairdo, and boots of clinging white suede. Everything is veiled by the falling snowflakes. Beside her is a figure in jeans, a denim coat, and a red wool cap, with a half-mile of scarf trailing in front and behind. Both of them are holding piles of books under their arms.

I walk up to them. "Hi. Can I give you a lift?"

Each girl takes my offer as applying to her.

"That would be great," says Irene.

"That would be very nice," says Veronika.

"Veronika Prst," I say, "meet Irene Svensson."

They grin at each other and I lead them to the parking lot. On the way I learn that Irene has had an accident, but she was not hurt. The Porsche will be repaired next week – in time for Christmas.

"Where are you going for the holidays, sir?" she asks me.

"Nowhere. What about you?"

It appears she's going to the Rocky Mountains. The Svenssons have a skiing cottage above Denver. "With your boyfriend?" I peer at yuletide Mississauga through the arcs made by the windshield wipers.

"I haven't got a boyfriend," says Irene frostily.

Both girls are sitting beside me so that the front seat is pleasantly crowded. There are two piles of books in the back.

"Where are you going, Veronika?"

"Nowhere."

"What are you going to do?" Irene asks Veronika.

"Stay at home and cry."

"You're boyfriendless too?" I ask.

"That's not the reason."

"So why?" asks Irene.

"I get homesick. Especially at Christmastime."

"I see," says Irene. The light of the night, sometimes polar bright, waxes and wanes as the wipers deal with each onslaught of snow, revealing and then obscuring Irene's knees bravely bared to the Canadian winter. Beside them is another pair of knees in denim, a small Czech flag sewn wistfully to one.

"I can't help it," says Veronika. "I always get awfully sentimental over Christmas. The last three years before ... before I came here, I was always with the band. The boys used to play rock Christmas carols, and I improvised the words – "

"Are you a singer?" Irene interrupts.

"Yes. That is, I was. Now I study English and religion and chemistry and I don't know what else."

"Why don't you sing any more?"

Veronika looks at me. I smile at her. She makes a wry face. "My English isn't good enough."

Through the arcs made by the wipers I glimpse a veranda festooned with coloured lights that blink on and off, intermittently illuminating Veronika's face, the red, green and gold bulbs announcing "MERRY XMAS."

Looking at her, I remember how I had opened the door and a rather wilted blonde had stumbled in. "I'm awfully sorry, are you Czech?" she had said.

"Yes, I am."

"Could I rest a while here?"

She had collapsed on the couch. She was all shiny – it was her Western clothes, two years out of fashion, bought on the black market in Prague for her Grand Tour to America. "Suzi Kajetanova gave me your address. She – "

And then she fainted. When I had brought her round, and got some whisky and Librium into her, she told me her preposterous story. "She ... Suzi ... tried to talk me out of it."

"Why didn't she come with you?"

"She said it was better to be a big fish in a small Czech pond than to get lost in the ocean. But the real reason is that she's terribly homesick everywhere she goes."

"So will you be."

"Maybe. But I couldn't stay there any longer."

I grinned. I knew that very few declare their true colours. Very few are bothered by ideology and ideals – other things upset them – and her story already sounded like an emigrant's tall tale. But I was a child of my country and my age and I knew that this story was not a myth, although Veronika herself was a child of the myth *des Zwanzigsten Jahrhunderts*. Her father a Jew, her mother an Aryan, a Caucasian. Simply put, the mother belonged to a race permitted by the benevolent Nuremberg laws to divorce Jews without bothersome bureaucratic delays. The mother rejected such benevolence; the father escaped the Final Solution. After the war they decided the world was safe for happiness and in 1951 they made Veronika. Later, in 1970, after the Soviet invasion, they chose not to get divorced again.

By this time Veronika was well on her way to fame – as the heroine in a musical version of a perennial piece of Czech summer-stock kitsch, *Nights at Karlstejn*. But the manager of the theatre explained to the director that organizations with an expressly ideological function such as theatre could not afford to hire children of mixed marriages for leading roles. The director lost his temper. "I'm no racist," he shouted back. "The concept of mixed marriages as defined by the Party," explained the manager patiently, "is not racial, but ideological. It simply means the marriage of two Communists, where one of the partners has been expelled from the Party and the other has failed to sue for divorce. So," he said ingratiatingly, "and I emphasize this, we are not parting with Veronika because she is a Jew, although of course that does nothing to increase her political reliability." "What do you mean?" exploded the rebellious director. But the manager was a tolerant man and went on to explain that this remark too had been ideological. Jews had been conditioned by a specific historical development and therefore they harboured, sometimes unconsciously, an incorrigible sympathy for Zionism. "You mean for their own nation, don't you!" objected the director. "How do you define 'nation'?" countered the well-coached manager, and he repeated a definition Stalin had once employed to exclude the Jews from the human community. "Considered purely historically, even Zionism is understandable. Centuries of pogroms, later the catastrophe of

Nazism – but the world situation being what it is today, Jews have become an objective obstacle on the road to – "

The director refused to listen to any more. "So I throw her out and I tell her it's because her father is an incorrigible – what? Jew? Zionist?"

"No no no," said the manager.

"But that's how they described him in *Rude Pravo!*"

"That was for the purposes of political agitation," said the manager, ever amiable. "And it was meant in *general* terms. Naturally her father is not a Zionist in any *organized* sense. Why, before the war he was even a member of the Anti-Zionist League of Czech Jews. Nevertheless, he *is* a Jew, and objectively – "

"So what then? An incorrigible Trotskyist?" the director interrupted him.

"That is too strong," said the manager. "Let's just call him a revisionist."

They got rid of Veronika for the objective Jewishness of her father. Suzi Kajetanova took her under her wing and gave her a place in her vocal backup group called *Boruvky*. Not long before, they had been called The Blueberries, but the authorities had forced them to change their name from English to Czech.

"Your English is excellent," says Irene Svensson.

"It's not good enough for rock," replies Veronika. "The audience here won't accept a singer with an accent."

I turn onto Spadina. The streets are alive with pre-Christmas bustle. There are crowds around Kensington Market. A man in a European lambskin hat is carrying an agitated carp in a net bag home for a traditional Christmas feast.

Irene says, "Would you like to come with me to the Rockies for Christmas?"

The good heart of Irene Svensson.

"There will certainly be enough of you there without me."

"There's room enough for thirty people to sleep in our cottage if necessary." "Cottage" is obviously a euphemism. "If you have a boyfriend, you can bring him along too."

"I don't have a boyfriend," says Veronika. "I'm a cast-off mistress."

"What's that?" laughs Irene.

"I had a boyfriend who ran away to Canada a year before I did," says Veronika. "But he didn't stay faithful to me."

"That doesn't have to be a reason to split up for good," says the great expert on sexual psychology Svensson. "Were you faithful to him?"

"Of course. I had an old-fashioned Czech upbringing."

"You have to be realistic about sexual relationships," Irene goes on. "You can't build a solid relationship on the basis of an unrealistic maximalism."

"I don't want anything to do with married men."

"I see," replies the expert.

But at the time it was a problem. Veronika had inquired at the post office and they had given her the address of a bungalow near High Park. The landlady answered the door, looked her up and down swiftly and told her the man she was looking for no longer lived there. Where had he moved to? Ask at the post office. They don't have any other address for him except this one, said Veronika. He didn't leave any forwarding address with me, miss. The door closed. "So I suppose I'll never see him again," she had said to me sadly and squeezed her hands between her legs.

I had an idea – inspiration, I suppose. I went to the house near High Park. The landlady obviously had instructions, and willingly gave me an address in Etobicoke. I arrived there around dusk. A brand-new subdivision of pretty little houses. The door was opened by a young woman in oversized glasses.

"Does Mr. Skvarek live here?"

"Yes, he does."

"You are – ?"

"Mrs. *Squareck*," said the young woman – Anglicizing the name – with the pride of the newly invested housewife.

I broke the news carefully to Veronika. She gritted her teeth. "And you say she was plain?" By this time we were on familiar terms. "Ugly? And with glasses?"

"Not ugly. Plain. If I meet a dozen like her in one day, I have the feeling I haven't seen a woman all day."

"So that's how he ended up, the pretty boy," Veronika said bitterly. "And in *Canada!*"

That was her epitaph for Oldrich Skvarek, and his name was never mentioned again.

"Can I invite you to our place?" Irene is saying. "My sister's showing a film and you might be interested."

"I can't," says Veronika. "I'm writing a test on Freud tomorrow."

"What's the film?" I ask.

"*Triumph of the Will.* By Leni Reefen-something."

"Maybe I will come after all, if I may," says Veronika, suddenly changing her mind.

"Sure," says Irene Svensson. "My sister says it's the first art film in the history of the cinema made by a woman."

22.6.52
Sicily

Dear Danny,

I guess you never expected to hear from me but I've got a chance to write because this buddy of mine here is leaving for Australia so he'll mail the letter from down there. Its been four years since I last seen you and a lot of stuff happened to me since. First they shoved me into a refugee camp just over the West German border near Regensburg and it was a bugger to get clear of. I didn't know anybody, didn't know any languages and couldn't locate my relatives to bail me out. When it got to be more than a year and a half and I'd just about had enough some recruiters came from the Foreign Legion so I joined up. I'm not going to write about how it was there, it was worse than in the books. We were in the Sahara and they gave us basic training for Indochina. There were six of us Czeeks all told. The training lasted for six months then we hung about for a bit and then they packed us onto boats for Indochina. On the way we stopped off in Spain and I said to myself they're not getting me to no Indochina so I jumped ship at night and swam to shore. I traded my boots and uniform to a tramp for civvies but they grabbed me anyway and I didn't know Spanish or any other language except a few dribs of French I picked up in the Legion. They got a French interpreter for me but I pretended I didn't know French either so they sent me here to Sicily to a camp for stateless persons. The place is crawling with SS men and Croatian militia and naturally they don't go around advertising it but when I found out and started arguing with them they beat me up so bad I nearly cashed in my chips. Thank God for that Latvian here who stuck up for me. He was in the German army during the war but he told me I'd have joined too if I'd been in his shoes. He's a real ass-breaker now so they don't dare touch me and also there's more of us here from the Legion including some Germans who fought in the Legion against Rommel. I put in to go to America (U.S.A.) but they didn't take me on account of my rotten teeth. So it looks like that leaves the Aussies but what the hell, anything is better than Sicily. Have to finish I'm running out of paper. I'll write you again from down under.

Your buddy,
Prema

•

"Well, anyway," says Dotty, and the seven-ringed Mr. Zawynatch covers her tiny paw with his large one. The tiny hand is also wearing a ring, with

something that looks like a scarab set in artificial amber. But her other hand
– with a wooden ring painted like a Slovakian Easter egg and a bracelet with
tinkling metal letters on silver chains – is gesticulating energetically as
though Dotty were a merchant in Kensington Market. "You know, it was
my first night downtown. I was cooped up with my mum for a week. She
had to have all the news and there was this constant stream of aunts and
cousins and nephews so it's no surprise I didn't make it into Prague until the
first weekend. That's why I dressed in my little red skirt and that T-shirt I
have, you know, the one with that naked bosom on it; come on, you've seen
me in it, haven't you?" Indeed we have – it's a T-shirt with a photograph of
naked breasts positioned precisely over Dotty's own. Mr. Zawynatch
laughs wickedly and squeezes the little hand in its captivity of rings against
the buttocks of the naked man on the front of Dotty's sweater. "Well," says
Dotty, and she doesn't mind a bit, "Prague is a very straight town and it was
just a bit daring, as you can imagine, but so what? I put a wig on too, not this
one, more like a kind of carrot-top, and I hailed a cab and drove straight
downtown. And would you believe it, right smack in front of the Hotel Jalta
I bump into Lida! You don't know her, but Lida always used to be my best
girlfriend, and now, my God! You *wouldn't* believe it! She had on exactly
the same T-shirt as me except that instead of the naked bosom, right here" –
and the little hand with the bracelet points to Dotty's own bosom, the tinkling letters flash and for an instant two letters are visible: s and h – "she
had this sort of reproduction of that famous woman, the smiling one,
what's her name? It's a famous painting. Come on, Brian, help me!"

Mr. Zawynatch says, "Painting? A smiling woman? Mona Lisa?"

"That's the one!" says Dotty, rumpling Mr. Zawynatch's hair. "Well,
you can't imagine what meeting her was like! We went straight into the
Jalta and gossiped about the living and the dead until we were blue in the
face. Then all of a sudden this guy sits down at our table!" Dotty rolls her
eyes and fluffs up her blonde Afro. "When I think back on it, I feel a bit like
Alice in Wonderland. To this day!"

"Why?" I ask, breaking into Dotty's effective pause.

"Why? Well because Lida just barely finishes introducing me and this
guy says, 'Come on over to my place. I'm giving a small party for two of my
buddies and the girls didn't show up.' Just like that! He didn't even know
me! I wanted to say no but before I could, Lida said 'Why not?' and I didn't
want to be a party-pooper. So we flagged a cab and on the way I asked Lida
if she still had her job as a nurse and she said no, she was working as an
interpreter now. Anyway, the guy was living in a house that on the outside
looked pretty ritzy but when we got inside – well, I couldn't believe what I
was seeing!" Dotty rolls her eyes again and goes on to say that the house had
wallpaper that looked like blue jeans, the latest scream, still a big novelty in

Toronto. A fireplace that big! – she spreads her arms wide and the bracelet tinkles but I can't read anything – with the sort of logs that burn with coloured flames, and Scandinavian furniture, very high tone, telephone nineteenth-century style – they sell them in Yorkville, says Dotty, very expensive, the kind with stars and stripes (her hand gesticulates and I catch a flashing C, N and U) like they had for the bicentennial. A colonial-style TV set with a remote control and a hi-fi stereo, quadraphonic beside it – all the very latest gadgets. And they played songs that were on the Top Ten a week before in the States! She looks around, then moistens her lips in a Pink Lady. No one says anything. Frank mutters something, and Mr. Zawynatch looks on proudly although this hardly seems an appropriate story for an engagement party. I have the impression, however, that Dotty is doing a precise balancing act, walking the very tightrope that Mr. Zawynatch wants her to walk, and when he sees her there he is putty in her fingers. So Dotty, cleverly stylized as an honest woman of easy virtue, sets her Pink Lady back on the table and continues:

"This guy's two buddies were sitting at the bar. And you should've seen the liquor in it! Chivas Regal, Gilbey's, Jack Daniel's, Cointreau, tequila – only the vodka was from Moscow. Well, we sat down at the bar and I took out my cigarettes and the guy who'd brought us there offered me a light – he had one of those gas lighters and as his sleeve went back I saw he had a snazzy new electronic underwater digital wrist-watch. And one of the other two said, 'I'd keep an eye on that watch if I was you, Bobby. You know how keen Korytenko is to get his paws on them. He's already boosted one from Pepik and probably from George too, so sleep with your eyes open.' I thought there was something queer going on, kind of a weird feeling, so I lean over to Lida and say under my breath, 'Lida, are these guys from any of the Western embassies?' And Lida starts to giggle and she says, 'That's a good one. Can't you tell? They're in the Secret Police.'"

●

We are sitting at the Svenssons' around an opulent table and Rosemary Svensson (née Rowentree from Tennessee, from the Bourbon Rowentrees on her father's side) is praising my excellent English – as all Canadians do out of politeness. I explain that it comes from having listened diligently to the BBC during the war. Kästrin, Irene's sister, wants to know why. She cannot understand why, during those two ancient wars, Korea and Vietnam, anyone would have listened to British radio. Rosemary, however, understands and there is a bond between us. The spirit of wartime alliance enters our conversation. "Where were you? In the army?" No. Unfortunately. I make a hazy reference to the resistance, then, in more detail, to how I was so brimming with English that I once unwittingly spoke in

English to the German Obermeister of the factory I worked in and what that led to. I want to tell her how I contributed, more or less through my own stupidity, to the war effort, but I notice the attentive look of Irene Svensson, reminding me of the scrutinizing and skeptical eyes at Edenvale College. I decide to remain silent about my improbable heroism. I will tell them, rather, how I played tenor sax in the Kostelec Dixieland band and how we swung American hits. The alliance intensifies and the suspicion disappears from Irene's eyes. "Oh yes!" cries mother Rosemary in delight. "When the deep purple falls," she begins, slipping into the melody, and I join in, "over sleepy garden walls ..." and the wartime alliance is permutated into an alliance cemented by old songs.

Mr. Svensson joins in too: "... and the stars begin to flicker in the sky...." His deep bass voice is all he has in him of music, except for the music agency he runs. The flames in the candelabra flicker like stars, real candles, real flames ... like the kind Nadia carried amid a knot of villagers through the woods down the slopes of Cerna Hora – the Black Mountain – to the midnight mass.... Rosemary, in the firm embrace of the nostalgia that inaugurates old age, is sitting at the piano and, of all songs, she starts playing "Lilli Marlene" – you mean it's a German song? She refuses to believe me. But the alliance is strong. Stimulated by the Châteauneuf-du-Pape (it reminds me of Prague and Esther, who drank the same kind of wine from a half-litre beer mug), I feel a strong sympathetic pull towards this rather angular Anglo-Saxon from Tennessee.... "Every star above," I intone, "knows the one I love, Oh Sue, sweet Sue ..." and Rosemary joins in. "Did you know that was a Czech song?" I ask in fun, but I underestimate Rosemary's American gullibility. "Oh really? I always thought...." Quickly I make up a story about how after the war, the First World War, an American Negro called Joe Turner wandered into Prague. To make it more interesting I attribute to him the authorship of the classical "Joe Turner Blues," and tell how he heard a polka called "*Zuzanka*," swung it, made up English words for it and then took it back to the States with him. "Do you know the Czech version?" asks Kästrin skeptically. I nod and begin, "*Hvezdy nad hlavou vi, ze mam jen jedinou....*" Nadia – in a thick skirt and thick stockings; in that distant primordial age on another continent in prehistoric time I sang "Sweet Sue" to her, accompanied by the whine of the drill ... she walks with a candle through the dark woods while I watch from the bushes at the edge of the path and then, from a distance, follow the knot of people from Cerna Hora to the blacked-out edge of dark Kostelec on that last Christmas eve.... I am filled with thick sentiment, as Rosemary is. "In America they sing a number of songs that were originally Czech," I continue, "they were brought over here by the emigrants. Like 'Clementine,' for example." "Sure," says Veronika. "Let's go," I say, and we start singing, Veronika naturally taking the harmony ... "*zkratka fine, Clementine.*" Rosemary laughs. "No kidding, is that a Czech song too?" Of course. Irene has understood and caught the spirit of my game. Mr. Svensson lights a cigar and listens, listens ... but not to me. To Veronika. The musical agency at work. Sigtone records. But it will come to nothing. I know. I've been in exile too long. "O, Susanna!" ... in the flow of time I get everything tangled up, that too is a long time ago, immensely long ago, and they are all dead, the Reverend Father Meloun preaches a sermon on the Infant Jesus as though he were describing a scene from a puppet play, I look at Nadia's face wrapped in a white shawl, her eyes burning like the black flames of an infernal paschal candle, riveted to the moonlike face of the Reverend Father Meloun.... "Jukebox on Saturday Night" ... "Chew Your Bubblegum" ... "*C'est si bon*" ... all Czech songs. Rosemary is astonished and surprised. Perhaps she is beginning to doubt me; her eyes are laughing.... Irene is enjoying the joke, Mr. Svensson has retreated like a squid behind a cloud of smoke. Irene says unexpectedly, "Why don't you try singing in Canada, Veronika?"

The song freezes on our lips.

"I have an accent," says Veronika unhappily, reluctantly.

"Nonsense. It can be trained. Isn't that right, Daddy?" Irene turns to her father.

From out of the cloud of smoke comes a noncommittal, "Sometimes, yes."

Irene drives her point home. "Why don't you record a demo with Veronika?"

"Well," says Mr. Svensson even more noncommittally.

"She's got as good a voice as any of your Sigtone stars. Why not give her a chance?"

"There would be problems," says Mr. Svensson.... "Ghost Riders in the Sky" ... that's Rosemary ... at the piano....

In the ferroflux room, Nadia and I daydreamed (we didn't even neck): when the pilot presses the trigger, the 20-mm Mauser cannon in the underwing gondola will spit out a few shots at the Flying Fortress, then the wings will shudder suddenly as the magazine, screwed tightly to the mounting bracket through countersunk holes that have been drilled too deep, begins to vibrate, the metal snaps, the ammunition no longer enters the breech and the cannon stops firing. The pilot will fly at the Flying Fortress, straight into the double string of lead from the tail-gunner's weapon. But his own wing cannon will be dumb, silenced by the fiendishly clever idea that I have thought up myself, an idea spawned by the courage of Nadia Jirouskova.

"What problems?" Irene wants to know.

"It's not a question of voice. You're as good as many singers on our label. But – "

"I know, the accent," Veronika interjects.

"But you've hardly got one at all," says the kindly Irene, "and a good coach...."

"Well ...," says Mr. Svensson uncertainly. I'm beginning to suspect what is behind his reluctance. Mr. Svensson knocks the ash off his quality cigar into a heart-shaped marble ashtray. "We already have a Czech group on our label, *Pro Arte Antiqua*...."

"... and they won't be able to prove anything," I said to Nadia. "The chief inspector leaves the gauge in a little box at the end of the line and I've already exchanged it for one of ours. The only one who knows about it is Ponykl, and it's in his own interest to hold his tongue. We'll simply drill all the holes about half a centimetre deeper, and if they find out about it all we know is that some saboteur secretly changed the gauges. Some unknown perpetrator."

"Unknown perpetrator," repeated Nadia with a giggle. The dime-novel expression obviously delighted her. "You worked it out real well, Danny. It's easy to tell you're a student."

She was gazing at me in admiration. I looked through the small dirty window of the ferroflux room into the plant. It was cold, and steam was rising from poorly sealed joints on the pneumatic hammer hoses. Sweatered women with iron rams pushed with all their might against the duralumin plates and from the other side men pounded the rivets with the hammers. The racket was infernal. A Messerschmitt Bf 109 appeared before my eyes, embroidered with patterns of lead ... and wreaths fashioned of those leaden pearls garlanded my heroism....

"And they'll never know why," I said flippantly. "Once we've disarmed the Krauts like that, the Americans will make short work of the planes."

"They'll blast them to smithereens!" said Nadia bloodthirstily.

"You bet they will, Nadia."

Outside the ferroflux room, Nosek began to jiggle the key lazily in the lock....

"... and there's almost nothing like that kind of music on the market here."

"So if you give a chance to an exile, the Czech government will give *Pro Arte Antiqua* to the competition, is that it?" I say.

"Exactly. Naturally I regret having to say this. But I have responsibilities to my partners. Those are the hard facts."

I look at Veronika. She is white, with rosy patches on her cheeks, like Nadia used to have. Tonight I have been overwhelmed by nostalgia, the wartime swing numbers, different responsibilities. How we are weighed in different ways. How we are always found wanting. How the world cherishes quite different values ... the only ones that remain.... E. M. Forster floats into the nostalgia of swing, nostalgia for poor Nadia. Last week I quoted him with fiery enthusiasm to a classroom of innocents with only the faintest hope that they would understand. When I peered at them over my notes I saw that Dianne, behind her *Passage to India,* was biting into a Mars Bar: "Ancient Athens made a mess – but *Antigone* stands. Renaissance Rome made a mess – but the ceiling of the Sistine Chapel got painted. James I made a mess, but *Macbeth* was born. Louis XIV – but there was *Phèdre.* Those who are, like myself, too old for Communism or too conscious of the blood to be shed before its problematic victory, turn to literature...." Not, I think, to the hard facts of Mr. Svensson, but to the fragile voice of the girl singing hard rock.... Irene begins arguing with Daddy, pinning him down with her beautiful faded eyes; Rosemary, transformed into a mother hen, tries to cluck them into reconciliation, the ordinary little flames on the expensive candles registering it all like the hands on a seismograph, candles ... flickering in the woods.... Nadia cleverly fell behind and entered the black-and-white darkness of the woods – she told them she had to "go" – and in that darkness there was I, like the Wild Huntsman, and the frosty, chapped but deeply warm kisses slid from the generous mouth of that bony girl from Black Mountain.... "Danny, I love you! I do! You're a real windsplitter." And I, who was touchy about any words that did not fit the style of swing, did not mind the old-fashioned country expression; I who was far, far from being a windsplitter at all, only someone driven through the world by those eternal forces that do not make the world go round at all but at best only complicate its hard facts ... for a while these forces knocked my fear, my guide, on its back, at least for as long as I stood with Nadia in the black woods, embracing the thin shoulders, scarcely feeling them at all through the huge wool coat. Fear did not come till that night, and it was the first but certainly not the last time I experienced it – and how often – fear from a heart of darkness, not from the Congo, but from a small, one-time kingdom in the geographical centre of Europe, that continental appendage to the great land mass of Asia – but there was only the cold skin of glowing cheeks and inside the mouth, warm, damp and safe ... then they called out to her, and she vanished with her candle into the black-and-white woods, the little flame bobbing up and down for a while longer, a will-o'-the-wisp cruelly awakened to a brief winter's flight ... very cruelly....

"I think there's been enough discussion," Rosemary announces firmly. "Let's sing some more songs!" and she starts in, too high to be able to sing the second verse: "Roll out the barrel ..." – Veronika remains silent. I join in so as not to spoil the fun – "We'll have the blues on the run...." Hardly.

Hardly in our lifetimes. Those are hard facts, hard crusts, each day closer to dust. Even Mr. Svensson joins in with his appalling bass voice. How can a concert impresario be so tone-deaf? But then kings are sometimes illiterate, and First Secretaries may sometimes even take democracy seriously. My mood does a sudden flip ... "sing out a song of good cheer...." Why not? *Dies illa* is approaching all the same. "That is a Czech song too," I say. This time I am serious. It really is.

Rosemary falls silent, as though someone had cut her off unexpectedly. She is offended. And offended by the truth, as so often happens these days, after having more or less swallowed whole an attractive pile of lies.

"That," she says stiffly, "is the song my poor daddy sang as he boarded the landing-craft on D-Day. That was the last English song he heard before he fell on the shores of France."

*Dies irae, dies illa* ... I wonder what philosophical lesson might be hidden in this battle of innocence with falsehood, a battle that is lost in the moment of truth.

A bell rings near the door. The movie must be about to begin.

●

We are all visibly startled. Dotty takes a sip of her Pink Lady. "Well," she says. "I thought I'd drop dead on the spot. You can imagine!"

We nod. The Pink Lady is finished, the seven-ringed paw of Mr. Zawynatch waves at the black waitress, flashing a turquoise the size of a miniature billiard ball. The waitress hurries off.

"I was scared stiff," Dotty continues. "Here I am, my first visit to Prague with a Canadian passport, just a week after I got rid of my Czech citizenship, and I'm sitting like a rat in a trap in a room full of Communist plainclothes policemen. And Lida says, calm as you please, that she's working for them now as an interpreter." The black waitress reappears, places a new Pink Lady in front of Dotty and a glass of Jelinek's slivovice in front of each of us, all paid for by Mr. Zawynatch. "Anyway," says Dotty, "there was nothing I could do about it, I was there, so I just said to myself there's no way I'm going to let these agents know I'm from Canada, because they obviously thought I was one of Lida's friends from work. But you can bet your life it was difficult. At one point I thought I was really up the tree. The guy who brought us there asked me if I was in the SS Youth! Well, what do you say to a question like that? Anyway, I almost blew it right there and then. I thought it was a joke, so I said no, I'm not in the SS but I'm in the sophomore SA. Lida made like she was choking on her whisky and said, 'Milena's a secretary in the Revolutionary Trade Union Movement.' So I saw right away that I'd made a blunder, but those fellows must have already been running with the wind because nobody noticed it. Well, to make a long story short, they never recognized I was from Toron'o!"

Mr. Zawynatch claps metallically. "Splendid, Milenka! First-class undercover job!" He is now entirely under the sway of his betrothed's personality. But I suspect Dotty may be pulling our legs.

"You can imagine I was looking for a fast way out of there. I could see the two at the bar were already pretty plastered and the one who brought us there was working hard to catch up. Well, just as I was trying to figure the best moment to tell them that I have an urgent date with my mum, all of a sudden he says, 'All right, let's go to it, shall we ladies?' Just like that. And fry me for an oyster! Lida stands up, pulls her T-shirt over her head and she's standing there in nothing but her bra! Can you imagine? I couldn't believe my eyes!"

Mr. Zawynatch looks around proudly. Mr. Pohorsky's mouth falls half-open. Frank frowns darkly. And without saying a word, we all raise our glasses to our lips and drink as one man.

"I was utterly shocked and who wouldn't be," continues Dotty. "But that wasn't all. Those guys jumped up and started stripping! I was even more shocked. I wanted to say something really nasty but I was so shocked I was speechless!" She stops, but continues at once. "Well, I must have blushed, because this one guy, who was standing there in nothing but his jockey shorts, says, 'What're you staring at? Don't tell me you've never had *Gruppensex* before!'"

"Did he actually say it like that – 'Gruppensex'?" I interrupt her.

"Everybody uses that word in Prague."

"Everybody?"

She gives me a hurt look and fortifies herself with the Pink Lady, annoyed at my suspicions. "Well, when he said that, I stood up," and she stands up, brushing Mr. Zawynatch's paw from her thigh, and gesticulates with both hands towards the naked man making love on her breast, "and I said, 'who do you think I am anyway, you pig!' and these three guys just stared at me in utter surprise. I turned around, crossed the room, opened the door, walked out and slammed it as hard as I could behind me – and then I began to run. Fortunately a cab was going by." We are all staring at her, and she sweeps us with an indignant look. "Well, don't you find that shocking? Can you imagine what those guys took me for?"

Her two little hands are still pointed at the scene on her T-shirt. Today her skirt is red, around her waist she is wearing a gold chain with the symbol of her sex on it, dangling directly over the spot it symbolizes. "What?" I say.

"They took me for a whore! Would you believe it?"

●

Toronto
Sept. 7, 1976

*My beloved Lida!*

*Since my return from Prague scarcely an hour has gone by when I have not thought of you. Nor can I forget your magnificent country, how contentedly the people live there and how well they are looked after. You know — we often talked about this at great length — that there are many things about this country that I really don't like. But it is my homeland and I only wish people here could have what they enjoy in your country. As soon as I got back I visited the secretariat of the Communist Party and asked to be accepted as a member. Comrade Slepidze who is head of the secretariat, promised me that they would process my application at the very next meeting. I can hardly wait till I can write you that I too am a comrade! And in fact even more so, because so far you're only a member of the Socialist Union of Youth. Of course, they have no such organization here. What they call the League of Young Socialists is a bunch of Trotskyists, half of them are Jews and I want nothing to do with them. Also I'm hardly the right age any more for a youth organization. But I'm convinced that by the time the comrades process our applications — mine in this country and yours in Prague — you too will be a member of the Party. It will certainly be no problem to transfer the membership from your Party to ours.*

*Oh Happy Day! as they sing in that popular spiritual. I'm longing for that day. Oh, my darling Liduska, you know what I mean by our happy day....*

Yours and only yours,
Booker

●

I tried to explain what little I knew about the German-American Bund to Nadia. She was appalled. "Mary, Mother of God! Did he really come back from America? To the Reich?"

"Maybe they gave him the boot."

She was speechless. The duralumin shavings cast a cold sheen on her waxy cheeks. Her large eyes glittered like two black paschal candles.

"That must've been it," she said after a while. "Not even a German would be crazy enough to come back *here* from *America*."

●

*June 15th, 1946*
*Kostelec*

Dear Dan,

*I cannot sleep, therefore I'm writing to you. I cannot sleep because I'm agitated, and because I am searching for an answer. Yet as soon as I find it a new question is always there in its place. Can one possibly go on like that* ad infinitum?

*Do you recall how I once wrote to you about the display window in the sweetshop? It's become fixed in my memory, although I sincerely desire to put it out of my mind altogether. But it's like a cancerous growth buried so deeply in the organism that it is beyond the reach of the surgeon's knife. You know that I have always argued against your skepticism, that I have always wanted to go along with what was* new *and* better *and* more *beneficial to people. You also know that my exclusive concern has always been the arts, because I believe that in the arts and sciences lies the final goal of man.*

*But the arts, after all, like all society, must seek the* new — *must seek the* better.

*Yesterday I was at an exhibition of Soviet art and some friends and I discussed it in the evening. Evening! We talked almost till morning, and I'm afraid we didn't part the best of friends.*

*Fiala defended* the show! *(Do you remember how he used to lend us Breton's manifestos during the war? How he said that our century marks the end of the realism of external forms and the only kind of art that has a right to life is surrealism, the realism of inner forms — Styrsky, Toyen, Yves Tanguy?) I thought the exhibition was simply awful. Groups of statesmen and generals rendered as though the painter had never even suspected that there had once lived a man called Rembrandt. It was just bad colour photography.*

*But so be it, I said. It's only official art, after all. Then I saw that picture, and I remembered it — it was sometime during the second year of the war with Russia, I had come home on a pass and we met at Rosta's. He had a magazine called* Signal *and in it we found a colour reproduction of a painting called "The Conquest of Sevastopol." Perhaps you recall it. The picture provoked a discussion of Nazi art, though discussion is hardly the word for it: we simply made fun of it. The fact is that we were* a priori *prejudiced against it. It was a battle scene of hand-to-hand combat between German and Russian soldiers. I remember counting seventy-three figures in all in the picture, and forty-two of them were Soviets, so they outnumbered the Germans, and there was an even more striking disproportion among the dead and wounded:*

for every wounded German there were at least five Russian casualties! In the Golden Section of the canvas stood an SS man shoving a bayonet into a Soviet soldier's stomach. All the Germans were idealized portraits of Aryan types; all the Soviets had button noses and degenerate criminal faces. Rosta was particularly amused at one detail: the Germans were clean-shaven, while the Soviets all had a three-day stubble.

Dan! You know how opposed I am to mysticism; "hypochondriacs, aesthetes, priests ... keep your mysticism to yourselves ... " and I agree with Neumann. But because I want to be honest with myself I cannot help feeling that this is not accidental, not just a coincidence....

At the Soviet exhibition yesterday there was a picture called "The Defence of Sevastopol" that seemed to me to be a copy of the one in Signal. Not a duplicate, but a copy in the sense of having an identical composition, style, technique, mood.

Except that everything was, naturally, the other way round. This time the Germans outnumbered the Russians, and there were also more dead and wounded Germans. In the Golden Section stood a Russian sailor and he was plunging his bayonet into the stomach of a man in an SS uniform. The faces of the Soviet soldiers were idealized versions of a Yeseninesque type; the faces of the Germans were almost caricatures. Dan – they were even unshaven!

At Fiala's place I finally lost my temper and asked him how he could possibly defend such an empty, idealized form of photographic realism, and he pulled Neumann out of his bookshelf: "Progress is beyond good and evil; how it affects its time depends on the organization and level society has attained ... ," and he went on to explain how the same technique and the same conception of art can have a quite opposite "social impact" (where have you heard that phrase before?), depending on whether the society is built on progressive or reactionary foundations. He left me speechless, but then I got a grip on myself and asked if he called that progress in art? And he quoted Neumann again: "Progress is everything new or transformed or returned to us, everything that proves worthwhile in more ways than it may eventually prove damaging." Nineteenth-century painting techniques, he said, can be progressive even today if they are returned to us, that is, used for progressive ends, and in the case of painting it means helping to lead people towards an understanding of the most fundamental tasks of our time. An aesthete, he said, might equate this with "destroying taste," but even were he right in the narrow, purely aesthetic sense the "damage" would be entirely balanced by the gain to society brought about by the positive influence of old techniques used for new ends.

But *what about the old Nazi category of* Entartete Kunst — *degenerate art? I asked. Fiala's answer to that was that in Nazi Germany the banning of modern tendencies in art was* reactionary *because it was done in the name of the* most reactionary *political theory. My head began to spin. And in Russia? I wanted to ask him if criticism of modern tendencies in the name of the* most progressive *political theory was* progressive. *But where, then, does that leave progress when it can clearly be anything, depending on the point of view of whatever theory something is returned to?*

*I walked home and, as usually happens, I recalled Mayakovsky, but too late:*

> I say to poets who feel guilty
> Stop scribbling your verses for the poor!
> Why, the ruling class's comprehension
> Of great art is not less than yours.

*Perhaps that could be an argument. I don't know. Fiala would only find something else in Neumann — it's awful, Dan, that for every response there's a counter-response.*

*At home I leafed through that article of Neumann's and I read:* "If we wish to act progressively, it falls to us to enhance progress in various ways, for example by enhancing democracy." *What is* "enhancing democracy"? *Is it not, for example, educating people to comprehend the new — even in art? And Neumann goes on:* "There is progress even in art: in poetry, the verse of Whitman and Verhaeren meant great progress, because it showed lyricism how to expand the richness of its form and content, and to achieve new expressiveness." *If this is so, can something that is* "returned" *straight from the easels of the SS painter or from the bourgeois salons of the nineteenth century be progressive?*

*I cannot sleep. I read in Neumann:*

> still beats
> the heart for reality, beauty, truth, fulness
> for the wonder of life and for good, for justice.
> The rest
> is literature and the past and twilight....
> a vain and profligate excavator in the shafts
> of language ...
> howling with the wolves....

*I do not believe in God, but I examine my conscience. "The wonder of life"; was there even a trace of it at that exhibition? And was not Whitman a "profligate excavator in the shafts of language"? Did not the surrealists give the sarcastic label "literature" to precisely those works which in verbal art are the equivalent of salon painting?*

*Oh Dan, answer! That display window haunts me!*

*Yours sincerely,*

*Jan*

•

The screening takes place in a large parlour on the ground floor of the Svensson residence. It is a panelled room with a view into the conservatory and the door leading to the hall is paned with beautiful glass that must be original Tiffany. Mr. Svensson has left us. Films, apart from those he finances himself, do not interest him. Rosemary said she couldn't watch it because it would remind her of her poor dead father. Through a perverse association, *Triumph of the Will* reminds me of my youth, the best years of my life. Seeing the formations of strutting troops on the screen lands me squarely back in Kostelec, a day after that midnight in the woods and Marie saying to me, "Your factory girl's a real sweetie." "She's not mine and you're a lot sweeter," I replied. "It's not that, it's just that I'm not yours," retorted Marie callously, pretending not to notice how the soldiers marching in the opposite direction were ogling her. "*Wir werden weiter marschieren, bis an das Ende der Welt,*" they sang rather wearily. "Marie," I said, "you're a monster." "But you love me all the same, Danny boy!" She laughed triumphantly and strode off haughtily away from the column of soldiers, towards the frosty light of the snow-covered town square. I look at the soldiers in formation on the screen. They appear rested, eager for conquest, not like those that marched through Kostelec. Cut to Rudolf Hess. A sweating face, the permanent shadow of dark stubble on the chin, arm sloping upwards in a magnificent exclamation point. Itzik Lewit used to sweat like that carrying cases of slivovice up from the basement. Where did he end up? At the end of the world? Irene's sister has invited to the screening some expert who teaches a course at Hunter College, ambiguously called "Women's Studies." The expert gives us brief instructions on how to look at the film. Parading SS men, horsehair plumes on staffs, a lyraphone, boots snapping up and down as if jerked by wires. In a recent interview, said the expert, Leni Riefenstahl denied ever having been a Nazi: *Triumph of the Will* is not a propaganda film, but a documentary. What it is depends on whether it is shown in a totalitarian or a democratic society. In a democratic society, it's a documentary. Therefore no one in a democratic society can reproach Leni for having made it. (I'm beginning to get an idea of what these "Women's Studies" are about.) Moreover, the expert points out, Leni said that she was a young woman at the time, and how could anyone blame her for believing in something that far more experienced men, indeed the majority of the nation, believed in? However, said the expert, *Triumph of the Will* is above all the first *art* film entirely filmed by a *woman*. Remarkable technical proficiency, the use of Eisensteinian montage, full of visual beauty.... Lines of arses stuffed into army breeches parade across the screen. They remind me of the Oberkontrolleur, Otto Uippelt, who had a pair just like that. They remind me of my youth in Kostelec. Associations – the essence of everything. Associations in time, in appearance, in theory, in the heart, omnipotent and omnipresent.

Someone twists and creaks on the chair in front of me. The luminous rectangle alive with the shadows of those now departed, in what was probably a violent and miserable death, casts ghostly light on a neatly combed head of hair. What kind of associations does the film arouse in Veronika? I recall her twice undivorced mother.

Veronika stands up, gropes about in the dark; a faint reflection from a Tiffany lamp in the hallway falls across her face. She follows it to the door and leaves the room.

The Leader and Chancellor of the Reich is speaking (why did he so mulishly insist on that bureaucratic title? Association too, probably. A poor German boy's notion of grandeur). The shot is taken from an angle that since Pudovkin's time has been associated with monumentality. A documentary, therefore, monumentalized by the technique of directors who believe in the opposite ideology. Is a monumentalized monument still a document? Perhaps I should ask the expert.

"You monster!" I shouted after Marie. "You beautiful monster!" Professor Bivoj was just walking past.

"Smiricky! At whom are you shouting like a gaucho?"

I gave the standard reply: "No one, sir."

"Then you ought to have yourself looked at, Smiricky," said Bivoj. "Speaking to oneself out loud is a symptom of a highly advanced state of absent-mindedness."

"I was just calling out to one of my classmates, sir."

Bivoj turned around. Marie could still be seen walking proudly away against the advancing column of soldiers. They were, appropriately, singing "*Lebe wohl, Erika.*"

"Does she look like a monster to you, Smiricky?" asked Bivoj.

"No sir, she doesn't."

"Then why did you call her 'monster' and add the quite illogical epithet 'beautiful' to it?"

"It was only a figure of speech, sir."

"And do you know what the technical term for that figure of speech is?"

I was stymied. He stood over me, as huge as an elephant. He taught us math.

"I'm sorry sir, I can't remember."

"Very sad," said Bivoj sadly. "A high-school graduate, and already the fundamentals have evaporated from his mind. Do you recall, by any chance, the formula for calculating the area of a sector?"

We were standing in the square, an endless column of grey soldiers filing past us in one direction, singing a medley of popular tunes, while people hurried home from church in the opposite direction. It was Christmas Day. And even though I had matriculated more than half a year ago, here was Professor Bivoj testing me in math on the town square.

Nadia passed us, escorted by her friends from Cerna Hora, and her burning eyes looked inquisitively at the enormous gentleman towering over me. She was walking arm in arm with another giant. Professor Bivoj was a mountain of flesh, a chess player and a sedentary man. Nadia's colossus was a mountain of muscle, somewhat pale after his appendectomy, but every inch a lumberjack all the same. A he-man.

So it was all up for me with Nadia too.

"What is the integral of the number three?"

The number three?

"Pointless," I said. The word had escaped my lips. Bivoj lifted his eyes in astonishment. *Lebe wohl, Erika!*

A ghastly debate follows the film, in which I do not take part. I listen, while through collective effort they unearth the intellectual aim of Leni Riefenstahl: that being to show the animal called man in all his militaristic folly, his churlish limitations and his herd mindlessness. As a beautiful young film-maker, Leni flirted with Marxism, or perhaps she only slept with Bela Balasz. If something is done well, it can have many meanings. In the covered entrance to their family residence Irene says goodbye to me.

"Did you enjoy the film?" she asks.

"How about you?"

"It was pretty interesting. A little long, though."

"I liked it a lot. All art that makes us think is valuable."

"Think?" She is curious. "What about?"

"About everything," I say. "What else is there to think about?"

"Good night," says Irene. The light from the Tiffany lamp transforms her into a Hollywood film close-up, from that era when actresses had to be beautiful and were always shot slightly out of focus to create the illusion of a corona around the head.

We remain silent, uncomprehending, although we comprehend, if anything, too well. Mr. Pohorsky chortles inappropriately and Dotty freezes him with a glance. The seven-ringed Mr. Zawynatch straightens his tie proudly.

"Imagine the gall of them! Thinking I was a whore!" says Dotty and sits down. "Next day Lida gave me a buzz at my mum's and asked if we could get together. Naturally I was anxious to know what was going on so I said sure, why not, and she came over and completely broke down in my bedroom. She confessed that she didn't have a job at all, that she didn't even work as an interpreter. She'd taken to prostitution for a living."

Once more she sweeps us with a look of innocent astonishment. Again Mr. Pohorsky chuckles imprudently, and Dotty raises her eyebrows.

"Well, and that's how I finally found out how they came to take me for a whore. It was because of Lida!"

She reaches for her drink and the tinkling letters on her bracelet come to rest on the table-top. Mr. Zawynatch begins turning the letters over; he too is curious to read the bauble's message.

What had Dotty really done before she emigrated to Canada? Why did Lida take her to that party so matter-of-factly? She must have known it wasn't going to be a sewing circle. And could Dotty and Lida's probable profession have awakened the masochistic pleasure principle in Mr. Zawynatch? But I don't mention these speculations. I don't want to spoil Dotty's chances. We all love her. We all want to see her gloriously wed to the seven-ringed owner of many stocks, bonds, lots of real estate and a large family house.

We go stiff with surprise. Mr. Zawynatch has straightened out the letters on the table and the bracelet yields its secret: THE TRUTH SHALL CONQUER.

●

I found out later what Veronika was up to. I should have had feelers to warn me to do something for the poor girl while there was still time, but I didn't. All I had was a writer's unscrupulous hunger for stories. So I merely listened to this funny girl Veronika, and her words became images in my mind. I saw the Tiffany doors from the other side, from the hall, and projected onto them by some malicious freak of optics I saw great fat arses, beautified by the *art nouveau* mosaic. The realism of the Third Reich's victorious art transformed by the green, blue and orange of Tiffany into goose-stepping cubist bullfrogs. And against that background a young man named Percy makes his appearance, named in memory of his maternal grandfather who, with the words of "The Beer Barrel Polka" on his lips, died, in the long run, for Communism. Smoking a pipe, he stares blankly at the parade of hips which the Tiffany optics have transformed from the *Paradeschritt* to the *passo romano* and from the *passo romano* to the goose-step and back to the *Paradeschritt*. All unaware, he looks at the vivid *Totentanz* flickering on the glass door-panes to the accompaniment of flutes and lyraphones, and suddenly the images slant sideways and dissolve to reveal a girl with long, meticulously brushed hair, old-fashioned tears on her pale cheeks, a traditional flower-patterned blouse under an unbuttoned denim coat, her bottom neatly enclosed in tight jeans, their cuffs trimmed with salt from the Toronto streets. Percy is astonished at the Melies-like special effect.

"Hi!" he says.

"Hi!" replies the girl, and she collapses in an armchair by the door, pulls a Kleenex out of her pocket and pats her tears dry. Shadows of the enormous arses are now parading across her hair, and vigorous male voices sing the Horst Wessel Song: "*Die Fahne hoch, die Reihen dicht geschlossen....*" The girl weeps.

"What's the matter?" inquires Percy, both moved and aroused. The girl hiccups, energetically wipes her eyes and the Kleenex comes away coloured with makeup. Percy asks, "Did the film get to you that much?"

The head shakes energetically.... *SA marschiert....* "No! It made me angry!"

"Why?" Percy has no idea who the girl is, or even who Leni Riefenstahl is. Insouciant Percy is aware of nothing, and knows less. Less than his grandfather from the Queen's Own Rifles who died to make Europe safe for Stalinism ... *mit ruhig festem Schritt....*

The girl pulls herself together, and tosses at Percy a classic "Got a cigarette?"

Percy smokes a pipe. But in a box on the coffee table there are cigarettes for Mr. Svensson's guests. Percy offers her one, lights it for her and the girl exhales a cloud of smoke in which the huge buttocks spin and whirl like dervishes.... *Kameraden, die Rotfront....*

"Never mind," says the girl. "It's just that I prefer films made by men."

"Why?" asks a surprised Percy.

"Men make films about women, that's why." By now she has regained her composure ... *und Reaktion erschossen....*

"I see that we have the same tastes. I'm Percy."

"Veronika," says the girl.

"But" – Percy examines the round face with its wide-set eyes and full lips and he is possessed by a cosmopolitan male sympathy – "but that film really got to you. You're all upset."

"I'm sorry. When someone gets excited about a Nazi film just because the Nazi wore a skirt...."

"Oh! A serious girl, are you?" says insouciant Percy with a knowledgeable air. The girl replies with mock anger, "No! I'm a funny girl!"

Percy is silenced. He stares again at the marching backsides, column upon column of them, as if blonde-haired Lenina couldn't get enough of them. Then he looks at the Tiffany doors which, he thinks, have never, ever revealed anything like this girl to him before ... *in unseren Reihen mit*....

"Did a woman really make that?"

Veronika does not reply directly. She says, "I'm a fool, because I shouldn't let politics get me going anymore. Not here in Canada anyway. But my father got tangled up in the laws laid down by those comrades." She nods towards the Tiffany doors where the black buttocks are twitching to the resounding chorus: *Kameraden, die Rotfront*.... "If you know what I mean."

"I have a vague idea," sighs Percy.

"So I'm terribly prejudiced, you see. I'm just a bundle of prejudices."

The instinct of the rutting male is aroused ... *und Reaktion erschossen*....

"Why don't we get together and talk about your prejudices sometime?"

"I'm not sure you'd enjoy hearing about them," says the girl and she vets him with a glance. Percy's clothes come from the most expensive boutique in Yorkville. Her eyes alight on the amulet hanging around his neck. She does not suspect that the peace symbol means nothing more to Percy than what it is, an accessory. It fascinates her. Her cheeks flush ... *marschieren im Geist*....

"Because I'm also prejudiced against *revolution*," and she looks sharply into Percy's innocent-infant face.

Percy does not understand that look. He does not suspect that her anger is aroused by the amulet, he does not know the amulet stands for peace, he does not know, as the girl does, that it can also stand for war if need be, a just war, for such is the nature of dialectics. Percy knows nothing of this. He does not even have an inkling.

Behind the Tiffany doors, for the third time, the *"Horst Wessel Lied"* thunders out its vigorous refrain, more rousing than ever,

> *Kameraden, die Rotfront und Reaktion erschossen,*
> *marschieren im Geist in unseren Reihen mit!*

"I don't suppose you understand German?" asks the girl.

"I'm afraid I don't. I know a little French, but no more than a little."

"I thought so. *Rotfront und Reaktion*. The Red Front and the

Reaction. Well. My mother was in some small way a victim of the former category, and my father of the latter. Fortunately, my parents didn't get shot. They were lucky. Their lives were simply made miserable, that's all. And I'd like to know what category I belong in, do you see?"

That was how she told it to me. But by that time it was all over.

•

I think of Dotty: W.W. Bellissimmo is delivering his opinions on the romantic relationship between Hester and Dimmesdale. He sharply condemns Dimmesdale, without attempting to examine his dilemma. I think of the luxurious villa in Prague that Dotty described to us, with its denim wallpaper and quadraphonic sound system, the Stolichnaya vodka from Moscow the sole representative of the world immediately outside its walls. I read: "Deep ruffs, painfully wrought bands, and gorgeously embroidered gloves, were all deemed necessary to the official state of men assuming the reins of power ... even while sumptuary laws forbade these and similar extravagances to the plebeian order." And then I see not a denim-papered room but an exhibition over a quarter of a century ago, in honour of Generalissimo Stalin's seventieth birthday. An airplane drones over night-time Prague, a red neon sign on its underbelly blinking the characters JVS 70. I see mountains of long-forgotten votive objects – embroidery work by ethnic embroiderers, Stalin's smile flashing from their handiwork instead of the traditional turtle-doves; a painting by an official state artist depicting, in the style of Dürer's *Assumption of the Virgin,* the Assumption of Stalin, his ascent attended not by saints but by symbolic figures of men and women, some with hammers, others with sickles, still others wearing eye-glasses; a T-34 tank with a gilded turret in honour of Stalin, the five-hundredth to roll off the CKD assembly line in Prague; a gingerbread heart with a coloured marzipan Stalin emblazoned upon it; Stalin as a hussar mounted on a mighty charger out of legend; and in the midst of all this national insanity, a shiny black railway saloon-car, a birthday present for Stalin, boasting its own conference salon and, on all four walls, paintings of Stalin as the focal point of four allegorical scenes; Stalin with an old woman, with Young Pioneers, with wounded soldiers and with men carrying hammers and sickles and wearing glasses. There too is Stalin's bathroom, much celebrated in the daily press, an alabaster tub with three gold taps, one for cold water, the second for hot water, and the third for perfumed water ... all for Stalin. I see Stalin as naked as a waterbaby, splashing about in lukewarm perfumed water. Oh Hawthorne, have you any idea what you wrote?

Bellissimmo, however, concludes with a stern verdict: *The Scarlet Letter,* entirely the product of its own time, has nothing to say to us today. It doesn't, he says, unilaterally condemn (in the holy enthusiasm of love,

Bellissimmo uses a phrase favoured in Communist Party Resolutions) Dimmesdale for his moral weakness, nor for his male chauvinism, allowing poor Hester to suffer while he went on hypocritically building his own career.... Bellissimmo is finished and he looks sweetly at the trombonist. I am still pondering on quadraphonia, on perfumed waters, on all those to whom I probably cannot and never will be able to say, "We be of one blood, thou and I." And then I think of George Orwell's hornless cows.

I stand up, try to begin my lecture, and I do not know where to start.

•

*August 21, 1945*
*From Kostelec*

*Dear Dan*
*I adres you with these few lines to let you know I am well and hope you are enjoying the same blesing at present. I'm getting maried. My bride is a distent cousin of mine a Slovak girl. They got a farm 17 hectares in Sofron near Kosice in Slovakia. I havent seen her yet except in a snapshot she's no beauty but I like her ok. The docters are giving me pneumotoraks and Dr Labsky says the change of air will do me good. They got cleaner air in Slovakia. Brother Olda got maried too if you heard about it. His wife's a Lithuanian chemical engineer and they got maried May 7 1945 when they first saw each other. It was love at first sight and she didn't mind that Olda stutters and is only a factory worker just like it dont bother me that my fiansay is no beauty and she's from Slovakia. His wife's a war victim says they ran away from the Germans all the way from Lithuania till May 7 when she fell in love with my brother Olda at first sight. They got maried in front of the Revolutionary National Commitee in Kostelec. My brother wanted to have you as witnes but you was with the soldiers, that was when there was still Germans in Kostelec, I seen you playing with the band on the platform on May 10 when they welcomed the Russians but by that time Olda was already maried. I couldnt go with the soldiers on account of they wouldnt take me because I already had pneumotoraks and I was spitting blood. The weding is on September 1st in Vihorka in the district of Sulirov and answer me by return of post if you can be my witnes since your an old freind. The parents would love to see you too. There's going to be food drink and all your heart desires, they got a 17 hectare farm. Let me know by return of post if you could come as a witnes. To conclude my letter with please exsept my warmest wishes and fondest memries.*

*Yours freind*
*Lojza*

•

In retrospect, it seemed to me nothing more than a rather insignificant over-
ture to fear. A platform had been erected at one end of the factory floor and
Mr. Zimmermann, the owner, was standing at a speaker's lectern from
which hung a swastika fastened to a tatty red backcloth. He was reading out
the news of the assassination in Prague of the Acting Reichsprotektor
Reinhard Heydrich. The proclamation was brief and menacing, and the factory owner, in a green herringbone suit, read it in a way that sounded neither sad nor threatening, and yet not so bland as to suggest indifference to
the fate of the Acting Reichsprotektor. The menace was provided by the
chief foreman, Ballon, who had come to the obsequies stuffed into those
classic dung-coloured riding breeches that the German military favoured.
On the sleeve of his neatly pressed shirt was a swastika, the kind worn by SA
units. When Mr. Zimmermann had finished, he turned the meeting over to
Ballon, and Ballon began haranguing us in German. His manner was that of
all such orators – the line of his ancestors and his descendants fades out
through the dimensions of time, into the past and the future, and is lost to
me in infinity. Since most workers didn't understand German, Ballon was at
a disadvantage – compared to others of his ghostly tribe – because his fiery
words had to be translated into Czech by the chief inspector, Mozol, who
although he could speak German was new to the art of interpreting. But it
didn't matter. Any language used for such purposes is internationally
comprehensible: the content, or lack of it, is interchangeable; the tone is
constant. Whether in German, Czech, Russian or the gibberish of the Great
Dictator, it always contains a threat, a threat delivered in the name of a
theoretical majority whose hard fist is about to crash down on the head of a
theoretical minority.

The others on the platform stood where they always stand (or sit) on
such occasions: in the background. The head accountant, Mr. Kleinenherr,
the only German from Kostelec in the factory management, wore a sphinx-
like expression. He was not a member of the Nazi party, perhaps because
before the war there had only been three Germans in Kostelec and one of
them was a Jew; they could scarcely have founded a party cell on that basis.
Had Mr. Kleinenherr lived twenty kilometres away in Braunau, where the
Germans were in the majority, he would likely have been a party member;
not that he would have burned for the Leader – he was a reasonable and
correct man – but when such parties ask you to join, it is difficult to refuse.
Beside him stood the three-hundred-pound Schwarz, whom the army had
rejected for obesity and because he was a specialist in Messerschmitts. He
was a dumb apolitical technologist and he wore a frown because he believed
the occasion demanded it. Dr. Seelich, the one-armed factory doctor, had

his eyes shut. He was an old lush and was probably sound asleep. Uippelt, also in riding breeches, stood with his legs apart. He wore a huge spidery swastika in his lapel and his pince-nez made him look very severe. Beside him was Gerta Ceehova, head of the personnel department, in the uniform of the BDM, the German Girls' League, for which she was somewhat too old now. She had attended the same grammar school as I had before the war but since the Occupation she had simply stopped acknowledging my existence because I was Czech. Representing my countrymen on the platform was engineer Zavis, who was sales director for the factory. He dealt exclusively with the Germans and spent most of his time travelling in the Reich, so you could call him a collaborator, though he was not a fanatic – it was just that he was indistinguishable from the Germans. And in the far corner stood the head foreman, Jerry Vachousek, wearing the deceptive expression of a village idiot.

Nadia and I watched the antics from the drilling section, and Ballon's Great Dictator gibberish reached us over the heads of Svestka and Hetflajs who were on the assembly line ahead of us. They were feigning intense interest but neither of them understood a word of German and at that distance Mozol's translation was incomprehensible anyway. A column of workers in blue overalls and sweaters stretched right up to the podium; most of them had apprenticed in textiles, hairdressing or the rubber industry, since there had been no heavy manufacturing in Kostelec before the Occupation.

Ballon's voice reached a climactic crescendo. He abruptly raised his arm and roared: "*Sieg!*"

The corpulent Schwarz, Uippelt and Gerta all shouted out "*Heil!*" Mr. Kleinenherr, Zimmermann and engineer Zavis said it half-heartedly. Dr. Seelich started and woke up. Jerry Vachousek didn't even open his mouth. Because there were only three to deliver the ritual antiphony with any verve it did not have the effect that Ballon desired. He stood a moment longer with his arm thrust forward and upward, evidently thought better of pressing the matter, turned red and as abruptly brought his arm down to his side. Those standing behind him followed suit. Mozol then called out in a raised voice:

"And now we will all sign the petition prepared here, stating that we condemn the assassination of the Acting Reichsprotektor, Obergruppenführer and General of the Waffen SS and Chief of Police, Reinhard Heydrich. Would you please come forward one by one ... and" – he wanted to finish appropriately, but he had no experience in public speaking – "and please maintain calm."

I saw the fellows up at the front of the assembly line under the podium look irresolutely at each other. "Come on now," Mozol coaxed. The gangly

Siska, a weaver by profession, walked over to the table where the petition was spread out, bent over, picked up the pen and signed it while Obermeister Ballon towered over him, the wrath of the Nibelungen in his face. Automatically the workers began to form a line. I didn't want to join in, but there was nothing I could do about it. I was not illiterate, nor did I dare show open approval of the Acting Reich Protector's assassination by refusing to sign. It could be a matter of life and death. I made a move to join the line.

"Dan!" Nadia whispered urgently behind me. "I won't sign it."

"For God's sake, don't be silly," I hissed.

"I won't sign it."

"Nadia, don't be crazy. It doesn't mean anything anyway."

"I can't do it, Dan."

But she got into line behind me and we began to shuffle forward.

"I really mean it. I can't sign it. My dad would turn over in his grave."

Absurdly, given the immediate danger, I recalled a verse from Jan's most recent letter. "Everything about them is steadfast; they are like the tree, born of the earth and the sun, and yet remaining what it is." It was a fairly accurate description of Nadia.

"I can't possibly do it, Dan, I just can't," she whispered into my ear. I glanced at the table. Between us and the petition there were now only Hetflajs, Svestka and two girls in sweaters, followed by Malina and Kos.

My God, what will I do if Nadia walks past the table without signing? Or does she intend to write in her *approval* of the assassination? What in the name of God will she try to pull off? Terrified thoughts raced through my mind, a tug of war between the fear that had us all signing that silly protest and my fear of looking like a coward in front of Nadia. Svestka had just signed and Hetflajs was ostentatiously preparing to do the same. I was sweating and my knees began to tremble when suddenly Nadia stumbled, gasped and then went limp, falling slightly against me so that I managed to catch her in my arms before she fell. Her eyes were closed. She was slumped helplessly in my arms, her face like chalk – which was the way it always was anyway – her large mouth clamped shut and her arms flopping back and forth. SA Ballon took his hands off his buttocks and said with almost offended consternation, "*Was ist das los?*"

"She's taken ill," I replied in German.

Meanwhile Vachousek had already jumped off the podium and grabbed Nadia by the legs. "Let's get her to the first-aid room, quick!" he said, and we loped across the factory with our limp load, leaving the petition far behind us. And then it hit me. What magnificence! What glory! The greatness of Nadezda Jirouskova! I held the skinny girl tightly in my arms and ran with her and Vachousek the foreman along the corridor to the yard and across the yard to the first-aid room. In the yard she opened her eyes and whispered, "There's nothing wrong with me. I just did it so I wouldn't have to sign."

She didn't have to explain.

Dr. Seelich stumbled out to the first-aid room after us, unbuttoned Nadia's sweater and the blouse beneath it; a pale blue slip appeared and Dr. Seelich stuck his one arm with a stethoscope under it.

A significant gesture. But I didn't know it at the time.

It took the one-armed doctor two hours to bring Nadia around. By that time the ritual signing was long over.

•

"What's relevant about the fact that Arthur Dimmesdale was a coward?" asks Larry Hakim, who does not and will not comprehend. "I don't understand, sir. On the one hand you say we're supposed to understand the novel in the context of the Puritan era, that means in the context of a religious ideology that's already dead, and on the other hand you claim that Dimmesdale's dilemma is relevant to now."

He's happy to have caught me in a logical trap. He senses in me a man from the far shore. At worst the students treat me with indifference because I have the reputation of being a soft marker. Perhaps they even find me mildly interesting. I am from a dictatorship, and dictatorship is a dirty word for them. But Hakim knows that it only takes the right adjective to make a dictatorship smell of roses. He must also have been taught that I am not a freedom fighter at all, but rather a revisionist, perhaps even a fascist – certainly a fascist, because a revisionist.

My heart hardens. I am ashamed. I ought to understand him, an American Arab who did not want to go to Vietnam just as I did not want to go to a concentration camp, nor later to the Gulag. He is a young man suffering from intellectual hunger, and the university establishment, grown hypertrophic with freedom, can only offer him alternatives, not clear answers. And so in the end his hunger for certainties is satisfied in the familiar soup kitchens, where he is offered not thick, nourishing volumes in which he may lose himself in a maze of footnotes, but thin brochures with brief, comprehensible, single-minded truths. Yet I too carry within me my own irrational Vietnam – and I feel an irrational distaste for this deserter.

"So you've studied Marxist dialectics, have you?" I inquire with professorial irony.

The brown eyes flash hatred. "Yes, a little."

"A little is not enough," I declare sententiously. "Otherwise you would know that the past and the present, and therefore also an understanding of *temporus actus* and *temporus presens,* are not mutually exclusive, but rather explain each other." I deliberately use Latin terms, which I otherwise avoid because I'm hardly ever sure of the proper case endings. "Open your books at page 90, if you have Norton's Critical Edition. Or just turn to the chapter entitled 'The Leech.' It's roughly in the middle."

Hakim reluctantly does what he's told. The class senses a conflict in the offing that promises to relieve the boredom and they eagerly leaf through their various editions; Wendy has forgotten her book at home and peers over the tight end's shoulders. Irene Svensson, of course, has the Norton edition and – in a grey dress with red maple leaves (another one I've never seen before) – is prepared to receive my next message. I read the message slowly and gravely:

"'Mr. Dimmesdale was a true priest, a true religionist, with the reverential sentiment largely developed, and an order of mind that impelled itself powerfully along the track of a creed, and wore its passage continually deeper with the lapse of time. In no state of society would he have been what is called a man of liberal views; it would always be essential to his peace to feel the pressure of a faith about him, supporting, while it confined him within its iron framework. Not the less, however, though with a tremulous enjoyment, did he feel the occasional relief of looking at the universe through the medium of another kind of intellect than those with which he habitually held converse. It was as if a window were thrown open, admitting a freer atmosphere into the close and stifled study.... But the air was too fresh and chill to be long breathed, with comfort. So the minister ... withdrew again within the limits of what their church defined as orthodox.'"

I read the baroquely complex, and therefore truthful and precise, passage and I am sustained by the mystical sensation that my spirit and Hawthorne's have touched, and together we are making fun of that serious-minded comrade, Mr. Hollingsworth of Brook Farm. Hakim frowns. He does not know that Hawthorne has already described him, that his youthful love of justice, "'when adopted as a profession, admitting it to be often useful by its energetic impulse to society at large, is perilous to the individual whose ruling passion, in one exclusive channel, it thus becomes. It ruins ... the heart, the rich juices of which God never meant should be pressed violently out, and distilled into alcoholic liquor, by an unnatural process, but should render life sweet, bland, and gently beneficent, and insensibly influence other hearts and other lives to the same blessed end. I see in Hollingsworth an exemplification of the most awful truth in Bunyan's book of such; – from the very gate of heaven there is a by-way to the pit!'"

Drunk on the juices of Hawthorne, I look victoriously at Hakim. "Do you understand?"

"Understand what?"

I look around the classroom. Everyone is paying attention, for a change.

"Don't you find it a rather exact description of the kind of thinking that exists in our time – thinking created by a new orthodoxy?"

"What you call new orthodoxy, sir," says Hakim, "is a scientific world view that – "

The voice of Allah. It has the power of great truths. Because they are great, they cannot stand up to microscopic examination. And apathy washes over me.

"There is no experience but experience," I say feebly. Hakim understands this as an inept reference to the religion of his ancestors. I look around the classroom. Interest is slackening off. Wendy has cajoled some bubble gum from Higgins and her freckled face is hidden behind a huge balloon. W.W. Bellissimmo and Vicky Heatherington have their heads together behind a copy of *The Scarlet Letter*. Maybe they're kissing.

Nothing, then, appears to be relevant in the tale of Hester and Arthur.

•

Nadia and I dreamed constantly of those Messerschmitts and the shower of metal from the Flying Fortresses ripping them to shreds in the air, like a hawk a sparrow, until the duralumin feathers fluttered to earth. Using the counterfeit gauges we drilled the new counter-sinks to within a tenth of a millimetre, doing it so quickly that Hetflajs and Svestka were in a sweat to keep up with us.

Next day foreman Vachousek showed up at the drills, something he never did; he stood silently behind me, watching me countersink the holes in the cross-brackets. Suddenly our dream of sabotage began to seem very silly. My hand trembled when I picked up the gauge. I measured the freshly drilled counter-sink: precise to within a tenth of a millimetre. I felt ill. Vachousek reached over, took the gauge out of my hand and examined it closely.

"Where'd you get this?" he asked.

"I – from the stores."

"You're lying!"

"No, I'm not!"

Though I tried my best, not even the Venerable Father Meloun would have believed me, the way I said it.

"Come with me."

He turned around and walked away. I followed. All along the assembly line I could see our cross-brackets already riveted to the duralumin panels, which themselves would later be riveted to the wings of the Messerschmitts, looking for all the world like an endless Golgotha. They couldn't be taken off now unless thousands of rivets were drilled out, and then what about the ruined brackets? The fellows on the assembly line looked like Roman legionnaires. At the final position on the line the gangly Siska stood with a screwdriver poised in his hand. On the table in front of him was a duralumin panel and the magazine drum of the Messerschmitt's auxiliary cannon. He was waiting for us.

He stopped and the foreman said to me, "Look at this." And to Siska, "Okay, Tonda, show him."

I knew what I would see. The retrained textile worker set his screwdriver in place and tightened the screw into the counter-sink with his mechanical screwdriver. Then he unscrewed it and held up the drum.

"Take a look!"

All you could say was that our idea had been a good one. Technically good, that is: there were tiny cracks in the metal of the drum.

"Come along," said the foreman.

Once again I walked after him. Later, of course, I thought of all the flaws in our story that I should have thought of earlier but didn't because I was playing the bold avenger for Nadia. An unknown perpetrator switching the gauges on me – the Gestapo was supposed to believe that? What a dumb fool I was! And even if they did believe me, since when had the Gestapo worried about such niceties? They would arrest the nearest fool and break his back in a swinging door.

I was shaking almost uncontrollably, but when we reached the foreman's glassed-in office I became bold once more.

"It was handed out to us yesterday morning, honest."

The foreman measured me with tired eyes. He sighed. "Look, student, don't try and pull that one on me. You may know Latin, but you haven't got a clue when it comes to the technical regulations. Show me the stamp on this gauge."

He rotated the gauge he had taken from me in front of my eyes. It was a shiny little object, identical to the factory-issue gauges, which Ponykl had turned out for two cigarettes (he took another one when he'd finished the work) and national solidarity. No one had checked our gauges before and it had never occurred to me that they would ever do so.

"I guess" – I swallowed and almost choked on my own saliva. My oesophagus felt like a drinking straw – "I guess somebody must have slipped it on me...."

"And Nadia Jirouskova had one slipped on her too?"

"Her too?"

"Must have been the Scarlet Pimpernel, eh?"

I didn't know what to say. The foreman stared silently into my eyes, as Professor Bivoj used to do when he failed me in math. Fool that I was, I had forgotten that a German factory is not a grammar school. And it was too late. My neck was already in the noose.

"Look here, student," said the foreman. "Whatever you do in this world, you've got to do it proper. And that goes for sabotage."

He must have seen how I was trembling. Perhaps he was even beginning to feel sorry for me. "Not that you didn't figure it out proper," he said. "Technically speaking." He took an ammunition drum from among the blueprints and tools strewn on the table. "This will drop off like a ripe pear as soon as the cannon starts firing. But before a single shot is fired, it goes through a bunch of different inspections, and then they give it a bench test. So even if your abortion did manage to pass all the factory inspections, it'd never make it past the bench. And what's the outcome of all this sabotage, you muttonhead, when the drum flies off during the test?"

I said nothing.

"You don't know, eh? Don't play ignorant with me. It'll cost the Reich a few lousy hours of lost work and a couple of hundred in ruined material. About the same as if a platoon field-kitchen gets a direct hit at the front. I imagine the Reich could take the loss without too much strain."

I still said nothing. For purely physiological reasons, I couldn't have spoken anyway.

"Oh, and there's something else will happen," said Vachousek. "They'll hang you."

For the first time in my life everything went dark before my eyes. I felt faint.

"So what are you going to do?"

"Maybe ...," I said haltingly, overcoming the cramp in my throat, "I could run away and – hide – with someone...."

"And leave Nadia Jirouskova to face the music, eh?" The foreman looked at me with contempt. "The great boy scout! When you disappear, the Gestapo will grab her. Just for revenge. And me too probably. Any hero who leaves other people floundering in the shit," he said, echoing Dr. Labsky, "is no hero by me – he's worse than a damned moron. And here you want to go and jump into some other poor slob's lap so when they do nab you, they'll string up you and the Good Samaritan."

"So – what should I do then, sir?"

The foreman picked up the drum and ran his fingernail up and down the metal grooves. "I reckon there's two things you can do. Both are risky. One's a risk to yourself, the other's a risk to more people. Which is it going to be, hero?"

I lost my nerve. "Mr. Vachousek, wouldn't – couldn't...."

"What?"

"Somehow, I don't know, but...."

"I take it you want to spread the risk around."

"No, not that, but...."

"There's no third way."

My teeth were chattering. The foreman heard them.

"Now that I look at it," he said, "there's really only one way. I can't have children on my conscience, not even when they do some damn fool thing only a snotty-nosed brat would try."

The words were balm to my fears, a tiny light in the dark panic into which I was sinking deeper and deeper.

"The first way would be to admit it upstairs and then try and convince them it was just your stupidity. In other words, stay close to the truth. Badly trained mechanical half-wit with two left hands, couldn't get it through his thick student's skull what a counter-sink's for. But are the Nazis going to swallow that? Eh? What do you think?"

I shook my head.

"The other thing," said the foreman thoughtfully, speaking more to himself than to me, "is to unfasten all the brackets. Too late to throw 'em out, there's too many already. That means we have to weld up all the counter-sinks and drill them over again."

"I'll do it!"

"Don't piss me off, student!" snapped the foreman. "Lucky for you the men slack off a lot, so the quotas are soft. If they get moving they can crack off a lot more in a regular shift than normal. Of course there's a couple of risks here. Ballon's a dope; he's satisfied if he sees everybody's busy. But we've got to figure a way to keep Uippelt from noticing. And in the second place, I've no idea what's going to happen to those re-drilled brackets when they start shooting. You know what calibre that cannon is, smart boy? Know what the recoil's like?"

Dumb, I merely shook my head.

"But I figure there's no way around that one. Here's two gauges. Bring me that other phoney one from Jirouskova. And drill like the devil, boy. You'll have to get it all done in the regular shift. Now piss off!"

He stared at me again with a mixture of pity and disdain. "And don't shit yourself in my office. Clear out!"

I almost ran back to Nadia. She had been watching for me, clearly terrified as well.

"Is Vachousek on to it?"

Her glowing eyes were bigger than usual.

"Y-yes."

I made a mighty effort to assume a mask of cool indifference. But the nerves in my face twitched, and I had to lean against the drill for support.

"Mother of Jesus!" said Nadia.

"There's hell to p-pay," I stuttered. "Here's the proper gauge. We've got to start using it again."

She grasped my hand and whispered, "Is he going to report it?"

"No. But he said if something isn't done about it, the – the Germans'll find out about it for sure."

Nadia held my hand, then suddenly dropped it, took the handle of the drill and started boring a counter-sink.

"Dan," she said quietly, "if they find out about this, I'm taking the blame on myself."

"What're you talking about?" I had mastered myself somewhat by this time and was slowly slipping back into the role of hero. "In the first place it was my idea, and in the second place it's ... you...." How was I to say it? That I simply couldn't let a girl take the rap for me? Once again dime-novel ethics were getting mixed up in the raw reality of the Protectorate of Böhmen und Mähren.

"I made you do it," she said.

"No, you didn't."

"Yes, I did. In your kitchen, remember? I said I just had to get revenge for my father. Then you came up with this plan. On account of me."

"You only – inspired me, Nadia."

Meanwhile SA Ballon had come on the assembly line and both of us busily set about drilling counter-sinks into the cross-brackets. Ballon came over to us, stopped beside Nadia, picked up one cross-bracket – one with sabotaged counter-sinks – turned it over a few times and then put it back. He didn't understand a thing about it.

"*Na, wie geht's?*" he asked Nadia. "*Fühlen Sie sich schon besser?*"

Nadia squinted at me. She couldn't understand German.

"*Sie versteht nicht, Herr Obermeister.*"

"*Also übersetzen Sie doch!*"

"He wants to know if you're feeling better," I said. She looked at the SA man, and her beautiful mouth widened into an insincere smile.

"*Ja,*" she said.

"*Na gut,*" said Ballon. "*Das freut mich. Was war das mit ihnen eigentlich?*"

"What was the trouble?" I translated.

"*Ich habe Tuberkulose,*" said Nadia.

Ballon raised his eyebrows. "*Was? Weisst das der Betriebsarzt? Kurieren Sie sich?*"

Nadia understood that he was asking if she was having it properly looked after. "*Ja, ich kurieren sich,*" she said.

SA Ballon clearly did not know whether to probe further into the state of his slave's health or simply pass her on to Dr. Seelich. He decided on the latter course.

"*Es wird schon gut. Nach dem Kriege wird man Sie in die Schweiz schicken. Ins Sanatorium.*"

Grinning like the *Triumph of Death* by Hieronymus Bosch, he gave the back-to-work order and left.

I turned to Nadia. "Why did you tell him you've got TB?"

"I couldn't say I was just pretending, could I?"

It struck me, all of a sudden, that she might be telling the truth. After all, she was almost a skeleton. I began to be afraid for her – oddly enough, for the first time. When I had been with Vachousek I had been terrified only for myself. Nadia had never once crossed my mind.

"What was that you said? That I – what was it?"

"Inspired me. I would have done something anyway. But you inspired me with the idea."

"You'd never've done it if I hadn't put you up to it."

Her words went through me like an electric shock.

"How do you know I wouldn't?"

"Because you got no reason to. The Germans let your dad go."

"But I – I still hate them."

"I know you do. But they didn't kill nobody close to you."

Was Nadia thinking purely in terms of a personal revenge? I found it strange. They didn't kill anyone close to me. Yet.... I thought of Rebecca. Strictly speaking she wasn't mine, in fact I hadn't even touched her unless you counted that one time, but we were just little kids then. I'd never even gone out with her. We were friends, I liked her, but she wasn't the only one I liked by far.

Rebecca was now in Terezin.

Against my will I said, "They killed Rebecca."

Nadia was taken aback. "You mean that beautiful girl in the cup?"

It was too late to recant. "Yes."

Nadia was silent for a moment, then said, "Even so, if I hadn't have, you know, you wouldn't have done nothing on account of her."

I don't know, perhaps I was sincere in trying to discourage Nadia from taking everything upon herself, but ... more probably it was the Hollywood in me. *Machismo.* The Kostelec version of the gentleman's code of honour. "I've already done something. You remember that gas dump?"

"Was that ... was that *you*, Danny?"

The painful uneasiness of a lie, because it was not me. "I – I didn't exactly blow it up. But I was in on it. I helped...."

That, at least, was basically true.

"Dan!"

For a long time she looked at me, then she dropped her eyes and began drilling.

"There, you see," I said. "I'm in it up to my neck anyway. It would be silly, if nothing else, to drag you in too."

She kept on drilling. Hetflajs came up and took an armful of cross-brackets – the one that Ballon had looked at, and others that were true to specification.

"Come on, get on with it, kids," he said nervously. "We've got fifteen more to do before the whistle."

He went off with his spoils. Foreman Vachousek had just arrived at their position on the line and I watched him take the cross-brackets, measure the counter-sinks, take one cross-bracket out, give the rest to Hetflajs and then say something to him. Then he walked away, with Hetflajs staring after him like an idiot. My God, he couldn't have let those fools in on it!

But I was the fool.

I glanced at Nadia. She was bending over a cross-bracket and tears were running from her eyes. She realized I was watching her and she turned those big, burning eyes on me.

"Dan, I want to be in it with you! And anyway I...."

"What, Nadia?"

"Nothing. I'm in it with you anyway. If they catch on to it, the Germans'll take everybody who worked on it. It's all the same to them."

Once again she was right.

•

Outside the gothic windows a melancholy snow is falling. I see hatred in the depths of Hakim's eyes. I look down at Hawthorne's book and slide my glance along the black lines of print: "When an uninstructed multitude attempts to see with its eyes," – I see Veronika in a spring dress, standing in a crowd on the Old Town Square of Prague – "it is exceedingly apt to be deceived. When, however, it forms its judgement, as it usually does, on the intuitions of its great and warm heart," – I see Veronika in a mob that is stoning squat tanks – "the conclusions thus attained are often so profound and so unerring, as to possess the character of truths supernaturally revealed."

I look up from the book. In Hakim's eyes I see the scorn the men of the future hold for the men of yesterday, men to whom today still provides a brief respite before they are branded the betrayers of Hakim's tomorrows. "Steer clear of the jugglers of concepts and feelings as carefully as you would avoid leprosy and the plague." Jan's poem, ruminated upon a thousand times. The classroom becomes uneasy. There is a pounding of feet in the corridors: eleven o'clock. Only Irene, in her grey dress with the red maple leaves, sits still, looking into her book, searching it for the key to the mystery of my soul.

I pronounce the formula: Class dismissed!

They all fly away.

Hakim slowly packs up his books – the muscular, swarthy young warrior who avoided a war because he did not believe in it, not because he was a coward. Hakim. I cannot imagine him destroyed by fear.

Associations are everything. That fatal Sunday afternoon long years ago returns. I shake my head, my eyes fall once more on the Gospel according to Nathaniel. "Is there no virtue ... save what springs from a wholesome fear of the gallows?" Should I perhaps point this Leninist *bon mot* out to Hakim? Speak to him of goose-flesh justice? He would not understand. How could he? He has, after all, "that beautiful detachment and devotion to stern justice of men dealing in death without being in any danger of it." He is not yet living in the empire to the east, in the kingdom of Mao or Fidel – or whatever other comic-book paradise he believes in. He does not know of the only final solution to the social problem, the one that Sinclair Lewis knew about. That there is no such solution.

Now I'm alone in the classroom. Irene too has left. Students are already beginning to drift in for McMountain's seminar on the Pre-Raphaelites.

If only one could say: Class dismissed! In the miserable school of life, where there is no curriculum, that is impossible.

And the snow is falling on the flat Ontario countryside. On the white expanse the Edenvale raven struts gravely, omnipresent, pecking for food.

●

*Toronto*
*Sept. 10, 1976*

*My darling Lida:*
*Last night I dreamed about you. You were lying naked on the red blanket –* REMEMBER? *– and I was lying beside you, but at the same time I could see us both from above, as one only can in dreams. And I felt your warm, moist body against my hot skin. We were like a beautiful domino. We are both young, Lida, beautiful, healthy and progressive. The whole future lies before us: personally, and for our countries and our people. Will it not be symbolic when we two marry? I only hope it may be soon. Don't worry, I understand that the comrades in your country must be careful when a Czech girl wishes to marry a Canadian. Often, the young Czech wives of Canadian citizens here become indifferent to socialism and social justice, because they don't*

*understand that the standard of living is so high here because Canada exploits the Third World. But you are different and anyway, as my wife, you will never be able to ignore our responsibility as comrades. I, who was born in imperialist Canada, can never ignore it. So, although I would be overjoyed if your country granted our request as soon as possible, I can understand why they are careful about permitting anyone to marry a foreigner. I can hardly wait for you, darling. Your hair, your mouth, your breasts, your....*

*Last week here in Toronto I attended a meeting where the representative of the PLO, Comrade Arafat, spoke. The fascist Zionist stormtroopers came as well and made so much noise that Arafat could scarcely speak! This is how the local imperialists conceive of freedom of expression! Finally there was a scuffle between us democrats and the Zionist hooligans and I have to admit that I could not hold myself back and punched a Jew's nose in. You know I was a welter-weight boxer in school and I also played football – not soccer, American football. So there aren't many that can get the better of me! The public was, fortunately, mostly on our side. Even in Canada people are beginning to realize where the truth lies.*

*I think of you constantly and in my mind I can already see myself in the Matrimonial Hall of the Old Town Hall in Prague – with you!*

*It certainly won't be long now – I firmly believe that.*

*I kiss you all over.*

> *Your*
> *Booker*

# CHAPTER THREE

... into my heart a tear drops, knowing well
the sea is greater than the land,
but in my heart, suddenly, profoundly, there comes to life
        again –
long-forgotten, dead for half an age –
a simple girl....

VLADIMIR HOLAN

Tragedy is simple, but comedy is complex because it touches human life in far more places than tragedy.

MADAME DE STAEL

●

# Twain

**V**icky protests. She takes *The Mysterious Stranger* literally. Life is not a dream, "a vagrant thought, a useless thought, a homeless thought, wandering forlorn among the empty eternities." Life has meaning. We are alive. We are more than mere thoughts. Sharon asks her what the meaning of life *is,* then. W.W. Bellissimmo hastens to Vicky's aid: Life itself! We live for life. But what does "living for life" mean, Sharon wants to know. The brown Indian girl Jenny Razadharamithan, who drifts into my seminars only very occasionally, says something in an English I cannot understand (and I don't think anyone else in the classroom can either), something that sounds like "life is a number." There follows a meditative silence (or perhaps they are only bewildered) before Wendy puts up her hand and says that the meaning of life is doing something that brings us pleasure. Vicky agrees, so does Bellissimmo. Sharon objects. Most people, she says, have to do things they don't really enjoy just to make a living. Silence again, broken this time by Higgins, the football player. There is one thing he doesn't understand – Mark Twain claimed that only thought exists, but *who,* Higgins asks, flattered by his own prowess, is *thinking* that thought? I let costly time pass, enjoying this discussion instead of earning my keep and leading the little children out of the age-old labyrinth of youth. Of Western youth, I correct myself. The closely watched pedagogues of Europe do not allow their charges to err. Where would I lead them were I an Eastern pedagogue?

I ransack my mind for memories of my own salad days. Perhaps the intensity of this quest for something that no one can ever find because it does not exist is the same in all ages and all systems. Fortunately most people soon lose interest in finding an answer. But if I were living in the East –

Hakim raises his hand and assumes my role as Eastern pedagogue. The social system must be changed, he states, so that each will, according to his abilities, be able to become fully capable of self-realization.

Dianne, the pragmatist, is unimpressed. "Okay," she says, "but even if everybody was capable of self-realization, what would the meaning of life be?"

Unfortunately no one has an answer. There is not a single religious soul in the classroom.

"Life *itself!*" Bellissimmo reiterates like a challenge. "We have to live it to the *full* ... the full and...."

"And usefully," says Vicky.

Should I stand up? Should I say: The purpose of life is to contribute to the rational organization of the world with all one's strength? So that the world will not be a picturesque jungle like America but a picturesque and ordered polity like – oh, I don't know what. Like a stained-glass window? Most of the time stained-glass windows merely depict the martyrdom of saints. Like a spectacle of mass gymnastics, thousands of boys and girls with hula hoops and medicine balls, ranked on a huge playing-field, dipping and swaying in unison to a single command? But who knows what those boys and girls are thinking? Perhaps getting to the toilet is really uppermost in their minds. Should I tell them to organize the world in order to eradicate, as far as possible....

Why don't I tell them?

I stop listening to the discussion and open the book at random. I have a vague belief in omens, as Nadia Jirouskova did. So, again at random, I place my finger on a line:

"'A stranger came next.... And he asked if what she confessed was true, and she said no.... She snuggled closer to the fire, and put out her hands to warm them, the snowflakes descending soft and still on her old grey head and making it white and whiter. The crowd was gathering around the pyre now, and an egg came flying and struck her in the eye, and broke and ran down her face. There was a laugh at that.... I told Satan all about the eleven girls and the old woman, once, but it did not affect him.'"

Marx, as always, was right. Man can go no further in theory than he can in life. I was never able, in life, to get beyond those funeral pyres; they always affected me deeply. So I cannot offer theories to these children of the plains. Let Hakim do it.

I do not entertain a scientific world view.

Had I remained in that country in Europe I might have evaded questions like Dianne O'Donnell's. I might now be celebrating what one is permitted to celebrate: Sundays at the cottage, mini-romances uncomplicated by the larger dramas of life. I might well be writing in such a vein. The desire to live exists, regardless of what Dianne thinks, so I would leave out of my picture of life what one is forbidden (in that country) to include, and perhaps, on occasion, what I left out would coincide with what I would not have wanted to include anyway. Perhaps. People would read my books and would perhaps even like them, for once upon another less orthodox time my stories gave form to their unscientific feelings. They would remain faithful readers even if I were brought to heel. After all, the scientific world view taught me how to maintain my balance on the edge of the permissible, and even after the required eliminations, something of those unscientific feelings would remain in my work. Libations to the gods of science. People in that country are forgiving. Sometimes I might even enjoy the satisfaction of feeling useful, of giving moments of pleasure to others. And I would avoid altogether themes that could not be written about with those eliminations.

But such things cannot be eliminated from the mind. Only from the page. And from time to time – after writing books full of cautious, utilitarian games, after all those winsome, tranquillizing little books – I would have to put together a book made up of the eliminations.

I am a little too old, however, to write for the desk-drawer.

And I would be afraid. Fear drove me from that country, a healthy fear of the gallows. And of its more sophisticated, more subtle and less bloody derivatives.

The raven is gravely pacing back and forth outside the window. I watch his pecking pilgrimage over the white snow of the Edenvale plain, in search of life's message.

•

Eisler marched across the factory floor towards me with a stride he thought appropriate to the execution of a *Werkschutzmann*'s duties. My heart pounded in my throat.

Foreman Vachousek hadn't put in an appearance since yesterday and I had no idea how the undoing of our devastation was proceeding. I had only noticed that Wagner, down the line, would rivet cross-brackets to the plates for a while, and then unrivet others. That night I had sweated so heavily I had had to change my pyjamas. The fear did not vanish with the morning. It was still there, stronger than ever. And now I was far too frightened to realize that the Gestapo would hardly have sent a half-wit like Eisler to arrest me.

He stopped beside me, opened his mouth and barked, "You're wanted to go to the station."

"Me?"

"You're Smiricky, right?"

"That's right."

"Oberkontrolleur Uippelt called. They're bringing some instruments by train and he wants you to pick them up at the station and bring them back to the factory."

"But – what about these cross-brackets here?"

"*Das da ist ein Befehl!*"

Nadia was listening. I smiled at her, which was almost as difficult as lifting a sack of coal, and set out for the station.

Uippelt was waiting on the platform.

"I'm expecting a lady-friend," he said matter-of-factly. "You will take her suitcases to my apartment."

Not a word about instruments.

"*Jawohl, Herr Obermeister.*"

"Here's the address. First I shall take the lady to my office at the factory, and you will wait for us in my apartment. I'll tip you there."

"*Jawohl, Herr Obermeister.*"

This time I didn't mix any English into what I was saying. Was he making a coolie out of me because he thought he had something on me? He paced up and down on the platform in his brown plus-fours; I waited by the men's washroom in my blue coveralls. The train arrived almost precisely on time. A woman leaned out of the window, waving, and Uippelt ran up to her. She disappeared and reappeared a few moments later on the steps, a Brunhild in a Tyrolean hat, a green dirndl skirt and cork-soled shoes. An army officer emerged from behind her, descended and helped her off the train. She had two blessed big suitcases with her. Uippelt turned to me and pointed silently at them. Then he took the Brunhild by the arm and they walked to the exit.

I lifted the suitcases. A hundred pounds each, maybe two. I put them down again. How could I ever drag these to the address he'd given me without dying from exhaustion on the way? There are worse ways to die, however. I heard the sound of someone groaning with effort behind me and turned around. It was Lenecek, from the factory, with two suitcases like mine. He had just set his on the ground and was staring around with a wild look in his eye.

"Hi," I said. He didn't reply. He was staring dementedly at something going on behind me. "A spot check!" he hissed. He seemed rooted to the ground. I turned around. A man in an ankle-length leather coat with a town police constable at his side was searching an old woman holding a large bundle tied up in a sheet. The constable was trying to pretend it had nothing to do with him.

"Oh-oh!" I said quietly. But this time I wasn't afraid. I was only a coolie. Lenecek, on the other hand, grabbed his suitcases and in undisguised panic tried to run with them to the men's toilet, but they were too heavy and he could only jerk them forward a few steps at a time.

The man in the leather coat looked around.

"*Halt!*"

Lenecek had managed to drag the suitcases forward four whole paces but it wasn't enough to get him to the toilet. It occurred to me that he must have been thinking of the public washroom somewhat as people in the Middle Ages regarded the church. The man in the leather coat, obviously bent on homicide, rushed after him. Hoping I might be able to distract his attention from Lenecek, I grasped the suitcases belonging to Uippelt's mistress, and though my knees were about to collapse managed to drag them towards the exit at a mild but obvious trot. As I had expected, the Gestapo man noticed, but he solved the problem masterfully. With an imperious right arm he pointed at me, he barked "*Festnehmen!*" at the constable and without missing a step pounded on after Lenecek who had meanwhile reached the toilet and was just turning the doorknob when the man in the leather coat grabbed him by the collar.

The constable reached me in the same instant and said disgruntledly, "All right, come along with me."

I dragged the suitcase to the Inspection Office, with the constable walking along beside me. He said under his breath, "What d'you have to smuggle so much in at once for? How in God's name d'you expect anyone to turn a blind eye to a load of goods like that? Even if Cvancara wasn't on duty today?"

So the Gestapo man was a Czech, a collaborator. A former textile worker in Kostelec, I now remembered, but like so many collaborators he had changed his name to spell it in the German fashion, Tschwantschara.

"These suitcases aren't mine," I said. "They belong to the Obermeister at the Messerschmitt plant."

This surprised the constable. "You don't say? And where is this Obermeister?"

"He went back to his office. At the factory."

The constable looked sharply at the suitcases, then glanced towards the toilet, whence Lenecek was dragging his baggage with Tschwantschara marching heavily behind him.

"Inside," said the constable, pointing to the door of the Inspection Office. I went in, dropped the suitcases on the floor and turned back to look out. The constable was hurrying out of the station in one direction while Lenecek approached from the other, his tongue hanging out. Behind him, Tschwantschara was shouting, "*Weiter, weiter! Aber dalli!*" He'd obviously absorbed enough German by now to be able to issue truncated commands. I watched Lenecek's calvary for a while longer. The platform was utterly deserted. Anyone with legs had vanished along with his provender. The distraction of Lenecek's conspicuous suitcases had probably enabled quite a few pots of lard to slip through the Reich's net undetected.

I turned back into the office. A moment later Lenecek appeared in the door, but he had only one of his suitcases. Tschwantschara himself, like Joseph of Arimathea, was dragging in the second one. This made him no more amiable, but as soon as he saw me and my two equally huge suitcases he beamed with delight. "Well, well, well," he said – in Czech, since he wanted to make a coherent statement. "It's a busy day for the travellers!"

I decided to let events take their course.

"And you must be going on quite a voyage, with sea trunks like that!"

He looked gleefully from my suitcases to Lenecek's. "*Also aufmachen!*" he commanded, once more in German.

Willingly I reached for the catches. Locked. I saw Lenecek open one of his suitcases a crack, but when he saw that Tschwantschara's attention was entirely absorbed by the lock on mine, he quietly closed it again.

"I said *aufmachen!*" Tschwantschara roared at me with enthusiastic menace.

"It appears to be stuck," I said.

"So we'll open it the German way!"

He lifted his rather scruffy boot and delivered a violent kick to the lock on the suitcase. His boot passed through the *Vulkanfiber* and remained inside along with the lock. He tried to shake his foot free but couldn't, and lost his temper. In a rage, he jerked his foot back and forth until at last he liberated it from its trap. But when he saw what was inside the suitcase, his mood brightened. Enshrouded in a lady's pink slip were three bottles of liquor that were clearly not the vulgar variety served in German tap-rooms. The dull crunch of a boot on a lock and the second suitcase lay open, revealing five more bottles and some tin cans resting on a satin nightgown trimmed with swansdown, like luxurious chocolates in a chocolate-box. The label on the bottles read "Cognac Martell."

Tschwantschara interpreted the contraband wrapped in lingerie in his own way. "Are you getting married?" he asked in Czech.

I deliberately replied in German, "*Nein, bitte.*"

For a moment longer he looked piningly at that wealth of alcohol; then he turned to Lenecek, who stood limply over his suitcases – which were still shut. Tschwantschara yelled at him so violently that the windowpanes rattled. "I said *aufmachen!*"

And Lenecek bent over and, almost shyly, raised the lid.

For a moment it looked like a murder. The sawed-up corpse in the suitcase, however, was happily not human but demonstrably porcine. A pink snout with a lemon in it was staring up at us.

"This is a piece of a suckling pig my uncle in Opocno slaughtered," said Lenecek nervously. "Legally."

"A piece?"

"Well, a piece or two," said Lenecek.

Tschwantschara leaned over the suitcases and studied the collage of pork for a long time. Then he straightened up, looked about, and pointed to a long table. "All right, take that piece or two and lay it out on the table!"

Lenecek knelt down once more, looking up at Tschwantschara as if begging for mercy. The Gestapo man straightened his shoulders and puffed out his chest, while Lenecek reached into the suitcase, lifted out a fat ham and timidly held it out to him. There was no mistaking his intention. Tschwantschara, however, glared back at him incredulously and shouted: "*Was? Auf den Tisch hab ich gesagt!*"

The unsuccessful briber made a quick about-face, and hurried to the table with the ham. Unhappily he set to work. In less than a minute the table was piled high with a mass of piggy legs, hams, loins, butts, trotters, and other less identifiable parts.

"A piece or two of suckling pig!" said the Gestapo man with studious irony. "From an uncle in Opocno."

"He – my uncle's on a diet, sir. So he gave it all to me."

"Well, let's see what we've got here." Tschwantschara grabbed the pig's head by the snout and placed it in the middle of the table. He pondered a while, as though studying a chess problem, then set two legs beside the head. He pondered some more.

Lenecek retreated to the suitcases and for some reason shut them. He was the colour of chalk. I recalled a recent news item in the paper about a butcher who had been executed for hoarding meat. I looked at the pig, but it too reminded me of things I would rather not think about. Tschwantschara went on with the anatomical brain-teaser.

It was a curious thing. A pig with two rumps was emerging under his hands. It also had five legs and three sides. Tschwantschwara was evidently pleased with this unusual creature. He placed the third hind leg by the two hams and turned to Lenecek.

"*Ein fünfbeiniges Schwein!*"

A five-legged pig. He said it as though it were a pleasant surprise.

"That can't be right, sir," said Lenecek. "My uncle must have got it mixed up."

"What do you mean 'mixed up'?"

"Well, a pig has only four legs, sir."

"So the fifth one doesn't belong there?"

"No, sir."

"And where does it belong?"

"Certainly not there," said Lenecek unhappily.

"No?"

"No." Lenecek stepped over the suitcases, hesitatingly crossed to the table, took one of the three hind legs and moved it from the twin hams to a position under the snout.

Tschwantschara looked at him questioningly. "That's a front leg, sir," said Lenecek.

"*Ach so!*" said the Gestapo man, looking at the creation. Then he took one of the hams and placed it under the snout along with the leg. "And that is a front ham, I suppose?"

"No," whispered Lenecek. "That is a – a hind ham cut in two. I mean an uncut ham has two halves. So when you cut them in two, there are four...." His voice trailed off. Thoughtfully, Tschwantschara supported his chin with his index finger and said, "Remarkable."

He held that position a long time, staring at the monstrosity. We stood there without saying a word. At last he reached into the pile of as yet unarranged pieces, pulled out another front leg and placed it under the snout so that the abomination now had three front legs, one of which was clearly a hind one.

"Is that right now?" he asked.

Lenecek raised a trembling hand above the enigmatic pig, hesitating. Uncertainly he took the hind leg that was lying between the two front ones under the snout and slowly carried it to the rear. There were already two hind legs there. He hesitated again. Tschwantschara leaned over the table and took one of the hind legs away. Lenecek, as if hypnotized, replaced it with the one he was holding in his hands.

"At last we've got it right," said Tschwantschara, as though delighted by the solution. "And this leg?" He held up the piece in his hand and looked at it closely. "Aha. *Ich verstehe*. It's not a leg at all, it's a tail!"

He looked inquiringly at Lenecek. Lenecek could think of nothing to say. Tschwantschara rammed the leg into the pig's anus.

The whole comedy smelled of the slaughterhouse.

"*Na, und was werma dazu trinken?*" He turned to me, bent down and pulled two bottles out of my suitcase. One was Martell, the other champagne. Tschwantschara savoured the dramatic pause, reading the French labels on the back of the bottles.

"*Was soll das sein?*" came a sudden roar from the direction of the door. We all jumped, especially Tschwantschara. Standing in the doorway, his little Hitler moustache bristling like the hair on a tomcat's back, pince-nez on his nose and brushcut like a cactus, was Uippelt. "*Was erlauben sie sich?*"

Brunhild was peering around him in her Tyrolean hat.

Utterly unnerved, Tschwantschara let the bottle of champagne slip out of his hand. It fell to the floor and exploded. A shard of flying glass struck him on the nose, drawing blood, but Uippelt ignored the wound and silently pointed to the suitcases.

"*Diese Dame hier,*" said Uippelt icily, "*ist Frau General der Waffen SS von Kater! Der Herr General hatte die SS Division Grossdeutschland bei der Kesselschlacht von Kiev unter Befehl. Jetzt erholt er sich in Paris!*"

Tschwantschara clacked his heels together, bent over and tried to shut the suitcases, but of course their catches had been kicked in and he couldn't. He turned to the constable who meanwhile had unobtrusively slipped into the room and, almost in a whisper, asked him for some rope. The constable helped him tie the suitcases shut.

With unexpected presence of mind, Lenecek took advantage of this interlude. As if the amorphous pig were also the property of the wife of the SS General von Kater, he reduced it in record time to its basic elements, put them back in the suitcases and scurried away with his hundred kilos of contraband pork. He seemed suddenly to have been endowed with superhuman strength.

Uippelt glowered at Tschwantschara as he struggled with the rope.

I saw that I was not going to avoid the coolie labour after all. But at the same time Uippelt's return and the black comedy I had just witnessed served to remind me that, when you're afraid, it's a good idea to do something physically taxing. It helps dispel thoughts of death.

●

August 10th, 1947
Kostelec

*Dear Dan!*
*Once after the war you gave me one of your manuscripts to read. I thought it was just another of your cynical jokes and didn't take what you'd written seriously. It was called* An Introduction to the Theory of

the End. *At that time you were interested in palaeontology and you had discovered the hypothesis of someone called Dollo – I think you called it overspecialization. It dealt with the mystery of extinction. Dollo, as far as I can recall, claimed you could paradoxically explain the dying out of some species by a too successful struggle for the survival of the fittest. It seems that some animals underwent a rapid development of certain anatomical features that seemed at first to give them an advantage: herbivorous reptiles grew to such a size that smaller carnivores could not harm them. The sabre-toothed tigers developed huge tusks which could pierce even the skin of a dinotherium. But sometimes things go awry and the development of advantageous features doesn't cease at the point of greatest advantage. The brontosaurus keeps on growing, the sabre-toothed tiger's tusks get longer. This growth continues* ad absurdum *until, according to Dollo, "there appear animals which are no longer adapted to survival, and these die out." The four-metre sabre-tooth's tusks curl round and close its jaws so that in the end it can only feed on mice. The brontosaurus reaches gigantic proportions and its brain, which is the same size as a cat's, can no longer manage the huge body; another brain develops in the pelvic region, but the two never manage to get coordinated and the brontosauri die out as a result of anatomical schizophrenia.*

*Thus far Dollo. You, ever the cynic, applied this to mankind. In the struggle for survival man's brain has grown, giving him an undisputed advantage, but once again this growth has not stopped at the point of maximum advantage. His rational abilities have grown, while his emotional and volitional capacities have remained unchanged. Thanks to this hypertrophy of the rational part of the brain, reality has become more and more complicated, leading to increasingly irresolvable conflicts of the reason with the emotions and the will, in turn producing individuals incapable of action – which can only be the product of the instrumental, not the reflective intelligence. Such individuals are no longer able to deal with life. Their numbers are increasing. Today there are already whole classes, or more precisely, whole strata of them. And when this overspecialization overtakes all mankind, Homo* sapiens *will die out.*

*I know you didn't mean it entirely seriously, Dan, but perhaps you happened on the trail of a disease that Marx and Engels were clearly aware of too. Fortunately all of mankind hasn't yet been afflicted – only intellectuals like us.*

> *We are the hollow men*
> *We are the stuffed men....*

*Leaning together,*
*Headpiece filled with straw. Alas!*
*Our dried voices, when*
*We whisper together*
*Are quiet and meaningless*
*As wind in dry grass*
*Or rats' feet over broken glass....*

*How accurately that puts it! Or old Rilke:*

wachen, lesen, lange Briefe schreiben
und ... in den Alleen hin un her
uṇruhig wandern, wenn die Blätter treiben....

*That is precisely what I have done. All my life. I have tried – like Rilke – to remain alert, to write letters, to listen to the wind, read poetry. And at the same time – and therein lies the irony of my fate – I have always lived among simple people unaffected as yet by a pathological hypertrophy of the brain, and I have seen them in situations where their humanity expressed itself most directly. I have never written to you about this, or even told you – but do you know what it is to ride through the streets the morning after a saturation raid and see a child flattened like a caricature against a half-burned wall by the terrible shock of the air wave? A crushed, distended bas-relief of charred flesh? And to see men in the barracks talking – but you know how – with tears in their eyes, see them look at that terrible work of art created by war, and faint?*

*I escaped from such things into poetry. When they drove us through the burned-out streets to the fire I would recite to myself into the howling of the siren:*

*The child gets out. The mother shrieks.*
*The dead men stand there dumb*
*On the platform of the Past.*
*The train is rushing on, rushing through time*
*And no one knows why....*

*Poetry was my refuge. And in recent days I have come back to it again and again. I happened across Neumann's poem: "Poetry is not a vain flight from earth and people." I felt it as a reproach directed at me, personally. In the war, when I was surrounded by people living, suffering, fighting, I escaped into poetry. In the last few weeks I must*

have read all of Neumann and I have discovered a poet I once felt
somewhat disdainful of. He used to seem dry to me, too declaratory
and full of propaganda. But that is only the surface; beneath that there
is great wisdom:

I love all things with simple relationships;
And I love such people most of all;
Pure they are, and comely, though I see them for the hundredth time.
They are made of primal stuff and taste of ripe beech-nuts.
Certain one is with them, safe and secure
As in a peasant's parlour, he still hale as oak.
They are not a kaleidoscope of brightly coloured shards,
That with each turn gives the lie to yet another star....

I know you're turning up your nose now, Dan, and thinking what a
naive fool I am. But I can no longer travel the route that you wrote
about, the route of rational hypertrophy. I feel the truth to be in
Neumann's wisdom. I must at last prove capable of drinking from that
well.

Yours,
Jan

●

I been there before.

The guests at Milan's housewarming party laughed at my account of
how I'd replied to a circular sent round the faculty by my colleagues Bill
Hogarth and Sugar Schwartz. To their question: "If a Marxism study group
is set up at Edenvale College, would you be interested in becoming a
member?" I replied with the final sentence of Sugar's favourite book: "I
been there before."

They laugh, and Barbara turns sharply to Milan. "What did Danny
say? Something funny?"

"Hellishly funny. But you wouldn't understand."

"What makes you think I wouldn't?"

"Because you've never been there before!" Milan giggles.

"I don't get it," says Barb evenly. "Did he say something about
Huckleberry Finn?"

"Who? There, you see, you haven't a clue what they are talking
about!"

Barbara shows no outward discomfort. She notices that our glasses have run dry and she takes them, her hands heavy with costume jewellery, over to the table where Milan has arranged an extravagant display of bottles – such as one would normally find only at receptions in socialist embassies. No one knows what finally swayed the court to grant him asylum. It may have been because the final hearing came shortly after the suicide of a young Polish girl who had preferred death to a forced return to Gierek's People's Democracy. Whatever it was, Milan is now a landed immigrant and he is busy building his future. Veronika is sitting in the corner by a brand-new stereo set, a huge set of earphones on her head and tears in her eyes. Barbara takes ice from a Thermos jug, pours amber whisky over it and comes back to us. Someone is telling a joke about the Prague policeman who drowned trying to stamp out a cigarette a passer-by had tossed in the river. There is loud laughter.

Barbara hands Milan his glass.

"I suppose he's telling jokes?"

"That's right."

"Well," says Barbara deliberately, "couldn't you translate them for me?"

"They're only word games. My English isn't good enough."

"Then how about making an effort? Your English is good enough for some things."

But Milan ignores her, selfishly soaking up the atmosphere of Prague, a city he voluntarily abandoned with the help of the Czechoslovak Travel Agency.

I watch Barbara, the shipwrecked victim of disparate love, as she walks back to the improvised bar, mixes herself a drink, sits down in an easy chair and takes some magazines off the coffee table. *Mlady Svet, Kino, Melodie,* even *Dikobraz,* all magazines from Prague. She leafs through them. The mélange of party functionaries and pop stars staring at her from their pages is quite alien. She gets up, walks over to the stereo and sits down on the floor. Two pairs of luminous knees in nylon stockings glow forlornly through the cigarette smoke. Great gusts of laughter break out, this time around Mr. Zawynatch, then subside; the company becomes more serious.

"We'll set the transmitter up in Ethiopia," Mr. Pohorsky is saying. "There are special atmospheric conditions there that mean it can be picked up loud and clear back home. At first we'll broadcast eight hours a day, then we'll bump it up to twelve. Give me two months, and...."

I turn away from Mr. Pohorsky, before he offers me a job. I look at the luminous knees and the two girls, their heads enclosed in oversized earphones.

Barbara is just removing hers. She gets up again, glancing in Milan's direction, but his spirit is elsewhere – perhaps in Ethiopia. She strolls over to the bookshelf, takes out a brand-new jigsaw puzzle and sits down on the floor.

I walk over to Veronika and point to the earphones. She exposes an ear.

"What are you listening to?" I ask.

"Milan's got some new records from Prague!" Her eyes glisten with a mixture of sadness and pleasure. "Do you know Ulrychova?"

"I know she exists."

"I knew her. She was sort of plump. But what a voice!"

I put on the magic headpiece and connect with Veronika's world. It used to be my world too. But only in part. The other part, literature, no longer exists there. It may not have been great literature, but here and there something was achieved, occasionally by someone who was in the same class as that gentleman who loved wearing white suits and was such a great pessimist. We carried on heated arguments about freedom, and as freedom slowly enlarged its sphere we filled it with small stories. I listen. It seems that a number of things, perhaps even a lot, can be done without freedom – that is, with the little freedom we are allowed until the day comes, as Plato envisioned, when we are all driven out of Utopia.

I listen. The sounds of electrified music and strings. What is the point of so much suffering, then? It is always out of all proportion to the end suffered for. The intensity of the need to express oneself is usually disproportionate to one's powers of expression. *Das Spiel ist ganz und gar verloren, und dennoch wird es weitergehen.* The game is hopelessly lost and yet it goes on. Poor Jan. Of course. If we hadn't babbled on so much about freedom – we who were then incapable of putting it to any profound use – perhaps we wouldn't be listening now to that great, beautiful and clearly un-normalizable voice which couldn't care less that everything it represents has more in common with *The Mysterious Stranger* than with organizations like the Union of Socialist Youth – the SS Youth as they call it now; a voice that has distilled from that little freedom, won (perhaps chiefly) by our truculent demands, a profound optimism:

> The train is rushing through the night
> In first-class they sleep till morning
> The signal light shines clear and bright
> But the engineer's missed its warning
> So what?

I close my eyes. What might she have sung twenty-five years ago, in the early 1950s, when my generation was just beginning adult life? I call to mind another voice, also great and beautiful, belonging to a girl called Venus Paroubkova. She sang:

> The victory fires burn about our land,
> Now gaze we boldly into sunny vistas
> And our wise leader, dearest comrade Stalin
> Lives with us, in peace and happiness....

Not that she really wanted to. When the variety show was over, she sang, "And that's the story 'bout the birth of swing, a drunken sailor on a fling, turned a stagger, into a swagger...." But on stage, she intoned in her great alto voice, obedient to the absolute command. And where is Venus Paroubkova now? Where is Jan, a deathly serious but minor poet? And where, after all, am I, Jan's frivolous raconteur of cynical tales?

Of the three of us I am without doubt the best off. I am alive, I am in Canada, and in this miraculous hemispherical headset I am now listening to another voice, a voice twenty years younger than Venus' but very similar, the voice of a singer who has, by chance, enjoyed a happier nativity, singing a song by an anonymous lyricist who was also lucky enough to have been conceived a quarter of a century after Venus, so they had both come to maturity when the old Stalinist imperative had temporarily lost its muscle.

> We are sad and we are gay,
> We've got the blues cause he's run away,
> So what? I say, so what?
> When headlong down the days
> The universe is rushing, rushing on
> At the crossing of absolute ways....

I suddenly find myself gripped by an intense sadness. The feeling does not set flowing the tears that, from the corner of my eye, I can see on Veronika's cheeks. The writer of those lyrics has fulfilled Capek's ideal: no one knows any more who wrote the song, but young girls still cry over it and in their hearts – perhaps – a fundamental truth remains in these unpretty times.... Nadia, her pale face on a rainy day in summer.... Sister Udelina had sent me for distilled water and as I walked along the dark, deadly corridors of the old orphanage which had now been converted into a hospital, I saw her wan face and the familiar feverish eyes beneath the granny-kerchief. "Nadia! What are you doing here?" "I been in for a pneumothorax," she said. She stopped, and the dead light from the hopeless grey windows stamped the hospital whiteness on her cheeks, ran down her sweater, flooded her grey, shapeless skirt, her thin legs in their cotton stockings and the men's lace-up boots. "Nadia," I said, "it's ... I'm glad you're getting treatment...." In the luminous grey my voice sounded foolish. "If they've prescribed pneumothorax, it'll soon be better ...," and my stomach heaved and turned from the awful sadness here, where yesterday, down through this crypt, Sister Udelina had wheeled a mere skeleton of a girl with a blue number tattooed across her forearm. "What ...?" I had whispered to Dr. Preisner. "Terminal case," he had whispered back. "Absolutely nothing to be done." I had glanced back at the skeleton in the wheelchair. Tears were streaming down the white skin stretched over her skull, flowing from almond eyes like Rebecca's, like Sugar Schwartz's. That was in summer, the year of our Lord nineteen hundred and forty-five. "The Americans brought her out of Buchenwald," Sister Udelina told me. "She wanted to come home. That's why we're praying to Saint Joseph – for happiness in the hour of death. Everyone wants to die at home." But the skeletal girl clearly wanted to live. The eyes staring out of the skull were intelligent. They knew that neither V-Day nor D-Day had anything to do with her case any longer. And the kind hands of Sister Udelina wheeled her away, into the white grave of a hospital bed in an ancient orphanage.

> So what? I say, so what?
> When headlong down the days
> The universe is rushing, rushing on
> At the crossing of absolute ways....

Sung by a great, beautiful, almost knowing voice, its only knowledge the sentience of the Hawthornesque heart, that mysterious source of wisdom in obtuse, unknowing man, seizing the words of the unknown lyricist who had achieved Capek's ideal:

> When feelings and thoughts and spheres intersect
> At the crossing of absolute, absolute ways.
> So what?

And I am sad, perhaps with the sadness of those who foolishly try to sever themselves from the eternal human condition. I hold all my writings in a second of memory – and where is this in my entire oeuvre, this essential truth distilled from a tiny drop of freedom? Nowhere, apparently. I console myself with the thought that I have made a small contribution to that drop from which others have distilled this absolute way, this intersection of truth. I console myself but there is no consolation. I am not one to be content with the fate allotted to the generality of mankind. A small share does not interest me. I would like to live eternally, perhaps because I have never lived enough, and I have never lived enough because I wanted to live eternally. It is a *circulus vitiosus* to which all scribblers, scribes and writers succumb. "I don't know," said Nadia. "That's what the doctor says too, but he's got to say it. I'm not afraid." But were you ever afraid, Nadia? I was. "Come with me," said Vachousek the foreman harshly, and I turned round seeking Nadia's eyes, she let go of the drill handle and reached out her hand to me. "Did you hear what I said?" snarled Vachousek and I pulled myself away, my legs as heavy as they must feel to the man being led from his death cell along the prison corridors to the yard where that hideous revolutionary engine is waiting, heavy with the full force of earth's gravity, to break his neck. I walked after Vachousek in a state close to unconsciousness. "Take a seat," said the foreman when he reached his cubicle, "because you won't be able to take this standing up anyway. We're in deep trouble. Uippelt took one of the cross-brackets from the welding room." I sat down, struggling in vain to say something. The foreman wasn't expecting me to. "It all depends now," he said, "on whether Uippelt figures out there's a whole bunch of them or not. I reckon he will. If there were only two or three bad brackets, we'd have chucked them out and not bothered to reweld them." He looked at me. He was serious, but whether he was afraid or not I couldn't tell. If he was, he didn't let on. "And then it'll depend on whether he decides those welded brackets will pass muster, or whether he decides to cover his ass. I reckon he'll cover." I felt as though they were already putting the hood over my head. The black cloth slipped over my eyes and the foreman disappeared from sight, nothing but his voice remaining. "And I hope it's bloody good and clear to you, student, that there's only one thing he can do to cover for himself so he won't be up to his neck in shit for letting a faulty component for a fighter get through!"

When I staggered out of the foreman's cubicle, the whole factory hall was spinning round me. I went into the toilet, my stomach closed like a fist and I vomited into one of the spattered bowls, then leaned back against the wall breathing heavily. "Hey!" It was Kos. "Stupid Malina here don't want to believe that snails are male and female both at once." "You're fucking right I don't," said Malina, "cause I seen them screwing." "So what you expect?" said Kos. "They screw in pairs, you silly prick. The male half screws the female and the female half screws the male. Explain it to him, asshole." And he turned to me. I hadn't the slightest desire to enlighten anybody just then, but what was I to do? My head was a maelstrom, I was overwhelmed by a longing to find – somewhere, somehow, in something – refuge, asylum, help. Spinning, thousands of tiny hands clutching at thousands of miniature straws that broke when I touched them. "It's true," I said. "Snails are hermaphrodites – both sexes at once." "That's fuckin' bullshit, you cow," said Malina. "Why should they be that way? What's the point?" "I don't know," I said. I felt wilted. "That's just how it is." "Aw, you're both fuckin' crazy as dingoes. There's no point to it," said Malina. "If they already had a pecker and a snatch in the same fuckin' body, they could go fuck themselves straight off, you yaks." "Such creatures actually exist," I said. "The tapeworm, for instance." Malina cast an unfriendly glance in my direction. "Don't try and fuckin' bullshit me, bullfrog." "So how d'you think a tapeworm screws?" demanded Kos. "You think everybody's got two in their stomachs, a male and a female?" "Gentlemen," said Ponykl, butting into the discussion. "Can't you see it when one of them tapeworms gets it up and goes to it! I wouldn't want two tapeworms fucking in my gut!" From the maelstrom in my head tiny hands reached out for straws, I thought of Nadia, I thought of Prema....

> White pages of the daily news
> It's black and white in print.
> So what? I ask, so what?

What would have happened then if....

> When headlong down the days
> The universe is rushing, rushing on
> At the crossing of absolute ways....

Veronika wasn't in this world yet, nor was Sugar Schwartz. Professor Hogarth was, but he was in Canada and he was only ten. He missed his chance to be gunned down on the Normandy beaches with "The Beer Barrel Polka" on his lips. "Nadia," I said, "does your fellow – is he still angry with me?" "Oh no. He's a good man. But you mustn't wonder at him. He was afraid of what might happen to me." I know, Nadia. I could tell by the force behind his blows. He was afraid for you. I was only afraid for myself, and my fear was as strong as the fear that powered Franta's fist. "He's waiting outside with a buggy," she said, then laughed. "I'm a real invalid, Dan. I can't even walk up the hill to Cerna Hora no more." She coughed. "If you have a mind to ..." – the coal-black eyes burning in the white cheeks on the slope of Black Mountain, that winter, that night, and for the first time since I had met her they searched me with a selfish demand, a personal desire all her own – "... come up and visit us some time. I'd really be happy...." No woman ever said anything quite like it to me again. She held out her hot hand. I looked through the window of the room where the skeletal girl had died that morning. On the road in front of the orphanage stood a horse harnessed to a buggy. A fellow as solid as a stump waited beside the horse, and when Nadia came out of the orphanage in her huge boots he helped her up onto the box-seat and gently wrapped a thick carriage rug around her shoulders. I looked from hell into paradise, and a terrible sadness broke me in two –

I take off the headset. This is unhealthy. I need an injection of Mr. Pohorsky, Brian Zawynatch or Dotty. I look around. Barbara is sitting gracefully on the floor in front of a jigsaw puzzle. Above her is a large gold picture-frame and inside it her own face, a huge blow-up procured in one of those special shops on Yonge Street. So Milan is treating it like a full-fledged love affair, with all the attendant ceremony. From the incomplete puzzle in front of her, Sherlock Holmes is slowly emerging. I walk over and become a witness to the ensuing conversation, because Milan has just approached from the other side and is clearly well into his cups.

"Well, well, Canadian habits. Puzzles."

Barbara lifts serious eyes to meet his. She can match him, sarcasm for sarcasm. "This is not a Canadian habit. I'm doing it because it amuses me."

Milan hands her a glass. The ice tinkles. "Here's a drink. That will amuse you more."

But Barbara rejects the proffered amusement. Reflectively, she sets a piece in place to complete Sherlock's knee. Then she raises her eyes to her boyfriend once more, exposing his ignorance with a line that Milan does not know just as he did not know the last line from *Huckleberry Finn*. How could he know it? When *Citizen Kane* last played in Prague, Milan was not yet in this world.

"You never give me anything I really care about," says Barbara, waiting against hope for Milan to understand. But he does not, nor could he, even had he time to think it over. He is called away. "Milan! Milan!" cry the men assembled round the makeshift bar.

Barbara watches him for a few moments, then takes another odd-shaped portion of the puzzle in her fingers and begins to look for its proper place.

So what?

I return to Veronika.

I lift the earphones and shout into the delicate little ear, "Where's Sir Percival?"

Veronika shrugs her shoulders and takes off the magic headpiece. She rubs away the tears with the palm of her hand. "I don't know."

"Aren't you going out with him?"

"More or less," she says. "I didn't want to drag him here. He'd just spoil the party. Everybody'd have to speak English."

I nod towards Barbara, still absorbed in her puzzle. "What about her? She's not spoiling it."

"I'm not a boor like dear Milan," says Veronika.

"He could listen to records with you."

"In Czech? It would bore him."

"Does he love you so little?"

Veronika takes a tissue out of her corduroy jacket and trumpets into it with verve. It helps to drive out the spleen. "Professors oughtn't to be so curious," she says, "I don't ask them about their Lolitas, do I?" How invigorating, this gentle breath of Czech flirtatiousness, this ancient antidote to the sadness of life. "I haven't a clue how much he loves me. A lot, I guess, because he must get terribly bored with me. I'm obsessed with Czechoslovakia."

"Don't you get bored with him?"

"No."

"Do you love him so much?"

Veronika thinks a moment. "It's more that he pisses me off so much."

The grey eyes concentrate sadness and self-control. She points to the table of near-empty bottles. "Vizee-vizee-vizee," she says, which is her way of indicating that she wants to imbibe. Clearly to the point of inebriation. She gets her whisky and then tunes me out, disappearing once more into the astronautical headset, transporting herself back home to Prague along a laser-beam of music.

•

*January 15, 1953*
*Braunau*

*Danny,*

*I know you won't mind, certainly not you. But you're the only one in Prague I can turn to. It's not so bad really but I don't want to write the Lewits and I can't even tell you why. Or perhaps I can. Anyway, I need a favour of you. David is under medication – I'm including the prescription. It's unavailable here in Braunau and I'm told you can only get it in Prague, but since it's from Switzerland I honestly don't know where you should start looking for it. I'm just depending on you to know. There is always a way to get things like that in Prague, so if you're still a friend – and I know you are even though I have a lot fewer friends than I thought until recently – you'll do it for me, won't you? I can't even send you the money for it, because I don't have much. I'm working in the textile plant here, and I always had two left hands when it came to manual training at school – perhaps I should say two right hands – so I never manage to produce any more than the norm. Anyway, many many thanks. Little David needs it badly, and I'm very worried about him.*

*I'm feeling somewhat better these days – I don't cry so much, and our living arrangements have improved a little. A very kind neighbour repaired our roof, or, to be exact, made us a new one, because the one we had when they moved us here could only be called a roof – what's the word? – euphemistically. Anyway, he's a maintenance man at the factory, but he doesn't talk about Leo, in fact he's never mentioned him once. Of course he knows about him, as they all do. And most people are kind to me, it's just that they're so curious. One fool who happens to be a foreman felt it was his duty to remind me that I must, through honest work, make up for what my husband – but you know the line. Mrs. Bobesova, who works with me on the throstle, gave him a real scolding and ever since then he's stopped lecturing me. I still can't believe that people say things like that to each other in real life, and not just in that make-believe world where they did it to Leo. Mrs. Bobesova doesn't pry, though there are enough women who do. But I'm used to it – almost.*

*Danny, my faithful goy, I'm only twenty-nine! I expect nothing worse can happen to me now. I'll probably just go on working here in this textile plant till I die, and in fact I really ask for nothing more than that. Only for David's medicine, and I know you'll get it for me.*

*And if you ever feel inclined, please write to me. Surely you can take some time from your busy love correspondence (I'll bet you use the telephone now but you can't call me, I haven't got a phone) to write to your faithful*

*Rebecca*

●

Someone knocks loudly on the door and before I can say "Come in," Ludmila Parkinson stumbles – literally stumbles – into my office.

"Dan! It's awful! They're trying to kill Rocky!"

"What? Who'd want to kill Rocky?"

"The radicals! Hakim was with them. Quick, we've got to help him."

The radicals? And Rocky, of all people? He's the only one in the English department the radicals feel close to. Last semester he accepted pictures instead of essays from them, and this semester, in his course on British romantic poetry, they say he's going to accept Plasticine sculptures so long as they express the mood of "Ode to the West Wind."

So why Rocky? Maybe it's just Ludmila's Ukrainian imagination. Everyone knows the Ukrainian imagination is overheated. Or is it? Ludmila only wants the best for everyone, but whenever she reads an editorial urging that dental care be included in the provincial health insurance plan she sees it as creeping Bolshevism, and starts packing her bags for Florida.

"Quick, Danny. We've got to help him."

She drags me by the arm and we run along the fluorescent corridor which at that time of day is empty. In the distance I can actually hear the pandemonium of many raised voices and the echo of violent blows.

"I was giving an English seminar in 250 and suddenly I heard a racket coming from 251. I knocked on the door, but no one opened. So I turned the handle, looked inside and...."

"What?"

"They were trying to strangle Rocky!"

We turn the corner. Two of Ludmila's students are standing by the doors of room 251.

"Where are Margie and John?" asks Ludmila.

"They've gone inside."

"What's this all about?" I ask.

Both students shrug their shoulders.

"Maybe he said something that upset the radicals," says Ludmila in a constricted voice.

"Surely his Contemporary Drama class can't be full of radicals?"

"But Hakim's in his course. And that black girl – Gwendolyn Washington."

I open the doors, and am greeted by a bizarre spectacle. Rocky is stretched out on the lectern, his black beard jutting up towards the ceiling like an exclamation point. Two students are holding him down by the arms, two by the legs, and Wendy McFarlane is pounding his stomach with her small fists. Wide-eyed Wendy a radical? But others are defending him. Jenny Razadharamithan is hitting Wendy over the head with a thick paperback, Bellissimmo is seated on the floor by a window with a bloodied Kleenex pressed to his nose. Vicky and two indistinguishable girls in jeans are grappling with Higgins the tight end and Gwendolyn Washington has her hands at Hakim's throat. It must be a factional struggle, then.

Suddenly everything goes dark, I hear a crunching sound and behind me Ludmila screams. Someone has socked me, and with my head spinning I stagger backwards out of the room. Ludmila slams the door shut behind me and leans her back against it. I feel my jaw tenderly and test my teeth with my tongue. None of them comes out.

From a nearby office a head with a Turkish pipe stuck in it pokes out. Doug McMountain. He takes the pipe out of his mouth and asks, with British sang-froid, "What in heaven's name is going on?"

"I'm not exactly sure," I say. "Ludmila says the radicals are staging an uprising."

"Nonsense," says Doug resolutely and steps over to the door, opens it and looks inside. Suddenly he is thrown back, and the chibouk is spinning on the floor along with a golf ball. He closes the door and adds calmly, "I'm going to call the campus police."

Crack! From inside the classroom come sounds of something hard bouncing off the blackboard. Doug and I look at each other. The fist and the golf ball that collide with our jaws do not come from the television world of papier-mâché violence. Two men in uniforms of the campus security force run up. "In there, hurry!" shrieks Ludmila.

The uniformed men open the door, and on the floor beside the lectern is a mass of bodies, male and female, covering a body underneath of which only the feet, shod in cowboy boots, are visible. They belong to Professor Rocky McBeth. The feet are twitching.

The policemen shoulder their way expertly into the turmoil and start flinging bodies aside. From the confusion of jeans and flowery blouses the tip of Rocky's beard appears first, and gradually the rest of him is uncovered. He stares in amazement at the campus police.

"What is the meaning of this!" he shouts in his youthful voice.

"Well, sir, what is the meaning of *this?*" asks one of the astonished policemen, pointing to the pile of bodies. Wendy is just extricating herself from the tangle and all that remains of her blouse are a few strips of cloth around her waist.

"This," says Rocky gravely and defiantly, "is a test in English 373. Contemporary Drama."

And so it is.

So what?

●

10 Sept. 56
Sydney

*Dear Danny,*

*Well it's been almost four years since I wrote you from Sicily. I was lucky because not too long after that I got permission to emigrate to Australia. They didn't care about my rotten teeth like the Americans did. I've been here pretty near two years and it's nice enough except that the local tea-swillers piss me off. You can't talk to them. They're a hundred years behind the monkeys as far as politics goes but the standard of living is high. Every day I have a slab of meat bigger than my plate so I've taken to fasting on Fridays, not that I've turned into an old maid or anything, I just need a rest from the meat. On Fridays I eat haddock – that's a kind of fish.*

*But to tell you what I'm up to. First I worked half a year in a sheet-metal factory, because I had experience in that from the nasty adhocu-pation. I made enough but some Czeeks on holiday in Sydney said*

*there was a lot more money in the oil fields of New Guinea so I signed
up for a year and went there illegally. The work was tough but I made
a pile and I saved it all because I lived and ate in a barracks and kept
clear of women so now I've bought this piece of land near Tibooburra
with the savings and I'm all set to take up farming. I always did like the
idea of being a farmer best, I guess I take after Uncle Martin, if you
recollect he was my father's brother, the one who inherited Grandad's
farm in Moravia. We always got slivovice from him, even during the
war when you and Dad got pissed that time, remember that? But I
could never have been a farmer back home because when we got the
Sudetenland back from the Germans and were passing out the land I
was doing my stint in the bloody army, then everything got took over
and nationalized. But here I'm a farmer in Australia and I own a
stretch of land as big as old Count Czernin's estate where you used to
spend your holidays, though here it's pretty normal. I'm taking posses-
sion next week and I'll drop you a line as soon as I get settled in.
They're supposed to bring the mail in by plane once a month. I'll send
you the address too as soon as I find it out. They say it's loosening up
back home, now that the Commies have had their congress in Moscow
and Khrushchev gave that secret speech about how rotten old Stalin
was, if you read about it. So maybe you can drop me a few lines too.*
> *Your old buddy,*
> *Prema*

●

It was a collective test, and the question was: "Improvise a performance in
the manner of Artaud's Theatre of Cruelty." At a special meeting called at
the request of the campus policemen, who feel affronted because Rocky has
accused them of violently disrupting his seminar and, in doing so, of violat-
ing academic freedom, Rocky admits that the test did get somewhat out of
hand, but he argues that the elements of Chance and Surprise are integral
components of the Theatre of Cruelty. The Theatre of Cruelty is moreover
visceral rather than cerebral, and of all forms of theatre in our time it most
faithfully mirrors our social experience.

"Well," says the Dean of Humanities. "Edenvale College naturally
supports experimental methods and new forms of research – but how do
you intend to assign marks?"

"The class decides the mark of every individual by a show of hands,"
says Rocky stubbornly, his beard once more beginning to rise.

"Well" – the Dean of Humanities releases a puff of fragrant smoke
from his pipe – "what are the – hmm – the criteria on which the class bases
its marks?"

"The same as in any other course," says Rocky, unshaken.
"Well," says the Dean, exhaling a ring of smoke. "I see."
What he saw, he did not say.

•

It wasn't that my head was aching, exactly. I felt a pressure inside it, and a strange feeling of having been wronged: was I of all people the one whom fate had chosen to mount the scaffold and die? And why? Because of Nadia. Because of my stupid desire – whim was more like it – to impress Nadia, to show off in front of a village girl who probably couldn't even spell properly. I stumbled along with the throng of workers pouring out of the factory, past the factory policeman Eisler standing on watch with his feet apart, and into the winter night. All the love I felt for the girl in the pale blue bloomers evaporated. A factory girl, Marie had said, and fool that I was ... but I had always put rashness before rationality. I should have known they would test the whole construction with live ammunition before mounting it on the Messerschmitt wing. The vision of those jammed 20-mm Mauser cannons and the Messerschmitt neatly riddled with a twin stream of bullets from the tail guns of a Flying Fortress had lost its savour and another, darker vision now took its place. In a recurring nightmare I saw myself in that prison yard, the executioner placing my neck in the loop, the click of the trap, the drop, the crack of cartilage.... After what Vachousek had told me, it was obvious that my vision of the disabled Messerschmitt was a juvenile adventure fantasy, while that second vision could easily become a reality.

The thirteen-and-a-half-hour shift was over. It was a quarter to eight on a freezing winter night. Terror drove me along Jirasek Street; all at once I thought of God. I had always had a rather odd attitude towards Him – though perhaps it was not as odd as I thought, but quite commonplace. I did not believe much in His existence, yet neither was I entirely sure of His non-existence, so I covered my bets by praying. In fact, it was simpler than that: under the tutelage of the Venerable Father Meloun, prayer had become my natural reaction to states of bliss, longing or fear.

I went right past the door of our apartment building and walked quickly to the town square against a biting wind. There was a faint blue light coming from the windows of the church, for they had been blacked out. By this time the church will be locked, I thought, but I'll stand by the door, and in the snow and the freezing cold I will pray. The discomfort will be my sacrifice to the Lord, as the Venerable Father Meloun used to exhort us – Don't stand when praying! Don't even sit! Kneel! Our aching knees remind us, however faintly, of the suffering of Our Lord on the cross, a suffering incomparably, immeasurably, inexpressibly more terrible – and the Venerable Father would roll his eyes heavenward. Very well, I thought,

I will suffer in the frost and the wind. But what if God wishes me to atone for his inexpressible suffering with a sacrifice considerably more substantial than frost-bitten ears? Hanging is not as painful as crucifixion but – once again my stomach heaved in horror. I was unable to drive the ugly vision out. A throng of spittle-drenched wretches, the Venerable Father had explained, are forced to carry their own crosses all the way to Golgotha, the place of skulls, to their own executions, and there, utterly exhausted and half-mad with fear, they are placed, no, flung down upon the crosses, their arms and legs pinned to the wood by mercenaries while they thrash and twitch and strive against the soldiers, though it cannot save them, and the executioner drives the nails through their wrists and ankles, and the agony when the legionnaires heave the cross upright and they hang from the nails by their tendons – oh God, Christ Jesus! For the first time I had an inkling of the suffering Father Meloun had tried to conjure up in that tragic voice of his. Our Father, Who art in Heaven. I reached for the handle on the church door.

It was unlocked. Was God trying to tell me the way lay open? My doubts remained but I walked up to the altar and there, kneeling before it in a black winter coat, was Uher.

I too knelt, not on the coconut mat that covered the centre aisle of the nave, but beside it, the better to suffer discomfort. Suddenly, looking at Uher, I had an idea – perhaps just one more of the straws I had been clutching at ever since Vachousek had spoken to me, yet it seemed my one and only chance of salvation. Far more realistic than a romantic escape to join those theoretical guerrillas in the woods above Kostelec.

Uher had been a year ahead of me at the local grammar school. He played football with the Kostelec Juniors and went out with Dasa Safrankova until she threw him over when her grandfather in Prague found her a rich husband. He graduated from grammar school at a time when they put you to work in the factory if you didn't have an influential uncle, and in a clerical position if you did, but Uher was admitted to a seminary in Zeleny Hradec and every so often after that he would show up in Kostelec wearing a theological student's dog-collar.

I watched him praying and forgot to pray myself, because I was scheming furiously. It seemed miraculously simple. Enter a seminary! The Germans would probably allow that. And then, if they found out about the sabotage, could they arrest a student of theology? Perhaps then they would even believe me when I told them it was not sabotage, just clumsiness. I began to mutter fragments of the Lord's Prayer, drawing small foolish draughts of cold comfort from the chalice of terror as the perspiration chilled my back. But could I get released from conscripted labour? Perhaps I could. Perhaps – might there not exist some private understanding between the Germans and the episcopal seat? I stared, hypnotized, at Uher's black back and his black head where – but perhaps I was only imagining it – his tonsure twinkled in the pale glow of the eternal flame at the altar.

He crossed himself with a flourish and stood up. I too crossed myself and rose from the cold stones of the church floor. You can't greet someone with the usual "Hi" in a church, so I nodded at him, he returned the greeting and I followed him out. At the door we both turned to face the altar, dipped our fingers in the font, genuflected and crossed ourselves with magic, majestic gestures. Then we entered the church vestibule where, above the kneeling stools on both sides, red lamps were burning under the votive pictures.

"Olda," I said in a half-whisper. "Can I have a word with you?"

"Sure. What do you want?"

In the light of the flames Uher's round, rural face shone ruddily over his dog-collar. He looked more like a puppet-show devil with a bristly brushcut than a future priest. Suddenly I felt embarrassed to be confronting him with such an unexpected request. But it was too late.

"I'm interested ... I'd like to ... I'm thinking of entering the seminary...."

He looked astonished. He clearly thought of me more in connection with the jazz band and girls – after all, he was from Kostelec too. But I had once been an altar-boy – up until grade four, not counting the time I filled in for someone when I was in grade seven – years ago.

"You?" he said. "What for?"

His question did not ease my embarrassment.

"I think I ... I feel the call...."

"You?" he repeated in amazement. "Isn't this a bit sudden?"

"I don't know. Maybe it's the war...."

"But you're in conscripted labour, aren't you?"

"Yes, at the Messerschmitt factory."

"Unfortunately, it's probably impossible. You'll have to wait till after the war," he said, still staring at me as though he couldn't believe his ears. "That is, if your decision sticks."

"But they accepted you, didn't they?"

"That was the year before last. Nobody from your year got out of conscripted labour."

"What if somebody put in a special request for me?"

"Who?"

"I don't know, the seminary. Or the bishop."

I knew I was talking nonsense. But fear is stronger than will, and incomparably stronger than intellect. Looking like a wooden Beelzebub, Uher stared at me inquisitively – almost, it seemed to me, cynically.

"In the first place," he said, "why should the bishop do that? Just because you made up your mind all of a sudden? Hang on a while. If you still feel so inclined after the war, no one will have to do any special pleading for you."

"But I really and truly want to...."

He interrupted me. "And in the second place, you have some pretty funny notions of what the bishop can do. Do you know how many priests in his diocese are in prison? Thirty-seven. And the bishop is intervening on behalf of all of them, negotiating with the Gestapo, handing out bribes, and the only one he's been able to get released is the Archdeacon Svehla, and he only managed that because Svehla is eighty and very sick."

Despite my fear, I saw that such arguments couldn't be countered by claiming a sudden supernatural calling. The straw I clutched at was being swept away, but I grasped at it desperately one more time. "Couldn't I at least enter a monastery, as a lay brother? Join some order ... ?"

"Which one?" demanded Uher sharply.

I couldn't have cared less. The thought of withdrawing to a monastery, any monastery at all, evoked even greater sensations of security than a seminary. At the same time, I was aware of the none-too-godly intent behind my display of piety, aware that once the danger was past I would come back again. I realized that this was a blasphemous breach of faith, and lost hope.

"Well," I said weakly, "what about the Cistercians?"

This was the fifth year of the Nazi occupation. The absurdity of such a wish hit me with full force. Uher was silent for a moment, then said, "You're in some kind of big trouble, aren't you?"

"Me? What gave you that – "

"You're not the first person who looked for sanctuary in a monastery. People have been doing it for about two thousand years."

"That's a load of – I mean it's nonsense," I said, for we were still inside the church.

"You don't say."

"No, I mean it! I'm not in any trouble. It's just that I ... I simply want to be a priest, that's all."

"Go on, admit it," said Uher. "If anyone can help, the Cistercian brothers can. Not that they can do a lot. The Gestapo are always sniffing around the monastery. They know very well the brothers are up to more than praying. But they'll do whatever they can."

Should I back down? Admit that he was right, that he'd seen through me? I looked into that satanic face. The collar below it had been starched a bright white. His mention of the Gestapo crackled through my brain like lightning, and I saw that it was too late. Even if the Cistercians were willing to take me in, an official request would have to be made, and that would take time. I'd have to join the guerrillas right away, that very night. By

tomorrow the mutilated cross-brackets would be in the Gestapo's hands –
and for the first time I saw the symbolism of the object of my amateurish
sabotage. But instead of Christian humility – am I already in Satan's
clutches, I wondered? – I played tough guy to the student of theology. I was
more convincing with Uher than I had been with Nadia. "You're wrong.
I'm not in any trouble. But I really want to become a priest. Like you." And I
looked him straight in the eye. "No one expected you to take up orders
when you were in the eighth form. And yet you did it."

He started to say something, then thought better of it. "But you're
probably right," I added. "It would be better if I waited till after the war."

A sardonic smile flitted across his face. Quickly I said, "And don't
worry. I'll bet you get over it before I do."

We stared at each other like two enemies. He had almost exposed me.
But why had he decided on the priesthood in the first place? Because of an
unhappy love affair? He hadn't been all that crazy over Dasa.

"If it's really the way you say," he said, "then there's nothing to worry
about. All the same, if you ever need any help with anything, come to me. I'll
do whatever's within my power."

He offered me his hand.

"God be with you."

"So long," I said, and added quickly, "God be with you."

Uher opened the massive door and vanished into the night.

I turned back towards the nave of the church. The sexton was striding
down the coconut carpet with a huge set of keys. The church was about to
be locked up. Once more it seemed to me symbolic – God closing the gates
of His tabernacle on me because I had in fact denied Him, as Peter had
denied Christ. Instead of humbly admitting to Uher that I had lied, that I
was in trouble, in awful trouble, I had succumbed to an inappropriate vanity, a sinful pride. And I had lied again, and even worse, I had shut myself off
from all access to God.

The sexton shook his keys pointedly. They rattled like bones. I
genuflected quickly, touching the four points of my body to make the sign of
the cross. I was not thinking about the four dear wounds of our Lord, but
rather of those holes I had countersunk too deeply. I stood up and, like
Judas, rushed from the church.

●

Mr. Senka is upset. He is standing in the lobby of Masaryk Hall, off Queen
Street, with Mrs. Santner. He is leaning over a table displaying her wares,
pointing to a book in his hand. The publisher's corpulent husband is slouch-
ing behind her, his nose florid from too much whisky. A small crowd has
gathered and is listening to Mr. Senka with interest.

"Don't try to tell me that," Mr. Senka declares in a loud voice. "Just read it yourself, madame, right here on page 19!" And he waves the book with its colourful cover depicting cubes floating in a blue sky; one of the cubes is sprouting a green tree. "Here it is. Listen to this if you please. Quote: 'I'd give the Virgin Mary herself a boot up the ass if it would save my bloody neck.' End of quote. Aren't you ashamed, madame, to put that in print?"

"I will not be a censor!" says Mrs. Santner, shaking her head. She is wearing a wig, which suits her better than her own hair, since she never has time to look after it properly. Not long ago her husband began lamenting this fact after his fifth whisky at the Benes Inn. He also complained that his wife had no time for anything else, either, only for her books. "That's what the author wrote," the publisher is insisting now, "and I will not censor what an author writes."

The Santners came to Canada after August, 1968; Mr. Senka left Czechoslovakia in 1939. The publisher does not realize that to Mr. Senka's prewar ears the word "censor" does not carry the same odious overtones that it does to hers. I knew her slightly in Prague, where she almost became a writer – almost, I say, because the manuscript of her overexplicit stories based on the lives of teenage girls was confiscated by the censor, who labelled it pornography. Mrs. Santner finally published the work in Canada, adding some stories that had been too risqué to include in Prague. The only émigrés who were not outraged were those who had come over for purely economic reasons in the 1920s and they were not outraged simply because they never read books.

Now, however, the diminutive, balding Mr. Senka is outraged by a book that Mrs. Santner has not written herself, merely published.

"You may not be a censor but you should be," he roars. "Enough is enough!"

"You have to read it in context," she explains. "After all, those words are spoken by an anti-Nazi revolutionary who's afraid the Gestapo will catch him. When people are afraid, they use strong language. It's a well-known phenomenon."

Her defence is too scholarly for Mr. Senka. "But this is a book, madame," he cries. "A book."

This time it is Mrs. Santner's turn not to understand. For her the word "book" has none of the sanctimonious overtones it has for Mr. Senka, for whom a book is a household object to be taken up only on very special occasions. Mrs. Santner's husband leans over her shoulder and whispers, "Now, Betty, don't let's get into an argument," but this only goads her on.

"I can't help it. In context, language like that has a valid function. That's the way people actually talk in situations like that."

"But they don't talk that way in *books*."

Each is partly right, according to his experience. A man with a slightly impacted face steps up to the table. He is wearing an armband that indicates he is an organizer of the event. He picks up the book and leafs through it, looking for page 19. A young man in a double-breasted suit steps in to defend Mrs. Santner. "She's right, Mr. Senka. Take *The Good Soldier Svejk,* for example. There are vulgar expressions in *Svejk* too."

Mr. Senka pulls his chin in, peers at this new apologist through his glasses, and raises a finger. "That may be, but that's *Svejk*!"

"So what?" demurs the young man. He is a member of the deeply democratic post-August 1968 generation. "If Hasek could get away with it, why can't this" – he tries to read the author's name – "Jan Drobek? Drabek."

Mr. Senka thrusts his finger under the young man's nose, causing him to jerk back instinctively. "And how would you like it if someone wrote, 'I'd give President Masaryk a boot up the ass?' Eh? How would you like that?"

"That's beside the point. All I'm saying is if Hasek could write like that, why can't Jan Drabek?"

Mrs. Santner is trembling, perhaps from anger but possibly from sorrow as well. Her eyes are glistening. When her husband got drunk at the Benes Inn he also said that his wife was like Charles Dickens: books are her children. Except that unlike Dickens she has each one with someone else. And so, in a fit of motherly love, Mrs. Santner commits a great faux pas. "Look, gentlemen," she says. "If someone were to write that he would kick President Masaryk in the ass, and it had some legitimate function in the book, then there's no way, no way at all, that you could object to it."

"What did you just say?" Mr. Senka's knees visibly begin to crumple. "Now, Betty," says her husband quietly. Mr. Senka turns pink, and opens his mouth. I expect a Jovian roar to emerge, but oddly enough the diminutive man speaks tremulously. "Why are you doing this to us? The Czech community is divided enough as it is, and here you are driving a wedge into it even farther! Instead of helping us to unite, you ... you...." He appears to be close to weeping.

"You see, Betty?" whispers the husband.

"You didn't understand what Mrs. Santner meant," says the young man. "She didn't mean that everybody should have the right to insult President Masaryk...."

"Then what did she mean?" sniffles Mr. Senka. "President Masaryk? In the ass? I, sir, am a liberal man. But I would never, as long as Peter Senka is my name...."

"But you said it first," says the young man. "I mean, it was you who gave that as an example."

"Me? Don't insult me, sir! I would never let a thing like that pass my lips. Kick President...."

There is a loud noise. The man with the armband has energetically snapped the book shut and banged it down on the table. "Mrs. Santner, I can't allow you to sell this book here. It's Communist crap. I've got nothing against selling books, but only the kind of books that President Masaryk himself, as Brother Senka here says, wouldn't be ashamed to have in his own library. Would you please put them back in the boxes and get them out of here?"

Now Mrs. Santner turns pink. Her husband, who has already obediently begun to pack the books back into their boxes, receives a rap across the knuckles as the publisher explodes: "Just a minute! You gave me permission to sell them yourself!"

"But I thought you were selling decent literature, not Communist trash!"

Mrs. Santner picks up the volume the organizer pounded the table with and brandishes it over her head. I wonder if she isn't getting ready to hit him with it.

"Communist trash? Do you know who wrote this book, Mr. Baur? A man who fled from the Communists in 1948. And it's an anti-Bolshevik novel. If you would just take the trouble to buy something from us for once, and maybe even read it – "

"I only buy books that can be read while eating, madame!"

"That's no literary – I mean that's no way to judge books," says the young democrat.

The organizer, however, sneers cruelly. "No offence meant, of course. If the Communists want to print something like that, let them. We're used to that."

Mrs. Santner, banned in Prague for pornography, wants to tell the man that his ideas are at odds with reality, but her voice catches and the organizer goes on. "We've learned what to expect from that lot. But insulting President Masaryk in a book published in exile!"

"But there's nothing in the book about Masaryk at all!" cries the publisher, her voice still unsteady. "This man here dragged that in!" and she points at Mr. Senka, who is holding his hand over his heart. "There's only a reference to the Virgin Mary – "

"And doesn't that amount to the same thing?" interrupts a woman in a mink coat who has remained silent until now. "Offences against religious feelings and national feelings are the same thing."

"Betty!" whispers the husband.

"No one is insulting anyone's feelings," wails Mrs. Santner. "Don't

you understand what it means for something to have a function in literature?"

"I don't understand and I don't want to!" replies the lady in the fur
coat. "The name of Masaryk is as sacred to me as the name of the Virgin
Mary."

"But," the democrat interjects once more, "the author writes about
Masaryk positively," and he rapidly flips through the pages of the book. "I
can't find it right away, but it's positive, all right. No, what I mean to say" –
he hesitates as though allergic to the word, for the expression "positive"
comes from a rhetoric he has long since rejected, the rhetoric of Marxist
literary criticism – "is that the book recognizes his achievements. The father
of the hero – "

"Of course the author likes Masaryk," Mrs. Santner says desperately.
"But you people don't know that because you don't read anything, least of
all anything that Masaryk wrote! You think Czech literature came to an end
a hundred years ago with Bozena Nemcova."

She has an unfortunate talent for faux pas. She forgets that the woman
in the fur coat, and Mr. Senka, and the organizer too for that matter, have
no way of knowing that Bozena Nemcova is now irrevocably associated
with the blinkered literary policies of the Communist Ministry of Culture.

"Unlike you," the lady in the fur coat snaps archly, "we hold our
national classics in high esteem. But you have been infected by your Communist education, if you don't mind my saying so. It may not be your fault,
but it's the sad truth. We believe our mother tongue is something sacred.
But the things your authors do with the language – 'bloody neck'!" she says
with disgust. "And I'm too ashamed to repeat the rest of it!"

"Also I think you underestimate us," says the lady's husband, a man in
a soft leather coat. "We read good modern literature too. And my wife is
right. Take the wonderful Czech of Capek or Vancura – "

"Vancura was a Commie!" retorts the young democrat angrily.

"Well," says the man in the calf-skin coat uncertainly, rapidly recon-
sidering and electing a neutral position. "Even so. But that's not the point.
After all, the Germans executed him."

"The husband of this writer," says Mrs. Santner, lifting a different
book from the table, "was executed by the Communists. Have you read it?"

"Now, Betty," says her husband.

"It sounds interesting," says the gentleman. "I'd like to read it."

"So buy it, then! Here's your chance! A measly four bucks!"

"Now just a moment, madame." The man laughs. "There's no need to
take me up on it right away."

"Why not? You said you'd like to read it. Now's your chance."

"Well now...."

"Except that you'd rather borrow it from your unemployed uncle, right? Or steal it from the public library?"

"Betty, for God's sake!"

"The libraries are always writing to us for replacements because somebody is stealing them right and left. And I'll bet it's not the Canadians."

"Betty, be quiet!"

The husband's command comes too late, and anyway Mr. Santner does not look much like the head of his household.

"This is impertinence!" snaps the man in the calf-skin coat. "All I've tried to point out to you is that the good writers, whether classic or modern, have always held their mother tongue in high esteem, and did not write about things that don't belong in books. And if you want to compare this Drabek of yours to someone like ... like" – he gropes about in his memory, but apart from the Communist Vancura not many writers' names have lodged there – "with someone like Karel Hynek Macha, who would never ever have written something like the passage you quoted us about the Virgin Mary – "

"Have you heard about Macha's erotic diary?" says Mrs. Santner abruptly. The gentleman is taken aback, for he knows Macha only as a Byronic Romantic poet, and so retreats once more to neutral ground.

"What of it?"

"Do you know that Macha writes about how he ..." – and here even Mrs. Santner hesitates, but she's too fired up to stop – "how he quote fucked the family maid – "

"Betty! For the love of God I beg you!"

" – from behind unquote?"

"You shall not divide our community!" Mr. Senka's sudden shout echoes above the bustle of the rapidly diminishing assembly. The publisher's bluntness has left everyone speechless and sent them scurrying. All except for the young democrat, who asks, "Does he actually say that?"

The husband is flinging books into boxes with both hands. The organizer takes a deep breath and bellows, "All right, that's it. Take your fiddle-faddle and clear out!"

"You can't do this," shouts Mrs. Santner. "I bought a ticket!"

The husband, his arms laden with boxes, scurries about trying to clear out.

"As organizer, madame, I'm responsible for the dignity of this affair. Your money will be returned, but you won't be allowed to stay in here!"

"Come on, Betty, let's go," cries the husband desperately from the exit.

Strangely enough, the publisher has calmed down. "Okay," she says, grinning sarcastically. "All the same, would any of you patriots care to guess how much Czech literature I sold here today? Eight bucks worth. Goodbye!"

And with this she turns her back on the organizer, provocatively thrusting in his direction that part of her body which started the discussion, and walks proudly out of the hall.

●

*Sofron, Slovakea*
*9 of May 1946*

*Dear Dan,*
*I adres you with these few lines to let you know I am well and hope you enjoy the same blesing at present and I am writing you because my daugter Suleika is having her first birthday today. She was born on the 9 of May on Liberation day so we killed some rams because relativs showed up from all the way from Saris and brother Olda and his wife from Lithuanea came too. Brother Olda runs a factry now. They got a lone from the bank and bought themselves a mill for knitting sweaters and they already showed there stuff at the exibition in Prague. They come in there own car. Its a Doge my brother bought from the American army. Suleikas a lot like me already. She didn't look so much like me but now she has a nose like mine a button nose as they say. The only thing is her eyes are far apart and mine are close together and also shes got brown and mine are blue but she takes after her mother whose got black eyes.*
*This country food is making me feel a lot beter and the fresh air. For now I am only helping out but the docter says I can work at harvist time so once a week I bake the bread and the rest of the time I just putter about, feed the poltry and put fresh straw to the animals. We got 4 horses and 12 cows not counting the poltry and the sow had 12 piglits. We will kill one when the crops is in by that time it will wiegh 100 pounds. Maried life is nice and its working out fine even tho I never knew the wife before we got maried and I seen her first a day before the weding. Shes an only child and when her old folks pass on I am in charge. Who would of said that one day I'd be a farmer. Shes a distent cousin but the docter says distent relations dont matter and the children wont be degenerated. You can see hes right from Suleika. Shes helthy and had an easy birth she was out almost as soon as the midwife come and shes real pretty with hair like a gypsies, it must be after the wifes father because the wife is blond and I have red hair. Her name is Suleika. Your probly saying thats a strange name and it is, its Georgian and its also in that song they sing everywhere now, the wife is real fond*

*of it and she wouldnt have any other name even if it is a strange Georgian name. But the main thing is shes helthy and the only thing I wory about is she might have weak lungs after me. We go to the movies once a week into town, we saw Sun Valley Serinade, a nice movie with Sonia Hynie and a Rusian film Ivan the Terrible which wasnt too nice but it was interesting too. To conclude my letter with please exsept my warmest wishes and fondest memries.*

*Your old freind*
*Lojza*

•

Niagara thunders mournfully
Thunders mournfully in the night....

A mixed chorus, dressed in jeans and sombreros, is singing, accompanied by guitars and banjos. The organizer has taken off his armband and, thus humanized, sings the harmony in a high tenor. The democratic young man, divested of his double-breasted jacket, in a check shirt, strums the same three chords, his eyes closed in an expression of bliss.

If your heart is torn by passion
there's no help for you in sight....

I'm sitting next to Margitka at the end of the row, because Margitka is dutifully holding the hand of her husband in the wheelchair. She has chocked the chair with two brightly coloured books so it won't roll forward – Mrs. Santner's total sales for today. Margitka has to read to her husband because the bullet that grazed his skull mysteriously damaged an optic nerve and he can barely see. I look at Margitka's gentle profile, so like those gothic statues of the Virgin Mary. I long to put my hand on her thigh, for the husband, after all, would hardly notice, but the woman in the mink coat who was so deeply offended by Mrs. Santner is sitting next to me on the other side so I restrain myself. I hear voices behind me whispering in English. Veronika is translating the Czech cowboy song into English: " 'Headlong into the abyss the water plunges and I see you, girl, floundering there. What a pity I can't embrace that beautiful delusion,' " Veronika murmurs in a sad voice. I turn my attention back to the stage program. It is pure camp. Later, when it was much too late anyway, she told me what happened that sad afternoon when I understood nothing and did nothing. She had told Percival that he could hear modern Czech folklore at an evening put on by the Czech Tramping Club of Ontario, and so Percy showed up in a Saville Row suit, expecting to hear electronic dulcimer music. What he heard instead was the Jingling Johnny which Mr. Sestak had made from an old crutch, some tin pie plates and assorted jingle bells; he would bang it rhythmically on the floor to punctuate the dynamic finale of the songs. Mr. Sestak also held the straying voices together with his thunderous bass voice.

"When you said folklore," Percy remarked, "I imagined something quite different."

"That's because your idea of folklore, darling, comes from the nineteenth century," Veronika replied. There was the softness of autumn in her eyes and she looked wistfully at the motley group on the stage, dressed in clothes from an army surplus store on Yonge Street. "This is folklore, too. It may be the only living folklore left on that side of the Iron Curtain. It's full of images of things like Niagara Falls and wild geese, moose and the Rocky Mountains, everything they used to imagine so intensely about this place." She fell silent. "You've heard of the Iron Curtain, I suppose?"

"It's a generally well-known metaphor. Didn't Churchill invent the phrase? One of those cold warriors, anyway?"

"It wasn't Churchill. I don't know who invented it. Some engineer from Moscow, probably, or maybe Prague. It's a metaphor made of barbed wire and booby-traps."

"I always thought it was just a way of speaking."

He took the girl by the hand. He felt ashamed, determined to read up on the subject. Who had written about such things? Orwell? Someone like that. Yet hadn't they told him in the courses he had attended in his chaotic student days that 1984 was a satire on America? On McCarthyism perhaps. He wasn't sure.

> The road to the west is long, so long
> And hopeless and vain is my longing....

"The song is about longing to go west," the girl explained to him.

"Why don't they learn some real country-and-western songs, now they're over here?" he asked. Veronika shrugged as he continued mechanically, "Maybe the American reality is too different from their dream of it."

"Reality is always different from dreams," the girl said. "And besides, the dream now is Czechoslovakia."

"If that's the case why don't they sing about Czechoslovakia?"

She pulled her hands out of Percy's grasp, took out her handkerchief and blew her nose loudly at the precise moment when Mr. Sestak brought his Jingling Johnny down upon the floor with a resonant crash.

"Because they're remembering the best of Czechoslovakia."

The humanized organizer, the democratic young man in the check shirt, two girls in sombreros and culottes, two guitarists, one man with a banjo and Mr. Sestak all sing:

> The west is calling me, and I cannot sleep
> But the way I have to travel is too long....

The stage boards rattle with blows from the Jingling Johnny and a thunderous bass voice carries the solo, while the rest hum like the wind over the prairie:

> The road is overgrown with grass
> I search in vain for the proper lass....

●

"Uippelt didn't come in for the shift today," said the foreman Vachousek.

"Why not?"

"Don't ask me. Ballon says he went to Hradec on business. On business, understand?"

"But what's that mean?"

Vachousek tapped the blueprint on his table with a pair of callipers. "Either nothing, or else big trouble. They got an assembly plant in Hradec. All those neat little parts we crank out here get put together there to make the Messerschmitt Bf 109."

When he pronounced the word "Messerschmitt" a vein jumped in my head.

"They also got those firing benches, you understand, student? Where they test-fire the cannons?" He stopped tapping the blueprint with the callipers and looked at me gravely. The back of my neck began to ache. "What — what are we going to do?" I blurted out.

"Nothing we can do except go on figure-skating. And hope we don't lose our balance," added the foreman. "The boys in the welding section will go on putting your botchery right, like nothing happened. And we could always try praying."

I said nothing. The foreman took a deep breath. "Now beat it, student."

Nadia welcomed me with wide eyes. I told her that Uippelt had gone to Hradec. "Isn't that a good thing?" she said. Dejectedly I told her what Vachousek had said and added that the nearest Gestapo headquarters just happened to be in Hradec.

She was silent, like a mouse. For the first time since Vachousek had hauled me over the coals I took a good look at her. In those few days she seemed to have grown even thinner and more wan, if that was possible. The siren howled. I had completely forgotten that the shift was almost over, though usually I waited impatiently for the siren's deliverance.

Nadia turned her drill off and came over to me. "Dan, shouldn't you ... while there's still time...."

"What?"

"You could hide in our attic. The war can't go on too much longer...."

I shook my head. "That's good of you, Nadia, but I can't hide at your place. Somebody might put two and two together...."

"Then I'll take you to my uncle's in Vrchoviny. He's got a mill there, and that's a safe place."

The reality of the danger was still not manifest enough to spur me to such a radical act. And besides that, I felt compelled to keep up the tough-guy act for her.

"No, Nadia. I can't get your relatives mixed up in this too. I've got places I can hide."

"Here in town?"

"No. Remember the warehouse? I've got friends. And no one'll ever connect me with them. We meet secretly."

The mention of the most awe-inspiring act of war heroism in Kostelec so far, the one that had already cost fifty people their freedom, filled Nadia with renewed respect.

"Oh well, that's different," she said, tying her kerchief. "But Dan, you let me know, all right? Not where you – I mean the fewer knows about it the better, but that you're safe, okay, Dan?"

All that seemed left of her now were the burning black eyes and white skin.

"I'd ... if I could...." She looked around. We were alone in the factory hall. "But I got to go. Franta's waiting for me at the gate." All at once she leaned towards me and gave me a kiss. "I still think you're really somebody, Dan. Even if our plan didn't work out."

She turned and ran to the exit, her huge boots clumping on the concrete floor. She ran like a boy, like a country girl.

I threw on my coat and went to the Skocdopoles'.

Prema was not at home. Mr. Skocdopole was sitting in the kitchen by the radio listening to news from the *Oberkommando der Wehrmacht*. When he saw it was me he took a "churchill," an illegal homemade frequency adapter, out of his pocket, stuck it into the back of the radio and tuned in to the BBC. He did everything with one hand; all that remained of the other was the stump of a forearm covered with a grey sock.

"Sit down," he said, pointing his stump at a chair. His face was florid and his nose looked like a red cucumber. The source of his colourful complexion stood on the table and Mr. Skocdopole pointed his sock-covered stump at it. "Have a drink."

It was home-brewed slivovice from his brother's farm in Moravia. Though the brother was younger than Mr. Skocdopole he had not lost his arm in the war and so had inherited the small farm. The state took care of Mr. Skocdopole. He was given a tobacco warehouse to look after, and all that was left of the rural life was the homemade slivovice.

I looked at his nose. I was unaccustomed to drinking, let alone drinking hundred-and-forty-proof brandy. The first glass made me tipsy. As I tried to focus my disobedient eyes on the legionnaire a drunken story ran through my mind, one that Prema had once told me – he had been tipsy with apple wine at the time. According to Prema, Brych the fortune-teller was responsible for his father's florid complexion. Although Reich officials had ordered Brych to close down his business – the Reich feared the influence of fortune-telling on public morale – he went on prophesying on the sly. He was a doleful man who drank a lot, and after the occupiers had ruined his business he often cast his prophecies while drunk as an owl. For years Mr. Skocdopole had been one of his most faithful clients, and it was even said that Brych had been responsible for bringing Mr. Skocdopole together with his future wife. Mr. Skocdopole had placed a classified ad in the paper which ran: "Legionnaire-invalid (arm) seeks wholesome girl up to 35 years old," and Brych used his crystal ball to evaluate the replies. Mrs. Skocdopolova proved to be one of eleven daughters, all of whom were pretty. Six had married Americans, one an Englishman, and three had wed Austrians, and they had all left the country except Mrs. Skocdopolova, who was the youngest and the prettiest. Her mother didn't want to lose her last daughter to foreign parts too so she answered the ad herself, and Mr. Brych's crystal ball told the bridegroom that the proffered bride was essentially a compliant creature. In that, the crystal ball did not lie: not only was Mrs. Skocdopolova the prettiest bride in Kostelec in living memory, she was also the most obedient woman in the world. She married the invalid without a whisper of complaint and became the kind of wife you only hear about in sermons. And Mr. Skocdopole, utterly content with his crystal ball marriage, had Brych tell his fortune each year on their wedding anniversary. Since nothing in particular had ever happened to him after he married, and since Brych's prognostications were so general that they always appeared to come true, Mr. Skocdopole's faith in Brych's crystal ball grew out of all reasonable proportion.

Then the Nazis closed down Brych's concession. It was just a few days before one of the Skocdopoles' wedding anniversaries, and when Mr.

Skocdopole came round for his yearly measure of crystallomancy a maudlin and glassy-eyed Brych, outraged at the Germans, predicted a death in the family. Mr. Skocdopole was terrified. After all those years of reassuring auguries he was unprepared for anything quite that drastic. The news so startled him that he jumped up in alarm, catching one of his buttons in the crocheted tablecloth and pulling the cloth off the table along with the crystal ball. He tried to stop the ball with the stump of his arm but merely succeeded in batting it over Brych's head, where it smashed to pieces against the copper buckles of the fortune-teller's antique *Book of Spells and Incantations*. In a fit of self-pity, Brych added gloatingly that death would strike down the head of the family, and that Mr. Skocdopole would not live to see the plums ripen.

That had been in January. Because Mr. Skocdopole had no reason not to believe Brych, he began to prepare for death, not in the Christian manner but simply by deciding to live the remainder of his life to the full. After all those years of happy marriage, however, with a wife who was pretty and obedient in all things, he had become so settled in his ways that he could only imagine the full life coming from a bottle. That year, in addition to the usual supply, his brother had to buy all the available home-brewed slivovice in the village at black-market prices, and Mr. Skocdopole embraced hedonism. He blossomed, his countenance was transformed into a cluster of tomatoes, and when the plums in the orchard turned blue they carried him off to the hospital from the town square where the police had found him running around the church crying out that a herd of wild white boars was after him.

He lay in the hospital, the plums ripened and dropped from the trees, he was given injections instead of alcohol, the snows came and Mr. Skocdopole concluded that the prophecy had been wrong. They released him from hospital on St. Nicholas' Day, and just to make sure he went on drinking until the New Year, but still he did not die. In January, on the day of the anniversary, he went secretly to Brych's, fearful that he had misunderstood the date the year before. But Brych was not at home and the new tenant informed Mr. Skocdopole that Brych had been arrested in the autumn and shot. Skocdopole's considerate wife had kept it a secret from him. The news was a relief to the legionnaire. He decided that Brych was wrong, not about the date, but about the person. From that time on he drank with moderation, merely to maintain his brilliant complexion.

The radio was announcing that the Red Army had conquered a village in Poland and that the Americans were retreating before a German offensive in the Ardennes.

"The bloody fools!" said Mr. Skocdopole. "The Yanks are playing tiddlywinks with the Hun and the Bolsheviks will be on our doorstep by spring." He squinted at me through infinitely bleary eyes and gestured with the stump in the sock. "Come on, drink up!"

I had rarely ever had a drink before, except for a few times at New Year's, and once, at Rosta's cottage when I tried to seduce Marie, I had drunk myself into a stupor. But now I was afraid. With one slivovice in me I grasped the stem of the glass and said, "Your health!"

Mr. Skocdopole repeated that paradoxical toast, tossed the contents of his glass into himself and I did the same. Almost at once my predicament began to appear less dreadful, a heroic death seemed desirable, the lanky Nadia the most buxom Mae West in the world and the opinions of the former legionnaire on military strategy extremely interesting.

"Do you think we'll be liberated by the Russians?" I asked.

"Liberated?" scoffed the one-armed hero. "We'll go from the frying-pan into the fire, that's what. And those gutless bloody Americans will diddle about just like they did back in 1918 in Russia."

The announcer on the radio was saying that a military commentary would follow. Mr. Skocdopole switched it off.

"Drink up," he said brusquely. "What do you think will happen when the Bolsheviks come in? Instead of tossing in the towel, Hitler is still giving the Americans a shellacking. So who is there to stop the Bolsheviks now?"

"Well, they're good. I mean as soldiers."

Mr. Skocdopole waved his stump. "Good my eye, boy! There's just a lot of them, that's all. Drink up. But that's what the Germans get for signing a peace treaty with the buggers in 1917. And if that wasn't enough, the Hun fought along with the Bolshies against the Russian democratic government. If it wasn't for the Germans and other jokers, there wouldn't be no Bolsheviks today. Nor Nazis either. Drink up!"

I took a drink. My fear had vanished. I had the feeling I was about to hear some great historical revelations. All I knew about the Bolsheviks was that my father was apprehensive about them. And that they had massacred Polish officers in the forest of Katyn. But that was what the Germans were claiming, so I didn't entirely believe it.

"Did the Germans really fight on the same side as the Bolsheviks after the Revolution, Mr. Skocdopole? Against you?"

"Of course they did, lad. Killed a few of them myself. Drink up!"

For a moment the legionnaire's matter-of-factness neutralized the restorative powers of the slivovice. "Who did you ... kill? The Bolsheviks?"

"Right, the Bolsheviks. But not the Russian Bolsheviks. We let them go. We played fair and square. After all, the Russians was on home territory and they was fighting against us. They was the enemy, of course, but they wasn't traitors. No, I shot our own people, Czechs. They was prisoners of war, originally, like us, but instead of fighting for the Whites they let themselves get sucked in by that propaganda, and ended up fighting for the Bolsheviks. So it was brother against brother. Look!" and he raised the stump in its sock. "And drink up, so I don't have to keep asking you."

"You lost that in a battle?" I asked admiringly, draining my glass.

"Indirectly," said Mr. Skocdopole. "It was near Pemza. I got bayoneted in the arm by a muck-shifter called Pospisil. I happened to know him. We was in the same company in the Austrian army and we both deserted to the Russians. Except that he was one of the first to join the Reds, after the revolution broke out. He used to come into our camp to spread Bolshevik propaganda. That's why he fought like a lion. The son-of-a-bitch knew damn well if they didn't win, he wouldn't get out of it alive. Drink up!" By that time his convivial imperative had become a mere punctuation mark. "Like lions they fought," he said. "All of Pemza was ours except for about a couple of hundred Czech traitors holding the centre of the city. The Acropolis, that's what they called it. The Russian Bolsheviks wasn't worth a piece of sheep dung – they had ten times the machine-guns we did, and all it took to make them shit their pants and run was a trick old Zizka used six hundred years ago when we were fending off the holy Crusaders back in the fifteenth century!" Mr. Skocdopole chuckled. "But of course they wasn't soldiers, they was just factory workers from Pemza. The only real soldiers was them turncoats of ours – "

"What trick was that?"

Mr. Skocdopole fastened his bleary eyes on me. "God's own truth it was my own idea. Have you ever heard about how Zizka loaded wagons up with stones and then let them run downhill straight at the Crusaders?"

That, of course, was one of the most advertised military feats in Czech history, and in our first year of high school Mrs. Trejtnarova used to pound the notion into our heads that the Czechs had really invented the tank way back in the 1420s. I nodded.

"The day before, we'd took over an armoured train at the Pemza station without firing a shot," Mr. Skocdopole went on. "The Bolsheviks turned tail, but they was Chinamen, so we let 'em run. Probably didn't know what they was doing. The train had a load of armoured cars on it. Drink up. In the morning we spread out around Pemza and the Acropolis was bristling with machine-guns and that's when I got the idea. So we filled one of them armoured cars with dynamite and fused it, I climbed in, started her up, got both machine-guns going and wired down the triggers so they'd keep on firing, lit the fuse, got her rolling and then jumped clear. You should've seen it! The thing went straight for them, the Reds was blasting away at it with everything they had, but that was high-quality armour-plate we plundered from the Germans and the bullets just bounced off her. And while they was busy crapping their drawers over this we stormed the hill and the Bolshies hardly gave us a look, they was too busy pouring lead into that car. Just when it looked like she was about to smash into the first breastwork, some sharpshooter hit the dynamite or maybe the fuse burnt down and *boom!*" Mr. Skocdopole flung out his stump, knocking over the bottle. But it was empty. He reached under the table and drew out another one. "Boom!" he said more quietly. "She blew to smithereens and we seen the Bolsheviks turning tail and running, except for those who was too scared to. We took the whole sector and only lost two men."

I felt good. Through the alcoholic mists in my mind I resurrected again the vision of a disabled Messerschmitt being blown to smithereens too, by the tail-gunner of a Flying Fortress.

"Yes sir, lad," sighed Mr. Skocdopole, "that was my last battle. Because later that same day Pospisil stuck me in the arm with his bayonet and the wound got infected, then gangrene set in and they had to amputate. But I still managed to finish Pospisil off, the traitor. And at first it just looked like a surface wound."

We started drinking from the second bottle; I gaze out through the gothic window of Edenvale College and, like a jinn from that long-since-emptied bottle, another story, also about infection, leaps out and I think of my father: fifty years after the battle at Zborov his leg was in such a state that they had to amputate it, but by then Father had a weak heart and he died on the operating table. Vicky is babbling on about the Mississippi River being the unifying structural principle of *Huckleberry Finn,* but my thoughts flee from the responsibilities for which I am paid to the opulent memories by which I live, to that ugly day in the spring of 1948 when in the morning mist I spied Mr. Pytlik, *Comrade* Pytlik as he had become, with a platoon of workers' militiamen, backed by the right of the workers' revolution, leading my dad off to jail – just as the Gestapo, backed by the right of might, had done with him five years earlier. Only this time the Kostelec jail was bursting with members of the Sokol gymnastic society, a couple of scoutmasters and two chaplains, and there was no room for my six-foot-two father. So they shoved him into the cellar of the old Mautner textile plant, locked the door and forgot about him. The cellar had only one window, high up near the ceiling, and it was covered by a thick grille choked with mud and cobwebs and dead flies. We didn't know he was there. We thought he was in prison.

Soon after that a rumour began to spread through a terrorized Kostelec: there was a corpse in Mautner's cellar – the Communists had thrown Brother Smiricky down there after beating him senseless in the secretariat. At first groans could be heard from the cellar – that was Brother Smiricky dying; then he had given up the ghost and was decomposing – there was a terrible stench coming from the grille, and the Communists couldn't even be bothered to bury the body.

Meanwhile Mother was going to the prison every day, and every day she was told that Dad wasn't there and sent away. She became convinced they had killed him and didn't have the courage to tell her.

Finally the rumour reached us too. Accompanied by a band of the more courageous Sokol women, Mother ran to the Mautners' factory to see for herself. I went with her. She knelt by the grille and, sure enough, the awful stench of decomposing flesh was drifting up through the clogged opening. "Joe! Joe!" Mother wailed. But there was no reply. Mother flung herself against the grille, and tore at it with her nails until her hands were running with blood. The Sokol wives were trying to pull her away from the mute window when a full division of revolutionary militiamen trotted up with Comrade Mr. Pytlik at their head – the rumour had just reached the secretariat as well.

Vicky has switched authorities and is now trying to persuade the class that Huck and Jim were homosexual lovers, for simplification is the fate of all overly ingenious theories, and I imagine to myself how the tactical meeting at the secretariat must have proceeded, since to martyr a director of the Sokol – a six-foot-two martyr at that – would have been politically inappropriate in those troubled days: a sentry runs up and announces that a mob is gathering in front of the factory; not only the Sokol women are there, but men as well. The situation is deteriorating and Comrade Mr. Pytlik puts the question: "All right, comrades, which one of you knocked him off? Come on, own up! That was a bloody stupid thing to do! It could have waited till things normalize!" No one admits to the hasty act, they merely stare at each other, most of them feeling rather ill at ease, for with the possible exception of Comrade Mr. Pytlik they are not killers. He begins to speculate: "D'you suppose he croaked out of fear? He always was a spineless son-of-a-bitch," and here he is talking from experience because he has already frightened my father once. At least he thinks he did; in reality my dad handed the diary over to him because the whole affair was embarrassing to him. Mr. Zillinger, the German bank manager, vanished a few days before the end of the war, leaving behind only a huge portrait of the Führer, brooding over a pile of rubbish in his office. It was in this pile that my father found the diary. He read it as though it were pornography, for not only was the widower Zillinger an accomplished debaucher of young women, he also wrote in detail about his conquests. But occasionally, among accounts of exotic couplings with gentle conscripts of the Luftwaffe School for Women Auxiliary Radio Operators, there would appear memoranda like: "Herr Pytlik came with the weekly report. Sent it to the Gestapo in Gratz." My father skipped over such annotations, partly because, in his innocence, he saw nothing sinister in the fact that Pytlik brought the bank manager regular reports to be passed on to the Gestapo, and partly because he was far too overheated by the more exotic material, for he had probably never encountered anything like it before. Moreover, it was too good to keep to himself for long, and soon he was reading the steamier passages in hushed tones to his companions in the Sokol restaurant on Saturday evenings. News of the diary's existence spread until it reached the ears of Herr Pytlik. Herr (in fact by this time he was no longer *Herr* Pytlik, but just *Mr.,* prior to becoming *Comrade*) Pytlik showed up at our door heading a unit of the Expropriation Guard, and in the name of the National Committee he demanded that Father hand over the diary. My father felt embarrassed. It was hardly likely that he even remembered those little notes in German that he had skipped over; he was only ashamed that someone had informed on him for reading depraved literature in public. So he handed the diary over to Comrade Pytlik, and thus the last trace of bank manager Zillinger vanished. The Expropriation Guard hung the manager's portrait of Hitler over the urinals in the public lavatory on the town square and the drunks took bets on who could piss on the Führer's head.

But my father was not a spineless coward, nor had he been done in. He was merely lying there unconscious, nearly dead from the gangrenous, suppurating war wound. When the revolutionary militia unlocked the door to the cellar they pulled out their handkerchiefs in unison, almost forced backwards by the same noxious stench which, in a milder form, had caught the attention of Judge Neuthaler five years earlier. The militiamen carried my reeking father out of the cellar on an improvised stretcher, the Sokol women began to sob, old Brother Vavruska, though he was wearing a homburg, saluted, and my mother flung herself at Mr. Pytlik with a cry of rage and scratched three long gouges in his revolutionary stubble that later became infected, probably because Mother had dead flies under her nails. The infection spread and Mr. Pytlik's whiskers fell out, but only on one side of his face, so that he had to shave his beard off. Later, when beards came into fashion, Comrade Mr. Pytlik had to go around as clean-shaven as an Englishman.

"They picked me for the execution squad. My arm wasn't looking all that serious yet," Mr. Skocdopole was saying. "We marched them to the woods outside the town, and Pospisil, the little weasel, actually tried to talk to me on the way, the traitor!"

Something yellowish glimmered and gurgled and a red cucumber appeared above it. I was in excellent spirits. I felt like a warrior among warriors. "What" – I hiccuped – "what did he say?"

"You'd never guess, lad. He says, 'You ought to be ashamed of yourself, Skocdopole, you a working peasant and taking up arms against a class brother.' Me? Ashamed? I fought for my country! For our Czechoslovak republic, while those turds, with that hoodlum of theirs, Lenin, cooked up a separate peace with the Germans and stabbed us in the back. They couldn't have cared a damn about the liberty of the nation. All they cared about was their own bloody so-called class interests!"

"You told him that?"

"Me? No. Drink up. All I said was: 'Shut your mouth, you goddamned traitor!' Then we shot them in the woods. And they called themselves Czech workers!"

Vicky has finished. I come to my senses and open the book. "I don't know," I say, still rather high on the marijuana of inappropriate memory, "what any of you consider to be the essential message of this magnificent novel, this remarkable literary improvisation which is held together, as a good bass-player holds together a band, by a technical device called the Mississippi. Open your books at page 222 in the Bantam edition."

I wait for a moment while they shuffle through the pages and my gaze wanders out the window to the black bird who may well be the proprietor of Edenvale College. He struts slowly, proudly over the dazzling plain, leaving behind him in the snow preternaturally large footprints. Once more my thoughts skip back to that drunken evening thirty years ago, now sunken into oblivion, into death. The legionnaire is no longer alive. "Fine bunch of Czech workers they were!" he said indignantly. "They could've shaken hands with the Nazis over a lot of things. We executed them, that's the truth, because they was traitors. But they did the same to us just because we fought for our country. Once – drink up!" he said and took a terrifying draught himself. "A body's almost ashamed to talk about it. If I wasn't so looped I'd never even mention this to you, boy. Sedlica – how old could he've been? Twenty-two at the outside. A farmer, too. A grenade knocked him out at Samara and they took him prisoner. The next day we took Samara by storm but it was too late. We found Sedlica in a little courtyard buried under a pile of rubbish, stabbed to death with bayonets. Czech workers! A fine bunch of rats they were! Filthy traitors!" The stump of an arm in a stocking gesticulated wildly, and then I heard nothing more.

Most of them don't even bother to look for page 222. They know that I won't do anything to them; I'm not interested in their marks; I'm a preacher, not a teacher. Perhaps they are hoping to hear another classic passage delivered in a comic accent. Only the faithful Irene Svensson, in yet a different outfit, pea-green with a yellow hem this time, opens her book gravely. "About half-way down the page," I say, and accent or not, I read the message: "'... I knowed it *was* the king and the duke, though they was all over tar and feathers, and didn't look like nothing in the world that was human – just looked like a couple of monstrous big soldier-plumes. Well, it made me sick to see it; and I was sorry for them poor pitiful rascals, it seemed like I couldn't ever feel any hardness against them any more in the world. It was a dreadful thing to see. Human beings *can* be awful cruel to one another.' "

I raise my eyes from the book, heavily, as though I had just loaded a wagonful of coal. Such beautiful children. Wendy with her kilt and bare knees despite the Ontario December outside, Irene like a picture from *Vogue,* the love-smitten mutt Bellissimmo, his hair recently transformed into a two-foot spherical Afro; but all I see is the red nose of the poor legionnaire, the woods outside Pemza, the foreman Vachousek ... he always appears ... in almost every memory.

When Prema arrived, I was completely smashed. Stiff, flat out, dumb. I woke up to an awful Sunday morning. My heroism had been absorbed along with his father's alcohol. Death was staring down at me from the gallows and I was dimly aware of being in my own bed at home instead of in the woods, hidden away with Prema's guerrillas. Or in the mill with Nadia's uncle.

Possibilities that, in any case, seemed impossible.

●

The telephone rings.

"May I?"

Margitka Bocarova.

"You may."

And it's done.

Margitka will be here in half an hour. I go into the bedroom, straighten out the sheet on my queen-size bed, fluff up the pillow, and in the bathroom hang up Margitka's pale blue towel with a picture of a pregnant Lucy exclaiming "GOD DAMN YOU CHARLIE BROWN." Then I go into the kitchen, take out a bottle of Jack Daniel's which I keep stashed away for these hours of special health care, and polish two glasses with a dishtowel. Margitka is very touchy about badly polished glasses; in fact, all forms of uncleanliness upset her. I make sure there is enough ice in the freezer, carry the Jack Daniel's and the glasses to the coffee table and take a shower. Then I get into my pyjamas and dressing-gown, remove the *Kama Sutra* from the bookshelf and begin to study the position that Margitka ticked off for me last time.

Margitka is a practical sexologist.

I begin to feel like a whisky. I used to be a near teetotaller, but here in this land of mixed drinks I have gone to the dogs. Jack Daniel's, however, is a sacramental wine. I go back to the kitchen and pour myself a straight scotch.

The buzzer buzzes.

I get up and walk over to the speaker by the door.

"Yes?"

Downstairs, Margitka pronounces the Sanskrit name of the position she checked off last week.

"Right," I say and press the button.

I open the door a crack and look towards the lift. In a few moments it pings open, but the first to step out is Cindy, a black girl from across the hall with no discernible means of livelihood. There is dancing in her apartment long into the night, almost every night. She winks at me with eyelashes that appear to have been made of black wire, says, "You men!" and disappears into her flat. Her men will arrive at about nine.

Margitka, dazzlingly white in her neatly pressed uniform, rustles towards my door. I usher her in, admiring her slender back and well-proportioned little bottom as she slips past. Progress does exist after all. In my parents' generation, forty-year-old women were usually three times that wide.

Margitka stops in the middle of the room and ostentatiously sniffs the air.

"I'm sorry." I hurry into the bathroom.

"You don't love me any more!"

"But I will!"

I bring in the sandalwood and spray it around the room. Margitka first encountered the scent in Chandler. She claims she fell in love with me while reading my translation of *The Lady in the Lake*. She was kidding of course — or talking nonsense, anyway. Nothing as childish as love exists between us.

It is true though that she read my translation of Chandler, because at the time she didn't know enough English to read it in the original. It is also true that she told me this at our very first meeting, but then the object of her love, or rather her ideal, was Miss Adrianne Fromsett. It is also true that I claimed Margitka was the spitting image of Miss Fromsett.

Which is true, even though she's a natural blonde.

Margitka first impresses one as the embodiment of a Platonic idea of cleanliness. An absolute, hygienic, aseptic cleanliness of apparel and body. When I got to know her better, I realized this was true of her soul as well.

Which, under the circumstances, may appear to be a rather odd assertion.

She smells of Lysol mixed with lily of the valley.

In the act of love these fragrances vapourize and vanish and she absorbs the aroma of sandalwood with which, at her request and in honour of Miss Fromsett, I saturate the atmosphere.

Margitka sits down in an armchair, her knees together, her skin shining pink through the white stockings.

Margitka is entirely white. Superficially, in her nurse's uniform, and underneath it, right down to her white skin.

White is wonderful.

She looks twenty-seven.

An average of three times a month, she cheats on her wheelchair-bound husband. With me.

So she isn't being that unfaithful, after all.

She doesn't cheat on me with anyone.

Or so she says.

"Danny," she says, "did you know that Lilka has run off on Rudy again?"

"You don't say! Who with this time?"

"Some Slovak from Calgary."

"That's what – the third time she's done it?"

"The fourth. The first was with Honza Popelka, then with Cincibus, then with that black fellow – I can't remember his name – and now with this Slovak. Fero Galuska."

Thus she begins her report on the sexual activity of the Czech community over the past ten days. We sip Jack Daniel's with ice, and for the next quarter of an hour I am regaled with details.

By that time my desire for Margitka is enormous. As is hers for me.

Yet I think that I am in fact interchangeable. So why hasn't she exchanged me for somebody else after these four years? Such are the mysteries of the organism.

She finishes her drink, gets up without a word and goes into the bedroom. I follow her. She pulls the white uniform over her head, carefully sets it over the back of the chair, unhooks her white brassiere and in the light of the thirty-seven bright storeys of the high-rise opposite – we use no lights, for that permanently lit Christmas tree provides our illumination – the miracle of the female body glows whitely. She removes her white stockings, steps out of her white panties and the whiteness of her white body contrasts with the golden-tinged triangle. She bounces onto the bed and stands on her head in the position indicated in the exercise she has ticked off.

We exercise.

Afterwards I go out to refresh our drinks and Margitka goes to the washroom and comes back redolent of sandalwood, takes a sip of her drink, arranges herself sensually on the bed, with me beside her, and says, "Who'd have thought I'd ever have a famous writer for a lover?"

"Is the famous writer famous enough in bed?"

"I've known better."

"Margitka! A virgin like you?"

"I mean from the movies."

I believe her.

"... D'you seriously think it's him?" Margitka once asked at the Benes Inn.

"The name is the same," Bocar replied. "Looks the same too: black hair, a round face, ruddy complexion, looks a bit like a farmer. And they used to call him 'The Priest.'"

"And he actually watched it happen?"

"What's so surprising about that? They're all pigs, aren't they? Of course he watched. It was his case. He was the one who arrested the fore-man Vachousek."

"... I suppose you never have pangs of conscience?" Margitka, in bed beside me, probes.

"All the time."

"So do I. It's awful. But what can I do?"

"Don't do it."

"I can't give it up."

"They sell chastity belts in Lovecraft."

"Don't be disgusting."

"I'd love to see you in a chastity belt. It would have to be white. Then I'd believe you when you say you're faithful to me."

"I'd have an extra key made at Simpson's, smart guy."

"With what? They only make one key for chastity belts and I'd have it."

"I'd get a skeleton key made."

"You'd have to undress so they could test it."

"So I'd undress."

"The locksmith would rape you."

"Only if he could unlock me."

We laugh.

"You've got such a dirty mind, Smiricky!"

"You've got such a bad conscience, Bocarova!"

That's the kind of game we play.

We did not play it at the beginning.

●

It snowed and snowed. A howling north wind swept the flakes into swirling gusts that buffeted me as I walked along Jirasek Street to church. Nadia was not there. No one from Cerna Hora was at church that morning. They hadn't made it through the snow. In the crowd of people in front of the altar I could pick out only the blonde head of Marie Dreslerova. After the service I waited for her but she came out with a friend. The wind lashed at their skirts and they held them around their knees and vanished giggling into the blizzard.

I had no desire to go home, for I felt almost safe in the streets. My head ached. I walked round the square. The wind whipped clouds of swirling snow through the square, pushing me along, freezing my ears. Finally I stumbled into the Beranek.

At a corner table by the window sat the boys in the band – Lexa, Haryk with Lucie, Benno with Alena, Fonda, Venca Stern, Brynych and Vlada Nosek, who played the alto sax with the band Red Music in Rounov. I walked over to them. They were laughing at something, but as soon as they saw me they stopped talking and stared. As I approached, I felt a wall between me and them. A prison wall. It was as though I no longer belonged.

"You're a fine one, you are!" was Lucie's greeting. "Begone from my sight!"

"What's going on?" They had clearly schemed up some joke to play on me. I had always enjoyed the banter, but today it brought me no pleasure.

"I'm quite put out," said Lucie.

"Why should you be?"

"You mean you have to ask?"

"Don't play the innocent, you cad," said Benno.

"Or the fool," said Lexa.

I was trying to join the fun, but I didn't feel like it. With a tremendous effort I said to Lucie, "I have a clean conscience. At least as far as you're concerned."

"You're blaspheming!" she replied.

"What's all this about?" I asked.

"Doesn't the name Nadia mean anything to you?" asked Lexa.

So that was it! I looked at Lucie, then at Nosek.

"I never said a thing," said Nosek, and he raised three fingers. "I swear on the Führer *und* Reichskanzler!"

"Do you admit that Lucie has every right to feel insulted?" asked Haryk.

I looked at Lucie again. Where had she found out about us? Nosek wouldn't have told her; he had character. Perhaps the women in the factory had noticed us. They saw everything. "I still don't know what gives you the right to feel insulted. If Irena – "

"Or Marie," said Fonda.

"Or Judy Garland," said Benno.

"Or et cetera," said Lexa.

"You mean you don't love Lucie?" said Haryk. "Now that hurts *my* feelings!"

"Your feelings?" I said.

"You bet! Don't you think she's good enough for you, if she's good enough for me? Look at that hair! That face! Everything below it!"

"Would you mind spelling that out?" said Benno.

"He's referring to her elegant attire, of course, you simpleton," said Lexa.

"Or those elegant legs," said Haryk. "What gives you the right not to love her, you impertinent sod?"

"Shouldn't you be jealous instead?" I asked him.

"What for, if you don't love her?"

"So what's there to be hurt about?"

"It's Haryk's masculine vanity that's hurt, isn't that right, sweet?" said Lucie, stroking Haryk's slicked-down hair.

Suppressing my real feelings, I played the thousand-and-first variation of a game we had played together as long as the band had existed. Then Irena entered the café. She was wearing a green hunter's overcoat, all covered with snow. She looked around, and sat down at a table at the other end of the room.

"All that's hurt, if anything, is his pride of ownership," I said. "He's monopolizing you like Bata monopolizes shoes."

"Danny's speaking from experience," said Benno.

"Is that so?" said Lexa. "Should I experience it too?"

"Go right ahead and experience!" said Haryk.

"May I feel under your skirt, Lucie?"

"Go right ahead," said Lucie.

"At your service," said Lexa and in a flash he ran his hand under Lucie's skirt. Lucie yelped and slapped him across the arm. Lexa backed away, caught himself by the wrist and roared, "Ow! My funny bone!"

"You get an F in anatomy," said Lucie. "That's usually found in the elbow."

"What's that? What's that?" cried Haryk. "You reached under there right up to your elbow? I'll have to check this out!" and in a flash he too ran his hand under Lucie's skirt. Once again Lucie yelped and grabbed his arm through her skirt. Haryk removed his hand, put his elbow on Lucie's knee and pretended to be measuring how far he had penetrated. Then he stood up and turned to Lexa.

"Sir, I demand satisfaction. You may expect my seconds!"

"Good God, when?" cried Lexa.

"In a year and a day."

"That's a relief," said Lexa. "I still have a year and a day of life ahead of me." I shivered. Lexa turned to Alena and pretended he wanted to run his hand under her skirt as well, deliberately doing it slowly so she could grab his hand. Benno grabbed it for her.

"Ah, another monopolist?" asked Lexa in a tone of astonishment.

"Isn't everybody?" said Benno. "Just wait till Nadia's monopolist finds out what Nadia does behind his back in working hours, and who she does it with!"

"An ugly situation," said Haryk.

"Fists will fly," said Benno.

"Teeth more probably," said Lexa.

I stood up. "So long, gentlemen." I turned to Nosek. "And thanks a lot for being so discreet about it."

"It wasn't him who told us, really," said Lucie quickly. "It was Marie. In rhythmics."

"And you had to pass it on."

"You'll have to admit it throws an odd light on your taste," said Lexa. "They say this Nadia weighs a ton."

"So long," I said again, and turned around and walked straight across the café to Irena who was still sitting alone at her table. My longing for her comforting presence was as great as my distaste for adolescent banter.

"Don't bother to sit down," she said. "It's not you I'm waiting for."

"Just a minute. I have to talk to you."

"But I don't have to talk to you."

"Of course you don't, Irena. But maybe you could do it as a favour. I won't be bothering you for much longer."

"Really? That's good news."

She didn't mean it to sound unkind, or even serious, but it wounded my heart.

"If you only knew the truth, Irena, you'd never say that."

"What is it? Heart-broken again? They told me in rhythmics that – "

"I know what they told you in rhythmics. But they don't know what they're talking about."

"Is that so? My impression was that they were very well informed."

I felt I could keep my awful secret no longer. I needed, as never before, to confide in this brown-skinned girl whom I had genuinely loved for almost six years, with the exception of Marie of course. And Nadia. "Seriously, Irena," I said, "you may never see me again."

"Now that's a line you've never tried on me before," she said. Then her large brown eyes, the colour of coffee-and-cream, opened with delight. I didn't even have to turn around. My confession was aborted.

"All right, so long, Irena," I said, and without another word I walked out past Zdenek, who was brushing the snow off himself.

"Why don't you go out somewhere, Danny?" my mother said to me when we had finished lunch. "It's such a beautiful day outside! You need to give your lungs an airing after a long week in the factory."

The blizzard had died down. A clear winter sun hung over Cerna Hora and the slopes glistened with fresh snow.

"I don't feel like it. I need a rest."

"Are you sure you don't want to come with us?" Mother stood there uncertainly, already in her fur coat. "We're going to call on Mr. Kudlacek, the head-clerk. Nadenka is having some company in as well, they said."

The name of the Kudlaceks' daughter drew my eyes back towards Cerna Hora. Black specks were already weaving down the slopes above the villas. Skiers. "No, Mom, you go on without me."

"Bye, Danny," said Mother and gave me a kiss.

I was alone in the flat. My throat tightened. What could I do? If only the Germans accepted Czechs in the army, I would join up and then desert to the Americans. I fell into a day-dream, gazing at the white slopes of Cerna Hora. Compared to the situation I was in now, being at the front seemed like the ultimate safety. It was absurd. But was it? I was in a cage. Illegal resistance activity in occupied territory requires greater courage than fighting in an army. Being in a cage is more terrifying than being in the front lines. Without knowing it, I was articulating one of the basic truths of our age. It crossed my mind that the war would soon be over, but a sudden superstition that defining the thought might bring about the opposite made me turn my mind to the past. Yet, there again, fear was dominant. It had been a primary sensation of early childhood, when I was terribly afraid to be left at home alone at night. And I was alone every Saturday night, when my parents went to the pub. The feeling of pressure rising from my stomach to my head would begin in the morning and intensify as eight o'clock approached. Just before eight my mother would put me to bed, give me a book, remind me not to forget to turn out the light. Then a kiss – like today – and the door would close and the key rattle. And I was locked into a cage thronging with monsters, ghosts and murderers. For a few moments afterwards I could hear my parents' steps on the stairs, then everything fell silent. I would begin to listen intently.... In the bedroom at the other end of the hall the parquet floor creaked. As I sat up in bed with the book open, the floor creaked again. Safer if I turn out the light. Won't see me in the dark. I turned out the light. Something tinkled quite clearly in the kitchen. Mad with terror, I switched on the lights again, slid out of my bed with my book and looked around the cage. Something snapped behind me. I spun around. Nothing. Again. Behind me. Again I turned around. Again nothing. With my heart in my mouth I tiptoed into the hall. Someone was smashing the furniture. I jumped for the door of the toilet, pushed inside and slid the bolt behind me. It was a tiny room with a little window above the toilet bowl looking into an airshaft. I sat down on the floor with my back against the side wall so that I could see both the locked door and the window. And thus I remained, determined to stay awake until one o'clock, when my parents would return. And I did, Saturday after Saturday, it must have been for several years. I never once fell asleep. On the other side of the door a carnival of spirits, and the slow, endless measuring of time by the striking of the wall clock every half-hour. I would count the strokes anxiously: nine, ten, eleven, twelve, infinity between them. The worst half-hour was yet to come. I couldn't let my parents find me in this humiliating state. An unbearable half-hour after midnight, the clock struck once, and I unlocked my door and fled to my bedroom, followed by what could only have been footsteps. I jumped into bed and turned out the light. For a long, long time I lay with my eyes half open, watching the glass panes in the half-open door. When a scarcely discernible glow appeared in the glass like a sunrise, it meant that my parents had entered the hall downstairs and had turned on the light in the staircase, although I couldn't hear them yet because we lived on the third floor. Sometimes the glow vanished again and there was no sound of our flat being unlocked, which meant that it had been another tenant returning from the pub. But usually it was my parents, the glow did not disappear, my father's heavy footsteps echoed through the building, one loud, one soft as he favoured his wounded leg. And at last, at last the key rattled in the lock, and I fell at once into a blissful half-sleep in the cosy embrace of safety.... I opened my eyes again. Before me was the white slope of Cerna Hora, the Black Mountain, black clouds massing in the sky above. It was starting to snow. The wind whistled around the eaves.

I was not safe at all. It was only a sweet dream of distant childhood, when everything always turned out well.

●

In the bar at the back of the hall an old-fashioned Czech good time is being had. Mr. Sestak has laid aside his Jingling Johnny and is sitting down at the drums. The democratic young man, wearing his double-breasted jacket again, has traded his guitar for an accordion, and the banjo-player is now torturing a violin. At the bar, cradling a glass of brandy and what is left of a huge sausage, the organizer is singing at the top of his lungs:

> Oh, them red-haired women
> They're the ones I love the best....

"Why don't you go for a spin, Margit?" Bocar suggests to his wife. He is clearly including me in the suggestion. I wonder nervously if he suspects something, but he never lets on. And Margitka swears she is terribly discreet.

The organizer sings:

> I ask her will she love me
> And she says no no no,
> But she's a red-haired woman
> And she breaks my heart in two.

"Are you sure you don't mind, Mila?" asks Margitka, the hypocrite.

"Don't be ridiculous."

We get up and Bocar grins at me from his wheelchair.

"Can I get you another beer?" Margitka's conscience is speaking.

"So I'll have to keep going to piss?" Bocar pounds the air-filled tires of the wheelchair with his fist. "This is some invention, Doctor." He means me. "An excellent way to shake all your vices." I feel I may be turning red, but Bocar, after a brief pause that seems pregnant to me, continues. "D'you have any idea how hard it is for me just to go for a piss? That's why I hardly drink anymore, Doctor. A good thing I have Margit!" He tries to pat her bottom, and I have the unpleasant sensation that he doesn't suspect, he knows.

"Aren't you fortunate?" says Margitka, and she blushes. It is one of her most charming traits, made possible by that alabaster skin, but now it is more embarrassing than charming.

"Of course I'm fortunate, a neat little piece like that!" And again he tries to paddle her bottom, and almost tumbles out of the wheelchair.

I take her quickly round the waist and we push our way in among the dancers. Over Margitka's shoulder I see Bocar waving at a waitress. Margitka reads my thoughts. "D'you think he ...?"

"I'd almost swear he does...."

We stop talking as Veronika and Percy appear beside us and I overhear a fragment of conversation in English: "I didn't say I hated playboys...."

"But who could have told him?" Margitka whispers. "Because I really am discreet. There are no Czechs living in your apartment building, and none work at the hospital...."

"Do I come to visit too often?" I ask.

"You've only been twice this year. Some of Mila's old cronies show up twice a week."

"But I'm not an ex-political prisoner."

"That's a fact," says Margitka abruptly. We dance silently. The gentleman in the soft leather coat, now wearing only a tweed jacket, slinks past us. He is dancing with the publisher and his hand is so far down her back that it would be euphemistic to say he is holding her round the waist. Can Mrs. Santner be so easily appeased? And if they threw her out why did she bother coming back? I can only conclude that she is doing it, as she does everything else, in the interests of her business, which is to say, for the good of modern Czech literature. Which means ultimately for my good as well.

"Mila was never a suspicious sort. Today's the first time he's ever talked like that."

"You must forgive her, my dear lady. Her nerves are in a bad way. She carries the entire load herself, no employees, you understand...." I turn around. The publisher's husband is circumspectly circling the dance floor with the pious woman, now minus her fur coat. He is clearly acting on orders.

"Someone must have spied on us," says Margitka unhappily.

"I don't think so. I think his suspicions are based on logic. How many regular visitors do you have who aren't former prisoners? He trusts them. Maybe it's naive of him, but...."

"Not in my case," says Margitka. "Or don't you believe me?"

"Of course I do. But he doesn't believe me."

"But he believes me."

We are silent. I observe that the hand of the tweedy gentleman has slipped even lower, if that is possible. Perhaps his arm is arthritic. I say, "Did you tell him what you'd been up to while he was in prison?"

"There was nothing to tell."

"And he believed you?"

"Of course he believed me."

"He must have had enormous faith in you. That kind of faith would move Mont Blanc over Stalin's Peak all the way to Venezuela. Ten years – that's somewhat abnormal, to put it mildly, wouldn't you say?"

"But it wasn't a normal love affair, with him behind bars and me on the outside."

"And he believed you when you said that for ten years you never ... with anyone ...?"

"He didn't have to believe me. He had proof."

"What kind of proof?"

"The usual."

"What's that supposed to mean?"

"You're a little slow today, Smiricky. Ah, but you've probably never come across anything like it in your life."

I finally understand. I almost sit down on the spot. I say, "You've never told me about this before."

"You never asked."

From nearby a sentence that must be a classic, spoken in English, drifts in on our conversation. "I've known lots of emigrant girls. But you're different...."

Percy is wooing Veronika. The sad girl's cheeks are flushed pink. For the first time since I've known her she doesn't look particularly unhappy. "I'm not an emigrant," she says almost gaily, "I'm an exile."

And rutting Percy replies, "What's the difference?"

"Elementary, my dear Watson," says the literary Veronika. "I can't go back home. Emigrant girls can. That is the only way I differ from them objectively."

"Would it be rough for you if you went back?" says Percy. He is intoxicated with desire.

"Oh God!" I hear Veronika say. "What have you been listening to all day, Percy? Have I bored you that much?"

"You don't bore me."

"Then it must be my English...."

"That's rather incredible," I say to Margitka. "How long did you go with Mila before...."

"Almost a year."

"And what did you do all that time, for God's sake?"

"We loved each other."

"How?"

"A lot, I guess, if I managed to hold out for ten years, waiting for him to come back."

"I mean technically, how did you do it? I'll bet it's not even in the *Kama Sutra*."

"I had no idea such dirty books even existed back then."

"So what did you do?"

"Something you would never even suspect."

"Surprise me."

"Nothing," says Margitka. "We went out together. In the literal, innocent sense of that phrase."

I realize that I am foolishly judging Margitka's youth from the pinnacle of my own adulthood. But when I was young....

"We were both in the scouting movement," Margitka remembers tenderly. "I was a Catholic and he was a sea-scout."

That makes me laugh. Margitka blushes at first, then laughs too.

"We've come quite a way since then," she says, suppressing her laughter. "But are you sure no one is spying on us?"

•

Darkness had almost come. The wind in the afternoon had blown more fiercely than in the morning. Frozen snow splattered against the windowpane, and the Black Mountain disappeared behind a mass of whirling whiteness. It was not four o'clock and yet it was almost dark, as it must have been over Golgotha. I imagined how they had nailed them to the crosses, and trembled. I longed to see the storm swell to greater and greater fury until it lifted all of Kostelec into a maelstrom of destruction. I longed to see King Kong rise over the crest of Cerna Hora and crush the entire town and all life in it, including me, with one mighty blow. And what if he were indeed to loom up over the horizon, step over the Jirasek Chalet, descend to the town with one giant stride and start to smash the buildings – where would I run to? He would come straight for me. I would run to the back bedroom but he'd pry me out with his finger ... and then I was fourteen again, sitting at the same window, and instead of King Kong I saw bombers coming over the crest of Cerna Hora, flying straight towards me, towards our house, releasing bombs filled with poison gas.... That had been in the autumn of thirty-eight, during the mobilization – the Munich Crisis, when angular concrete anti-tank barriers called "Zizka's spurs" blocked the roads and people hastily lined up in front of shops that sold gas-masks. My parents had already owned a pair for several years. I had tried one on in front of the bedroom mirror and imagined I was a deep-sea diver or a man from Mars. It was fun then, but later, in September of thirty-eight, I was afraid. I no longer minded being at home alone, but there was still no lack of occasion for fear. I had read the pamphlets on mustard-gas Father brought home and was convinced that the mask wasn't enough; they would drop mustard-gas on Kostelec and we would be helpless.... But other people didn't look frightened, they behaved quite normally. The odd thing was, I behaved normally too.

My father may have been afraid, if only for me – however it was, I was the only one in my class sent inland during mobilization. Mother and I went to live with my grandmother in Kolin. We had a huge suitcase, and we each carried a tin case with a gas-mask over our shoulder. The train was jammed with people, all carrying their gas-masks, and I couldn't get my mind off mustard-gas. We should have had anti-mustard-gas suits but we didn't. The very first day in Kolin, in the high school I was to attend until the crisis had passed (though I sensed that it would not pass, that there would be a war), the bald-headed principal in his stiff collar asked, "And why do you want to register him temporarily with us, madame?" "If anything were to happen...." My mother swallowed. "Kostelec is in a fortification zone...." "Don't you think, madame, that it makes little difference? Kolin is an industrial town. We may expect air raids. However, if you wish ..." and I was trapped once more in a cage, this time a cage called Kolin. I seemed to carry my cage around with me.

That first evening we went with Grandma to a neighbour's to listen to the radio. Hitler was supposed to speak. Everyone said it would be an important speech, perhaps announcing whether or not there would be a war. The neighbour was an engineer called Blazek, and he, his wife and two acquaintances of theirs with a little boy were all sitting around the radio set. The boy was playing with a tin aeroplane and making buzzing noises and they had to keep shushing him up. A terrible hissing and crackling was coming out of the radio. Then Hitler began to speak. Though I could understand German quite well by this time, it was the voice itself rather than what it was saying that terrified me. I remember thinking, If that is what his voice is like, war is inevitable. I looked at Mother, at the engineer, at his two friends, at Grandmother, and all of them were rapt, staring at nothing in particular. Only the little boy with his aeroplane was buzzing quietly to himself. The room was almost dark. There was a lamp with a cloth shade in the corner and there were blackout blankets over the windows. The brightest light came from the dial of the radio. The voice grew more and more frenzied. It was cadenced into what seemed like stanzas and punctuated by thunderous outbursts of shouting. What was it the principal had said? We may expect air raids – that's why the blankets were on the windows. My father's pamphlet on mustard-gas ... *Hier stehe ich!* roared Hitler. *Und dort steht Herr Benesch!* A deafening roar, then a single voice shouting, *Sieg!* And a tumultous *Heil! Sieg! ... Heil! Sieg! ... Heil!* The doorbell rang, the sound running up and down my spine like a series of tiny explosions, Mrs. Blazkova stood up and said, "That'll be our little Jirka. She's been at Sokol," and she left the room. The siegheiling disintegrated into indescribable pandemonium. Weren't any of those howlers afraid of war? Engineer Blazek turned off the radio. No one said a word. The unexpected sound of a fresh girlish voice came from the doorway: "Good evening!" I turned around. There stood a girl about as old as I was, holding in her hand a net bag that contained a black sweat-suit and a white T-shirt. "This is our Jirinka," said Mrs. Blazkova, and the girl laughed politely –

●

"They got me because I was scared," Bocar is saying. "I chickened out and told them everything – not that there was a lot to tell, it was more like we were trying out for a conspiracy badge. Lord Baden-Powell would have loved it. Luckily Margit had the flu that day so they didn't grab her too. And nobody spilled enough to incriminate her."

It's after midnight and the democratic young man is still persisting on the accordion, alone. The organizer is dozing with his head on the bar; Veronika, sad once more, is hanging on Bocar's words. For – how absurd is the passage of time – Veronika was just a little girl playing with dolls when the new Communist regime banned the boy-scout and girl-guide movements. Now she is playing with a playboy and translating Bocar's strongly idiomatic talk into fluently idiomatic Canadian English for him. Margitka has her hand on the tire of her husband's wheelchair, the story-teller between us. Mr. Pohorsky, on the other side of Margitka, is resting his hand unobtrusively on the arm of her chair.

"*Wie sich die Konspiration der kleine Moritz vorstellt,*" Bocar goes on. "The scout leaders called five patrols, including two from the girl guides, to a secret meeting in Stromovka Park where they gave out instructions for carrying on under the new circumstances."

"Didn't you even plant a look-out?" asks an astonished Mr. Pohorsky.

"You bet your sweet life we did. But the look-outs were supposed to report on suspicious-looking persons, and the Commies sent along a couple of completely unsuspicious types who didn't look suspicious till it was too late. To make a long story short, we were jumped by about two hundred completely inconspicuous gentlemen in leather coats, with even less conspicuous German shepherds which our look-outs must have thought were seeing-eye dogs. Before you could say Joe Stalin they had us all gift-wrapped in their knacker wagons, including our leaders. And it was the leaders who chickened out first."

"Ah, fear," observes Mr. Pohorsky thoughtfully. "I know it well."

"Naturally we all tried to cover up at first. So they played a little psychodrama on us. They took us into the interrogation room twenty at a time. 'You confess?' they asked the first little scout. 'I haven't done anything!' 'Take him away!' and two big goons grabbed him under the arms and dragged him off. The interrogators didn't say anything and neither did the rest of us. After a while we heard a bang from next door."

"Were they beating him up?" asked Mr. Pohorsky.

"For God's sake, Pohorsky! And you call yourself an ex-political prisoner? It was a shot, naturally. Anyone who wouldn't confess – bang! And that would be that!"

Veronika is horrified. "Did they really shoot him?"

"Be patient, girl," says Bocar. "In a little while the two goons came back and stood behind the interrogator. He called the next one forward and said straight out, 'You confess?' This fellow didn't have such a ready answer. I could see his knees starting to quiver. But he didn't confess, he just shook his head. His name was Novak and he had a lot of badges. The interrogator just nodded, the two apes moved in, Novak stiffened but they hustled him out the door and a minute later – bang! As they say – from somewhere a roscoe. Anyway, the two apes came back, never said a word – one of them shoving his roscoe into one of those shoulder holsters they wear in

American movies, but before he did it I swear to God he blew the smoke off the barrel."

"But it's ...," interjects Veronika.

"What?"

"It's so ... so incredible!"

"I said be patient. Then it was my turn. As the interrogator eyeballed me, I caught a whiff of the gunpowder. I'm ashamed to say I didn't even wait for him to ask me if I was going to confess or not. I blurted it out all by myself."

"I don't blame you," says Veronika, horrified.

Percival is impatient. "What's he saying?"

"Just a moment, don't translate yet! So far they'd only bumped off two, but everybody after me confessed, except for one girl who called herself Akela. And when the hulks hauled her off into the execution chamber, she fainted. But she didn't confess."

"And – did they kill her?" says Veronika, catching her breath.

"They gave her the same as they gave the two ahead of me."

"Was she the last one?" asks Mr. Pohorsky.

"In our group of twenty, yes. All the rest of them came clean. The interrogator made up a rough confession, then he translated it from Russian for the court, and tidied up the style. The final version was published in all the big newspapers. It said we were trying to ideologically influence young people despite the ban on all forms of such influence – excepting the scientific variety, of course, since scientific socialism taught that if you were a Young Pioneer it was your duty to report anyone to the cops who didn't appear to believe what Comrade President Gottwald said."

"I've got to translate this for Percy," says Veronika. "He won't believe it. He hardly believes anything like that."

Mr. Pohorsky scowls. "Is he a lefty?"

"You might say so," admits the girl, "but not that way. I'm going to translate it for him."

"Just a second," says Bocar. "First tell him that in the end even the ones that got shot confessed."

"Are you making fun of me?" Veronika sounds hurt. She finds this mixture of humour and horror distasteful.

"They were the ones who were making fun of *us!*" Bocar roars with laughter. "It was just a kind of practical joke – black humour in action. They didn't bump anyone off – not that they wouldn't have liked to. It just wouldn't have looked good if all of a sudden a bunch of boy scouts and girl guides had died of pneumonia while in custody. So the goons took the heroes into the basement and on the way back they fired off a blank outside the door. Meanwhile the other goons in the basement worked their powers of persuasion on them until they were all persuaded – except for Akela and one other, but it didn't make any difference, they got twelve years too, like the rest of us."

Veronika looks silently at Bocar. Percy takes her by the hand. "It's okay," says the girl, "it was just a practical joke, only...."

Later, on the day when I understood nothing, she told me about her unobtrusive ten-minute disappearance that evening. A man had suddenly appeared in the bar; Veronika had turned pale, excused herself and made a bee-line for the new arrival. They had gone outside together.

"So you ditched me," Veronika had said to him. "And I went to all the trouble to get myself into this wilderness on account of – at least partly on account of you."

"Look, Nika, you've got to understand...."

"I don't understand. How could you leave me for such an *owl?*"

"Well, it was taking so long ... I thought you'd never make it out of Czechoslovakia – "

"You thought, eh? Then why did you tell your landlady not to give out your new address to any woman?"

"That wasn't because of you – " and the young man by the name of Oldrich Skvarek caught himself, but too late.

"Well, well. So I wasn't the only one you dumped."

"I ... I was lonely, you know. A foreign country...."

"Well, let me tell you, Oldrisek," Veronika said with deliberation, "being dumped like that was a new experience for me. It still makes me feel sick."

"Look, Nika, you'll ... there'll be others."

Veronika stiffened. "D'you see this?"

"What?"

"It's a hand. They call us 'ethnics' here. We're supposed to have a lot of quaint old-fashioned customs."

"Yes?"

"So why not live up to that image?" And she gave Skvarek such a wallop that his cheek puffed up on the spot. It was not an ethnic wallop. It was a very North American one.

"Devilish," Mr. Pohorsky is saying, "but very clever. I've got nothing against borrowing a trick or two from the Commies when it comes to that. Fear is a powerful weapon, and that's why *our* next project is going to put the fear of God into the Party." And he briefly outlines the plan: on the Ethiopian airwaves, the citizens of Czechoslovakia will be exhorted to buy at least ten boxes of matches each. Even if only every fifth citizen does so, that will mean about twenty-five million boxes, the Communists will have to manufacture new matches fast and this will throw a monkey-wrench into their five-year plan. If, instead of ten, every fifth citizen buys twenty – "

"What are they going to do with all those matches?" I interrupt. "Strike them all at once? If they don't, it won't have any effect at all. People just won't buy matches for another year, that's all."

"They're going to break them to form a V and they're going to put those Vs in front of the doors of known Commies."

"V for VD?"

Mr. Pohorsky treats the remark as an expression of my political ignorance. "Of course not! V for Victory, naturally. Winston Churchill's wartime slogan."

"What precisely do you expect to achieve by all this?" the Vancura enthusiast asks gravely.

"It's the psychological effect we're after," says Mr. Pohorsky. "Picture it for yourself. The Commie goes out the door in the morning and he sees a capital V made out of a match on the doorstep. The first couple of days he thinks there's nothing in it, but then he starts wondering what the hell is going on. In a month or two it'll drive the weaker ones to suicide and the stronger ones will end up in the asylum."

He looks around at the assembled company. There is not a single person here cruel enough to spoil his pleasure.

"And where will the Party be?" Bocar pounds his tires with roguish glee. "Up shit creek!" And his Jovian laughter awakens the organizer. From the direction of the bar we can hear a wilted voice singing:

> Oh, them curly-headed women
> are the ones ... I love the best....

●

– the girl had smiled. She was wearing a blue skirt, tennis shoes, and a yellow T-shirt that revealed her small breasts. For a brief moment, I forgot all about Hitler. She sat down in the corner on a tabouret, her knees pointed towards me, and although I knew that war would break out in a few days the girl in the T-shirt caused me delicious pain. That whole week, before they signed the Munich agreement and Mother and I returned to Kostelec, I walked to and from school with her, and she has remained with me always. A tiny drop of joy in a medallion of black fear ... how she entered the dimly lit room in her yellow T-shirt, carrying a net bag, and greeted us politely....

I could hear a bell. Someone was ringing the doorbell. My reverie was cruelly disturbed. Cerna Hora swept in and out of sight through the mad swirls and flurries of snow and pushed the soft glow of memory from my mind. It was getting dark. My instincts told me the Gestapo had arrived.

The bell rang again.

The flat was quiet. I held my breath, listening. I could hear the click of iron-shod boots outside the door as the Gestapo shifted from one foot to the other.

If I don't open, they'll smash the door down.... So Uippelt has reported me. Uippelt, an American!

There was no possible escape. We lived on the third floor.

Suddenly I longed to have it over with. Better to be under lock and key, knowing where I stood, than this uncertainty.

I got up and crept into the hall. It wasn't logical – I wanted to give myself up but I went to do it on tiptoe. We had an old-fashioned peep-hole in the door. Holding my breath, I carefully slipped the cover back a little and looked out.

Nadia was standing there, covered with frozen snow.

I flung the door open.

"Nadia! What are you doing here?"

"Dan! How come you're not hiding?"

"I'm ... not going till tonight," I lied, rashly as always, and thus shut the door on deliverance, on the asylum of her uncle's mill. But there were clearly forces in me stronger than the fear of the Gestapo.

She was standing there in her granny-kerchief and a secondhand winter coat that could have been either a man's or a woman's, probably a kind of unisex of the highland proletariat.

"I was awful afraid for you, Dan."

"Come on in."

"Are your parents home?"

"No, I'm here alone."

She came in and I closed the door behind her. She stood on the coconut mat.

"I better not tramp this mess in," she said awkwardly. "I brushed myself off in the hall, but the snow's froze."

"It's only water. Take off your coat."

I helped her out of her winter coat and hung it on the coat-rack. Underneath it she had a blue cotton blouse with yellow polka dots. Probably her Sunday best. I'd never seen her in it before.

"I'll take my boots off too, Dan, all right?"

"You don't have to."

"But you've got carpets everywhere. I'd just make a mess."

She knelt down and began to struggle with the bootlaces with blue fingers.

"My fingers are froze," she said.

"Wait, I'll unlace them for you."

And so I helped my first lover out of her heavy, lace-up, hobnailed mountain boots that clicked on the floor like Gestapo jackboots. I had to get down on my knees to do it. When I finally got them off, I took hold of her feet in their ski socks that had been washed and darned a thousand times. They were like ice.

"You're frozen right through!"

"Like an icicle."

For the first time I noticed that her teeth were chattering slightly and her thin shoulders were trembling beneath the polka dots.

"Nadia – I was looking for you this morning in church."

"We didn't go this morning. There was a storm. But I couldn't stand it, Dan, wondering all the time if you were hid proper or not."

"You came down here in that storm?"

"I couldn't stand not knowing."

I looked at her. I was still too young and silly. She looked like a little puppy yanked out of the waters of a frozen pond.

"Come on into the room, I'll make you tea. And put on a pair of slippers." I began to rush busily about the flat. I brought Mother's winter house-shoes and dressing-gown from the closet, wrapped Nadia up and sat her on the ottoman in the living room. Then I hurried into the kitchen, put the kettle on the stove and took some prewar tea out of the pantry.

She appeared in the doorway and made straight for the stool by the stove. Huge, burning eyes.

"What – whatever would you have done? It's just pure chance I happened to be home...."

"I wanted to know for sure if you were hid or not. Or if your friends couldn't hide you I thought maybe I could take you to my uncle's."

"Nadia, you're wonderful – "

"Do you have a place? Where?"

She was afraid for me. That much at least I could read in the burning eyes. I had never experienced anything quite like this before. I remembered Irena that afternoon in the Beranek. The kids in the band. They all seemed like children to me....

"There's nothing to be afraid of. But I won't tell you where it is. The fewer people know – "

"That's true," she said quickly. "But you'll let me know, won't you? That everything's all right?"

"Sure I will. You know I will."

The tea-kettle began to sing. I poured boiling water into the teapot and took a tray of jam tarts out of the pantry. I poured the tea into a large coffee-mug, set it beside Nadia on the stool and put the tray of tarts on the coal-box.

"Aren't you having any too?" she said.

"I'm not cold."

"I can't drink all this by myself."

"But you can eat it all."

The frozen face thawed out somewhat in an embarrassed smile.

"I know I eat an awful lot, but your mum bakes them so good!"

I laughed. "Anyway, I've got nowhere to sit. Except on the coal-box."

"So come on!"

And I sat down on the coal-box. Nadia moved the stool over to make room. I shifted the teapot and the tray of tarts and poured myself a cup. We drank the tea and Nadia put the first of the small tarts into her huge mouth.

"How are they?" I asked.

"Delicious," said Nadia. The old Nadia. "How many can I have?"

"As many as you want."

"What if your mum finds out, Dan?"

"I'll tell her I was hungry."

So Nadia took some more. She looked around the kitchen. It was almost dark outside now, and the kitchen was whitely luminescent. A copper coffee-mill gleamed on the cupboard.

"I like it here an awful lot."

"Nadia," I said, "did you tell Franta where you were going?"

She lowered her eyes to the tarts and took another one. On her finger she had a thin silver ring with a stone shaped like a forget-me-not.

"Franta went to Volesna to visit his aunt. She's real sick. He's coming back by the morning train and going straight to the factory." She raised her burning eyes to me. "So I didn't have to tell him anything."

I was foolish, inexperienced. All I knew how to do was talk, as Marie never tired of pointing out. In fact I had only once come close to anything like this moment of twilight illuminated by the coffee-mill on the cupboard that shone like a beacon of memory. That had been in a mountain hotel, but Alena's father had been lying in wait for us. I was still stupid and green, but not so green that I didn't realize it would not stop this time at boots, tea, jam tarts – or even at the kissing that would follow when the tea had thawed Nadia out. The coffee-mill shone like a monstrance. Fear vanished. At the bottom of my mind I knew it would return, but not right away. I felt a promise of something like happiness – that the future did not exist and would not exist for a while, because I would soon die a beautiful death, having known, briefly, something greater than death. And then perhaps, for I wouldn't, I didn't even know how to, be careful, for another seventy years, death might be cheated, the unequal struggle of *Homo sapiens* against nature might be extended by one more new life – All this flashed through my thick student's head as Nadia swallowed the last tart. I stood up and said, "Come on into the living room, Nadia, it's warmer there."

She stood up obediently and followed me in her ski socks like a kitten. The white dusk of the winter's day, not quite over, was reflected in the crystal chandelier. The same dusky light lit her face, her two round, pitch-black eyes. She walked straight to the ottoman, sat down beside me and her big, soft, damp, chapped mouth was on my lips and we were kissing. Then she lay down, I beside her, on her –

How I carried it off I don't know. Amateurishly, that much is certain. I found my way through cotton and calico, did battle with some elastic and pulled it down over lean, hot hemispheres. Nadia helped me, and together we carried it off with the help of God. But that was not really the point. The point was that, face to face with death, she gave me what she had and what she felt was the ultimate gift she could give. She gave me herself, since she had come of her own free will. She was afraid for me. She wanted to hide me in her uncle's mill.

We lay on the ottoman, a heap of calico, cotton and yellow polka dots on a blue background. Nadia was still wearing her knitted stockings and her ski socks. They gleamed faintly, like two yellowish-grey puppies, into the night which had descended. A half-moon was out. Nadia snuggled up against me, in an embrace of love unlike any I had ever known, and nothing else mattered....

●

A familiar figure is stomping up and down at the bus-stop. The air is bitingly cold, and the Ontario wind whistles down Yonge Street. I stop the car.

"Hi, Frank! Can I give you a lift?"

"Great. Thanks."

He slides in beside me. He has on a winter coat that looks as though it's made from a blanket, and a flat cap.

"Bleeker Street, just off Carlton."

"It's right on my way."

We drive south along Yonge through the wind and snow-dust. The shadows of the windshield wipers pass back and forth over Frank's gloomy face. Though I hate the silly question, I ask it anyway: "How are you doing?"

"Like the Tommies at Dieppe."

"What happened?"

"I got fired."

"What for?"

"I didn't watch my tongue."

This unexpectedly Eastern European answer surprises me. My reply is more North American. "What did you do, have a fling with the boss's wife?"

Frank shakes his head. "No, I told them straight out what I think of their programs, and they gave me the sack – the place is crawling with Reds!"

"That can't be true."

"They're not in the Party, naturally. But otherwise they're typical Commies, typical armchair Bolsheviks."

We approach a dazzlingly illuminated intersection. The neon signs are blinking. I stop, Frank lights a cigarette. The display window of a bookstore shines into the night, filled with bestsellers in garish covers. In an Eisensteinian montage, bold golden letters proclaim: ANGELA DAVIS: THE LIFE OF A REVOLUTIONARY. The green light pops on and we continue on our way.

"What programs are you talking about?"

"It doesn't make any difference at Universal TV. They're all bent to the left, some of them right round the corner and out of sight."

I shift gears and we pick up speed. It's half past one in the morning, a north wind, almost no traffic.

"If you had to wallow in it all the time like I do," Frank continues, "you'd end up believing you'd be better off back in Prague. To hear them talk, you'd think there was nothing but repression here. Our boss wrote a scenario for a soft-core porno film, but he couldn't get tax exemption status because there weren't enough Canadians in it. He wanted to give the main role to that American who played in *Deep Throat*. When they turned him down he started screaming censorship."

"The government is certainly depriving us of a lot," I say.

Frank chuckles gloomily. "So I told him that if people like him have their way we'll end up with women's rights, dykes' rights, whores' rights, queers' rights, abortion rights, junkies' rights, killers' rights, everything in the bloody book except human rights. The bastard accused me of being a fascist and fired me on the spot."

"You could always report him to the Human Rights Commission," I suggest.

"Get serious," Frank retorts.

"Then why don't you just stick to your camera?"

"I can't help it," says Frank. "I came to Canada so I could say what I want, so I say what I want."

I stop at the next set of lights. Across the street a group of male prostitutes are skipping about with their clients, wobbling on high-heeled boots of silver and gold leather sewn with bronze symbols, pants stretched tight over lean hips. The rings glint in their ears. A night full of Eisenstein.

"They deserve a dose of Bolshevism!" says Frank.

"But gays are legal over there too."

"Not out in the open like that, they're not."

We drive on. The desolate wind grows stronger, lashing frozen snow-dust against the windshield for the hard-working wipers to deal with.

"Don't worry, something will turn up. I don't know a single Czech who hasn't found a decent job here sooner or later."

"Maybe the ones that came out after the Boatmen invaded," snorts Frank, "because they're all Commies too."

"I thought you were post-invasion yourself, Frank."

"The hell I am. I got out before, in sixty-six."

"What for? Things were starting to look good then."

"I'd had my fill."

Of what, I wonder. For several years he had been an assistant camera-man at the Barrandov Film Studios, and he had ended up shooting documentary films – an excellent job. He had had a car. What more had he wanted? "I was tired of keeping my mouth shut," Frank is saying. "So when I first came here, I was shooting it off all the time. I had illusions. You know what I thought, back home? I thought it was the capitalists who were running things here. I found out the hard way. I ended up spending most of my time washing dishes. Turn left here, this is Carlton."

I make a left turn. Frank goes on, "Did I ever get a shock! My first real job lasted a week. It was a good job, too, with a private producer. But of course he was a Commie, naturally. The day after I got the job he started trying to indoctrinate me. Said this film we were making was revolutionary. And he was right about that. A pile of shit like the world has never seen. It ran for three days and the guy went bankrupt. I told him I wasn't interested in filming revolutionary shit and he said nobody was forcing me, I chose freedom and I could have it. He fired me. Here we are."

I slow down. Bleeker Street is run-down and full of derelict town houses. I stop in front of one that used to be a shop but is no longer. The window is boarded up and plastered over with ragged weather-worn posters. DON WRIGHT FIGHTS FOR WHITE RIGHTS is the slogan under a picture of a tin-pot Don Juan with a sloping forehead and a moustache.

"Good night. And thanks."

"Good night."

Frank unlocks a rickety door beside the boarded window. I start up, turn back into Carlton and then drive down Yonge Street towards the large, brightly lit hotels.

•

A weak light appeared in the glass panels of the door. At first I didn't realize what it meant. We lay there beside each other, half asleep, the hot skin of

Nadia's belly warming my hand, her hot face my face. Then I was touched by an ancient fear, and the import of the pale light in the glass door became shockingly clear.

"My parents!"

"Mary, Mother of God!"

I skidded to the floor trying to get into my trousers. Somehow I managed to pull them on. How long did it take my parents to reach the third floor? As a child the time had seemed endless, but it couldn't be more than two minutes.

Behind me, Nadia was struggling with her clothes. I flew into the hall, flicked on the kitchen lights and hurried back to the hall, switching on the light there just as the key was turning in the lock.

"Are you home already?"

"Why, it's almost six," said my mother and gave me a kiss. She looked into the kitchen. "Danny! You forgot the blackout!"

I turned quickly to set that right, but my mother beat me to it. She ran over to the window and pulled the blackout blind down.

"Whatever got into you? Do you know the trouble it might have caused us?"

"I completely forgot about it," I replied stupidly. Mother glanced at the coal-box. The teapot, the tray with a pile of tart-crumbs and two cups were still there. She looked at me questioningly. At that moment Father's voice came from the hall: "Whose clod-hoppers are these? They've made a bloody mess out here!"

We both looked into the hall. Nadia's unlaced boots were standing in a puddle of water.

"Do you have a friend visiting?" asked my mother.

"Yes. That is, a girl ... a colleague of mine from the factory ... she brought me...."

Mother stiffened. My father looked at me roguishly. "Well, in that case, begging your pardon!"

"Colleague?" My mother looked starchily about the empty kitchen, and noticed the door to the living room. It was closed, with darkness behind the glass panels. "Where is this ... colleague ... of yours?"

"In the living room."

"It's dark in there," said my mother, raising her eyebrows.

"They were saving electricity," said my father and winked.

Feverishly I wondered if Nadia was dressed yet. She had never been completely undressed and she'd had no garter belt or other such paraphernalia, only elastic garters above her knees. Perhaps she was ready by now. There was silence on the other side of the doors.

In a very unnatural voice Mother said, "Aren't you going to introduce her to us?"

"Sure, if you'd like," I babbled.

"Good manners and morals demand it," my father said and gave me another terrible wink.

I went to the door and opened it a little. "Nadia, my parents would like to meet you...."

For a moment nothing happened, then out of the darkness came Nadia. I had never seen her look that way before. She was as red as if she had been sunburned at the seaside, and one of her knitted stockings was twisted into a spiral. Otherwise she had managed to get everything in its place. But the situation was clear all the same.

"Good afternoon," she said.

"Good evening," my mother said with heavy emphasis, as though it were two in the morning and not six in the afternoon.

"This is Nadia Jirouskova," I said.

"Delighted," my mother said, but she did not proffer her hand. "Mrs. Smiricka."

We stood there like badly carved statues of the saints, Nadia incandescent. She was lovely at that moment, thin though she was, like an undernourished Cinderella. Father, a libertine in theory, was obviously aware of her charms because unlike my mother he proffered his hand and shook Nadia's warmly.

"Delighted, Miss Jirouskova," he said, leering like the villain in one of Chaplin's comedies, and, adopting a tone of voice he had learned from amateur theatre productions, he added, "of course you'll stay for supper, won't you?"

"Oh, I couldn't," said Nadia. "It's awful late already."

She deliberately avoided the combined stares of my mother and father, and as her eyes darted about she noticed the empty tray. "Anyway, I done enough mischief today already – " She stopped short, and the blood flared up into her cheeks again.

Mother raised her eyebrows so high they almost met her hairline. "Mischief?"

"I've ate all your tarts. Dan only had one...."

"Come now, we're not about to die of hunger here," said my father, and he grinned raffishly. "We'd be genuinely delighted if you could stay."

Mother flayed him with her eyes. Nadia noticed. She said hastily, "But I got so far to go home. It's time I was on my way."

"And where do you live?" asked Mother.

"On Cerna Hora."

"Well, in that case you *do* have rather a long way to go," she replied, as haughtily as Lady Windermere.

"Specially now in winter."

"You're going to walk all that way? In the dark?" inquired my father in genuine astonishment.

"Oh, I'm used to it. I walk to the plant at four every morning and this time of year it's still dark at four too."

Mother was silent. The factory girl from Cerna Hora had left her speechless. This was something she hadn't expected of me. She was quite happy to talk to me about Irena, the alderman's daughter; she knew I was crazy about her and it didn't bother her. Nor did she mind Marie Dreslerova, because she thought the two girls were fighting over me – never suspecting that it was I who was making an effort on two fronts at once. Neither Irena nor Marie, however, spoke in Nadia's unschooled Czech – and Cerna Hora was a place they visited only to ski.

In a foolish attempt to ease the situation I declared, "Nadia and I work together at the factory."

"On the *drehmaschine*," she said.

"The what?" my mother said with faint disgust.

"On the drills," I said.

"Are you conscripted labour too, Miss Jirouskova?" asked my father.

"I – don't know," Nadia replied hesitantly, and she blushed again. "The work office shifted me from Mautner's textile mill to the factory."

"Did you – work on the drills there as well?" My mother was obviously fighting down her distaste.

"Oh no! They only got drills in the repair shop. I worked on the throstles."

"Ah, I see."

An embarrassed silence. "They're for making thread," Nadia added.

Once again we stood like wooden statues.

"Well, I'll take Nadia home, I guess," I said. "So she won't have to go alone."

"Now? All the way to Cerna Hora?" and Mother's eyebrows shot up again so abruptly they were almost lost in the curls on her forehead. "Supper is at seven," she said emphatically.

I had never seen her like this. She was certainly not the kind of woman to stand on formal ceremony as she was doing now. But for the first time she had almost caught her only son in bed with a girl. And, as Marie had recently pointed out, a factory girl, at that.

"Oh, there's no need for Dan to go along," said Nadia quickly. "I won't keep you no longer." And she quickly knelt down on one knee, stuck her foot into a boot and nimbly began lacing it up.

We stood over her — a rudely carved Holy Family. At one point she glanced up at my father, who was leering at her like Mack Sennett, and she blushed again. Her fingers got tangled in the laces.

At last she stood up. I helped her into her shapeless coat and pulled on my overcoat while Nadia was putting on her scarf. For the first time I noticed that it was the same kind of woollen scarf that our cleaning lady wore in the winter. Red-faced, she blurted out, "Thanks for everything and goodbye!"

"Please don't mention it," said Mother in that unfamiliar voice and Father, with that leer still on his face, added, "Pleased to meet you! Come again," and he almost didn't finish because of the look my mother turned on him. I had no trouble guessing what they would talk about when we had left.

"Bye for now," I said.

"Be sure to be back by seven at the very latest," replied my mother in beautifully articulated tones.

And we left the flat.

Nadia ran down the stairs and the metal on her shoes clacked. She didn't speak until we were outside the building, where the wind and the blizzard caught us and spun us around. "That was awful embarrassing, Dan, to have them catch us like that."

"So what?"

"You'll be in for it when you get back, Dan."

"Aw, come on, Nadia! I'm not a kid any more."

"But you'll catch it all the same."

"I'm old enough."

"But your mother, she didn't like me at all. Course you can hardly blame her...."

That made me angry. "Well I do!"

"But you're a man. And you're young."

I didn't know what she meant by that. "Father liked you though," I said. "I thought he was going to jump you."

"Don't talk so ugly, Dan."

I was taken aback. Ugly? And I knew that I loved Nadia. And that I wasn't afraid.

"Come on, Nadenka," and I took her under the arm. "You've got to get up early in the morning."

We walked silently for a while, against the wind and the driving snow. Then she said in an anxious voice, "What time do you ... what time do you have to be...."

"Where?"

"You know, where they're supposed to hide you?"

I had completely forgotten that I was supposed to join the guerrillas that night. And I had forgotten my fear. "Not till after midnight. I'll take you home."

"No, Dan. You got to be back for supper at seven. And you got to save your strength."

"I've got strength enough. You've given me so much that I have enough to last until – until the war's over."

"Don't fool yourself! All that does is wear men out."

It took me a moment to realize what she meant. I was flooded with violent jealousy – jealousy of her he-man Franta Melichar. Christ, I hadn't even noticed if she was a virgin or not. She probably wasn't, if I hadn't noticed. Absurdly, a wave of love swept over me. So she wasn't. So she was more experienced than I was. What of it? I tried to feel jealous again but all I could feel was contentment. That I had a girl like her. A pretty girl with funny boots. I was filled with tenderness.

"But you really better not come with me. At least not all the way to the top."

"Don't you want me to?"

"You oughtn't. I know you're strong," she said, and I swelled up, though my strength was strongly relative. "But you aren't used to it and I am."

"I can last the course."

And I did. But she, unexpectedly, did not. We clambered up the hill along a steep, winding, snowbound path through the woods for at least an hour, and all at once Nadia began to breathe very heavily and she said, "Dan, I have to rest."

We stopped. She was wheezing, gasping for breath. It frightened me, and trying to drive away my fright I said, "You see! You play the strong one and before we're finished I'll have to carry you."

"Don't be angry, Dan!"

"Oh, go on with you. I'm not angry."

She was still breathing heavily. The half-moon had already set, the sky was hung with glassy winter stars and around us crowded the soughing black woods. In a white face, two round eyes burning. We were utterly alone, in the winter, in the woods, in the night.

"In this – in this storm – it's hard – anyway," Nadia gasped.

"Look, stay home from work tomorrow, Nadia, okay? I know Dr. Labsky and he'll write you a certificate for three days if I ask him to and you won't even have to go and see him. At the factory I'll tell them I was at your place today and you've got a fever."

"But" – she gasped – "but you said you wasn't going to the factory any more!"

I had forgotten again, of course. Suddenly the whole business of hiding out with the resistance seemed stupid. And my fear too. Even if they arrested me, I would not be alone. Perhaps I could stand it. And I would plead stupidity, which was really what it was anyway – certainly not sabotage. The only true thing I had said that day was that Nadia had given me strength. I decided to tell her the truth.

"I was just bluffing, Nadia. I'm not going to hide anywhere. It can't get so hot."

"Dan! Uippelt knows all about them cross-brackets!"

I have never got very far with the truth. I began to romanticize again. "But you know that Uippelt's an American German. He's probably got no love for the Nazis."

"I hope you're right," she said faintly, but it was clear that the idea of my flight into some mythical forest did not fill her with pleasure either. I continued to reassure her for a few minutes and by that time she was breathing normally again so we continued.

About two hundred metres from the village, where the wood came to an end and the steep path became almost vertical, Nadia knelt down in the snow and began to tremble. The unexpectedness of it frightened me. Though she was extremely thin, she had always seemed terribly strong.

"I don't know what's come over me," she wheezed. "My knees won't hold up...."

I looked around. The bare summit of Cerna Hora towered over us, and above it the stars. The village was not yet visible but I knew that it was just over the brow of the hill. The black outline of a stone cross stood out against the sky. In the valley, like a dark, dappled bull's-eye in the white slopes around it, lay Kostelec. Suddenly, I felt desperate.

"We're almost there," I said. "Don't you want me to carry you?"

"Why you – couldn't carry me. I'm – heavy. Nothing but bone." She tried to laugh. She stood up, and we dragged ourselves up that awful ascent. I supported her and soon I was puffing like a broken steam engine. But it was worse for her. In the end I had to carry her. Not in my arms but on my back, as one would carry a child. She was not heavy at all, but I wasn't used to carrying loads either and I thought I would collapse. With gritted teeth, however, I finally crawled to the top of the Black Mountain.

I carried her as far as the stone cross and there I let her slip gently to the ground. She leaned against me. An icy wind beat against us. It was only a short walk to the village, and we staggered the remaining distance holding each other up. We stopped in front of the cottage. It was a mountain cottage, with small windows and firewood stacked up to the thatched roof. When Nadia opened the door a mottled cat came out and meowed. We kissed, and the cat rubbed against our legs.

"Good night, Nadia. I – I love you."

"I'm awful fond of you, Dan," she said.

The wooden door shut behind her. I stood there for a while longer. An oil lamp lit up the window; they didn't have electricity in Cerna Hora yet. Light seeped out around the edges of the makeshift blackout curtains.

I turned around and slowly retraced my steps over the crest of Cerna Hora. The stone cross stood out blackly against the starry sky.

●

*10 October, 1952*

*Hi D'Anielli!*

*Greetings from you'll never guess where – our native hick metropolis. The most important news: Molly Dreslerova is walking around with what they would have called in the first boorjoie republic a bun in the oven, except that the phrase doesn't exist any more because it's slang and as Comrade Stalin, the Generalisssimmo (I'm lost: do you write it with three 's's and two 'm's or the other way round? I always was weak in spelling) writes in his work, which is scientific, as the title itself makes clear – On Marksism and Lingwistics – slang was invented by the boorjoisie to prevent the working class from learning how to speak properly, thus keeping them out of the better type of jobs. But our working class is educated now so they don't use the expression "bun in the oven" any more, they just say she's knocked up.*

*A less, but still important bit of news: they sewed Rosta Pitterman up, not for a political delict, as the honoured custom is now, but on a morals charge, which is rather unusual in these stormy times. And I had thought of him more as a politico than a sexual pervert. Anyway, he always was a little odd, so I'm not surprised they brought him to justice. He knocked up a minor, which as a teacher he's forbidden to do, someone called Ruza Rehackova from Cerna Hora who used to pose for him, though she's not yet sixteen. Since the crafty bugger is already married they couldn't sentence him to a lifetime of wedlock as they would if he'd been single, so he only got five years in a corrective institution.*

*Which reminds me: I didn't mean to be misleading. Marie's not really about to become an unmarried mother as you might surmise from the con-text because her name is now, at last, Kocandrlova. It took him long enough, though. I know you were so madly in love with her that the heavens (and certainly Kocandrle) must have been offended, but if it'll make you feel any better, you weren't alone. I was in love with her too, but even more secretly than you and, if you can believe it, even more platonically.*

*Another important piece of news: my wife Jana's also anticipating a blessed event and she says it's definitely mine. So I'm believing her, even though I am a little surprised, by which I don't mean to suggest, for God's sake, that you should think ill of my wife Jana. But truth to tell, we don't have as much fun together as we used to now that I'm spending most of my time at party meetings, on volunteer work brigades, komandyrovky and agit-prop activities. If I ever do show up around home, it's such an extra-ordinary event that Jana always puts on a tremendous meal and since I'm so hungry after all those institutional meals I gorge myself and then I'm not much fun for Jana. So even though I can't really remember our having any fun together in the last two or three months, I'm going to be a father anyway. What the hell. Matrimony is a union of mutual trust, as Stalin – who else? – probably said somewhere.*

*But to get on to the most important thing of all: what am I doing here in the first place? Well, it was for agit-prop. We put on a program at the Kovotex National Enterprise, formerly Messerschmitt Aktiengesellschaft where you frittered away your youth working for the Reich, even though in the end your work wasn't worth bugger all to the Reich. We presented the new ruling class with a literary variety show written by some other comrades and myself. I went to the brown coal mines at Kladno for inspiration – into the Marie Majerova pit to be exact – but in the end I got most of my material from Vilimek's Magazine of Humour which my landlord had stashed away in the attic before the war. The program was of course mostly serious and there were beautiful songs – none of your low-brow stuff like "Give Me Five Minutes More" but numbers like "Where Are You, Suliko My Star?," a ditty popularized by Comrade Stalin, the Generallisssimo. They also recited poems by Comrade Stanislav K. Neumann and Comrade E. F. Burian. My satirical skit bore the inspired title, "At the Housing Department." Somehow or other it was out of place in that otherwise serious and highly artistic program, which is probably why the audience rewarded it with such stormy applause – so that I wouldn't feel badly that it wasn't as beautiful as, say, Comrade Neumann's poem on the joys of Marxmanship. Or could it possibly have been because all those years of exploitation have left our working class with somewhat jaded tastes? It may well take another twenty years and at least three Comrade E.F. Burians with their poems on the delights of building socialism to raise its taste up to the point where it will be willing, for example, to give Comrade Neumann's poem the same amount of applause as my poor skit.*

*But our program was only the opener to what the evening was really* about. It was, in fact, the ceremonial signing of a petition during which it was demonstrated that not only do Czech workers know how to sign their own names but they are also very well aware of what *they are signing*, so they would sign it anyway, even if they didn't know what it said, because they were told to. It all goes to show how politically mature our Czech working class is, in spite of having had its taste so debased by the boorjoisie to the point where they could actually enjoy "At the Housing Department."

What they signed was a petition demanding the hardest but nevertheless the most just punishment for the traitorous Comrade Slansky and his clique (you can strike "Comrade" out, Comrade, and don't put anything in its place: that's contempt for you. Ever hear anyone say "Comrade Bata"?). Anyway, the ceremony itself was uplifting and we had an excellent view of it. We stood in the very same large factory hall where you once sweated for the Reich, on a stage with a speaker's dais and a portrait of Comrade Stalin in front of it in a very pretty art nouveau *kind of frame*. The Comrade Factory Director read a report on the heinous crimes of Comrade Slansky's gang (you can strike out "Comrade" again, I don't know why I keep sticking it in — habit, I guess). It was a rather colourless effort, but no matter, speechifying is not within his field of competence. For that he's got Comrade Hetflajs, leader of the workers' militia, who showed up, as befits the occasion, in a spanking new boiler suit and an extra large pistol. He laid it on so thick about Slansky's Titoism and revisionism and Zionism that we were all in a rage at Comrade Slansky's gang (ohmygod, strike out the "Comrade" again). There was a slight problem in that a comradely delegation from the C.C.C.P. was present, and so that they could savour the situation everything had to be translated for them into Russky, which was taken care of by Comrade Mozol, head of the technical control department. Oddly enough, even though he doesn't speak Russky very well and the microphone was acting up too so that you couldn't understand a word, I could still get the drift of his speech, more or less. Comrade Hetflajs finished very nicely, by shouting out, "Long live Comrade Stalin!" who is indeed certain to, which is not entirely the case with Slansky's gang (you don't have to strike anything out now).

Then Comrade Mozol stepped up to the microphone, which by now had conked out, so that Comrade Mozol had to raise his voice and say, "And now, all of us will sign the petition we have ready here, stating that we demand a just but hard punishment for Slansky and his gang of traitors. Come forward one by one ... and ... and ..." – he searched for *a way to end the speech on a dignified tone, but since he's no speech-maker he simply said — "and maintain calm!"*

*For a while the comrade workers just sat there looking at each other, but then hard but righteous wrath must have started boiling in them — and one tall fellow with a head like a pinecone stood up, bent over the table and signed. Then the others followed suit, standing neatly in a row as if they were lining up at the butcher's for meat, and one after the other, with their heavy proletarian's hands (the women with a lighter hand, although heavy and proletarian still) they signed the just demand of the Czech and Slovak people whose collective will is a beacon to our government. The dignity of the entire evening was scarcely disrupted even when a young woman comrade fainted and some official from the Union of Youth had to carry her off to the first-aid room, unfortunately before either of them had a chance to sign, so that the petition had to be sent off to the president minus their two names, which is regrettable — not of course for the president, he has nothing to regret, you understand, but for the young comrades. I guess the crimes of the Slansky gang were too much for her.*

*You're probably wondering, you old son-of-a-bitch, whether I'm still glad I threw in my lot with this crowd. If you can ask a dumb question like that after this report, then you're not only stupid but ignorant as well. But now that I'm a part of the Party, I have to try to influence the other comrades, so they will be aware as I am how much work still awaits us before we build socialism of the kind that Comrade Stalin, the Generallissssimo, is leading us towards (I know there's probably too many s's in it, but Comrade Stalin deserves only the best).*

*Yours ever, Vratislav*

*P.S. Molly really looks great, even though the bun in her oven is a gargantuan one.*

# CHAPTER FOUR

In each breast there is only one heart-beat
And there's only one road you can go
And if you're afraid to walk down it
You will never arrive at your goal.

Love's map is erratic and lawless,
Its ways rose-coloured and wild —
If you wish for a future that's certain
Be not by love's vision beguiled.

If you don't know the weight of earth's burden
When the bell tolls its knell in the gloom,
Then your life is a tissue of fancy
And as dry as the dust of the tomb.

JOSEF KAINAR

Change has rarely ever changed things.... Perhaps it is not
true that history repeats itself: it is only that man remains
the same.

WALTER SORRELL

●

# Crane

*March 7, 1954*
*Kostelec*

**D**ear Danny,
 *I assume you followed the dressing down I received in the
press; now not even dogs in the street will give me the time of day. I
was taken to task for using slang and argot because it deforms the
Czech language and devalues poetry. But I am quite capable of standing up to such admonitions. Language has its roots in how people
speak. Seal it hermetically into books and it loses its sap, it dries up. Of
course, you can try to compensate for this by over-writing with complex syntax and decorative flourishes, but that is artificial and like
everything artificial it soon wears thin, loses its fashionable appeal,
and dies. The only authors whose work remains alive are those who
transfer language to the page in its natural form. It may be stylized, of
course, but never prettied up!*
 *But that's not the worst thing. I decided to go and work in a factory,
influenced by the poetry of S.K. Neumann:*

*I love all things with simple relationships*
*And I love such people most of all;*
*Pure they are, and comely, though I see them for the hundredth time.*
*They are made of primal stuff and taste of ripe beech-nuts.*

*The absurd thing is, it was these very lines that some of the critics beat me over the head with. They said the heroes of my Monologues were simply the bourgeoisie in proletarian dress; that in my work proletarian relationships, their psychology, etc., are just as decadent as relationships between people in the do-nothing class. They said there was too much sex in my work, and almost no politics. They even accused me of disguising my true political colours, and as proof that I see the workers falsely one critic quoted a passage from Neumann:*

*They are not a kaleidoscope of brightly coloured shards*
*That with each turn gives the lie to yet another star....*

*But, Danny, I really did go out among them. I made friends with them, gained their confidence, studied them. This time I grasped the opportunity that I had let slip during the war, and I discovered that they only appear to be simpler than we are. In reality they are just as complex as you or I. They differ from us in nothing fundamental. The difference lies in our ability to verbalize our own complex nature – this they do not have. But isn't verbalization of what remains unexpressed precisely one of the fundamental responsibilities of a writer? They say: Everything about them is steadfast. But what is that everything? In many ways they seem to me more cautious or lethargic than steadfast. Perhaps that's a result of centuries of experience, or an aspect of the age we live in, I don't know.*

*I don't know in the least what all this means for me, for my work, for literature.*

*I only know that in this world everything is always just a little bit different from what we think it is, Danny.*
*Yours sincerely,*
*Jan*

●

My one good fortune is that I didn't choose this profession, I was forced into it by circumstance. It is fortunate too that circumstance forced me into a profession which is so well paid, and which demands my presence at work for only a few hours each week and only eight months in the year. The most fortunate thing of all, however, is that because I did not choose this profession of my own free will I need not torture myself about its significance.

My colleagues do torture themselves. They speak to me of their research almost with embarrassment. To them it seems pointless beside my novels. They haven't read them, of course (my novels have not been translated into English yet, and my colleagues belong to a race that does not excel in foreign languages), but the fateful slogan "publish or perish" has branded them for life with an existential respect for the printed word.... I try to reassure them that the discoveries of Mr. Webster concerning minor textual variations in the work of a certain forgotten Elizabethan playwright, which indicate errors in the dating of his plays, are a more concrete contribution to the sum of human knowledge than all my novelistic impressions put together. They think I'm merely being kind, but I mean it. Nit-picking analysis that illuminates sources, influences and relationships is something immensely concrete, and concrete things have a lasting worth. I am not at all sure this is true of my own works. In them, it seems to me, I have tried to second-guess life, to interpret it, to conjure it up out of fantasy. The trouble is that students are also more interested in conjuring life out of fantasy than they are in examining its concrete details.

During my lecture on the main features of literary impressionism, the class came down with sleeping sickness. Towards the end of the hour, when I was neatly summarizing in several concrete points the chief characteristics of a naturalistic vision of the world, Higgins put his hand up. "Sir, wouldn't it make more sense to talk about the actual novel? I enjoyed it so much."

Had I chosen this profession of my own free will, my professorial self-esteem might have been severely shaken. But since circumstance had chosen it for me, I was merely annoyed with Higgins, and retorted that if he liked *The Red Badge of Courage* so much, he could give a paper on it himself.

Higgins may have liked the novel, but when it came down to giving a paper he too obviously considered it his academic responsibility to give an interpretation of it rather than talk about it, and to this end he borrowed from the best-known authorities. So now he is trying to demonstrate to his audience, which as usual is not particularly quick in spirit, that *The Red Badge of Courage* is not in fact about war at all but rather about the emotional and intellectual maturing of a young man and his progress from idealistic illusion to knowledge and from innocence to a full experience of de-idealized reality.

Once again my first reaction is annoyance. "So you say it's not a novel about war."

"No, it's not. It's about the maturing of a young — "

"Nor about fear?"

"Yes," admits Higgins, "it's about fear, among other things."

"But not about war?"

Higgins falls back on his *auctoritates*.

"No."

"But you will admit that it takes place in the middle of a war?"

"That ..." – Higgins hesitates – "is not the basic thing. The basic thing is that it describes the development of a young man from – "

"Read this," I interrupt, and quote. " 'He saw a man climb to the top of a fence, straddle the rail and fire a parting shot.' " This passage has always reminded me of the end of poor old Hroch as he knelt with the *Panzerfaust* beside the badly damaged bunker: a tall SS man jumped down from a German tank and very calmly – the air was alive with bullets – took a step forward and aimed, and a tiny flame spurted from the barrel of his gun. At that distance no sound could be heard. Hroch slumped to the ground, the SS man leaped back onto the tank and the vehicle rumbled off. A parting shot.

I look at Higgins. On his face there is nothing more than the defiance of one subscribing to a truth he considers self-evident.

"Well, what about this?" I suggest. " 'The orderly sergeant of the youth's company was shot through the cheeks. Its supports being injured, his jaw hung down afar, disclosing in the white cavern of his mouth a pulsing mass of blood and teeth.' "

Once again there is no response. "Elementary, my dear Watson," I say to myself. There is nothing at all in Higgins' experience that relates to this text, so he can only understand it in terms of my professorial dicta – that the naturalists were naturalists because they revelled in horrors, and that the aim of impressionistic authors was to create powerful visual effects, for which the horrors of war were eminently suitable subject matter. Higgins has not, as I have, carried a man in a German uniform on a stretcher through a parched May afternoon. He has not helped to lay him out on the operating table. He has not seen Dr. Capek poking his spatula around in the mass of blood and teeth hanging where the man's lower jaw should be. He has not heard the gurgling coming from the wide cavern of his mouth. Dr. Capek played around for a little while with that terrible protrusion, then said to me, "This needs a battle surgeon. To tell you the truth, I don't know what to do with it." Then they put the man to sleep, and Dr. Capek tried something. The man died on the operating table. He may have suffocated in his own blood.

Still nothing? Try the story, Higgins, about the letter Wilson gave to Henry for his family, which he awkwardly demanded back when the danger was over? Nadia – how I lied to her, because shame was stronger than fear, but then again, fear was stronger than shame; Henry – his mad, galloping, somersaulting thoughts, his self-justifications, his instinct for survival....

There's no point in going on. It's not Higgins' fault that the Gestapo never made it as far as Canada. I should instead respect his parents for not letting them. And for landing on the beaches of Normandy where they too saw gaping caverns for mouths....

So all I say is, "You still think it's not about war?"

"Well, okay, it's about war too, but that's not the basic thing. What you've quoted are typical naturalistic details. But basically the novel traces the emotional and intellectual maturing...."

If it were not a story of the soul, it would only be an ordinary sea narrative. I give up. I look at my watch: twenty minutes more. So I put the question, "Don't you think, at least, that you might regard it as a novel against war?"

Higgins thinks it over and shakes his head. "No. Crane is not condemning war. He treats it as an integral part of natural catastrophes – "

"Dianne?" I interrupt, turning to the Irish girl waving her hand impatiently in the air.

"It *is* an anti-war novel," she says with almost personal conviction.

"What makes you think so?"

"Because he presents us very graphically with the horrors of war. And this arouses disgust for war in the reader."

"But it's not clear whether Henry is fighting for the North or the South. Don't you think ... ?"

"It doesn't matter," says Dianne, shaking her head. "War is awful for soldiers, no matter what army they belong to."

Again I find myself in a classic impasse: a point of view formed by direct experience of war, face to face with ideas shaped by the atmosphere and fashions of an age and its television.

"There are wars that are just," I say, quoting the Great Stalin, "and wars that are unjust – "

"Sir!" Wendy McFarlane's excited voice interrupts me. "Name me a single just war!"

She takes my breath away. The unacknowledged citation of the Generalissimo has genuinely upset her and her cry has caught everyone's attention. No one yawns. Vicky puts aside her bag of potato chips and Wendy repeats, "A single one!"

Oh God. I lower my eyes. I see Rebecca in my mind, the only survivor of the large Silbernagl clan: those Jewish girls! My father, embarrassingly saved by his fetid leg. Anger rises in me – not at Wendy with her knees naked in the Canadian winter but at the blunt stupidity of the blind march into the trap. And I see Prema, and hear Nadia's voice saying, "I hate them. My poor father's probably with God in his Truth."

I raise my eyes – black Gwendolyn is fighting on my side: the Civil War was a war against the slave merchants, even though the motives were largely economic....

"But why isn't it clear what side Henry is fighting on?" asks Wendy, slightly embarrassed.

"Because Crane was a racist. He couldn't have cared less about the fate of the black slaves. *The Red Badge of Courage* insults me! I can't understand why we're reading such *trash!*"

I can't get angry at Gwendolyn, even though she has unwittingly applied to Crane's work canons that the critics once used to embitter poor Jan's life, not to mention my own. But that was in another country, and besides, those whores are....

*Trash.* Caverns of mouths. A sharpshooter straddling a fence. History is cruel, even the history of literature in the cruel hands of green youth. And even crueller in the hands of old men, red as maple leaves in autumn. Old men should be pale....

"Class dismissed."

●

"Get a load of this," said Prema. He turned his back to the street to conceal what he was up to and pulled something from under his jacket. He showed it to me. A parabellum. Prepare for war.

"If he hadn't cleared off, I'd have pulled it on him."

If he had, we might well have been where I almost ended up four years earlier (if I hadn't managed with the help of Mr. Skocdopole's slivovice to avoid the unique fate of becoming a guerrilla from Kostelec, so forgetting all about my desire to live in the mountains). President Benes had died two nights earlier and the new Communist government had introduced something like an undeclared state of martial law throughout the country. I was standing on the street corner by the Granada Hotel with Prema, Benda, and Vahar the greengrocer. We had our heads together, and the three of them, to my horror, were talking about an underground resistance organization.

I had come from Prague just for a visit, with no idea that they'd set up any kind of organization. I had run into them on Jirasek Street, and Prema had quite matter-of-factly let me in on the conspiracy. It was the same as the one I'd got mixed up in four years before simply by taking pictures of Prema's heroic act of sabotage against the Nazis. Only the adversary was different. This time it was the Communists. The decisive factor in each instance was the circumscription of freedom, but with my smattering of university Marxism I could not really understand what a worker from a tobacco warehouse, like Prema, needed intellectual freedom for.

We were standing there, our heads together like true conspirators, when from behind us came a voice: "What's going on here, gentlemen?"

Malina. The same Malina from the old Messerschmitt factory days, only now he was wearing the uniform of the new National Security Corps, the SNB, which had replaced the normal police force.

"What's it to you?" retorted the greengrocer rebelliously.

"You'd be surprised, you donkeys!" replied Malina. "See this uniform?"

"So what?"

"Don't this uniform mean nothing to you, turkey?"

"No. You're just bullshitting."

"What're you talking about here?"

"What's it to you?"

"You'd be surprised," said Malina. "You're carrying on anti-state talk. You don't have to be a fucking genius to see that."

"A good thing you don't," said Vahar, "because a genius you ain't."

Prema, who was standing beside me, slipped his hand inside his jacket like Napoleon.

"Cut the insults, okay? Otherwise you come with me, you mutton-heads," said Malina.

"Must be the uniform that does it."

"You watch it, or you'll be smiling on the other side of your face!"

"Why shouldn't I smile? I feel great! Socialism at last...."

"That's it, Vahar, you're coming with me!"

Something clicked softly under Prema's jacket. Nervously, I decided to intervene.

"Come off it, Malina," I said. "As a matter of fact, we were just talking about women."

"Women, my eye. You baboons was talking politics."

Between the men's room in the Messerschmitt works and that uniform there lay a historic watershed. Faithful to a beautiful tradition, I said, "That's a load of crap. We were talking about tight pussies."

"Don't give me that bull," said Malina threateningly. But his officiousness was clearly weakening.

"We really were. I've got this incredible chick in Prague, see, but I can't get into her."

Now he was genuinely interested. "So how do you go about it?"

Prema removed his hand from under his jacket.

"Can't be done. I told her to go have an operation."

"You mean you can do that, operate on them like that?"

"Sure. The only problem is they might make it too big, and then you're in real trouble. There's no way you can satisfy her then."

"Malina could," said Benda.

The officer laughed. "Tough bananas, you chihuahua. Why not just get another girl?"

"I may have to. If the operation doesn't work, I'm stuck with her, and then what?"

"Give her to Malina," said Benda. "He's got one like King Kong."

Malina laughed again without trying to deny Benda's claim, but then he realized that he had let things get too intimate. "All right, you fucking studs," he said with conciliatory gruffness. "If you want to talk about women, go to the Beranek. We got orders to stop any assembling on the public streets."

"Who's assembling?" said the greengrocer rebelliously.

"Don't worry, Malina, we're leaving," I said quickly. "We won't make any trouble for you."

"It's not trouble," said the officer, "it's a question of public order." And he walked away proudly.

It was then that Prema said, "If he hadn't cleared off, I'd have pulled it on him!"

"And we'd have been in the shit," I said.

Prema flipped open his jacket. He had an underarm holster attached to his suspenders. He probably got that idea from a film. "He'd have stuck his tail between his legs and run. I know him."

"Sure," I said. "Straight to the police station. Then what?"

"We got to be ready for anything," said Prema.

Later, in the same room where Dr. Labsky had tended to his burns four years earlier, Prema explained what he wanted of me. He said they had enough people for the physical struggle. Now they needed someone with an education to draw up their program, invent their slogans, and write their appeals to the public. He pulled open a drawer. There was a small duplicating machine inside.

"Write us a leaflet."

"What kind?"

"Doesn't make any difference. For instance, you can say that there's no butter because the Russians carted it off."

"Ah, I see."

I sat down and took out my pen. If I had said no to Prema, I would have felt like Malina in his new uniform. But I wasn't very enthusiastic about writing anything, about butter or anything else. I had no desire for any new adventures in the resistance, and moreover I wasn't altogether sure what was happening around me.

Prema was an old friend. I remembered the afternoon when I had risked my trousers to take pictures of his work of destruction, destruction that had won a place on a plaque of honour for seven citizens of Kostelec. We were bound together by a powerful bond. I couldn't betray that.

And so I wrote:

*A question for the Minister of Supply:*
*where is our Czech butter?*

*Our answer:*
*in trains heading for the Soviet Union!*

*Czech children are going without*
*while the comrades in the Kremlin butter their bread with our butter!*

Prema liked it. "Brief and to the point," he said.

Slightly embarrassed, and feeling an incipient fear, I watched what I had just tossed off being multiplied with each turn of the handle: *A question for the Minister of Supply.... A question for the Minister of Supply.... A question for the Minister of Supply....*

"Come tonight at nine," said Prema when he had made about a hundred leaflets. "We're going on the air."

My stomach heaved. I simply wouldn't be stupid enough to get involved again.

I was there at the stroke of nine. Some things are stronger than fear.

Prema opened up his wardrobe. Inside was a huge transmitter. "Christ, where'd you get that?" I gasped.

"I stole it when I was in the army up by the border. I knew it would come in handy someday."

I remembered something. "You still have that machine-gun you had during the war?"

A wry, confident grin crossed Prema's Mongolian face.

"Don't worry," he said, "the wavelength and time is already set. But my cousin Robert doesn't understand Czech. That's where you come in. I want you to send in English, *Ziss iss layda kollink svan.* That's the way me and Robert set it up when he was here in the spring. And he's supposed to reply, *Ziss iss svan kollink layda.*"

"What then?"

"What then?" said Prema, taken aback. "Well, you just say that we're going to send on the same wavelength in a week."

I breathed a slight sigh of relief. In a week I would be back in Prague and Prema would have to find another assistant. How to find one in Kostelec was his problem. I had not betrayed him.

And so I transmitted, "This is Leda calling Swan." My voice mingled with the potpourri of voices calling out in Russian, German, Patagonian, in languages I didn't understand. And from somewhere in that Babel a swan was supposed to answer. But it didn't. Robert, a son of one of Mrs. Skocdopolova's ten sisters who had married an Englishman, had probably forgotten about the agreement. Or maybe they wouldn't believe him in England. A tailor who knew of a secret transmitter in Eastern Europe? Prema and the greengrocer were sitting tensely beside me. On the table, a pile of leaflets about butter. This is Leda calling Swan. The swan was silent.

We packed it in at ten.

"Are you sure it was today?"

"Dead certain," said Prema. "I wrote it down."

"Did you understand him right? You said he couldn't speak Czech."

"We spoke German."

"Since when can you speak German?"

"Well, I can't too well," admitted Prema, "but it was today for sure."

We locked the transmitter back into the cupboard and went into the kitchen. Since that memorable evening four years earlier nothing had changed. The florid Mr. Skocdopole sat at the table with a sticky bottle of home-distilled slivovice.

"Have a drink, boys!"

Only the greengrocer and I accepted his invitation. Prema did not drink. He kept to the vows of the conspiracy. Mr. Skocdopole drank to the memory of the president who had just passed away. It was no doubt a very long memory; by this time he was in a prophetic mood. As I listened to him, it occurred to me that he might perhaps be more successful as a prophet than poor old Brych, the fortune-teller on whom he had once depended so completely.

"I tell you, boys, we're in for a time of it. First there was Masaryk, then the Nazis came. We barely squeaked through that one. And now Benes is dead, and the Bolsheviks are here. It's the end."

"We're going to fight back," said the greengrocer.

"We can't fight back alone. The West has abandoned us to their tender mercies. Just like before. But we were strong then and the Bolsheviks weren't very well organized, just shifty and prevaricating. Now they've got the whole shebang in their hands. It's going to be terrible. Drink up, boys!"

He responded to his own command and we followed suit.

"I tell you, boys, I've got the willies. You've no idea what we're in for. But I do. When I recall" – Mr. Skocdopole poured himself another drink – "Sedlica, for example. Knocked out by a grenade at Samara and they captured him." Mr. Skocdopole's voice cracked and he began to tell us the story I had first heard that dark night four years before, about the legionnaire who had been bayoneted and buried in the rubble by Czech Bolsheviks. Only this time Mr. Skocdopole added a detail he had kept from us four years before, or else I had been so besotted that it had dropped from my memory. "You know" – the old man almost sobbed – "you know, boys, what they did to him before they finished him off? It boggles the mind. I'd never've thought it possible if I hadn't seen it with my own eyes. Drink up!"

Even though I'd sworn I wouldn't end up as I had that other night, I did what he said. With the stump of his stocking-covered arm the old legionnaire wiped a tear from his nose. It looked like a red cucumber.

"They cut off his balls, boys! While he was still alive! Czechs! And they did that to a fellow Czech!"

Both of us automatically took another swallow.

"If they could do a thing like that when they weren't even organized, can you imagine what they'll do now?"

The yellowed whites of his eyes glinted at us through the cigarette smoke. I was right back where I'd been four years earlier. It was high time to get out of Kostelec again.

•

It seems that Veronika is already one of the family. With her hair all nicely blow-dried she is standing beside Percy in a pale blue dress, smiling at the Svenssons' guests, to whom he is introducing her. Another clever Czech girl about to marry well, I muse. I draw within earshot and stop. This Czech girl is playing a dangerous game with the ritual introductions, a treacherous bit of absurdity, sawing off the limb she's sitting on.

"Meet Veronika Prst," Percy is saying in the appropriate tones to an elegant lady in a long gown. "Veronika is from Czechoslovakia."

"How interesting!" declares the lady in a corresponding tone. "How long have you been in Canada?"

And Veronika, her voice perfectly pitched, replies with a sweet smile, "About a century."

The lady does not register the slightest surprise, and offers the proper ritual response: "How do you like it in Canada?"

"Not at all," she answers cheerfully, with a sweet smile.

"How nice!" the lady replies, and then, "Oh, excuse me, there's Molly Smith. I simply must say hello to her. See you later!"

"I hope not!"

Veronika, in short, is playing with fire. I feel annoyed at her for making fun of these good people who have done nothing to hurt her. At the same time, she is banking on the fact that Percival is too drowsy with love to object to her game.

Percy is talking with some gentlemen. I try to see Veronika through his eyes. Why has he chosen this sad girl from Prague, who is pretty enough, to be sure, but no prettier than Percy's sister and several of her friends? It is a mystery, of course. Once upon a time, in the era of friendship among nations, a certain Mabel came to Prague, a black girl from Chicago, who strummed on the guitar and sang progressive songs about banks of marble. It was nothing special, but one day I discovered that the palms of her hands were pink, and I immediately translated "Banks of Marble" into Czech. Pink-palmed, chocolate-coloured Mabel had cast a spell on me, though not for long. Can it be that Veronika's slight accent has the charm of those pink palms? I hope that Percy's delight in Veronika is not just skin-deep, as mine was in Mabel.

And the silly girl goes on sawing the limb. She invents new variations.

"See you later!" someone says.

"Don't bother coming back!" she replies, with an Ultra-Brite smile.

Here and there tiny clouds of doubt cross the faces of people chatting with her, but either they are too polite or they think that the poor immigrant girl doesn't know enough English to realize what she's saying. The poor dear.... And so pretty.

"I'll see you later, Veronika. Prst, is it?"

"You bet, honey!"

"Are these the games people play in your country?" I hear someone say behind me.

I turn around. The grey eyes of Irene Svensson.

"Do you think Percy notices?" I ask, instead of replying. "I have the impression that Veronika cares very much about your brother."

"And do *you* care very much about Veronika?" Irene asks gravely. And mysteriously.

I smile. "I feel a little like her father. She's got no one in Canada...."

"Fathers are usually in love with their daughters."

"You've been reading Freud!"

"So what?"

She stands before me in her protean dress, against that same Tiffany background I used to dream about when I was a young man intoxicated by Hollywood kitsch. She is smoking a cigarette. Marijuana. That absurd distance between Kostelec and the Svenssons'. All in one brief lifetime.

"So nothing," I say. "It's just that she's from my country and she's young enough to be my daughter."

"So am I."

"So what?"

"Don't you know so what?" she asks. Then she turns around and walks away. Sweet Jesus. She has slender legs and shoes with golden heels. She is straight out of a professorial dream about the most beautiful girl in the class.

And this is the twentieth century, in which everything is possible. Why not something nice as well?

And are not these the games people play, in Canada as well as in Kostelec?

●

I had heard that Irena was in Kostelec, and I longed to see her before I left for Prague. It was shortly past noon, the day after we'd made the transmission, and the sun was shining. Prema hadn't showed up; he was probably making the rounds with my embarrassing leaflets and sticking them under people's doors. An unpleasant thought. I needed to see Irena.

She was married now, but I hadn't met her husband. I didn't love her anymore; I had got over it when Mother fell seriously ill and Irena suddenly started being nice to me. Once she had even come to our place and offered to mop the kitchen floor for us. While she was doing it, I stopped loving her – it was a sudden thing. But I didn't tell her, and she wouldn't have cared anyway because not long after that she fell in love with a university lecturer who was said to be quite a snazzy dresser. Later she married him. Now she was an elegant woman living in Prague, and I had run into her a few times as she was out strolling to or from a game of tennis, racket in hand. We would chat amiably and go our separate ways. Then once I was on the train to Prague with Haryk and we were telling funny stories about the girls we had known and I told him how my love for Irena, a love that had lasted many years, had abruptly and inexplicably come to an end one day when I saw her mopping the floor. We laughed about it while Irena's aunt, who was in the next compartment, heard every word. Naturally she told Irena and Irena was hopping mad. I had not spoken to her since then: Irena was a closed chapter, though pleasant to browse through again once in a while.

I turned into their apartment building, walked up to the third floor and rang the bell. Alena, Irena's younger sister, answered the door. She was startled to see me.

"Oh, it's you," she said quietly. "Look, come some other time, can you?"

"What's up?"

"I can't tell you now, but come some other time. And telephone first!"

"Good afternoon," came a voice from behind Alena. She clapped her hand over her mouth in the comic sign for trouble. The man who emerged from the living room could not see this because her back was to him.

"Good afternoon," I said, greeting him.

"Mr. – ?"

"Smiricky."

"Ah, Mr. Smiricky," he said. "Come in." I should have listened to Alena and not asked any questions. But it was too late to back out.

Irena was sitting on the living room sofa in a trouser-suit. I had never seen her dressed like that before and she looked good. But she was not in a benevolent mood. She didn't even respond to my greeting.

"Whatever is the matter, Renka?" said the gentleman, who I supposed was her husband. He certainly was a snazzy dresser; he reminded me of Grau, the phys-ed teacher Irena had been crazy about in third form. A big hunk of beef. "Our guest said 'hello,'" said her blond hunk.

"Hello," said Irena, unaffably.

"Do sit down," offered the gentleman. So I sat, and the man settled into a club-chair. Alena sat down at the opposite end of the sofa from Irena. There was an awkward silence. I had obviously come at a bad moment, but what was going on?

"Would anyone like tea?" asked Alena finally.

"How about our guest?" said the gentleman with unmistakable irony.

"Don't bother just on my account," I said.

"Why, surely we're not going to sit here with nothing to drink," said the man, "even if we have nothing to say."

"Let me make it," said Irena, and she rushed out.

He gazed out of the window, as though lost in thought. At her end of the sofa, Alena was trying to stifle a laugh. I crossed my legs, kicking the coffee table as I did so. The sound was like a pistol shot.

"Excuse me."

The man continued staring out the window.

We sat there in thoughtful silence for about a minute. It seemed more like ten. The kettle began to sing in the kitchen.

"I'm glad of the opportunity to meet you," I forced myself to say, just to break the silence. "Irena – told me about you."

"Hmm," said the gentleman, slowly rotating the chair to face me. "Did she tell you a great deal about me?"

"Well – some," I replied uncertainly.

"Isn't that a coincidence," he said. "She told me about you too. In a manner of speaking."

The way he said it made me feel extremely uncomfortable. "Well, we were ... friends ... in high school," I said uneasily.

"So I gather," he said.

"Did she tell you a lot?" The conversation was quickly turning sour. Alena looked as though she could hardly contain herself.

"Not nearly enough," he said drily.

Irena came back into the room with a teapot and four cups on a tray. She set the tray on the coffee table and poured the tea, spilling some into my saucer. We took our cups and began to stir the tea with our spoons. The delicate clinking of silver on china only emphasized the silence. I tried to divert the conversation to safer ground. "Are you down for long?"

No one replied.

"Our guest has asked a question," said the gentleman.

"Then answer him!" snapped Irena.

"I could almost have sworn," said the gentleman, enunciating deliberately, "that he would much prefer it if you answered him, Renka."

"We're going back to Prague tomorrow."

"Aha." I took a deep swallow of tea and gasped. It was terribly hot. The husband sipped noisily. Someone's stomach growled. We were silent.

"Of course you could always remain here another few days, Renka, if you wish," said her husband, breaking the silence. "Shall we say until Sunday. Would that be long enough for you?"

"I don't want to stay," said Irena.

"No? There's so much here to catch up on."

Irena said nothing. Alena bit her lip.

"On second thought, you go to Prague, Renka, and I'll stay here until Sunday."

What kind of queer bird was this? Whatever was going on, I judged that it would be best to make a rapid departure. I stood up and said, "I must be going now – "

"I won't hear of it!" said the gentleman, standing up too. "*I* shall go! *You* shall stay here! And Alena will go with me, won't you, Alena? We shall go to the café." He turned to Irena. "Will an hour, say, be sufficient? Or would two be more like it, Renka? What do you think?"

"Oh for God's sake, Ota!" said Irena.

"Alena?" said the gentleman.

Alena stood up.

"I'm going with you!" said Irena.

"And what about our guest?" he said, as though family honour were at stake. "He came to see *you*, after all, did he not?" And he turned to me.

"Yes," I said, "that is, I only thought Irena might happen to be home...."

"You see, and she was home," he said unctuously. "Unfortunately, not alone. We shall put that right immediately."

He took Alena under the arm and began dragging her out. Alena could control herself no longer and burst out laughing. "Ota!" Irena said angrily, "If you go...."

The gentleman flashed her a toothy smile and pulled Alena out of the room. The hall door snapped shut. Irena turned her back to me on the sofa, one leg folded under her.

We were silent for a while.

"Obviously I came at the wrong time," I said.

"You're incredibly observant!" Irena turned around and drank some tea. She scalded herself and angrily dashed the cup back on the saucer. "I feel like...."

"What?"

"Oh, nothing. Wasn't it enough that you...." She fell silent.

"That I what?"

"That you bugged me all through high school, and afterwards too. And now you have to make trouble in my marriage!"

"Me?" I said righteously. "Why, I haven't taken the slightest liberty since you got married!" I paused, and added maliciously, "Renka!"

She bowed her head, then threw it back, tossing her hair beautifully about her, and said, "Because you don't care for me anymore."

"How can you say that – Renka!"

"Because I know it's true. And drop the Renka, will you?"

"Do you still believe what your aunt told you?"

"Why shouldn't I?"

"It was noisy in the train. She misunderstood."

"My aunt happened to understand very well. 'I saw her mopping the floor, and suddenly, I stopped loving her.'"

"Loving shmoving," I said. "We're older now, and more experienced. But desire – that's something else...."

"That's all I need! He's jealous enough as it is."

"But there was never anything to be jealous of – we never did anything."

"He has just read this." She pulled a typescript out of the bookcase beside the sofa. It looked familiar. I opened it. Of course. *Seven Years I Served You....* My opus on Irena. I had finished it about two months before she mopped our kitchen floor, and had given it to her for her birthday. It may have contributed to the fact that she started to be so nice to me.

"But this proves we never got up to anything. Otherwise I'd have written about it, wouldn't I?"

"And what about the others?" Irena asked drily.

"Oh, I see."

Holy smokes! *Seven Years* was a chronicle of my unsuccessful attempts to seduce Irena; but it was also a list of Irena's undoubtedly successful adventures, insofar as I knew about them. And, in all modesty, I was well informed. Grau, Zdenek, Kocandrle, Dr. Capek, that marathon runner from Prague.... It also included information about where Irena had really stayed when her father thought she was away from home with the Kostelec track team or with her girlfriends on a trip. Each revelation was followed by a rather indigestible analysis of my state of mind. "Well," I remarked, and closed the book.

"How can you be so calm! My marriage is breaking up because of you! If you hadn't written it all down, Ota would never have found out!"

It seemed to me that the prospect of a broken marriage held no particular terrors for her. And she immediately confirmed my impression, because the next thing she said, quite amiably, was, "Would you like something to drink?"

So we had grown up at last, I thought. Tea – how many times had I had that at Irena's. But something to drink ... like this, the two of us alone....

"What have you got?"

"How should I know what's in the house?" She stood up and walked over to the sideboard. The alderman had a decanter of cut glass and, beside a bust of President Masaryk, a half-circle of tiny glasses. I remembered them from earlier times. Irena poured the drink into two glasses and took a sip from one of them. "Kummel brandy," she said, making a sour face. "Who cares. As a painkiller, brandy works just fine."

We drank. Irena drained back the whole glass. At first I only took a sip, but when I saw how she was drinking I downed mine as well. Irena filled the glasses again at once.

"Let him have what he wants!" she said.

"How do you mean?"

"When he comes back, let him find his wife defiled. By alcohol, of course."

"Is that all?"

She looked at me with her brown eyes. Memories flew out of them like sun-tanned angels. She had certainly grown up. It made me feel somehow pleasantly sad. "I'm not about to surrender the last bit of charm I have for you."

"One thing I don't understand," I said. "Why's he trying so desperately to get us together when he can read for himself what an also-ran I am?"

"Because you're a persistent also-ran," said Irena. "Read the last paragraph. You've probably forgotten it."

I opened the manuscript and read: "And what of the fruits of these seven years? Three kisses and two thousand five hundred and twenty-five unforgettable days. What wondrous gain! We are young! A year from now, I will count my profits again...."

Embarrassing. I looked at Irena. She was holding her empty glass against her cheek, watching me to see my reaction to those breathless hopes.

"Do you see?" she said. "He's been trying desperately to pry out of me what profit there was in that last year, the one that's not in the report."

"There wasn't any profit. I ended up in the red, as usual."

"The problem is, I don't have that in writing."

She filled my glass. Memories washed through me.

"That guy of yours must be a real prude," I said. "Retroactive jealousy is a new one on me."

"If it was only retroactive I wouldn't mind! He's jealous – what's the word for it? In advance."

"Your real mistake, Irena, was marrying him and not me."

"You never asked for my hand, darling. You always wanted everything but."

"I was a minor then. I had no financial security. I still don't. And you know I was always trained to be responsible."

"Trained, but untried," said Irena. "You'll never know what responsibility is. And you'll also never be secure."

"I will too," I said. "When I become what I will become."

"And what will you become?"

"Nothing. That's exactly what I want to be. Nothing."

"You're nothing already."

That made me sad.

"Drink up, poor little thing," said Irena, like Mr. Skocdopole. "You're mine and you always will be."

"That I am," I said, swallowing my drink. "For you I'll always be nothing."

"But you'll be *my* nothing." And Irena tossed her glass back. "That's something, isn't it?"

"It sure is!" I said enthusiastically. "If nothing is yours, then it's some nothing. Dear at any price."

"That's what you are! Dear at any price – you should cherish that!" said that fine, brown-eyed young lady.

"I do. Drink up!" I commanded. We both tossed back our glasses. I was in seventh heaven. Not only had the alcohol dulled the ache, it had also roused my former love from its apathetic adult slumber. But it was a different love. We were grown up. It was sad. And gay. I knew that her improbable husband was probably standing on the other side of the door with his ear to the keyhole. I said, "As far as your charm goes, Irena, you'll never lose that for me as long as you live."

"Then how come in spite of all that charm you stopped loving me?"

"I didn't, Irena!"

"But my aunt heard you say so."

"Your aunt heard wrong. I was wrong, too, when you were scrubbing the floor. I still love you. And I always will, forevernever."

"Damn," said Irena, "which glass do I pour it in, the left one or the right one?"

"Try the one in the middle."

Irena poured the liquor right into her lap. "Damn, damn," she said, wiping it with her hand. "I'm a little ... glazed over...." She hesitated, the decanter in one hand and a glass in the other, and then she drank directly from the decanter and handed it to me. I drank too.

"I love you, Irena," I said. "For me you'll always be charming."

"I know. And you know how I know? How I know it for absolute certain sure?"

"Because you believe me," I suggested.

"Blather!" she said. "It's because I never have and never will let you — fuck me."

She had certainly declared a great truth, but she would never have put it that way when we were kids. She used to be touchy about language. Now we were grown up, I suppose, though it hardly seemed like it. Those merry, drunken eyes looked at me. "You know, Danny boy? That's what Molly Dreslerova always used to call you, wasn't it? Danny boy ..." and she imitated Marie's caressing voice. The decanter was almost empty. I drank a little and, following the gentleman's code of ethics, gave the rest to Irena.

"In purely romantic affairs like ours, Danny," she said unsteadily, "one rash, thoughtless act and charm flies out the window. That's the way it always is, always is...." She put the decanter on the coffee table. She turned pale.

"Know what, Danny?"

"What?"

"I feel rotten."

"Drink up!"

"Some advice!" she said. "Anyway there's nothing left. We've already drunk it all up."

"It's all gone."

"All gone. Don't you feel rotten?"

"Not yet. But don't worry, Irena, I will."

Irena clutched at her stomach.

"I do now!" She grew even paler. "Jeepers creepers!" she moaned, as she used to in those distant, not-so-distant times. She fled from the room.

Someone unlocked the door in the hall. I stood up, stumbled and fell back into the chair. Into the room ran Alena. She stopped when she saw the state I was in, and put her hands on her hips.

"Now that's what I call style."

Someone thrust her aside.

A handsome, blond hunk of beef. He had no charm at all.

He reached out for me.

●

"Russia is not somewhere I'd want to live," the woman director is saying. "But Fidel is different from – "

"He has more whiskers!" Veronika has abandoned all self-control. The director assumes a long-suffering smile.

"Certainly. I admit that things are far from ideal in Cuba" – an unmistakable tone of contempt and aggression, those terrible twins, creeps into her voice – "but things are indisputably better than they were, and they are fighting for values that are *worth fighting for.*"

"Why aren't you willing to fight for the values you have here?" cries Veronika.

The director replies with a question: "Are there any values in this society worth fighting for?"

●

And away I flew. He grabbed me by the collar and heaved me down the stairs so abruptly that I almost missed the bannister. Irena had sure married a fine one. An uncivilized hick. Even if he was an assistant professor from Prague, he was still a hick.

I blundered out of Irena's old tenement house and bumped straight into Mr. Skocdopole who was running towards the woods with an overstuffed briefcase. In his haste, he was waving the stockinged stump of his arm in the air, and when we collided he poked me in the eye with it.

"Good-day, lad," he said when he saw who I was. "You don't happen to know what that scallywag of ours has been up to, do you?" I sobered up on the spot.

"What's happened?"

"They come to get him. Two of them." The legionnaire was panting heavily. "A good thing they don't know about his room off the hall. They rang at the kitchen door, pounded on it like they'd gone bonkers. So he must've heard them and jumped out the window."

"Where did he go?"

"If I only knew! They sat there for an hour, said they'd wait for him. But then that friend of his called round for him, the one that has the greengrocer's...."

"Vahar."

"That's the one. So they grabbed him and went away. One of them said there's more people mixed up in it, but he claims Prema's the ringleader. You sure you don't know about it?"

Lord God, why are you punishing me? For what?

"Mr. Skocdopole – did you go into Prema's room after they left?"

"Of course I did!" He looked around and conspiratorially opened the briefcase. Prema's parabellum was lying on a pile of egg-shaped grenades, and beside it was a garden trowel. "He had this stuff in his desk drawer. I'm going to bury it in the woods."

"Didn't you find any leaflets in his room?"

"Leaflets? No." He looked at me suspiciously. I swallowed drily.

Mr. Skocdopole set off again at a run. I looked after him, his stocking-covered stump describing ominous circles in the air. Then I turned and hurried home at a similar tempo.

There was a surprise waiting for me there.

"Prema is here!" my mother whispered in the doorway.

When I entered the room he stood up gravely from the ottoman and said, "G'day."

"The shit has hit!" I greeted him.

"Did they find anything?"

I told him what his father was up to. When he heard about the gun he said, "Shit! I should've taken it with me. I took the leaflets instead, like a fool. That's what happens when you panic."

"So where'd you put them?"

"I met Vahar. I passed them on to him, told him to go burn them."

"They've nicked Vahar."

"Shit!"

The crimson light of the sunset infused Prema's Mongol face.

"We've got to do something about the transmitter," he said. "If they find it they'll never believe my old man didn't know about it."

I felt myself losing heart. Outside the window the sunset bathed the slopes of Cerna Hora in red light; on its summit glowed a white point: the stone cross. Angrily I realized that I would do anything Prema asked me to. The sky above the mountain was clear blue, tinged with delicate crimson.

"We'll take it apart at night and hide it in the cottage," said Prema.

"They'll search it."

"So we'll bury it in the woods. But I'll have to let my dad know."

How? We racked our brains until we came up with a plan. I left Prema in the room and went to Hadrnice, the part of town where Benda lived. Half an hour later little Jirina Bendova ran to the Skocdopoles' with a note. We hoped that no one would pay any attention to a small girl. It worked.

But that evening Mother didn't want to let me out.

"They're arresting people all over town, Danny! Mrs. Vavruskova said they've arrested Mr. Krocan and Dr. Bohadlo! I'm not letting you go anywhere!"

"That won't help me," I said cynically. "The only thing that can help me is if we do what we plan to do."

"For the love of God, Danny! Are you mixed up in something?"

"No, of course not. We just have to arrange a few things, that's all."

"I'm not letting you go."

It was a difficult situation. Then Father entered the argument. "Leave him be, Mother. He's grown up; he knows what he's doing."

Prema stood to one side, embarrassed.

"He doesn't! That's just it, he doesn't know what he's doing!"

"I do know what I'm doing, Mother."

I knew I was doing something foolhardy. But what good was knowing that? *Ich hatte einen Kameraden* –

In the end, my mother gave in. Or perhaps she understood that staying home with Mother was no protection anymore in this great age of ours. We hurried through the back streets. It was, unfortunately, a light night, with a full moon. Our shadows, clearly outlined, ran before us. We approached the Skocdopoles' from the rear, from the riverside. The moon was reflected in the water like a silver five-crown piece. Or perhaps a round loaf of bread. We climbed over the fence and through the window that Mr. Skocdopole had left open according to the instructions reliably passed on by little Jirina. Mr. Skocdopole was waiting for us in the kitchen door and, behind him, his dutiful wife.

We went through the hall into Prema's room. Since receiving our message, Mr. Skocdopole had been active. The dismantled transmitter lay on the floor in three duck-cloth sacks. The duck-cloth was Prema's old tent, once procured for the purposes of waging guerrilla warfare. It was finally about to see action.

"It weighs a *ton*," whispered Mr. Skocdopole. "I'll take the lightest part. It's hard to carry with just one arm. Mother'll carry the tools."

Prema went over to the window and lifted the blackout blind that was still there from the war. The moon lit up his narrow face.

"It's bad," he said. "When's the moon supposed to go down?"

"Not till morning," said Mr. Skocdopole. "But never fear, lads. They started arresting people this afternoon. They're rounding up Sokol people – they're the main target, and then People's Party members and Czech Socialists. They haven't the guts to touch old legionnaires yet, it would make for a lot of bad blood. That's for later. We've got the advantage because their hands are full and people are keeping indoors. With just a touch of luck no one will nab us."

He wiped sweat off his brow with the sock, but he looked calm. His dutiful wife, on the other hand, was trembling. Oddly enough, my own fear disappeared, perhaps because I had something to do, perhaps because I didn't care anymore. Perhaps my long training with fear was beginning to show. I didn't feel as trapped as I had that other time four years before –

"I'm just wondering," said Prema, "how they could've figured out – "

"By all accounts, I'd say they put the screws to someone," said Mr. Skocdopole. "A couple in the teeth and anybody'd sing."

"It must have been Sagner," said Prema, thinking. "They got Vahar after me, Benda was still home in the afternoon – "

"Lads," Mr. Skocdopole interrupted, and there was anxiety in his voice. "I hope you haven't kept lists or anything like that. That wouldn't be too wise. Not at all – "

"Don't worry, Dad. Our group's been together since the war," said Prema.

"Does anyone know about me?" I asked.

"No," said Prema, looking at me with his infinitely honest eyes. "Only Vahar. But he's tough. They'd have been back for this here long ago if he'd talked."

He pointed to the sacks. That was logical.

"But I can't figure out why Vahar came back here."

"I don't know, lad," said Mr. Skocdopole.

Prema pulled the blind aside again. The moonlight fell on his nomadic face. Mr. Skocdopole spoke. "We better be going. We've got a hard night ahead of us. It'll be a piece of work, burying that."

"Let's go," said Prema.

"Wait!" With his good arm Mr. Skocdopole reached around to the rear of his trousers and pulled out a fat flask which could have been called a pocket flask only by stretching the imagination. "Let's drink to it!" He gripped the bottle to his chest with the stump of his arm and uncorked it. "Cheers!"

"Cheers."

He took a big swallow and then passed the bottle to me. I drank. It was slivovice. I drank deeply and then passed the bottle to Prema. The familiar warmth of that eternal friend and slow killer spread through me. I was not afraid. Surely the greatest danger threatening us was jail, not the gallows as it had been before? Or so I thought. Long live adventure!

Here I was again, helping people who were hatching plots against a regime that I, infected with university Marxism, as yet had nothing against. But what is university abstraction confronted with legend ... I saw Nadia in her lace-up boots walking across the meadow towards me – my heart is thumping – and hiding in a thicket at the edge of the meadow, his pockets bulging with hand-grenades and the parabellum, is Prema, a hat like Masaryk used to wear on his head ... and Nadia is striding in long strides across the green meadow, among the long shadows of the high pines ... what is university abstraction compared to that bright day when, his arm scorched by gasoline....

"All right, let's go," said Mr. Skocdopole. We threw the sacks across our backs. They were heavy, but fortified with slivovice, memories and our own past, I stepped out into the moonlit night after Prema and Mr. Skocdopole. Mrs. Skocdopolova followed with a shovel and grub-hoe.

Without incident we walked through the outskirts of Kostelec like a line of geese, three hunchbacked shadows, followed by a tiny woman carrying something that cast another shadow like a cross. A curtain of mist floated across the moon, and fog rolled out at us from the streets at the edge of town. "So far, so good, boys!" whispered Mr. Skocdopole, when out of the fog emerged Mr. Hornych, the local constable. He saw us and pretended he hadn't. Majestically he walked past Mr. Skocdopole bent under his load, and hissed out of the corner of his mouth, "They've arrested Brother Kaldoun!" And majestically he vanished into the fog. The round-up was on.

The last houses at the edge of town were swallowed up in the incandescent whiteness behind us; we took the bridge across the river and struggled up the steep slope towards the woods. At the edge of the trees we halted. Mr. Skocdopole wiped the sweat from his forehead again with the sock and pulled out his field flask.

"Jesus, boys, I don't have the staying power I used to!" He took a huge, gargling swallow. I recalled Samara, the battle of Pemza, that executed Czech proletarian, that distant battle ... and now his own son fleeing from his country. I realized with astonishment that Prema was actually leaving. Leaving the land for which Mr. Skocdopole had sacrificed his arm. This paradise on earth. But a paradise to the eye only. Almost every country is a place of beauty, and I realized that this one was beautiful because of certain people who were a part of it – were, are, will be, are no longer – and because of all the places associated with them, beautiful places. For Cerna Hora, for the sun flashing gold on the rocky peaks, for copper fish swimming in white coffee, for V for Victory, for Nadia's slender legs and her men's workboots. For nothing else. If such things do not exist, what is a country for? What good is a country where the people are compelled to – when fleeing from it is the only – Mr. Skocdopole handed me the flask. Imitating him, I took a deep, gargling draught. I passed the flask to Prema. He took a drink and gave it back to his father. We left the dutiful wife out of the round. She stood silently behind us, a shovel over one shoulder and a grub-hoe over the other, their hafts crossing behind her head.

We climbed up through the woods. The dew on the spiderwebs glistened in the moonlight. Owls hooted. We reached a clearing overgrown with blackberry vines, and Prema and I started to work. The one-armed legionnaire and his wife couldn't help us with this. As we dug, he unfolded his plan.

"You'll spend the night at my brother-in-law's in Karlin. You'll leave the day of President Benes' funeral. I reckon they'll pull all their cops in to Prague and the borders should be clear. Pepek ought to know best. He'll tell you what to do."

We dug till the sweat was pouring from us. An owl flew silently by overhead.

"Tonight you'll walk to Stare Mesto and catch the express. But don't board it from the platform, get on from the other side where the hedges and fields are. I'll buy you a ticket here. You'll find me in the train." The legionnaire's voice was quite different from what it had been that time over the sticky bottle. "I'll get off at Hradec."

"Okay," said Prema.

At last all three sacks were buried. We covered the site with blackberry vines – not a very good job of camouflaging – but we had no strength for more. When the work was done, the four of us stood over it as if we were paying our last respects to the dead.

"It's too bad," said Prema. "She could have done a lot."

Mr. Skocdopole took a drink.

"Yes, lad, it was a good idea." He sighed. "But you were dreamers. This time there's no getting out of it ourselves. We're done for. I know the bastards too well. Drink up!"

We stood there in the fog, silvered by a moon as big as a round loaf of bread with its white bottom turned towards the earth.

"Prema!" Mrs. Skocdopolova could stand it no longer. "I'll never see you again!"

"Sure you will, Mum," said Prema, embracing the tiny woman. She kissed him, her whole body sobbing. Reluctantly she let him go.

"So long for now, Dad," said Prema.

"Goodbye, lad," said Mr. Skocdopole, offering Prema his good hand. The scene seemed shrouded in unrealities, as though I were watching a film. Mr. Skocdopole wiped an eye with his sock. I shook hands with Prema.

"I'll see you soon. I'm going to Prague tomorrow too. I'll get your uncle's address."

"Good," said Prema.

He turned away. Mr. Skocdopole took another drink as Prema strode off decisively through the blackberries, and vanished in the fog.

I gathered up the shovel and the grub-hoe and carried them back to the Skocdopoles' house. Mrs. Skocdopolova sobbed all the way home.

When I walked home along Jirasek Street, the yellow rays of the rising sun were pushing through the pale fog. All of a sudden a clutch of people in blue boiler suits, carrying guns, emerged from the fog, led by a man in a long leather coat. Comrade Pytlik – formerly Herr Pytlik. Among them was a tall limping figure. It was my father. His hands were tied behind his back and he was as pale as Hamlet's ghost.

•

Veronika has done a thorough job of it. Percy's friends have dragged him off somewhere and Veronika refuses to let the bartender help her. She has five glasses in a row in front of her and she is pouring whisky into the first, gin into the second, then vodka, then sherry, and into the last glass, cognac. Mr. Svensson's guests continue their conversations but they keep glancing over at the pretty girl in the pale blue dress.

Her experiment is something to watch. Veronika takes five straws from a tall glass, puts one in each of her five glasses and then sticks all the straws in her mouth. She winks at the Svenssons' guests with heavily mascara'd eyes and becomes one of the heroines in *Daisies* – before metamorphosing into a scene from another much older film, one she has obviously never seen. She sucks up the contents of all five glasses at once as her eyes roll back in her head. Mr. Svensson's guests begin to neglect their conversations.

Percy arrives. It's about time. "Poor little Angela," Veronika is babbling, "has to wear glasses! A trip around the world wearing glasses! It's exactly the same here. I don't think I'd enjoy living under a dictator – "

"Nika! You're drunk!"

"But somebody like Che...."

I leave her in Percy's care and walk across the room. Irene Svensson's grey eyes watch me stonily from the conservatory. Mr. Svensson is talking business in a huddle of men:

"... is business. Their domestic affairs...."

"... Ellington at that price? Out of the question, I'm afraid."

Arches of time tensed to the snapping point. Is this still me? It is. So much can fit into a single life.

•

Next morning Nadia didn't come to work. They put an old man by the name of Varecka to work on her orphaned drill, and he immediately began to break all records for speed. Alarmed, I tried to think of a way to slow him down so that Ballon wouldn't notice. When Hetflajs came for the cross-brackets, there were three times as many as usual waiting for him.

"By God, you fellows are really cracking 'em through today!"

Old man Varecka smiled; perhaps he was flattered. As soon as Hetflajs had carried off the brackets I said, "For Christ's sake, that Hetflajs is breaking his back for the Nazis!"

"What's that, what's that?"

"I said the idiot's overdoing it."

"Right you are." Varecka pressed the drill into the duralumin as though it gave him a thrill.

"Grandad," I said. "I'm trying to tell you something. You're screwing up our quotas."

"What's that, what's that?"

"There's a girl normally does that work. If you keep on like that, they'll raise our quotas and she'll never make any money."

"But I always work this way." Once again, he pressed the drill into the duralumin with all his might and didn't let up until the bracket was finished, which took him about half a minute. A natural serf. I wondered if he might be susceptible to political argument.

"Look, old man," I said, "if everybody worked as hard as you, the Germans would have won the war long ago."

"But they haven't!" Varecka rejoined.

"No thanks to you!" I retorted angrily. Varecka raised the drill out of the cross-bracket, leaned over to me and bared his brown teeth, most of which were in a state of advanced decay. "You're right, boy! But don't take no account of me. I don't mean dick. The Russians – that's who's driving 'em out. London says they're already in Prussia. So they'll be here any day now!"

With that, he attacked the cross-bracket once more. I gave up. I went back to work at my standard pace, as Nadia had taught me, and wondered where my fear had gone. The creature was still lurking at the bottom of my stomach, but it was much smaller now. Yesterday, as I lay with Nadia, I had conquered the nightmare. I felt euphoric. I could survive everything, even if they nabbed me, even if they hanged me. No, not that. Fear has big eyes, I said. I reminded myself that I could always play the idiot, in line with our national tradition. With a contemptuous glance at the old man, I switched off my drill and went to the toilet.

Wrapped in clouds of home-grown tobacco smoke, Kos and Malina were debating the existence of Atlantis. In one compartment Ponykl was writhing on the toilet, shitting and fouling the air. Two tool-makers were arm-wrestling in another one. Franta Melichar was pissing into one of the urinals.

I hesitated. I had never actually spoken to him, but I knew who he was and Nadia had said he was kind-hearted. I thought he must be a bit of a chump as well and I felt proud of my illicit love. Although rumours of the necking sessions in the ferroflux room had reached Lucie's ears, as far as I could tell, Franta suspected nothing.

He buttoned up his fly and turned around, a robust young man with a ruddy, highland face.

"Cheers," I said. "What's with Nadia? How come she's not at work?"

"They told me she was to the doctor's this morning. I come to the factory straight from Rounov, so I don't know."

"Why I'm asking is they put some ass-breaker in her place and if she doesn't come back soon he's going to screw up our quotas."

Franta looked at me with blue eyes full of worry. I felt a sense of triumph when I thought of how I had slept with his bride-to-be yesterday. I felt elated.

"I'm worried about her," he said. "They said she was coughing blood."

"What?"

"Coughing blood. That's why she was to the doctor's this morning."

"Guard!" said someone near the door in a raised whisper. All those who were able immediately leaped to the urinals and undid their flies. I managed to grab a toilet seat, and I squatted on it with my trousers down around my knees. My elation evaporated.

Eisler strode in. He stood with his legs apart, looking around. "Smiricky!"

And fear gripped me again, as though yesterday had never been.

"Here."

"Herr Oberkontrolleur Uippelt wants to see you," said Eisler. "And make it a fast shit, boy! The Oberkontrolleur is expecting you at his home. He says you've already been there once and you know where he lives."

My heart began pounding. My position, with my trousers down, ceased to be a camouflage.

Sept. 15/76
Toronto

*My darling Lida!*
*Today my missive will be short, for I can hardly write. No sooner do I sit down and pick up my pen, than I am overwhelmed by such desire for your white body that I am compelled to go down and cool my ardour in the translucent waters of the pool. But I want at least to share with you a wonderful experience I had last week. Comrade Jiri Krupka — yes, the virtuoso — played with the Toronto Symphony Orchestra and delivered a breathtaking rendition of Dvorak's concerto for violoncello. As you know, Lida, I play the trombone quite passably, so you can imagine how deeply moved I was by that exquisite music, all the more because it was played by an artist from the same country that harbours you! An artist from the land of progress, and how I hope that one day — soon — we will be able to say the same of Canada too! As he played one could almost hear Comrade Krupka giving thanks for the remarkable care and attention your society gives to its artists.*

*I know you'll be eager to hear what Comrade Williams, our music critic, wrote in the CPC newsletter last week: "Comrade Krupka, with his masterful grasp of that piece by Antonin Dvorak, a progressive composer of the nineteenth century, is living proof of the towering superiority of socialist art over the hollow virtuosity of artists who live under capitalism. Here, in the aggressive, competitive struggle for artistic survival, they strive to outdo each other in formal brilliance, while the humanistic content of their art falls by the wayside. Such is not the case with Comrade Krupka. He penetrates straight to the heart of Dvorak's composition, and interprets its message simply and comprehensibly."*

*I couldn't agree more.*
*I think of you always, my darling. Soon you will be mine!*
*I kiss you everywhere.*

Yours,
Booker

Uippelt lived a short distance from the brewery in a turn-of-the-century villa which had formerly belonged to Dr. Strauss. It stood in a run-down English park, rising out of the snow and fog like an oddly asymmetrical outcropping of pink rock. The little roof over the veranda was held up by a pillar shaped like a naiad, whose breasts wore little mounds of snow. Someone had drawn a vertical line in chalk over her smooth, stylized genitalia.

The blood was clanging in my head, despite my attempts to persuade myself that if Uippelt had wanted to turn me over to the Gestapo he wouldn't have summoned me to his home. I rang the bell. For a long time nothing happened. I looked across the hillside, desolate and covered with snow, at the town with its white rooftops. A huge raven was striding around a sandstone cupid in the snow-covered flowerbed. It stopped, cocked a beady eye at me and crawked.

The door opened. In the doorway stood the wife of General von Kater of the Waffen SS who I suspected was, once more, fully occupied by war operations. "*Kommen Sie herein,*" she said.

I went in. The hallway hadn't changed since Dr. Strauss's time, with the same huge picture by Benes Knupfer of a greenish sea with a mermaid perched on a spur of rock, and the same wooden bear, its arms outstretched, to receive the patients' canes and umbrellas.

"*Otto ist in seinem Arbeitszimmer im ersten Stock,*" said the general's wife. She gestured with a white hand towards the staircase and then left me. I started up the stairs. The hall was gloomy, almost dark. I knocked on the carved wooden door. "*Herein!*" With my heart flipping about like a fish in a net, I entered Uippelt's study.

He was seated not behind the wide writing desk, which was remarkably bare, but in a black leather upholstered club-chair in a dark corner of the room. A golden grape design glinted on the violet wallpaper. His polished SA boots competed with the cold black gloss of the expensive leather that had once cradled the ample figure of Dr. Strauss. It was scarcely ten o'clock in the morning, yet an open bottle already stood on a low round table in front of him. The Oberkontrolleur held a thick cigar in his hand, probably another import from the SS General in Paris.

"*Kommen Sie näher,*" he said. Not a hint of English.

Stiff as a mummy in my blue boiler suit, I edged closer over the deep Persian rug and stopped in front of him. Uippelt straightened his pince-nez and looked me up and down.

"*So!*" he said. "*So sieht also ein Saboteur aus!*"

The blow was straight to the chin. I felt my legs sag. The little eyes behind the pince-nez fixed me with a cold Gestapo stare.

"*B-bitte?*"

"Very cleverly worked out," he went on in German. "A simple trick, and you might have been able to put the best fighter plane in the world out of action."

"I...." My voice caught. I coughed and felt a faintness coming on. "I don't know – what you're getting at – "

"I'm talking about the German Industrial Norms. The counter-sink is a half-centimetre too deep."

He poured himself a drink and with a gargling sound tossed it back in a way that reminded me, surprisingly, of that hero of battles long gone by, Mr. Skocdopole. What could I say? He knew everything.

"Well, all right," he said in English. "Sit down somewhere and have a drink."

I was staggered.

"That chair – over there!" Uippelt motioned towards an armchair that stood a little to one side, under a painting of Moses holding the tablets of law.

I grasped the chair, dragged it over to the stool and mechanically drank something. What it was I couldn't tell. Alcohol.

"It was a good idea, but you don't know the inspection regulations," said Uippelt. "Either you thought it up, or that skinny girl did. But I doubt she could have. It requires a technical imagination."

The piggish eyes were almost twinkling behind the pince-nez.

"Of course she must have known about it. I'll bet it impressed her no end."

My stomach heaved at the thought of how thoroughly he had seen through me. I half stood up from the chair. "But sir, she ... if you like – "

My legs gave out and I fell back. The glass skipped to the floor. I leaned over and picked it up, but as I tried to set it back on the table my fingers trembled so violently that I knocked it over twice more.

The Oberkontrolleur watched this bit of theatre with delight. "I believe you're scared shitless," he said.

The human organism is full of mysteries. His remark made me angry and I shot back, trying to affect a tone of scorn, "I did it because I was stupid. I never gave a thought to the consequences. And that girl knew nothing about it. The faulty counter-sinks are all my work."

The Oberkontrolleur poured out another drink for me, and one for himself.

"Okay, okay. Don't get excited," he said. "I went to Hradec on Saturday and tried it out. The welding held. How long it will hold and how much stress it will stand I can't say, but it definitely passed the bench test."

He sat back and shrouded himself in silence and smoke. As I stared at him my faith in the existence of an objective world abandoned me. He went to Hradec for *that*? Of course – he was an American. Still, I couldn't believe it.

The gloss of the leather, the etched, *art nouveau* windowpanes transported me and the SA American to another world, beyond this world.

But I was still me, and we were both sitting in Strauss's villa, where an SA man had not replaced a picture of Moses with a portrait of the Führer.

"Mr. Uippelt ... why...?"

He stood up, hitching up his breeches. He was obviously fond of beer. The SA uniform fit him like a glove.

"Let's just say you're not the only one who's ever done something foolish with no regard for the consequences." He walked over to the large panoramic window with the etched glass borders. Beyond him lay Kostelec, black beneath the white snow. The dark silhouette of the Oberkontrolleur stood out sharply against the background of that pleasant but cold town, like a raven. His back was to me.

"All right. If you want to do something for your country or whatever it is you do it for – I'll give you the chance. It won't be anything as spectacular as putting a Messerschmitt Bf 109 out of action, but who knows? All you have to do is go to Prague to pick up an instrument for the factory. At the same time I want you to go to a certain address and hand over an envelope."

He turned to face me, but he was still just a black silhouette against the white brilliance of Kostelec, framed by the frosted glass. I could not make out his features. "That will be all," he said.

I almost ran back to the factory. I could feel the pink villa looming out of the winter fog behind me like a scene from a romantic painting. My fear was made of bone china and it shattered around me. The prospect of future danger in Prague did not alarm me. I was free and easy again, and I began to look forward to Nadia's return.

Then I realized that the real reason I was happy was that the sabotage had not worked.

But I was a hero.

Some hero.

Even so I rejoiced.

●

Snow is falling, the white flakes glistening. The pale letters MASARYK THEA shine weakly into the street. The rest of the sign is covered by a banner with a crudely drawn clown leering down like the corpses of Edgar Allan Poe's mariners. Above the gaping head, a red sign glows: BINGO EVERY NITE! Beneath it, people are drifting into the theatre for the pre-Christmas revue.

They are all here. Dotty in a mini consisting of something that looks like peacock feathers, Zawynatch, her fiancé, in a beige herringbone suit; Gladys Hlavackova, a lady of charity tailor-made for caricaturists, casting her lifelines year after year to adventurers washed up upon these inhospitable shores. Margitka in white, pushing Bocar in his wheelchair; the pious lady in sealskin, her husband in a calf-skin jacket; Mr. Senka; the organizer with the armband; the husband without his publisher wife; the publisher with the wealthy Mr. Seymour; Milan in *le dernier cri;* the democratic young man in the checkered, off-the-rack suit; generations of emigrants layered upon one another, thrown fortuitously together by the unfortunate course of events in a distant land. Pauperized, re-established, industrious, hungry for money, sentimental, hungry for freedom, limited, intellectual, mean, merciful. All kinds. Indestructible. These are the traitorous emigrants against whom the Prague press rails. A lady, a most sweet lady, steps up to the microphone. Sweetly she announces that we are about to hear the sweet sound of our national songs, sung by our little girls, Jennifer Brabcakova, Pearl Cerychova, Rosemary Novakova and Heather Siskova. The girls mount the podium.

They are pretty, plump little things, wearing folk costumes from different regions: Kyjov, Domazlice and Chicago-Toronto. Their boots are fashionable and North American, for the local ladies cannot make boots in the folk tradition. One of them, the prettiest, has the latest thing from one of those glitzy Yonge Street shops, gold boots with bright green hearts and eight-inch soles. She is exactly that much taller than the others. Then they begin to sing in their fresh, youthful voices:

> *Tchece fota tchece-e*
> *cches feleski machajir*
> *Neechal simha necha-al,*
> *stcharo tchavny frachajir*

Their voices drift apart, and they sing as though the words are in a foreign language. One of them turns red. Then two more blush. They haven't rehearsed much. One falls silent, then a second, then both of them join in on the melody. The triple first part echoes throughout the large hall hung with garlands and bounds across the marzipan map of the Czechoslovak Republic, with Karpato-Ukraine still a part of it, and above it the lone second voice belonging to the pretty girl in unisex boots from Yonge Street wavers uncertainly.

> *Neechal simha, nee-chal,*
> *tchopse ty fis kchomu-u*

*ccho tchy retsi nocho-schi*
*tcho naschecho tchomu-u....*

The motley, traitorous émigré community listens in rapture to the message delivered in a strange mutation of Czech, filtered through oceans and across vowel shifts. Mr. Pohorsky, the saviour of the nation, blissfully taps his long-nailed index finger on the armrest of his chair....

Not long ago he called me and asked me to drop round and meet Bondy. I thought I was about to be offered a part in the Ethiopian radio caper, but there was more at stake than that. Mr. Pohorsky, always one step ahead of his creditors, frequently changes his place of residence. I first called at one of his old addresses in the Portuguese section of town, and it was only through a complicated series of telephone calls to several acquaintances that I discovered he was now lying low in the Polish district of Parkdale. When I found Pohorsky's digs at last, in a foul-smelling little rooming-house, Bondy was already drunk. I thought it was because I was almost an hour late but, as I later came to realize, no matter how early one arrives it is impossible to find Bondy in a state of sobriety. He is a tall, handsome Semite who, without stretching the imagination, might bring to mind those mass-produced plaster casts of the Saviour they used to sell in the official State shops for religious supplies in Prague. In fact, he may have been capable of performing Christ's first miracle, for water seemed to turn to wine in his stomach.

"Agree with everything he says," Mr. Pohorsky instructed me in the doorway. "He's in a great mood and we mustn't spoil it. Then we'll go ahead and do it the way we want. But he's got a good idea...."

The idea was an organization founded only an hour ago in Mr. Pohorsky's bachelor flat. Bondy had invented a name for it, the National Liberation Army of the Czechoslovak People — a title they both hoped would help gain them recognition in the UN, in which case Mr. Pohorsky would become their representative at the General Assembly. Bondy admitted glumly that if he took the job people might say there were Zionists behind it.

I expressed skepticism about getting into the UN at all, but Mr. Pohorsky wouldn't hear of it. "They let the bloody PLO in, why shouldn't they let us in too?"

"The PLO established their credibility by doing something — hijackings, bomb attacks and such like. Have you ever heard of anything like that going on back home?"

This was precisely where Bondy, who for tactical reasons could not take a seat in the UN, came in.

"The only reason why things like that don't go on back at home is because they've got no weapons," he said. "That's why we're setting up a national liberation army. Weapons are on the way."

"Are you going to incorporate?" My question was intended to be facetious, but meanwhile the wine had changed to whisky and the idea caught Bondy's fancy.

"The Czechoslovak National Liberation Army Incorporated?" he intoned, to see how it sounded.

"It's a great title," Mr. Pohorsky reassured him.

Imitating Bondy's meditative tone, I said, "The Czechoslovak National Liberation Army and Co.?"

"That sounds stupid," said Bondy.

"You're absolutely right," agreed Mr. Pohorsky rapidly. "Let's leave it the way it was: Incorporated."

"On the other hand," I said, "almost every company in Canada is 'Limited'. How about 'The Czechoslovak National Liberation Army Limited'?"

"That sounds even stupider!" said Bondy.

"You're quite right, Egon," agreed Mr. Pohorsky. "So we won't bother incorporating it at all."

"Of course it always makes a better impression in business circles if your company's incorporated," Bondy mused.

It proved a difficult problem to solve. We fell to thinking once more. I said, "Incorporation won't be as important in the UN as it would be on the stock market. What you actually accomplish will carry more weight."

Mr. Pohorsky looked uncertainly at Bondy.

"Right!" exclaimed Bondy. "We won't incorporate it at all, we'll just arm it to the teeth. Now what do you think of this?"

He reached under Pohorsky's bed – where, as guest of honour, he was sitting – and pulled out an executive attaché case made of soft leather. The monogram, EB, looked like real gold. He put the case on the bed and snapped it open. There, on the plush satin lining, lay a splendidly shiny automatic rifle. But it was rather small. It looked as though it had been tooled by a jeweller.

"Is that a toy?" I asked.

"Sure," said Bondy, as he lovingly removed the weapon from its silken resting-place. "For grown-up kids!" And he began the litany: "Shooting speed one hundred and twenty-five rounds per second. Muzzle velocity...." A lecture on weaponry followed. The automatic rifle was the latest top secret model being supplied to crack units of the U.S. Marines. Bondy did not explain how he came by it. But his California factory manufactured computerized valves that were said to be used on nuclear missiles, so he undoubtedly had contacts throughout the munitions industry.

Mr. Pohorsky made some impressively rapid calculations. "Incredible – a hundred and twenty-five rounds a second, that's seven thousand five hundred a minute! With that you could mow down a whole infantry division in three minutes. If you had ten of them, you would wipe out a division in eighteen seconds. If you had a hundred, it'd take less than two – "

"That is if you hit one man with every bullet," I said.

"Right!" Bondy hiccuped.

"And even if it does fire seven thousand five hundred rounds a minute," I went on, "where does all that ammunition go?"

We looked at the tiny weapon. Bondy turned the gun over in his hands, until the barrel was aiming straight at Mr. Pohorsky.

"It's a smart design," Mr. Pohorsky said nervously.

Bondy pressed a lever and pulled a magazine out of the stock. It was stuffed with bullets, like a sack of fish roe.

"This can't hold seven thousand rounds," he said. "I guess you have to load it a few times if you want to fire for a whole minute."

"So that's it," said Mr. Pohorsky. "Still, it wouldn't take more than a second. A one-second blast from that thing would be enough for any enemy."

Bondy slid the magazine back into the weapon and held it out ready to shoot, like Patty Hearst in the famous photograph. He described a half-circle with it. "*Ratatatat!*" he roared. Then he laid it on the bed and explained that he intended to arm only a single company with it at first, but it would give them the fire-power of a whole battalion. From his attaché case he pulled out a handful of dog-eared brochures published by different firms in the U.S. Most of them were about guerrilla warfare and one had even been written by a general of Fidel's, who also held the copyright on it. Bondy told me that along with the automatic rifles we had just seen, he would have a company of napalm flame-throwers, bazookas and non-recoil cannon. He already had a bazooka in his garden. He would take over the military leadership personally, and land the whole company by parachute in the Brdske woods near Prague.

Mr. Pohorsky smiled ingratiatingly. "Can't you just see it? We'll be in Prague inside an hour. With the element of surprise, Prague is ours!"

I asked what they would do when the surprise wore off. This led to a discussion. Mr. Pohorsky reckoned that, with the possible exception of its political officers, the whole Czechoslovak army would support them and the civilian population would of course back them up to a man. Simultaneously he would use the situation as a bargaining card in New York to gain at least observer's status in the United Nations for his Liberation Army. I reminded them that they could hardly expect the Soviet occupation army to go over to Bondy's side as well. They had thought of that too. The company would provoke a conflict between the Czechoslovak and the Soviet armies and that would be Pohorsky's cue to request UN intervention. Either that, or the Russians, fearing an atomic conflict with the U.S., would withdraw from Czechoslovakia entirely.

They had it well worked out. The company was to parachute out of special stratospheric aircraft that fly above the range of anti-aircraft missiles. I objected that there was nothing to prevent the Soviet occupation army from blasting the company to bits as they floated down from the stratosphere. No, they replied, the company would sky-dive, not opening their parachutes until they were two hundred metres above the ground.

I was charmed by this heavenly vision, like something out of an etching by William Blake. Bondy took out a map of Prague and its environs with several tactical variations of the attack drawn on it. He had even arranged for food supplies to be brought in, and should the company have no opportunity to make contact with the Czech troops, there was a whole squadron of helicopter gunships in West Germany ready to ensure an orderly and safe retreat. The men chosen for the rearguard action were to be provided with cyanide capsules.

"Do you think you'll find enough volunteers in exile?" I said.

Mr. Pohorsky laughed. "At a sober estimate, there's about twenty thousand men in exile of military age, counting the post-1968 wave alone." As always, he knew his figures. The post-February, pre-Nazi and older exiles would form the first, second and third line of reserves. He estimated that if only one in every three hundred young men of Czech origin were to volunteer, they would easily have men enough for ten companies. "And let's say we do fall short, we can still take up the slack with mercenaries, and recruitment in the field. The people back home are more up for it because they have to struggle against communism every day. The recruits will be taken to a training camp in the U.S.A...."

The meeting ended when Bondy was finally overcome by the whisky and fell asleep. We no longer had to agree with everything he said, and so Pohorsky got drunk too and began to call me by my first name. I tried to be moderate but, even so, by the time I left for home I had offered to join the National Liberation Army as a volunteer, and since I had already served in the army as sergeant in a tank division, Mr. Pohorsky immediately granted me a commission as a first lieutenant and put me in charge of a platoon of amphibious tanks – which were likewise to come plummeting out of the stratosphere to rescue a beleaguered nation.

The motley, traitorous émigré community listen in rapture to the message filtered through oceans and across vowel shifts. The saviour of the nation blissfully taps his long-nailed finger in time to the rhythm. The girls, now in a pure, four-voice unison, encouraged by the response in the hall, their voices fresh and high, sing in second-generation Mississauga Czech:

> Tcho naschecho tchomu-u
> pchot nasche okcheenkcho
> ccho som sa napshakchal,
> sifa cholupjeenkcho....

●

Nadia didn't come to work on Tuesday either, and old man Varecka succumbed so completely to his neurotic compulsion to work that the cross-brackets began to pile up behind Hetflajs and Svestka. As I had feared, Ballon noticed. He stood watching for five minutes with his hands behind his back and then strode away.

"You're pushing it too hard, old man!" I whispered angrily. "There's going to be trouble."

"Trouble? With these quotas I'll be making a hundred crowns more than when I worked on the die stamper."

"We'll see about that on Saturday!" I replied. I was incensed.

My prediction was right. Ballon returned with a stop-watch and stood over Varecka for five minutes, while the old man just about popped his eyes trying to dazzle him with an even greater output. At last Ballon pressed the stop-button energetically and roared, "Wie ist das möglich? This fellow here is new and he's working five times faster than you and that girl who's off somewhere pretending to be sick."

"We're not very good with our hands," I yelled back in German. "And he's exceptionally skilful."

Old man Varecka didn't understand German; he heard only shouting, and he cringed.

"Na! Werma sehen!" roared Ballon and stomped off again.

"Wh-what's going on?" said the old fellow timidly.

"I told you there'd be trouble. You insisted on working flat out, and now he thinks you're working too slowly."

"But I wasn't even half trying!"

It was only now that he showed what he could really do. But he did himself a disservice. Ballon came back with the time-and-motion man and they checked everything again, whereupon Ballon announced that I should report to the outdoor detail for work because two of us were no longer necessary on the production line. And at the end of the week old man Varecka was only given six and a half crowns extra, since they had raised his quota; as a bonus, he got a ration-ticket for a quarter of a litre of some unspecified alcohol.

But before I could report for outdoor detail, Uippelt called me in to run his special errand. In Prague I handed the letter over at an address that I had had to memorize. I had to ask, "*Wohnt hier Herr Seifert?*" and the gentleman who opened the door replied calmly, "*Jawohl*." That much I did for my country. I spent the afternoon in the Café Lloyd in the faint hope that, sometime before six, Karel Vlach's big band would show up to play. In vain. I took the seven o'clock train back to Kostelec. At the station I ran into Machane. He had been conscripted to work in a laboratory in Prague but because he was afraid of air raids there he spent ten hours on the train each day travelling to Kostelec and back. He got up at three-thirty in the morning and got to bed at midnight each night. But he had learned to sleep in the train, which was what he did most of the way back, so I had a lot of time to think.

Next morning Nadia still hadn't come to work. I went looking for Samec, the foreman of the outdoor detail, to ask for an assignment. But neither he nor anyone else on outdoor detail was anywhere to be seen. There was only an inconspicuous, wizened little man rolling a huge barrel across the yard.

"You don't happen to know where Samec the foreman is, do you?"

"In the can," said the little man, without stopping.

So that was where I went, hoping also to find Franta there.

In the toilet, the usual company was smoking the usual home-grown tobacco, and Kos and Malina were holding a seminar on the subject of Siamese twins. Kos claimed that they only had one stomach between them, so if they liked different food they could never agree on what to eat. Malina said he reckoned it was all just an old wives' tale.

"Like shit it's an old wives' tale! I heard that one of 'em can hold his booze and the other gets pissed after a single glass."

"What happens if the one who can hold it really gets plastered?" I asked. "Can he give the other alcohol poisoning?"

"Of course he can," said Kos. "But then they'll both croak because the live one's joined to a corpse and he'll get poisoned by the corpse's poison and die."

"What a pile of fucking crap, you dodos," said Malina.

"They've got problems right across the board," I said. "I read about one pair, they were girls, and one of them got married."

"And what about the one that didn't?" asked one of the listeners.

"I'll bet they covered her with a sheet," said Kos.

"Bullshit!" said a pimply lad from the welding stamp. "He scuppered 'em both! He could only marry one because otherwise it'd be bigamy, but he scuppered 'em both."

"No, he didn't," I said. "The unmarried one died a virgin. The autopsy proved it."

"Tell me another one, you camel!" said Malina in a burst of temper. "What woman would fucking stand for it! Lying beside them two having it off every night and not wanting to join in? She'd have to be a fucking saint!"

"That's right. It's all stories," said one of the guys from the paint shop, Habr.

Absorbed in a game that seemed like poetry to me, I declared, "What is so odd about that? It was like with the stomach. The unmarried one had exactly the same sensations as the married one, but she didn't have any of the work."

"You fucking rhinos!" said Malina.

"Did the married one have any kids?" Kos enquired.

"Two, I think."

"What about labour pains? Did they both of them feel it?"

"Yes."

"Next, you pony, you'll try and tell me that the fucking virgin had one of them!" said Malina hotly. "A real live fucking immaculate conception!"

I wanted to expand on this refinement but Kos got in ahead of me. "She'd have to be the bloody Virgin Mary, you cow!"

Malina frowned at Kos and spat generously on the floor. "You bunch of fucking heifers."

Someone said that the Virgin Mary maintained her virginity only until she gave birth; a paint-spattered theologian claimed that she remained a virgin even after that. Kos said that the Virgin Mary was no virgin at all, that she'd only been able to convince St. Joseph she was because he was a kindly old boob, and that Jesus' real father was St. John the Baptist, who snuck in to see Mary disguised as an angel. Habr declared that he wasn't going to listen to blasphemous talk, but instead of resolving the problem by walking out he punched Kos on the nose, and they began to fight. Through the smoke I finally caught sight of the foreman, Samec, and asked him what I should do.

Samec considered my question and said thoughtfully, "First take a shit, since you're already here. There's no particular rush. Then go back to the yard and see Nejezchleba. He's the little old wrinkled man rolling a barrel around. Tell him I sent you and he's supposed to show you what to do."

I pushed my way through curtains of smoke to the urinals. Franta was standing there looking dejected. I told him that Ballon had thrown Nadia and me off the drills and that when she got back —

"She's not coming back. She's got TB."

It took a while for me to realize what that meant. At first I was almost glad, thinking, at least Nadia won't have to work in the factory till the end of the war. Then all at once it hit me. And I began to be afraid for Nadia.

•

In the corner, over a glass, a sullen Frank.

"They got Maslo. Remember he told us about that wild chase he had along the Queen Elizabeth Way? Well, he's in hospital."

"Who got him?"

"Probably a hired killer. He called Pohorsky."

"Who, the hired killer?"

"No, Maslo. He just gurgled something into the telephone. When Pohorsky got to him he was lying in a pool of blood."

"Why didn't he call for an ambulance first?"

"Can't trust them. The Commies are everywhere."

Frank looks around, as though they are here too. But at most there are only have-beens here. And one Canadian — Percy. Frank relaxes.

"Maslo says he heard a shot and realized that someone was shooting his lock off from the outside. He ran to the door but when he got there the fellow was already inside. He had a pistol with a silencer. Maslo says he heard something like a fart and then he passed out. When he came to, he had a bullet in his shoulder. A shade more to the left, and he would have got it right in the heart."

"Did he get a look at the killer's face?"

"No, the guy was wearing a stocking mask. It must have been someone from the embassy, or else a hired killer. But if it was a hired killer he wouldn't have needed a mask. They always get hired a long way from the scene of the crime...."

So the dangerous scout leader almost got rubbed out.

Dotty makes her entrance. Today she has outdone all expectations. What the T-shirt with the painted breasts merely hinted at is now transparently obvious. She is decked out in a dress of gilded mist — underneath it, from the waist down, a petticoat; but above the waist she is clearly braless. "That's why I'm glad I'm a citizen of Canada," she is effusing. "I'm sorry to say it, but Czechoslovakia is a racist country." Beside her, Mr. Zawynatch, in a glowing herring-bone suit and a vest with stylized hearts on it, affects nonchalance. He is bursting with pride at Dotty's braless bosom. "That's also why I appreciate Brian here," she continues, "because with Brian it's all copacetic."

With great effort we pry our eyes away from the gilded mist and look at Mr. Zawynatch. He flashes a gold and white smile. "Some of my best friends are blacks."

"You see?" says Dotty admiringly. "I was engaged once and my fiancé was a real nice guy so I said to myself why not come clean with him? The beans might get spilled one day anyway. So I told him I was a spook. You know, that my dad was black. The guy says he doesn't care because it doesn't show on me anyway. See what I mean? Just like that Jewish joke where they're going to lynch all the Jews and all the barbers, and someone says, 'Of all the nonsense. Why barbers?' "

"Perhaps it was a slip of the tongue," I say.

"That was how I was willing to take it too. But of course he blabbed about it at home, and his family put a bird in his brain."

"You mean a bug in his ear," Mr. Zawynatch corrects her gently.

"Or a bug in his ear. Trying to get him to think that we should break up! They said we could have a black baby! According to genetics they say it's possible."

"If he wasn't a racist then it shouldn't have bothered him," I say.

"He claimed" – Dotty's voice rises breathlessly, her anger roused – "his friends wouldn't believe it was his baby! They would think I got myself knocked up by one of those black bastards that hang around the nightclubs I used to hang around!"

The breasts with their attractive little bull's-eyes bob up and down under the gilded mist. We can't take our eyes off them.

"Well" – I breathe out after a while – "strictly speaking that's not racism. Strictly speaking your fiancé was afraid people would think he was a cuckold."

Dotty is taken aback. "Well, anyway, that's a prejudice too. Afraid his stupid friends would think there was somebody standing in for him, with him allegedly in love with me!"

●

As I stood in the corner by the welding section watching for Nejezchleba, I thought of the bright little roses in Nadia's cheeks, how her eyes glistened and burned, how she sat in the kitchen and looked into the cup, gobbled down the tarts....

"*Hasta nix zu tun?*" Eisler's voice croaked behind me. I looked around for something to do. A metal barrel stood by the wall of the welding section. I bent over and started rolling it away. Eisler watched me for a few moments, then turned and strode with an air of self-importance to the gatekeeper's lodge.

From around the corner appeared the inconspicuous, wizened little man, also rolling a barrel and bearing straight down on me. As soon as he saw me, he stopped and cried out, "Where are you going with that, young fellow?"

I stopped too. "Are you Nejezchleba?"

"That's me. Where are you going with that barrel? That's my barrel."

"Samec sent me. You're supposed to teach me."

"Teach you what? What am I supposed to teach you?"

"I don't know. Your work, I guess."

"My work?"

"As far as I know."

"Samec told you that? That I'm supposed to teach you my work?"

This Nejezchleba was beginning to annoy me. I saw that Eisler had changed direction and was now heading for the door of the can. The factory was humming in the winter afternoon, manufacturing war technology for a doomed army. And that grinning spectre with a scythe on Black Mountain....

"That's what I'm saying, isn't it?"

"Then get yourself a barrel."

"Can't you see? I've got one already."

"Look, young fellow, you put that right back where you found it! That's one of my barrels!"

So I bent down and rolled the barrel back. Nejezchleba rolled his right behind me. When we reached the welding section I asked, "What am I supposed to do then?"

"I already told you. Find your own barrel. There's usually a few near the crane. And don't go rolling it in here neither, nor around the canteen, nor around the main warehouse. Find your own place!"

Nejezchleba stood the wooden barrel behind the metal one and got ready to roll the metal one away.

"Where are you going?"

"This one goes to the main warehouse. I've got another one there, a green one, and I roll that to the canteen. And the striped one at the canteen goes to the paint shop, and from the paint shop...."

And thus, at last, he explained the methodology of the outdoor detail to me. You found some barrels – at least three, but preferably more, ideally each one conspicuously different: large, small, metal, wooden, brightly coloured, colourless. If one were to constantly roll the same barrel around all the time, the *Werkschutz* might notice. Nejezchleba was a real expert in his peculiar field. He was doing it for the third year in a row, and it looked as though I too was guaranteed fascinating work for the duration of the war.

Fate decided otherwise.

●

•

The little girls offer us another bouquet of vowel-shifts that pass for singing, Mrs. Ruzena Smrk-Pine plays the Slovanic Dance, Priscilla Kouba – a freckled Scottish lass who takes after her mother, and looks a lot like Wendy McFarlane – dances the highland fling in a kilt, her legs pumping up and down as though strings are attached to her knees, but as stiff as an icicle from the waist up. Brother Senka delivers a speech on T.G. Masaryk which, unlike other speeches about other great men I have heard in Prague, does not quote the man at all but still manages to be empty. Then a sweet, beautifully coiffured (Beauty Salon Kroupa) lady steps up to the microphone and announces that the moment we have all been impatiently waiting for is here at last. Thanks to the miracle of technology – and with the kind assistance of Brother Pilnacek, owner of the Praguesonic TV and Stereo Shop – we are about to hear the beloved and unforgettable voice of our first president, liberator of the nation, Thomas G. Masaryk. Everyone falls silent. "Brother Pilnacek, if you please ..." and the pretty arm describes a pretty arc....

Silence. A child at the back cries out and is shushed. Brother Pilnacek presses a button and from the oversized, deluxe stereo speakers comes the voice of – Mickey Mouse.

It is a cynical joke played by Chance or the Lord God who, it would seem, works in favour of the Bolsheviks. The lady maintains professional calm, an apologetic smile flashes across her sweet face. Brother Pilnacek struggles with the lever, but a malicious deity is holding fast to the other end. The child, entranced by Mickey Mouse, stops its crying. I try to decipher the message that is screeching through the hall. It is more unfathomable than the words on Dotty's charm bracelet.

The mouse babbles on for an embarrassingly long time. God knows what the flageolet voice is saying. Brother Pilnacek thrusts a screwdriver into the back of the machine and pries at something.

A click. At last. The hall breathes a sigh of relief. The beloved voice will now speak, that we may know. The mouse is silenced, and in its place – King Kong. The child at the back, terrified, starts crying again. Brother Pilnacek drops his screwdriver. A sigh arising from the traitorous band of émigrés is accompanied by another sweet smile from the lady. King Kong's voice thunders in stereo out of the speakers – his message hopelessly encoded in frequencies too deep for the human ear.

All seems lost. But wait! Brother Pilnacek, who fought at Tobruk, has not given up yet. The screwdriver is brought into action again, poking and prying. Brother Pilnacek perspires, and – at last – the lever is in the right position! That elderly, slightly whinnying voice pronounces the final words of the message: "... our democracy must be ceaseless reform, ceaseless revolution. But – a revolution of hearts and heads!"

And the voice from the depths of a totally dead time dies away; its absolute demands were smashed by another revolution, which dealt impressively with many a heart, and more than one head. A voice from the pleasant fairyland where principles such as Judge Others By Yourself once held sway. The lady maintains an angelic expression. Brother Pilnacek removes the tape from the machine like an archbishop raising the host. A pious silence follows, a sepulchral silence into which, like a jack-in-the-box, Brother Kocman leaps, his Sokol pin from the Ninth All-Sokol Festival gleaming in his lapel, and in a high tenor voice full of feeling and immense nostalgia he begins to sing the Czech national anthem: "Where is my home...." Unfortunately Brother Kocman's voice is too high, and to compound the misfortune he has started off in the highest register. Everyone stands up. Some make an attempt to stay in the same octave as Brother Kocman, but they drop back from those unattainable heights, their voices trailing off. Others begin an octave lower – and drown in the depths, until all that remains is that high tenor voice singing in unison with a soprano belonging to Sister Zdislava Warwick, an ancient voice teacher at the Royal Conservatory.

Yet all at once I am happy. Have I ever experienced this before, this sensation of being an integral part of a small entity? I feel the total absence of threatening respectability, the close humanity of our ridiculous nostalgia, our searching, erring desires, our equality. Here there is not the bullying pomp of state-financed, organized enthusiasm, only a little dialectic cabaret produced from our own resources. In the euphoria of the moment I too try to join in song, and end, like the others, disastrously.

•

"There's this company in West Germany," Dotty is saying, "and they make special compartments in cars, see? Custom-made to fit the size and shape of your body, fits like your skin, the customs officers'll never find it. Naturally it's uncomfortable and you have to strip naked to squeeze into it, so you come into the free world like a new-born babe, but of course they have new clothes waiting for you across the border. It costs you fifty thousand marks, but that includes a trip by their agent to Czechoslovakia, where they take your measurements, and then a second trip with the special car to get you out. Well, it's a lot of money but it's worth it."

"Money is not an object," says Mr. McEachen, his tailored New York suit and rings competing in decorative impact with Mr. Zawynatch's. His original name was Macecha but no one could pronounce it properly. "That's not what worries me."

"I'll bet you think," says Dotty, "that your mum would be ashamed.

Don't worry. They are very discreet. The agent looks the other way when the customer strips."

"That's not the problem," says Mr. McEachen apprehensively. "As a young woman, my mother used to model for artists, painters. That picture I have over the fireplace, *Freedom Guiding the Legionnaires*, by Master Slabinoha, that's her – Freedom. I mean from here up" – he motions from his own waist upwards. All of us, involuntarily, squint into Dotty's golden mist, including the gentleman who wants to smuggle his mother out – "it's all visible. My mother, if you know what I mean, has nothing to be ashamed of."

"So what is it, then?" asks Dotty. "If you *want* them to take a peek, they will. You're the customer."

"The problem is she's too fat now," says Mr. McEachen gloomily. "Two hundred and eighty pounds. It would be hard to conceal a compartment big enough for her in a passenger car. I seriously doubt it could be done."

No one reassures him. It is clearly a problem of considerable technical complexity.

"It could be done," says Mr. Zawynatch finally, "if they took one of those big station-wagons...."

"That would make it more expensive," says Dotty. "They normally operate only with standard-size cars."

"Money is no object," repeats Mr. McEachen. "But a station wagon is – what's the word – hollow behind. Empty. Where would they put the compartment?"

Once again we are silent. None of us has a technical mind.

"Well, that's their problem," decides Mr. Zawynatch at last. "If money is no problem, then nothing should be a problem."

Mr. Zawynatch's faith in the power of money is not blind. Dotty is a bargain no matter what it may have cost him to win her. Besides, I am beginning to suspect that Dotty is taking love seriously.

"There could be another problem," says Brother Pelikan, a post-1948 emigrant who, before the so-called Victory of the People, was student president of the People's Party of Charles University in Prague, where he studied philosophy. "And if the company hasn't taken it into account in their design you should ask for a discount."

Brother Pelikan is only in Toronto on a visit. Otherwise he lives in New York, where he has given up philosophy and now owns a chain of nightclubs.

"Speaking from personal experience," he says, "I can tell you, Mr. McEachen, that your good mother could get herself into very embarrassing difficulties with that type of transport."

"But Mr. Pelikan," says Dotty. "When you defected the company wasn't even in business yet."

"I know," nods Pelikan. "But we had similar ways of getting out. I used one of them and I can tell you I almost ended up dying the same death as Tycho Brahe."

He has caught our interest, and begins his tale. At that time the old Prague-Munich express was still running. It was in those first few turbulent days after the February 1948 Victory of the People, and friends hid Pelikan in the restaurant car where they had prudently prepared a small space in the roof of the wagon, just big enough for one person. The cook was an accomplice. Pelikan squeezed himself into the hollow space like a bog-man and the cook screwed him in so tightly he couldn't budge. Because he was thinking of a thousand other things before his departure, he forgot to go to the toilet. No sooner had they screwed him in place than Murphy's Law came into operation.

"There was a tiny hole right next to my eye where they forgot to put a screw," says Mr. Pelikan, entering into the spirit of that long-ago escape. "And as if the devil himself had ordained it, who should sit down at the table directly below me but Hubert Stein with some fancy lady. You probably don't know who Hubert Stein was...." Dotty shakes her head. "A colleague of mine, at least until the *putsch*. President of the University Communist Party organization. And he probably had other less visible functions as well," adds Mr. Pelikan, "since that was the day after Gottwald gave his speech announcing the Victory of the People on the Old Town Square and here was Stein already on his way to Munich. It stands to reason he wasn't emigrating. Anyway, a bit of hard luck. I said to myself: Pelikan, dying of a burst bladder is not an undignified way to go. If Tycho Brahe could do it, so can you. But – have you got the will-power Tycho had? Can you hold out?"

Pelikan held out until they reached the border. There the train stopped for an hour and a half while a thorough search was carried out. All that time, Stein and his fancy lady were drinking champagne right below him. Pelikan was beginning to think he was about to meet Tycho Brahe's fate. He gritted his teeth, but as the train jerked into motion, the pressure in his bladder proved more powerful than his will, and its contents began to flow forth, forming a puddle underneath him. When he looked down through the screw-hole he saw that the liquid was dripping, drop by drop, straight into Stein's Château Melnik.

"I prayed," remembers Mr. Pelikan. "Stein could still have pulled the emergency brake. But his fancy lady saved me. 'Hube,' she said, 'Hube, is it raining out?' So they both looked out of the window, and there's not a cloud in the sky. 'It's coming through the ceiling,' said the lady. Hube stuck his hand out and let a drop fall on his palm and then – you'll have to excuse me, it's rather disgusting – and then he licked it. He looked up and said, 'Funny rain. Tastes like sea-water.' And both of them looked at the ceiling, straight into my eye through the screw-hole. They couldn't see me but I could see them. And someone outside shouted, *'Furth im Wald.'* We were in Germany. I was saved."

The cook came running up and unscrewed Pelikan, but he was so stiff from lying in one position all that time that he couldn't hold on; he came crashing down onto the table between Stein and his fancy lady from the Ministry of the Interior, all wet and wilted. Stein knew that Pelikan was beyond the reach of his jurisdiction, so he could only comment acidly, "Well, well, well, if it isn't our democratic hero! So scared he's pissed himself!"

"What did you say?" cries Dotty. "It wasn't because you were scared at all!"

"What did I say?" Pelikan grows serious and shakes his head. "If I'd known then what would happen later, I wouldn't have said what I did. I said, 'Look, Stein, I pissed myself on my way out of there. But one day you're going to be so scared you'll shit yourself in fear and you'll have nowhere to run to.' Yes" – he nods his head sadly – "barely four years later they hanged him."

This denouement plunges McEachen into gloom once more. He seriously doubts whether he can expose his elderly mother to such martyrdom. Her nerves are not what they used to be. She has requested permission to visit him three times and been turned down. Why? They almost always allow senior citizens to visit the West, says Dotty, surprised. "I don't know," says McEachen unhappily. "They said it was because I was politically active. As long as I stay politically active, they won't let her go. All I can do is try and smuggle her out."

"There's one other way that's a lot safer," says Dotty. "But it takes longer – up to a year."

"What one is that?"

"Have the old lady marry a foreigner."

McEachen wilts. "She's nearly eighty. Who would have her?"

"There are people around who will do it," says Dotty. "It costs money, though."

"Money is no object. Could you find someone?"

"Sure." Dotty glows with willingness. She explains that the whole business is somewhat complicated. The hired fiancé first has to visit Prague as a tourist and there he has to accidentally, as it were, meet the bride. Then he returns home, writes letters.... Dotty unfolds the minutiae of her complex and time-consuming plan.

"Sexy? Passionate?" Mr. McEachen sounds doubtful. "The old lady is nearly eighty and weighs two hundred and eighty pounds...."

"No problem," says Dotty. "We'll choose someone fitting in age and weight. Czech brides are a real catch," she says.

She has no idea how right she is.

•

I missed Nadia. Rolling barrels may have been far better work than drilling counter-sinks – I had physical exercise, and could stay in the toilets as long as I wanted, if I managed to avoid Eisler's inspections – but each time I returned to one of my two barrels, which is all I had managed to find so far, and saw old man Varecka slaving away because now it was all he could do to fill the quotas that had been raised through his own stupidity, I became bitterly aware of that skinny girl's absence and wondered how she was.

By the end of the week I was obsessed by thoughts of Nadia. On Sunday morning it occurred to me that although the tuberculosis had stopped her from working she might still come to church, but she didn't. So she must be seriously ill. The church was empty without her. It was somewhat enlivened by the presence of Marie, except that she was there with Kocandrle. They were standing side by side in the choir, looking painfully moral as they sang the hymns and recited the credo with daunting seriousness.

But Nadia wasn't there. I could imagine the cottage with the logs stacked up under the low eaves, the tiny window set in the log walls, the mottled cat, and I couldn't stand it any longer. After lunch I left the house and started up Cerna Hora, not knowing exactly what I was going to do there, or rather knowing very well that I would do nothing except gaze at the cottage which Nadia's presence made somehow special, different from all the other houses in the village. No more than that – because her fiancé would almost certainly be there and would probably find my concern for Nadia's health exaggerated. And Nadia would probably blush.

The fiancé was there. It was a sunny day, white all around, and when I reached the stone cross I saw Franta splitting firewood on the porch, in a checkered shirt with his sleeves rolled up. A little way off from the village, on the hillside below the Jirasek Chalet, people from the town were skiing and sleighing. I didn't want Franta to see me. I was in my skiing clothes, so I moved closer to the black figures on the snow-covered ski-run above which the wood-trimmed stone restaurant towered. I stopped behind a scrub-pine bush and gazed at the cottage. I was almost blinded by the reflection of the sun in its tiny windowpanes, so I moved to one side. In the window the cat stared out at the white expanse of snow. Franta left the cottage with a water bucket, crossed the path to a neighbouring building, set the bucket under a pump wrapped in pine boughs, and began to pump. The screeching of the handle echoed across the snow and mingled with the hallooing of the skiers. Nadia was somewhere on the other side of that window, perhaps in bed. What did they do together, I wondered. What did Nadia talk to Franta about? I couldn't begin to imagine. All at once I found that I could scarcely even imagine Nadia – only her masculine mountain boots, her worn and formless sweater and threadbare skirt, there for ever in the cottage with her man who, wearing only a shirt although it was freezing, was carrying a bucket full of water back to the cottage as though it contained nothing but air. But why not? Someone had to stay in these villages. It had never for a moment crossed my mind that I would remain in Kostelec. Kostelec was just a way-station. I was born there, and because I was not yet of age – but mainly because there was a war on – I couldn't leave. As soon as the war was over ... I didn't know exactly what I would do, apart from a vague dream of going to America. I could not understand how someone could spend his whole life in Kostelec and not even try to do anything about it. But clearly there were people like that. The fellows in those bull-sessions in the toilet would never think of going anywhere else, or doing anything else. Kostelec, the factory – these were for them absolute givens. Perhaps it was also because they had certain skills: Ponykl was a welder, Kos and Malina were fitters; they were lathe operators, painters. I had no skills at all, except playing on the sax, though I didn't think I was good enough to make a living at it. Not in Prague at any rate. I was probably good enough for Kostelec. School had taught me almost nothing because almost nothing had excited my interest except books, and even then not the books we were expected to read. Perhaps that was why I liked them. And Nadia? She had no skills either, except for housework, but then she was a woman and that was enough. Franta would marry her – here I caught myself out in a contradiction, for although I was obviously crazy about her, standing staring at her cottage with the smoke drifting out of the chimney, I had never thought of marrying her. The smoke from the chimney meant Nadia was probably getting supper ready in the oven – they almost certainly had a woodstove in the kitchen – and I remembered how I had felt that time when I fed her my mother's tarts, and how we had washed the dishes together....

I heard a swishing sound behind me and the shrieking of girls' voices. I turned around. A little way off lay an overturned sleigh. Beside it sat Marie in ski-pants and a Norwegian sweater, and on the other side of the sleigh another girl, who was lifting a pair of glasses out of the snow and checking to make sure they weren't broken.

"Help!" called Marie, laughing in my direction.

"What's the matter with you?" I said. "So you fell on your bum. It must be like falling on a bunch of pillows."

"How would you know?" said Marie. She stood up and started dusting the snow off that part of her body.

"Women have more subcutaneous fat than men," I said. "That's what old Starec told us in fifth form. Particularly in the rear quarters."

"You added that bit. He didn't say rear quarters." Marie came up to me and turned her back. "Feel it."

"What?"

"Go ahead, feel my bottom!"

What was going on? So pious in church and now this? The other girl was slowly rising out of the snow. She squinted short-sightedly at us and pulled out a handkerchief.

"Do you mean that seriously?"

"Don't take it the way you're obviously taking it. Just think of it as a lesson in practical anatomy. Go ahead, feel!"

I felt. Marie's bottom was as firm as a gym mat. Not much subcutaneous fat there. But it was resilient.

"It's bouncy," I said.

"But not like a pillow."

"More like an inflatable pillow," I said, feeling it again. But Marie pulled away and turned to face me, her cheeks all red from the frost, a blue cap on those golden curls.

"What are you doing here?" she asked.

"Nothing. Out for a walk. Run along and play now."

She regarded me inquisitively, then looked past the scrub pine towards the cottage. A thick plume of smoke was now curling up from the chimney. They were probably putting pine branches on the fire.

"How come you're treating me like a stranger all of a sudden?" Marie asked. "I'll bet you know somebody over there."

"What are you talking about?"

"It's obvious." Marie looked at me steadily. Of course, I had no skis with me and I was here alone. "You aren't the sort to be out walking alone on Cerna Hora just for the heck of it."

"Why not?"

"It would break too many psychological laws, Danny boy!"

The second girl came up to us. She had her glasses on now. She was probably the same age as Marie but she looked thirty. Marie introduced us. Hana Klegrova from Hradec. When she heard my name she began to laugh.

"That's him?"

Marie giggled. "Yes, that's him."

"What's this all about?"

"We mean it's you," said Marie.

They were both laughing, and I was annoyed. "D'you find me so amusing?"

"As a matter of fact we do," said Marie.

"You write amusing letters," said Hana. "I mean, I've heard you do. You haven't written any to me yet."

And I won't either, you owl, I thought.

"He'll make up for that," said Marie. "He's such a writer!"

"I don't have time now. I'm busy working for the victory of the Reich," I said. "Give her some of your letters to read. You probably have already anyway."

It was obvious that she had, but I didn't care. They happened to be rather fine letters.

"Me?" said Marie in mock astonishment. "If anybody showed her it was Jarmila Dovolilova. That's Hana's cousin."

"No one gave me anything," said Hana. "But all the girls say how beautifully you write."

She had an acid tongue.

"Well, so long," I said. "Run along and play now, children."

"Look at that!" said Marie. "See how cold he is? And he's just finished patting my bottom! He's got somebody else."

Both of them began laughing again. Two people were approaching Nadia's cottage, an elderly man in a lambskin cap and a woman in a kerchief. They knocked and Franta appeared in the doorway. As they all disappeared into the cottage the cat ran out into the snow and stepped gingerly into a drift. "He has somebody new here!" I heard Marie's merry voice say. "He's been carrying on with a factory girl, and now he's taken up with a villager."

"You're in an exceptionally good mood today," I said wearily.

"You guessed it, Danny boy."

"Is it because your boyfriend's not around?"

The girls looked at each other and giggled.

"Look," said Marie, and she became more affable again. "Since my fellow isn't around today, how'd you like to buy me a beech-nut coffee at the restaurant? I'm cold." She made her teeth chatter.

I looked at the cottage. Another elderly man stood at the door and Franta let him in. I realized that I was cold too. I looked at Marie – how well the cold suited her. Her blue eyes shone in the glow of her golden hair.

"Don't always be staring off over there!" she said.

"I'm in love, Marie."

"I know. With me," she said.

Was I? Marie was beautiful, I had loved her for at least five years. But now, at this moment?

"And with Irena too, naturally," said Marie. "But more with me."

I said nothing. The problem puzzled me. I was certainly not indifferent to her. But Nadia ... that afternoon on the ottoman ... her thin, naked belly ... those pathetic big boots of hers....

"And with that village girl too, and so on," Marie was saying. "But that's no reason why you can't buy your old love a beech-nut coffee."

She was right, and in any case it was bitterly cold. The sun was low in the west. Beech-nut coffee it was.

The restaurant was humming with life. They were selling wartime coffee, linden tea and a green soft-drink. They also had some tarts for ration coupons, but none of us had any. At one table Vrata Blazej and two clerks from Barton's cotton-mill were playing a noisy game of euchre and at another table Jarka Mokry's crowd were playing pinochle. A few families were there with their children, and some local villagers drinking the light wartime ale.

The girls giggled constantly. On the way up the slope Marie had fallen down five times, four times deliberately and once accidentally when she tripped over a root poking out of the snow and went sprawling flat on her face. She stood up holding her nose and began whimpering.

"Cry-baby," I said. "There's nothing wrong with you. You fell on your subcutaneous cushion. Both of them."

Normally a remark like that would have made her touchy. She would have accused me of having a filthy mind, or if she had been feeling particularly well disposed she might simply have asked me to cool my imagination. But something was going on; she thrust her bottom out at me. "Want to pat it again?" she said.

"He wants to touch your nose," said Hana.

"Very well," said Marie, and she proffered her nose. Both of them began to laugh again and then, as if on command, both of them fell over in the snow. Pure merriment.

Over the beech-nut coffee, Marie pulled out a pocket mirror, though God knows where she kept it in her ski clothes, and thoughtfully examined her face.

She and Hana were whispering together and tittering secretively.

"You really are in a good mood today," I said.

"It's because an enormous stone has fallen from my heart," Marie said.

"What kind of stone?"

"An enormous one."

"But not a material one," said Hana.

"It is partly material too," said Marie.

What could they be talking about? Trouble at school? Marie was still going to school, in the eighth form, though she didn't attend very frequently because they were always closing it down due to fuel shortages.

"You just barely squeaked through in math, is that it?" I said.

"Just barely," Marie agreed. "But what's material about that?"

"The cane," I said. "Your father would use it on that very material part of your body, the part I touched today."

"I hope you'll write a beautiful letter about it," said Marie.

I longed to be let in on their secret. Did it have something to do with Kocandrle? I remembered how he and Marie had sung with such conspiratorial concord that morning in the choir.

"I'll bet you were unfaithful to your boyfriend," I probed.

"I beg your pardon!" cried Marie in mock anger. "What do you take me for? And if I were, it could only be with you."

"No great stone had to fall from your heart because of me," I said. "He tolerates me."

"I'll have you know that it was partly because of you," she retorted.

"What d'you mean, Molly?" said Hana.

"I wouldn't want him to stop loving me," said Marie.

"Who, your boyfriend?" I asked.

"Not him, you."

"They don't stop loving you for that, if they really love you," said Hana. "If they love you, they love you."

"Till the end of time!" said Marie, and they started laughing again.

"You're talking like the oracle of Delphi," I said, growing irritated.

"*Ibis, redibis, non moriaris in bellum,*" said Marie.

"You've got an F for failure, Dreslerova," I said. "*In bello.*"

"Please, sir, I'll study harder next time," said Marie. "I've been a little preoccupied with other things lately, sir."

Suddenly, as though a leaf of time had been torn from the future and fluttered into the present, I saw what it would be like in ten years. Or twenty. Where would these giggly girls be then, this beautiful Marie? Where would Nadia be? Irena? It made me sad. They would look like my mother, they would have their own giggly eighteen-year-old daughters, but they themselves would no longer be giggly. The fun would be over. I knew of no forty-year-old woman who was that close to laughter all the time. I began to fear that it would soon be all over, and I longed to go on playing this game with them for a long time yet.

"Hana, your boyfriend is here," I heard Marie say.

I looked around. The boys from the band had burst into the restaurant with their girlfriends and there was a strange fellow with them. They looked round, saw us and came over.

"Look at him, the snake-in-the-grass!" said Lucie by way of greeting. They were all in ski outfits, but each of them wore a different hat, Haryk a flat straw boater, Benno a derby and Lexa a top-hat.

"Get thee from yonder forbidden fruits!" Haryk intoned at me, pointing at Marie.

"The cheek!" said Lexa indignantly. "His true love a mere stone's throw away, and here he sits, plying another with coffee."

"You mean she lives in that cottage?" asked Lucie.

"The one with the thatched roof."

"I hear she's quite a dish," said Benno.

"You know about her already?" asked Marie. "About this village girl?"

"He's been corrupting her for at least a month," said Haryk.

"Wait. A month ago it was a factory girl he was corrupting. Or was it she corrupting him?" said Marie.

"It's the same one," said Haryk. "A factory girl from the village."

"Underneath the mountain."

"From a cottage underneath the mountain."

"At last I see the light," said Marie, turning to me. "You'll have to forgive me, Danny. You're not fickle at all. I thought the factory girl was someone else."

"She's one and the same person, madame," said Haryk.

"Gentlemen," said Lexa, "shall we talk of something else?"

"Like literature," said Benno.

"You know that doesn't interest us," said Haryk. "Unless of course it's erotic."

"Hana, we really must go," said the stranger. "It's almost dark."

And so I was left alone with Marie. The stranger took his Hana off to Hradec in a Praga car that ran on wood-gas. The boys and Lucie had Benno's four-seater bobsled with them – Marie had her own sleigh. In spite of that morning's piety, Kocandrle had not materialized.

We walked with the boys as far as the wayside cross and there the foursome got on the bobsled. The boys pushed forward with their feet, edging towards the steep slope of Cerna Hora.

The sun was red by now, and low over the horizon. Kostelec lay far below us, behind a delicate veil of mist rising from the woods. The windows of the castle burned as sunlight reflected off them. I was filled with the sensation that life was magnificent, that youth was magnificent. I recalled suddenly how a week earlier I had had to carry Nadia home over the crest of this hill, but even that merged effortlessly into this new sensation – the afternoon in the park, on the ottoman, her large damp mouth, youth. I gave the bobsled a push, Lexa shouted, "Let us pray!", the bobsled dipped over the edge of the slope and shot away into the blue shadow that lay across the path down by the woods, Lucie shrieked, and they were transformed into a long, black, shrinking shape that swept in a slow arc along the path and suddenly vanished into the woods.

"They won't stop till they reach town," said Marie behind me.

"Neither will we," I said, "but I'd like to."

"But I wouldn't," said Marie. "Know what I mean, Danny?"

"Of course I know," I said, pretending to be sad, though I felt great. "But what you want is nothing compared to the laws of gravidity."

In the golden-red light of the late sun, Marie blushed.

"I mean gravity," I said quickly. "Ever since I became a worker my intelligence has suffered."

I turned and sat down on the sleigh. Marie sat down behind me and caught me around the waist. I felt her soft breasts in the Norwegian sweater pressing into my back, her hair smelled sweet and her thighs squeezed against mine from the outside. Someone was climbing up the path. We waited for him to go by, for he was taking the path we would take.

Then I recognized him. It was Franta. He reached the edge of the slope and looked at me.

"Hi!" I said.

He stopped. It seemed as though he wanted to say something to me. He looked careworn. I thought quickly of Nadia but I had my tender cargo behind me and it was no more than a brief thought, a squib of a prayer as the Venerable Father Meloun would have said.

Franta did not even reply. He hesitated a moment, then walked on.

"Let's take off, Molly," I said. "Let us pray!"

"No blaspheming – we don't want to crack up," said Marie.

And off we went, swishing down the steep slope like the bobsled before us, through the pure, frost-filled mountain air towards the blue shadow of the trees. The woods rose and blocked our view of Kostelec, with only the burning castle and its tower still visible above the tips of the firs. We began to drag our left heels in the snow and slowly, like the bobsled, we banked towards the woods, the castle was swallowed up in the blackness, and we shot into the dark.

The white snow-covered path wound through the darkness, down, down, first to the left, then to the right, above it the pale blue-grey sky streaked with banners of red and black cloud. Here and there a star shone. Marie was silent, holding me tight from behind, because she had to, and the intense feeling of life grew until it was an inexpressible certainty. As we wound down through that magnificent forest Marie said, with her fragrant mouth right on my ear, "Danny...."

"What?" I roared to the forest.

"Don't shout," she said gently. "I'm fond of you. I'm so happy today."

"Why? Because that enormous stone fell from your heart?" I shouted back.

"Don't shout," Marie said, "don't shout."

"What kind of a weight was it?" I cried, more quietly now.

"You wouldn't understand," she said tenderly.

"Why not?" I shouted, and at that point there was a six-fold echo. The sleigh had slowed down and the echo called back to us: "Why not, why not, why not, why not, why not, why not?"

"Because you're a man," she whispered in my ear, "and there's nothing you'll ever be able to do about that."

God knows what she meant. The sleigh slowed down, we came out of the woods. To our left the first villas of the town began to appear. The sleigh finally came to a stop. I didn't get up right away. Neither did Marie. Then she suddenly squeezed me tightly, with her arms still around my waist, and stood up.

It was dark by now. When I stood up too, Marie was just a slender silhouette, her face white against the darkness. In the shadow of night, her golden hair had become platinum.

"You'll walk me home, won't you?"

"You don't think I'd leave you to the tender mercy of some lonesome tough, do you?"

Marie laughed, then turned and walked up the slope, along the path leading to her villa. I joined her, pulling her sleigh along behind me.

"Are you really fond of her?" she said. "That – factory girl?"

I was silent.

"She's a fine girl," I said finally.

"I'd be glad if you were happy. You can't be happy with me because, well, I've got a boyfriend."

"I know you do."

She turned her white face to me. She seemed to grow darker.

Suddenly it hit me. Christ! So that was why they were singing so piously. Now I understood. She must have been afraid of confession. Such a pious girl! And that was the great weight that had fallen from her heart. Partly material! Of course. So Marie and her fellow.... But I realized that I wasn't jealous, as I might otherwise have been, from her talk and her blushing – and I thought of Nadia.

Ah well. Those platonic, babbling loves were a thing of the past for me too. Marie was no longer a virgin. Nor was I.

We climbed up another slope, which almost brought us to her house.

"I really want you to be as happy as I am," she was saying quietly. "And if you were, then I wouldn't be jealous. Otherwise I would be, since you love me."

I stopped. The blackout blinds on the windows of her virgin-white villa were down; a tiny hole glowed like a star.

"Don't you love me, Marie?"

"Of course I do," said Marie sweetly, and then she did something, I don't quite know what it was, but it simply became very clear that I was to embrace her. I did, and she went soft in my arms, her cold damp mouth was against mine, her warmth came through the cold and I found the tip of her tongue. We kissed for about five minutes, or maybe ten. An awfully long time, measured by the breathless long kisses of those young years. Then she did something else, again I wasn't certain what, but I released her gently and it was over. She took the sleigh by the cord, unlocked the gate with a large key that, like the mirror, she had pulled from the secret recesses of her clothing and, on the other side of the gate now, she turned and whispered, "Night, Danny!"

"Night, Molly."

She stood the sleigh on its end under the veranda steps and ran up to the door. Again she turned round, laughed the way she had at first on Cerna Hora but sweetly, executed a deep curtsy, and blew me a kiss. The door closed behind her.

I stared at the villa for a while, as I had stared at the cottage. Smoke was coming out of the chimney. An intense sensation of life filled me and at the same time, I realized, a sensation of safety as well, without which the feeling of life may not really exist at all – the affair with the cross-brackets had been smoothed over, the war was rapidly approaching its end, Nadia, Marie.... I turned around. The close winter stars were glittering above the woods.

Full of happiness I slowly descended the path into town.

Coming towards me was a man. When I was almost on top of him, he stopped. Then I recognized him.

It was Nadia's fiancé, Franta. An absurd thought: Marie's fellow was also called Franta.

I heard something. "You bastard."

Then the stars in the sky blended with the stars in my head. Something inside it cracked.

And I woke up, with my head in great pain, in the hospital.

●

Sofron, Slovakia, 6.5.52.

*Dear Dan,*

*I adres you with these few lines to let you know I am well and hope you
are enjoying the same blesing at present. They are coming round agi-
tating for us to colectivize but the old man says only over his dead
body. Half the village has already joined up. The comunists are swine
to take property away from people like that when they never done
nothing to earn it themselves. I dont deserve this, I got that property
honest by maraige and now I am going to lose it again and be a beggar
or else I'll have to go back to baking. They promise the heavens and
the earth and then goble everything up but now more than half the village joined and the ones that didnt are afrade. They say they are going
to arest people and I wouldnt want to get locked up. What would my
daughter Suleika do then. Thats a Georgian name in case you ask
yourself what kind of a strange name is that. So what can we do except
be glad of what little we got left. Bravko weighs almost two tons now
and in a month we are going to slauhter her and we will have meat for
half a year and saussage too. You should come for a visit since you
couldn't make it for the weding nor the chrisening of my daughter
Suleika. My daughter is the only thing that gives me plesure in this
misery. You aint seen her yet but she will be five soon she dont look
much like me except for the button nose. They say she has gipsey hair.
Must be the old man because I am a red head. We dont go to the
movies so much now I havent got time for things like that now what
with the comunists trying to take away everything that properly
belong to me. We saw a movie called Katka about a girl who went
from a vilage to a factry it was nice and funny too. Also saw one about
Muchurin the fellow who grew strawberies as big as oranges but that
was only just a movie because its imposible to do that in real life. The
best one I saw was Rome at 11 o'clock where a balkony with girls on it
collapses and all the girls were prety, only I didnt understand when she
took of her coat and she had a T shirt with something wrote on it that
wasn't translated. They have prety bad subtitles. To conclude my leter
plese exsept my warmest wishes and fondest memries.*

                    *your old freind Lojza*

●

I had been in the toilet almost since morning. The men in the seminar were
exploring the question of whether English was spoken in Australia or, as
Malina was insisting, Australian. Confronted with the existence of neighbouring Austria, he stubbornly defended the existence of a language called
Austrian. Kos asked him if he thought that in the protectorate they spoke

Protectorian, Malina called him a fucking marsupial and the discussion ended in a free-for-all.

Eisler didn't even bother to intervene. It was the end of February 1945. Long columns of German peasants were streaming through Kostelec; four years ago they had gone east to colonize the Ukraine. Conditions in the factory were almost idyllic. Eisler had had his last fit of cockiness at Christmas, when SS Panzermayer and his division broke through the American lines at Bastogne and rolled into Belgium. Eisler stormed into the can and ranted and raved at us. "*Das ist der Wendepunkt! Jetzt kommt des Führers Geheimwaffe!*" and he drove everyone out, including those who had an authentic reason for being there. But then the SS division ran out of gas; Eisler retreated to the porter's lodge and there he sat from morning till evening, absent in spirit. At four o'clock he would turn on the radio and listen to the news from the Führer's headquarters. When it was over, he would switch the radio off, pour himself a coffee and rum from a Thermos flask, and by the time the evening siren went he was usually as tight as a bale of barbed wire.

Nowadays there was scarcely room to move in the toilet. Even the cautious Nejezchleba had given up his barrel-rolling and I kept it up purely for the sake of the exercise. We were waiting for the war to end.

Franta emerged from a cloud of smoke and made straight for me. I was suddenly worried that Nadia had got worse.

"There's trouble, boy," he said. "The Gestapo picked up Vachousek last night."

The idyll was abruptly over.

"You think it's because of ...?"

"I don't know what else it could be. Nadia's gone to her Uncle Venhoda at the mill. She can keep low there till the war's over."

I was so stricken with panic I didn't even notice that Franta had stopped talking. A moment later he said, "Nadia's afraid for you, boy. If you want, you can go to the mill with her. There's easy room for more."

"I – I wouldn't want to get her into any more trouble."

"It don't make any difference now. You're both in it, so we got to help you both."

At the mill with Nadia. Franta looked at me gravely, without a smile. But an exaggerated fear had gripped me, and the positive aspects of the offer did not come home to me. Instead, I mechanically repeated my old excuse: "That's very kind of you, but it would be better if we each went to a separate place. I'll hide at – a buddy's."

"Do whatever you like, but be careful," he said. Then he turned and disappeared. In the smoke and stench he looked like someone from another generation, although I was as old as he was. I was ashamed.

I walked rapidly across the yard to the administration building and knocked on the door of Uippelt's office. "*Herein!*" he barked from inside. There was some kind of conference going on, but it looked more like a drinking session. Several bottles stood on the table and all the Germans from the Messerschmitt factory except Mr. Kleinenherr and Gerta Ceehova were there. The corpulent engineer Mr. Schwarz had tears in his eyes and Dr. Seelich appeared to be asleep. Schilling, who owned the factory, was smoking an English pipe. Even the collaborator Zavis was with them.

I thought at first I had made a mistake in going there, but almost as if he had been expecting me Uippelt said, "*Da Sie sind endlich. Hier ist der Passierschein und hier die Bestellungskarte.*" He wrote something quickly on a piece of paper.

I left at once. The note was in English. *Go to my place and wait for me there.*

But he'd forgotten to include the key, and the general's wife had left town. I waited for him on the open veranda of Strauss's villa for almost two hours, numb with cold. Most of the snow had melted, and only patches remained in the ditches and depressions on the hillside sloping down to the river, but the air was damp and chilly. I watched a raven angrily peck at something in the leaves and then gravely walk away with it in his beak, disappearing behind the villa. Perhaps the thaw had cast up the carcass of some tiny animal.

Uippelt came hurrying up and took me directly to his wallpapered room. The town, emerging from the long winter, glowed optimistically in the panoramic window. The Obermeister walked over to the liquor cabinet and poured us both a generous drink.

"Do you know anything about that fellow Vachousek?"

"No. Only that he found out about the – "

"Nothing apart from that? Did he belong to some group?"

"I don't know. I thought – he might be in yours – "

"He has nothing to do with that."

He turned to the window and I saw him take a drink.

"Do you think ...?"

"I have every reason to," he retorted. "In any case, you'd better keep out of sight."

He looked at me. It was an odd feeling to have this man – a Nazi – as concerned for my safety as Nadia was.

He quickly quashed any illusion of altruism.

"Because if they got you, I doubt you'd be able to keep your mouth shut."

He had good reason for thinking so. Not long ago I had almost fainted in this very room. All the same it angered me.

"I can take a lot!"

The little eyes behind the pince-nez half closed and an ironic smile twisted the mouth behind the Hitler moustache.

"Don't kid yourself, baby," he said in English. He poured me a drink, and went on, "It's not worth it. It's just a matter of a month, two at the most, that's all." He turned to the window again and looked out at Kostelec. I said nothing now. I could hear the muffled industrial hum of the small town under the brow of the mountain.

"*Das Leben ist ein grosser Irrtum,*" said Uippelt in a Zarathustrian tone. Life is a great mistake. But mistake or not, I was only interested in staying alive. The biggest mistake of all would be to let myself get done in, now, so close to the end of the war.

"What do you think of National Socialism?" he asked. It was a rhetorical question, because he immediately supplied the answer. "I know what you think of it. After it's all over everybody knows the score. But in Detroit, in the thirties, it was different." He paused, then – "That was at the height of the Depression."

He stopped and looked out at the pleasant town. But his problems were not mine, and I was wondering if Prema knew of a place to hide. Uippelt turned around, went back to the liquor cabinet, and poured out the rest of the bottle. The lethal liquid sparkled golden in the cut glass, and reflected in his pince-nez.

"So," said the Oberkontrolleur, "*ich fuhr ins Paradies.*"

I was headed for Paradise. Those were the last words I ever heard him say.

I left quickly and ran to the Skocdopoles'.

●

I sat in the dusk in Pejskar's cottage and looked at the meadow sloping down to a narrow footpath that disappeared into the woods on the far side. A low full moon hung over the trees, a pale, pale green. Spring was here. The end of March. I had been hiding in the cottage a month already. Twice a week Prema brought me food from my parents.

The cottage stood by itself in a valley on the other side of Cerna Hora. There were no buildings around and the only approach was visible from the windows, that is if no one came through the woods. But the Gestapo had better things to do now than crawl about in the underbrush trying to nab a conscripted student who had deserted his post in the labour system.

I was safe. Twice, Prema, Vahar, Benda and I had gone out to cut wires, but it was mostly for the sake of doing something. Once a small line of tired German soldiers had straggled along the path below the cottage and

I had got scared and climbed out the back window to hide in the woods, but they didn't even notice the cottage. Otherwise I was bored. Pejskar had a pile of dime novels in a cupboard, all of them westerns. After the fifth one I lost interest. Then because I had nothing to do I wrote one myself, called *The Revenge of the Godless Gunman,* and I sent it via Prema to Nadia in her uncle's mill. I awaited her praise, but when she wrote back she told me about the tarts her aunt was making, and added at the end, "Dan, you scribble awful. I couldn't read a word you wrote about that godless german."

A figure emerged from the woods and walked briskly along the footpath towards the cottage. I recognized Prema.

We sat in the dark by the window. The moon had almost set and an owl was circling the cottage.

"Are you dead sure it wasn't because of those cross-brackets?"

"I'm positive," said Prema. "They let Sagner and Tichy go yesterday and both of them claim Vachousek was in their group. They're all Social Democrats. It looks like the Gestapo aren't taking things that seriously anymore so we don't have to be too worried about them. It's others we have to be worried about." In the heavenly peace of the moonlit valley, Prema's voice sounded like the voice of doom.

"What do you mean?"

"Well, get a load of this."

He pulled a piece of paper out of his pocket, unfolded it on the table and smoothed it out with his hand. I struck a match.

DEATH TO THE GERMAN OCCUPIERS!
COMRADES! *The Red Army Liberators are on the way!*

The match went out. I struck another one and looked quickly at the conclusion of the leaflet:

... *be prepared to liquidate the bourgeois so-called anti-German resistance groups directed from London....*

There must have been a draft in the cottage for the second match guttered and went out too. I didn't bother striking a third. I looked at Prema. Bathed in the pale green light of the moon, his Mongolian face was deadly serious.

"That means us," he said darkly. "*So-called* anti-German groups."

In the emerald night he reminded me of his alcoholic father, the stump of his arm in a sock, telling long-forgotten stories. I changed the subject. That note of gloom did not belong to the end of the war.

"Why didn't the Germans let Vachousek go too?"

Prema shrugged his shoulders. "They claim he was the leader of the group. He was connected to Prague."

I couldn't help being sarcastic. "And he was being directed by London through Prague."

"Yeah, like us," said Prema. "But Dr. Benes in London is the legal Czechoslovak government."

We were silent again. Outside the owl hooted. A veil of mist covered the moon.

"Do you think they'll do him in?" I thought of the sardonic foreman who had in all probability saved my neck. Now he was in trouble himself.

"Hard to say. Some of the Gestapo just don't give a shit any more. Others are going wild."

"That would be bloody rotten" – I couldn't begin to express the depth of my gratitude towards the foreman – "if after all that he gets it in the neck now."

We were silent again, until Prema announced that he was going to sleep. We lay on couches in the dark, the hoot-owl still circling outside the window.

"What are you going to do after the war, Prema?"

"First I'll do my hitch in the army," he yawned, "then we'll see. Maybe I'll take a gander at the rest of the world. Go to South America, you know. Always wanted to be a farmer, it's in my blood. They say you can still get land cheap in South America. Course, you've got to clear the jungle and burn...." His voice died away. He was asleep.

That night I decided to return home. The danger was clearly over so there was no point in sticking around the cottage. The next day I waited till dark, because it still didn't seem wise to go back in broad daylight. Strange thoughts were running through my head. All of a sudden, I wasn't looking forward to the end of the war: I couldn't get Prema's leaflet out of my mind. Was it possible that there were people who, as soon as they were rid of one paradise, would want to plunge headlong into another one? *Ich fuhr ins Paradies....*

People. I recalled Nadia, Marie, Irena, the boys from the band, Franta Melichar. Kos and Malina. I thought of Hetflajs. The foreman Vachousek. And old man Varecka, and his hundred a week more.

But who am I to say what a hundred a week more means?

Nadia knew. Even so....

I stared out of the window at nothing in particular. The sun was low over the edge of the woods. Green was already appearing in the meadow, and the woods behind it cast a wide shadow. From the edge of that wide shadow a small, narrow shadow appeared and grew longer. Someone was walking towards the cottage.

I stopped trying to peer into the heart of an insoluble mystery and focused my eyes.

Walking across the meadow towards me was Nadia, wearing a man's raglan coat bought round about the time I was born.

# CHAPTER FIVE

Thou whose hand crushes all things great,
Thou, who condemns to death
youth and spirit, but not base crime,
Whose eye lingers with delight
on the torments of the innocent, the triumphs
of rogues and murderers, whores, on the frippery
of criminal politicians, on the dens
of all unassailable gangsters, lo! my faith:
Be Thou damned, Al Capone of the Universe!

FRANTISEK ZAVREL

The daydream is the true basis of all literature.... Reality is
not what happens to be most real to us at the moment. It is
what we perceive in our moments of greatest intensity.

COLIN WILSON

•

# Fitzgerald

Sydney<br>August 7, 1959

**D**ear Danny,

*I've finished with farming and here I am again in Sydney. I couldn't find work in a factory so I'm working outdoors. As far as I can recollect, last time I wrote I told you I'd bought a farm. The owner's wife died and he sold it to me cheap. I thought it was a bit strange, but then I said to myself after all he's got no kids and he's already too old (67) to work it himself. Well, now I know it wasn't age that got to him, it's just that you get so damned lonely here. At first I liked it — beautiful countryside though it's different from back home, eucalyptus trees, colourful bushes, kangaroos, he even had a tame one there. But there are no people, just rabbits. I spent most of the time mending the fences so the rabbits wouldn't get in and eat everything up. I used to listen to the radio but there was never much interesting on. I got myself some cows and I had a real beaut of a horse, a riding horse, used to ride it all day. It was such a huge spread of land it felt bigger than our whole country. But there wasn't a living soul*

*anywhere, just kangaroos. Weren't even any aborigines – they're the
local blacks, ugly as sin but you can get along with them okay, but
there weren't even any of them out there, so the loneliness started to
get to my brain. The old man sold it to me because when his wife died I
guess it got to his brain too. But I didn't feel like getting married. None
of those dumb, tea-drinking Aussie women would ever think of moving out to the bush, so I'd of had to marry an Eyetalian, and you can
forget that, they carry on like a bunch of monkeys. Anyway, I finally
started to go a little stir crazy from it all, and even the tame kangaroo
ran away. Then I started having all these dreams about Kostelec, how
we used to hang about on Jirasek Street, remember that? And about
Vahar – I'd heard they locked him up because of those leaflets about
the butter but Mother wrote that they let him out long ago and now
he's working at Messerschmitt's or whatever the hell they call it now,
Kovo Techna or something. And how we used to try and sneak looks
at the girls in the local swimming pool and how Rosta Pitterman made
a fool of himself because of the one that you liked. What was her name
– Marie? What's she doing now? Do you ever see her? Anyway it
nearly drove me crazy and in the end I was sleeping more than I was
working and the farm was going down the drain. I also used to dream
about Dad. You probably heard he died this year. The Legionnaires
went to his funeral but they weren't allowed to wear their uniforms –
so Mother wrote. Well, he's got that over with, but it's still a miracle he
lasted till he was 64 what with all that drink and him being an invalid.
She also wrote about Vachousek – makes me glad I'm here. I guess I
would've ended up the same way if I'd of stayed home.*

*Time to finish. I've got a thirst and there's no beer in the house. Here
they sell beer in cans, even in the bars. That's the Aussies for you.
They're a hundred years behind the monkeys. Haven't even got a public health system not to mention pensions. Write me, if you're not
afraid, about what's new in Kostelec and with the boys, Vahar and
Benda and that lot, and Marie and Irena, the alderman's daughter, the
one you was in love with. I don't suppose you are any more. Time flies,
old buddy, and we're getting older and I guess the girls are too.*

*Your old mate,*
*Prema*

●

A cold wind is blowing across the steel-grey waters of Lake Ontario; dirty
waves slap against the sides of the Svensson yacht. The boat lurches up and
down and I'm worried about being seasick.

Irene has invited me and five of her classmates for a winter excursion on the empty lake. It is something of an adventure. All the other sailboats are wintering in their slips at the yacht club docks, looking like coffins with canvas lids, and we're on the water alone, the prow of our barque pointing south, towards the shores of America. As we set sail before the wind, a bright green monoplane rose into the air from the tiny airport on the western tip of Toronto Island, circled the island once and headed straight for us, passing a few yards above the mast. Irene waved.

"That's Bobby Harkins. He's nuts about flying."

He must be if he's up in this weather. Irene is nuts about sailing, and has persuaded a hired helmsman to take the boat out. The wind on the lake is so brisk that it has driven us below, leaving the mariner at the helm, drinking, mariner-fashion, from a flat hip-flask. Now we are sitting inside the cabin on upholstered leather benches, bottles steadied in special depressions in the table, the leaden winter sky beyond the round portholes. Wendy was the first to get stoned. Bellissimmo had cast an uncertain glance in my direction, pulled out a plastic sandwich bag full of marijuana, rolled a cigarette and, with even greater uncertainty, offered it to me. So here we are, marijuana'd, aboard the *Jane Guy,* or perhaps it's the *Pequod* ... the wind out of the north ... sea-spray dashing against the Plexiglas porthole ... in fact I've always been seventeen ... I have searched all my life for the Southern Passage on a schooner from the Miskatonic University Expedition; I have sailed to Tsalal, Kerguelen, to Ultima Thule....

Wendy is pissed, stoned, and bristling with spirit and literary lore.

"Hey, Nicole! I mean Irene! Is it true that the trains begin their run in Chicago for your sake?"

Her paper on "Fitzgerald's Use of Period Objects" was the usual picture gallery put together at the expense of mutilating countless *New Yorker*s and *Cosmopolitan*s, borrowed, I fear, from the Sigmund Samuel Library. But she has read her Fitzgerald, as novelists ought to be read, thoroughly. She relates his books to the world around her.

The Fitzgeraldesque Irene Svensson is sitting beside me in an appropriate sailing jacket and white pantaloons and, as always, like Nicole, she stands out from the blue-jeaned uniformity around her. The rich are different from you and me. They have more money. She is wearing a captain's cap atop her Vidal Sassoon haircut.

"Sure. Half-breed Indians toil on Brazilian coffee plantations, also for my sake."

"You haven't got it right, Irene," I say.

"You've read that passage to us three times. I know it by heart."

"It's like it was written about you!" says Wendy.

"Ever-grateful Czech musicians fiddle for peanuts for my sake," I say.

"Hare-brained Soviet dancers break their legs, also for my sake." Irene does not laugh at this. The others don't understand it, except perhaps for Hakim, but he understands it in his own way.

"Isn't she just like Nicole?" babbles Wendy.

"Irene is not schizophrenic," I say.

"But she's beautiful!"

"Stop it!" says Irene. Here, in the cabin of the family yacht, she is in a setting that perfectly reflects Wendy's fantasy. Bellissimmo, who is in love, notices this.

"And rich," he says respectfully.

"I'm not beautiful," says Irene truculently in self-defence.

"So what are you?"

"I'm just...."

"Well-dressed?" I suggest.

"And beautiful!" Wendy insists with deep conviction.

The yacht lurches, Wendy grabs the table and gazes slightly cross-eyed at Irene's pink face. "I think Irene is the most beautiful girl in Edenvale."

"Oh shut up, Wendy," says Irene and she punches a button on the television remote control box.

"You talk like a lesbian!" says Vicky, who has not succumbed to Irene's charms, perhaps because Bellissimmo *has*, even if only slightly.

"Maybe I am a lesbian," says Wendy.

"Are you a socialist?" I ask maliciously. Hakim glowers at me.

"I guess so," says Wendy. "I'm a Buddhist for sure."

A woman with a face like a monstrous white mask appears on the television screen. Only her mouth is moving. She is pleading in monotone the cause of revolution, women, blacks, prostitutes and the proletariat.

"Do you think she's had a face lift?" asks Wendy.

"Of course," says Irene. "She probably hired a whole team of plastic surgeons."

"... *and thus turns us into commodities which are sold....*"

Irene turns to me. "Would you buy her?"

"I wouldn't take her as a gift."

"Maybe you'd be making a mistake," says Irene. "She's a Vanderhouten of the Philadelphia Vanderhoutens. She's not rich, she's superrich."

Hakim looks at the mask. I have no idea what is going on inside his head – nor what could be going on inside the mask. "Svensson," I say, "don't you remember what happened to Dick Diver because he married Nicole of the Chicago Warrens?"

"I do," says Irene, and she looks directly into my eyes with an odd stiffness. "But he didn't marry her because she was from the Chicago Warrens. He loved her."

•

I had a concussion, the bridge of my nose was caved in, a tooth was broken and two ribs were cracked. Franta had accomplished all this with a single, legendary blow predicted first by Marie and later by the boys in the band. I lay in a large ward in the surgical wing along with two skiers with broken legs, two appendectomy cases and one accident victim, brought in when the methanol tank on his car exploded. The window gave me a view of the snow-covered slope of Cerna Hora, the skiers and the children sleighing, and provided an opportunity to meditate. I was devoured by a bad conscience, the quickened voice of the Venerable Father Meloun. What a bastard I was! Lying there in bed I attempted a moral evaluation of the past few days' events. First I seduce Franta's Nadia; I fall for her so badly that I am drawn again to the top of Cerna Hora, only to forget about her in an instant and fall for Marie. Theologically, Franta's intervention could only be explained as divine retribution, the finger of God become a highlander's fist.

A single blow to the nose had done it. The rest was accomplished by gravity and an icy rock I fell against. I was knocked as cold as a stone and Franta was frightened and ran off. Mr. Dresler found me on his way back from the café. He quickly phoned for an ambulance, so that Marie learned of my fall at once. Naturally she was curious to know what had happened and so she was the first – not counting my mother – to visit me in the hospital. By that time I had completed my moral autopsy and had come to the conclusion that I couldn't betray Franta. In spite of being an agent of divine retribution, he had, from the secular point of view, committed the punishable offence of assault with intent to injure and I wasn't that big a rat. So I told Marie that I had slipped on the ice. Marie, of course, had been talking to Dr. Capek beforehand, and she reacted to my version of the event in her inimitably sweet way. "Nonsense, Danny! I told you factory girls have violent lovers." "What are you talking about, Molly?" I asked with very unconvincing surprise. "I told you I slipped." "Is your nose going to be that way for ever?" asked Marie, and she touched the tip of it, which had puffed up like a tomato. "Why should that bother you?" I shot back. "It looks terrible," said Marie.

"Well, so long, Danny boy," and she stood up. On her way out she bumped into Irena who was coming in the door. They greeted each other rather coldly, and then Irena was sitting beside me, her brown eyes wide. "Well, he certainly fixed you! Is your nose going to stay that way for ever?" "In the first place I don't know what you're talking about. I fell, that's all. And in the second place, they're going to put a spring in my nose so – " "How come you don't know what I'm talking about when everybody else does?" "It's all gossip," I said. "I slipped on the ice." "Ondra says," said

Irena, Ondra being Dr. Capek whom she was crazy about though he was not crazy about her, "that you couldn't possibly do half that damage to yourself just by slipping on the ice." "Ondra's just a country doctor," I said angrily. "After the war I'll get plastic surgery and a nose that'll make you fall harder for me than you have for Ondra."

"How corny," replied Irena. "And since you've got such a great imagination, maybe you should try using it on your girlfriend. If her lover made such a mess of your nose, just think what *she* must look like now. I really feel sorry for her, even though infidelity disgusts me," she said righteously. And with that pharisaical declaration she got up and left, only to bump into Lucie and the boys from the band on her way out. "Holy cow, look at that nose!" said Lucie. I was clearly a remarkable piece of work. As soon as they leave, I thought, I'll have to go to the washroom and look at it in the mirror. "Like a fig!" said Haryk. "Squashed," added Benno. "What will you do, sire?" asked Lexa. "With a nose like that, you can scarcely expect to attract the attentions of the fairer sex." "Two of them have said as much to me already today," I said. "Lucie is the third." "What do you mean, the third?" said Lucie, in surprise. "I like it. It's exactly what you needed, Danny." "I shall donate my nose for transplant," said Lexa. "See what a friend I am?" "With your nose," said Lucie, "he'd be even less handsome than Benno." It went on like that for a quarter of an hour, until Sister Udelina came in and shooed them out. I was almost curious to see who they would bump into in the doorway, but the only other visitor was Dr. Capek on his evening rounds. He too was interested in the nose and who had done it. I repeated my story about slipping on the ice and he said that, personally, he couldn't care less what story I made up but he could not jeopardize his professional reputation by diagnosing a moderately serious physical injury, caused beyond all doubt by a second person, as something I'd done to myself. But if I didn't want to tell the truth, he said, he would say that I had been attacked by an unknown assailant, probably drunk, because he had to report it to the police. Just as I was about to conclude that Dr. Capek was a man of character after all and not a gossip, regardless of how offensive I found him because of Irena, he disabused me; he rose from my bed, winked at me rakishly just as my father had recently done to Nadia, and said, "I hope the sin was at least worth the beating." And with that he left the room.

This sequence of scenes naturally was an enormous source of amusement to both the skiers with broken thigh-bones, because they knew me and they knew all the girls who had come to visit. The group irritated me. I also began to worry that Franta might actually have beaten up Nadia too when it finally dawned on him that she had been unfaithful to him.

So I lay there with my thoughts and I could hear the distant shouts of skiers on the hillside, most of them children since very few adults could go skiing on a weekday. The sun was setting in the west and a pink line of clouds had formed above the horizon. Someone coughed in the doorway. I glanced in that direction, and every reflex in my body told me to jump out of bed and run. But as my body twitched in response, a pain shot through my ribs and into my head and I collapsed helplessly on the pillow.

There stood Franta, his lambskin hat in his hands, his lowering eyes searching the beds. He was looking at the two broken legs suspended from the ceiling on a cord.

Then he caught sight of me. Terrified, I fumbled around for the bell to call Sister Udelina. There was no one to help me but a roomful of immobilized cripples.

"G'day," Franta greeted me.

I opened my mouth and a sound that might have been a question escaped.

"I won't keep you long," said Franta. "You're probably tired."

He came right up to the bed and stared at me.

"I come to say I was sorry," he said. "Nadia wouldn't have it any other way."

I was flabbergasted. Was he coming to apologize for the fact that I had slept with his bride-to-be? Was he *that* much a Christian?

"I overdone it," he said. "I couldn't hold back. I was mad at you for dragging Nadia into a risky business like that."

My incredible mistake dawned on me. And that all things are pure to the pure of heart....

"When Vachousek told me on Sunday, I was so mad I could've tore you apart like a snake," said Nadia's fiancé. "If they ever lock Nadia away, she'll die. With her TB she'd never make it through the concentration camp. You got to understand that I lost control...."

"I understand," I managed to say eventually.

"I would've just told you off, or maybe hit you a couple – "

"But you did!"

"I know, but with my fist. I should've just slapped you. I could knock a cow out with my fist."

Franta looked like a bull and I felt like a very small calf. "I – I'm real sorry ...," he mumbled, as though he were at confession.

"Don't be sorry," I said. "I" – I was infected by his earthy common sense – "I guess I had it coming."

He chuckled, running his eyes along one of the ropes from which those broken thighs were suspended, up to the ceiling and down again. Then he turned to me again and held out his large hand.

"Well, if you're not all that mad at me, let's shake."

The wide eyes looked straight into mine, and I could see nothing encoded in them.

I gave him my hand and immediately regretted it, for the bones cracked. It was the capstone to my punishment. "So God be with ye," said Franta, and with a final respectful glance at the legs in plaster casts he picked his way among the beds and left the room.

It seemed to me that I loved him. And I wondered if I could really be in love with Nadia, if I felt no jealousy towards Franta. I pondered these mysteries and everything seemed to be just as it should be.

Or was I just a bastard? What about Marie? What about Irena? And all the others? I squirmed uneasily on the bed, thinking of Nadia's bare belly, of the snow-covered hillside and the cottage, and of Marie. I couldn't make sense of it, and I felt wretched.

Sister Udelina came into the room and noisily began pulling down the blackout blinds. Then she turned on the lights, came over to my bed, reached under her apron and brought out a letter in a blue official envelope. "The postman brought you this!"

•

*June 12, 1961*
*Kostelec*

*Dear Dan,*
*I don't know if you still read poetry or not. You never were a great poetry reader anyway. As far as I can recall, you only knew a few lines from Seifert and Nezval by heart and, if you don't mind my saying so, it was their most banal work. Undoubtedly you also used them for extra-poetic purposes. But have you at least glanced through some of the collections that have come out recently? You should. Of course I ask this for selfish reasons, because these new collections, along with the rediscovery of Kafka and what is happening in literary criticism, are for me, if not an answer to the questions which, as you know, I have been asking myself ever since the war, then at least a confirmation that I was headed – perhaps instinctively and with many a twist and turn, but headed nevertheless – in the right direction.*

*Do you remember that notice board at Rupa's in Kostelec? And the criticism that came down on my head – today I'm tempted to put the word criticism in quotation marks – when I published my first collection of verse? That lay on me like a heavy stone. I did not treat everything lightly like some of my friends. After many sleepless nights – I'm not exaggerating, even though you probably won't believe me because you've never lost any sleep over trifles like literary problems — I have, I think, a clear mind at last.*

*You know that although I am not and never will be a communist, I have always thought it important for us to build a better — by which I mean a more just — society in our country. The only thing is that "better" must not mean better in some things and worse in others. Does that seem to you like maximalism? Your beloved Hemingway once wrote: Revolution is a wonderful thing. For a time. Then it degenerates — and so I concluded that perhaps equally as important as carrying out a revolution, possibly even more important, is preventing it from degenerating. Notice that I continually use words like "possibly" and "perhaps" — that is because I am trying to keep my subjective and private inclinations from getting in the way of objective and general things, things of concern to the community.*

*But it is true: you can only justifiably call a society better if it's better in all its aspects. In the period immediately after the revolution — five years at the most, I would say — before the organs of revolutionary power consolidate — some important areas may perhaps be objectively "worse." Legality, for example. Revolution is a violent measure and eo ipso it contradicts formal legality. In this immediate post-revolutionary period posters are probably more important than pictures, fables that simplify and instruct more essential than Kafka who complicates and raises doubts. But all this must necessarily be transitional. It must not last so long that it swallows up entire human lives. Otherwise the revolution would annul itself.*

*If bourgeois and feudal art was capable of giving profound expression to man's complexity, then socialist art cannot afford to turn its back on that complexity and depict only the surface, or even worse, try to make the surface look better, "paint it over," as they say.*

*I once quoted you lines by S.K. Neumann over which I puzzled for a long time:*

*I love all things with simple relationships*
*And I love such people most of all;*
*Pure they are, and comely, though I see them for the hundredth time.*
*They are made of primal stuff and taste of ripe beech-nuts.*

*Today I would like to quote some other lines to you, also about simple people:*

*In a little butcher shop a man*
*Stuffs the intestine with meat and a woman*
*Closes the ends with match-sticks. The water in the pot boils.*
*The woman is singing to herself. The steam*
*Rolls out into the grey yard*
*Where children are pulling apart*
*A dead cat, the man stuffs*
*The intestine (his wedding ring occasionally*
*Flashes), evening descends.*
*The children poke with sticks*
*At the cat full of worms*
*Pink and living, living*
*Immensely, evening descends*
*Pink and living; the wedding*
*Ring flashes occasionally with that*
*Pinkness, the woman sings to herself*
*(The circle on her hand is*
*Dull) and the board heaps up*
*With sausages as pink as*
*Early evening in this small butcher*
*Shop....*

*Do you understand me? Neumann is abstraction. Kolar is concrete-*
*ness. Verifiable truth. A real picture, not a poster. What do we really*
*know about "primal stuff"? Who knows how complex are the rela-*
*tionships of people whose relationships are "simple"? Anyway, I have*
*already written you about this: is not their "simplicity" rather our*
*own lack of awareness, or our own laziness to make the effort, even*
*with people like that, not only with evidently complicated intellectu-*
*als? Were not the old Czech authors Baar, Svetla, Nemcova, wiser in*
*this? They knew how to look beneath the painted simplicity and ver-*
*balize the labyrinth of the spirit.*

*But perhaps you have no patience with poetry. I'll remind you once*
*again, therefore, of your paleontological theory. If the relationships of*
*simple people in the twentieth century (or in any other age) were*
*genuinely "simple," in order to be scientifically precise we would have*
*to call them "primitive": corresponding to a lower level of the*
*development of intelligence. But primitive people cannot be the*
*intended product of a socialist society, because it is impossible to*
*develop in that direction: it would go against the laws of evolution. In*

literature (and in politics) it is precisely this "painting over" that corresponds to such primitive relations: the substitution of slogans for knowledge, the escape from the concrete to the abstract. Thus it is, in the true sense of the word, a reactionary art. The soul of man in this century carries within itself the entire history of mankind, and therefore it cannot be made to resound with an art that primitivizes it. The coat of paint over the surface wears thin. An art which is not effective is worth nothing.

Therefore the literature of socialist society, if it is to be better, must be more complex than the older literature. It must reflect human complications with greater precision, more subtlety, from more points of view. And it can do this precisely because such a society has got rid of — or should get rid of — the crudest complications, that is, complications springing from relationships of ownership, from exploitation, and so on. More and more, therefore, can be devoted to the relationships of the heart and mind, and not to speculations about property laws.

Here this is starting to happen. Some of the things which are coming out now stand to become part of a genuine socialist literature, even though it does not always call itself socialist. It is socialist, however, for it is a human literature.

Please forgive this show of emotion; I always seem to wade into it. But these things are terribly important to me. They contain the meaning of my life and — you can laugh at this if you want — if I cannot find or if I cannot at least freely seek the meaning of this life, I will be of no use to this society, or to any other.

The revolution was intended to free man, not only from physical poverty but from spiritual poverty as well. Perhaps even more from the latter, for the spirit is the essence of man. It was intended to create a society which is in every way better — or perhaps worse only to the extent that it is more difficult (and in that sense "worse") to be a person who is concrete (that is, complicated) than it is to be a person who is abstract (that is, a so-called simple person). In short, the revolution must improve everything. If it improves only something, then it was not a revolution but a Machtübernahme. You think this is an absolutistic demand? Maximalism? Anyone calling himself a revolutionary must be a maximalist. If he is not, then he is an ordinary, irresponsible gangster. He is a scoundrel without even knowing it.

I greet you from my heart, Dan. Forgive me, in this depoetizing age, for having become so poeticized again.

> Yours sincerely,
> Jan

•

Our barque is bobbing about in the north wind on Lake Ontario. The marijuana has now seeped into the minds of all my charges, including Hakim. On the television, Comrade Vanderhouten is still holding forth and in the great tradition of Sinclair Lewis is offering her viewers the sweet smell of revolutionary hatred, directed against depilatories, against imperialist aggression in Angola, against discrimination against women miners in the hard coal-mines of Louisiana, against sexless dolls for children.

My Edenvale flock has no interest in Vanderhouten, her loves or her hates, but I am fascinated by the mask. It sets the wheels of old paradoxes in motion. Dr. Agostinho Neto, says the moving mouth, and the Popular Movement for the Liberation of Angola which represents the true aspirations of the Angolan people.... The trouble is that I have seen, with my own eyes, in my own country, T-54 tanks representing the aspirations of a certain building remarkable for the number of corridors in it. Squat, dangerous-looking chariots of war.

Outside the round porthole, the foam-capped waves of an ancient Indian lake, the moon to which Chingachgook prayed torn to shreds by the wind. Fidel's hoodlums in those squat vehicles of war, spurred on by the hope of rapid promotion, making mincemeat out of the imperialist soldiery of Jonas Savimbi with the help of the latest version of the oft-improved Kalashnikov. A ludicrous and bloody thought. I feel Hakim's eyes upon me. Is he reading my thoughts? Does he see into my conscience? But my conscience is clean. I will not swear by answers that exist in only one version – the Kalashnikov. Thirty years ago these same weapons, although as yet unimproved, converted the men of the Muslim SS Division Handschar led by General der Waffen SS Sauberzweig into human mincemeat. An uncle of Hakim's may even have ended up in that bloody steak tartare. Naturally this has nothing to do with Hakim's faiths. It is just that in this flow of thoughts, in the flow of our inner time – as convoluted as the subject of a modern novel, impossible to rearrange into a lucid *fabula* – in this *Zone,* everything appears to arrange itself into those odd, strange contrasts so typical of the human situation. As though I had set Hakim beside that pretty girl whose name I once lent to the geisha in the coffee cup. The wheel of life, Fortune's wheel, the carnival-ride of existence.

My Nicole, Irene Svensson, lays her small hand on my arm. "Are you interested in this?"

I shake my head. "I'm not listening."

"A penny for your thoughts!"

A classic opening line of girls in Victorian novels. What am I thinking of? I'm not really thinking at all.

"I'm a living stream of consciousness," I say.

"Aren't we all that?" asks the girl, who has learned about the nature of human consciousness not only from me but also, and in greater detail, from Professor Steiger in Psychology 235.

"It's just that in each of us the stream is cluttered with bric-a-brac ... empty bottles, sandwich papers, silk handkerchiefs, cardboard boxes ... cigarette ends...."

"But the principle is the same."

"Yes, the principle is the same."

"So what's afloat on your stream?"

"There, you see? You're not interested in the principle, you want to know concretely."

"I already know the principle. I don't know concretely what...."

What I am thinking about.

"Not Ulysses," I say. "My thoughts don't flow in the channels of classical myth."

"Well, you're not writing a novel," says Irene. "Joyce was. There is a *real* stream in you now...."

A stream, a river ... could it be because Vanderhouten is now defending the right of homosexuals to take part in military service? A telephone rings in the February night. Allen here. Listen. I'm calling from the airport. I'm in Prague. What a surprise! And so we got together, all night and into the morning, talk, talk, talk. Perhaps poets love shooting the breeze even more than writing poetry. I was the only one he knew in Prague. That was because I'd once translated *Howl* into Czech and a part of it had been published in the literary monthly *World Literature*. (He was unaware that I had changed the word "Trotskyites" in the original to "revolutionary" in my translation, and I had not tried to explain why to him. Fortunately the censor was too lazy to compare my translation with the original, or perhaps he couldn't read English. Thus do Trotskyites become revolutionaries, and a beatnik becomes a progressive poet.) And we gabbed and babbled till morning and everything ended up in a naive American poet's notebook, along with ideas for metaphors and lists of neologisms. Later a comrade from the state police confronted me with the notebook, leafed through it and said, "How do you explain this, Comrade? Here he writes 'And then we sang the Horst Wessel song.'" Easily — but not to an employee of the State Security Police because he is preparing material for yet another metamorphosis for Allen from a progressive poet back to a beatnik, from a revolutionary to a Trotskyite, and from both to a reactionary. Between my two glimpses of the same notebook, first in Allen's hands and now in the hands of this secret police bureaucrat, the progressive poet had committed many a sin. He had even been declared King of the Majales. Was he now to become a fascist for the benefit and in the eyes of the State Security Police? Why not? He would join the exalted company of Jean-Paul Sartre, George Orwell, General de Gaulle, P.G. Wodehouse, Bertrand Russell and President Tito, perhaps even T.G. Masaryk, who all, at one time or another, were labelled fascists, regardless of the true state of affairs. The only mystery that remains is, why bother to conceal the nakedness of power with a whore's G-string of ideology?

Perhaps all human activity in the end betrays a tendency towards art-for-art's-sake.

"How do you explain that, Comrade?" the State Security officer had asked patiently.

"We were drunk," I confessed truthfully.

It was my misfortune to have come up against that rare animal, the educated secret policeman. "*In vino veritas,*" he replied.

So I shifted to his level. We talked about mental associations liberated by alcohol. We had sung quite a number of political songs, I said, for example "*Los Quatros Generales,*" so....

He looked into the notebook and considered. The four anti-fascist generals were clearly recorded there as well, but the comrade interpreted it in the only way appropriate to the powers that be.

"Yes, that revolutionary song is in fact mentioned. But how do you explain that immediately afterwards you sang the Horst Wessel song, and after that" – his eyes plumbed the pages once more, he thought hard, and the magnificent coherence between the three songs, two of which he hadn't originally intended to mention at all, was revealed to him – "you even sang the '*Internationale?*'"

Associations? Not a very clever way to explain it. So I said, "And right after the '*Internationale,*' as far as I remember, we sang 'Annie Laurie' – "

"And how do you explain *that?* Is it not disgusting and disrespectful to sing the anthem of the international workers' movement between a fascist street-song and a cheap American hit?"

He must have known only the swing version of "Annie Laurie." I toyed with the idea of giving him some folkloric explanation, then thought better of it.

"But, Comrade, isn't the very fact that we sang such a garbled mixture of songs proof enough that we were drunk?"

All in vain. He flung a current legal formula back at me: "Drunkenness is not an extenuating circumstance!"

And *in vino veritas.*

"When you write a novel," asks the contentedly stoned Wendy, "d'you know right from the start what the message will be or do you write it all out first before you see what the message really is?"

"Both," I answer. "You just go ahead and write, but you already know what the message of the novel is going to be."

"That's illogical," says Irene. "If you know from the start what the message will be, then regardless of what you do, you're writing a novel à thèse."

She has become erudite, but I must disappoint her excessive faith in logic.

"Every serious novel — and I'm not talking of hack-writing — is à thèse. But the thesis is always the same, except in novels à thèse."

Irene says nothing. The murky water of the lake lashes the portholes. The boat pitches and tosses and the wind and waves outside the expensive hull make a terrifying clamour. Hakim speaks up. He talks, as always, as though I were beneath contempt. "That's a nice-sounding wisecrack. But that's all it is — just a wisecrack."

I tame my anger. His uncle was probably part of that human mince-meat.

"The most truthful truths about anything, including life," I reply, "usually come in the form of wisecracks."

"For example?"

"I know that I know nothing."

"What is this thesis?" Irene retorts quickly.

"It's very old. Dr. Johnson once said that writers who cast about for something new will scarcely ever be great, for great things could not have escaped the attention of earlier observers."

"That's the thesis?"

"No. The thesis is: *Homo sum. Humani nihil a me alienum puto.* Terence. It's almost two thousand years old."

But at that age everything old is still new, while at the same time everything is growing old. Meanwhile they are discovering their own America. Irene, a furrow between her eyebrows: "But if Dr. Johnson is right — if people have already discovered and said everything before us, then what's the point?"

"Perhaps because so much that is human is still alien to so many people."

"All wisecracks," scowls the Sorcerer's Apprentice, Larry Hakim. "Sometimes it's proper that some things human are alien to some people. Being reactionary is also a human quality, but — "

"Right, Hakim," I interrupt the disciple. "But, as you very well know, truth is a dialectical process. Once they asked Evelyn Waugh if a good artist can be a reactionary — "

"Another wisecrack?"

"Haven't you noticed that all good wisecracks are based on dialec-

tics?" I say. "They are. And Waugh replied: 'An artist *must* be a reactionary. He has to stand out against the tenor of the age and not go flopping
along; he must offer some little opposition.' Some little opposition,
Hakim...."

And while they were scattering them literally to all the corners of the
earth, except to the East whence they had driven them out, Allen, on his
farm in Pear Valley, was making songs from the poems of William Blake,
picking out the melody with one finger on his harmonium. I arrived there
one evening. Allen came out and gave me a moist kiss. Seated on a pile of
straw, I described what had happened that time after they expelled him. A
joint was making the rounds, soon to become a soggy butt. It was passed to
me by a young fellow with an endlessly blank stare in his eyes, who looked
like Charles Manson; the young fellow had received it from a girl who was
the embodiment of that hackneyed phrase – she moved as if in a dream; she,
in turn, from a pale man with rolled-up sleeves whose forearms were oddly
puffed up; he from a young woman in a stiff rural shirt with large, drooping
breasts hanging down around her waist, and a tittering five-year-old girl
peering out from under her skirt; she had taken it from a man who didn't
touch the joint, but merely passed it to her from Allen. The sun shone
warmly through the mist rising from the stooks of hay; the countryside of
Upper New York State fell away into the distance in a series of theatrical
stage flats just as it does in Central Bohemia. Two dogs followed by a baby
pig chased each other around the mounds of hay and the piglet tried to imitate everything the dogs did; it even tried to bark. That evening the woman
with the large breasts cooked goulash made of grass and purée of hay. A
large stereo tape-recorder stood behind the harmonium broadcasting
Allen's songs (later they became hits and the money from them flowed back
into this phalanstery); men, women and children of all four sexes, Allen told
me, shared a common bedroom, but I could choose: either I could sleep
with them or they would erect a tent for me. I chose the tent. Over the herbal
purée they sang the wonders and delights of the simple, bucolic life – somewhere a toilet was exuding a foul stench, far worse than the can at the
Messerschmitt factory – the rustic beauties of farming, the gentleness of cattle, the glory of self-sufficiency – and Heinz ketchup was the only edible
thing with the grass goulash – while the girl moving as if in a dream spoke to
Allen in Patagonian. It's her inner, private language, said Allen, no one else
understands it but her, and so you can say anything, any words, she will
understand them, and he said, "*Es kuta malabhad al nekreysol*," and the
girl understood, her comely pale face glowed with a smile. It was transparent. She was scarcely twenty. She went about in a long sack-like dress on
which she had sewn incomprehensible, disfigured cabbalistic signs. Her

father's a lawyer in Tucson, said Allen, but she left home and lives here with us. I can't tell you how much I enjoy this life on my farm. In the night, towards morning, a storm broke and rain seeped into the tent. I was angry. Should I sleep in the kitchen? That awful stench from the can. We have a flush toilet but we only flush once a day, Allen had said, because there's a shortage of water here. So if you have to go, don't flush it. I went in the woods. A light shone through the soaked canvas. Someone scratched at the flap. Four o'clock in the morning. Are you okay? Allen's kind voice. I'm okay except I'm wet. Come on, it's dry in the shed. We went. There was a rustic shed by the barn, under its roof a mound of rotting manure and hay. Allen lit a joint and it passed back and forth between us, soggy and covered with spittle. We looked towards the eastern horizon where a strip of pale blue light was beginning to pry its way through the rain and watched as a white band appeared beneath a blackened raincloud, the rising of the sun. I'm so happy here, said Allen, so happy that I feel selfish. While people are dying in Vietnam and in workcamps, here I am living the good life. The soggy joint burned down, he lit another, rays of sunlight extinguished the rain, and the morning mist began to rise from the manure pile, from the mounds of hay, from the meadow, the stench from the toilet exploded forcefully into the air, and it seemed to me that I was dreaming a dream, my bladder full, about a shithouse all choked up with shit, pissed upon, fecalized until it could hold no more, and suddenly I felt as though Allen were unabashedly enthroned on an enormous shithouse world, and meditating thus: You see? America! Isn't it marvellous? Isn't it marvellous when you get rid of the thin skin of idiot civilization? I always think to myself that the general idea of revolution against American idiocy is good and I guess it's a good thing, like in Cuba, and obviously Vietnam. But what's gonna follow? – the dogmatism that follows is a big drag. And everyone apologizes for the dogmatism by saying, well, it's an inevitable consequence of the struggle against American repression. And that may be true too, meditated Allen on his enormous shithouse of the West. The sun was already high in the sky, the farmers of Pear Valley were still dreaming their drug dreams, a cow mooed desperately in the barn, a goat bleated anxiously, the piglet stood helplessly in front of the closed barn doors and tried to moo, bleat, open the doors, and then simply oinked and ran playfully off after both dogs who were chasing a butterfly. That may be true, Allen, yes, except for the fact that in my little country over there, there was no American repression, and all the same dogmatism came, and it was terrible, you're right, we even had the gallows, you kind, considerate king of the shithouse in Upper New York State. A writer must be a reactionary ... offer some little opposition. The first farmer staggered out of his farmhouse, a pony-tail of hair hanging down his back; he stretched, yawned, listened to the cow mooing in the barn, picked a shit-caked bucket out of the manure pile and disappeared into the barn. The cow set up a terrible racket, the little pig scurried out squealing and wealing and a while later the farmer emerged spattered from head to foot with milk. And out of the farmhouse, as in a dream, came the girl in the sack, *O hare maranthula kerguethule kramvluelez....*

•

*March 2, 1944*
*Cerna Hora*

*My dear Dan,*
*I take the pleasure of writing you these few lines, hoping they will find you as they leave me enjoying the blessing of good health at the present. I'm thinking about you all the time and I don't want you thinking I told Franta, it was the foreman Vachousek who told him not me and he got angry and said you was iresponsable and it didn't make any differents when I told him it was me put you up to it in the first place to get revenge for killing Dad. I kept on at Franta all day but he seen you that afternoon with a young lady and he come into the room and said just look at him dragging you into this mess and now he's carrying on with some peace of fluff like nothing was happening. And it didn't make any differents even when I told him the foreman (Vachousek) said the danger was probably over when Yplt never did nothing about it and he said it don't make any differents and he walked up and down the room then he went down to Machane's for salt and seen you again with that young lady and that was what did it and I couldn't hold him back. I was feeling very poorly in bed with a fever so Franta made me tea then he said he was going out to take the air and walk his anger off. When he come back he was all upset and kept saying I think I killed him! I think I killed him! I was frightened but I was so weak I couldn't even get out of bed but I sent Franta to Uncle Venhoda to find out and Franta kept saying I'll turn myself in! I'll turn myself in! So I told him to go to Uncle Venhoda's first and tele-phone from Jirasek's Chalay down to the Hospital because you'd probably be there and I was afraid for you in case Franta really did kill you. He's strong and he can hurt people without even wanting to. And he was angry at you but otherwise he likes you and he always asks what we talk about all the time and so I told him how you told me about the Soler System and how the nearest star is about 300,000 years away and so he said do you think you'd come for coffee some day if he asked you. Of course that was before the Foreman (Vachousek)*

told him all that stuff. Then he got angry with you. A great weight fell
off my mind when Uncle Venhoda telephoned the hospital and they
said you was alive and only hurt a bit and Franta still wanted to go and
turn himself in but I said he'd just cause all sorts of extra trouble even
to you because they'd want to know how come he beat you up and
what would he tell them? I was also afraid if he turned himself in folks
would talk it up and Franta might get to know about us and then he
might even really kill you even if he only wanted to give you a hiding.
So I told him its better no one knows who did it and all you have to do
is go to him and tell him your sorry because he's clever and he'll know
you didn't mean no harm that you was only mad at him. But he kept
on with it and finally he said, You're such a saint and I'm a hot-
tempered man but I know anger's a sin so I'll go, but I can't go till the
day after tomorrow, because tomorrow I'll have to work days instead
of nights, so I can go to the hospital in the afternoon cause evenings
they don't let you in. So now he's off at the morning shift and I'll give
this letter to Manka Krpatova she's my friend and I know she'll see
who the letters to but she won't tell Franta. She's never told him nothing about me and I never told Olda nothing either (about her). She
knows that when a girls young she has to kick up her heels while she
can then she gets married, children come and other troubles, I know its
a sin but when I'm so fond of you, dear Dan, and before the wedding
I'll confess and then I'll stay faithful to Franta he's very kind and not
hard-harted at all he really only did it because he was angry. If I could I
don't know what I'd give to be able to visit you in the hospital but I'm
still in bed and weak with a fever. I'm taking pills and so I'm getting
better again and maybe I'll see you again if you want to as I do.

To conclude my letter please accept my warmest wishes,

Yours,
Nadia Jirouskova

•

Veronika told me about it.

She was not aware that he was standing over her. With the earphones
on her head she was aboard a train bound for disaster and so what? In
Milan's apartment in Toronto she was back in Prague, at home in her little
room behind the kitchen with its window onto the small courtyard, listening, until she heard Milan speak behind her. She couldn't understand him
with the earphones on, so she took them off. He said, "So you are crazy
about music, Nika?" He stood over her, swaying slightly. He was drunk.

"What did you say?"

"That – that it's nice looking at you there – listening to music...."

She looked around. The flat was empty except for a cloud of smoke near the ceiling, which was slowly sinking to the floor.

"Oh, dear! Has everyone gone home? Where's Barb? I thought she was staying with you."

"Barb?" Milan looked around sheepishly. "That's odd. Maybe she's in the bedroom."

She stood up and went to the bedroom door. Milan lurched after her. The bedroom was empty. She turned around, and it struck her that something had changed. In the frame where there had been a large blow-up of Barb's face at the beginning of the party, there was now an equally large blow-up of Suzi Kajetanova. A note was pinned to her lips, and torn paper dangled from the frame, probably what was left of the original enlargement of Barbara which someone had obviously ripped out.

"Milan! You are a jerk!"

She stepped up to the frame and unpinned the note. She read it out loud: "Bye, bye, Bluebeard! Barb."

She looked at the portrait of Suzana Kajetanova. She was well informed about the Great Suzi's lovers, so as far as she knew, this had to be a platonic love affair from Milan's days as a rock fanatic in Prague. But Barb would have had no way of knowing that. Veronika lifted the torn blow-up and discovered that there were two – there had been one underneath it. She straightened the second one out and received a slight shock. The girl staring at her out of the blow-up was herself, although Milan had never had anything to do with her, just as he certainly had never had anything to do with Suzi. It was made from a snapshot that Percy had taken at another party. In the original picture, Milan had stood beside her; to make the blow-up he had cropped himself out, had her enlarged and then used it to cover up a part of the past called Suzi. The irrecoverable past. The bonehead, the platonic dunce! And finally, the present called Nika covered by the current Barbara. Veronika lifted Barbara's picture and stuck it back in the gold frame.

"Milan, you really are a Bluebeard."

"You think so?"

"You're the epitome of male chauvinism."

She pulled all three portraits out of the frame and rolled them into a tube.

"What're you doing that for?"

"Your true beloved ran away from you because of that exhibition, you fool."

Milan waved his hand and almost lost his balance. "Let her! Anyway, she was a bore. Just a dull, Canadian ... bore."

"And I suppose she saw you as the great entertainer?"

"How's a guy supposed to be enter-entertaining with a wet blanket like her?"

He stumbled, and she had to hold on to him to keep him from falling.

"Poor little Milan! So utterly misunderstood by those dull Canadian women!"

"They're all dreary old cows. They're all boring ... boring!" He squinted at Veronika and, following the rules of the game, added, "You're different from all the rest, Nika."

"That's what I call a talent for observation. But you put Barbie's picture over mine. How come?"

"I – I was mad.... When you fell for that little drip of a Canadian – "

"And you only left Suzi underneath me in case I decided to hang on to my Canadian drip?"

A drunken attempt to embrace Veronika.

"Nika! I love you. From the very first.... It's just that ... I never got round to – to telling you before."

"And what about Suzi?"

"That was just long-distance love."

"And Barb? She a long-distance love too?"

"Well, not exactly – "

"So clear out and find her."

That made Milan angry. He wanted to say something, but he seemed to be having difficulty. "F-f-f-...."

"What?"

"Fuck Barbie!" he finally exploded.

Veronika raised an eyebrow.

"You'd better, buddy!" she said.

Then Milan fell flat on his nose. Veronika watched him for a while struggling unsuccessfully to get back on his feet.

"You really are drunk as a loon."

There followed a brief, uneven struggle between a sober girl and a drunken fellow who shared the common goal of getting the other into bed, each for a different reason. The girl won.

She returned to the living room and looked at her watch. Just two. She was in no mood to go home alone at night. Though young, she was an experienced veteran of many a Prague party where both party-exhausted sexes would lie strewn about on the floor, the couches, the carpets, sleeping together like logs, without it necessarily resulting in either collective or individual love-making. She yawned, went into the bathroom, and found Milan's bathrobe. She undressed, put the bathrobe on, went back into the living room, listened to Milan's saw-like snores emanating from the bedroom, threw her clothes over a chair and lay down on the couch in the bathrobe. The room was overheated, so she didn't need a blanket.

And because she was young and tormented by nostalgia, she fell asleep the instant she put her head down, and she heard nothing when, ten minutes later, someone unlocked the front door. Someone heard the loud snoring and stopped in the doorway. The moon was streaming in the window and its light fell on Veronika's unmistakably feminine clothes draped over the chair. Someone stood motionless for a while, and then whispered, "You really are a Bluebeard, you son of a bitch!" turned around and quietly closed the door.

Veronika slept soundly, dreaming of trains.

●

Compared to what it was in the ancient, gilded age, my fame has shrunk to about a twentieth of its original magnitude, reckoned by the number of books I sell. But because the Party, in its infinite wisdom, has transformed me from a rare bird into forbidden fruit, that miserable one-twentieth is enough to make my countrymen drive their Datsuns and their Pontiacs from far and wide in this vast, snowbound land to take their places in a lecture hall at the local university (there is at least one university in even the most snowbound outpost in the country), to listen to the latest gossip from Prague and hear my comments on contemporary literary works from the old country. There is no end to the sources of gossip. Some of it even comes from diplomatic sources, and it makes for quite a cabaret. As I see it, all the contemporary prose works coming out of Prague appear as the outpourings of people suffering from clinical dysfunction of the intellect. At the same time I have discovered two things I was not aware of at home. The first is that literary criticism is a rather simple, very amusing trade, and how right Hemingway was when he said, "Look, if you can't write, why don't you learn to write criticism? Then you can always write. You won't ever have to worry about it not coming nor being mute and silent. People will read it and respect it...." The second is that stiff literary censorship can trim even the greatest of the great down to official size. In our present age of normalization, however, we have come a long way from those wooden cowboy stories from the age of socialist construction, and those clipped geniuses, though the *forms* have been reduced, now have control of their pens, and no longer simply splatter ink all over the page. They have some slight knowledge of the West, they are aware of the techniques of a craft which, before they were trimmed down to size, they had hoped would "render the highest kind of justice to the visible universe, by bringing to light the truth, manifold and one, underlaying its every aspect." Cut, trimmed and pruned back, they abuse these same techniques to render invisible the tricks they play on the visible universe, so that they may bring to light those limited, isolated aspects of truth through which they heap flattery on the worldly powers that be. In such a world, writing serious literature means writing rubbish; and writing rubbish means writing serious literature. "If ... conditions are such that a writer cannot publish the truth ... he should write and not publish. If he cannot make a living without publishing he can work at something else." Hemingway again. Under such circumstances, therefore, a writer is left with that holy trinity of possibilities: making a living at something else and writing for his desk drawer; writing for children; or writing rubbish. Writing serious work (and under these circumstances it can only mean writing rubbish) is the only betrayal of his country (and his art) that a writer can commit.

Thus I sermonize unmarxistleninistically to the public gathered in a lecture hall at McMahon University. Not all of them understand me, that much is clear. Some of them left Czechoslovakia at a time when literature was not yet important, because it was not a threat to the state, because the state was not that kind of state. They listen politely, but my gibberish from the era of the construction and the final destruction of socialism is remote from their experience and perhaps incomprehensible. Our batracho-myomachian battles for the right to place a male hand on a naked female breast on the printed page do not excite them. And why should they? These are really just cabaret sketches aborted by the terrible midwife of those times, the gallows. It is madness degenerated into mere imbecility.

Here and there, however, among these politely attentive countrymen, there sits a girl – they are mostly girls; women always love literature more than men and the exceptions only prove the rule – who is genuinely excited because I know all about things which no one really needs to know anything about, about a city called *Praga Normalisata*. No one? These girls need to know. For you see, I also know about their real country, the one they carry in their hearts, about the light that seems to shine only in dictatorships, for in democracies it is outdone by the glare of glossy magazines. The real religion of life, the true idolatry of literature, can never flourish in democracies, in those vague, boring kingdoms of the freedom not to read, not to suffer, not to desire, not to know, not to understand. They fasten their eyes on me, these Veronikas driven out of paradise, they devour my stories of the ephemeral heroes of pre-Dubcek fame, and of literary prostitution under conditions of normalization. Paradise is not something objective but a product of subjective circumstances and conditions; its saints are time and Epictetus. It is a product of tender youth, of whatever one associates with it. With hungry desire in their eyes, they listen, these Veronikas, to my good-natured (it is not in my nature to be self-righteous, to reproach or to hate – thus did the Almighty make me) lampooning of new works by old heroes whom they once read (and still read; they have their books sent here), about which they debated in those classic bull sessions, over Gamza, Oran and Georgian brandy, books for which they lined up from daybreak in queues utterly unknown in these longitudes, first in the street and then inside the store so that they could have the books autographed by some master of the pen, serenely smoking a large cigar – perhaps even with a dedication, if the Master would be so kind: my name is Veronika. And how could the master refuse? All masters are fond of women.

I won't tell them that even literature becomes a whore, for in conditions of normalization everything and everyone becomes a whore, and out of solidarity the whore is forgiven. I won't tell them how with historical training a prostitute becomes subtle and genteel, and when the circumstances of an age fall out of memory she appears like a virgin bride. And the work remains, the conditions it was written in pass away, dirty hands become dust – only the work remains. I won't tell them that. But will any work remain? I won't be able to tell them that.

When the cabaret is over, they come up to me just as they used to over there, and I smoke a large cigar, that phallic symbol of serenity. The Veronikas are seven or eight years older, but lovely as ever in the intensity of their love for the literature and the country that we bear in our hearts alone, a love which can be neither beaten down nor taken away. They give me the books for autographing, books that come now from the workshop of the former singer Mrs. Santner who, amid the smoke of many cigarettes, typesets them herself. But here and there older editions appear, editions printed in paradise, brought with them to this desert island. Falling apart, spattered with wine, they have been read over and over again, my only literary awards. And they say, I once spoke to you in Trebic, do you remember? But you probably don't remember me. I am ashamed to say I can't remember. The puppet in the pulpit is conspicuous and even the most stunning Veronika is lost in the crowd and vanishes from the puppet's eyes and memory – until she surfaces once more, like an ornamental jewel, on the other side of the ocean, in the middle of the bee-heavy Manitoba prairie, on Fisherman's Wharf in San Francisco, on the plains of Colorado – the Veronikas, everywhere, exorcizers of Orwellian nightmares, of the inconsolable pan-prostitution that accompanies the establishment of Communism ... those sinful saints....

Thus do sentimental thoughts chase themselves around my head. I recall them again in the house of Professor Abraham, an agent – according to revelations from high places in Prague – of, simultaneously, the Gestapo, the CIA, and probably the Japanese intelligence service as well. In reality he is an expert on capricorn beetles.

•

"I was somewhat taken aback," says Dr. Toth, the freshest of the exiles, having arrived only last year. "A day after I got back to Prague from England I was scanning *Rude Pravo,* as I do each morning, and the leading article caught my eye because it had a rather unusual headline. Now the headlines for leading articles, as you certainly know, are something rather ritualistic, petrified. It is always, 'For the better fulfilment of,' or 'For a higher crop yield,' or 'Against' – against intervention, against non-intervention, against the wrong type of intervention. This petrified formula signifies lack of content, that is to say, it promises boredom. This leading article, however, was called 'The Story of a Traitor,' which signified concreteness, that is to say, it promised potential entertainment. Who are they going to tar and feather now? I thought to myself. And one always hopes one knows the person because the process of tarring and feathering is most interesting when it happens to someone you know. So I put my glasses on and I read: 'Our society gave the doctor everything he needed, and often things he did not need, but merely wanted. And yet, despite this, the doctor started down the road to treason. Last week in London, where he was sent by our government to attend a conference on electronic technology, he declared to the capitalist press that he would not return to Czechoslovakia. As a reward for such treason, a cosy place, naturally, was waiting for him at Leeds University where he has already begun lecturing.' I stopped reading there. There was something both familiar and unfamiliar about the story. Because, you see, I too had been at that self-same conference in London and had just returned home but there had been another Czech there and if one of us had committed treason it had entirely escaped my notice. So I read it over again from the beginning: 'Our society gave the doctor ... on electronic technology ... last week in London....' Everything fit, except that I could not bring myself to believe I had overlooked a third Czech delegate. In any case, that would even have been technically impossible, for we were required to meet each evening with the head of the Soviet delegation, to give him a report and receive instructions for the following day, and I did this in London, precisely according to instructions. But I was always alone with the comrade; no other delegate went there with me. So I read further. As you know from experience, the art of editorial tarring and feathering consists of a general first paragraph, usually followed by a second paragraph which is specific. So I read on, but contrary to good custom, the second paragraph too was abstract. It merely fleshed out the homily on the theme of everything our society had given to the doctor and what the doctor had given back to our society. Once again it struck me as both familiar and unfamiliar. It was also boring. I jumped ahead to the final sentence of the editorial, and my vision went dark and spotty ... I read it again, and a third time, looked into the mirror, then went and read the sentence a fourth time. If I had not forgotten how to read altogether, the sentence was quite clear and it ran: 'And thus did Dr. Ctibor Toth, from the State Institute for Research in Electronic Technology in Prague, become a traitor.' I reasoned in the following way: in the State Institute for Research in Electronic Technology there is only one Doctor Ctibor Toth. Me. This Toth was in London last week at an international conference on electronic technology. According to *Rude Pravo* he remained there and committed an act of treason. I, however, am sitting in my office in Prague and reading about myself, who, according to the paper, am lecturing at Leeds at that very moment. This is not amnesia; it's geophysical schizophrenia. But because I am a very real and realistic man a third possibility occurred to me. Someone had falsely informed the editor of *Rude Pravo*."

"Or the editor of *Rude Pravo* made it up himself!" thunders a man resembling a ball of flesh, who is sitting at the opposite end of the table stuffing himself with canapés.

"That was another possibility, yes. The question, however, was why?" Dr. Toth looks foxily at the spherical man. "Please realize, sir, that as a fully screened specialist and non-Party member, I was a highly valued person. I, sir, just like you, *timeo communistes et dona ferentes,* but unlike you, I had never got mixed up in anything. I hung my flags out and decorated my windows with portraits of the statesmen *du jour.* Thus I was of use to them no matter what the general line happened to be; no one need fear that I might be an embarrassment or a source of trouble should they recommend me for whatever job or function needed doing or filling. And suddenly – this public execution. It was illogical."

"It's pointless to expect logic of the Bolsheviks!" snorts the rotund man.

"I'm afraid you're wrong, sir. True, there are, as you say, many things it is pointless to expect of the Bolsheviks – as you call them: truthfulness, morality, decency. But logical, that they are. They are even logical in all their illogicality. Even these, these illogicalities, are useful to them, and thus they are, in that sense, logical. No, no. There must have been some rational explanation for the editorial. The question was, what?"

"Had they mixed you up with someone else?" asks Professor Abraham.

Dr. Toth shrugs his shoulders. "I stuck *Rude Pravo* into my pocket and was about to walk out when who should come into my office – and on tiptoe, like a conspirator – but my secretary. 'Dr. Toth,' she whispered. 'It was unwise of you to come back! Do you need somewhere to hide? And you'd better leave by the back way and not go past the hall-porter. Novotny's working for State Security.' Novotny, you should understand, was our hall-porter, not the former President. But I only waved my hand and said there'd been some mistake that could be explained. She greeted this, I must say, with extreme skepticism."

"Smart woman!" roars the rotund man. Dr. Toth laughs.

"In the *Rude Pravo* building I had my identity card checked by two gunmen, but my name did not surprise them. Perhaps they don't read *Rude Pravo*. Thus I easily gained access to the editor who had signed the article, and without a word I showed him my citizen's identification card. He looked at it and said, 'Sit down, Comrade Doctor. What can I do for you?' I thought perhaps he might not even read his own leading articles, so I pulled the *Rude Pravo* out of my pocket, pointed to the place and said distinctly: 'I am this Dr. Toth!' The man was somewhat taken aback. He rubbed his cheeks and read a little of the editorial, then it seemed to me that he sighed with relief. He said, 'Aha, I have nothing to do with this, Comrade Doctor. This came from the Ministry. I only put it in this particular issue of the paper. If you have a query about it, you'll have to go to Interior.'"

Dr. Toth falls silent and the rotund man thunders, "You should have lambasted him one, the Bolshevik swine!"

"Perhaps," allows Dr. Toth. "On the one hand, however, I am a peaceful man and on the other hand the thing interested me more intellectually than it did emotionally. Also I will admit that his reference to the Ministry of the Interior made me rather nervous. You see, it confirmed my suspicion that this was not just some editorial error, but that the whole thing was part of a higher plan. Therefore I was extremely chary when, after a somewhat exhausting march along many corridors of the Ministry headquarters on Letna, I was shown in to the official whose pen — and I did not know yet whether his head was involved as well — had spawned the article. His name was Sedlacek."

"I'll bet it was!" retorts the rotund man.

"That, at least, was the name he gave. He heard me out, frowned somewhat, thought for a while, and then the telephone on his desk rang. He picked it up, put it to his ear, said nothing, hung up and asked me to repeat everything."

"The tape recorders buggered up on them!"

"So I repeated everything, and once more he listened to me silently. He acknowledged that since I was in Prague and not London there might have been a mistake. I corrected him and said that there most *certainly* had been a mistake and he admitted this. But how could such a mistake have occurred at all, I asked him. He replied that the mistake had taken place in London because they had received the news from the embassy there, and that the matter would be looked into. Would he print a retraction in *Rude Pravo*, I wanted to know."

The rotund man splutters.

"Exactly," says Dr. Toth. "For a while I had the distinct impression he was going to ask me to repeat everything once more, because he remained silent for a long time. Finally he said, 'Look at it this way, Comrade. The few people who know you personally will certainly realize it's not true that you're a traitor, and those who don't know you and read the editorial — well, it might have an edifying effect on them. Listen to this' — and he began to quote sentences from the second paragraph of the editorial, the homily: 'Although the doctor was of upper-middle-class origin, our people gave him their full confidence and made it possible for him to study at the university.' I interrupted him here and made bold to point out that here too the data was imprecise. My father had a small greengrocer's shop with no employees so that he died from overwork at the age of forty-six and because he was classified as bourgeoisie I was not accepted at the technical school and therefore had to apprentice as a practical electrician and study engineering at night, and I got my doctorate at night school as well. He interrupted me and said that as an edifying example it was more emphatic the way he had put it and the end justifies the means. Apparently Lenin said that. 'But what will the people who know me think? Won't it be obvious to them that the article contains erroneous information?' I shouldn't have asked. He looked at me and he looked at the article and suddenly it was as if a kind of direct rapport had materialized between us. Ladies and gentlemen, I felt most strongly at that moment that he would have much preferred to have me in Leeds and that in fact it was sheer arrogance on my part not to be there. I began to be afraid, but I wasn't quite sure yet of what."

"The man was right," says the host. "Your very presence in Prague was an affront to the reliability, if not the truthfulness, of the Party press."

"You were a living provocation, man!" roars the rotund man. His laughter is infectious, a chain reaction in a nuclear rocket dump.

"You're right," smiles Dr. Toth. "And what would you do, sir, if you were in Sedlacek's place?"

"I'd have you locked up till hell froze over!" cries the rotund man gleefully.

"Perhaps. However...," says Dr. Toth. "On the way from Letna back to the office I mulled it over. The whole thing reminded me of a detective story I once read called *Murder by Hypothesis*. A corpse is found, that of a certain lord. It is mutilated beyond recognition but identifiable by the clothes and the contents of the pockets. The detective pins the murder on a poor tenant-farmer who is condemned to death and hanged. Of course shortly thereafter another body is found and it too is identified as Lord

Brougham, this time incontrovertibly, by his fingerprints. In the end, the lord's younger brother, I think it is, determines that for reasons I've forgotten the lord had gone abroad incognito. The first corpse was someone else, and when the lord returned he had the misfortune to run into the detective who had 'successfully' solved his murder and been promoted. The detective then really did murder the lord to get him out of the way and save face. Well, on my way from Letna to the office, I began to wonder whether or not I might not be, to a certain extent, in the same boat as the twice-murdered lord. And very soon my suspicions began to take on substance."

"Did they arrest you?"

"No. They merely took away my service passport. Fortunately, however, their affairs are, shall we say, in some disarray. So they left me my private passport. On the other hand, they installed a new bugging device in my flat that was far more sophisticated than the old one. When I discovered it I began to be genuinely afraid."

Dr. Toth refreshes himself with a sip of coffee, glancing around Professor Abraham's room, which is dominated by President Masaryk on a beautifully painted horse and President Benes doffing his diplomat's homburg. I am intensely aware of how safe we are in Canada. There is almost certainly no microphone hidden in that hat, and no laser beams radiate from Masaryk's eyes.

"In time," continues Dr. Toth, "the fear became an obsession, a nightmare. I would wake up in the middle of the night, bathed in sweat. Once, in a dream, I called out for help so loudly that I woke up my neighbour. In those pre-fab high-rises you can hear everything through the walls. She knocked on my door insistently until I finally opened up and explained to her that I'd had a bad dream."

"Was she at least worth the sinning?" chortles the rotund man.

Dr. Toth strokes his moustache thoughtfully and says: "With your permission I'd prefer not to expand on that – you see, I'm now engaged to a certain young lady in London. But despite the tender understanding the nightmares persisted. I began to feel like a rat in a trap. I had almost given up all hope of salvation when I got a final desperate idea. I concluded that the disarray in their affairs – indicated by the fact that they had left me my private passport – was perhaps a faint source of hope, and therefore I applied, through Cedok Travel Bureau, to go on a skiing trip in the Austrian Alps. And believe it or not, they granted me my request without raising the slightest difficulties!"

"A bloody balls-up!" hoots the rotund man.

"That's one possibility," says Dr. Toth. "The second one is that Sedlacek found out about it and guessed why I wanted to go skiing in the Alps. As he certainly must have discovered from my records, I am an absolute non-skier. Besides, the people who were shadowing me must have reported that I was buying everything for the trip, because naturally I had no skiing outfit of my own. And perhaps Sedlacek decided that would be the simplest solution. It would make the editorial essentially true without making it necessary to liquidate the mistake physically in Prague, even if it was physically impossible to prove in Leeds. In short, one fine day two months ago I was standing in a brand-new skiing outfit with a brand-new set of skis and equipment in front of the Cedok Travel Bureau waiting for the coach to come and pick us up."

•

I found an empty compartment and eagerly fell to reading the newspaper. The article was on page two. JUST PUNISHMENT FOR ANTI-STATE GROUP. The train jerked into motion, the lights of Wilson Station began to slide past the window and I read breathlessly. A metallic strip of sky appeared over Kobylisy reflecting coldly from the dome of the Liben gasometer. I read of inveterate enemies, of the treacherous plots by seditionaries, and of the capture of a gang of reactionaries. It was my first encounter with the vocabulary of the new age. It was the autumn of Year One and at the head of the list stood *Premysl Skocdopole*. Seven names followed and right at the end stood *Josef Benda, for aiding and abetting*. They were arranged according to the length of their sentences. Prema's name was followed by the remark *in absentia*. I read the biography, the obituary, the lexicon entry on my old mate from the main streets of Kostelec, my fellow gangster from the tobacco warehouse, that hero who brought about the death of seven innocent people, that nomad of romantic longing. Three men entered the compartment and began talking about something but I ignored them and read on, read how the traitor Skocdopole had run away to a hostile foreign land to escape his hard but just punishment. In Year One the term "hard but just" meant four years in prison; two years later, it meant the gallows. The men on the seat opposite were talking quietly together while I read that somewhat distorted biography. How he came from the family of a legionnaire decorated with bourgeois and imperialist medals for murdering Bolsheviks. How during the occupation he became instrumental in establishing a bourgeois so-called resistance group (this was also my first encounter with the very particular semantics of that expression "so-called") which, however, was less concerned with struggling against the Nazi occupiers than with conserving its strength for the post-war situation in order to play a role in re-establishing bourgeois rule. After the war, the document went on, this traitorous group (in my anger the anachronism in the adjective escaped me; later we all simply got used to it) continued to meet, and immediately after the People's February Victory it resumed its anti-state activity (nor did the inappropriateness of the verb occur to me in my excitement). They set up a printing press in Skocdopole's flat for the production of warmongering handbills, the remains of which were found in a stove belonging to Vahar, also sentenced, who had tried to destroy them. Rather than accepting the responsibility for his traitorous activity like a man, Skocdopole chose a cowardly flight from his country. Vahar also tried to escape, but he was caught by the organs of State Security and remanded in custody. In a house search, the organs found a large number of incriminating documents, among them a complete list of all members of the terrorist band.

I stopped reading. Fortunately Vahar had not written my name down. Had he been more thorough about it, he could have radically altered my life. I looked out the window at the late-afternoon countryside sliding by, at the tree-lined roads and the small silent prewar cars puttering along, at an old-fashioned farmer driving two tired cows harnessed to a haywagon out of the field. But in my mind, Prema was just getting up from a table where a map lay spread out, his face with its Mongolian cheekbones grave, the room dark because the blackout blinds left over from the war were drawn. A train timetable lay beside the map. The plan was simple and as far as we could tell a good one. Trains were still running to Germany and the uncle confirmed Mr. Skocdopole's guess that on the day of President Benes' funeral they would pull all units of the border guard into Prague for extra security. About a kilometre this side of the border there is an up-grade and the train slows down. Prema would jump out and go the rest of the way across the unguarded border on foot. It would be two in the morning. We sat looking at the timetable in the cousin's flat. There was an old radio on the cupboard with a nostalgically preserved card on one of the knobs, also from the days of the protectorate, warning that listening to foreign radio stations was punishable, in extreme cases, by death; it was on now so the neighbours couldn't hear what was being said. But at last there was nothing more to say. I stood up, so did Prema, I offered him my hand and everything he had done came back to me in a flash: the burning warehouse, the radio transmitter – so successfully liquidated with the help of the one-armed legionnaire that the state police had no idea of its existence, otherwise they would certainly have mentioned it in this article instead of the rather unsensational duplicating machine which they had transmogrified for effect into a printing-press. After our liberation, however, Prema had not reported his part in the spectacular destruction of the gasoline warehouse; I had kept quiet about it and so had Dr. Labsky. A great historical silence surrounded Prema. He would go down in the history of Kostelec as an incorrigible traitor, a congenital murderer and a seditionary. I looked into his narrow Mongolian eyes, doubtless inherited from some ancient Tartar warrior on horseback who had raped one of his great-great-great-great-grandmothers. "Well, so long, and good luck," I said. "*Ahoj*," Prema said. And so we parted for ever. In the doorway I turned around for a last look. Prema stood in a cone of yellow light, studying the map and the timetable, thin, muscular, in a dirty shirt. Hero, traitor, friend. I turned and walked out of the cousin's flat.

I raised my eyes from the newspaper. One of the men on the bench opposite was staring at me. It was Uher – black hair, round face, ruddy complexion. Looking like a farmer.

"Hi," I said.

"Hello," said Uher, and he glanced at his two colleagues. There was something not quite right about him, but I didn't know what it was, nor did I know what to talk to him about. I hadn't seen him since we'd met that time in the church. Then I realized what was wrong. He wasn't wearing a clerical collar.

"Well, how are things?" I asked. "Have you got a parish?"

He made a face that was almost a frown. "I gave all that up right after the war. Didn't you know?"

I was surprised. "Why'd you give it up?"

He scowled, then grinned mockingly. "Look, I was in the seminary for the same reasons you wanted to go there. I wanted to get out of conscripted labour."

Again he glanced at his two companions, who were looking me over rather oddly. This was my first encounter with such looks. I didn't believe him. I remembered how he had knelt before the eternal flame in the freezing church and how I had deliberately knelt behind him on the cold stone floor in order to imitate Christ.

"But you were religious, weren't you?" I said.

"Me? Don't be silly!"

"Well, you used to go to church."

"As a novice I had to."

For some reason he irritated me. Perhaps I wanted to avenge myself for that embarrassing experience several years before, an experience I had only myself and cowardice to blame for.

"You used to go to church even when you didn't have to," I said. "Do you remember how we met there one night?"

But in saying this, I had put the ball right onto his racket. "Of course I do. But if you also remember, you were trying to convince me you wanted to go to the seminary. Are you in the seminary now?"

"No, I'm not!" I found I was trembling with anger. I began to dig at him. "I had a better reason for going into a seminary than you did. I committed sabotage in the factory along with a girl – Nadia Jirouskova – and we were caught." And then, God knows why, I added, "Prema Skocdopole was in on it too. When you refused to hide me in the seminary, he hid me in the Pejskar place. You knew him, didn't you?"

Uher turned red. "He was – "

"This is who he was!" Besides the anger, there was indignation in my voice. I didn't want to sound like that, but I couldn't help it. I pointed to the verdict in the newspaper and recited with heavy ridicule: "'the initiating member of a bourgeois so-called resistance group'! Isn't that great stuff?" I was almost shouting, possessed by a foolhardy animus. It was Year One and I was not yet familiar with all the dangers. "I happen to know that group. The only bourgeois in it was me, and I wasn't even a real member. I only knew about them."

Uher and his two colleagues exchanged very strange looks. Uher said, "That group was connected with the London government, and the London government was a bourgeois government."

"Who gives a shit about the London government!" I shot back, blinkered by political blindness. "Those kids were all workers. Skocdopole was never anything but a labourer. They booted him out of school because he refused to learn German. The language of the occupiers, remember? And it was a real resistance group, and not 'so-called'!"

I pushed back against the hard seat, trembling with anger. Something else, however, was finally oozing through the anger, something familiar. His companions were very odd indeed. They were eyeing me like two male sphinxes.

"If you knew the group," said Uher drily, "then you probably also know they were only playing games. All they ever did was cut a couple of private telephone lines. Some resistance. That's why it's 'so-called.'"

The new sensation filtering through my anger was overpowered by a fresh onslaught of indignation. "Skocdopole played games all right – with matches!" I shouted. "And he was so good at it a whole German warehouse full of gasoline went up in flames!"

The three of them stiffened. In a very queer tone, Uher said, "So that was Skocdopole?"

"You're damned right it was!"

"Do you have any witnesses?" said one of the companions sharply.

"Ask Dr. Labsky about it. He treated him because his arm got burned by gasoline. I arranged for Labsky to see him."

"Why didn't he claim it after the war?" asked Uher.

Why? I didn't really know. Perhaps because of the seven who had lost their lives as a result. But Prema hadn't claimed other things either.

"I suppose because he didn't want to make himself out to be a war hero like so many others," I said acidly, and I couldn't stop myself from adding, "he also wrecked a tank at Homole."

"That seems like a lot of heroic acts for one ordinary man!" the second colleague shot back, just as sharply.

"Only two," I said. "Otherwise, you're right, he only cut wires. But if blowing up a gasoline warehouse isn't resistance activity, then I don't know what is. Writing nasty leaflets about other resistance organizations? That was something he never did."

"He has now!" barked the second colleague. "But even back then he was getting ready to oppose the power of the people later on!"

Clearly they knew a great deal about the case of the Kostelec traitors. This thought chilled me. Even so I said, "I wouldn't know anything about that. He never said anything to me about it at the time. All I know is he did more damage to the Germans than anyone else in Kostelec."

"Do you know how many lives it cost?" put in Uher.

"I do. But in case you've forgotten, there was a war on."

I felt very uncomfortable. I realized what it was that was percolating through my anger, slowly snuffing it out. It was fear, my old friend.

"Just like the assassination of Heydrich," said one of the colleagues. "A typical, irresponsible bourgeois act of resistance." Here was some kind of scholar, I thought; in Year One, I had not yet met many brochure-educated scholars. "They sit around, safe and sound themselves, but a disproportionate number of civilians pay for it with their lives."

One last time, anger rose to drown out fear.

"Skocdopole *was* in danger," I said. "But it's true that instead of turning himself over to the Germans and accepting the responsibility for his terrorist activity like a man, he chose to hide like a coward."

They recognized the reference and drew in their breath. Uher narrowed his eyes. "Did you have any contact with him after the war?" he asked.

My instinct for self-preservation finally triumphed over my anger. I realized that like a fool I was manoeuvring myself into a position dangerously similar to the one that had once led me to ask this defrocked hypocrite for help.

"No. Right after the war he spent two years in the army and I've been in Prague since the war ended."

Uher didn't reply. His companions glared at me for a little while longer and then they began to discuss their own affairs again. They were talking about the Revolutionary Trades Union Movement. Very entertaining.

I left the compartment to go to the toilet, and on the way back I stopped in the narrow corridor and looked out the window. It was almost dark, and the train was passing through a deciduous wood. A yellow leaf stuck to the window right in front of my face. Uher appeared in the door of the compartment and started off towards the toilet as well. I held myself against the window to let him by; he squeezed past me, then stopped. I could tell he was hesitating. Obviously something left over from the seminary had won out inside him, for he said quietly, "Let me give you some good advice, Smiricky. Keep a closer watch on your mouth."

I looked into his eyes. I could not see much Christian love there. "This is no idyll we're living through," he added.

"So I see."

If there had been any Christian love there, the last traces had vanished. "And keep your sarcasm to yourself. You might end up paying for it."

He turned and lurched down the swaying train to the toilet. There was something about the way he looked from behind that spoke for itself. But it was nice of him to warn me. Leaves swirled outside the window, the train emerged from the wood, and a red strip of sky was reflected in a pond, making it glow as though it were full of blood.

He was religious once, no matter what he said. I remembered how he had knelt down there in the night in front of the eternal flame and prayed. On a weekday. In Kostelec. And the seminary was in Hradec. He was lying when he said he was never religious. He was.

●

"It was a very odd skiing trip, very odd indeed," says Dr. Toth. "There were only three men, all the rest were ladies. And I was the youngest of the lot. To be more precise, it was a skiing trip for old-age pensioners. I don't think there was a single woman there under seventy-five. But they all had skis, oh yes, even though they were wearing dresses that left their varicose veins exposed. Some of them even had grandchildren along to carry their skis for them, and one of them was suffering from Parkinson's disease. We had to help her into the coach and I put her skis in the luggage compartment myself. Every one of them had paid in advance for two weeks of skiing instruction in the Alps, including use of the ski-jump."

The rotund man laughs thunderously.

"It was a very specific form of socialist emigration," says Dr. Toth with a smile. "All of them, with the exception of one lady and the two old men, one of whom was eighty-two, were going to Austria. Their children had come to the border to meet them, in one case from as far away as New Guinea. The children picked them up at the customs house on the Austrian side of the frontier so the coach went on empty except for myself and one old lady whose brother was waiting for her at Linz. She cried all the way there. Originally she and her husband had intended to flee the country together but the day before the trip he had fallen seriously ill and she wept because she now had to return to Czechoslovakia and she knew she would never see her brother again. She was seventy-eight and they had spent every penny of their savings, and even sold their furniture to buy ski equipment and pay for the course. She would be ninety-eight and her husband a hundred and five before they could save up for another trip like that, she sobbed. But I'm getting ahead of myself," says Dr. Toth. "On the way to the frontier, I had a growing feeling, a premonition, you might say, that there was something I ought to do. I didn't realize what it was until we got to Tabor, where there was a lunch stop. Then it hit me. I went into the bathroom and tore all the names and addresses of friends in the West out of my notebook. Among them was the address of a young lady who was to play a particularly decisive role in my story, and still does. My premonition turned out to be correct. The Czech border police searched us so thoroughly that they even took the ski-poles apart and in certain select cases they carried out what they call a complete body-search. There are ladies present, so I won't go into details. After the search, they sent a man and woman – husband and wife – back to Prague. They had tried to smuggle out a family photograph in a gold-plated antique frame for which they had no customs clearance papers. You can imagine the scene that caused!"

"Skinning them alive is too good for them!" roars the rotund man.

"They also went through my notebook very carefully," Dr. Toth goes on, "but they discovered nothing amiss. So I found myself happily on the other side of the border, where all those children were waiting. Once again, you can imagine the scene that ensued when the children of that dishonourable couple discovered what had happened. They had come all the way from Ecuador to pick them up."

"Cut off their balls, fry them and force them down their throats!" roars the rotund man, disregarding the ladies present. The entomologist's wife shakes her head sadly and Dr. Toth, with dignity, takes a sip of coffee.

"And you went straight to England, did you?" asks the hostess.

"Not right away," says the doctor. "I went to the ski resort in the Alps and from there I telephoned my fiancée and invited her to join me. It seemed silly to let two wonderful prepaid weeks in the mountains go to waste. So Wilma came and we spent there what I might call our pre-honeymoon."

"You old dog, you," thunders the rotund man. "And did you practise the *Geländesprung* with her?" He guffaws. "I mean on the slopes, of course."

"I didn't," smiles Dr. Toth. "I scarcely managed to learn the snowplough. On the other hand, Wilma and I did unravel the mystery."

"What mystery?" asks the hostess.

"Of that lead article in *Rude Pravo,* the one that caused all the trouble," says Dr. Toth. "The false report of my defection was sent to Prague by the cultural attaché in our London embassy, a man called Cehyna. You may ask why. Well, the reason was a classic one. He was jealous of me. He had made an unsuccessful effort to win Wilma's hand; he got nowhere so he tried at least to stop me."

"But what could he have been thinking of?" asks Professor Abraham. "After all, he knew the report was false...."

Dr. Toth nods his head. "He knew his cohorts well. The good fellow came to the same conclusion that I did in the end: my presence in Prague would contradict the report in *Rude Pravo* and the party would resolve the contradiction not by publishing a retraction in the press but simply by liquidating that presence in Prague. In short, he thought they would do me in, or at least put me on ice, as the saying goes."

We express amazement, but Mrs. Abraham asks the question we all have on our lips: "How did you get to know all that? Did this Cehyna confide in Wilma...?"

Dr. Toth shakes his head. "Deduction, madame. Fact number one: Cehyna was in love with Wilma and she did reject him. Fact number two: as soon as the editorial appeared in *Rude Pravo,* Cehyna applied for political asylum in England. Fact number three: Sedlacek told me at the Ministry of the Interior that the report of my treason came from the London embassy. Conclusion: Cehyna sent the report with the intention of ruining me, and saving himself by defecting."

For a moment, we are all speechless. Then the rotund man explodes in a general damnation of Bolshevism, moving on to a particular damnation of everything related to it, all at a voice-level of several hundred decibels. He even includes in his attack countrymen who send money back to the Bolshevik homeland. The hostess defends the practice: she has recently sent over some money to allow her cousin's sick daughter to buy Swiss medicine. The rotund man declares that he would rather let his own mother croak than add a single penny to Bolshevik coffers. To change the subject, the entomologist begins talking about the construction of a new Czech cultural centre for which they have been raising money for twenty years. Work can finally start, he announces, because of a generous gift from a factory-owner from California called Bondy.

An unfortunate remark, for the rotund man begins shouting again. "Another bloody rat!"

"I beg your pardon!" cries the hostess. "Why, he's such a patriot! Such a philanthropist!"

I glance quickly at Mr. Pohorsky. He is sitting between myself and Dr.

Toth and ought to be the first to defend the supreme commander of his troops. Oddly enough he does not intervene and looks extremely nervous. The rotund man is a burning juggernaut of indignation.

"You know what he makes in that factory? Things he calls kitchen gadgets. He exports them to the Soviet Union and they turn around and use them as important components in their submarines. He's a scoundrel and he only gives money to Sokol to square it with his conscience! The rat! I don't care if he donated a whole herd of swine for the Pork Feast every year; he's beyond the pale as far as I'm concerned! He's a bastard, a scoundrel and a two-faced traitor!"

I listen to this preternaturally loud voice and wonder at the power of nature that created it. Professor Abraham tries to defend Bondy – the products that Bondy makes, he says, are exported under American government contract – but the rotund man outshouts him. An elderly gentleman tries to edge in with the argument that if Bondy refused such state contracts he would have to shut down his factory, and because he employs Czechs almost exclusively many of our people would be out of work. But the rotund man is not a materialist and easily shouts down these base arguments as well. Finally his stentorian roar alone fills the room and makes the house shake, and we cringe, for the acoustic effects of his voice are like the Chinese bell-torture.

I look at Mr. Pohorsky. He has turned grey and is sitting with his foot in a puddle of spilled coffee, his leg trembling. Poor Mr. Pohorsky. The rotund man, in his Olympian rage, has smashed yet another of his patriotic dreams to smithereens.

•

*May 15, 1959*
*Kostelec*

*To hail with labour, Daniel Josefovitch!*
*So I've made my first voyeurage to the land where tomorrow means yesterday – literally. Everywhere there is order and enthusiasm and above all cleanliness. Take, for example, the fact that in the public toilets you're not allowed to throw used paper into the toilet so it (the toilet, that is) won't get dirty. In every closet they have special baskets for the used paper and at the same time, to prevent asphyxiation, they have provided a little slot-machine which, for a kopek, gives you a blast of beautiful, fragrant Air de Moscow so you won't pass out. The sheer inventiveness of it! Things are so perfect you can scarcely imagine them getting any perfecter. It's also a bloody bore.*
*We probably would have bitten each other's heads off from boredom if it wasn't for a certain Czech artiste who says she's a former*

girlfriend of yours – which claim, of course, might be made by almost everyone in the theatre, including the dressmakers. This artiste, however, demonstrated a remarkable talent for landing herself in the merde, which of course in this country of perfection almost never happens. Scandal is virtually an unknown concept, so kind are people to each other. Just in case she was telling the truth and really was your girlfriend, she's a certain Jana Honzlova, so you won't confuse her with anybody else.

The Soviet Union welcomed us with a magnificent experience right out of the classics (of Russian literature, I mean, not Marksizm-Leninizm). On the way to Moscow by train, our tiny troupe stopped to do a guest performance in the little town of Glogotsk in the gubernia of Moscow, and on Saturday afternoon my wife Janka decided that she'd run out of shampoo. So I set off into Glogotsk in quest of shampoo. Through some caprice of urban planning, our hotel had been built all by its lonesome about two kilometres beyond the furthest outskirts of Glogotsk. So I set out across that wide and endless plain and about half-way there I encountered a steppe-brother and even when he was yet some way off I could tell he didn't have a kopek to pay for Air de Moscow. But I didn't faint, and when I got close enough to the steppe-brother to be heard I gave him a wide berth and in my perfect Russian asked him the way to the GUM department store. The steppe-brother merely jerked his thumb behind him and said, "Follow the muzhiks!" by which, I took it, he meant that the steppe-brothers and sisters would be streaming into the local GUM from all sides and I couldn't miss it. And so I walked on, and about twenty metres from the first building on the outskirts of the town I caught sight of a muzhik in bast shoes lying supine on the ground. I walked up to him and at first I was startled because he looked dead. But when I bent over him I saw he was merely sleeping with an empty vodka bottle stuck in his mouth. I had to consider him a sad relic of the past. But he looked eighteen at the outside, so he couldn't have experienced the past, and therefore was an atypical case because in the Soviet Union alcoholism has been eradicated. And I continued. A short way on I spied another muzhik, likewise looking as though he'd passed away, this time in a sitting position with his back against a lamp-post, and beside him in the ditch, again, was an empty vodka bottle. I looked around and a little farther on there was another one sprawled out on the steps of a tenement house. A babushka was just coming out the door. She stepped on his chest, the muzhik passed wind rather loudly and so startled the babushka that she trod on the empty vodka bottle, fell, hit her head on the steps and collapsed in a heap beside him. Then a comrade with a seeing-eye dog came out of the same building and walked over both of them. And as I went on, I began to see muzhiks everywhere, about twenty metres apart, each with an empty bottle beside him or stuck in his mouth, and every one, to a muzhik, was sound asleep. Well, that's what I call discipline! Perhaps this was some kind of vodka relay race, I thought, or perhaps the chairman of the Glogotsk branch of the Party had passed away and they were all drowning their grief. And because everything else in the Soviet Union is great and gigantic, that line of sleepers wound its way through the streets for a good three versts. At last I saw one who was just about to lie down, the bottle in his mouth, and then I began to encounter comrades who were still conscious and wobbling about at regular intervals, each one with his head back, sucking on his bottle. I was so absorbed by my study of this peculiar side of Soviet life that I didn't watch where I was going and bumped into a muzhik who was just pulling the cork out of a still virgin bottle. I looked at the door he had come out of and over it I saw a large neon sign: U M. The G had burned out.

Then I understood at once what the steppe-brother who had money neither for Air de Moscow nor for vodka had meant when he said, "Follow the muzhiks!"

What a wise and omniscient people!

I went into UM for the shampoo and downstairs in the hall I saw a circular counter with two comrade salesgirls inside. They were up to their waists in rouble notes, and away from them, into the depths of UM, stretched an orderly line of muzhiks, each with three roubles ready in his hand. Each muzhik stepped up to the counter, one comrade salesgirl took his roubles and tossed them somewhere on the floor beneath her, the second one handed him a bottle, he took the cork in his teeth and the next muzhik stepped up and handed over his three roubles. Everything took place in silence, without the slightest disorder or disturbance.

What a happy and disciplined people!

I really wanted to tell you about Honzlova but all those unforgettable impressions have set my consciousness streaming. Anyway Honzlova told us about yet another interesting line-up and I'm beginning to get the impression that standing in lines is one of the characteristic features of your socialist society, just as those dehumanized superhighways full of cars are a characteristic feature of your capitalist society. To make a little more money, Honzlova and a couple of other artistes accepted an engagement in Riga – that's in Latvia or whatever the name of it is – to sing at some local Walpurgisnacht. It was basically an obscurantist celebration of the summer solstice, but at the same time a people's festival, so the two cancel each other out, making the celebration acceptable from both the ideological and the popular points of view. Honzlova had a curious experience there. She said, "You know, man, it looked like all of Riga and the surrounding gubernia was there. There's a natural amphitheatre on the shore of the Baltic Sea. On one side there's a podium where we sang our medley of songs, and the other three sides are lined with pine trees which reinforce the sand dunes by the edge of the sea and at the same time mark the outer limits of the amphitheatre. But the trees were rather far apart and that, as I found out later, has interesting ideological-functional consequences." Not that Honzlova's particularly educated – it's just that she learned words like "functional" from an architect she had an affair with, who was eventually liquidated for "formalistic functionalism." He designed a building for a district secretariat of the Party (the Communist, not the People's) with Stalin's head on the façade and he wanted to place the archive with everybody's personal file in a room inside the head. As a result, Stalin's head was to be hollow, and one of the comrades justifiably interpreted this not functionally but symbolically, and the architect got ten years. The other word, "ideological," she picked up from the air. "And we sang our little medleys in that amphitheatre," Honzlova told me, "but even though we had a PA system we were drowned out by the Latvian audience, who were singing because they had brought along very functional wagons carrying huge vats that looked like septic tanks, except that inside there was beer, terrible swill," said Honzlova, "but a lot of it, and they were chewing away on a highly distinctive Latvian cheese, even stronger than the beer. And they gobbled and guzzled away under a night sky as bright as an Arctic summer, thousands, maybe even millions – if there are that many – of Latvians, and each wagon with its vat was drawn by a mare decorated with red ribbons and leafy green branches. But all of a sudden, I had a queer feeling that something important was missing. I looked around, but everything was there. Professional folk ensembles, mass participation, the people getting deservedly drunk after honest toil, beautiful folk decorations of green boughs, beribboned mares, banners flapping from the flag-poles in the night breeze – but something was not quite right. Suddenly, I knew what was missing. There were no ikons of the statesmen! What an oversight! Or was it deliberate? I set out to look for them myself because I couldn't believe that a down-to-earth, folkloristic people like the Latvians would not love their Russian leaders and pay them the homage that is their due. So I walked around the entire amphitheatre and out through the pine trees on the east side, and there I found relief. On the other side of the pines there was a wide green meadow, every detail standing out sharply in the white Latvian night; and at the far end, about two hundred metres from the amphitheatre, were two huge billboards, like the ones with the eyes of that bankrupt eye doctor in the Valley of Ashes." Honzlova had picked up that allusion from a certain translator of American literature who, instead of sticking to his trade, had written his own novel, the fool, out of sheer, unadulterated, anti-socialist ambition, and subsequently had to emigrate to Borneo for his own personal safety. "Except," said the girl, "it had no eyes. It was a black silhouette on a brilliant red background, a deluxe rendition of Comrade Lenin, including his cap which was suspended above his head, also in profile, like one of those silhouettes pasted on white backgrounds that they do at local fairs, except this one was incomparably more grand. An endless line of Latvians was moving slowly towards the left-hand corner of the silhouette and likewise, from the right-hand side, an equally endless line walking back to the festival. I thought they must be paying their respects to Lenin, as they do in Moscow, and I felt moved to do the same so I joined the line and started slowly shuffling forward. The Latvians were giving me a lot of queer looks but I put it down to the fact that in the light of the midnight sun I looked almost beautiful," she said modestly, "but then I noticed that as far as I could see I was the only woman in those huge lines and ideologically that seemed pretty surprising. When I finally got to the corner of the billboard with the silhouette I expected to see the Latvians on the other side standing with heads bared. Imagine my surprise," she said, "when I saw them baring another part of their anatomy, a specifically masculine part. I suppose you can guess why. The pine trees were too far apart to provide any shelter and there was too much beer." From this you can see how the Latvian designers took to heart the slogan, "Economy begins at work." They hadn't built any public comfort stations for the amphitheatre because they figured that the billboards with Comrade Lenin would do just as well, thus making both ideological and functional use of it and saving the state money. Oh, and they weren't looking at Honzlova so queerly because of her feminine beauty, although there was that too, but because the women had their own silhouette, of Stalin, on the west side of the amphitheatre, through the pines.

What an economic, functionally-minded people!

And while I'm on about our mutual pal, I have to tell you that she upped and fell in love. A really beautiful man (as my wife Janka says) latched onto her, something between Yesenin and Comrade Khrushchev, so beside him her feminine charm faded right away. And he was a real nobleman, a grand duke! Of course they don't recognize that *title in the U.S.S.R., but it belongs to him by right of inheritance and I feel reasonably certain that Honzlova latched onto him because of the title, for she's not at all susceptible to masculine beauty. She won't look at me.*

*Well, the poor girl was walking about in a dream and wherever she went she carried on about how the grand duke loved her so much that he was willing to take advantage of statutory sexual equality and leave the Soviet Union to go and live with her in Prague. Imagine that! Leave the U.S.S.R.! What love!*

*Utterly inexpressible!*

*But the girl had her ups and downs with him. First of all a militia-man caught her trying to sell her underwear on the black market so she could buy a beaverskin coat for the grand duke in GUM. So they gave her a warning. Then the corridor supervisor in the hotel she was stay-ing at, quite within her rights, opened the door of Honzlova's room at two in the morning and found her in bed with the grand duke. Such immorality! She got a second warning. Well, bad luck comes in threes, and while she was putting on her make-up for a date with the grand duke, her eyebrow tweezers fell into the toilet. As she was groping around for them, her hand discovered a solid object. She tried to pull it out but it appeared to be fastened to something so she gave it a proper yank and out it came. And you'd never guess what it was – or would you? A microphone.*

*I have no idea what it was doing there, but knowing the high level of Soviet technology, it wasn't there for nothing.*

*Naturally, enough was enough. The corridor supervisor came rush-ing along to her room, and instead of going on her date Honzlova got taken to the KGB (that's the Soviet travel agency specializing in Wonders of Siberia tours); and from there they sent her under police escort to Prague, for the wilful destruction of hotel equipment which belongs to all Soviet people. Serves her right. She does have to yank at everything she gets her hands on.*

*The grand duke remained behind in Moscow, and no sooner had Honzlova fallen afoul of The People than he fell in love again, this time with Tronickova, the wig mistress. She's the one whose left leg is shorter than her right, but to compensate her right shoulder is higher than her left. Again rumour has it he's willing to move to Prague with Tronickova. Imagine that! Leave the Soviet Union!*

*Which brings me to the end, and I implore you: Go to the Soviet Union! Ja drugoy takoy strany nyeznayu, and you don't either!*

*Yours,*
*Vrata Cenkovic*

*P.S. I managed to get that shampoo in Glogotsk. It turned Janka's hair pink, flecked with blue.*

*One more P.S. You ask why I don't quit the Party? Partly from cowardice and so I won't lose out on jobs, partly from the sincere conviction that our imperfect society can be made like Soviet society only through the Party, and therefore the Party needs people like me, who can be blinded by nothing and see clearly how beautiful it is in the Soviet Union, and who love the place and honour it so much that out of respect for it they would never dare to allow themselves to imitate it at home.*

*And another P.S.*

*Marie Dreslerova sends her greetings to you in Prague. She says you're a fine one for never visiting her. If you're afraid to, she says you needn't be. Franta is already settled in his ways (she says) and every Monday, Wednesday and Friday from eight to eleven (you can set your watch by him, says Molly) he goes to the Beranek to drink beer and play cards, and Molly is home alone with her daughter whom she can always send to Biloves for mineral water.*

*P.P.P.P.S. (This is the way you're supposed to write it says Janka (my daughter, not my wife).) Molly still looks great. But it's probably some kind of organic anomaly, because we all get old, for God's sake.*

*P.P.P.P.P.S. Or maybe Molly is immortal.*

●

Explain it to us!

It is almost dark. On the horizon above the lake there is a brilliant yellowish white, bitterly cold strip of sky, the kind that can only be seen over this wild, secure continent. It separates the dark grey water from the grey-black clouds above it. To the south, Rochester, though invisible, has begun to suffuse the sky with illumination.

"It's difficult," I say. "Man is incapable of contentment. It's probably his best and therefore his most human characteristic."

"But why don't they fight? Isn't it because they *are* content?" Hakim scowls at me.

It's difficult, Hakim. Not by bread alone, but mostly by bread. My *exempla* may be too subtle for you, for so far you exist in a black-and-white world. Not by bread alone but predominantly by bread. The immense, cruel, Darwinian injustice of nature, accepted once more as the principle of society, is painful only to those it affects directly. It hurts only those it hurts and some of those very few who do not live by bread alone. But can I say this to Hakim – or to Sugar Schwartz? Her Circle for the Study of Marxism is cultivating Hegelianisms, not storytelling. I look through the round porthole at the bright, icy horizon. (How the telephone rang in the night – but I no longer fear it, nor have I for a long time. Mr. Smiricky, the writer? Yes. This is Lida Lewis; I'm supposed to pass on greetings from Gott, you know, the pop-singer. She identifies herself: married to an American and therefore able to travel freely back and forth from East to West. Another foolish distinction you will not understand, Sugar. If you leave on your own you are a traitor. If you prostitute yourself through marriage, you are not. I said that to myself in anger and saying so made me a Marxist. I was not describing the uniqueness of Lida Lewis' case, but the generality of a legal phenomenon. All right then, Mrs. Lewis: what is Gott doing? What's he singing these days? Everything's fine again, Mr. Smiricky, they're making money again, Kotak too, and they don't even censor their lyrics very much now – they just mustn't be too gloomy. Everything's okay again. And what about Marta, I ask. Which Marta? You know, Marta Kubisova, Dubcek's favourite. Oh, Marta! Well, she's finished, says Lida Lewis, they won't let her sing at all. So everything's okay again, I say with unforgivable (forgivable) malice and hang up, silencing the attractive little voice from Prague, now living in Santa Monica, California. I wonder if she too sat that day by the statue of the saint who died at the stake and swore she would never, ever forget? But that was seven years ago, in 1968. Apathy, our mother, our salvation, our ruin. So Marta will never sing again?)

Just take a simple sociological sampling, Hakim, and you'll see: the statistical majority struggles only for more bread; the statistical minority struggles too, for more non-bread. And that holds true even for this society, which has miraculously survived so far on this wild continent, where except for incurable diseases and muggers there is no longer anything dangerous. Anything. Is anyone afraid of the President or the Prime Minister?

And in that society over there?

*Exempla?*

The years of wonder, that miraculous brief flowering in the sixties of a less circumscribed freedom, were on their way. Once we were having a conversation in a Prague publishing office about local hippies and hooligans and what to do so that they either would not exist or would cease to be the way they were. Re-educate them? Let them have their rock and roll and win them over through music? (But I always thought that they were necessary just as they were, like bacteria in the lower colon or pike in the pond. But it was still the late fifties and the years of wonder were only on the horizon, so I kept that opinion to myself.) Over in the corner sat a silent visitor, the playwright Kach. He said nothing but when the Marxists brought up the theory of Dr. Striz of the Dobris reformatory who had introduced a system of rehabilitation based on trust, Kach spoke up. "I'm astonished at you, Comrades! What's the problem? What's all this about a system of trust? Just before the war they had a problem with hooligans in Moscow. They called them *stiliagi*. So Comrade Stalin gave an order: Round 'em up! Off to Siberia with them! And that was the end of the *stiliagi*." For a minute the Marxists were speechless, but then the discussion got under way again. The years of wonder were on the horizon: the generalissimo's solution no longer held any appeal.

Do you know who Chroma was, Sugar? How could you know that? Not long ago you said at lunch, "Regardless of how things are, we have to give Fidel credit for one thing: he got the Mafia out of Cuba. That's something we weren't able to do."

*Exemplum:*

Chroma, swelling with pride, persuaded me to come home with him. He wanted to show *him* off to me. We went down by the laundry stairs into the basement. His tiny father was sitting in the kitchen, coughing occasionally, in a striped sweater, his small feet in dandyish boots, legs propped up on the table like an American. "Just got back from the nick!" Chroma whispered to me proudly. "Been sent down twenty times!" Mr. Chroma senior was a safecracker by profession, or rather by conviction, because the trade was clearly not that lucrative. I looked about the damp, steam-filled kitchen, dry-rot fungus sprouting in one corner. Chroma, in that outsized suit provided by Masaryk's welfare system, looked with respect at the diminutive toff whose pantlegs had crept up to reveal shining white calves. This is how he remained in my mind's eye. His obituary? His end was swift and easy, like your kin, Sugar, except that he was not lamented by rabbis, his name did not appear in the roll-call of martyrs of the nation. His name would embarrass genuine patriots. The efficient bureaucracy of that dictatorship invented a less familiar Final Solution, and overnight they were rid of safecrackers. They disappeared down the trap door of history. In Bergen-Belsen, in Buchenwald, in Dachau ... what the pre-Munich republic could not get rid of ... all at once there was no more crime. There was only the Gestapo.

The Czechs have it in their blood. In their nervous system. In their subconscious, Hakim. That's why they don't revolt. Where the apostles of the Slavs, Cyril and Methodius, once stood, today on cathedral rooftops stand the pagan gods "Watch-your-tongue" and "Keep-an-eye-out."

I look away from the steel sky above the land of Chingachgook.

"The Czechs are a strange people," I say to Hakim. "But they're not naive. They're like hay fever, suppressed by a decongestant. As soon as you stop taking the pill, the hay fever comes back full strength. That's what the Czechs are like. Their second revolution – "

"What do you mean by the second revolution?" asks Irene, a furrow of thought between her eyes.

"The one in 1968," I say. Hakim is again wearing his disdainful, know-it-all expression. "The Czechs are a funny nation. An ungrateful nation. Anyone who stuffs them full of bread will get no thanks for it. As soon as they forget to take the decongestant...." *Revolution for the Fun of It.* But perhaps we are only kidding ourselves. Perhaps the second revolution is just a counter-revolution; perhaps it is a good thing to replace freedom with police order, which over time transforms bureaucratic decrees into natural laws in human consciousness. "Man will be free by not trying to be free. He will make a dialectical leap from Engels to Epictetus.... *Do not desire that everything happen as you wish, but desire that everything happen as it in fact does happen*, and you will be free...." My eyes wander again to the wildly free landscape around this lake. The steely horizon is already dotted with stars. Perhaps clinging to freedom is really no more than an atavism after all, even the uncompromising clinging to artistic freedom. Perhaps it is the expression of a minor rather than a major talent ... perhaps a great talent is capable of that Epictetian leap into the realm of freedom ... I think of Shakespeare, indifferent to the fate of Essex, to the cruelties of a professional queen. I think of the novelist Nabal, who now lives in his district town, away from the compromises of Prague, rewriting his once-explosive saga from black to white, from minor to major, from negative to positive, all with the same technical wizardry. ("He's such a mouse," Lida Lewis told me. When the phone went dead she thought we'd been cut off, and she rang again. We met later in the Marika Café on Bloor Street. "He realized he was in a bottle and it was pointless to try to get out of it. So instead of running about the field, he's simply running about inside the bottle. But even so he still runs very nicely. Just imagine how he'd run if they let him back on the field again!" ... Yes, he would run beautifully.) *If a writer lies to them only once, they won't care for him anymore.* Like all witticisms it's only half true. Or is it perhaps only true for this wild continent? Is that witticism true for that continent over there? And are there not readers — who are otherwise expected to vote in any way, at any time, for anything, and so what? — who, when it comes to books written in bottles, can filter out the wine which was meant for them from what was intended as a libation for the gods? The clear stars glow in the western sky. Greatness of talent is often inversely proportional to the stridency of the demands for freedom. Shakespeare silent before the iniquities of his age. But then we have Kafka, and his Milena who wrote: "He had to die because he did not know how to make compromises and take refuge, as others did, in intellectual deceptions...." But that is merely Milena's hypothesis. Kafka died because he had tuberculosis. He didn't take refuge in intellectual deceptions, because he had never been in a bottle.... I awake. Where was I? "... so that man will be free because he will not try to be free. He will be as free as the reptile who does not try to fly, but merely creeps and crawls in the dust and the dirt...."

"But sir!"

The sweet, whiskied voice of my Wendy. She puts her hand up as though she were still in class.

"Yes?"

"Birds *did* develop from lizards!" she cries. "I take Science 203, Introduction to Paleontology. There was this lizard, an ornitho something."

"Ornithosuchus!" Bellissimmo comes to her rescue. He is probably taking Science 203 as well.

"Yes — something. They hopped about from branch to branch until feathers grew on their behinds. And it became the first bird...." She turns trustingly to Bellissimmo, and he says glibly, "Archeopteryx!"

I am grateful to this little Scots girl, as I have been many times before. Perhaps way back then in that year of wonder feathers began to grow on our behinds....

It's getting late now. The wind has died down. The Svenssons' yacht has stopped pitching and yawing and is now merely bobbing up and down as it glides gently into the slip. It is dark; the huge radiant beehives of downtown Toronto stand like luxurious lighthouses of a wild civilization. The helmsman brings the boat up safely to the dock, and we disembark. Bellissimmo and Vicky disappear towards the luminous beehives, and Wendy too vanishes, with Hakim at her side. "Good night, Miss Svensson," says the hired mariner, and walks past us into the night. We move slowly towards the parking lot.

Around the corner, Irene stops.

"Let's wait here till he can't see us."

We wait. Irene in a glossy leather coat with beaver-skin trim over her sailing clothes.

"Do you want to go back?" I ask.

"Don't you?"

The dream of a randy old professor come true. Almost all dreams come true when it's too late.

The yacht is rocking in the water gently and seductively, knocking against the bumpers on the dock. It sounds like a slow tom-tom, like a sound effect from a clever scenario. The mast nods back and forth like an inverse pendulum, like a pointer offering a choice of stars. Which one will you choose? The most beautiful, of course.

"I do," I say to Irene Svensson.

And she opens the hatch to the cabin.

•

An ear-splitting din pours from the loudspeakers in every corner of the hall, including the one where I have taken refuge, as far away as I can get from the Teutonic decibels produced by Hucil and his Czech orchestra, who have stuffed themselves into plastic lederhosen and Tyrolean leg-warmers. Hucil is even singing, and like so many musicians he can faithfully imitate any language without having properly learned a single one. So he can sing better than all the Bavarians here, who are waving their huge beer steins to the rhythm:

*Vor der Kaserne, vor dem grossen Tor....*

The Bavarians weep tears of joy into their beer and here and there one of them joins in with a braying voice, "Lilli Marlene," the remembrances of time past:

*stand eine Laterne, und steht sie noch davor.*
*So woll'n wir uns da wiedersehn....*

I'm certain of it. I've seen the woman with the two-litre beer stein somewhere before. She's waving it aloft and singing, an enormous – not fat, merely enormous – German woman in a green-trimmed dirndl, a Tyrolean hat and reddish hair, waving the stein and singing:

*bei der Laterne woll'n wir steh'n....*

The song enters her, illuminates her, rids her of excess poundage. Suddenly she becomes a plump, full-blooded German *Mädel,* a *Mädel* in the uniform of the *Bund der deutschen Mädeln* –

*Wie einst....*

"*Entschuldigung,*" I say, "aren't you Ilse Seliger? *Aus Kosteletz?*"
The faded German eyes focus on me, then begin to push their way back, back through the jungle of time....
"Jesus, Mary *und* Joseph! It's Smiricky! Smiricky the sax player!"
"*Ego sum,*" I say, "*et amavi te, puella –*"
"Shut up, *du*" – and the metacarpal bones of my right hand almost snap. Perhaps as a punishment for that lie. Perhaps she has really crushed them. And it was just a *pia fraus –*

"*Naja*," sighs Ilse Seliger later. Her married name is now Schröder. "I remember that one. *Sehr gut.* Some Frau General von Kater used to come to see him all the time. Her husband was at the front. A fine little tart, that one. I wonder where he ended up?"

Naturally, we reminisce about people from that closed chapter of which we were a part. Once we're done with that, we shall tell our life stories. I seem to be genuinely in love with the enormous Ilse now, though, back then, when she tried to indoctrinate me with National Socialism on the train back to Jaromer, I hated her sincerely.

"I'm not so sure she really was such a tart," I say. "She was free to travel back and forth between Paris, Berlin, Vienna, whenever she felt like it. I have the feeling she was acting as Uippelt's courier. Uippelt was a spy."

Ilse's sweet little mouth opened wide in astonishment. "Uippelt? Why he was always so *echt deutsch!*"

"From a certain point of view he was a traitor," I say exploratorily.

The eyes in the fleshy face above the little mouth look at me just as questioningly. "Why don't you say it outright – you mean from my point of view?"

"Would I be wrong?"

"From my point of view then, no."

"And what about today?"

"*Schau mal hier,*" says Ilse, then stops and listens again to Hucil's voice pushing itself through the outsized speakers. She holds up a fleshy finger as though she wants to draw my attention to the song. Of course, I understand. It's an odd thing how songs have so often answered the great questions of my life. Perhaps even more often than books, or wise men. The crooners' wisdom thus answers for Ilse:

> *Es geht alles vorüber,*
> *es geht alles vorbei....*

The Toronto oom-pah-pah band is condensed nostalgia.

"Do you remember how we once took the same train to Jaromer?" I say, in a tone appropriate to this nostalgia.

"*Naja,*" says Ilse. "Well you certainly must have been in love with me then, *nicht wahr?*"

"Oh, hopelessly! I was afraid of you."

"There was no need for that." Ilse places the palm of her hand on the back of mine. "Oh, I was *ein Ideologe* all right. But I was no informer."

"I had no way of knowing that," I say. "So I was scared."

Ilse sighs, takes her hand off mine and grasps her beer stein. "*Die Welt ist einer toller Platz.* I really latched on to the proper passion to match my schoolgirl stupidity. But believe me, Daniel," and again she places her hand on the back of mine. "After the war I – *wie sagt man das?* – I went into myself. Don't remind me of it. But really, I had no idea what was going on at the time. You don't believe me, do you?"

I look into her eyes. She looks back at me, good-naturedly, sincerely. But I reply, "Let's just say you didn't know for certain, and you didn't know any details but, basically, you went along with it."

She lowers her eyes. "*Verzeihung.* You're right."

"It's nothing. It's normal," I say. "As long as our experience is confined to theory, we behave like animals. It's only when we have our noses rubbed in blood that it makes us vomit like human beings."

"Well, I certainly got my nose full," Ilse sighs. "Our group was captured by the Americans and they showed us Buchenwald, fresh."

"Don't remind yourself. *Das ist* long ago *vorüber.*"

"In one sense. But all right, we won't talk about it, *einverstanden?* So what happened to Uippelt?"

> *Nach jedem Dezember*
> *kommt immer ein Mai....*

To Uippelt? I remember that day in May, 1945, when I was out walking with Irena....

"They killed him."

"Who, the Gestapo?"

"Something like that," I said ... sabotage, Uippelt, my heroic errand to Prague – in the euphoria of those May days right after the war everything evaporated from my head. Beside Irena and in that atmosphere of safety after the war I didn't think about such things at all, especially not at that particular moment, for we were hurrying to the movies to see *Sun Valley Serenade*, my first re-encounter with the world of my dreams. Zdenek was supposed to be waiting for us in the theatre, but even so, I had Irena all to myself on the way. She was wearing a pretty summer dress and she easily deflected my witty barrage of seductive words. Suddenly, out of context, she said, "Look at that! They're marching off the quislings!"

And so they were. Young lads in confiscated *Afrika Korps* uniforms, wearing large red Revolutionary Guard armbands. In the first row was the corpulent Velcl, owner of the warehouse that Prema had blown up, though they hadn't locked him up at the time. He had done business with the Germans. Someone probably knew something about him or, on the contrary, knew nothing. Next to him was Gerta Ceehova and beside her the former *Werkschutz* Eisler. They had all had their heads shaved, but Gerta, the tallest of the threesome, was the only one who looked impenitent. Velcl was crying. Eisler marched with conscientious rigidity, wearing an expression that made him look as though he expected at any moment to be hit in the face. Behind them, in columns of three, were other shorn heads, male and female, in that strange unisex of revolution. I managed to recognize Dr. Seelich, who was limping badly on one leg, and engineer Zavis, who was handsome even when shorn. Ballon wasn't there, he had vanished in time. But in the second-last row marched Uippelt and without his pince-nez he looked like a little pig. They had only shaved off half his Hitler moustache, a joke favoured by the Revolutionary Guard. And I blurted out, "He doesn't belong there!"

"D'you mean Zavis?" asked Irena sentimentally.

"No, the one with only half a moustache, Uippelt."

"But he's a German!"

"Yes, but he...."

I poured out my story of heroism. Irena was highly patriotic. It impressed her.

"Danny! You've got to tell them right away! Down at the Town Hall. They've made a mistake!"

"Right now?"

"Of course right now! An innocent man is suffering!"

"I'll do it tomorrow morning, Irena."

She stopped and measured me with severe, coffee-brown eyes. "Not tomorrow. Do it right now! You're a fine one, letting an innocent man suffer...."

"But I'd miss the movie!"

It seemed like a reasonable argument to me, but not to Irena. She blew up. "You go to the Town Hall at once, Danny Smiricky, or I'll never go with you to any movie ever again!"

"Then I'll go right after the movie!"

"Right now!"

She spun round indignantly and walked rapidly towards the cinema. I trotted after her like a whimpering dog. It was soon clear that there was no hope for me in that role, so I stopped and called after her, "All right, I'm going, Irena."

Without even turning around, she said, "We'll meet you afterwards in the Beranek."

Sure. So off I went.

Somewhere in the bowels of the Town Hall the mayor or the President of the National Committee or whatever he called himself must have been present, but the place looked more like an army barracks. The lads in *Afrika Korps* uniforms were playing at war. They'd even set up a system of passes, which finally gained me admittance to Mr. Pytlik. This was before my father brought Herr Dirigent Zillinger's incriminating diary home, and so, filled with innocent trust, I announced to Mr. Pytlik that there had been a botch-up and that along with real collaborators the Revolutionary Guard had managed to arrest a hero of the resistance by mistake. I also described my conspirational errand in Prague and quite logically Pytlik asked how I'd got together with Uippelt. So there was a lot to tell. Not that I was reluctant: I enthusiastically recounted my story of the sabotage and how Uippelt had found it out.

"Who else was working with him?" asked Mr. Pytlik sternly, as though he were interrogating me. I looked at the red star. The Red Army wore it on their caps, but Pytlik had stuck it in his lapel. It had an oddly numbing effect on me.

"I don't know. He didn't mention any others and I didn't ask. It's better not to know too much."

Mr. Pytlik nodded in agreement. "And you haven't the slightest notion who else might be in on it?"

"I thought the foreman, Vachousek, might have been, but Uippelt claimed he wasn't and he said they arrested Vachousek because of those cross-brackets."

"And was that the real reason?"

"I don't know. He still hasn't come back. Do you know what's become of him?"

"No, we don't," said Mr. Pytlik. "But just because Uippelt said he wasn't in on it doesn't necessarily mean anything. He could have been covering up."

"That's a fact," I said. "Perhaps Vachousek could testify to it if he comes back."

"Testify to what?" asked Mr. Pytlik sharply.

"That Uippelt was in the resistance."

"Oh, that. No, we'll check that out ourselves."

"Aren't you going to let him go?"

Mr. Pytlik laughed. "It's not that simple. We have to verify what you've told us."

"But how? No one knows it but me and him. Except – wait a minute – I told it to Skocdopole – "

"That's...."

"His father runs a tobacco shop. A legionnaire. Skocdopole was – he was active in the resistance too."

"But you only *told* him? He wasn't in direct contact with this Uippelt?"

I admitted that he wasn't and Mr. Pytlik declared that it wasn't enough. I remembered the unnamed person in Prague to whom I'd given the envelope and Mr. Pytlik wrote down his address and stood up. "That's a better tip. As soon as we can get through to Prague, we'll check up on it."

I stood up too.

"And – are you going to keep him in custody in the meantime?"

"Those are serious things you've just told me," said Mr. Pytlik. "We have to screen all this information carefully."

Screen? That was the first time I had heard the word used in that way. "Couldn't you let him go on his word of honour?" I said.

"A German?" said Mr. Pytlik in severe astonishment.

"No, that is, *I'd* give my word of honour. I mean I'd kind of vouch for him...."

"For a *German?*" asked Mr. Pytlik even more severely.

"Look, I'm certain he was working for us. Naturally you don't have to believe me. But I know it for an absolute fact."

Mr. Pytlik wrapped a fatherly arm around my shoulder and walked me slowly out of the office. "Look here, I believe your intentions are honourable. But you're still young. You have no idea how hypocritical people can be."

He was right about that. I went to the Beranek and there I experienced one of my many bitter disappointments – Irena did not show up. Zdenek had probably convinced her to go home with him after the movie for a little dalliance. I waited in the Beranek until I was certain there was no hope, loitered around a little longer on Jirasek Street and then went home to bed.

That night I dreamed about Uippelt and Irena. Irena was scolding me for doing nothing, although I had done what I could. Or had I? Pangs of conscience began to gnaw at me, and first thing in the morning I went to the old Hycman's cotton mill where they had locked all the collaborators up. I got there before six. Ponykl, in *Afrika Korps* gear, was standing guard at the door holding a submachine-gun.

"I've got to speak to one of the quislings," I said when he dramatically blocked my way and pointed the submachine-gun at me.

"It ain't allowed."

"But he's there by mistake. I'm just going to act as his witness."

"Bullshit, man! No one's there by mistake!"

"This one is. He saved my life." All at once I remembered – why, Ponykl had been mixed up in it too! "And your life too, man!"

"What're you talking about?"

"D'you remember how you made me that false counter-sink gauge on the lathe?"

"So what?"

The question of the century.

I explained. I also reminded him how the welders, directed by Vachousek, had saved the situation. Ponykl was less sure of himself now, but when I mentioned Vachousek, he misunderstood.

"How thick can you get, man! Vachousek was no quisling! And he ain't here, either. God knows if he's even alive."

"Not Vachousek – Otto Uippelt, the German Oberkontrolleur."

Ponykl twitched visibly. "Uippelt?"

"That's the one. Let me in there."

"Oh man, there's been a real balls-up," Ponykl said, and I began to sense what he meant.

My worst fears were confirmed. When a self-styled officer finally escorted me to the cellar, Uippelt was lying there chin up. There was a drop of blood on his half-moustache.

"Someone gave him a bit of a tap and he fell down a little awkward," explained the self-styled officer. "Hit the back of his head on the steps. An unfortunate accident."

"You're goddamn right it's unfortunate," I said. "He was our man. He wasn't a quisling at all."

"Who was supposed to know that?"

"I spent a bloody hour telling them all about it yesterday in the Town Hall."

"Nobody told me anything about it. Some of the comrades interrogated him last night and that's when he got the tap...."

But it still hadn't dawned on me yet. I was simply angry and I felt stupid and helpless. I turned to look at Uippelt. They hadn't even closed his eyes. He was staring blankly, minus his pince-nez, at the damp ceiling of Hycman's cellar. His bare feet were splayed out and he was holding something in his clenched fist. I pried the stiff fingers open while the self-styled officer looked on. A little red star fell out of his hand. The kind the Red Army soldiers usually wore in their caps. Very slowly its desperate message came through to me. But Mr. Zillinger's diary had not yet come to light. I turned back to the corpse. I saw again in my mind's eye that afternoon with Kostelec framed in the panoramic window ... his black silhouette ... the five-legged pig ... General von Kater's wife ... an address in Prague ... rewelded counter-sinks on the cross-brackets ... a few apparently heroic acts.

The grey Prussian eyes stared at a damp spot in the ceiling. So I tried at least to close them. I was not very successful.

"*Na siehst du,*" sighs Ilse. "The world is a crazy place."

It is.

So what?

•

*November 7th, 1960*
*Israel*

*Daniel!*
*Do you still exist? Sometimes I get the feeling you belong to another
historical era. But perhaps that's because I've been living for more
than a year now in the Herschel kibbutz. Little David is attending
what we would have called fourth form back home and everything
that was is no longer. But don't think that I've forgotten you. I can still
see you as if it were yesterday, bringing the medicine for David from
Nosek. In those days it was almost an act of heroism. I don't suppose
you know how the cadre chief interrogated me because of you, but I
refused to tell him who you were, and by that time they weren't so certain of their own certainties anymore so nothing much ever came of it.
At least as far as I was concerned. Somebody saw you coming to see us
that night and, as you know, informing on a Zionist is always an
expression of progressive thinking, in any age.*

*But a fine Zionist you befriended! When we arrived in Jerusalem
they took us round all the historical landmarks, including the museum
of the first kibbutz that was founded by the Zionists sometime before
the First World War. Even then they had to defend themselves because
there were people here who had this homicidal Pavlovian reflex whenever they saw a Jew. But the first Zionists were devout people and the
idea of bearing arms went against their nature so they hired Arab gunmen to defend them. As you might guess, the gunmen didn't exactly
overwork themselves, so that in the end a few young Zionists said to
heck with purity of religion and got themselves rifles. One of them is
still alive; he's about eighty now and works as a guide in the museum. I
asked him something in English and he answered right back in
Hebrew. As you know, I only took Hebrew lessons from Mr. Katz and
I never learned it as well as I did Latin in the third and fourth forms.
And in those long years after Mr. Katz died (the poor fellow, or rather
the fortunate fellow: he died the day after arriving at Terezin and he
never made it to Auschwitz. He had a very bad case of diabetes and
they didn't provide insulin at Terezin) in those long years my
embryonic knowledge of the language of my forefathers simply evaporated from my mind except for a few letters. When I admitted not
knowing Hebrew to this eighty-year-old warrior, he flew into such a
rage that I thought he was going to take one of those historical
muskets off the wall and if not shoot me dead on the spot then at least
disfigure my Semitic beauty (I was touched by what you told us about*

*the Japanese cup that time you came with the medicine. Unless of course you just made it up. You always were a great one to tell stories and nothing is sacred to you except perhaps friendship, and then more likely the female variety) and the old man shouted, "What's to become of Zionism with all the young people nowadays too lazy to learn Hebrew!"*

*As you know, in Kostelec we didn't have a very clear notion of what Zionism really was. But here, Daniel, I've found out. It's out-and-out communism! On the kibbutz, anyway, the only difference being that we're here voluntarily. In Herschel, my first job – and don't laugh, it's true – was feeding the hogs. No, that is not a slip of the pen. The thing is that here on the kibbutz there are Jews who come from that kingdom we both know so well, where the national dish is pork, dumplings and cabbage, and since they were not exactly pillars of piety, they decided to set themselves up with some pigs. Of course there are also Jews of the true faith here and when the Jews from that faraway kingdom got ready for their first ceremonial slaughter, fratricidal war almost broke out, ending in the victory of the true faith: the pigs were slaughtered but not consumed. They were buried down by the river instead. Later one blasphemer dug one of the corpses out at night and roasted a leg under the bridge, but the guardians of tradition smelled it and the backslider almost ended up like that false prophet from Nazareth, what was his name? The Arab cousins honour him as well. Oh yes, Christosvoskres.*

*But then the number of people in the kibbutz from that faraway kingdom and neighbouring kingdoms began to increase and the pro-hog party grew in strength until at last it won the right to observe the ceremonial feast of the slaughter. Not inside the kibbutz, of course. And so a traditional procession was born: when a pig is slaughtered the pro-hog comrades put him on a kind of stretcher and carry him, singing "Who cares if it debase us, we're going to fill our faces!" (which some claim is the national anthem of that faraway kindom of Porkdumplingsncabbage). The procession marches three kilometres away from the Herschel kibbutz to an olive grove, where they all stuff themselves to the gills. Unfortunately I don't go in the procession with them, not out of piety but for very practical reasons (chronic colitis that I picked up at Auschwitz), so I can't tell you exactly what goes on. But old Ashkenazy claims that it's a Jewish version of the Black Mass. Apparently they even hold orgies there, which at my age (I am, I think, a hundred and seventy-six) doesn't interest me, although it might interest you. It could also be that old Ashkenazy is making all this up because he is a very lecherous old man. He sits on the porch every evening, where everyone can see him, with the scriptures open in his lap and they say he only reads the Song of Solomon, ad nauseam, but of course he doesn't think it's ad nauseam.*

*What else is there to write about? David is doing very well at school, though I don't suppose you could care less, but there is really no other news. He wants to be a doctor and if he keeps on as well as this the kibbutz is going to send him to university.*

*And it's beautiful here, in fact I feel as though I'm on a permanent vacation. The climate is good for me, and everything that has been has been and will never, I believe – I hope – come to pass again. And of all that has been, you are one of the few things that I like to think back on.*

*In fact I feel so wonderful here that I'm almost afraid, and it's silly because there's nothing to be afraid of. But I suppose that's just a kind of neurosis. Everyone who was there is a little bit* meshugge.

*Write me, Daniel, about your young ladies and your literature, which in your case always overlapped considerably.*

*Or have you, heaven forfend, started to write novels of socialist construction? Ah, but that can't be, especially now, when it's gone out of fashion.*

*So write me, for sure!*

*Yours,*
*Rebecca Silbernaglova von dem Teecup*

•

A group of young Jews in concentration camp costumes was demonstrating outside the O'Keefe Centre. Limousines pulled up to the main entrance and disgorged Toronto high society, dressed for a gala occasion. The demonstrators were passing out leaflets but there were few takers. Only occasionally would a hand reach out. Most of the guests walked past the costumed youngsters with stiff smiles, as if they were all ambassadors of the Soviet Union. Percy had his eye on Veronika. She was the only one of the Svensson entourage to accept a leaflet, and she even greeted the demonstrators with hands clasped over her head. They were holding up a banner that said LET MY PEOPLE GO. High above their heads, on the marquee, there was a sign in glowing lights:

AT THE O'KEEFE CENTRE TONIGHT:
THE RED ARMY CHORUS

Veronika's wilful silence made Percy nervous. They took their seats in the front row and Veronika handed him the leaflet. He tried to read it but couldn't concentrate. He glanced furtively at the sad girl sitting quietly next to him in a black dress, her hair in a smooth knot, her lovely profile immensely serious. Behind her was a mélange of formal suits, hot pants and *décolletage*. The girl had a handbag of black beads in her lap and her slender hands were folded on top of it. On one finger she wore a ring with a little flag. Percy was quivering with love and anxiety.

The lights went down. A military march was struck up and a troop of male and female vocalists paraded onto the stage wearing high boots and smiles. Veronika called them "Colgate smiles." In powerful voices, they sang a song that Veronika alone in the Svensson entourage understood:

> *My za mir! I pyesnyu etu*
> *ponesyom, druzya, po svyetu.*
> *Pust ona v syerdtsakh lyudyey zvuchit*
> *smyelyey, vpyeryod, za mir!*

A strange scene flashed into Veronika's mind – men in high boots, like the ones on stage, but playing harps, their hands gliding sweetly over the strings. The scene would flash into her mind for an instant, and then disappear again. She must have seen it somewhere. Perhaps at those cinematographic seances held by Percy's sister Kästrin. Veronika felt an immense aversion to high boots. She looked around. Behind her, white bony knees below a pair of hot pants, a diamond brooch in the shape of a huge red star. She turned to Percy. My little idiot, she thought. You're not going to like this, but I have to do it.

> *Nyebyvat voynye pozharu*
> *nye pylat zyemnomy sharu*
> *Nasha volya tvyorshche, chem granit!*

You fools, why they're laughing at you all.

The choir rearranged itself like wooden marionettes. A corpulent functionary stepped up to the microphone accompanied by an interpreter.

"*Dorogiye kanadskiye druzya!* Dear Canadian friends!"

She did not listen to the speech. She knew its melody, sung over and over again, a million times. A loathsome song. She waited. The melody reached a climactic high C, and as the dear Canadian friends rattled their diamond bracelets while they applauded, Veronika reached for the thing in her handbag. The waves of applause died away, the conductor, in neatly tailored riding breeches, turned his back on the Canadian friends, flung his arms apart and the full-bodied voices of the Colgaters shook the O'Keefe Centre.

Percy noticed Veronika pulling something out of her bag and felt a stab of fear. An assassination attempt on Wallace last week – but it was something flabby. Not a metal object, probably just a handkerchief. He exhaled in relief. The song thundered on and Percy turned back to watch the choir. There was no variety in their singing, and he didn't understand them, but the melody excited him. He caught himself tapping his foot. Then he heard a strange, quiet sound beside him and he looked at Veronika. She was blowing up some kind of balloon. He didn't understand right away, and the girl inflated it so adroitly that in no time it looked almost big enough to carry her away. Then he understood. Glowing red letters on white rubber spelled out the message:

RUSSIANS GO HOME!

Veronika lifted the balloon high above her head. In the row behind her the bracelets rattled but the voices on stage sang on without a quiver. Percy was overcome with panic and shame. He had no idea what to do. Mr. Svensson, who was sitting on the other side of the girl, hissed, "Stop it, Veronika! It's embarrassing!"

And in a clear, unmuted voice, but with a hint of tears in it, she replied, "I'm glad you say so, sir!"

Veronika stood up, the balloon in her hand raised high above her head. It reflected the light from the stage. The girl turned to face the audience and from among the rattling bracelets came scandalized whispers and shouts of, "Sit down! Put it down!"

But Veronika stood motionless, in the posture of the Statue of Liberty, in her hands a strange torch and in her eyes an emerald light.

Mr. Svensson got to his feet and reached up for the balloon, but Veronika was taller than he was, and he was forced to jump. At that instant the song ended and the applause erupted but it was perfunctory. The comedy act in the front row had attracted attention. Mr. Svensson jumped again and grabbed the balloon. By now the hall was quiet. And into the silence there came a high raucous noise, like an extended raspberry. The balloon had a noise-maker in its neck. Mr. Svensson stood there helplessly with the bleating thing in his hand. He put his finger over the noise-maker and the rasping stopped, but at the same time the balloon also stopped shrinking. The red letters still declared their message to the hall. Mr. Svensson, his cheeks flushed, turned round and round so that the inscription could be read from all sides. Even from the stage.

A man in an RCMP uniform unstuck himself from the exit and marched towards Mr. Svensson with an expressionless face.

"If you'll allow me, sir!"

He put out his hand and the befuddled Mr. Svensson gave him the balloon. The noise-maker screeched briefly and was blocked by a large thumb. Like Veronika, the man from the RCMP raised the balloon high above his head, and set off slowly and deliberately down the long corridor to the exit, his progress followed by the entire audience in O'Keefe Centre.

Someone began to laugh hysterically beside Percy. Mr. Svensson sank indignantly into his seat. "I'm sorry, Percy," said Veronika, and she stopped laughing. On the stage, the conductor gestured abruptly with his hands and the voices broke into another resounding song, to the accompaniment of the sweet harps in Veronika's mind:

> *V zashchitu mira vstavaytye lyudi!*
> *Ryady tyesnyey, strana k stranye!*
> *I pust nad mirom silnyey orudiye*
> *prizyv nash ryeyet: Nye byt voynye!*

The professional resolve of the chorus on stage was intruded upon by a weak bleating sound from the main exit. The man from the RCMP had taken his thumb off the noise-maker on his way through the door.

• 

Nothing there had changed. In the back of the café, where the lights were kept on even during the day because the light from the large windows on the square could never adequately dispel the gloom, men in crumpled suits were still playing billiards, and along the wall, at tables covered with green felt, sat the card sharks. Vrata was sitting at one table, one of a foursome of euchre players including Kocandrle. They didn't notice me at all, for their eyes were on the cards. Vrata, unlike me, was bound physically to Kostelec by roots of nostalgia. He came back at least twice a month and would spend the whole weekend sitting with his motionless card-playing cronies. But in all the years that had passed since Prema had escaped, I had been back perhaps twice. For me Kostelec was a phenomenon of time, not of place, and the time machine had not yet been invented. There is only the one we carry about in our heads, and I didn't have to go to Kostelec to use it.

This time, in fact, I had come back out of spite. I wanted my presence to embarrass the local patriots who couldn't forgive me for writing that musical comedy. Though they were all firmly anti-Communist, they very much agreed with the Party when it honoured my operetta with the traditional collection of negative epithets. Mayor Prudivy's widow had even written an article in the local Party newspaper, which borrowed its hostile phraseology verbatim from the Party's central organ, and attacked me for impugning the honour of the girls of Kostelec. I knew more than she did about that honour and I did full justice to it in the operetta. Nevertheless the realistic representation of my incessant and silly small talk with Irena, made possible years after the fact by my vivid aural memory, won me the reputation of being the foremost pornographer in Kostelec, defaming the good name of the countryside where Bozena Nemcova had been born. Once Mr. Moutelik had told Rosta on the train to Hradec, "Did you know the National Committee's going to put up a monument to that smart-ass friend of yours in Kostelec?" "You don't say!" said Rosta incredulously, and Mr. Moutelik – no longer a wholesaler, now merely a sales clerk – opened his eyes wide, threw his arms apart and said with gusto, "A sandstone prick ten metres high and three metres thick." He had no idea how he was overestimating me. What would they have done to me, I wondered, had I really allowed my imagination to soar?

My operetta was in fact a profession of love to that lilac-bowered town, to its beautiful girls and its vital, funny people. Instead of gratitude, however, I was honoured with anonymous threats to knock my teeth in, ostentatious silence, and the noses of those same beautiful girls lifted in the air and sailing by me as though I were a wax puppet, his hat raised in his hand, frozen in that pose forever.

And so I went to Kostelec deliberately, in the hope that my presence would add splendour to the unveiling – not of a huge phallus but merely of a monument to the Red Army on the twentieth anniversary of the Liberation.

I was not invited to take a place on the tribune, so I mingled with the crowd. It was a gala affair. They had even invited a Commander of the Soviet liberating army, General Jablonkovsky, leaner after twenty years, but even more bemedalled. He was a somewhat saddened old man. Now he was sitting in the front of the restaurant by one of the etched glass windows with his tiny Soviet wife and an uncommonly pretty, big-eyed girl. I didn't know who she was.

Kos and Malina were playing billiards at one of the tables, and Machane was kibbitzing with them. After twenty years at the game they had not improved. Kos got four hits, Malina followed with three. They too looked almost the same, except that they were balder and plumper and Malina was wearing his policeman's uniform.

I stepped up to the table.

"Hi, gentlemen!"

Kos was just getting ready to shoot, but he straightened up. All three looked at me.

"Hi," said Malina after a pause. "What you up to?"

"Nothing."

"Just goofing off, eh?" Kos began rubbing the tip of his cue with blue chalk. The three balls on the green felt were ideally positioned. Malina looked at me with steady eyes straight out of the Messerschmitt can. These three had certainly not seen my operetta.

"Right," I said, "I'm living like a pig in clover."

"The word around town is they locked you up," said Kos.

"What would they do that for?"

"I heard it's because of something you wrote. Some anti-state theatre play or something. I never seen it myself," said Kos. "But you always was a silly son-of-a-bitch so it'd be just like you."

The endearing conversation warmed my heart.

"They must have got me mixed up with someone else," I said. "I was in Australia."

"Come off it, you pony!" said Malina.

"I was interpreter for the Czech Quartette. I brought back a kangaroo embryo."

"You're a horse's ass!"

Ah, certitude of home! Time passes you by....

"You don't believe me? I've got a kind of pocket at home, sewed for him out of rabbit fur. He lives in there and I feed him milk from a baby-bottle."

"An embryo, eh?" said Kos. "Drinks from a bottle, eh?"

"Kangaroos can do it," I said. "The mother kangaroo gives birth when the young are still embryos."

"D'you want a sock in the snoot, you elephant?" said Malina.

"No, I don't," I replied. "Kangaroos are what they call imperfect mammals. The embryo's three centimetres long when it's born, and they crawl up the mother's fur into her pouch and grab onto her tits."

"Out of the pussy and into the pouch, eh?" said Kos contemptuously.

"I didn't want to put it that crudely. I might get a bad name in my own home town," I said. "But that's the idea."

"How'd you like to eat this fist, you fucking kiwi?" said Malina.

They thought.

"How come they get born so small?" asked Kos. "Only three centimetres long, eh?"

"I don't know why. I guess so the kangaroo won't have labour pains."

Kos made a wry face. "I'll bet women'd go for that, if you could arrange it."

The silent kibbitzer Machane made a face too. Only two of his teeth were showing. "Son-of-a-bitch," he said to Kos. "Can you imagine coming out of your ma only three centimetres long and crawling up her tummy ...?"

"Sure, but women'd have to have pouches!"

"You're all a bunch of heifers, you asses!" said Malina.

"You could make pouches out of plastic," said Machane.

"Sure, but the embryo'd suffocate under her dress."

"So women'd have to go around naked – "

"How'd you like to lose your teeth?" said Malina.

"Maybe they could carry it around in their breast pockets," I said.

Kos chuckled. "And the pocket would have a hole inside so it could go straight to the tit!"

"Watch your tongue, you magpie!" said Malina.

The magic of home, untouched either by time or by socialism. I looked towards Vrata's table, where Kocandrle was just taking a trick off Vrata and Vrata was moaning, the way he always used to. I turned to the main entrance. General Jablonkovsky was talking with the big-eyed girl in Russian. I overheard a fragment of her Russian. She spoke with a Kostelec accent. I walked out of the café onto the square.

The unchanging magic of home. I could hear the organ playing in the church, because it was May. A May mass. Voices indistinguishable from those twenty years before were singing a hymn to the Virgin Mary. The only difference was that there were no clusters of late-comers, who could not get into the church, gathered around the main entrance as there would have been twenty years ago. Fear had done its work.

But Kostelec Castle was still firmly enthroned on its rock, with a new red roof. The windows, as always, were golden in the rays of the setting sun. Around the square little clutches of girls loitered in spring dresses and blue jeans – that was different – and groups of boys, some with guitars.

Suddenly I remembered the multiple postscript of Vrata's letter. It was Friday evening, and Kocandrle, exactly as the message had said, was playing cards in the Beranek. That meant Marie was at home alone. The May evening wafted that Maytime witch into my soul; nothing had changed, not even I, for I remain physically and mentally in that splendid state of puberty, just as this splendid town, this church, has remained unchanged since the twelfth century. I walked quickly along Jirasek Street where more groups of girls and boys were hanging about, turned past the Granada Hotel and walked across the tracks near the station, past the house beside the river where Irena had once lived and where Marie had spied on us from her aunt's house on the other side of the street, across the bridge, past the brewery and up the path to the spot where Marie and I had stood with the sleigh one prehistoric evening and then I had pulled it up the slope to her house, the house I was approaching now.

The summit of Cerna Hora, fringed with dark woods, glowed pink and yellow-green in the sunset. On it a white spot was visible, the stone cross. The Dreslers' house was newly stuccoed, and the upper-storey windows reflected the sunlight. A glassed-in entrance hall, as middle-class and mysterious as ever, and beyond that the mysteries of Marie's private chamber to which I had never gained admittance. I had only seen Marie emerge from there, blue coat, golden curls, V for Victory....

I pressed the bell and peered into the mysterious glass house.

The glass shone, someone inside opened the door and Marie stepped out onto the veranda.

Golden curls, blue eyes, large red strawberry mouth. She had on a close-fitting white cotton sweater, and beneath it those magnificent breasts, the most beautiful in Kostelec. She was wearing jeans, filled breathtakingly with slender thighs and stretched tightly across her little-girl bottom.

How had Vrata put it? *Maybe Molly is immortal....*

"Good evening," said Marie. "You must want...."

•

We are back on the boat once more, alone this time, and the cabin smells of wood, Irene and the faint aroma of perfume. She is sitting across from me on the leather-upholstered bench, and directly behind her the red signal on the roof of the Toronto-Dominion Bank is winking through the porthole. A low table is between us. The only light comes from an intimate wall lamp beside a curtain sprinkled with golden stars that divides the cabin proper from the sleeping quarters. The stars glitter brightly. Irene is nervous. The yacht rocks gently back and forth, bumping intermittently against the wooden wharf. A muffled tom-tom.

Will it really happen? Will that professorial dream come true? Why? *Sic visum Veneri?*

I get up.

"Well – "

"No! You wait here!"

Irene disappears behind the golden stars.

A switch clicks.

So, in this the children of the new world are traditional. At the outset, they must shroud everything in bashful darkness. I wait for the little voice, echoing with nudity, telling me to fling aside the curtains –

– Irene flings aside the curtains and I sit down. Literally. She has a red strip left by an elastic waistband around her white stomach. Otherwise she seems made of alabaster. She glows like the white goddess in *Trader Horn*, and around her head a golden halo of blonde hair and in the female centre of her body a magnificent golden thicket, almost – my breath catches in my throat – like her hair, covering the sweet fissure with golden down –

"You'll catch a cold," I say.

"No I won't," she replies, and doesn't know what to do next. She has not reckoned with my immobility. I ought to stand up and commence the work. But it's much more pleasant to sit and look at this stunning alabaster girl.

For an absurd recollection has taken my breath away.

"Well," she says, evidently embarrassed. "Aren't you going to do something?"

"So you're still a virgin?" I ask.

A dermatological phenomenon envelops that white body. It flushes red from the face right down to the toes, to the toenails which are painted a ridiculous emerald green. The arms, which until this moment have been hanging relaxed beside her body, execute an involuntary motion and she adopts the classic Venus pose. Then she regains her composure. "Yes!" she declares defiantly.

"Well," I say, "put your clothes on."

"You – don't you like me?" her voice trembles.

"Of course I like you."

"Then – why don't you" – the small voice, trembling terribly, drops until it is almost inaudible – "take your clothes off too?"

"Because I want you to like me."

Lifted by an errant wave, the cabin rocks slightly and a golden beam of light from an illuminated skyscraper sweeps through the porthole. Irene's breasts tremble slightly as she asks, "Are you ashamed?"

"Aren't you?"

She nods and the dermatological phenomenon reoccurs. "If you'd take your clothes off too, I wouldn't be."

"That's precisely why I don't."

"But why?"

"I'm not nineteen anymore like you."

The yacht rocks again. The circle of gold from the Toronto-Dominion Bank flushes her white body beige.

"But ... I love you ..." says Irene. "Please!"

I shake my head. An absurd memory hangs in my mind like an opal set in a green monstrance. I shake my head again and say professorially, "Put your clothes back on, Svensson!"

Her hands have ceased to obey her. She doesn't understand me. What has she come up against? Her experience, oddly enough entirely theoretical, cannot tell her. A heroic decision, and so complete its failure. She asks me a touchingly concrete question from the depths of her theoretical experience: "Are you – impotent?"

"No, but you're going to catch your death!"

She stands a few moments longer in the half-dark, beautiful beyond belief. She is still trembling, but in anger now. "Oh, shit!"

She turns around, her bottom like a white pearl, and disappears behind the stars. A switch clicks angrily.

I lie back against the leather upholstery and take a communist cigar from Cuba out of a box belonging to her father. I light it, blowing a thick cloud of smoke across the shaft of light cast by the Toronto-Dominion. The sky beyond the porthole is cheerfully bright. I feel like one link in a chain of repetitions, spanning generations, economic systems, faiths and stupidities.

The stars part, and Svensson, in high dudgeon and more lovely than before, makes her entrance in her white trousers and sailor's middy. She tosses her head indignantly. She sits down and takes a cigarette from her father's box.

"Still a virgin," I say.

Svensson drags half the cigarette into her young lungs and says, "I hate you!"

"Please don't!"

"Couldn't you have told me?"

"What?"

"That you're impotent."

I laugh. "You mustn't simplify things, Svensson. The same behaviour can have different causes."

She inhales the second half of the cigarette and looks at me uncertainly. But she is far more self-assured when dressed.

"Don't you love me anymore?" I ask.

She ponders. "Are you some kind of pervert?"

"Does it bother you so much, Irene?" I say, and love her. "Do you love me?"

"I hate you!" she says, but it's obvious that she is more curious than hateful. "Are you a pervert? Tell me."

"No, I'm not. It's just that I'm about to turn fifty, Svensson. With you I can go back to a time when I was nineteen too."

Another dose of nicotine. She is trying hard to understand me. But she is a child of her generation, and an irrepressible logician. "What's the matter, didn't you fuck when you were nineteen?"

"Now, now, Svensson. Is that how a virgin should talk?"

"Well, did you or didn't you?"

"Do you?"

She looks at me sharply.

I look at her.

We look into each other's eyes as though we are trying to hypnotize each other. People can never keep that up for long and remain serious, as long as there is no real hatred between them. Irene and I begin to laugh at the same time.

"Oh, you're just an old lecher!" says Irene. "But – why didn't you make love to me?"

"I don't know," I say truthfully. "Isn't it nice here, on this splendid yacht? Don't I feel great here? With this beautiful girl, now naked, now dressed?"

"Should I get undressed again?"

"Don't you feel more like yourself when you are dressed?"

"Oh, you are an iceberg!"

"I'll thaw out," I say.

"But when?"

"One of these days."

She pulls her knees up to her chin with her arms and in this typical teenage position she utters the classic lament of her uninhibited generation: "It's such a drag to be a virgin!"

"Such agony!"

"You're a boor!"

"It is agony. I know from my own experience. When you're a virgin you suffer. And then there are all those mysteries."

"Fuck mysteries! I know them all. I've read all the books."

"Not everything is in books. For example, I saw something today for the first time in my almost fifty years."

"What's that?"

"You have it on you."

Involuntarily she looks down at her blue shoes.

"You can't see it now," I say. "You could when you were in the buff."

"Haven't you ever seen a naked woman before in all your fifty years?"

"It's taken me fifty years to see a natural Scandinavian blonde," I say. "I seem to have had better luck with brunettes, and all the blondes I knew were dyed. Except for one, but that was a long time ago. I was still a virgin then – "

"And what is it? What did you see on me?"

"I'm going to tell you a story about it. It's nicer that way. So listen. We almost drove ourselves crazy trying to figure it out."

"You and the blonde?"

"No. Naturally she already knew it. I mean me and a friend of mine. We were both so madly in love with her that we weren't even jealous of each other."

"Did you both have sex with her together?"

"Unfortunately not. She was in love with a third party and wasn't exactly crazy about us. This friend of mine was a painter and the girl's name was Marie. My friend painted her, and once he did her in the nude too but strictly from fantasy. In those days girls were not as shameless as they are today."

"You're mean!" says Irene, just like the girls in Kostelec.

"I only mention it so you'll understand why it was such a mystery to us. Are you listening? So listen." And I tell Irene Svensson the old story that has probably kept her virginity intact today. The intimate light from the lamp makes her Scandinavian hair sparkle, the wind from Lake Ontario sings like the Melusine on Cerna Hora. I begin my story: "Rosta brought all kinds of monographs home from the library, but the earlier painters weren't realistic enough. We examined hundreds of Venuses and Naiads and Aphrodites and Modiglianis and Renoirs, but we couldn't find it any-where – "

●

"... to talk with Daddy? He's not home. He's playing cards at the Beranek."

Golden curls, blue eyes, large red strawberry mouth. No V for Victory but a white cotton pullover. No ribbed knee-socks but jeans. Otherwise it was Molly. Complete. Immortal.

"I'd like to speak with" – the word stuck in my mouth, but there was nothing I could do; that was the proper expression – "your mother."

"Marie's not home either," said Marie, "but she should be back any minute now. If you'd care to wait ...?"

"And you are ...?"

"I'm Dana," said Marie.

"Well, if I might ...?"

"Yes, come right in."

The Marie called Dana stepped aside, I walked through the gate, up the steps to the veranda and through the open glass door to the undiscovered chambers of my far-off youth.

In the hall, Marie went ahead of me and opened another glass door. "Right this way."

I found myself in a sitting room that had clearly once been Mr. Dresler's room. Mr. Dresler had suffered under the illusion that he was descended from some unknown aristocratic family and he had had an expert on heraldry draw him up a family coat-of-arms. This coat-of-arms was carved on the backs of two enormous armchairs upholstered with cracked leather. On an equally enormous writing desk stood a photograph of the late Mr. Dresler, who looked very unlike Marie, and a photograph of his wife, who was also deceased. Marie had her mother's blue eyes, but otherwise there was no resemblance. She must have been the beginning of a new dynasty, or perhaps someone else had fathered her. On the left-hand wall there was a glassed-in bookcase, gleaming with the golden spines of some leatherbound volumes, probably the collected works of Master Alois Jirasek because this was his native district. There was a studio couch against the opposite wall, which in this setting of studied, glassed-in aristocracy had the same effect as a football on an altar. And there was also a small set of bookshelves full of what looked like textbooks. On top of the bookshelves was a picture of the new comedy team, Suchy and Slitr, cut out of a magazine, and on the wall above an oil painting by Rosta Pitterman, called *Idea*, depicting Marie. Not the one called Dana.

"Dana?" I asked. "Or Daniela?"

"It's really Daniela," said Marie, "but it's too long. Won't you sit down?"

She stood in front of me in her blue jeans, and the setting sun conjured alluring shadows from her snow-white pullover. Daniela. Could it be that Marie had remained faithful to her old love, even though in those days she had not loved him very much? But time is merciful to unloved ones. We learn to appreciate them when it is too late. Like everything else in life. It is always too late for everything in life.

"Would you like coffee or something?" said Marie.

I shook my head and sat down in one of the huge armchairs belonging to the nonexistent clan of the seigneurs d'Essleur. "My name is Daniel too," I said, "but everyone calls me Danny."

Eyes like blue pebbles opened wide. "So it's *you*? Well, Marie will be delighted! At least, I think she will."

"Just who do you think I'm supposed to be?"

"Why, you're Danny boy – oh, gosh...."

"You seem to be well informed about me."

"Oh gosh, don't tell on me! Marie doesn't know?"

"Just a moment. What am I not supposed to tell on you and what doesn't Marie know?"

Marie ran her fingers through her golden hair.

"Would you like some coffee?"

"I don't want coffee. Sit down and confess."

She sat down on the corner of the second throne, the coat-of-arms with a swan and a star directly above the golden fleece on her head. "Well ..." and she ran her fingers through her hair once more.

"What doesn't Marie know?"

"Oh, that I've read your letters."

Instead of getting angry with her, I felt a glow of warmth. So Marie had kept them. There were no doubt some very silly things in them. The girl, in an attempt to put her peccadillo in a brighter light, said, "They're very pretty letters. Sort of ... funny...."

They weren't meant to be funny, but Marie, called Dana – I hoped after me – belonged to a less sentimental generation.

"I meant them seriously."

"Oh, I know you did!" she said quickly. With a shameless curiosity unfamiliar to our generation she added, "You must have had a terrible crush on Marie!"

"I still do," I declared proudly.

The forget-me-not eyes flashed and Marie said saucily, "Well, Daddy is going to be delighted!"

Immortal Molly. She had not exactly been a genius. She had barely passed in mathematics and in Latin she could not fathom *consecutio temporum* to save her soul. But *in eroticis* she had always been a great sage – which means: she had a feeling for the humorous side of things, while I did not.

"Don't you go telling him now. He's never ever suspected it."

The forget-me-nots flashed with wicked delight. "If you won't tell Marie that I've read those letters...."

She was obviously my daughter. Only in the spiritual sense, of course, but she was mine. Kocandrle had only given her his surname.

"Fine. A gentleman's agreement?" I said it in English and had to explain what it meant. She was studying French in school. It turned out that her late grandfather had insisted on it. Ah yes, the Count d'Essleur.

"What else do you know about me that you shouldn't?"

"Well, I know that Uncle Rosta said that one scene in your musical, the one that – "

"I know the one you mean."

"It's based on something that really happened. That's the scene with the song that goes: 'I look across the street at night, I see you in the candlelight, the only trouble is you're not alone.' "

"Uncle Rosta is right."

"Almost everybody in Kostelec has seen it," she said, almost sadly. "They say the whole thing is based on stuff that actually happened."

"Haven't you seen it?"

She shook her head. She was definitely sad. "I was eleven at the time, and then they banned it."

Of course. I realized that Marie too had stopped growing old at seventeen. I looked at the oil painting on the wall, capturing that moment.

"Why do you keep it a secret from Marie that you've read those letters of mine?"

"Because it's more interesting when – "

She stopped.

"Out with it!" I said sternly. I was her father, after all. "More interesting when what?"

"When Mum and Dad get into an argument."

My, my.

"An argument? What has that got to do with my letters?"

"Well, you know, they sometimes have arguments about Daddy not making enough money and then losing too much at cards and Daddy always says, 'Why didn't you marry your Danny boy, then, if I'm so dumb!' And if Marie is really angry she sometimes says, 'That wouldn't have been such a bad idea for *other* reasons, either!' That always makes Daddy fit to be tied."

Sadly, I wondered what other reasons there could have been. Apart from having once patted her bum – and she'd invited me to do so – those "other reasons" were sheer fantasy.

"I still don't see what this has to do with my letters – "

She interrupted me. "Well, from those letters it certainly doesn't look as though much ever happened."

"What do you mean by that?" I said in a strict, paternal tone.

"You know what I mean."

"How could you ever dare think such a thing about your own mother?" I said, pretending to be shocked. "Your mother is a saint and the stork brought you."

She exploded with laughter and I couldn't keep a straight face. I felt wonderful.

"You seem to be quite the sly one," I said. "What do you think about all the time?"

"Surely you must remember those letters. What did you think about?"

She was my daughter all right. I rumpled her golden hair with my fingers. Out-and-out incest. Of course, as is always the case with me, purely spiritual.

"Have you got a boyfriend?"

"Yes, sure."

"And what?"

"And nothing," she said. "He could write letters too. Only he doesn't."

"Then what does he do?"

"He loves me."

I lit a cigar. A droplet of recognition slid into this delicious feeling of happiness, a recognition that these recurrences with their variations are perhaps our only form of immortality – nothing else. *Verbleibe doch, du bist so schön!* That verse from the era of the protectorate surfaced in my mind, yet it had nothing to do with a historical sense of time. Marie called Dana brought me an ashtray, sat down on her high-born grandfather's throne, crossed her legs under her and looked at me inquisitively.

"Is it really true that you and Marie never had anything going? Never ever? Never ever ever?"

"Never ever ever," I said. "Except, of course –"

"Aha!" she said with naughty delight. "I knew it!"

"I don't know what it is you know, because you certainly don't know this."

"Well, you kissed, didn't you?"

"If only that were all."

The forget-me-not eyes nearly popped out of her head.

"You did *more?*"

"At confession it was called 'touching,'" I said, because I had remembered Marie's one and, alas, only invitation on the slopes of Cerna Hora. "But if that were all!"

"Well, but there's ... nothing beyond that except...."

"That," I suggested.

"Yes."

"You're wrong," I said. "There was a certain bet."

"With Marie?"

"No. With Rosta – I mean with Uncle Rosta."

"A bet about what?"

I exhaled a thick cloud of smoke. In the rays of the setting sun it was golden. Like Marie's hair.

"You've got exactly the same hair as Marie," I said.

"Don't try to change the subject!"

"I'm not. On the contrary."

"Then don't keep me in suspense!"

Should I tell her? After all – but in the embrace of incest the former scandal suddenly appeared in the light of eternity, that is, without guilt. Not as something decent people don't talk about – because "decent people" do not exist – but as something tender and beautiful, because in the passage of time the foolish excesses of youth are transformed into ethereal things. A comic attempt to peer into the mystery of eternity, forever locked away in that commonplace sanctuary, hidden from man and his science.

"Since you ask so nicely...." I exhaled another cloud of smoke. Once again it glowed with the gold of that distant evening and its electric light-bulb. "We racked our brains about it for days. Rosta brought all kinds of monographs home from the library, but earlier painters were never realistic enough. We looked at hundreds of Venuses and Naiads and Aphrodites and

Modiglianis and Renoirs, but it was never there...."

I paused, a long pause.

"What wasn't there?"

"If you listen, you'll find out. Don't interrupt me."

Just then a key rattled in the lock.

Both of us sat up and looked towards the glass door. I could see radiant golden hair and the blue shadowy outline of a figure in a spring dress.

"Dana? Are you home?" said Marie's voice. The door opened and there she was exactly as Vrata had described her. The ravages of time had absolutely nothing to show for their efforts.

•

"*What* wasn't there?" Irene asks. "The navel? They did paint the navel in those days, didn't they?"

"I'm not talking about the navel," I say. "We saw navels enough at the swimming pool. By then women *were* wearing two-piece bathing-suits. Not as scanty as today, but you could see their belly-buttons sometimes."

"Well, what *was* it?"

"I can only tell it as a story. Any other way it wouldn't be as nice. Almost everything is nicer when it's told as a story."

"Well, tell it, tell it!"

"I'm trying to," I say. "It began when Rosta found out, God knows how, that the Dreslers' water supply had been temporarily cut off and that Marie was coming to the Public Baths. Like all young girls, she loved the water. Rosta came to get me while the band was rehearsing at the Port Arthur Restaurant and he said, 'It's now or never!' Incidentally, this shows what a pessimist he was about his future chances with Marie."

"Were you an optimist?"

"I was a skeptic. I dropped everything, right in the middle of practice, and we rushed over to the Public Baths. We waited out of sight around the corner until we saw Marie. She had come, all right. It was winter and she had on a very pretty coat with a hood with white fur trimming. I called it *Fau für Viktoria*."

"What's that?"

"It means V for Victory. When the hood hung down behind it made a big V."

"And did she win?"

Did she? Yes, I suppose she did. What is victory in our lives? Recurrences with variations, the exquisite interment in time. The line of a family, not aristocratic, drawn out between two mutations. Probably she didn't win. There is no victory. Even God himself may blunder, thwarted by a silly invention called freedom.

"I don't know," I say. "But don't interrupt me. This story really begins even before Rosta learned that Marie was going to the Public Baths. It began with a conversation in the washroom of a certain factory, and that gave us a hint that it was technically possible. But in the first place it was too risky, and in the second place the Dreslers had a bathroom of their own. As we talked about it endlessly, it gradually began to obsess Rosta and he came to think of it as an artistic problem, a creative problem. And the only way it could be solved finally was by a kind of autopsy. That's why we decided to take the risk, now or never. As soon as Marie disappeared into the baths, we rushed in and each of us rented a compartment. When the attendant wasn't looking, we both nipped into the same one."

"Was there a hole in the wall? And anyway, how did you know which compartment this Marie was in?"

"Shows you're thinking. We couldn't have known, of course, but it didn't matter. Each of the compartments had a roof made of large squares of pebbled glass. You could see through it, but it blurred everything slightly, as though you were looking at it through a cloud, or surrounded by a halo of light. Kind of impressionistic, or like in old movies when the camera-man would have the lens just slightly out of focus during the close-up of a face. Like Hedy Kiesler in *Ecstasy*. Anyway, everything on the other side of the glass seems to be radiating some kind of aureola. Now, in each compartment the panel of glass in the corner could be raised to let the steam out. This was the key to our plan, and we wasted no time in carrying it out. I stood under the panel; Rosta climbed up on my shoulders, pushed it open and pulled himself up through the opening. There was a catwalk running along the wall above all the compartments – Prema had told us about it in the factory washroom. Rosta sat on the walkway and helped me up. As the steam came out of the compartments it condensed, so the catwalk was extremely slippery. It was also awfully narrow."

"You're making this up," says Irene. "It's like a scene from a screwball comedy."

"Svensson," I say, "kindly remember this most banal of all truisms: the most incredible comedies are written by life."

"My life is more like a railway timetable."

"Just wait till time intervenes. The alchemy of time transforms everything into comedy. Everything. Even crucifixion. But listen, damn it! Anyway, we both got up on this catwalk and with our backs against the wall we edged ourselves very cautiously along above the compartments till we got to the one where Marie was taking a bath. It wasn't far, just one away from where we were. In the intervening cubicle there was a fat man with a bald head who looked, through the glass, like the moon in a fog. He was playing with a red toy sailboat. We were soon over Marie's compartment – that is,

Rosta was. I was sliding along after him, so I couldn't see her yet – except a bit of her naked leg was visible over the edge of the partition between the compartments. I could see a point just above her knee, and it was beautifully out of focus and beige-coloured in the greenish water. And before I go any further I have to say that we never did get to know what we'd come to find out, because something happened – "

"What kind of story is this? What are you telling it to me for if you didn't find out? This story lacks a final effect!"

I laugh. "And what should the final effect be, Svensson, according to Edgar Allan's theory?"

"Stronger than all the ones that come before it."

"Right. And if the author cannot think up a final effect that is stronger than the effects preceding it, he should leave the ending what?"

"Open."

"Correct. Like Pym who, plunging into the abyss of the watery whirlpools, sees a mysterious superhuman figure, white and terrible – "

"Oh God!" Irene sighs impatiently. "What abysses did you plunge into? And was there a white figure?"

Into what abysses? *Vanitas vanitatum, ubique semperque vanitas?*

"In this story," I say, "the only effect stronger than the one we expected would have been gold itself. But then it would be a fairy-tale. This is pure realism. Let's call it national socialist realism, since it happened during the war. So it couldn't have been gold, therefore life left us an open ending. We didn't find out. I, however, did – "

"Well, did you or didn't you?"

" – but that was in another country, and besides, the girl wasn't alive at the time. Look, just listen, Svensson. All of a sudden, Rosta's feet slipped on the catwalk, and right before my eyes, with a tremendous crash of glass, he plunged into Marie's cubicle like the devil into hell. I could hear a great splashing of water down below, Marie screamed, and I saw Rosta hanging by his hands from the frame of that broken panel of glass, the blood spurting through his fingers. But by that time I was beating a hasty retreat along the catwalk and down into our compartment. I grabbed my clothes and, God knows how, I climbed back onto the catwalk and got down into the next compartment, which we had also rented, and jumped into the bathtub. I was in such a panic that I forgot to take my underpants off. There was a terrible commotion coming from Marie's compartment. That girl certainly knew how to scream, I can tell you. Then I heard someone, the attendant I suppose, banging on the compartment door, and a confusion of voices as people rushed into the baths from the waiting room. I thought it might seem strange if I didn't put in an appearance too, so I ran into the corridor – in my wet underpants, but no one noticed. Everyone was naturally interested in

Marie, who was standing there wrapped in a large towel, her teeth chattering but not from the cold – she was honestly and truly terrified. Not surprisingly, considering that a half-naked man had just fallen into her bathtub. And she screamed, Irene, how magnificently she screamed. I have never before or since heard a woman scream like that. And the attendant burst out of the compartment literally dragging Rosta by the ear, and the blood was pouring out of him. Not just from his hands – he was cut badly on the stomach, and he had a – " I stop.

"What did he have?"

"Well, he had a hard-on."

"This isn't a screwball comedy," says Irene. "It's hard-core porn."

"Maybe it is. But that's the way it is in this world. It all depends on why you tell it in the first place."

"And why are you telling it?"

" 'For the joy, the grief and the sadness of life and death,' Irene."

●

"Well, this is a surprise visit if ever there was one!" said Marie.

"Aw, couldn't you have stayed away a little longer?" muttered Dana.

Marie looked inquiringly at her daughter, and then sharply at me. "Why longer?"

It was an embarrassing situation for both Dana and me.

"We were talking about – things," said Dana.

Marie's eyes, still merry, examined the intangible situation that hung in the air like the smoke from my cigar.

"You can go right on talking in front of me, pet."

"It wouldn't be the same."

"Whatever were you talking about?"

"Oh you know – about life."

"And weren't you talking about Marie as well?"

Dana and I looked at each other.

"But only nice things," said Dana.

"And decent I hope, too."

"Well I don't know about that," Dana retorted slyly. "He was just starting...."

"Well, go on, 'he,' " said Marie to me, and she sat down in the armchair where Dana had been. She had a short skirt on and her white knees were the same as always. "Just pretend I'm not here."

"That's all very well," I said, "but you *are* here."

The blue eyes swept in another half-circle from me to Dana and back again.

"So it wasn't exactly for schoolgirls, I take it."

"You know what, Marie?" said Dana. "I'll leave you both here alone and he can tell you what he was about to tell me, and if it's suitable, then you can tell me, okay?"

And she got up to leave. Marie said, "Go and make something for supper. You must be hungry, 'he,' aren't you?" and she turned to me and then back to Dana. "And his name is Uncle Danny."

"I know. He's named after me," said Dana saucily and disappeared through the glass doors into the recesses of the house.

"What were you telling her?" asked Marie, as though we had last seen each other the day before at the pool.

"It was nothing, Marie," I said. "I was telling her how Uncle Rosta once fell into a bathtub."

"With me in it."

"I hadn't got that far yet. I mean, I hadn't intended to mention that fact."

"She would have guessed," said Marie. "Even if I could imagine how you could *not* mention me in that story, which I can't. Don't underestimate my daughter's intelligence. At least not that type of intelligence. That way she takes after you."

"Like her name?"

Marie looked down and smiled mysteriously.

"It's obvious," I said. "She's not called Rostenka, nor Alberta, nor Cenka nor Leopolda," I said, naming the ones who had once followed the lure of the great V for Victory. "And she's certainly not called Frantiska."

"You forgot Rudolf and Gustav," Marie teased.

"Who was Gustav?"

"He used to play the alto in Kovarik's band in Olomouc."

"Him? I didn't know that...."

"Oh, indeed! And how!" sighed Marie. "But he was out of mind before you had a chance to take note of his existence. And besides you were in love with Irena at the time, so I was free to do what I wanted."

"I never loved Irena, Marie. I always loved you."

"I know, because you told me. Many, many times."

"You didn't believe it?"

"Yes, I did. Why do you think our little reiteration is called Daniela?"

"Then why didn't you marry me, Marie?" I said entreatingly.

"And have Dana turn out schizophrenic?"

"But I'm not — "

"You, Danny boy, are a magnificently split personality. Not just two ways, but fifty ways. Even when you were lying, you were telling the pure truth. To both me and Irena. Maybe the truth was even purer in her case."

"It couldn't have been!"

Marie laughed. The setting sun turned her mouth into a strawberry. Is not speech, I thought, the essence of all human delight?

"I believe you," said Marie. "Gentlemen always prefer blondes."

"But seriously, I loved you, Marie."

"And seriously I loved you too. Why do you think I wouldn't marry you?"

"I know," I said in mock sadness, "because of the schizophrenia."

"That too. But the main reason was that you were such an unreal lover. I didn't ever want to lose you in some idiotic reality." How could anyone ever have believed that women are stupid? They are wiser than men. Men are merely clever. If that. "But surely you didn't have to go on about such dubious episodes from your youth in front of Dana."

"Where you're involved, Marie, I can't hold back."

Marie crossed one leg over the other and I felt just the way I used to feel.

"Not that Dana isn't well informed," said Marie. "You did carry on about it in that musical of yours. And then Dana turned up your letters, so it would be naive to try and keep anything from her."

"She told you that? That she read our correspondence?"

"You're something of an expert in the psychology of teenage girls, Danny," Marie said. "Fortunately they have a lot on their mind at once, and she left a postcard from one of her boyfriends in Prague among the letters. She must have used it to mark her place."

"But Marie," I said slowly, "that means you read the letters too. Molly!"

Marie stopped. Had the western sky flushed red in the sunset? She said, "All right, I read them, I admit it. It's kind of elevating. When I feel that we're getting old, they prove to me that we're not. They're full of exactly the same nonsense as your great theatrical masterpiece. You know, 'Danny boy,' you haven't changed a bit!"

She looked at me with merry, forget-me-not eyes.

"I haven't!" I cried proudly. "And I don't want to! Not changing means remaining faithful. And seeing things always with fresh, unexhausted eyes. The only change is change towards the worse. It's a law of nature."

"My goodness!" said Marie. "I thought you were just a storyteller and here you are a philosopher!"

"Supper's on the table!"

In the open doorway stood Marie, called Dana after me.

•

We had supper in a white cubist kitchen designed in the 1920s. Through the French doors leading to the garden we could see Cerna Hora, a copper moon above it. We talked about everything in a grand farrago of gossip and reminiscing: Irena; her prudish husband; Zdenek, who had tried to hang himself over Irena but the rope broke, and then he tried it again over some girl from Prague; the boys in the band and their marriages, infidelities and tribulations; Rosta and his wife, about whom Marie spoke with delightful acidity; Marie's lazy brother, who had joined the Party and was district secretary in charge of physical fitness – whose only work, said Marie, consisted of reporting once a month on the athletic progress of the young sportswomen in his jurisdiction for which he was getting eighteen hundred a month and an eighteen-year-old private secretary. Is she pretty? You're asking a lot for a soft touch like that, aren't you? And we gossiped about the doubtful paternity of several children of our older friends, whereupon Dana pointed out that she had noticed she had a double incisor like mine, and Marie, with exaggerated emphasis, told her that Kocandrle had had one too but had knocked it out playing hockey in adolescence; which must have been a lie, because Kocandrle never played hockey in his life. I asked what time Franta usually came back and Dana stood up and said she would unlock the back gate and wash the third plate as soon as she heard the key in the veranda. We felt good together. We were, in a way, an unreal family, and I didn't want to go home. And anyway, where was home? But midnight was approaching and the father of the real family would soon be returning from his card game. So I got up and Marie and Dana walked out to the veranda with me. They stood there like two Maries, a physical schizophrenia, two girls with golden crowns on their heads, bathed in the silver light of the May night. I waved to them. Then the house disappeared in the dark.

When I had turned onto the main path below, at the point where the sleighs from Cerna Hora always came to a halt, I heard the light footfalls of someone running. I looked around. It was Dana, bringing me the box of cigars which I had dangerously left behind.

"Uncle Dan," she said, "what wasn't on those Modiglianis and Renoirs and was on Marie?"

"I won't tell you," I said. "Marie didn't think it would be suitable. And anyway, you probably have it too. So think about it."

And I turned to leave.

"I'll find it in the letters all the same," said Marie called Dana after me.

"You won't find it there," I said, turning around for the last time. Marie, called Dana, stood there in jeans and a white cotton pullover luminescent in the dark, and in the moonlight her hair was more golden than the halo which once, long ago, the Venerable Father Meloun had placed on the Virgin Mary's head in the grammar-school assembly, with his own hands, freshly painted by Charita. She was standing before me and her head was burning like pure gold.

"You won't find it there," I said. "Marie never found out I was in the bath-house too. She's always thought I only knew the story from Rosta. Goodbye, golden head!" I said and walked towards the town.

And that was the last time I ever saw Marie and my spiritual daughter.

●

*September 23 1954*
*Sofron, Slovakia*

*Dear Danny,*
*I adres you with these few lines to let you know I am well and hope you are enjoying the same blesing at present. The harvist is over for this year so now I have more time to write to you. This year the harvist produced a yeild of I guess about 1 1/2 to two hunderd per hectaire. Our Unified Peasants Cooperative was judged the third best in the district so we'll be getting twelve to thirteen crowns per unit. I wrote an artical about it in the* Ludove Pravo *and got payed 70 crowns for it. It didnt take me more than two hours to write and that makes 35 crowns a hour. How much do you make? My artical had 40 lines and when they printed it had fifteen so I reckon that 35 crowns a hour is good pay. Im going to write a artical in the spring about how the sowing went.*

*Our co-op has 70 head of cow and 3 pair of horses and we make folk lore easter eggs and hemp rope on the side. Every members got his own little plot of land where he can grow whatever he likes. I grow mainly potatos. And thats because now the leaders are saying that all over potatos havent grown too good because of bad weather and enemy agents in the co ops so I hand my spuds over and make a good profet and help the state out at the same time. I feed the pig with leftovers from the pub that the husband of my brother-inlaws cousin runs.*

*I should write something about the family as well. You know my daughter Suleika, that's a Georgian name, is 8 this year and she looks a lot like me with my nose but with little girls it dosnt matter. Her hairs as black as a gipsies after her old grandad. Shes in the second grade at the elementary school and she can already sign her name and count to twenty and even she uses a Soviet thing called a abracadabrus to help her. We are very happy with her especialy my wife only we'd like more children like her but so far my daughter Suleika's the only one. My wife wanted that name acording to the song Where are you Suleika My Star. My old father died this year. He was in jail for three years for anti-state talk. He wouldn't join the co op. He was a reactionery and killed his own 2 horses when they arested him. He died in prison but he wasnt so old. My old mother is still alive but she is failing.*

*My brother Olda and his Lithuaynian engineer wife are now raizing angora rabits and they give the skins to the factory in Kostelec that they used to own. They are still independant exsept that now they dont exployt anyone like before which is why they nationalised there factry two years ago in 1952. It was the last one in the district and my sister-inlaw the Lithuaynian engineer started raizing angora rabbits without exployting any workers. I hope to God they dont nationalise this one because they arent exployting anyone anymore.*

*We got a fridgerator and I'm also on the list to buy a television which is a great thing for culture that was impossable in the old days of private enterprize. The chairman of our co op has a new Spartak car and some of the members have Java motorcycles. I want to buy one soon too, one with a sidecar so I can take my wife and Suleika to the fares and other places we could never get to before.*

*We also have a better cultural life here in the district town. Theatre troops come on tour to the local theatre where we seen a play by the playwrite and poet Jan Vrchcolab So Grate A Love and which was very nice even when the sad heroin kills herself because nobody under-stood her. We also go to the movies two or three times a month and we seen Mr. Habetin Goes Away which was pretty good except that it wasnt so interesting and also My Freind Fabian which I didnt like because I got no use for gipsies who steal chickens from our co op until I caught more than three of them myself and handed them over to the local police who put them behind bars. Gipsies are robbers and fleabags and ignerant and all they know is getting drunk and fighting and playing the fiddle. Also we saw the film Mr. Angel on Holiday with Marvan which was very nice. But I still think actreses was prettier in the old days like Barova or Mandlova or Hayde Mary Hatayer they were fine figures of a woman. Maybe I shouldnt write that in case my wife reads it. Id be in for it if she did. In conclusion plese axsept my warmist wishes and fondist memries*

> *your old freind*
> *Lojza*

•

She walked across the field in a man's raglan coat that had probably been made about the year of my birth. Even from a distance her eyes shone with a light they say does not exist. She looked like "The Bride of Death," a picture I remembered from an old book of fairy-tales. The terrifying Schweiger had painted her long before she was born. A monstrous red sun stood over the black woods, and on the edge of the black shadow cast by the black woods a gaunt white face and from those eyes that black light which set fire to the Pejskars' cottage. She appeared to be limping. I looked out at her from the window, where she could not see me. Not even with the laser beams of those eyes. I was hidden behind the golden conflagration of the sun in the window-panes. I did not move. I burned in that fire, a ridiculous actor in a bungled act of sabotage, Danny the crackerjack, the wind-splitter. I did not move.

She was already quite close. Her boots thumped on the wooden steps of the cottage. I could hear her heavy breathing. I opened the door.

We embraced. Beneath the old raglan coat I felt scarcely anything at all. When I let her go, she said, "I have to sit down first, Dan. I'm properly bushed."

She was. She looked as though someone had painted her face: little circles of red appeared on her white cheeks, like a wooden carnival doll.

She shivered.

"I'll start a fire if you'd like."

She nodded, and was racked by a fit of coughing.

"And I'll make coffee – I mean Melta. There's no real coffee here." I started a fire in the pot-bellied stove and soon the heat was spreading through the wooden room.

"Dan, can I stay the night here?"

The question startled me. "But – what about Franta?"

"Franta went to see his aunt in Rounov and he's going to stay there until at least the day after tomorrow. His aunt's very poorly and she's got nobody to look out for her. And he's not working in the factory no more – almost nobody is...."

"Of course you can stay, Nadia."

She took the awful raglan coat off. Underneath it she was wearing the same grey sack-shaped dress and a fustian blouse with little flowers on it. From the ample pockets of the raglan she took some tarts her aunt had made. So we drank Melta and ate the tarts. The fire in the pot-bellied stove crackled, but Nadia shivered as though she was still cold. We were silent, until she said, "That young lady you was on the sleigh with – is she your girl?"

"She's just a kind of – friend, that's all. She goes with someone else."

She lowered her eyes and looked into the chipped cup. "My father's not coming back. I just know it. But maybe that Miss Silbernaglova will get through. Young people can take a lot more. When they're healthy," she added.

I had completely forgotten the china cup in our kitchen – that had been long ago, sometime in the winter. And I had forgotten the story I had made up about Rebecca.

"Rebecca will come back," I said. "She's got a strong constitution. She was on the Kostelec junior swimming team."

"Will you marry her?"

"Well, I" – the question made me feel like a fraud – "I mean who knows whether she'll even want me? God knows what she's had to go through there."

"But you went together, didn't you?"

"Well ... yes, a little."

A strong feeling of humbug and immorality almost robbed me of my voice, although it was all slightly absurd. It was she, after all, who was engaged to be married. I was as free as a bird; I had lied outright about Rebecca. Even so I felt like a swine.

"Franta and I are getting married just as soon as the war's over," she said. "We already been to catechism, and we're only having the banns read once, because the priest knew us since we was kids."

I tried to change the subject quickly. "And are you feeling better, Nadia? You wrote me you were taking some pills."

"Yes," she said. She took a drink from the cup and then, with her burning eyes fixed on the worn table-top, she said, "But you know, Dan, I'm going to die soon anyway. I won't even live to have children."

"That's – that's nonsense, Nadia!" I almost shouted. Her remark felt like a blow to the stomach. "You'll be taking a cure after the war's over."

"I'm not afraid, Dan," she continued calmly. I looked at her wide-eyed while she went on as though she were talking about the weather. "Everybody has to die. Only it makes me feel sad, you know? That I won't ever see you again, and that I'll leave Franta behind alone, and we won't even have kids."

"Nadia!"

I choked back tears. But not because I was moved by my own fate, as I had always been before. All at once I knew that Nadia was right. The moon took the sun's place behind the window, the red spots disappeared from her cheeks. Her face was as white as a winding-sheet. Deep, dark shadows under her eyes. And more and more, that terrible black light radiated from them. She was beautiful and terrifying. And she went on talking, more to herself than to me. "Franta'll be all right, he can marry again. He's still young. And Father is in the arms of God now anyway. I'll see him sooner than I figured."

"Do you – " I blurted out, and then stopped. But I had called her back from her world, where I did not belong at all, where I have never been and could not be, though I tried hard enough and often enough later in life.

"What, Dan?"

"I mean, I'm glad that you ... that you believe that, that you ... have such faith...."

She looked at me, but she didn't understand. "I'm a believing Catholic, like you."

I nodded, with that ghastly feeling that I was a fraud, a fool, a bastard. I couldn't find a word for it.

"Maybe I'll have to go to purgatory first," she said, "but I hope not to hell. I go to confession twice a year and I never deliberately hurt anyone" – and she hung her head – "except Franta – but – I couldn't help that."

I was overcome by a painful longing to tell her that she would certainly go to heaven, because if she didn't where would they send everyone else? For others hell is too little, or if it is not, then heaven is not good enough for her. Except that there's no heaven. Nor hell. Nor eternal life. At that moment I was certain of it. Where would that sadness have come from if death were just a kind of mutation? In this ugly universe it was impossible for anything beautiful to be immortal. After all, the universe is based on cruelty and indifference. There is no justice in it at all. It is empty, and at the most there is a gangster presiding over it somewhere, some Al Capone of the universe – that was a phrase by a poor poet whose wife had died of a brain tumour: Al Capone of the universe. And Nadia was dying. Thus I blasphemed, overwhelmed for the first time in my life by the sadness that is the lot of all things living, because the gangster invented death, and left himself out of the reckoning. I didn't tell Nadia any of this. But I could not bring myself to tell her she would go to heaven either. In this regard, at least, I could not lie.

"That's my fault," I said instead, "not yours."

"Oh no, Dan. A woman can always help it. If she doesn't want it to happen, then it doesn't happen."

She shuddered.

"Are you cold?"

She shook her head. "I got a fever. Can I – can I go to bed now, Dan?"

She was sick. I got out the blankets, made her a bed on the couch, if it could be called a bed. She stood up and said, "Don't look now, Dan."

I turned away and put more wood on the fire. The cracks in the stove threw a fiery dance of light on the wooden walls. The wood crackled. "You can look now," said Nadia.

I turned back. She was lying on the couch with the blanket pulled up to her chin. She had spread the raglan coat from the year of my birth on top of the blanket. On the dirty pillow, her lovely white face was framed by her hair.

"Come to me, Dan. And don't be angry with me."

How could I have been angry with her? I took off my clothes and got under the raglan beside her. I took her in my arms. She was by now terribly thin, poor innocent Nadia.

In the night I woke up. The full moon was high in the sky, but at first it seemed that I was staring into absolute darkness. A black darkness. Then I realized that Nadia was not asleep and was looking into my face.

"You're fond of me, aren't you, Dan?" she said when she saw I was awake. "I'm awful fond of you. But you know, Dan, when I'm with you I have thoughts – sinful thoughts...."

"What do you mean, Nadia?"

"That it's – but it *is* a sin. A great sin. And because of Franta too. But I...." She sobbed. It was the first time I'd ever seen her cry.

"Don't cry, Nadia! It's not a sin at all. And even if it was...." Jesus the merciful, I went on, but only to myself, because I believed in nothing. Jesus of the pure heart. Of the pure heart!

"It *is* a sin," she sobbed. "You know it yourself. You're a Christian!"

O Jesus, who they say taketh away the sins of the world.

"But you wrote me yourself, Nadia, that a young girl has to kick up her heels – "

"That's just a saying, Dan, but she shouldn't let it go right to – she should resist the temptation. Only, Dan, you know something, Dan?"

"What, Nadia?"

"With you it doesn't seem like temptation, Dan. You're – my – you're so – so wise, Dan."

Me? Wise? Jesus the unjust! Jesus the foolish, the simple-minded, the evil, delighting in our blindness –

"I'm just stupid, Nadia."

"No you're not. You've been to school, haven't you? But you're fond of me, aren't you?"

"I am. I'm very fond of you, Nadia."

She put her big, hot mouth against mine and my fingers slipped into the grooves between her tender, fragile ribs. I remembered those badly carved statues of Christ done by the folk artisans on Cerna Hora, with chests like slat boxes. Nadia was departing. Whom the gods love. Jesus the incomprehensible. Within me there arose fury, regret, a suffocating, strangling regret. Nadia forgive me, said a voice in my head, a familiar voice, overheard somewhere before. Forgive me, daughter, for having created you. Forgive me, all you who are tortured. I, a miserable sinner, confess to you, Nadia, that I have sinned greatly. The all-powerful, the little-merciful, unwise –

I fell asleep and dreamed that I was riding on a small horse of the steppes towards a large pagan moon, regarding it from the depths of a dark cave, that from a dreamless sleep of the diluvium, the alluvium and the Tertiary, a question was forcing its way into my brain, and it is still the same question here beneath this prairie moon, or on the filthy couch in the Pejskars' cottage, and not even God himself can answer it, much less the gods of this world, an insubstantial question, yet heavier than Jupiter – I fell asleep in the embrace of the dying girl – I fell asleep and perhaps I never woke up –

In the morning Nadia had a fever. I walked her through the woods to Jirasek's Châlet on Cerna Hora, but I stayed at the edge of the woods so no one from the village would see me that early in the morning. I had to support her all the way, for she was weak and had several long coughing fits.

I watched her as she walked slowly away over the crest of Cerna Hora in her highland boots and that huge raglan coat, past the stone cross to the buildings at the edge of the village.

And then I only saw her once more in my life.

And then I only saw her –

# CHAPTER SIX

The merely poetic destroys poetry....

VLADIMIR HOLAN

If the Axis powers were to lose the war, most of the real
Fascists who survived would go over to Communism. Then
we would bridge the gap that separates the two revolutions.

ARGENTO SOFFICI,
*Ideologist and Minister in Mussolini's*
*Italian Social Republic, 1943-1945*

•

# Conrad

*Toronto*
*September 18, 1976*

**M**y darling Lida!
   *I'm infuriated, and perhaps I shouldn't be writing to you at all,
since you deserve only letters of love from me. But both of us know
that the world is a struggle between contradictions, so perhaps it will
give you some pleasure if I write about my indignation and hatred. My
best friend Lincoln, whom I've told you so much about, who grew up
with me and who is one of my closest soul-brothers, has read Solzhenitsyn! Can you imagine? And not only that, he believes him! He even
tried to persuade me to read him too! When I told him I didn't know
why I should bother with such filthy rubbish he told me I should learn
something about the other side of socialism! Why? I asked him, and he
didn't understand! Why should I learn the so-called truth from a fascist like that, and anyway nobody but him has ever seen it! The truth I
have seen with my own eyes is enough for me. I have been to Prague
and I have seen that magnificent city for myself and those happy,
cheerful people in the theatres and beer halls. I know you – and even*

365

*though you were born there and have lived there all your life, you've never seen anything like Solzhenitsyn described either.*

*So Lincoln has been a great disappointment to me, my darling Lida. Tonight I've more or less calmed down. You see, I went to a restaurant where the comrades from the Toronto organization meet, and Comrade Smith, our distinguished political organizer, gave me a long, explanatory lecture on the whole problem, in which he made very short and uncompromising work of Solzhenitsyn. His words are so full of truth that not even ten Gulag Archipelagos could prove them wrong. "I have searched my map in vain for some Gulag Archipelago," said Comrade Smith. "It's humbug! No such archipelago has ever existed anywhere. It is sheer fabrication and lies from start to finish! It exists only in the hate-filled mind of A. Solzhenitsyn, the author of that useless book. There is no need to look for the Gulag Archipelago. It has to be forgotten!"*

*That is the truth. Traitors like Solzhenitsyn, however, are so consumed by rage that even if no Gulag Archipelago existed they would dream one up just to be able to blacken the truth about the world of socialism.*

*So please don't take it amiss, dearest Lida, if today I write you nothing of what I would like most to write to you about. I would love to embrace you, to imbibe the liquid warmth of your sweet body – and I know you feel the same. Whenever I recall being together with you in Prague, the centre of my being swells with the great power of my love for you....*

> I kiss you everywhere, everywhere,
> *your*
> *Booker*

•

Irene has poured thick ketchup over her french fries and she passes the bottle to Dianne. Dianne uses it for the same purpose and passes it on to Bellissimmo, who first applies it to Vicky's potatoes, then his own, then flips the bottle across the table to Ted Higgins. The ritual is repeated: Higgins gallantly anoints Wendy McFarlane's potatoes. Jenny Razadharamithan refuses the ointment; she is eating something equally ritualistic that looks like a fried tie. Hakim too refuses it. He treats his french fries with mustard before smothering them in emerald-green slime.

Apart from french fries, the shiny, chromed, automated and utterly sterile Edenvale cafeteria offers triangular slabs called Fried Fish (with french fries) and an acidic mixture of carrots, peas, potatoes and ground hamburger going by the name of Beef Stew. From the automatic dispensers of Canteen Canada one may purchase five different kinds of triangles, called Ham, Ham and Cheese, Tuna, Cornbeef and Chicken Salad sandwiches, and four types of artificial pastry. A shiny percolator dispenses a liquid called Coffee which causes heartburn and into which the students put a powder called Coffee Master. The Coffee Master gives it the colour of that long-ago Irena's eyes. Either because they don't have any money (they squander it in the three Edenvale pubs on three drinks, beer, ale and lager, which all taste the same and have the same threshold of inebriation: in my case three bottles) or because they are watching their figures, their lunch consists day in and day out of french fries and ketchup. They treat their pimples with an ointment called Propa Ph that costs a dollar seventy-five. Irene eats this uniform lunch in order not to stand out from the rest. I do it because I am probably perverted. I like french fries with ketchup.

Over this Edenvale banquet we continue the debate begun before lunch in the lecture room, where Bellissimmo had been reading an endless, carefully prepared paper. He did not have time to finish it then, and he does so now from memory:

"Each of the three stations on the way to the interior symbolizes the regression of the ego faced with the reality of the jungle. The jungle is described in the same terminology that Freud used to describe the id."

I don't know who – if anyone – understands Bellissimmo. Be that as it may, Hakim sticks to his view that *Heart of Darkness* is a social critique of European imperialism, and Irene takes up a position in the middle: I agree, she says, with Guérard who says that the novel is above all about a journey into the centre of a soul. The experience of Kurtz may be generalized: he accepted freedom and thus became human. But he did not realize all that was entailed in *being* human –

Will Hakim rise to confront such an outpouring of idealism?

He does.

"Kurtz," he replies drily, "is an ordinary imperialist lackey. He robs the blacks at the same time as he pretends to be civilizing them. But in the end Kurtz himself defines the real aim of this civilizing: 'Exterminate all the brutes!'"

Jenny Razadharamithan offers a commentary that sounds as if it's about comets and appendicitis, and thus for a while she silences the others, who have been taught to respect the idiosyncrasies of non-Canadian peoples. After a minute of silence Wendy says, "But then why is it so kind of strange?"

"What's kind of strange?"

"Why didn't he write it clearer? So we could understand it?"

"Because he was a *bourgeois* writer." Correct, Hakim. And even more correctly, he adds, "He instinctively understood some of the social evils of his time, but he could not demonstrate how to solve them."

"Why not? They all say he was a brilliant stylist," says Wendy. She is genuinely confused.

"But he wasn't a brilliant thinker. He painted a picture of Belgian colonialism in its – "

"Then what's the Russian doing there?"

A minute of silence.

Wendy breaks it herself. "The Russians didn't have any colonies in Africa. Did they?"

The presence of a Russian in a Belgian colony in Africa in the nineteenth century is really quite odd. Before I can say anything, Higgins speaks up: "In the notes at the back of the book it says, 'Conrad was aware of a certain obscurity.... He wrote to Garnett, "My dearest fellow ... your brave attempt to grapple with the fogginess of *Heart of Darkness,* to explain what I myself tried to shape blindfold, as it were, has touched me profoundly." ' That means that Conrad himself did not know what he was writing."

He lifts his head and looks around as though annoyed.

"But what is the Russian doing there?" Wendy insists.

"Him? Why ... he's there to make it more interesting."

"The book is an investigation of the instincts that reside in the human soul. The instincts of the ego in contrast to those of the id."

Jenny Razadharamithan points out that a sewing machine is rolling up the hill. Hakim cannot explain the Russian at all. Two minutes of silence.

Then a bewildered Dianne asks, "Well sir – what do you think?"

What do I think? That nothing is what it seems. "Nothing is what it seems."

They stop dunking their french fries in their coffee and wait to see what profound truth will emerge from me this time. Or what lie, as far as Hakim is concerned.

And what do I know about it? What did Jozef Korzeniowski know about it? Why did he pride himself on his ignorance of Russian, and of the Russian classics? Why, in that story of jungle horrors, is there a Russian present?

I run my eyes over the gallery of students. They are a random cross-section of this country and of human destinies, chosen by no one, or at most by the upheavals of this century. I look from one to the other, and in the accelerated time of thought I try to penetrate their mysteries. Dianne, desperately struggling to understand the fleeting wisdom of critics who are more obscure than the obscurity surrounding the heart of darkness. She will get married; become a housewife. Something of these effort-filled years will stay with her. Bellissimmo, son of a Neapolitan labourer. He will never understand even *Uncle Tom's Cabin*, but he will become a sharp Italian lawyer supplying his overworked father with a reason to brag and disentangling more than one Mafioso from legal embroilment. Vicky Heatherington, happy little soul. She couldn't care less about the mystery of *Heart of Darkness*. Ever-ebullient Wendy, whose heart and mind are touched by the work itself, but never by secondary sources. One day, perhaps, she may do artwork for the Sears catalogue – the raven in a negligée. Ted Higgins, proudly non-intellectual, rejecting every explanation beforehand ... perhaps he will become a writer. Jenny Razadharamithan will vanish in her yellow sari into the exotic aromas of the Indian quarter near High Park. And Larry Hakim, holding the skeleton-key to everything – an easy-to-understand ideology? And finally my Nicole. Is she the one student in the class capable of penetrating beneath Korzeniowski's skin? No. Such an effort, I'm afraid, will interest her only as long as she is interested in me. She raises her faded eyes to meet mine: "You said Conrad hated Russians because they were responsible for the death of his family. Perhaps he was using the character of harlequin to ridicule the Russians. Harlequin seems like such a ridiculous figure."

"Very good," I praise my girl, and she wriggles with pleasure. "Harlequin is really the key to *Heart of Darkness*. Marginally, of course, it is also critical of colonialism, and you can see it as a parable of the id overcoming the ego if you like. But it is not primarily a novel at all. It is a prophecy."

Hakim? Hakim scowls. "About what?"

"About the Soviet Union."

He makes no reply, waiting to see what easily refutable nonsense I will try to put forward. Dianne's brow furrows. "But the Soviet Union didn't exist then, did it?"

"That's why I said it was a prophecy."

"Isn't that too far-fetched?" I meet the eyes of my Nicole and smile.

"Mr. Higgins quoted from a very interesting letter here. Conrad wrote *Heart of Darkness* 'blindfold.' A favourite trick of clairvoyants, that is, of prophets."

"But he meant it metaphorically," objects Irene.

"It was a metaphor for the state of mind in which he wrote the novel. He wrote it in a state of clairvoyance."

"I'll be damned!" says Bellissimmo.

And I, a well-paid professor, indulge in some light-hearted charlatanism which may not be charlatanism at all, for there are so many things between heaven and earth.

I also fail to mention that this prophecy has an entirely down-to-earth historical basis: abominations tend to repeat themselves in variations that are embarrassingly similar. *Ab initio orbis terrarum.*

●

The fellow came up beside me and undid his fly. I felt him staring at me as he urinated. He stood there with his fly open, but nothing was coming out of it. I glared angrily into his face. It was a fellow I had noticed from the podium, a blond man with a light moustache, in an Esterhazy jacket, about thirty-five. A bachelor out on the prowl. Sitting at a table, a glass of wine in front of him, his fingers holding a cigarette and tapping to the rhythm of the boogie. Observing him over the neck of my tenor sax, I had noticed that he never took his eyes off me.

This in itself was nothing strange. The Boulevard was frequented not only by girl-hunters but by *aficionados* of jazz as well, usually a little wanting in intellect, often with a rather poor ear for music, but utterly obsessed with their ostentatious passion. They never danced, and this one was no exception. They would listen avidly as we embroidered our wildly syncopated patterns; the Boulevard was one of the last oases of this out-of-favour music. So there was nothing unusual in the fact that he had been staring at me as though he wanted to eat me up.

Now he was standing beside me, not urinating, and still gaping.

"Hi, there," I said challengingly.

His reply took my breath away: "Hello, Smiricky. What's Nadia up to?"

Who could it be? God! – then immediate uncertainty again – that crew cut, that little moustache –

"Vachousek!"

"Shut up, student!"

I was so astonished I pissed over my trousers.

My old foreman!

Why had he become a zoot-suiter – so late in life?

Then I was frightened. The answer was obvious. Holy Christ!

Blond hair instead of a chestnut brown crew cut. A blond moustache instead of a clean-shaven upper lip. An Esterhazy jacket instead of a – and it was nineteen hundred and fifty.

I lowered my voice. "I thought they'd done you in!"

"Not yet," said Vachousek in a soft voice.

We had both misunderstood each other. "I meant the Gestapo, not the Soviets."

"Oh, the Gestapo...." He looked around; no one was in the toilet. He bent over and looked under the half-doors of the two cubicles; they were empty. He stood up straight again.

"A close shave," he said. "Lucky for me they picked Dresden for the execution, and the Americans chose the same place for their famous air raid. What you up to these days, student?"

"Studying."

"Haven't they chucked you out yet? I mean, since you play here...."

"I'm just working the side. I squeezed through political vetting."

"Good for you."

A zoot-suiter came in and pushed his way to the urinals. Vachousek buttoned up his fly and walked out without a word. The corridor outside the toilets was jammed with bodies, and I could hear the hum of conversation and laughter from the dance-floor. A familiar-looking gentleman was leaning against a column in the corner, the type that would intervene whenever the zoot-suiters' dancing began to look too much like the newsreel clips of debauched behaviour which they occasionally showed in the movie houses as a warning.

The foreman offered me a cigarette. We lit up.

"D'you still mind that heroic number of yours?"

"That would be a hard one to forget. I've never been so shit-scared since."

"Not even when they was vetting you?"

"Political screening's not a matter of life or death."

"Hm," said the foreman. "Look, I'd like you to understand I didn't stop you from going through with it because I was scared myself."

"I know you weren't. The whole thing was a botch-up from the start."

"There was that, too," said the foreman. "But we had bigger things to worry about than jamming the machine-guns on a couple of fighters. Did you know the Germans was making components for the V-3 in the same factory?"

"What?"

"D'you mind them funnels they was welding out of heavy metal?"

I vaguely recalled one session of the washroom seminar when Ponykl claimed the thing he was welding, which looked like an oversized mortar, was part of a rocket. Malina called him an ant and said a huge hunk of metal like that would never fly. Ponykl claimed that it could and that it would be the biggest rocket in the world and that they were going to shoot it all the way to America and bomb New York with it. Malina gave him a smack and called him a stupid goat and a fucking muttonhead.

"That was the *Vergeltungswaffe* Number 3," said the foreman. "Might have changed the whole course of the war for the Germans. We'd just about managed to piece together their whole production pattern right through Europe. The last thing we needed was to have the Gestapo move in and start poking around asking questions because of your little game. While you and Nadia was fooling around with your bloody counter-sinks, Zavis had located practically every factory that was making components."

"Zavis? I thought he was a collaborator?"

Vachousek took a long pull on his cigarette and enshrouded himself in smoke. A strange fellow, Vachousek. He looked more like Bull Macha, the king of the Boulevard zoot-suiters.

"That was part of his cover, wasn't it? Part of the craft. He was the main buyer for Messerschmitt, so he could visit all those factories without arousing the Gestapo's suspicion. But it was still bloody risky – we wasn't up against amateurs," he said, looking me in the eye through the smoke. "And we ain't now either."

The familiar-looking gentleman unstuck himself from the column and started walking towards the toilets. I nodded in his direction. God knows why, but he reminded me of Hitler. Vachousek registered my nod, laughed out loud, patted me on the shoulder with his broad foreman's hand and said very loudly, "That was a good one, wasn't it, student?"

The gentleman walked by us with vigilance on his face, but he had clearly excluded us from the sphere of his suspicions. The door to the toilets closed behind him.

"I'm only in Prague for a day or two," said the foreman, more quietly now. "How would it be if I stayed over at your place?"

I felt the cold breath of that winter afternoon before Nadia had come. Evening in the empty church, where the now godless Uher had prayed beneath the eternal flame, and then Mr. Skocdopole hastening towards me: "You don't happen to know what that scallywag of ours has been up to …?" I felt my stomach tighten. But I couldn't turn him down. None of the various socialisms in my life have been able to teach me how to do that.

"Wait for me after the last set," I said.

We played "Ain't Nobody's Business If I Do." I had a big, two-chorus solo in it, and the pleasant world in which I lived then – a world I shared with Lizeta, and if she wasn't around, then with Geraldinka, and if she wasn't around, then with – that world evaporated, and the slow foxtrot rhythm merged with the memory of an old invalid tapping out the beat unrhythmically with the stump of his arm in a sock … the burial of a radio transmitter … Hitler's voice coming out of the radio and Jirina entering the room … nights spent locked in the toilet listening to the footfalls of furniture-smashing ghosts … the organizing principle of my stream of consciousness, a sensation James Joyce or Virginia Woolf probably never knew … "Ain't Nobody's Business If I Do." Over the neck of my tenor several pairs of eyes followed me, including Geraldinka's, who was there with a fellow in a cone-shaped coat. All at once she stopped dancing. Perhaps she heard the menacing wind blowing through my long solo, the Melusine of a winter afternoon before an imaginary execution, my "Mousetrap Blues" ... "Goin' to church on Sunday, then a cabaret on Monday ... ain't nobody's business...."

He was waiting for me outside the Boulevard. I was living at the time in a villa belonging to an elderly writer in the Podbaba district of Prague. According to the new housing regulations the house was too large for him. The writer belonged to the circle of Lizeta's admirers, and because he had connections and was a national artist he had arranged for a private printing of her poetry. Lizeta repaid the old writer by arranging in turn for me to rent a room from him, one with a separate entrance, thus allowing him to keep the villa. It was through this separate entrance that, unobserved and at one o'clock in the morning, I brought my old foreman Vachousek, now quite clearly a diversionist and an undercover agent. I preferred not to ask which intelligence service he was working for.

In fact I didn't ask him anything. The Uippeltian principle held to by the unlikely *dynamitero* of the Velcl warehouse came back to me spontaneously. I told him about Nadia, then about Uher and how he had given me some friendly advice on the Prague-Kostelec express. About Prema and his escape plan, which by all accounts seemed to have worked. That didn't interest him so much, but Uher did. I told him that the former theological student was now an official in the headquarters of the Revolutionary Trades Union Movement. By his smile I could see Vachousek had his own opinion about that.

"So you're our man, then," he said. It was half statement, half question.

Their man? No, I was not their man. That series of bungled heroic acts of mine had cured me of the desire to be on any side. I had also outgrown the need to show off in front of girls. I was my own man and had no intention of trading my solipsistic freedom for the freedom of some Sartrian activity.

"Well," I said, "I'm not against you. But I'm not against them either."

"Neutral, eh?" I detected a suggestion of disdain in the foreman's voice. "You wasn't neutral during the occupation."

"I'm inconsistently neutral," I said. "You can see that for yourself, can't you?"

"The way I see it, you're as consistent as you ever was."

Was I? Or wasn't I? Why the hell am I sheltering him? Why had I been unable to refuse Prema's request to toss off some idiotic manifesto about shipments of butter to the Soviet Union? Why, for the sake of Nadia's beautiful eyes, had I almost brought down a few Bf 109s and got myself hanged? Stupidity, that's why. Nobody's that stupid anymore.

"I just can't say no to the girls and my buddies," I said. "I'm a bourgeois. But you're a worker. I'm surprised that you're opposed...."

Nonsense. Here I was, a bourgeois, yet clearly I had not escaped being influenced by the categorical imperative of absolute dividing lines. Vachousek hadn't been conscripted into working by the Nazis as I had. He was a real worker. Then how come a worker was – but then, why not? Is every saxophonist –

"What's so surprising?"

"I don't know ... that you're mixed up in ... in this."

"I'm an old social democrat, know that, student?"

"Sure, but this is American business you're doing, isn't it?"

He took a sip of the Gamza. I had poured him out a generous amount.

"Think so? You really think it's only America's business?"

"You're right," I admitted. "I'm just shooting my mouth off without thinking. But the fact is that the Americans are no socialists."

"And the Communists ain't no democrats. So take your pick. Whichever suits you."

I said nothing. I had never thought of it that way before. I had never thought of it before at all, I had only tried to find ways of getting safely around it.

"I see what you mean."

"You see what I mean," said the foreman. "And since you can't say no to your buddies, or to women, you're going to let me sleep here tonight and tomorrow night, and then I'll clear out. No questions asked." He said this last phrase in English, with the pronunciation of a pupil in a beginners' course.

Bitterly I realized that I was trapped again, and that this time there was no Uippelt and no Pejskar's cottage to fall back on. Now there was no end in sight; on the contrary, things were just beginning. Unless ... unless I let him spend the night, then next morning went to a certain street and ... ratted on him. Then I'd let him come the next night, but instead of me waiting for him in the elderly writer's villa, it would be Uher....

But a bourgeois is incapable of going further in life than he can in his thoughts. I read that somewhere in the Marx I crammed to get through political vetting. As he almost always is, Marx was right. With a feeling of helplessness, I realized that tomorrow night the only person waiting for Vachousek in the writer's villa would be me.

And it was. The second night we didn't have any philosophical conversations. We spoke about more interesting things. About women, naturally. About how Nadia had married Franta Melichar. About how Marie had married Franta Kocandrle. About how Gerta Ceehova had finally been transported back to the Reich, because they couldn't prove she had ever informed on anyone and her only sin was excessive enthusiasm for the wrong dictatorship. About how Ilse Seligerova had disappeared somewhere in the Reich but Mr. Kleinenherr had stayed behind and they had even given him some decoration for his work in the resistance. Then Vachousek spoke at great length about a certain Heather who was living in Regensburg, in Germany. He called her Hetser because he couldn't pronounce the English, and said, "Only thing bothers me about her is when I talk to her I have to bite my tongue. Hetser. What kind of name is that?"

I admitted he had a point.

We talked about women's names. We agreed that Marie, Irena, Heidmarie, Jessica, and Dianne were nice names. Neither of us liked Ruzena. Only I was fond of the name Nadia, and Vachousek said it was no wonder. I wondered why he didn't like Heather. He said he liked it, but it was so fucking hard to pronounce.

He had become more vulgar, and an ageing zoot-suiter. But he pronounced even the vulgarities gently, at least when speaking of Hetser.

He didn't get much sleep that night; we rambled on about women far into the early morning.

At first light, he disappeared.

For ever.

●

"The prophecy is a prophecy about the Russians and Russia. You cannot understand *Heart of Darkness* unless you put it beside another of Conrad's novels called *Under Western Eyes*. Has anyone read it?"

From across the bitter cups of coffee, thickened with enormous doses of sugar, from across the remains of ketchup-smeared french fries, the eyes tell me dumbly that no one has. Not even Hakim or Irene. I know my Nicole well enough to know that immediately after lunch she will vanish into the library and borrow it. "No one?" I say, as if disappointed. "Why do people write books in the first place? They want 'to render the highest kind of justice to the visible universe, by bringing to light the truth, manifold and one, underlying its every aspect.' This particular kind of torch-carrying, however, is an incurable disease, and one of its symptoms is an attempt to improve the world. But men and women of the pen rarely succeed at this, because they are not men and women of action. Still, they feel – quite mistakenly – that all you have to do is show men of action the truth, and they will understand and know that the men of the pen are their allies. But the men of action, to act at all, have to ignore this manifold truth. To silence it with their own, singular, one-and-only begotten truth. Simplified truth. That is why 'those who can, do, those who cannot and suffer enough because they can't, write about it.' Does anyone know where that quotation comes from?"

Again the eyes peer innocently at me over the coffee, but at least I detect in them a thirst for knowledge. Unfortunately, I know that knowledge will come to them through deeds rather than words.

"Faulkner, *An Odour of Verbena*. But let's return to Conrad. In *Under Western Eyes,* there is a sentence that is the key to understanding why the Russian harlequin is found in *Heart of Darkness.* 'We Russians are a drunken lot,'" I quote. "'Intoxication of some sort we must have.'"

"The harlequin doesn't drink," says Ted Higgins. "Not in *Heart of Darkness.*"

"'Of some sort.' Look," and I open the book which I have filled with unacademical marginal notes. "Marlow has just met the Russian and the Russian makes him swear to hurry and free Kurtz from a certain as yet unspecified danger. He is in the grip of some unnatural excitement; one moment he is at a height of exaltation, and then, 'in the twinkling of an eye was in the uttermost depths of despondency.' Marlow asks him, '"Don't you talk with Mr. Kurtz?"' And now pay attention to what the Russian replies: '"You don't talk with that man -- you listen to him," he exclaimed with severe exaltation.' With severe exaltation," I say. "And he doesn't talk to him, he only listens. Dig around in your minds, dear children. Who in our time aroused severe exaltation in people? With whom did one not speak? To whom did one only listen?" The innocent eyes. Of course I did say "in our times." I commit the fallacy of personal experience. For these beautiful children "our times" began with the death of James Dean, no, Janis Joplin.

"How about modern dictators," I say. "Since the harlequin is a Russian, let us take Joseph Vissarionovich as an example."

"Who?" asks Wendy.

I tell her who, and continue my indoctrination: "Marlow, however, is utterly and completely a man of the West. Regardless of how much thought he gave to it, the harlequin remained a mystery to him. I quote: 'His very existence was improbable, inexplicable, and altogether bewildering. He was an insoluble problem. It was inconceivable how he had existed, how he had succeeded in getting so far ... he was gallantly, thoughtlessly alive, to all appearances indestructible....'"

On the margin of the page there is my comment, which I don't read to them: "*Sie kamen Welle an Welle.* Wave after wave they came. We mowed them down like rye ripe for the harvest, but they kept on coming, the rear lines climbing forward over the heaps of dead bodies. In the end, we couldn't get ammunition fast enough to keep up with their Hurrah! and we had to pull back. We were better. We had better officers and better men, if you don't consider a mindless but invincible advantage of numbers as better...." Heinz. The drummer in Hucil's tinpot oom-pah-pah orchestra, the only one who felt at home in lederhosen. I continue out loud:

"Marlow, then, doesn't understand the harlequin. And the harlequin 'nodded a nod full of mystery and wisdom. "I tell you," he cried, "this man has enlarged my mind."' Which man? Why, Mr. Kurtz. A man who enriched the traditional cannibalism of the simple savages with 'a ritual so terrible that it cannot be spoken of at all.' A leader of men, whose final principle became 'Exterminate all the brutes!' by which he meant his 'subjects.' A man with whom you don't talk, but to whom you merely listen. In *Under Western Eyes,* Miss Haldin says, 'There is no harm in having one's thoughts directed.' Harlequin is an embodiment of her words. He is a perfect 'subject' of dictatorships, a perfect grain of sand. He does not look for truth; he looks for a prophet to reveal it to him."

I stop talking. Do they understand? Vicky gets up, goes to the automatic dispenser and puts a quarter in it. I follow her pilgrimage for bread, then say, "Into the heart of Africa, against the background of West European colonial exploitation, Conrad transplanted the problems of Russia and the future of Russia."

Vicky returns with a piece of bloated substance that calls itself Apple Pie on a paper plate. I notice an incipient smirk on Hakim's face. Is my interpretation nonsense? In what way is it more nonsensical than those with which Bellissimmo primed himself for his paper? I take the text and read: "'I did not envy him his devotion to Kurtz, though. He had not meditated over it. It came to him, and he accepted it with a sort of eager fatalism. I must say that to me it appeared about the most dangerous thing in every way he had come upon so far.'"

•

At last I realize what is odd here. It's an ordinary New Year's Eve party, but everyone seems to have been specially screened and selected before escaping into exile. There are radiant young women with children acquired in Canada, veterans of reconnoitring expeditions into the plundered interior of the House of Fashion on Wenceslas Square, which is perhaps why, wearing the dresses they now wear, they look like the models in a Simpson's catalogue. It is not just Dotty, who stands out like a gaudy tigress in her orange and green striped pantsuit. It is not just Brian Zawynatch, dancing in the grand style of the Budapest cafés, the sheen on his suit flashing from emerald to pink and pale blue as he whirls round and round. There is also Dr. Cizkova, mother of three and proprietor of a lucrative false-teeth business, a starry-eyed, eternal sixth-former. There is Georgiana Akoratova, blonde, beige and blue, who went from being a politically unreliable medical student to being a factory owner's wife in Canada because her husband, a politically unreliable industrial-school student, took out a patent in Canada on something evidently patentable. Georgiana is foxtrotting kitty-corner across the dance-floor, her blonde head like a sunflower, her eager eyes without a trace of nostalgia, also radiant with a little "Made in Canada" boy. Are they phantoms? Is this reality? Even Bocar in his chrome-plated wheelchair is a manly Ironsides in a checkered jacket. And Margitka, in transparent white chiffon over a smoke-grey slip, is hopping about with a sun-tanned Perelin who has just opened a clinic for cats and got himself a "Florida Tan."

Is it natural selection? Or can it be attributed to those nice little bastards, the screeners and arbiters of political reliability? And are such people, the cadre chiefs, perhaps an instrument of that phenomenon called natural selection? Or is it just that all these roses simply longed to hear the mournful roar of forbidden Niagara and, unlike the majority of the nation, had the courage to slip out when the nice little bastards left the gate ajar for a brief moment?

On one corner of the stage Mr. Sestak is pounding his Jingling Johnny on the floor and Wimpy Sedlak is singing a solo:

> In the lonely light of evening
> Hounds are howling at the moon;
> And the tramps are leaving Revnice
> Marching smartly to this tune.

I play a strange game: I look about the crowded dance-floor and try to find an ugly girl. If I were interested in men, it would be an equally hopeless quest. I see Percy, driven by the Jingling Johnny, trying in vain to follow Veronika's ethnic sense of rhythm, and Veronika is transformed – she is Marie who once, a long time ago, in a small autumn village in the mountains, danced a wild Charleston and you could see her garters. Even Mrs. Santner the publisher sparkles with a glamour usually concealed beneath ratty hair and food-stained pullovers. Her head is crowned with a new chestnut-brown wig, her eyes are rings of black cabaret make-up, her legs golden pantaloons and her body a blouse created from the constellation over the Hollywood Bowl. In Canada she has sacrificed her beauty on the altar of literature, but today, to her extraordinary advantage, she has said to hell with the altar and is kicking up her heels as energetically as that member of a younger generation, Jarmilka Vokurka, who is holding the hand of Fascist Frank Obnova, dressed in a mauve-tinged tuxedo rented from Formal Wear. The publisher's devastated husband is sitting behind Bocar, and Bocar, slightly lit on rye, is giving him some advice. "What kind of crap is that, man? The hell she's got nothing in her head but books! May the good Lord shake you out of your socks when you find out what she's really got under that permanent-wave. Every single goddamned one of them has only one thing on her mind. Why don't you look after her better, you gimlet? You're just using those books of hers as an excuse to drink!"

> ... then with faithful friends around you
> the valley welcomes you again....

But the husband is not making excuses. I know from my own experience that Santner really has nothing whatsoever on her mind but books. When I tried to find out if she was an exception, I ended up doing her a service quite different from the one I had originally hoped to provide. Although she had told me – not in hints and suggestions, but straightforwardly – that I interested her simply as an author, I was still, at that time, nurturing a hope that she might discover in me qualities more interesting than the saleability of my novelettes, and I had offered her various forms of assistance including licking stamps and dragging mail-bags full of books to the post office. So I could not very well refuse her when she said, "Well, Don Juan, if you want me to like you, you can keep a very important rendezvous for me. I can't make it myself because I promised to lecture the Ladies' Auxiliary about 'Women and Other Animals in Czech Literature,' and a courier is flying in at seven. He'll be waiting for us at eight in Union Station and at nine he's got to catch a train. I can't cancel the lecture, because I'm silly enough to believe that I can teach these dames how to read, not just listen to me blithering on about a subject I know something about – but more from the non-literary point of view, though, of course, I'm not about to tell them that."

"How will I recognize the courier?" I objected, nettled because that evening I had been mentally prepared (I had not known about her lecture) for something better than hanging around Union Station waiting for some nondescript emissary to show up.

"By instinct," said the publisher, "and also by a bag he'll have, stuffed with things. He didn't give me any more details when he phoned from Montreal. But he says he's got an extremely important manuscript that the parents of a friend of his smuggled from Prague to Denmark, where he met them. Otherwise I don't know anything about him. He's not in my index of readers, so he's probably just some stupid fool. Judging by his voice I'd say he's not very old, but voices can be misleading. In any case, his name is Prochazka."

I implanted the name – which is common enough in Czech – in my memory and set off to meet this literary emissary of the Prague underground *samizdat* network. It was a miserable evening, with snow, rain and a harsh wind off the lake. The plane into Toronto must have been delayed, because at eight o'clock there was no one waiting in the main hall at the station with a bag stuffed with things. There were a few bagless teenagers, and a couple of blacks who had bags – but as far as I know no Prague students from Africa had yet turned the Soviet invasion to their own advantage. Otherwise a crowd of people waiting for no one flowed through the hall. Several old women with minor rose gardens on their heads had managed to snatch places on the bench among the long-haired teenagers and pimply girls on a school outing, stuffing greasy potato chips into their mouths with filthy fingers, spilling crumbs down the fronts of their blouses and shouting at each other so loudly that it was impossible to understand the announcements coming over the loudspeakers. The old women who hadn't managed to get a place were sitting on their suitcases. There was no sign of a white man of about thirty, with a stuffed bag, who might have given up his seat to an old lady because he had not yet become adjusted.

But then, over by the variety shop, a head wearing a baseball cap peeked out from behind the revolving postcard rack and looked around. The gesture could only be described by referring to a phrase about vigilance and alertness made famous by President Gottwald. Immediately, however, the head alertly and vigilantly withdrew again behind the postcards.

I walked over to the rack and pretended to be selecting one of those magic-realistic views of Toronto in which the city looks the way we used to imagine New York, an endless mountain range of neon-embroidered skyscrapers, not an endless village. I gave the rack a half-turn and looked straight into a pair of alert and vigilant eyes. The man in the baseball cap hastily took a garish folder of views of Niagara Falls from the stand, but his hands were trembling so violently that the folder fell open and a long tongue of waterfalls drooped to the floor like an open accordion. The man nervously began trying to gather it up, but the tongue tumbled out again and then he dropped the whole folder. As he bent to pick it up I saw behind him, in the corner, a bag stuffed to bursting with Things.

"Mr. Prochazka?" I asked. He straightened up abruptly and Niagara Falls spilled out of his hand and dangled there for a third time.

"Vot?"

So I said it again.

"Nou."

He began once more to push the long tongue of Niagara Fallses back into the envelope. But his bag was stuffed with things and the word "Vot" did not seem to indicate a WASP. He could have been Russian, but as far as I knew, the word had a different meaning in Russian. For a few moments longer I watched the trembling hands struggle with the intransigent accordion and a mean trick occurred to me. I asked him, in a language that I hoped at least sounded like Russian, "*Gaspadin priyechal iz Denmarku?*"

It was ludicrous but the cascade of illuminated waterfalls plunged to the floor once more. The young man said, "Aye dont anderstant."

He was obviously my man. In Czech I said, "You're Mr. Prochazka, aren't you? You called Mrs. Santner from Montreal."

"No, I didn't." The man with the bag had involuntarily spoken in Czech. He recovered his self-control and added, "Aye dont anderstant."

I said, again in Czech, "But you did call. You said that your name was Prochazka and that Mrs. Santner was supposed to wait for you in the hall of Union Station and that you would have that" – and I pointed to the bag – "with you."

He jammed a hand into the pocket of his wind-breaker and something in the pocket thrust forward, pointing at me. It must have been a pen, because it made a sharp protuberance in the jacket.

"You moof – aye shoot!" he said in a panic-stricken voice.

"Are you all right?" I asked. "Mrs. Santner can't come. She had a previous engagement. So she sent me. You're supposed to give me the manuscript."

The pen in the pocket began to tremble. But the young man, since he had already decided to shoot if necessary, clearly reckoned there was no point in keeping up the pretence any longer. He said in Czech, "What manuscript?"

"The one from Prague."

"And who are you?"

"I'm a friend of Mrs. Santner's."

"Anyone could say that."

I sighed. "Look, I can't help it if you didn't agree on a password. All Mrs. Santner told me was that you would have a bag stuffed with things – those were her very words – and that your name was Prochazka."

Uncertainty appeared on the narrow face. But the pen was still aimed at me.

"Prochazka?" It sounded like a genuine question. I made a sardonic face to suit the situation.

"Maybe it's just a cover name."

"What's your name?"

"Smiricky."

It was clear he didn't know what to say next. A boy in a furry jacket stepped up to the rack, dribbling potato-chip crumbs over himself, and spun it around for the fun of it. The man with the pen in his pocket stiffened.

A perfect impasse.

"Look," I said, "if you want we can call Mrs. Santner at the Ladies' Auxiliary. You can talk to her yourself."

The emissary glanced around. There was a line of telephones directly opposite the variety shop. They were perfectly visible from all directions. He hesitated, then said, "All right, call her. And then leave the receiver off the hook and go and stand over there by the ticket counter." And he nodded towards a small group of people lining up to buy tickets.

"Okay."

I walked over to the telephone, dialed the number of the Institute and said to the woman who answered, "I have to talk to Mrs. Santner. It's urgent."

As she walked away to get the publisher I could faintly hear in the background the voice of the expert on Czech literature. Then the publisher's voice broke off abruptly, and a few moments later she was at the phone, her voice so characteristically hoarse from all those cigarettes that even Prochazka might believe he was really speaking with Santner. I told her what was going on and then, precisely according to instructions, I left the telephone off the hook and joined a line of people buying tickets. The young man threw the bag over his shoulder to cover his back and, with his eyes on me, he picked up the receiver and spoke into it. His conversation with Santner seemed endless but he finally hung up and came towards the ticket counter. He walked right past me without even looking at me, muttering out of the corner of his mouth, "Where can we talk?"

"Anywhere."

I saw that he did not share my feeling of security, so I added quickly, "We could try the cafeteria."

"Are you absolutely sure we're not being followed?"

Whatever else I might have thought, I had to admit that the priceless manuscript was at least in reliable hands. So I laid aside my habitual frivolity and gave in to the conventions of conspiracy.

"I'll go first," I said, "and you watch to see if anyone's tailing me. I'll sit by the window, and when you come in, I'll watch to see if anyone's tailing you."

If anyone had been following me for those eight miles between the publisher's house and Union Station, I must have shaken him as I walked across the hall. The agent who had shadowed Prochazka all the way from Montreal had clearly lost his way in the station too.

We sat by the large cafeteria window, which gave us a strategic view of both the hall of the station and the cafeteria itself, where there were only two old ladies wearing pink cornucopias on their heads, and a pretty black girl absorbed in a paperback called *Helter Skelter* about the Sharon Tate murders.

Prochazka, still speaking under his breath, said, "I have to apologize. My real name is Novak, Peter Novak."

Well, such things do happen in conspiracies. I had a fleeting memory of how, those many years ago, I had sent that appeal into the ether: "Leda calling Swan, Leda calling Swan." Perhaps Prema had got the names mixed up then too. But Prema had been a seasoned hand in the anti-Nazi underground, not a raw amateur. I asked Novak what the manuscript was like. Superb, almost eight hundred pages, author can't get it published in Prague, not in the Party. Wants to publish it under his own name, not afraid. Ever published anything before? No. It's such a scathing indictment that they wouldn't publish it even under Dubcek. A novel. Haven't had time to read it. But the parents of this buddy of mine say it's fantastic. An eight-hundred-page savage indictment.

He refused to hand the novel over to me in the cafeteria. He cast suspicious, sidelong glances at the artificial pears on the old women's hats, then asked me to take him somewhere where no one could see us. So I led him down to the toilets.

Although there was no one there, the emissary insisted that we each lock ourselves in a different cubicle to effect the hand-over. Then it turned out that he had no small change, and I had only a dollar. So he assumed a convincing pose in front of the urinals while I went back to the cafeteria to get change from a quarter. The black girl had only two dimes and when I suggested she keep the nickel she was insulted. The old ladies were already on their way out, but they insisted on turning their handbags upside down, and about five minutes later I returned to the toilets with the two necessary coins.

Meanwhile, however, someone had occupied one of the two cubicles. Under whispered pressure from Novak, I took up a position similar to his and we waited for the man in the cubicle to finish. Then I realized that it would be bad tactics for both of us to wait outside when one of the cubicles was empty. Novak saw my point, took the money from me, zipped up his fly and locked himself in the empty cubicle. After standing by the urinals for a while longer, I realized that it would make more sense to wait beside the other cubicle. But it was too late; before I managed to move to this new position, an old man in ear-muffs came into the washroom and got there ahead of me. Back I went to the urinal.

The unknown interloper flushed the toilet, and spent the next five minutes doing up his trousers; when he finally emerged the old man with the ear-muffs caught the door before it snapped shut, and saved himself a dime. Then, to my anger, I realized I had given both my dimes to Novak. There was nothing I could do now except wait for the old man to finish. As I had anticipated, he took his time about it, to the accompaniment of powerful acoustic and olfactory effects. I thought I could repeat his trick with the door and thus avoid having to get my dime back from Novak, but when the old fellow finally emerged he stood directly in front of the cubicle struggling with his recalcitrant fly and the door snapped shut before I could catch it. He took a look at my Harris tweed overcoat, muttered something in disgust, tore the tab of his zipper off, cursed, pulled his threadbare raglan coat around him and walked out.

"Give me the other dime," I said through the door of the other cubicle. "I gave you both by mistake."

The voice from the other side said, "Right, just a moment." Then a long silence, followed by, "I put it in my pocket somewhere. Just a moment."

Meanwhile a gentleman in a distinguished bowler hat and an overcoat that looked tailor-made rather than off-the-rack entered in a great hurry. I jumped in front of the door of the empty cubicle and fished around in my pocket and pulled out a quarter. The gentleman had a handful of change ready and was shifting back and forth uncomfortably from one foot to the other.

"Have you got any change?" I asked, because there was nothing else to do.

"I'll see." The unfortunate fellow opened up his sweaty hands and took two dimes and a nickel from the pile of coins, but I knew that if I entered the cubicle now Novak would never have the nerve to slip me the manuscript.

So I took the change and nodded to him. "You go ahead."

But the bowler hat did not lie: he was a gentleman. British.

"Eheugh, neheugh, neheugh," he objected. "First come, first served."

"Really, you go ahead."

"No, please. I can wait," he said mendaciously, but within the traditions of his code. We bantered politely back and forth for a few moments until an alarming sound emerged from his bowels. I stuck one of the dimes in the slot and energetically motioned him inside. Urgency overcame good breeding, and in a short while embarrassing but irrepressible sounds echoed from within.

I wondered if I would ever be able to deliver the precious manuscript to Mrs. Santner. Fortunately, unlike the old man with his folksy protractedness, the British gentleman relieved himself in record time, emerged, stood in front of the door to politely express his gratitude to me so that it again slammed shut, and went over to wash his hands. I put the remaining dime in the slot and tried to turn the handle. Nothing happened.

I shook the door. Still nothing happened. The gentleman turned on the electric dryer and I rattled the door again. I pressed the coin return button and retrieved the dime. Of course. Roosevelt. The lock wouldn't accept American dimes.

The gentleman finished drying his hands and noticed my difficulties. "Anything wrong?" he asked, in the tone of one willing to return a favour.

I explained the mechanism's patriotic caprice. He reached into his pocket and pulled out an encouraging pile of change, but Murphy's Law was operative. I went to the cafeteria with the gentleman to exchange the American dimes for Canadian.

When I returned, someone else was sitting in my cubicle. Stoically I walked over to the hand dryer and read the instructions. After some time, the new patron flushed the toilet and stepped out. He was a wino and slightly unsteady on his feet. When he got out he turned around and began fiddling with something on the coin box. I stepped over to him, as the gentleman before had to me, and asked in the same tone of obliging interest, "Anything wrong?"

He turned his wine-damp eyes on me and slurred, "Damn ting got stuck!"

I bent over the lock. The wino was tugging at a thick black thread emerging out of the coin slot. Fortunately the thread was strong. Gingerly I said, "Wait a sec. Let me try it."

He moved aside while I tried to liberate the dime that was tangled up in the thread somewhere in the depths of the box. But the machine clung to it firmly.

"You're right, it's got stuck," I announced to the wino.

"You bet, sir," he replied good-naturedly. "Can you spare a dime, sir?"

"You just used one up."

"Not for shit. For booze. Will you give me a starter?"

To get rid of the wino, I made him a gift of the useless American dime. The liquor stores weren't that patriotic; they might even give him a bonus. The wino wandered off and I went on tugging carefully at the thread. But it was no use – the machine wouldn't let go. I lost my temper, jerked the thread, and it broke. Well, it didn't matter. Just to be certain I had changed two quarters in the cafeteria and I now had a supply of dimes.

Without thinking, I put one into the slot. That is, I tried to, but it was blocked by the thread. Angrily I tried to force it in, but it stuck fast. The door was locked as tight as Ali Baba's cave.

Without much hope, I tried to pull the dime out by the protruding edge, but I only succeeded in breaking my fingernails. I uttered an unliterary colloquialism out loud. I had no intention of suffering like this any longer for mere literature.

Novak's voice came darkly out of the other cubicle. "What's going on?"

"The coin jammed in the slot. I can't get into the other cubicle."

Novak said nothing.

"Look here," I said, "this is absurd. Come out and you can give me the manuscript. There's nobody here, it'll only take a second and we can clear out."

I waited. Silence. At last Novak said, "You come in here."

And so I went into his cubicle. As I was closing the door behind me, I caught sight of two more patrons in checkered woollen shirts. The faint hope that they had only come to urinate was soon dashed as both of them flung themselves with extraordinary verve at the door of the unoccupied cubicle, and discovered that the lock was jammed. One of them applied a metal-toed boot to the mechanism, without result. Novak and I were jammed up together in the tiny compartment. A good deal of the space was taken up by the bag stuffed with things.

"We're up shit creek," I whispered into the emissary's ear, which was directly in front of my mouth – in dangerous situations even the most literary person returns to the bosom of the people. I looked around hopelessly for another way out. On the wall, at the eye-level of a seated patron, was a philosophical poem:

> Some come here to sit and think,
> I come here to shit and stink.
> And I come here to scratch my balls,
> And write this bullshit on the walls.

I turned from the quatrain and looked at Novak, who was perspiring. "What now?" he whispered.

Still feeling close to the people, I replied, "I'll be buggered if I know."

A lumberjack's fist was banging on the door. "Hey, mister, hurry up!"

I was delivered from the bosom of the people by a literary association and whispered in English into Novak's burning ear, "Hurry up please its time."

"What?"

"Closing time."

Something flashed in the crack between the door and jamb. I peered out and looked straight into a human eye. The encounter was followed immediately by a jubilant shout: "Hey, Mike, it's a coupla queers. They're cornholin' each other."

"What did he say?" Novak's teeth were chattering.

A second eye appeared above the first.

"Hey sweetie, what's his cock taste like?"

"Don't make him a baby, miss."

Olympian laughter from the throats of the people.

"It's okay," I said. "They're just making fun of us. Grab the bag and let's go."

"Wait a minute!"

The door was shaking under a barrage of heavy fists. "Till they force their way in here?"

"Hey, you homos! We wanna shit. Shittin' comes before fuckin'!"

More blows.

"Let's go."

I grabbed the bag and opened the door. Novak backed up, the toilet bowl came between his legs and he sat down on it. When the lumberjacks saw me with the bag, they both began to roar with laughter. I left the emissary to his own fate and hurried towards the exit.

"Fuck off, lady!" I heard one of them say, and from the corner of my eye I saw them each grab Novak by an arm and heave him unceremoniously out of the cubicle.

We met again in the cafeteria. The drastic experience had broken down Novak's conspiratorial orthodoxy and he consented to complete the transaction with the irreplaceable manuscript from occupied Prague in the café. I had to bring two coffees and doughnuts, however, and we sat down in the farthest corner of the room even though we were the only ones there, except for the black girl who was utterly hypnotized by murder and therefore safely preoccupied. Nevertheless, Novak began pretending that the foam rubber doughnut was very tasty, at the same time rummaging about in the bag under the table with one hand. Then something touched my knee. "Take it," muttered Novak. I groped around under the table until my hands found a thick manuscript.

"Stick it under your coat!"

I obeyed, and buttoned up the coat. I must have looked like a pregnant goalie, but Novak relaxed. He swallowed the rest of his doughnut and said, "I haven't eaten since morning. They only served drinks on the plane from Montreal."

"D'you want another doughnut?"

"You'll have to lend me the money. I've run out of Canadian money. I've got some Danish crowns, though. I'll send you a cheque from home."

"That's okay."

I got up, holding the precious manuscript under my coat with my left hand, and returned with three doughnuts.

I sat down. The emissary flung himself upon the elastic pastry with gusto. I ran my hands over the folder.

"There's at least a thousand pages in here. I don't know whether Mrs. Santner will be able to publish it or not."

"She puts out Czech books, doesn't she? In Denmark they told me they publish Czech books in Toronto."

"Haven't you ever read any of them?"

Novak was taken aback. He swallowed the last half doughnut and licked off his fingers.

"Well, you see, I don't read Czech anymore. My Czech just isn't that good. You know how it is, you talk English all the time and hardly use Czech at all. And I only read English books now. Doesn't she publish books in English too?"

I said she didn't and Novak suddenly looked at his watch and jumped up in agitation. His train was leaving in five minutes, he announced, and he didn't have a ticket yet. We raced to the ticket counter and on the way I lent him twenty dollars. He rushed up to the wicket and said to the girl, "Kitchoona von teekit."

"One way or round trip?"

"Vot?"

"One way – or return?"

"Kitchoona," said Novak again. The girl measured him with a look and then made him out a ticket.

"Vodor?"

"I beg your pardon?"

"Vodor. Train to Kitchoona. Vot dor?"

"Gate Two," said the girl without twitching a muscle in her face. She was clearly accustomed to hearing the language spoken in a wide variety of ways.

I ran with him to Gate Two, where we said a hasty farewell. He never sent me the cheque. Of course I treated it as his remuneration for the great service he had rendered to Czech literature, and anyway Santner paid me back with a cheque she entered in her books as a gift to a business associate and thus deducted from her taxable income. I added some money of my own and bought her three bottles of Jack Daniel's, which she consumes to help her maintain her high level of efficiency. But she offered me nothing in return except the chance to do a reader's report on the Prague manuscript.

Something is better than nothing. So I read it for her. It was a genuine novel. It must have been written, or perhaps begun, at least half a century ago, because some of the pages were quite brown and almost all of them had yellowed considerably. It was called *White Flesh,* and judging by the contents, the author was the type of person whose faith in the authenticity of Ossian would not die even if Macpherson were to rise from the dead and confess to the fraud. After the experience of the last quarter of a century, I had to admit I wouldn't really blame him.

Unfortunately, this author did not believe in Ossian but in the popular Jewish custom of preparing matzos with the fresh blood of murdered Christian virgins.

The manuscript was a real pearl. Among other things it enabled me to realize my long-standing desire to read the legendary *Protocols of the Elders of Zion*. The author used the *Protocols* in a scene involving a rabbinical exhortation that covered almost a hundred densely typed pages. The exhortation, from beginning to end, consisted of literal quotations from the *Protocols,* and the author had not even bothered to write them out; he had simply pasted pages torn from a book, of which he had evidently several copies, onto pages of typewriter paper, numbered them accordingly and inserted them in the manuscript at the appropriate place.

I also discovered that the work was built up in several different layers which had been created at various times, written on different typewriters and incorporated into the plot in various ways. They were all dramatized essays purporting to reveal the Jewish origins of important personages, of whom I would never have suspected such a thing. Judging by the degrees of yellowness of the different pages, I estimated that the oldest was an essay on Eduard Benes and his wife (née Steinova; I didn't know that either), whose Jewish father was called Bernstein. Of somewhat more recent vintage was the well-known story that Adolf Hitler was an illegitimate son of one of the Rothschilds, begotten upon one of the Rothschild maids. Even fresher was the de-Aryanization of Ferdinand Peroutka (Perlmutter) and the newest of all was a proof of Dubcek's origins (Dreifuss). In spite of this, they did not publish Kropacek's novel in Prague. Every regime, in short, trembles before the naked truth. I wrote Santner a warm recommendation of the book to avenge myself, and she in turn castigated me for wasting her time. She had taken my reader's report seriously and read seven whole pages of the manuscript before she discovered that I was pulling her leg, by which time she had wasted almost three whole minutes. Later we received a letter from Kropacek, mailed in Munich by some Western tourists who had smuggled it out of the country. He requested that we send his advance in foreign currency coupons and the remainder at regular intervals every January and July the first, in the same way. I sent him a copy of Marx's anti-Semitic tract on the "Jewish Question" via a legally married Czech girl, along with a letter which said that we would publish his book only if he were to round out his rogues' gallery of Jews with something on Engels. About two months later the chapter actually arrived, mailed once again from Munich. I learned that Engels' real name was Ehrlichmann and that he debauched young working girls in his factory. Santner told me I should write and ask him if he would consider rewriting his book with a little more emphasis on the debauching of young working girls. Pornography sells very well, and since hers was a mail-order business, no one would have to risk the public shame of being seen buying it in a Yonge Street porn shop. From the profits, the publisher claimed, she could establish a non-profit poetry list.

When another legally married Czech girl went to Prague, I sent a new letter to Kropacek expressing my regrets that Mrs. Santner could not, unfortunately, publish his book because her business is supported by funds from the CIA, where Jews like Ford and Moynihan and that Semitized renegade from the Church, Kissinger, have the final word. Some time after, Kropacek's final message came through the Munich channel asking us to throw the chapter on Engels out and send the manuscript to the Molodaya Gvardiya Publishing House in Moscow. Santner did so with great relish.

She comes up to us, quite out of breath from tripping the light fantastic, and she brings another beauty along with her. Have all the ugly girls in the world died out?

"This is Jirina O'Reilly," she says: an olive-skinned, Czecho-Italian Lollobrigida, of less promotable shapeliness but with Slavic melancholy in her eyes to compensate and dressed like a naughty little angel. "And this is her husband, Jim." Husband Jim is an uninhibited, repulsive, bald-headed fellow in jeans. He looks intently at Bocar's crippled legs and asks him in English, "What happened? Multiple sclerosis?"

"Would you like a punch in the teeth, smart guy?" Bocar replies in Czech, with feeling.

And thus, a pleasant tone is struck.

●

*Prague*
*February 7th, 1966*

*Dear Dan,*

*What do you think of the events? I should feel joy, but instead I feel a kind of anxiety. Of course, what's happening is marvellous. At long last they have stopped speaking in phrases, at last the government is asking the people what they think, at last one can read the newspapers again, and perhaps at least even the political prisoners will see justice.*

*The only thing is, Dan, I don't know.*

*Do you recall that anti-snobbism campaign at the beginning of the sixties? It was perfectly clear to both of us that it was not snobs they were attacking, but literature; it was simply that the cultural department of the Party was afraid of certain authors. At that time I wrote an article to the effect that I wasn't afraid of snobs; I was only afraid of censorship.*

*I still believe that. It is true that I myself did not have a great deal of sympathy for some authors whom the Party was afraid of, but if I demand freedom for myself, I must demand it for everyone.*

*But Dan, why are they all so self-assured and one-sided? Why do they turn literature into a steeplechase and scorn every horse that does not come from their stable? Have you ever read Vetvicka's reviews? I don't know him personally. Apparently he is a young critic and they say he is clever. Perhaps he is. But today, when I read his disparaging remarks on the poetic and cleverly feminine novel of Alena Obdrzal-kova, I recall Raymond Chandler, whom you love as well: "Show me a man who cannot stand mysteries and I will show you a fool, a clever fool — perhaps — but a fool just the same." It seems to me that this applies precisely to Vetvicka. I have no wish to do him an injustice, but he seems to me the same type of inquisitor as the socialist realists were, only his dogma is different. In the 1950s our enemies excluded everything from literature that was beyond the grasp of the most primitive worker. Today, Vetvicka expels everything that deviates from the taste of the most avant-garde aesthete. Naturally what he praises is often good literature, whereas the critics of the fifties almost always praised trash. But both of them exclude what lies between: that is, most literature. And have you noticed Vetvicka's tone? That too is identical, except that it has a different timbre. A haughty, contemptuous irony. At first it may well seem that his irony is founded on solid analysis, whereas the other had its roots in that well-known side of Marx's character. But Vetvicka's irony is simply more elegant. Behind it, too, there are labels and every label testifies to a lack of human insight. The critic sees the work not as the testimony of someone who is trying to do his best in that most difficult of all vocations (vocations in Salda's sense, not in the sense of the Wages Control Index), but as some kind of cadre material on the basis of which they have to choose candidates to fill leading posts. With the socialist realists it was "decadence," "incomprehensibility," and "formalism." With Vetvicka it is "cliché," "convention," or "undigested Robbe-Grillet."*

*Undigested Robbe-Grillet? I cannot imagine a more Czech, more contemporary novel than Alena's evocation of Prague in our present time, as seen through the eyes of a young hairdresser. Is originality of form the only important thing (insofar as originality alone is important at all)? Is this not just socialist realism, which in the same way maximized the importance of content, turned inside out? In reality there is an altogether different dialectic at work in art. Form is almost always, to a greater or lesser extent, borrowed, and for that the critics have labels like "epigonism" and "influence." What gives that form the taste of newness is content. Of course the basis of that content is the individual* uniqueness *of man, who lives out what everyone lives out: his unique variation on the general theme. This is precisely what Alena's novel is to me.*

*And ultimately it's not even a question of aesthetic arguments. Once again your Chandler said, "No mystery writer I have ever met ever thought what he was doing was not worth doing; he only wished he could do it better." I agree: just read the biographies of writers, Dan, the least and the greatest. We all shed blood. And the snobs – I can use this term today because the socialist realists are silent – the snobs treat us like charlatans, if not outright criminals, when our work is not successful. Except that it usually seems to me they can't hear.*

*What I mean is, they do not have good ears. They cannot hear what literature has in common with music and what makes it art. It is no problem to define the technical procedures, to analyse and praise them; stream of consciousness, achronology, the narrative point of view and consistency in the categories of narrative forms. But what is all that without the ancient and unacquirable talent of mimesis? That secret ability, inaccessible to the reason, to awaken in the reader the joy of recognition: precisely this has happened to me too (your Hemingway), it was exactly like that, even though it wasn't like that at all, and therefore it is precisely like that (now). Ecce the dialectics of art! A truth more truthful than truth. Everything else, as Henry Miller wrote, is* literature. *Stream-of-consciousness writing was invented long before Joyce by Dorothy Richardson, but it was she, not Joyce, who fell into obscurity. Why?*

*In the end, every art is a mystery. And also, there is not just great art and non-art, with nothing in between; there is also minor but not at all dishonourable art. Once again, your Chandler wrote to Erle Stanley Gardner, "To say that what this man writes is not literature is just like saying that a book can't be any good if it makes you want to read it. When a book, any sort of book, reaches a certain intensity of artistic performance it becomes literature. That intensity may be a matter of style, situation, character, emotional tone, or idea, or half a dozen other things. It may also be a perfection of control over the movement of a story similar to the control a great pitcher has over the ball."*

*Please understand: I am not asking for mystery writers to be treated with the same respect and to the same extent as great poets, and I don't expect Vetvicka to declare Alena Obdrzalkova a genius. But I cannot bear to hear people who have put all they know into a book spoken of with contempt or even with ridicule. No one can do more, not even Joyce or Nathalie Sarraute. Faulkner once said that all novels are shipwrecks. Derelicts. And he was right. There is something that falls* short of perfection in every book, without exception, something influenced by the age, even something ridiculous; just like everyone, without exception, has weaknesses and is trapped in his age and environment, and may even be ridiculous. But if he is an honourable man and if it is an honourable book, no one has the right to ridicule it or heap contempt on it. Genuine lovers of literature will instead feel sorry that the author was not up to some things, and will look for the remains of the golden treasure in that shipwreck on the bottom of the sea of criticism. Such treasure is there, Dan, far more often than the snobs know, or are prepared to admit.

But usually they don't even bother to look for it. And Dan, I'm afraid in the end they may spoil everything. And I don't just mean literature. I wrote a reply to Vetvicka's review, and the editors sent it back to me. They said that this problem is not important at this particular time. One editor even told me that given the situation today my article would play into the hands of –

Dan! Do we really have to worry – today, when at last everything can be said – about those whose hands the truth plays into? Or, more exactly, the opinion that I consider to be the truth?

If only I could get rid of the feeling that there are a lot of Chandler's clever fools among those whose intentions are all good. Unfortunately I cannot.

How will it all end, Dan? I am genuinely afraid. Why, those clever fools could very easily bring down overnight everything we have been trying to build up for the past twenty years.

Ach, Dan!

Yours,<br>Jan

•

Although he has a Czech wife, the bald man fortunately understands no Czech. His olive-skinned Czech wife, however, turns pink. As for Bocar, life has taught him to deal more or less good-naturedly with the most thoughtless remarks, and so after his incomprehensible retort in Czech he enlightens the bald man in Jachymov English:

"Not sclerosis. I'm just lazy. I no like to work. So I sit in wheelchair and beat my wife she work for me."

The Lollobrigida flushes a shade deeper, but the bald man is not only insensitive, he is slow to comprehend.

"Really? You mean it?"

I take advantage of the tension to ask the Lollobrigida to dance.

She dances beautifully.

"Is your husband always that blunt?"

She lowers her eyes. "He's – against conventions. I know he carries it too far. It's just that he belongs to that generation."

"Obviously."

"But he's not one of those – he's a student. He's not a drop-out."

"What's he study?"

"He's taking courses in Arabian and psychology. He's thinking of taking art history too. Last year he took genetics and Chinese...."

I stop asking questions. The bald man looks at least thirty-five. Of course he may simply have burned himself out on marijuana. Last year he took genetics and Chinese, the year after next he'll probably take theology, Marxism and travel. When he graduates he'll be fully qualified for welfare. I inquire no more about him. I'm prejudiced against him already. No more questions. Then she asks, ashamed for her husband, "What really happened to that man in the wheelchair?"

"He's lazy, so he simulates paralysis."

"No, seriously."

"He was shot with a revolver. The bullet severed his spinal column. Almost the same thing that happened to Governor Wallace."

"Was he – a politician?"

"No. A political prisoner."

Slavic sadness wells in her eyes, but a different sadness from that flowing from the grey pupils of Veronika Prstova.

"Did it happen – in a concentration camp?"

"Hmm," I say. "Bocar is one of life's little ironies. One of this century's little ironies. Have you noticed that blonde woman?" I nod towards Margitka. The Lollobrigida lowers her eyes to signify affirmative.

"That's his wife. They went out together before he got locked up. They were about eighteen at the time. She waited fifteen years for him and when he got out, they got married."

"That was – she was – really...."

"Hats off," I suggest. "What they used to call abiding love."

"They must have had a truly wonderful relationship – and then to marry him as an invalid...."

I grin wryly, cynic that I am.

"Not at all. Bocar came back from the camps in one piece, they got married and flew to the Tatra Mountains for their honeymoon. Margitka had scrimped and saved for fifteen years so they could afford it. And they had an unexpected stroke of good luck on the plane."

Margitka and Frank the Fascist, in his mauve-tinged tuxedo, jive past us. Anyone would say she was a well-preserved housewife.

"Some enterprising fellow hijacked the plane to Munich, and Bocar saw that as divine providence. Like many people, he got religion in the camps, and Margitka had always been religious. They met in the scouting movement – she was a Catholic, he was a sea-scout."

The Lollobrigida does not laugh at this. "But you said they shot him – "

"I didn't say when. Anyway, they got off the plane in Munich, and since Margitka had some relatives in Canada they were here within a month. The problem was that the only experience Bocar had was as a uranium miner, so to take advantage of this he applied for a job in the Elliot Lake mines. He honestly owned up to his ten years in the mines, thinking it would improve his seniority. It didn't. They have a regulation at Elliot Lake: no more than ten years in the mines, no matter where, and it's a hard-and-fast rule because the Canadian government is open to public pressure, whereas the Czechoslovak government takes its orders from Moscow, which *de facto* owns the mines. Anyway, Bocar got sore, answered a want-ad and became a Pinkerton man, hoping he would end up as a guard in a Canadian pen so he could get his own back on the communists he was sure were locked up in there. But he was wrong again. He ended up guarding a luxury apartment building and he hadn't been Pinkertoning for more than a week when two thugs tried to burgle the penthouse. Bocar stepped in on them, the thugs pulled out their guns and – to put it in the only appropriate way – they pumped him full of lead."

"That's dreadful!" The Lollobrigida is clearly sincere. She has that rare ability to feel compassion for people who mean nothing to her.

"Fortunately, Bocar had insured himself heavily after his arrival in Canada. Since he was a Pinkerton, the premiums were so high that they would have swallowed up most of his income, if the Lord had not inter-vened again. Bocar loved Margitka very much, though, and his nightmares were straight out of *Rude Pravo*: he was afraid that if anything happened to him, Margitka would be all alone in the cruel capitalist world without visi-ble means of support and would have to take to the streets." I grin. "But thanks to the special brand of socialism she had experienced, Margitka had already learned how to be independent, and while Bocar was still in prison she had become a registered nurse – at night school, naturally – and so it was not difficult for her to get accredited and find a job in Canada. And because registered nurses in Canada don't have to toil and moil quite as much as they do in Prague, Margitka is beautifully preserved. Would you believe she'll soon be forty-three?"

"She's very pretty."

"However, as far as piety and other such fiddle-faddle goes," I say, and perhaps I blaspheme, "if Bocar considered the hijack as the intervention of divine providence, what should he consider the intervention of the gunman?"

"As a trial," says the Lollobrigida quietly.

"Are you religious too?"

She shakes her head. "No, I'm not. But life itself is mostly – a trial."

"To what end?"

"I don't know." She lowers her eyes.

I don't enquire any further. Perhaps I shall ask the publisher. Or Margitka.

If life is a trial, then Margitka hasn't exactly stood the test.

She had come to me, in the role of a Veronika, after some literary evening and asked me to autograph a copy of my translation of *The Lady in the Lake,* published in Prague. I looked at her closely, and as I was handing the book back to her I said I enjoyed autographing books like that most of all, books that people had taken the trouble to bring with them all the way across the ocean.

"I didn't bring it with me. My parents just happened to send it to me."

I was disappointed, but even so I told her she looked like Miss Fromsett, and she was flattered. Give me a call sometime, I'm in the book. She called in a week. At our very first meeting we became – as the romantic euphemism has it – lovers.

That was in the spring. Bocar was in the hospital for a three-day check-up and she could stay with me overnight. Thus I learned her melodramatic story from her in bed. When the doctors had told her that Bocar would not only spend the rest of his life in a wheelchair, but would also be incapable of physical love, it was too much even for her and she broke down. But she did not break down in the usual way. Margitka has never lived an ordinary life.

"How then?" I had asked her.

"Like this. My breakdown is called adultery."

"An odd way to break down."

"*You* find it strange?" she almost shouted.

"I'm not criticizing you."

She turned over and burst into tears. "Fifteen years I waited for him. Do you know what that is for a young girl? Even if she's a *pious* young girl? Fifteen years, and night after night with a rosary in bed instead of your boy?" She sobbed into the pillow, in a room with a view of the beautiful lake. I didn't entirely believe her, but I let her talk. "Then he came back; a couple of days later that miracle with the airplane; and three months after that – crippled for life. And so I broke down like this."

"No one could hold it against you, Margitka."

"Bocar could."

"Does he know about it?"

"I'm careful. And there's only been one before you. A doctor in the hospital where I work. That was no problem to keep secret. Night shifts and that."

"You're not seeing him anymore?"

"He's opened an office in Calgary."

In the next flat Cindy was partying. The hi-fi was blaring out "Oh Happy Day" at full volume, fashionable shoes pounding out Afro rhythms on the parquet floor ... "When Jesus washed our sins away...." Cindy had no carpet.

"So you don't use a rosary anymore?"

"I do. And I go to confession. But I'm doing this to God deliberately. I'm trying Him out to see if He really is cruel enough to punish me for it on top of everything else."

"Al Capone of the Universe?"

"What's that?"

"One of the many names of God," I said. "It was coined by a certain Czech fascist poet whose mistress died of a brain tumour. I recalled it in connection with a girl – "

... when Jesus washed our sins away....

– the swinging spiritual took me back to a medieval chapel. A tiny rural organ wheezed and the Venerable Father Meloun shook his aspergillum over a pasteboard coffin decorated with black paper lace, and in his kindly, rural voice intoned tunelessly:

Out of the depths, O Lord, I call unto Thee
O Lord, hear Thou my voice!

I wept helplessly and without shame, but no one paid any attention to me. Everyone was weeping. The widower in a black Sunday suit that was too small for him, Uncle Venhoda with a fringe of grey around his bald, weathered highland head, Aunt Venhoda and those seven neighbours from Cerna Hora who had walked seven kilometres through the winter blizzard to the Kostelec Municipal Cemetery because Nadia had wanted to be buried near her father. An absurd wish. Her father was not resting there; her father had probably not been laid to rest anywhere. But in the municipal cemetery stood a provisional plaster-of-Paris monument to the martyrs of war, and among them, along with the names of the victims of Prema's act of sabotage, was the name of Antonin Jirousek from Cerna Hora. The gold leaf had already fallen from the names. It was scarcely two years after the war, and the names could no longer be deciphered.

> If Thou, O Lord, were to weigh our iniquities
> Who, O Lord, would not be found wanting?

The funeral notice had reached me in Prague, addressed in Franta's blacksmith's hand, with SPESHAL DELIVRY in large capital letters written on the corner of the envelope. I caught the morning express and alone in the compartment I wept and wept, although I had not thought of Nadia in almost a year. I felt sorry for myself, for that pleasant memory, the lost paradise of the black mountains where I had sojourned only briefly, but I could not live there. The countryside swept past the window, as comfortless as the Sunday afternoon, and the compartment was cold. When Nadia had told me that day in the hospital that she was coming for pneumothorax treatments, when she had shyly invited me to come and have coffee with them sometime, the buggy outside the window, and Franta had covered her with a horse blanket, Nadia, now only big, feverish eyes surrounded by a woollen village shawl, I disregarded her kind and loving invitation and I never saw her alive again. Now I was shaken by weeping, too late. I saw Nadia, now only in my mind, sitting by the tiny cottage window looking out over the hillside towards the white stone cross, but I no longer appeared on that bare line between heaven and earth, beside the cross, and the cross materialized out of autumn mists and then poked out of deep, undefiled drifts, and snowdrops bloomed at its foot, and the sun-blessed mountain grass billowed around it and then, once more, the mists enshrouded it and the snow diminished it. And I never appeared. She died. At home, in Franta's rough-hewn embrace, leaving nothing behind her – no child, nothing, only me and her homespun husband, that obituary notice, memories of some of the things she would say which to this day sound in my ears like the wind howling down the chimney, the Melusine of reproach. "It's delicious!" The wind of class reproach, a simplification somewhat adjusted. How she would lick her lips with her unfussy little tongue, how she was simple as a clarinet counterpoint in a village band and yet full of surprises, how slyly she had feigned unconsciousness, how, that time in the ferroflux room, she had displayed the wisdom of a beautiful mayfly who is crushed under foot before she can fulfil the one meaning her life has. But no. Nadia's life had a different meaning. It was more than mere biology –

"Al Capone of the Universe!" said Margitka. "That's awfully blasphemous."

"But it fits, doesn't it?"

"I don't know. Aren't most of us gangsters?" said Margitka. "Maybe we have the kind of God we deserve."

"We have no God."

"Maybe that's what we deserve."

The Venerable Father Meloun sang:

> But with Him there shall be salvation
> And great shall be His forgiveness....

I wept. Out of the depths I call unto Thee, O Lord, I said vainly, defiantly, unhappily, desperately, sentimentally, too late. I would never see Nadia again. I took a taxi from the station and got to the cemetery just as Uncle Venhoda and a small knot of people from Cerna Hora were entering the chapel. The coffin was already closed and only the paper lace reminded me of Nadia and her fustian Sunday blouse with the little flowers on it. Two wreaths of artificial flowers were leaning against the catafalque, and two wide ribbons on them: FAREWELL – FRANTISEK. FAREWELL – THE VENHODA FAMILY. And the Venerable Father Meloun sang sadly, kindly, out of tune:

> *Quaesumus Domine, pro tua pietate*
> *miserere animae famulae tuae Nadezdae*
> *et a contagiis mortalitatis exutam,*
> *in aeternae salvationis partem restitue....*
> *Per Dominum....*

"I don't know," says the Lollobrigida. "But if we didn't treat life as a trial – it would be impossible to go on living."

"You must be either a Christian or a Communist."

Her eyes full of Slavonic sadness.

"I'm neither," she says. "I don't believe in God and I've never been in the Party."

"You don't have to belong to the Party or the Church to – "

"It's just that – I simply don't know."

I don't enquire any further.

They lifted the coffin onto their shoulders, the husband, Uncle Venhoda, two neighbours. The Venerable Father Meloun took up a position behind the coffin with a tiny sexton behind him, and I joined the insignificant little band of mourners. We walked slowly along the snow-covered cemetery path up a gentle incline. It was snowing thinly, the flakes falling on the black coffin, on Uncle Venhoda's bald head, on Franta's brushcut, where the first grey hairs were showing. Kostelec became a theatrical backdrop: the castle, Cerna Hora, the blackwash of winter sky, the bleak snow. They placed the coffin on clay-smeared planks set across the open grave and slipped the straps around it. The little sexton removed the planks with an experienced hand and the four bearers lowered the light pasteboard coffin into the pit. A woman who might have been an aunt offered me a wilted winter flower on a plate. I threw it into the hole after Nadia. I was no longer crying. I squeezed Franta's hand but I don't think he could have seen me, his blue eyes almost lost in the puffy red skin around them. I started back to town on foot, alone.

"What's so surprising about that?" says Father Hunak. "Sometimes God will make use even of a scoundrel for His own ends. Have you forgotten about the one on His right hand?"

"Of course, you're right. Did I tell you he was originally a theology student?"

"A defrocked priest?"

"He never made it to the priesthood. I met him in church once during the war when I was looking for a way to hide from the Gestapo. After the war he quit the seminary and took up – but you know the story better than I do."

Father Hunak, a black crow among the Bohemian waxwings at the New Year's Eve Party, is committing the sin of intemperance. Beneath a greasy clerical collar, little rubies of red wine sparkle and slowly seep into an already badly stained dickey. Bocar is holding Margitka by the hand and the acoustical backdrop to this unexpected homily is provided by Mr. Sestak's Jingling Johnny.

"There, you see, sir?" The priest raises a mayonnaised finger. "I didn't know that. So that's why they call him The Priest. Caught like a fish in God's net. Let us pray he may never escape."

"You can lay odds on it, Reverend, that particular fish will always get away," says Bocar. "And if the good Lord is merciful to sons-of-bitches like him, then what I will do, Reverend, is leave your church."

"The Lord God is big-hearted," declares our eccentric spiritual father. "None of us can hold a candle to Him. Even with all our virtues. But what I'm telling you is as true as He's above me. He came through at the last minute, but he came through! That's what counts!"

The guard rousted him out at three in the morning and he felt sick because he thought they'd be dragging him off to interrogation again and he knew it would end as always, with a bloodied mouth, because he knew nothing at all and even though – "God forgive me this sin against the

Seventh Commandment" – he crapped out and confessed to everything, he could not, stunned as he was by the going-over, figure out what it was they wanted of him, what it was exactly he was supposed to confess to. He learned at last that he was supposed to have passed on espionage intelligence encoded in the sermons of Father Urbanec to a Catholic girl-guide who then carried it to the Apostolic nunciature. They wanted the code from him. "I've never even managed to solve a cryptic crossword in my life, let alone decode anything." And he told how the security cop, who for unknown reasons was called The Priest, was waiting for him in the corridor and told the guard that he would take the prisoner off himself. And they walked for a long time up and down through the silent night corridors of the Pankrac prison, until they finally came to a certain corridor, "and, gentlemen, I was scared to death, because the corridor led to Death Row. All sorts of things were going on then and, may the Lord forgive me, I was scared shitless because I thought they'd decided to string me up without a trial. Just like that. And what would have happened? One more good-for-nothing vanished, without even a wife and kids to wonder what's become of him. And I stopped, or rather my legs gave up on their own, and I started babbling to myself, 'God help me, God help me!' And the security cop stopped too and said, 'What's the matter with you?' and I blurted out, 'I want a priest!' 'What d'you want a priest for?' the cop says. 'I have to make my peace with God!' I say and the cop smiles a kind of strange, terrifying smile and he says, 'What for? Nothing's going to happen to you. I'm taking you to the death cells so that you can help another poor chump make his peace with God. His need is greater than yours.'" Father Hunak takes a drink and shudders. "Gentlemen, I've relived it a thousand times in my mind, and I still feel the shivers go up my back every time. You see, I couldn't help thinking it was a trap. After all, it wasn't their practice to let condemned prisoners receive supreme unction. Horakova asked for it – and she was a VIP – and they refused." The priest takes another drink. "But that explains it. Uher used to be a divinity student. It always used to baffle me. But he got caught in the net. At the time, though, I thought they were just playing games with me. They'd got some security cop to play the condemned man and as soon as I'd heard him confess they'd either make fun of me or at worst they'd nail me for carrying out forbidden religious rites or something like that. That cop, The Priest, must have known what was going on in my head, because he said to me, almost in a whisper, 'Don't worry. I'm doing this on my own hook. I knew him. We're from the same village. This is one last favour for him, the silly bastard. I'm doing this on my own, you understand? It's just as risky for me. More. You're down for ten years, and they're not going to change the verdict over a little thing like this.' I tell you, gentlemen, I was relieved. I was expecting to get twenty-five. And I believed him, I thought he must be one of the higher-ups and he must know, so I just nodded and on we went."

The Priest led him past the cells filled with prisoners awaiting execution, until they came to the last one. The Priest unlocked it, said, "You've got ten minutes, make it snappy," he gave him a push inside and locked the door.

"He was sitting on the bench, sunken cheeks, skinny, you know, the last night before your execution I don't imagine anyone would be man enough to sleep. I had administered extreme unction before, but nothing like this had ever happened to me before. I had never heard confession from someone condemned to death. And I don't even recall what he confessed to, so even if I would, I couldn't reveal any of his secrets to you. It felt more like I was the one who was dying. He did the talking, and he was quite relaxed, but I was trembling so violently I didn't notice when he'd finished, except that suddenly it was quiet. I stuttered out a Latin absolution and I commended his soul to God. From the theological point of view I would say my presence was irrelevant. It was a confession from desire. The Church acknowledges such things: if a priest isn't handy and the dying man sincerely desires absolution, God grants it Himself. I was there in body alone. In spirit I was beneath the gallows, I saw it before my eyes, a terrible device, and I couldn't get it out of my mind, so I just made the sign of the cross on his forehead and his mouth and chest and then the door creaked open and the cop dragged me out. 'Well, is the spirit at peace?' he asked. I couldn't say a word. 'Not yet, I guess,' the cop says and he looks at his wrist-watch. 'In about three hours.' Pfui! What a time that was. Praise be to God on High we survived it!"

"The motherfuckers!" Bocar hisses. "Pardon me, Father — as you were telling your story, my knife opened up all by itself in my pocket and I cut myself. That's why I cursed."

I raise my eyes to Veronika and Percival. From the stage, the sound of the Jingling Johnny, the banjo, guitars and voices.

> And that's the story 'bout the birth of swing
> A drunken sailor on a fling
> turned a stagger
> into a swagger....

Prominent among the singers is Milan, who has become the epitome of nostalgia. How old was he when Captain Uher led Father Hunak into foreman Vachousek's cell? He was probably swimming through the amniotic fluid into this world at the time the poor foreman left it, as a soul freshly absolved of all sin –

> ... the story 'bout the birth of swing....
> ... O Happy Day!....
> ... *my za mir! I pyesnyu etu*....
> ... in a yellow submarine....

Veronika takes up the job of interpreting, Percy cocks a loving ear; Margitka looks at me inquisitively; Jirina O'Reilly brings a pair of frank-furters on a paper plate to her bald husband who is sitting with his feet parked on the table between two unfinished bottles of wine, picking his ear; Father Hunak dribbles wine down his dickey; Bocar lays a hairy hand on Margitka's thigh. Graveyard, churchyard, garden so green, Nadia's a little seed, but where is her soul, love? With God above? With God above.

Nadia. Nadia. Nada.

•

The debating circle of Kos and Malina was standing around a lad with a face as green as an unripe plum. He was new in the Messerschmitt works, having just come from Dresden, where the factory he worked in, along with the workers' barracks, had been reduced to ashes and rubble. Of the eight or so boys who had come back he alone had registered at the work office. Gerta Ceehova must have been surprised when they sent him to the factory. There was a mass exodus from the Reich at that time, but aside from there being hardly any work to do, nobody was exactly lining up. Most people simply lay low, but Vozenil was an orphan and had no money. They couldn't send him back to the Reich, because the Reich was shrinking too rapidly, so he showed up in the Messerschmitt works and Gerta assigned him to outdoor detail, which by that time had grown to the strength of a battalion. Thus he spent most of his time in the can, boasting of his exploits.

As a veteran of several heavily bombed cities, he was an expert in hor-rors. The last five years of his life had been one long horror, but he had come through it all with no visible damage to his mental health. His green com-plexion was in fact self-inflicted, the consequence of one of his many efforts to make himself sick and get off work. Advised by a black worker from Algeria, who as a French prisoner of war had been assigned to the same air-craft factory, Vozenil ate an unidentified pill that the fellow sold him for a hundred marks. It was supposed to give him the symptoms of a stomach ulcer, but instead he merely turned green. There were no other effects. Not even an exhaustive examination in the hospital (this unprecedented dermatological phenomenon had interested the doctors) turned up anything pathologically wrong with Vozenil's organs. He had to go for a check-up once every two weeks, but the colour of his skin did not get him off work. The Algerian refused to give him his money back and Vozenil got into a fight with him. A month later the factory, the camp and the hospital lay in ruins, the Algerian had perished and Vozenil was tranferred from Hamburg to Berlin.

Now, in the washroom of the Messerschmitt plant, he was bragging about his stint in the capital city of the Reich, where he had been promoted from *Hilfsarbeiter,* a common labourer, to *Feuerabwehr,* doing a job he called *Feuermelder,* or fire warden. It sounded to me more like recollections from *King Kong,* except they hadn't run any American films for three years. All night one week and all day the next, Vozenil would stand on the roof of an observation tower during air raids and report firebomb strikes by telephone to the captain of the *Feuerabwehr,* who would then dispatch the fire engines as directed. It was a highly important function, and *Hilfsarbeiter* of the lesser Aryan races were assigned to the job only because it was also highly dangerous. The life expectancy of a *Feuermelder* in battle was, Vozenil said, a minute and fifteen seconds, so there was a rapid turnover.

The green *Feuermelder,* however, had been as indestructible as Popeye the Sailor Man.

"I was strapped to the railing of the tower," he said, his green face as expressionless as a frog's, for it seemed the Algerian's pill had also paralysed his facial muscles, "but if the bomb dropped any closer than fifty metres, it'd take you right out along with the railing. Worst of all was those flying torpedoes. Exploded in mid-air and the son-of-a-bitch would whip you off that tower like foam off beer."

"Were you ever whipped off?" I asked skeptically.

"Twice. But I was lucky both times. First time I landed in one of them water-tanks they laid out around the city to put fires out with, and the second time I went through the window of an apartment house across the street and landed in one of them double beds, the kind with the canopy over it."

I glanced at Malina to see if he would object. But clearly he had been trained so well in our many discussions of the curiosities of this world that nothing seemed strange to him anymore. After all, there was a war on. So I said, "You really were lucky. Was the couple in bed?"

"They was down in the shelter."

"That was lucky too. You might have killed them."

"Easy," said Vozenil. "I was blasted off the tower by a flying torpedo and I could've been moving at a couple of hundred kilos an hour easy. Lucky, sure, but then the luck ran out. The building collapsed and they died of hunger in the shelter 'cause they couldn't get through to them for three weeks."

"Bullshit," said Filipec, a welder who had also spent two years in the Reich. "They never spent no three weeks trying to dig through to nobody. Soon as they seen the rubble was impossible to get clear, the ones underneath was given up for dead."

"Just let me finish, man," said Vozenil, "I never said they spent three weeks trying to get through to them. Three weeks later there was another air raid and the same building took a direct hit and the bomb crater revealed the drama."

Malina was finally stirred to respond. "What drama, you dromedary?"

"Cannibalism," said the green veteran. "First they polished off some old woman who had a heart attack during the first air raid. Then they ate each other."

"More bullshit," said Filipec. "How many of them was there?"

"About seven."

"So the one who ate all the rest of them must've held out if he had so much meat down there."

"Maybe he was a vegetarian," I suggested.

"Rot," said Kos. "When you're dying of hunger, principles go to hell. You'll eat anything."

"But not any*body,* you fucking worm," said Malina.

"Easy," said Kos. "Pirates did it all the time."

"But these wasn't pirates," said Filipec.

"So what? They was Nazis, wasn't they? It's all the same."

"Wrong, gents," said the green man. "One of them actually survived. They found him surrounded by skeletons. Only in the second air raid he took a direct hit. They only found him from the waist up. The rest of him was mush."

We fell silent, inhaling the smoke of home-grown tobacco. I was trying to imagine the incredible adventures of Vozenil against the very real backdrop of burning cities. And that was just the beginning of his horror show. Filipec said, "It's still bullshit. You say the building collapsed. So how come you wasn't killed in that wedding bed?"

A naive objection. Vozenil had the durability of a Buster Keaton.

"It didn't collapse, it just sort of crumbled. The bomb knocked out the concrete foundations down below and the whole building just kind of slid down like lava. And I slid down with it in the bed, like I was in a sleigh, and I ended up across the street in front of a store that sold musical stuff."

"The man is fucking indestructible!"

"I was lucky, and everybody was surprised because I tell you, boys, there was awful things happening. There was this frog by the name of Oriol — he got flattened against the wall of a department store by a flying torpedo. The wave of air pressure just sort of splattered him out like a pancake, except it was five times bigger than he was normally. He looked like a giant five metres tall, hanging up there."

"You mean normally he was only a metre high?" I said.

"All right, ten metres," shot back Vozenil. "I didn't bloody measure him. They tried to scrape him off but they couldn't so they left him there. And there he was, hanging over the city like a bloody ghost. Boys, it was terrible."

"You're a numbskull, you fucking chihuahua!" said Malina, coming alive.

"Or once," continued Vozenil calmly, "I was on the watchtower, it was daytime and the Americans was on a bombing run. They call them Flying Fortresses and they can sure fly all right but they ain't up to much as fortresses. Anti-aircraft gunners was picking them off one after another, and so was the Focke-Wulfs. They was just mowing each other down. They flew in these three-layer formations and the Focke-Wulfs dived at them from above, *zooom! zooom!* and they always shot some of these Forts down or else the Americans shot down the Focke-Wulfs. But mostly the Focke-Wulfs made Swiss cheese out of them formations."

"D'you want one in the mouth, cow?" Malina asked. "You siding with the Nazis?"

"What d'you mean, siding with the Nazis, you sloth?" said the erudite Vozenil, affronted. "I'm just telling you the straight facts. The Americans got nothing to beat the Focke-Wulfs. Only one that's up to it is the Spitfire."

"Messerschmitts are better than Focke-Wulfs," said a lad from the paint-shop. "That's what London says."

"As fighter planes," said Vozenil, "because they can manoeuvre better. Focke-Wulfs are better up against the Forts because they're smaller."

I was more interested in the story, so I interrupted the technical debate. "What about these Focke-Wulfs?"

"I was just about to tell you that," said the veteran. "I was standing on the watchtower one day when all of a sudden, about ten metres away, this American comes floating down on a parachute. He was a nigger. I waved at him, but he was scared shitless and didn't notice me. It's no picnic to be floating down into Berlin on a parachute with the city on fire underneath you, I can tell you. Not only that, all of a sudden I see this one Focke-Wulf pulling out of a dive to go back upstairs and make another — "

"Another hole in the cheese," I said.

"Right. Only the pilot catches a glim of the parachute and starts aiming at him to shoot him down, and right there and then a torpedo goes off right between the Focke-Wulf and the nigger. The explosion takes the Focke-Wulf and whips it like that" – Vozenil used his hand to indicate the unplanned course of the fighter and unintentionally hit Malina in the stomach. Malina yelled, "Have an eye, you fucking elephant," but Vozenil continued without missing a beat – "and smashed up against some buildings. But that nigger, I tell you, boys" – and he raised his green face to the ceiling. It was snowing damply outside the window – "that explosion caught his parachute and he went flying way back up into the air and then about three kilos farther on he came down on the zoo."

"Where he was eaten by a lion," I said.

"Wait a minute," said Kos. "Didn't it blow you away too, if it did the fighter?"

"I got knocked into a water-tank. And I tell you, boys, the water in it was almost boiling, because phosphorus bombs was falling all over the place."

"So that's where your brains got boiled, you narwhal," said Malina.

"Don't believe me, then," said Vozenil. "You never been anywhere except Hicksville where you come from, that's why you think you're so smart."

"And you probably think I'm stupid, you bloody great rooster."

They debated this distinction for a while and then the lad from the paint-shop asked Vozenil about women. No one objected, for women were even more interesting than the horrors of war. But it turned out that the love life of this green veteran was distinguished by gore as well.

•

The meeting was arranged by Jirina O'Reilly because she had known Jiri Krupka at the conservatory. They had been colleagues. But it's now clear that it was a mistake. Krupka's description of the present dictatorship in Prague has left O'Reilly unmoved. By Krupka's account it's a very special kind of dictatorship employing highly sophisticated forms of terror: the National Committee in Chlumek did not allow the cellist to buy a rococo hunting-lodge which he wanted to convert into a weekend cottage. The purchase was blocked by the local schoolteacher in an unlikely alliance with the local pastor, both claiming that the lodge was a historical building that should serve everyone. "The teacher is a Commie and the pastor belongs to that quisling outfit *Pacem in terris,*" cries the virtuoso, "and the lodge was already a ruin. In a couple of years it would be a pile of rubble. If a private individual doesn't renovate a place, the public will ransack it for stones to build pigsties in their garden plots. And it's the same with everything. I told them that too, on the level, and you'd never believe what they did to me."

"Couldn't have been much, if they let you out," says Lojza Vrabec with a clear undertone of hostility. Vrabec provides a crop-spraying service to farmers in the Canadian west. He has five special airplanes for the job, and a manager, because he's a fanatical pilot and he flies the planes himself. Lojza has it in for members of the Party and he does not make the recommended distinction between those who are genuine Communists and those who merely belong to the Party.

Krupka, however, ignores his innuendo.

"They squeezed some money out of the district and repaired the lodge! Now they only allow people in organized groups to visit it, and only on Sundays!"

"So in fact you helped bring about a good thing."

"Do you have any idea what a joy it would be to compose music in a place like that? At one time Count Spork, or whoever it was, lent the lodge to Myslivecek and he wrote one of his finest symphonies there."

The O'Reillys are having the same kind of difficulties as Veronika: Jirina has to translate everything for her husband, who studies languages but does not speak them. But she does not have Veronika's linguistic talents and she translates "hunting-lodge" as "castle" and the bald-headed perpetual student, lounging comfortably in a beanbag chair, raises his bushy eyebrows.

"What would you need a castle for?"

The cellist understands a bit of English and so he explains that it was not a "castle," but a "little castle." A "very tiny castle." But this explanation does nothing to correct the bad impression O'Reilly has received. "Why would anyone in a socialist country want to live in a castlet?"

"What's wrong with that, when they're always going on about giving full support to artists?"

"My wife is an artist too but I'm sure she'd never want to live in a castle, would you, Jirina?"

Jirina is embarrassed. She runs her slender violinist's fingers through her hair, today pulled back in a bun, and replies evasively, "The idea never occurred to me."

"How much do you make here, Jirina?" Krupka almost snaps at her.

"Well – it depends," says the violinist. "About eight or ten thousand a year." Jirina has no permanent job. She has only recently joined the Toronto Musicians' Association and because the conductor of the Toronto Symphony Orchestra likes her playing she is occasionally called in to substitute for members who are off sick. The conductor has told her privately that she plays better than half his first violins, but that he can't fire anyone without reason simply because he finds someone better. That's how it is, he says, this is capitalism. I'd have the union on my back, and they don't fool around. Until someone dies, all I can offer you, unfortunately, is substitute work. Apart from that, Jirina gives private fiddle lessons to the children of rich families in Rosedale and Forest Hill. In Prague she had been a member of the radio orchestra, and because she had rhythm she also played a swinging fiddle in a semi-professional country-and-western group. But then the bald fellow hitchhiked over to take a gander at socialism and Jirina succumbed to the charm of an exotic personality. Now, with her occasional work, she is supporting this exotic personality and keeping him at school, and Krupka has unwittingly touched a sensitive spot.

"Ten thousand dollars?" exclaims the virtuoso with envious satisfaction. He converts the sum to Tuzex currency in his mind and multiplies it by the price of Tuzex coupons on the black market in Prague. His calculations tell him that Jirina makes a quarter of a million a year. This is his second trip to the West. "And how much does your husband make?"

"He's a student."

The cellist stares in astonishment at the student in his mid-thirties. In the meantime, O'Reilly has got up, walked through the curtain that divides the sitting-room from the kitchenette and gone to the fridge for beer. The curtain is a monstrous homemade affair of beer-bottle caps and tin buttons with imbecilic slogans on them, the kind the local kids wear on their jackets. When we arrived, Jirina announced proudly that her handy husband had made the curtain, the bookshelves and the table all by himself. The bookshelves are made from prefabricated parts, but the table looks as though it might actually be made from scratch. On the other hand, he has had neither the diligence nor the skill to varnish it. Confronted with such evidence of her husband's abilities, I felt very sorry for Jirina. She was as proud of her student as if he'd just completed a triple doctorate.

Krupka takes his eyes off the curtain, looks sharply at Jirina and, in a way that makes me wonder if he and the Lollobrigida were not hitting it off before disaster hitchhiked into her life in Prague, says bluntly, "He's taking his time with these studies, isn't he?"

"He" – Jirina swallows – "had to interrupt them. He was called up by the army, to go to Vietnam...."

What she omits to mention is that he interrupted his studies after spending eight years in five universities, and now, after a year's break because of Vietnam, he's been studying four years in Canada. Unaware of this, Krupka replies with compassion, "Oh I see. Well, in that case, the main thing is he survived."

"He wasn't in Vietnam," says Lojza Vrabec. "He's a draft-dodger."

"He's a what?" says Krupka, hearing the expression for the first time.

"Instead of going to fight against Communism," I say maliciously, to put this loyal citizen of the Czechoslovak Socialist Republic in the proper humour, "he went to Canada."

As I had expected, Krupka looks at Jirina in great puzzlement. Jirina turns a shade darker and begins to look even more like Lollobrigida. The draft-dodger comes back through the curtains with a bottle in his hands. We have all run out of drinks, but O'Reilly hasn't been paying much attention to his guests. Jirina says quickly, "Would anyone like more beer?"

We all mumble assent and the flushed Jirina jumps up and hurries through the curtain. Krupka looks with disgust at the draft-dodger as he collapses back in his bean-filled throne (two hundred dollars or two Ninth Symphonies at substitute's pay). A cuckoo-clock cuckoos into the silence. Jirina brought it from the tenement house in Vinohrady where she was born. It cuckoos three times, although it is nine in the evening. Another consequence of O'Reilly's manual dexterity.

"Are the Commies still locking people up?" asks Lojza. His aversion to the draft-dodger is equal to his aversion to the cellist who is still living off Communism instead of running away like an honest man when he has the chance.

"Oh sure, they're locking people up," says the virtuoso. "But most people think they've got it coming to them. They're doing it mostly to Party members."

Jirina has returned quietly with the beer and Lojza turns to her. "Translate that!" he insists.

She does what she can. O'Reilly wants to know what they lock them up for.

"Usually some internal Party disputes," says Krupka, who is elsewhere in spirit, for his attention has just been attracted by the wall where the cuckoo-clock is hanging. O'Reilly has papered it with a wallpaper featuring comic-book heroes. Krupka, I imagine, is wondering whether his mistress in Prague would go for this instead of the denim wallpaper she had asked him to get after she saw a picture of Janis Joplin's house in *Mlady Svet*, the weekly youth magazine. Before this evening's debate turned to politics, he told us about his two-day odyssey in search of the denim wallpaper, ending with his discovery that it could only be had in a special shop in the Dominion Concourse for three times the price of the most expensive normal pattern. So Krupka bought an electronic pocket calculator, in a sale, to bribe the official at the passport office so that he would look kindly on him in the future, and decided to tell his mistress that denim wallpaper was no longer in.

"One gang kicks another gang away from the trough and the ones that have been cut off go around screaming that they've been treated unjustly and, because they always have been and always will be bastards, they start locking each other up." The cellist turns and addresses the draft-dodger directly. "Not like in America, where you can go right ahead and criticize the government if you damn well feel like it, and bugger all happens to you."

O'Reilly's reaction, despite Jirina's sanitized translation, is precisely what I expected.

"It comes down to who you are," says O'Reilly. "Like if you're a black, for instance, you don't even have to criticize the government and all kinds of stuff can come down on you."

"Oh sure, they write about that back home too. All the time. 'Racial discrimination' they call it. I don't know what they're talking about. In New York, wherever you go, it's full of niggers. I don't mean Harlem. I mean the banks, city hall, when something got in my eye there was a nigger doctor in the hospital, in the hotel white waiters are breaking their asses to get decent tips from niggers – "

"... 'blacks,' " Jirina translates euphemistically.

"You should translate it 'niggers,' " I point out to her. "Or maybe 'shines.' Or 'darkies.' "

Her sad eyes reproach me. I feel ashamed.

" – and one fellow showed me – he was a music critic!" – Krupka makes an exclamation mark with his voice. Music critics probably represent the pinnacle of authority for him – "showed me some rag that the – "

" – niggers," Jirina translates obediently, but she lowers her eyes.

"– put out at Harvard – *Harvard!* – University. *Rude Pravo* is nothing! *Tribuna* is nothing beside that one. So don't, *please* don't try and tell me about the suffering of the bloody niggers in America today! Wherever you look there's nigger queers, all dolled up like fashion plate models – "

"You should try visiting some prisons. They're full of blacks too," says O'Reilly, pulling out a high card. But the cellist has his own experience of negroes and trumps the card with ease.

"The officials know what they're doing when they lock them up. I know their kind. Prague is full of them too. They're supposed to be students, but the only thing they study is our girls and our booze. Not long ago a bunch of them beat up a poet in the park in front of the Main Station, robbed him blind and hurt him so badly that he had a concussion. I'm no racist, but they're bad."

Despite Krupka's disclaimer, O'Reilly now knows whom he's dealing with. He speaks quietly, as though instructing an unwitting savage. "Most American blacks come from socially underprivileged classes. They are desperately poor – "

But he has come up against a thoroughly screened and schooled veteran of the system: "Oh yes, I've heard that one too. It's exactly the same as what they call class origin back home, except it's the other way around. If they feel like it, they can destroy every honest, talented man just by claiming that he comes from the bourgeoisie. And if they feel like it, they can pardon any crook by saying his father was working-class, drunk, and unemployed."

Jirina prunes down Krupka's direct argument in her translation, so that O'Reilly hears: "Every criminal is excused if he comes from a poor background."

O'Reilly nods. "That's right. American justice is class justice and that's why you're quite justified in considering the inmates of American prisons as political prisoners."

Krupka lifts his eyebrows in astonishment and looks at his former colleague.

"Jirina! What kind of goddamn bird-brain did you marry?"

"Oh shut up, please."

"Now at last I understand why you had to come all the way across the goddamn pond to find a husband! You'd never find an original like that in Prague nowadays. He really believes that shit!" The virtuoso's voice rings with uncounterfeited astonishment.

"What's he saying?" asks O'Reilly.

"Don't tell him what I said. Just say that if American justice is class justice, then what is Czechoslovak justice?"

O'Reilly listens to the translation and replies, "But at least in your country it's *open* class justice. America has *hidden* class justice."

Now it's Lojza's turn to explode. "You're goddamn right it's open! They've got a double standard as big as a barn. Have you ever heard of Apolena? Your wife knows the story." Lojza speaks in fluent Canadian prairie English and with the unfailing talent of a raconteur he unravels a little-known tale from the annals of class justice. It concerns Apolena, one of the few genuine, and not merely self-confessed, agents of the CIA in Czechoslovakia. During a border crossing, Apolena and an accomplice were discovered by the border guards, young soldiers with machine-guns who were anxious to shoot themselves a leave of absence and maybe even a medal for gunning down enemies of the people. But Apolena and his accomplice had both been through a tough training course at the hands of an American marine by the name of Crack McCracken; they shot from the hip; one of the border guards was killed on the spot and the other got away. But the soldiers had two animals with them, hybrid offspring of a wolf and a German shepherd, and these excellent creatures eventually overcame

Apolena and his accomplice. And a great trial took place. The post-mortem showed that the bullet which had shortened the border guard's life came from Apolena's pistol, while his accomplice had missed altogether. Nevertheless, the accomplice got the rope and Apolena got a mere twenty-five years. In the summing up the judge revealed his line of reasoning: there was hope for Apolena's rehabilitation but none for the accomplice's. Why? Because the accomplice's father had been a bookseller, whereas Apolena was the son of a foreman in a large Prague steelworks. In some mystical way, punishment would bring Apolena to see the light, whereas it would only harden the bookseller's son in his ways. So the accomplice swung, and they let Apolena go during the great amnesty of the early sixties, and after the fraternal invasion in sixty-eight he lit out for South Africa, where he reportedly joined the police force.

"That was logical," I say. "The gallows can educate everyone as long as the rope doesn't break."

Krupka is evidently impressed by the story. He chuckles and files it away in his memory for later use in Prague and other capital cities of progress. Any sense of humour O'Reilly might have had, however, has been wiped out of his nature. As if he were engaged in student common-room banter, he remarks, "That's exactly what goes on in American courts. If you're black or a pain in the ass politically, you'll get a far higher sentence for the same crime than if you're white and have money or political pull."

At this Krupka abandons any thoughts he may have had of protecting his beloved colleague's feelings. "And what about Angela Davis?" he asks in a needling voice. Both sides now trundle out the usual arguments. Thesis: In Prague, with a mere fraction of the evidence that the District Attorney had against Angela, she would have been hanged, regardless of her sex. Moreover they probably would have drawn and quartered her because she came from the black bourgeoisie. Anti-thesis: The District Attorney was unable to make his case convincing enough to persuade a prejudiced white jury, but even so Angela had to languish in prison for almost a year, during which time her eyesight was ruined. The synthesis in such debates is always lacking. Thus another thesis: The evidence against Slansky and company in the early fifties was not only controverted, it was even declared later, by official sources, to have been entirely made up, the only problem being that in the meantime Slansky and the rest had been hanged. Antithesis: The difference between Angela and the Slansky gang is merely one of quantity, not quality; in both cases innocent people were kept in jail. But the cellist does not appreciate the qualitative equivalence of poor eyesight and a broken neck and he begins shrieking at the innocent Jirina: what kind of bird-brained, asinine fool have you gone and married? Poor Jirina does not translate this, merely rephrases it: of course they didn't hang Angela, whereas they did hang Slansky. I add that even theoretically you can't consider the difference between the gallows and eyeglasses merely quantitative, because the gallows leads to a change in state from biological life to biological death, which is no less a radical change from quantity into quality than, for example, the familiar transformation of water into ice or egg into chicken, an example put forward by Engels in, I believe, *The Dialectics of Nature*. O'Reilly at long last begins to suspect me of being ironic, and he leaves the secure terrain of pure theory to give a classic example from history: Sacco and Vanzetti. Now it's the pilot's turn to lose his temper and he too begins screaming and shouting that he is fed up to *here* with Sacco and Vanzetti and that there were thousands of Saccos and Vanzettis in Prague. The controversy is quickly transformed from a discussion into a battle between two belligerent cohorts with well-armoured minds. O'Reilly introduces another classic example: the Rosenbergs. The cellist relieves Lojza and declares with absolute certainty that they were Soviet agents and the pity of it is that they didn't fry more while they were at it. Jirina stops translating; the cellist struggles on in broken English, helped by the pilot. O'Reilly cringes down in the bean-filled chair and only his bald red pate is visible: there are plenty of political murders in America that never get written up in the newspapers; the police shoot every Black Panther they don't like — So how come Eldridge Cleaver came back? Homesickness, is O'Reilly's opinion. But then why does Cleaver declare that America with all its horrors is better than Communism with all its tender mercies? Because Cleaver wants the courts to treat him leniently. But why did he come back *at all*? I just told you — he was homesick. Looking at it logically, I say, that means East, West, American jails are best, isn't that so? O'Reilly throws a beer bottle at me angrily, I dodge it, Jirina gets up and goes to sweep up the broken glass and wipe up the beer.

"He went back because he wasn't a complete asshole deserter like you, you shit!" Krupka shrieks. He says it in Czech. He has experienced gooseflesh socialism on his own skin. The unsuccessful buyer of a baroque hunting-lodge is almost choking from an excess of emotion.

To induce the bald deserter to break the cuckoo-clock as well, I point out: *Entia non sunt multiplicanda praeter necessitatem,* and when I register a murderous look I add: "Mr. Krupka's explanation is simpler and more probable, so it has to take precedence over yours, Mr. O'Reilly."

"And I'll give you an even simpler explanation, you imbecile!" cries the pilot. "Eldridge probably had jail coming to him in Korea too, except that in Korea they don't give you steak once a week. Maybe he farted in Kim Il Sung's mausoleum and for that they get the rope in Korea. Of course, since he's black, maybe he'd only get life in the uranium mines, or wherever the Koreans send their tough cases for softening up."

Forced into a corner, O'Reilly resorts to the *argumentum ad hominem.* "You're a socialist, aren't you?"

"Who told you a thing like that?" asks Krupka, horrified.

"Well, you said it yourself, yesterday in the *Star.*"

There was in fact an interview yesterday in the *Star* with Krupka. Just before his tour of Canada, Krupka had played in Moscow at an international competition of cellists, held in honour of the anniversary of the birth (or perhaps it was the death) of V.I. Lenin, and therefore he was newsworthy. The usual short circuit took place in the mind of the Canadian reporter and he asked the virtuoso a stupid question: "As a socialist artist, do you feel you have creative freedom?" Naturally Krupka could not publicly object to being labelled a socialist artist, nor did he feel like expatiating for the media on what he felt about freedom; it was simply not very wise. Therefore he answered with a laconic "Yes." Now, in private, he speaks from the heart.

"Naturally I'm about to go shooting off at the mouth to the newspapers about what I really think!"

"Did you support Dubcek when he was in power?" says the balding deserter, moving in on the attack.

"I did!"

"Dubcek was a communist!"

"But he was a decent man." The argument is too much for the ideological O'Reilly. "His only trouble was he was too stupid. But at least under Dubcek the truth could finally be told. All the muck and filth came out in the open."

O'Reilly reaches an arm out for his beer and remembers he threw it in the corner. Jirina jumps up and runs to the icebox. O'Reilly says in his debating-club tone, "What you've just said only confirms that the Russians had to intervene."

"It was that old fool Dubcek's fault." Krupka has not understood O'Reilly's remark.

"The Kremlin's political analysis was correct," says the student thoughtfully.

Krupka catches his drift. He turns a russet red.

"You support the invasion?"

O'Reilly shrugs. "It was painful but necessary."

Two men bellow at once. Lojza, in a rage: "Listen, you piece of shit, shut up or I'll do it for you." Krupka, in despair: "Jirina!"

All of us – including O'Reilly, who has a fresh bottle of beer in his hand

– look at the bald man's wife and breadwinner. She is lying in a graceful bundle of misery in the corner of the room on a pile of colourful patchwork pillows, sobbing quietly; O'Reilly's hand with the bottle in it drops and the beer spills on the floor. He pulls himself out of his chair with an effort, but he does not, as I naively expected, go over to his wife. He goes into the kitchenette for another bottle.

So I walk over to her and begin to comfort her. The result is that the weeping is qualitatively transformed. Her shoulders shudder in a spasm of sobs. "Now, now, there now girl," I coo. I can smell the lacquered, fragrant hair. "Don't listen to them. It's all just silly talk."

"He – " she sobs, "Patrick doesn't really think that way – but he's so – so inexperienced – and he's awfully touchy about Angela Davis – when he's not upset he's quite reasonable – "

"I know," I say, and add untruthfully, "He's a fine fellow – I understand him."

A new onslaught of sobbing. Then a loud bellowing as Lojza greets O'Reilly coming back into the room with another beer.

"Just wait till the blacks start a revolution in America! People like you will be the first to hang!"

He may be right. O'Reilly's father is the main shareholder in a chain of hamburger joints. But I underestimate the thoroughness with which he has been indoctrinated.

"We," says O'Reilly, "will be no loss."

"I couldn't agree more," says Krupka. "You betrayed America when she needed you most."

"We did not betray America. She was betrayed by the ones who sent us to fight in Vietnam!"

"Against Communism!" roars Krupka. "Anyone who is given the opportunity must fight! It's his sacred duty. And you fled from the battle."

O'Reilly turns pale. He feels on thin ice here. I see that Lojza the pilot is waiting for his chance to strike. O'Reilly immediately gives him an opening. "Why should I fight for something I don't believe in?"

And Lojza: "You don't believe in it because you're chicken."

"That's not true. But I will not go to drop napalm on innocent people."

"Don't give me that bullshit. You deserted because you were scared shitless."

"Have you ever seen photographs from Vietnam? Have you seen those burned children?"

"Of course I've seen them," says the pilot. "You were afraid you were going to burn too. Leave the children out of it."

But O'Reilly insists. "I will not kill children!"

"And I tell you, you numbskull, that if all you had up against you in Vietnam were children, then you'd have gone. But you were up against the Viet Cong, and you chickened out – "

"I was not afraid!"

"You were up to your ears in shit. Now you're making a bloody virtue out of it."

"Don't insult me!"

I cannot resist the temptation to add my two bits' worth of Marxism to help grind down O'Reilly's pomposity.

"I have to admit that Mr. Vrabec's arguments sound convincing," I say, as though I were moderating a college debate. "In the world, and in life itself, the material forces are the ones that decide, the physio-biological movements. In the sphere of the ideological superstructure, we dress them in all kinds of ideological arguments. So why not admit it? To fear for one's life is human. It is equally human to be ashamed of one's fear. And so you displace the fear with another, far more noble motivation *ex post*. There are always enough justifications lying around."

O'Reilly has learned to recognize my baseness and he glares at me. But my argument is too high-flown for Lojza the pilot. "Don't butt in, doctor. He's a piece of chicken-shit."

"And a traitor," cries Krupka. From the mottled pillow in the corner Jirina sobs loudly. O'Reilly finally realizes that he is not alone and that he can use his wife in his own defence. So he retreats from ideology into social convention.

"I think we've had enough," he says in his best salon voice. "I must ask you to leave my apartment."

We get up. Lojza the pilot, like the hero of a gangster serial, walks up to the bald deserter and with a strong right hand grabs him by the scarf around his neck.

"*Your* apartment, you say? What's yours about it? Nothing but that Czech girl over there, who's carrying the load of all this herself, you goddamned freedom fighter!"

"Is that true?" asks Krupka.

"Just ask him!" growls Lojza, and lets go of the scarf.

"Jirzhina and I both believe in the equality of the sexes," wheezes the half-choked O'Reilly. "As soon as I finish my studies – "

"As soon as you finish your studies, you pipsqueak, Jirina will be a goddamn great-grandmother. I only hope she has those kids with someone who deserves her more than you do."

The gentle girl on the pillows is mortified. By the bitter insistence of

Lojza's tone, I conclude that he can't think of a better candidate for the paternity of Jirina's children than himself. I feel a sudden surge of desire for him to succeed. But such things are strange. *Sic visum Veneri—*

•

*3.3.68*
*Boolongong*
*near Perth*

*Dear Danny,*

*I haven't written for a long time, three years I reckon. Time really flies. We hardly turn around and here we are 44 already. Now I work mostly digging ditches, at my age I guess I can't expect ever to find better work. Sometimes I'm up to my waist in water, but I'm making a lot, last year I went to Tahiti for a holiday. There's beautiful women out there and I almost got married except that the guardian angel stepped in at the last minute and I changed my mind. You've got nothing to talk to them about, they make good servants but not wives. So I said to myself what would you say if I was to tell you that with things back home what they are I might set out across the old pond and drop in on Mom. She's 71 and I'd have a look around, see if maybe there wouldn't be work for me at home. The word here is that this Dubcek is giving an amnesty for political offences so maybe if you could ask about it somewhere, maybe at the court. I got four years in abcentium, but a Czeek here claims it ought to come under the statute of limitations since it's been exactly twenty years. He used to be a lawyer but now he's an insurance agent and he insured my house. If I sell the house and put my savings together I'll have enough for the trip there and back to Australia in case I can't hack it back home anymore but first you'd have to ask to make sure they wouldn't lock me up or I wouldn't go back at all. This Czeek says you can't believe anything they say but I'll take your word on that, after all those years you know them better than I do. I do mostly manual labour here and I could easily do that at home too, I can drive a truck and a car and I've learned English, which might be good for something. But first you have to check things out. I'd sure hate to end up in some stinking prison at my age. Mom writes once a month, she's pretty old now and her handwriting is so shaky I can hardly read it. I heard Benda still isn't married, the silly fool, Czech women sure aren't like the Aussies or the Eyetalians or the Slants so why he don't latch onto one is beyond me. I heard Vahar moved away where they don't know him because of the time he done in jail. Your buddies from the band was in jail too, wasn't they, that tall blond fellow Lexa I think his name was and*

Haryk, and I heard Lucie is in the bughouse, Mom wrote that she took up drugs and he divorced her and married somebody younger. I still remember her, she was pretty, but when Haryk got locked up she copied out music for orchestras to support the kid and she often had to work all night and so she got addicted to drugs. It's a bugger of a thing and it's starting up here too but I want to stay clear of it. I don't even drink. Poor old Dad frightened me off booze for good so I only drink beer and I smoke like a chimney – Dad and his tobacco shop. Mom sends me postcards of Kostelec and I pin them to the wall over my bed. One of them shows the square and the savings bank and you can see Dad's old tobacco shop on it and Rupa and the Hotel Beranek where we used to play billiards. It seems pretty much the same there except for some new apartment buildings, otherwise just like old times, the castle and the church and the vicarage and the old courthouse with the stocks where you locked up that fat guy for a joke, the one that used to play trumpet, and the brewery on the other side and Cerna Hora and the Jirasek Châlet just like old times. You can even see old Velcl's warehouse on one of the postcards and I've got those snaps you took as it was blowing up; that was a great job you did. I hear Dr. Labsky is dead. It's a pity, he was a good man. Here the doctors are only out for money, not like Labsky, and the insurance is lousy. Last year they almost bled me dry because I needed dentures or whatever they're called – false teeth. It cost me such a packet I couldn't go to Tahiti this year. But if you'll check this thing out for me I'll sell my house and that'll be enough for a boat ticket (it won't get me on a plane) there and back. I'd try and get on some freighter, I hear you can work off part of your passage. Otherwise I don't hang around much with the local Czeeks here, they're all full of politics and I've grown out of that, but you understand. Dad lost his arm and in the end they pensioned him off sooner than they should of so he didn't even have enough for his booze, he got 350 a month and Mom got nothing because she never worked, Dad wouldn't let her. It's a good thing the relatives in Moravia didn't forget about them, now they've got this co-op, so they sent Dad a nice supply every autumn just like they done when they was private so at least he had his slivovice to make him feel a little better. And what good did it all do? I wouldn't go through it all again. So anyway could you check that out for me if you know where to, maybe at the court, and if you think it's not too big of a risk, I'd show up sometime around the end of the year.

Your old buddy,
Prema

●

In the parking lot in front of the apartment house Krupka says, "Did you see that scarf? Saks Fifth Avenue. I've got one exactly like it in Prague. My brother-in-law brought it from Paris."

We are standing among the cars and above us, like a hive full of well-fed bees, the endless high-rise shines into the night. Golden windows on the tower where O'Reilly's enchanted princess is withering away greet their black sisters on the shore of Lake Ontario. Above the summit of the tower, in the stratosphere, hangs the Canadian moon.

"How could a girl like that marry such a moral cripple?" says the pilot emotionally. "Such a pretty girl! And she's Czech!"

I sense that the pilot will try very soon to correct the situation. I cross all my fingers in the pockets of my raglan.

"You know how it is," replies Jiri Krupka, in the wise tones of those who know how it is. "She was lured away by the attractions of America. The *dolce vita*. But in Prague she could have had all the boys she wanted. I knew her there. She could have had handsome men, politically influential men, or both, all wrapped up in one. But Prague is not America."

"But such a lazy goddamn good-for-nothing! And a Czech girl! A Czech girl!" wails the pilot. "And she marries a goddamn American *Commie!*" he laments, and his voice flies up to the clear Canadian stars. Lojza is speaking of Communism from unique personal experience. Sestak told me about it. Once upon a time Communism didn't bother him. He was an enthusiastic member of a civilian flying club run by the armed forces and when he was drafted he got accepted in the air force. He went into it full of dedication, for his ultimate aim was to become a MiG pilot. Not that he cared about guarding the peaceful sleep of our women and children, as the official propaganda had it. He just wanted to fly faster than sound.

But why else do we have the cadre chiefs, those sweet little arbiters of political reliability, as Danda the cornet player in the Boulevard used to call them? The cadre chief in the pilots' training school discovered that Lojza's father had fought against Franco in the Spanish Civil War, and that, in the fifties, made him suspect of leftism; he had been jailed for a brief term and expelled from the Party, before being released and rehabilitated. The way the cadre chief saw it, Lojza's father had once been found guilty by Party decision, therefore his factual innocence was a betrayal of the same Party, and they were not prepared to entrust a supersonic fighter to the son of someone like that. So they transferred Lojza from flight school to the infantry and he appealed in vain for justice. He did his hitch in the infantry and as soon as he was discharged he went straight back to his old flying club. There, unaware of his demotion, they welcomed him back as a freshly trained military pilot, drank to his return, and the comrade instructor said, "Hey Lojza baby, the captain here is going on a hop to Brno. Gas him up a machine and roll it out on the tarmac for him so you don't lose your touch."

The airport was five kilometres outside Bratislava. Lojza baby said nothing, went into the hangar, gassed up an aircraft, started the engine and taxied it out onto the apron where his friends were waiting, headed by the instructor and the captain with his flying goggles on. They watched Lojza taxi across the tarmac towards them, but Lojza didn't slow down as he approached. He leaned his right hand into the throttle, the aircraft snarled indecorously. The captain jumped onto the apron and raised his arms in the signal Stop! but the aircraft whizzed past him, lifted into the air, skimmed the tops of the trees at the end of the runway, banked southwards, cleared the poplar trees lining the highway and vanished. Twenty minutes later Lojza touched down on the runway of the Vienna Aeroklub.

And now he is fertilizing the grain-rich fields of Canada; he owns a fleet of five dung-dispensing Cessnas and is in love with an enchanted princess. He lifts his weather-worn face to the prairie moon and talks with intense feeling: "That slimy bastard is the goddamn epitome of all that's Communist! That chicken-shit, lily-livered, deserting son-of-a-bitch. He'd make a first-rate tooth-puller in Ruzyne prison. I can just see him. I hate their goddamn guts!"

Then he quickly leans close to us. "And you know what I'm going to do? It's been haunting me for years, but now I'll do it just to show Jirina!"

"What are you going to do, murder him?" I ask. "I wouldn't if I were you. You'd just give them a martyr. An opponent of the war in Vietnam murdered by a revisionist and a defector."

"The jerk isn't worth the effort," says the pilot. "And Jirina will get rid of him herself. She's not stupid, just temporarily dazed. Happens to everyone. I'm going to do something far better. Listen!" Once more he looks at the blazing stars and his face lights up with a blissful smile. "It's about three minutes by air from the Austrian border to the place where they have their bloody May-Day military reviews in Bratislava, and that reviewing stand where they always put those pot-bellied dignitaries, ours and the Soviets, on display. They're highly visible from the air because they give off a metallic glow from all the goddamn Orders of Lenin they wear on their tits. Perfect for drawing a bead on. You know what I'm going to do? I'm going to rent the biggest goddamn crop-duster in Vienna, fill it full of liquid barnyard waste into which, in addition, I will personally shit, and when the pot-bellies are up there reviewing their march-past, I'll fly across and drop my load of Canadian napalm right on top of them from a height of about five metres. Before they know what hit them, those heroes of the Soviet Fucking Union will be walking shit-houses!"

We stand there a while longer, dazzled by the vision of the foul-smelling generals of the Occupation Army. Then we say goodbye and part. Lojza roars off towards Don Mills in his MG at an illegal speed, and I take Krupka back to his hotel. On the way he asks me whether Saks Fifth Avenue has a branch store in Canada, and then he wants to know where he can buy those women's panties with "Yes," "No," and "Maybe" on them. He says that not a single girl in Prague has them yet and his mistress wants a set. This reminds him of the problem of the denim wallpaper. He has already abandoned the idea of taking back the whitewall tires that the director of the concert agency wants for his Saab because he would have to pay for the excess weight on the plane. So he says he'll at least take the boss's daughter some genuine Levis, and either a bubble umbrella or a Mexican poncho made of rattlesnake skins for his wife. We drive down beautiful post-midnight Bloor Street and in front of the conservatively smiling black door-man at the Sutton Place we say our farewells.

Next morning Krupka flew to Cuba. He gave one concert at the Che Guevara Artificial Insemination Station, another at the Vishinski Sugarcane Plantation and a final one in Havana, where El Jefe himself came to hear him. After the concert a short time was spent with the leader in cordial conversation.

•

"The future of Russia is the future of the world," I say, and this arouses Hakim's interest. Of course, I mean it otherwise than you think I mean it, Hakim.

"D'you think that Russia will attack the States?" asks Wendy. Bellissimmo is scowling and smoking a cigarette, and Dianne is taking notes.

"That won't be necessary, I guess. I was thinking of the future of certain social phenomena that are traditionally Russian."

"I thought you mean revolution," growls Hakim.

I know that's what you thought, Hakim.

"Let me put it this way: phenomena that in Russia followed the revolution. Open your books to page 56." And I quote Marlow's story again:

"'"Kurtz got the tribe to follow him, did he?" I suggested. "They adored him," the harlequin said.' And now pay particular attention," I urge this handful of apprentices, but I know that the words of the quotation will not evoke in their minds that face and the heavy moustache which, ever since the razor was invented, has always hidden something: an inferiority complex, vanity, a longing to be different, or the same.... I quote: "'The tone of these words was so extraordinary that I looked at him searchingly. It was curious to see his mingled eagerness and reluctance to speak of Kurtz.' Mingled eagerness and reluctance," I emphasize. "Whose portrait is

Conrad actually painting? Don't forget I told you that *Heart of Darkness* is actually a prophecy."

"You're thinking of Stalin?" Nicole replies.

"Judge for yourselves," I say and go on reading aloud: " ' "He came to them with thunder and lightning, you know – and they had never seen anything like it – and very terrible. He could be very terrible. You can't judge Mr. Kurtz as you would an ordinary man." ' " I pause. "In party vocabulary, a phenomenon like that is called 'the cult of personality.' "

"Do you mean the Communist Party?" Wendy asks to be certain. Her silliness rouses Bellissimmo: "Naturally, chicken-brain!"

"Well, I just wanted to make sure, gigolo."

"Now, now children," I say. "Listen. Listen to the harlequin: ' "You can't judge Mr. Kurtz as you would an ordinary man. No, no, no!" ' Do you hear the passion? But I'm getting ahead of myself. Listen to the harlequin: ' "Now – just to give you an idea – I don't mind telling you, he wanted to shoot me, too, one day – but I don't judge him." ' 'Shoot you!' Marlow cried, and the harlequin related how Mr. Kurtz had wanted to shoot him for some ivory that belonged to the harlequin. Mr. Kurtz declared that ' "he could do so, and had a fancy for it" ' – do you hear that? a fancy for it! – and the harlequin adds ' "there was nothing on earth to prevent him killing whom he jolly well pleased. And it was true, too. I gave him the ivory." ' You don't talk with Mr. Kurtz, you listen. You obey. You can't judge him as you would an ordinary man. But once again, Marlow does not understand. He has a Western explanation for such a personality: ' "Why, he's mad!" ' The harlequin 'protested indignantly. Mr. Kurtz couldn't be mad. If I had heard him talk, only two days ago, I wouldn't dare hint at such a thing.' "

The cafeteria has emptied and only the secretaries from the Humanities Department are conscientiously taking their afternoon coffee break. Hakim speaks, his voice the old familiar mixture of contempt, doubt and hatred – and at the same time, of something that draws him to me, because both of us are members of a strange élite; we are concerned about things that neither Wendy nor Dianne care about, that Vicky has never thought of, and that Nicole takes an interest in only for reasons that are very ancient, and very feminine.

"But all that stuff can be applied to any tyrant in history. Like Shakespeare's heroes. Like Richard the Second – "

"Don't forget that the harlequin is a Russian," I say. "And notice how Conrad emphasizes this key conversation between a man of the West and a man of the East. The very fact that Marlow is individualized by a name of his own, while the harlequin is generalized by the lack of a name, indicates the intellectual aim, though it may be unconscious. Listen. Marlow observes Kurtz's house from a distance through a telescope. There is an ornamental fence around the house with decorative knobs on the ends of the posts. Now listen: 'Now I had suddenly a nearer view, and its first result was to make me throw my head back as if before a blow. Then I went carefully from post to post with my glass, and I saw my mistake. These round knobs were not ornamental but symbolic; they were expressive and puzzling, striking and disturbing – food for thought and also for the vultures ... those heads on the stakes....' "

"Disgusting," says Wendy to relieve the tension. I say, apparently unconnectedly, but there is a connection here and its name is Hakim, "In the novel *Under Western Eyes* there is another key passage. I'll read it to you." And I read: " 'In a real revolution the best characters do not come to the front. A violent revolution falls into the hands of narrow-minded fanatics and of tyrannical hypocrites at first. Afterwards comes the turn of all the pretentious intellectual failures of the time. Such are the chiefs and the leaders. You will notice that I have left out the mere rogues. The scrupulous and the just, the noble, humane, and devoted natures; the unselfish and the intelligent may begin a movement – but it passes away from them. They are not the leaders of a revolution. They are its victims: the victims of disgust, of disenchantment – often of remorse. Hopes grotesquely betrayed, ideals caricatured – that is the definition of revolutionary success. There have been in every revolution hearts broken by such successes.... My meaning is that I don't want you to be a victim.' "

Hakim's black eyes flare with wrath, an inner passion – I recall other burning eyes, belonging to a girl with a name that lent itself to wordplay: ... Nadeje, which means hope ... Nadezda ... Nadia ... Nada ....

Your head on a post one day, Hakim, or perhaps it will only be a broken heart ... even violent revolution may one day become civilized ... people like you will be the first to hang War ... ah, innocent Hakim, you beautiful vessel of Arabian longing, so sincere, so Leninistically exploitable with the help of the *reservatio mentale*....

•

Veronika told me about it that afternoon. The tour of the famous Soviet poet Vokurovski was sponsored by Mr. Svensson. This time she did not hold it against him, because Vokurovski, she said, was our man.

But with Percy in mind she dreamed up a small, partially pedagogical experiment: on the mantel of the Svenssons' fireplace she displayed several books, printed in Russian but not in Russia, and she said, "Now let's see what happens."

She also told me a story related to the experiment, about someone called Franta Novosad, an accountant and mystery writer in Prague. In the distant past, Novosad had written novels under the pseudonym Sheila Siddons. In the fifties he was compelled to stop writing and he became an accountant. He cautiously poked his horns out again in the 1960s and gained a certain popularity with a series of novels published under the pen-name Josefa Novakova. The hero of this series was a police lieutenant called Honza Fialka, an entirely improbable character both in the way he talked and behaved, and in the type of adventures he got mixed up in. He spoke just like Novosad's first detective, Inspector Wollstonecraft of Scotland Yard, whose diction was a faithful reproduction of Sam Spade's translated into vernacular Czech. Fialka's Prague was indistinguishable from Las Vegas. It was populated by dope dealers, and roulette was the hottest game in town. Like Wollstonecraft and Spade, Fialka worked more with his fists than with his head, and though he got hit on the head with a revolver butt at least three times in every story, it never softened his brains, so they never promoted him. He remained a lieutenant. In the first two years after the Soviet invasion, Novosad's luck took a turn for the better; his books were read almost like protest literature. Then his career was once more temporarily suspended by an article in *Tvorba* titled "Intellectual Poison in the Guise of Entertainment." Although the author of this article, Dohnal, was a Party hack of boundless servility, he was also unfortunately intelligent enough to recognize Novosad's sources. He pointed out that Fialka, a so-called officer of the National Security Corps, was in reality the blood brother of the dissolute Sam Spade, whose "philosophy" genuine officers of the public security forces could have nothing to do with. Novosad, his brain softened by the American manners and mores he had soaked up from his incessant consumption of pulp novels, tried to defend himself by writing a letter to the editor of *Tvorba,* which consisted largely of quotes from Chandler characterizing Marlowe: "Down these mean streets a man must go who is not himself mean, who is neither tarnished nor afraid...." But at that time the editors of *Tvorba* were only printing letters which they wrote themselves. The editor-in-chief quite correctly treated Novosad's letter as a provocation, and told the manager of the restaurant where Novosad worked that Novosad thought his socialist homeland was depraved, and its honest workers people with tarnished hands who lived in fear. Novosad was fired from the National Restaurants and Dining Rooms Enterprise, and his books were removed from all public libraries and burned. A scholarly work by a more-than-untarnished candidate of science, Slava Vypsouk, called *The History of the Mystery Novel: A Marxist Point of View,* met the same fate; the work, like its author, was more than untarnished, except for the fact that on page 477 there was a footnote which read, "In this country, attempts, with little success, were made by J. Novakova and F. Novosad to imitate the American 'hard-boiled egg' school, the latter having published in the 1940s under the pen-name Sheila Siddons several novels whose spirit and language were quite derivative of Mr. Ngaio Marsh, and especially of his anti-Communist pamphlet *Five Red Fish*." This learned work of Czech scholarship went into the chopper not because of the minor errors of fact, but because it was decreed that the names Novosad, Novakova and Siddons were to be utterly expunged from the history of Czech literature.

In the lean years between the Siddons era and the J. Novakova period, Novosad became a highly specialized crook; Veronika's story concerned this particular period in the life of the man who was now helping to dig the new Prague Metro. He stole English and American mystery novels which he then lent for a fee to a fairly extensive clientele, mostly in the national health service. He had launched his career as a book thief in a fashion worthy of Inspector Wollstonecraft: when the authorities shut down the United States Information Service in 1948 he stole the key from an employee, and the night after they had closed and sealed the agency he broke into it and stole everything that had anything to do with crime. At the time his bold act cost the careers of two fledgling security police officers, who were accused of having made such a haphazard study of the inventory that they failed to notice documents important enough that the Americans thought them worth stealing. No one ever thought of connecting the burglary with Wollstonecraft.

In the late 1950s, Novosad, who was then working as an accountant for the National Restaurants and Dining Rooms Enterprise, made contact with a certain department in the Ministry of the Interior in charge of delegating waiters to serve at parties given by Western embassies and consulates, and he managed to bribe his way onto that well-screened list. From time to time, therefore, he would don a white shirt and tails and distribute drinks on the premises of a Western embassy; afterwards he would submit reports to the secret police on the behaviour of the Czech guests. Happily, their behaviour was always impeccable, and Novosad was never compelled to do anything in pursuit of his passion that he could not square with his American conscience. The diplomats attributed the massive disappearance of mystery novels from their embassy libraries to their invited guests and tactfully said nothing about it.

But Novosad exploited his connections with the Ministry of the Interior in a far more daring way. The Ministry also had a vast number of American crime and pornographic novels scattered through its collection of literature, all of them confiscated from shipments of books sent to private Czech citizens by relatives in the West. Systematically, and using a variety of different ruses, Novosad visited his contacts in the cream-tiled headquarters of the Ministry, and with Tuzex coupons (purchased from customers at the restaurant) for bribes he managed to get acquainted with an ever-increasing number of Ministry employees, until there was hardly a person in the Ministry to whom he did not have access – including the Minister, who became a customer of Novosad's book-lending service without being aware that a considerable number of the books he borrowed belonged in his own library. If Western intelligence agencies had contacted Novosad at that time, they might have found in him an answer to Kim Philby. Novosad, however, kept his double life a perfect secret.

The acme of his criminal career was a job in Moscow. Sometime in the late fifties, during the early days of rapprochement, the Supreme Soviet permitted the Americans to hold a book exhibition. At that time Novosad made his first (and last) trip to the motherland of socialism, and he did so with an ambitious purpose: to steal from the American exhibition a complete set of Mickey Spillane, who at that time was the most famous practitioner of the genre. Novosad knew that the exhibition would not be open to the general public, just to ticket-holders, and that furthermore these tickets would not be on sale, but distributed to only the most politically reliable cadres throughout the entire monstrous country. But he also knew that within those most reliable of cadres, a sufficient percentage could always be found who were open to the notion of bartering. He filled his suitcase with such a quantity of ladies' underwear, Italian pumps and plastic raincoats that the customs officials at the Moscow airport suspected him of fetishism. He was rescued by an alert fellow passenger who declared that the women's things belonged to her but that she simply hadn't enough room for them in her own suitcase. This favour of hers cost Novak half his supply of barterable goods, but even so the remainder was enough to secure him two tickets of admission to the American exhibition. On his first visit he lifted the complete works of Spillane and three J.D. Carrs from right under the nose of the deliberately unobservant American employee and a very vigilant Soviet plainclothesman. On his second visit he trimmed the stand of the rest of its detective literature. In the week remaining until his flight back to Prague he combed the second-hand bookshops of Moscow, where he managed to steal all the practically unavailable Russian mystery writers from the pre-revolutionary period, three nineteenth-century Ukrainian translations of Gaboriau and one Agatha Christie in Uzbeki.

Novosad's story seemed to me unique, an intellectual anomaly, but Veronika thought otherwise. She felt that book theft had become the national disease of the Russian intelligentsia which, thanks to the Soviet occupation, was beginning to appear in Czechoslovakia. Novosad was merely the first swallow.

The great poet Vokurovski emerged from the customs area at the Toronto airport accompanied by a miniature, pale man. Veronika had not the slightest doubt about his function; she was merely interested to see how he would pass himself off.

He presented himself as Vokurovski's interpreter.

"My name is Ramses," he said. "I translate Vokurovski."

"Oh, so it's you who did those marvellous translations!" said Rosemary Svensson delightedly, and then she caught herself: "Oh – but I thought – it was – wasn't it W.H. Auden who ...?"

"I mean," said Ramses, "I translate vot he say, zen vot you say. He talk, you talk, I translate."

"What he's trying to say," said Vokurovski, with barely a trace of an accent, "is that he's my interpreter."

"Zat's right," said Ramses.

In the car from the airport Vokurovski managed to seat himself in the back between the two women, and they stuffed Ramses into the front with Mr. Svensson, and Percy who was driving. Ramses did not protest, because he could still hear what was being said in the back.

Vokurovski revealed himself at once to be a perspicacious tactician. He asked a few conventional questions about what films were showing in Toronto, and Veronika immediately knew why. Rosemary began naming a few of the romances, westerns and comedies that were on at the moment and Veronika, as if it were an afterthought, added that *The Confession* by Costa-Gavras was also in town. At the same time her eyes met Vokurovski's and the longing in them was unmistakable. It was not exactly a longing for romances.

"You'll have to take me there," he whispered to her later at the party. "I don't know Toronto. But first I'll have to get rid of this pharaoh here. For three hours at least."

"How? Should I try flirting with him?"

"He's not interested in women. Get him drunk. It's the only thing that works."

Veronika looked around. The eyes of the little pharaoh were watching her intently over Rosemary's shoulders.

With Percy's help, she manoeuvred Vokurovski over to the fireplace, and then struck a picturesque pose with one bare arm outstretched along the mantel. Veronika had elegant arms and Vokurovski was not like Ramses in such matters. He noticed the books almost at once.

He looked around in horror and whispered:

"Good God! D'you think I might – borrow them?"

Veronika exchanged a look with Percy.

"You can have them," said Percy. "Veronika put them here for you."

Vokurovski looked at the girl with inheld breath, then burst into loud, effervescent laughter while whispering under his breath, "Is the pharaoh watching?"

"I think he is," said Veronika. "Wait a while. I'll fix things for you. Come on, Percy!"

She and Percy walked over to the little group standing around Ramses. Rosemary was bubbling ecstatically on the subject of the pharaoh's homeland.

"I've been to Russia twice. The last time we were there we visited several cities in the Arctic. Amazing! Magnificent! Simply gorgeous!"

"Yes," said Ramses. "I know it."

"I often wonder why we can't build such magnificent cities in our own northland."

"You don't got so many people like ve," said Ramses politely.

"That is true. However – "

Veronika barged into the conversation like an elephant. "Those cities were built by millions of prisoners, Mrs. Svensson."

"Oh, really?"

"De young lady exaggerating a little," said Ramses icily.

"A little," admitted Veronika.

"Well," Rosemary was drowning in embarrassment, "well – of course we don't have so many – criminals – in Canada."

Meanwhile Vokurovski judged that the conversation had distracted his watchdog sufficiently to allow him to act. He turned to the fireplace and reached out to take the books. Just then, an uninitiated guest, Professor Tomkins, stepped up. Vokurovski was startled, and because, despite Percy's reassurance, he still felt that what he was about to do was essentially theft, he made a deep bow and in that position pretended to examine the inside of the empty fireplace.

"Have you lost something, Mr. Vokurovski?"

Vokurovski straightened up. "N-no, I was just looking at the inside of this fireplace. It's odd, isn't it?"

Professor Tomkins looked at the fireplace. "It looks like a perfectly ordinary fireplace to me."

"I've never seen one like it in my life," said Vokurovski desperately.

"Really? And what's so odd about it?"

"Well, that is – in Russia we don't have fireplaces and – you see – this is my first trip to the West ...," the poet lied, beating a bewildered retreat.

"Well, in that case, it's ... logical ... I suppose," said the equally bewildered professor. "If you'll just excuse me ...?" and he moved off.

Vokurovski looked around again. Veronika had her claws sunk deeply into the secret policeman.

"Apparently you're a writer?" she asked him.

"Only translator, Miss. Member of Translator Section of Union of Soviet Writers."

That interested Rosemary. Translation would surely be a safer subject than Arctic cities; so she murmured, her tone at precisely the correct pitch, "Is that so? How interesting!" And asked the inevitable question: "What kind of books do you translate?"

"I am translating in African literature."

"Is that so? How interesting! Can you really speak all those languages ... Swahili ... Xhosa ...?"

"I am translating from English translations. To Russian."

"Naturally," Rosemary reassured the translator. "How many books have you translated?"

"For matter of fact – I work now on first my translation."

"Oh, I see...." Perspiration was beading on Rosemary's brow. "How – "

Veronika interrupted her. "My goodness, you must be a damned good translator if they accepted you in the Writers' Union even if you haven't translated anything yet."

The pharaoh's eyes narrowed viciously. Veronika withstood his gaze. Rosemary recalled how interesting it was that it had rained yesterday.

Back at the fireplace, Vokurovski was bracing himself for another attempt when again he was interrupted. He reacted in the same fashion, if anything with more exaggeration, as the interloper was his host, Mr. Svensson.

"Have you lost something, Mr. Vokurovski?"

"No, I was just looking at your fireplace."

"Would you like me to make a fire? As a matter of fact, I'm finding it rather chilly in here myself."

"Oh no, please don't bother."

"No trouble at all. I like making fires. But first I'll have to...." Mr. Svensson lifted the precious volumes from the mantel and looked at them. "Look – these might interest you. I believe they're by Russian authors."

And he handed Vokurovski the books by Mandelstam, Solzhenitsyn and Zamyatin.

Vokurovski made an amateurish attempt to feign bored interest. With a trembling hand he took the volumes from Mr. Svensson and without even looking at them he said, "Yes, they're Russian writers." He conquered his excitement and even managed to hit a note of irony that was, however, inaccessible to Mr. Svensson: "Of course they're not very widely read in Russia."

"I guess my daughter must have bought them. You can keep them, if you find them interesting. I'd be honoured."

What happened next took Mr. Svensson's breath away. The poet glanced around, then rapidly stuffed all three volumes under his shirt.

"Isn't that a bit – uncomfortable?" inquired his astonished host.

Too late, Vokurovski realized that he had acted impetuously. He turned a brilliant red and stammered, "It – it's a kind of – of old Russian tradition. From czarist times – almost second nature...."

"Is – that so?"

Meanwhile Rosemary had stopped commenting on climatic phenomena and was imprudently backsliding towards more dangerous topics.

"What I really don't understand, Mr. Ramses, and perhaps you could answer this, is why Mr. Vokurovski needs an interpreter at all? Why, his English is" – she hesitated, then lied politely – "almost as good as yours."

And her guileless American eyes lingered on the secret policeman's evil face. Before the pharaoh could offer an explanation, Veronika said, "Don't you see? That's precisely why!"

Which, of course, did not make Rosemary any the wiser.

Vokurovski spent the next two weeks trying to get Ramses drunk so that he could slip away to see *The Confession*. But the secret agent vigilantly cut down on his drinking. The day before Vokurovski's departure, Veronika's telephone rang. It was the excited poet begging her to pick him up at a certain address and drive him to the cinema where Costa-Gavras' film was playing, because he didn't know Toronto and he had spent all his pocket money on gifts for his girlfriend in Moscow, so he couldn't afford a taxi. Later, in the car, Veronika gathered from the very disjointed ramblings of an over-excited Vokurovski that the pharaoh's vigilance had been beaten insensitive, rather than actually broken, by a Czech girl who, at a party arranged by the chairman of the Department of Slavic Studies, had monopolized the agent's time. She had been eccentrically dressed and she had spoken to the agent in a strange Russian that sounded like a bad translation from English, but she was so persistent that he began pouring drinks into himself to help withstand her incessant verbal barrage. And he didn't make it, said Vokurovski happily to Veronika, and then bade her farewell with a quadruple Khrushchev and rushed into the cinema.

Dotty probably never suspected what a great service she had rendered to Russian culture.

•

According to the curriculum, our history teacher, Mrs. Trejtnarova, was responsible for introducing us to the doctrine of race. She did this theoretically, while Herr Doktor Schwarzkopf took a more practical approach: he measured our heads with a metal L-square. But he tarnished his scientific reputation in our eyes when he failed to recognize that Benno was half-Jewish on his mother's side and, on the contrary, declared that there was a prominent *nachgedunkeltes nordisches Element* in his physiognomy very like that of the Reich's propaganda minister Herr Doktor Josef Goebbels. Later we asked Mrs. Trejtnarova what *nachgedunkeltes nordisches Element* meant, and after consulting her dictionary at home she translated it slavishly in our next history lesson as "latterly darkened Nordic element." Naturally the phrase caught on for Benno and all the other not entirely pure Aryan students at school. That was at the time of the early victories, before the grammar school was totally Aryanized.

As for the girls, Dr. Schwarzkopf did not measure their heads, but rather their pelvises. He would take them into his office one by one and whatever it was went on in there, they made a great and giggly secret of it, so we concluded he had measured their busts as well. We were wrong.

Mrs. Trejtnarova was already an elderly lady. She couldn't speak German very well, but since history had to be taught in German, she spoke to us in the language of the Reich. *Reichsdeutsch* was also the prescribed language in mathematics, but there Bivoj dealt with the problem by declaring that all sums would be calculated mentally. This meant that the first half of the math lessons resembled a yoga meditation and the second half, when he tested us, a pantomime. His explanations were limited to wordlessly writing complex equations on the blackboard with utter disregard for our feeble-mindedness, and when he tested us, instead of the usual liturgical triad – "Can you solve it?" "No." "Sit down." – we did the calculations mentally and wrote the results on the blackboard. Our minds were usually blanks and our answers were usually wrong. To ask a question, Bivoj would raise his hairy eyebrows to an unnatural height, the one being tested would shake his head, Bivoj would wave him away from the board and then write an F in his notebook with a flourish.

It worked in mathematics, but history was impossible to teach using the deaf-mute method. Over the holidays they would send Mrs. Trejtnarova on a two-month ideological re-education course – *Ideologische Umschulung*, they called it – where, instead of teaching German, they dictated over a hundred pages of world history interpreted in a completely new way. Before the war Mrs. Trejtnarova's lessons consisted of detailed descriptions of famous battles, and even more detailed accounts of royal banquets, with the greatest care of all lavished on descriptions of what she called historical life and institutions; they were really lectures on women's fashions in the Middle Ages or the Renaissance. Once she became so absorbed in what she was saying that she began to describe the minutiae of ladies' undergarments at the time of Louis XVI – all the girls sat there as red as boiled crabs, but Mrs. Trejtnarova simply didn't notice. It was the same during oral tests. I once gained notoriety for an account of the battle of Crecy which was limited to a vivid atmospheric and acoustic description of how the breast-plates glistened, the armour clashed and the wounded groaned, and Mrs. Trejtnarova remained blissfully unaware that I had neglected to mention the date, who had fought whom and, most important of all, the death of John of Luxemburg – because I had no idea he had died in that particular battle. Mrs. Trejtnarova gave me an A and held me up as an example.

But she didn't teach like that anymore. There were no more battles or banquets or historical bloomers. Very slowly – at about three words per minute, to give us time to copy it out and to last her till the end of the period – she dictated from the sheets of paper they had originally dictated to her at the *Umschulung*. We learned that the most cultured nation in Europe in ancient times were the Germanic Vandals, because they had uprooted (the German term for it was *ausrotten*) the Jewish merchant colonies in North Africa. Moreover the Romans themselves were more than half Germanic; and those healthy wars against the Germanic tribes in the north, during which *eine gute Rassenmischung,* or racial mingling, took place, were of great benefit to them. The French resulted from a mingling of Germans and Englishmen, and the Czech language was in fact literally translated from the German, because the Slavs were incapable of creating on their own a language as rich as Czech. One proof of this was the word *Schraubenzieher,* screwdriver, which in Czech is *sroubovak*. Thus the new history marched forward until it arrived at the present with the claim that *"der Führer und Reichskanzler Adolf Hitler wurde in Braunau geboren"* and *"der Reichsmarschall Hermann Göring hat sich im ersten Weltkrieg als Jagdflugzeugführer auserordentlich ausgezeichnet."* In this revolutionary conception of history the Czechs came out of it relatively well, certainly better than any of the other Slavic peoples. They had the greatest *Zumischung vom germanischen Blut*. Jews, on the other hand, were *Ausschuss*. The new historians could not find a good word to say about them.

German people, according to this version of history, represented the best possible combination of the best possible races and were characterized by a tall body, a narrow skull, blue eyes and fair hair. When Mrs. Trejtnarova dictated this to us, Lexa put his hand up and asked in German, "Please, miss, why is Herr Propagandaminister Doktor Josef Goebbels so small and his hair so black?"

The question embarrassed Mrs. Trejtnarova considerably. In truth everything that went on in history classes was done because of Ilse Seligerova who was German and who, in that period of early victories, still went to school with us and not to a German grammar school as she did later. Mrs. Trejtnarova was afraid of her, and so when Lexa asked the question she stuttered and stammered until she recalled the recent query concerning latter darkening and replied in her clumsy *Reichs deutsch*, "Herr Doktor Goebbels is latterly darkened – and – and – and – latterly shrunk. But he still has a German element, for example he writes German very beautifully."

That too became part of our folklore. It had happened shortly before Christmas. We celebrated New Year's Eve at Haryk's place, because his parents had gone to get soused at their brother's, who was a wealthy landowner. We managed to accumulate a large number of bottles, most of them a wine we called Château Vomitella, two suspicious-looking liqueurs, one bottle of artificially coloured *Eierkognak* – a sort of eggnog made at home out of grape-oil by Jarka Pila from Cernice – and one small bottle of pre-war Meinl rum which Lim got me in exchange for three issues of *Erotic Review*. Lucie was wearing a dress with a deep, rectangular *décolletage* so that whenever she leaned over one had a good view of her solar-lamp-tanned hemispheres. Right at the outset of the evening, therefore, we began to talk of science and ideology.

"Say, Lucie, how did he measure them?" asked Lexa.

Lucie straightened up. Although she knew very well who and what was meant, she asked uncomprehendingly, "Who and what are you talking about?"

"*SS Rassenforschungsoberführer Herr Doktor Schwarzkopf*," said Lexa, who was talented in languages, "and lactiferous glands."

Lucie looked even more uncomprehending than before. "What's that?"

"That," said Lexa, "is what we can see when you bend over."

Lucie made a deep bow, almost to the ground, because she took classes in rhythm. She said, "I don't see anything."

"But I do," said Lexa.

"What?"

"Your bust," said Benno. "How did Schwarzkopf measure your bust?"

"With a tape-measure, of course," replied Lucie. "If Lexa meant my bosom, he should have said so in the first place and not gone showing off with some disgusting natural science terms."

"He doesn't know that word," said Benno. "He only knows the colloquial term for it."

"What's that?" asked Fonda. "Breast?"

"Breasts," said Haryk. "It's plural. There's two of them."

"He knows an even more colloquial word," said Benno.

"Benno!" said Alena.

"Chest?" asked Fonda. "That can't be plural."

"Thorax," said Lexa. "But I didn't want to say the word I know because it might have made Lucie rubricate."

"You could have gone right ahead," said Lucie. "If you'd made me rubricate, I'd have slapped your face."

"How did he measure your thorax?" asked Benno. "For length, or circumference?"

"Benno!"

"He didn't measure it," said Lucie. "He photographed it."

We were silenced. At last it was clear why the girls had made such a secret of Schwarzkopf's racial study. Lucie had already drunk two *Eierkognak*s, and like all girls – then anyway – she was not used to drinking.

Lexa broke the silence. "In your bra?"

"He took pictures of us naked, if you must know. Anyone who refused he threatened to report to the Gestapo for sabotaging the scientific research of the Reich."

We were silent again. We could see Schwarzkopf examining the girls' racial features, all right. Ilse Seligerova supposedly had the biggest breasts – if only because, as a German, she had all the best racial features.

"He says you can measure racial features best of all from photographs, especially when they are projected on a screen," Lucie went on. "He says you measure the width of the hips, the shoulders and the waist, divide that by the distance between these," and she pointed at her breasts, "and then multiply it by the distance of the navel from what's down below it. Then you look up the results on a table and according to that you determine the racial type."

"What kind of *Rassentypus* are you, Fräulein?" asked Lexa.

"He told me, but I forgot. It was an awfully long word. Something like ... *niederhochbohmischmehrischrheinlandischeblondmittelrundbrustiges* somethingorother."

Benno said, "I'm a *nachgedunkelter Nordischer Element*. Like Gaybells."

"You're more like Gayring, Benno," said Haryk. "A latterly darkened Rotundgerman."

"I'm not a German, I'm a Czech Jew," said Benno.

"But originally you were. Originally we were all Germans, before we began fornicating with Jews and Slavs."

"And what were the Germans originally?"

"They were monkeys, of course," said Haryk. "Germans descended scientifically from the monkey, and the other less educated races were created by the Lord God from Eve's rib."

"Rubbish! Eve had them with the serpent," I said.

By that time two bottles of Château Vomitella had gone down, and the game loosened up. Benno stood up on the couch, let his arms hang down around his knees and let his mouth drop open. "I came from a chimpanzee crossed with a garter snake." He looked like an idiot. "Scientifically, they call me a *nachdunkelter Rotundjewgermane*."

"More like a *Bellygermane*," said Lexa.

Benno made himself erect and thrust his stomach forward.

"*Grossbellygermane*," said Haryk.

Benno puffed himself out further and Lucie jumped up on the couch with him. "And what am I?"

She assumed a picturesque pose – in her case any other kind was impossible – bared her upper teeth and crossed her eyes.

"*Roundbrestige Toothshegermane?*" suggested Lexa.

"How do you say cross-eyed?" asked Haryk.

No one knew.

"Lucie's dominant feature is not her thorax," said Lexa, "but her hair. *Peroxyde Toothshegermane*."

"I don't dye my hair!" said Lucie. "Just a little. But I do have false teeth. Look!"

"*Falschzahnige Blondgermanin etwas peroxidiert*," said Lexa, the linguist.

"How would you translate that?" asked Benno.

"A rather false blonde German woman with peroxide teeth."

"That's wrong!" said Lucie. "And what are you?"

"And how would you say *Grossbellygermane* in Latin?"

That stopped us. Our knowledge of Latin had dissolved in the alcohol. Lexa stood up and went to look in Haryk's Latin dictionary.

"And what are you?" Lucie asked me.

I had no particular outstanding features. I took a drink of rum.

"*Badluckgermane*," said Lucie. "No woman will have him."

"Whereas he wants them all," said Haryk. "*Whorechasing Badluck-germane*."

"I beg your pardon!" said Lucie indignantly. "I'll tell Molly Dreslerova you used that word about her."

"Only because of gaps in my knowledge of the language, Lucie," said Haryk. "All right: *Mädeljagender Pechgermane*."

"Translation?"

"Wench-chasing bad-luck German."

"I'm telling Molly you said she was a wench."

"Girl-chasing," said Alena. It was unusual to have her participate in our word-games other than by scolding Benno. But the Château Vomitella was doing its work.

"Girl-chasing fuck-up German," Lexa corrected her. He had finished consulting the dictionary. "And Benno is *Venterogermanus Giganteus Goeringi*."

"And what am I? What am I?" cried Alena, and began marching around the room in a goose-step with her right arm in the air. "What am I?"

"Come on, Alenka!" pleaded Benno.

"*Heil!*" shrieked Alena. The Vomitella had gone to her head. "*Siegheil! Himmelherrgottheil!*"

"*Grossarschige Heilgermanin*," said Lexa quietly.

"What's *Grossarsch* mean?" cried Lucie.

"That's when the distance between these here," said Lexa – he touched Lucie on the tips of her breasts and she slapped his hand away – "is added to Benno's circumference and multiplied by six."

Alena was not listening. She was marching around the room and shouting, "*Siegheil! Donnerwetterheil! Scheissheil!*"

"*Ich bin ein nachgekleinerter Zwerggermane*," said Haryk, and joined Alena, and heiled along with her, but at the same time marched around on his knees so that Alena towered over him.

"*Dame zu hoch!*" sang Lexa to the melody of the Horst Wessel song. "*Die Liebe ausgeschlossen!*"

I was possessed by linguistic inspiration, probably from Pila's *Eierkognak*, and I sang raucously, "*Für so 'nen Zwerg – das ist ganz aussichtlos!*" And thus I made a discovery that was valuable for my later literary career – I found the surest way of guaranteeing inspiration: I reached for the rum.

"Hey, it fits the melody!" said Fonda, who was the most musical. "Let's try it again, okay?"

Alena and Haryk stopped, Haryk remaining on his knees. Lucie jumped off the couch and sat in her short yellow skirt on Haryk's shoulders so that she had one leg on each side of his head. He grasped her knees. Benno and Lexa took each other around the waist and danced a Tyrolean dance. I quickly thought up another verse and the rum was transformed into rhyme. Fonda gave us an A and we started in:

"*Die Dame hoch – die Liebe ausgeschlossen –*"

Haryk struggled to his feet so that Lucie was even taller than Alena. He wobbled about and Lucie caught him by the ears.

"Yow!" he shouted, right at the break.

"That's it!" cried Fonda. "Sing it there every time, Haryk!"

We began again: "*Die Dame hoch – die Liebe ausgeschlossen!*"

"Yow!" Haryk's yelp was right on key and perfectly timed.

I sang on: "*Für so 'nen Zwerg, das ist ganz aussichtlos!*"

"Yow!"

Lucie squirmed around on Haryk's shoulders, her short skirt slid up high over her knees and I was visited once more by inspiration. Not that I saw anything – it was purely innocent inspiration. Without missing a beat, I sang the next solo line: "*Schaff dir 'ne kleinere – mit lila Unterhosen!*"

"Yow."

"*Den triffst du wohl – viel leichter in den Schoss!*"

"Yow! Yow!" roared Haryk.

"Wait! What are you suggesting?" cried Lucie, who was still sitting rather immodestly on Haryk's shoulders. Haryk was now holding her by the thighs. "Lilac underpants?"

"I just put that in for the rhyme," I said. "I mean the rhythm."

"I should hope so. Lilac is a disgusting colour."

"So what colour do you have on, Lucie?" Lexa asked. Lucie made a face and shot back, "None!"

Lexa took this up and suggested an improvement to the verse. I noticed that the bottles with the suspicious-looking liqueurs were empty and that there was only a little Château Vomitella left in the bottom of one bottle.

Fonda sat down at the piano and played through the Horst Wessel song in swing. Lucie slipped off Haryk's shoulders so deftly that we were unable to ascertain the colour of her knickers; we only saw that she had a black garterbelt on. Fonda swung Horst Wessel for a while, gracing it with Kansas riffs. "Let's go, gentlemen."

"Lucie, hop up on me," pleaded Lexa. "I'm taller than Haryk!" He knelt down on the floor.

"Let Alena get on you!"

"Let me get on you!" cried Alena, and before Lexa knew what was happening she was sitting on his shoulders. Her knickers were pale blue.

"Now, Alena!" said Benno.

"Led be alode!" said Alena.

Lexa made a desperate face and began to huff and puff like a weight-lifter. He finally struggled to his feet, staggering, and Alena grabbed his ears as Lucie had before.

"*Ein arschbelasteter Schweingermane,*" said Haryk and he offered his shoulders to Lucie. She swung herself up on them, her black garters visible once again. Alena had the hem of her pale blue petticoat showing.

Fonda hit an A and swung a few bars of introduction full of Kansas riffs and then we started singing like the Mills Brothers coupled with the Boswell Sisters. Benno played nose trumpet and I beat on a tambourine with

*Souvenir de Grado* written on it, which I had taken off the wall. We played with supernatural alcoholic verve in the magnificent rhythm of swing:

> *Dame zu hoch – die Liebe ausgeschlossen,*
> The lady is too tall – love is out of the question,
>
> Yow!
>
> *Für so 'nen Zwerg – das ist ganz aussichtlos!*
> For such a dwarf – that's hopeless!
>
> Ya – yayow – yow!
>
> *Schaff dir 'ne kleinere mit keinen Unterhosen*
> Get yourself a shorter one with no underpants
>
> Yooooow –
>
> *Der triffst du wohl viel leichter in den Schoss!*
> You'll find your way into her lap much easier!
>
> Ya – yaya – yaya – ya!

We were sixteen, we were young and free in that awful dictatorship, and we had no respect for its glories. I often recalled that New Year's Eve afterwards – once, in particular, when an employee of a different dictatorship had me on the carpet for the same song. And it seemed to me that freedom is purely a matter of youth and dictatorships. That it exists nowhere else, perhaps because we are not aware of it. Just as we are unaware of air until, in the gas chamber of life, it is replaced by those crystals, tasteless, colourless, odourless....

●

Veronika told me about it later, that afternoon. Percy was facing unpleasantness at home. After Veronika's private demonstration at the concert, which had netted his father twenty thousand dollars' profit, and after her antics at the party in honour of the Russian poet, Percy was having difficulties. And to him, blinded by love, Veronika herself began to seem blinded, dazzled by a black light. He took her on a long trip up north. Fields and pastures surrounded by fences swished past the Jaguar, "No Trespassing" signs everywhere. It was early spring. It seemed to Veronika that the colours of distant autumn had already begun to seep through the grey-green Canadian grass. Here and there in the beautiful, empty countryside a structure that seemed straight out of Dali's dream appeared, like a monument to Le Corbusier. What possible use could it have been serving in that pleasant melancholy wilderness? A church, a transformer station, a county court-house – white, glassed, chromed monuments in the empty, almost endless land under the grey-blue sky. Above these cubistic cairns, formations of green geese were flying north.

They came to a wharf where a handful of drunk Indians were waiting with a load of crates. A small ferryboat landed and they got on; the Indians carried the crates on board, opened one of them and began pulling bottles out. A week's supply, said Percy. They can take the ferryboat free, a government subsidy. They also get treaty money. What's that? asked Veronika. Compensation for the land that was stolen from them. This island is their reservation. They can rent the land here to whites, but they can't sell it to them. People from the mainland build cottages here.

Then a village of wooden huts with mongrel dogs, gutted cars on their backs, skeletons of snowmobiles, Indian boys in running-shoes playing baseball, the painter's log cabin. A great artist, said Percy. The painter showed them the fruit of his labour for the past two weeks. He had an ornamental style, the Woodland school, Percy said, stylized caribou, elk, dogs, squaws carrying papooses on their backs, symbols of the sun, fire, water, good and evil. The inherited world, quite dead. Percy gave him two hundred dollars for a picture of the sun. The painter walked them down to the wharf, where they waited for the afternoon ferry to take them back to the mainland. They said goodbye, the painter turned round and wobbled slowly back towards the horizon, divided by two long fingers of smoke which high above the cloud-shrouded sun dissipated into nothing.

"He's constantly in that state," said Percy. "And it's our fault...."

Veronika took the picture and leaned it against the railing of the ferryboat. "It's beautiful," she said.

"For those two hundred dollars the painter can remain in a state he considers happy for about three weeks."

The girl lifted her grey eyes from the picture and looked at the grey shoreline, at the village, outlined by the two columns of smoke, at the distant, retreating figure.

Then they drove back to the city through the pleasant sadness of a Canadian evening, the red Jaguar flashing by the white cairns, the sun like a ruby in the pink velvet of its own setting. Percy talked about Indians, how they live aimlessly, without work, with no meaning to their lives, from one week's shipment of beer to the next; about how little papooses die five times more frequently than white children, how they are mowed down by tuberculosis.

"It's just horrible."

And Veronika – rather coolly, it seemed to him – said, "I'm sure it is."

They drove on silently for a while, but Percy did not give up. He wanted to return the girl's eyesight to her, set glasses on that charming nose of hers through which she could see his world too, a world, it seemed to him, that she was blind to. Even he himself, he realized, had really only seen it for the first time when she appeared in it. And so he spoke of Indians and then of Eskimos: "We completely destroyed their natural way of life. Now they survive on welfare, and instead of living from hunting and fishing they eat canned food and Coca Cola. Their ancient customs are forgotten...."

And the girl said, "Hmmm."

He didn't give up. At that time there had just been a prison riot somewhere and the newspapers were full of articles and interviews. Veronika had read them. It seemed to her that the prisoners were in the right. The monotonous life inside the four walls of a prison could hardly be a cheerful one; not even the guards are free of the power of those walls, and flare-ups and fights are inevitable. She did not consider every murderer a monster, but she felt that murder was always a monstrous act, to be murdered a monstrous death. Yet in those interviews with murderers suffering from claustrophobia those who had died a monstrous death were somehow forgotten. Perhaps this was fitting: they were already at peace, they were sleeping the eternal sleep, they no longer existed, nothing concerned them anymore. But she could not forget the dead —

"... there is a desperate lack of social amenities in the prisons. People are always getting beaten up. And women prisoners are even raped by their male guards...."

She looked at the velvet horizon and said wearily, "They are always doing something to improve the conditions."

"Not enough! Not by a long shot!"

"It takes time."

"It's already taken a damned long time as it is."

They drove onto a four-lane highway. Percy stepped on the gas. The girl talked wearily, it seemed to him: "All it takes is time. That's all. Over *there*, you need the courage of a test pilot if you want to change things."

Percy was disappointed. He felt the prick of incipient malice. "Well," he hesitated, but then went on, "it's not entirely safe to want social change in this country either. Can't you be just a little objective, Nika?"

He was interrupted by the wailing of a siren. An Ontario Provincial Police car passed them and slowed in ahead of them, its red lights flashing. They pulled in and stopped. A young policeman with a carefully trimmed moustache and a well-scrubbed face stepped up to the Jaguar.

"Do you know you've been doing ninety, sir?"

A smile flickered across the girl's sad face. Her lover squirmed with embarrassment.

"Oh, well ... I guess I just didn't ... look at the speedometer...."

"You realize it's not safe, sir?"

Percy admitted it. Humbly he accepted the ticket. The girl smiled at him. When the police car drove off, she laughed out loud.

Percy was hurt. Not a great deal, however; he fought against it. Veronika chuckled. "I was afraid he was going to hit you. He looked real mean. Sir," she added.

"All right! So he did call me sir."

She held up two fingers. "Twice."

"Okay. So it was twice. So what?" He added, "A cop is a cop is a cop."

"Who told you that, Percy? You can't have read it. You don't know how to read."

This made him genuinely angry. "Okay, okay, okay!" he almost shouted. "I'm just an empty-headed playboy from a rich family. I'm also in love with you, wise lady, and the tragic fate of your country moves me to tears."

"You couldn't care less about my country, darling," said the girl with a smile, but sadly. Percy, however, was far too angry to hear the sadness.

"And what about your new country?"

"I couldn't care less about it," said Veronika.

By now they were speeding again, but Percy's rage was slowly dissipating. He declared, not quite as seriously this time, "That's what I call emigrant gratitude."

"Exile gratitude."

"All right, exile gratitude."

The girl said quietly, "Only I love my new country. I've never felt so safe as I do here now."

And a family of raccoons ambled out onto the highway. Percy swerved to avoid them and went into a skid. The girl did not have her safety belt fastened, and she flew forward and bumped her head on the front windshield.

Percy was an experienced driver and there were no cars on the highway. The Jaguar was soon proceeding as if glued to the road. The girl rubbed the bump on her head with a Kleenex. He looked at her out of the corner of his eye and was flooded once more with a feeling he believed to be love.

"Let that be a lesson to you, Nika."

Veronika thrust her tongue out at him. "You're an incurable innocent, Percy," she said sweetly.

They were getting close to the city. There was a sense of ease between them once more but Percy was still not satisfied. Something remained unspoken, unresolved. As long as they did not reach an understanding about – about what, he did not know, exactly....

"Didn't you once tell me that people can only learn from personal experience?"

She nodded.

"That's why I took you to that island, Nika. So it would become part of your personal experience – "

" 'To make you *emotionally* involved,' " she said.

"I knew very well what he was getting at," Veronika told me that afternoon. "Better than he did himself. And I did feel sorry for those children with tuberculosis, I really did. But what did he feel sorry for? Nothing! He only started taking an interest in those children because he fell for me, and his radical chic friends told him I was a reactionary. And his daddy is angry at him because I'm spoiling his business and creating scandals. But I swear to God, Danny, I'm not blaming him because he can't feel sorry for my mother – he never knew her – or for those children – he's too young for that – or for our country, because for him it's more or less an abstraction. And anyway, our country isn't suffering that much. I also don't know what's harder to bear, homesickness or anger. I just don't know," she said that afternoon. "I don't even know what I really want. But whatever it is, Percy is not it. At least I don't think he is. I don't know."

And I, that afternoon, had no arguments to offer.

She looked at Percy in the seat beside her and sighed, "I must be a lousy teacher. You really don't understand anything!"

Percy frowned. "I'm sorry about that. I guess I'm just mentally retarded."

She moved closer to him, because she wanted to fill that empty space with something. "Let's talk seriously, Percy, okay?"

"I'm talking seriously."

"Okay. Do you know what you've been doing to me all day, darling?"

They were already driving past the first houses on the edge of the city. Percy shrugged and said, "Well, I was trying – "

"You were insulting me, Percy."

"Nika! How can you say that?"

"And you did it so gently that you didn't even know you were doing it."

"I'll say I didn't. All I did was – "

" – was try and show me that Canada isn't the Utopia that you think I think it is."

Red neon lashed twice across the girl's face. She had a swollen bruise on her forehead.

"All right," said Percy crossly. "But honestly, don't you think that just a little?"

Orange and green neon. Then a golden point of light in the grey eyes. She said, "Yes, I do. After everything I've gone through in my short lifetime, I honestly do think that Canada is too good to be true. Or, if it is real, then I don't think it will last long. Perhaps it's an imperfect Utopia – "

"I would say it's very imperfect indeed," said Percy, stepping irritably on the gas. The conjunction of Utopia and his own country seemed to him shameless nonsense. The girl said sadly, without irony, "Sure. If you shoot the Prime Minister, you still have to go to jail for it. And you can stay on ice for at least ten years – "

"For God's sake, Nika, don't be such a demagogue!"

He felt desolately that they were still exactly where they'd always been. The island, the painter, the whole long day, everything had been pointless. He accelerated. They sped past the low houses on the upper reaches of Yonge Street, the lights and the neon signs now making a wild kaleidoscope of Veronika's face.

"And it made me so angry," she said to me that afternoon. "Why, they have no idea what words mean. When a cop taps them on the head they call it 'police brutality,' even if they spit into his face first. But I don't know. I have no idea what goes on in Canadian jails. But I do know that if you shoot the Prime Minister they won't hang you for it. Is that being a demagogue? Tell me, is it?"

"Of course not, Nika," I said.

Her excitement was out of all proportion to such a meaningless argument. She seemed to be gasping for breath.

"At the same time," she said, "there are young illiterate Portuguese girls here slaving away in their factories and nobody could care less how much they make. The main thing is that the Indian kids have enough milk. Their social conscience is a fashion, it changes every year. Mini-skirts and Eskimos, midi-skirts and murderers with claustrophobia."

"Don't get so worked up about it," I said. "Fashion or no fashion, Indian children don't have an easy time of it and illiterate Portuguese women are at least better off than they were back home. And this *is* home for the Indians."

Veronika swept back a lock of hair from her forehead. "I know, Danny. But what about me – when it's all so...."

"What?"

"Oh, nothing," she sighed; she stood up and looked out of my window at the beautiful lake. Light planes owned by wealthy sportsmen were chasing each other around in the sky like dragonflies.

"Oh well," said Veronika. "We should leave it to the horses to figure out, they have bigger heads." She turned to me. "Except you'd need a head like a brontosaurus to figure that one out."

"That wouldn't do, Veronika. The brontosaurus had a brain smaller than a cat's."

"Really? Oh well, let's stick with the horse," she said. "Goodbye, Mr. Chips. I have to go."

She offered me a small hand, and looked into my eyes. All at once I saw again – heard again? Rather saw again – her voice in the students' common room commenting on the song about the girl who was waiting for death, about a long, black limousine ... why should I be the one whom fate has chosen now....

"*Me*, Percy, a demagogue! *Me?*" Veronika said in a rage, turning in the car to stare at him.

"Well, sometimes you are."

"And what about those friends of yours?" she cried. "All you have to do is mention the word injustice and Angela Davis pops out of their mouths!"

They flew south along Yonge Street, the evening exodus from the city flowing in the opposite direction. Percy said, "You're the one who ought to sympathize most with Angela. She was a victim of political persecution, just like you and people from your country."

Veronika was overwhelmed by a feeling of impotence, and she tried to drown it in anger. "Angela is a Communist. She represents a system that destroyed my father. How can you expect me to sympathize with her?"

And her tears flowed.

... I watched her from my thirtieth-storey window as she walked to the bus stop in her denim jacket and bell-bottom trousers with flowers embroidered on the hem of the cuffs, a red ribbon in her hair. She looked tiny from that height. I knew nothing at all about her. She was perfectly Canadianized, elegant by Canadian standards, spoke English almost as well as Czech, and she walked independently, with long strides....

They argued long and bitterly. Veronika was hysterical. "... not only do you know nothing about *me!* You know nothing about *anything!* About anything that's *important!* There is an iron curtain of *trivia* between us!"

"All right, that's enough!"

"... so let the Eskimos go back to their hunting grounds and invite the Russians into your theatres. In the end the only happy people in Canada will be the Eskimos, as long as they keep to their hunting grounds and stay illiterate! Maybe. I can't even say that for certain."

"When you get hysterical like that I can't understand you at all!"

"... the biggest shock you ever had in your life was when the doctor pulled you out into the world and slapped you across the bum! You're just like all your friends! I hate you all!"

"So why don't you go back to your Czech friends?"

"That's exactly what I intend to do!"

"Go ahead, then! What are you waiting for? I'm not keeping you. Go!"

She looked at him for a brief instant, then she turned and slid out of the car like a grass snake, and without looking back she walked away with long strides in her jeans with the flowers on the cuffs. Her ribbon reflected redly in the light coming from the windows in that Canadian evening.

"God, he pissed me off!" she said. "I know he can't help it and he is right about some things. But so am I. Except I'm a woman and should have been wiser. Which means I should have backed down, like wise women have done since the dawn of time. But he made me so – "

"I know," I said. "I understand. And I think you were wise. Except for the fact that you've lost a lot. Couldn't you make up with him? Then he'd marry you and as soon as decently possible you could get a divorce and you'd have alimony. That's what wise women have always done. Not since the dawn of time, but ever since alimony was invented."

"Oh sure," said Veronika. "But anyway it's too late for that now. He's going off to give his nerves a rest at the Club Med, where young girls go who want to get married, the ones with the kind of wisdom you just described. Oh well, I have to go now."

The bus came, a black man stepped aside to let the white girl enter it ahead of him and the red ribbon vanished.

●

*7 Apr., 1961*
*Prague*

*Gratings, fallow countryman,*
*I can't help it, I just have to blow my horn re Jana my daughter. Not only is she pretty, after her mother, and handsome, after me, with dimpled cheeks after her uncle (though that sometimes puzzles my mind because the uncle is only married to Jana's (i.e., the mother's) sister), but it now appears that she is terribly clever as well. Who she gets that from I can't say at the moment. (My family and Jana's – the wife's – were always decent, honest people, and poor.) Maybe it's some kind of mutation.*

*The fact remains that Jana, now in her first year at the conservatory where she is girding her loins for a career in acting even though I had always secretly (and out loud too) hoped she'd become a dentist, so I wouldn't have to depend on the national health in my old age, which would and will be ghastly now that Jana's about to become an actress. Where was I? Oh yes, in her first year at the conservatory she made a play, as it were, for the famous poet, playwright and public and private man of affairs, Jan Vrchcolab, and she did it so cleverly and he fell for her so hard that every day until the late hours of the night he stands drooling beneath our windows while she leads him around by the nose and delivers interim reports to me about what she's up to.*

*What she's up to is this: he's already written a screenplay for her in which Jana will play the leading role, and I, exercising my parental authority (Jana isn't sixteen yet) have approved all but one scene of it, the one where she was supposed to run starkers across a meadow and "skip" into a pond, as Vrchcolab puts it in the scenario. Well she won't be "skipping" anywhere, not even in a bathing-suit. But so I won't seem foolish or old-fashioned, I told Jana to tell him she's bothered by the scene because it's a direct steal from the film classic* Ecstasy, *where there's a very similar scene, and that he should rewrite it to have the heroine in an astrakhan fur coat and high felt boots queuing up for Lenin and when her turn comes, skipping into the mausoleum. According to Jana, Vrchcolab said it wouldn't work and the meadow would have to stay because the whole film takes place in Czechoslovakia and there is no Lenin here and Prez Gotvald's body went all putrid and they had to bury it. So I informed him that the meadow could stay in the film if he thought it was logical to have Jana walking across it, in the astrakhan fur coat and the high felt boots in the middle of a hot summer. Why not? After all, Eisenstein edited harp-players into a scene from the Congress of the Bolshevik party even though it would have been more logical to have accordionists. So finally, with Jana as the interlocutor, we arrived at a compromise. Jana will walk across the meadow in a medium-length mini and he will edit Hedy Kieslerova into it from that famous scene. He says that's done a lot now in film, that is, you quote from the classics and it's supposed to stand for what's going on in the main character's head. Maybe people won't interpret it wrongly, but my principle is: no daughter of mine is going to show herself naked in public. Especially not for such a ridiculously low fee!*

*In the 2nd place he's writing a play for her. The conservatory is going to perform it as an anniversary piece, and all Jana's friends will have exactly the same size role as she does – that was her wish – so they'll all have a chance to act – of course Jana just a bit more than the others. I'm curious to see how Vrchcolab deals with a request like that but he'll figure something out. After all, he knows his dialectics.*

*In the third place, he wrote a cycle of sonnets. He printed excerpts in* Literarni Noviny *and then the whole thing appeared in the weekly magazine for working women* Vlasta, *and I tell you they're real gems! They rhyme! And the similes! Among other things he compares Jana to a bedewed flower! Doesn't that display the precision of near-genius? The only thing I don't quite understand is why "bedewed," but Jana says it's a kind of metaphor to suggest that she doesn't let him touch her physically. That's what she claims, and I more or less believe her. I wouldn't let him touch me physically either.*

*In short, I'm happy.*

*As I think of the poems the famous poet has penned about my daughter Jana, I recall how fortunate my encounters with him have been. I'm one of the few people alive, I suppose, who recollect his now almost legendary performance, away back in '47, for his Excellency Sir John Nichols when The British Society held a special evening to welcome this particular peer to Prague. I don't know why you weren't there too, since you belonged to that society, whereas I didn't. My presence was a mistake. We were having a meeting next door in the Bridge and Euchre Club and when I was walking back from the WC a gentleman in a tuxedo stopped me and asked me something very politely in English. Because my mastery of that language is somewhat imperfect, he put me in an embarrassing situation and, so as not to completely deny the man an answer, I replied "Yes," in English. And he bowed to me and beckoned me to come along with him, and on the way he asked me something else and for the sake of variety I replied "Nou" this time. Then we entered a room and there was an assembly of ladies and gentlemen all in tuxedos, and ladies with dresses that mostly started from the breasts down, and you could smell cigar smoke and this gentleman led me up to the podium and asked me something else and again, so I wouldn't look stupid, I said "Vell." By this time we were already standing on the podium with me in my tweed jacket, the one I play bridge and euchre in, and it's got leather patches on the elbows so I won't wear them out when I'm playing cards, and down in front of me the room was full of these half-uncovered ladies and the gentlemen dressed to the tens and they all had these awkward smiles on their faces, probably because of my tweed jacket. The gentleman beside me gave a brief speech in English and finally he turned to me and said, "Velcame to Prag, Sir John!" and the people began to clap politely. So I waited politely till they finished and then I said, in Czech this time, "There must be some mistake. Blazej's the name."*

*And it was a mistake. This Sir John fellow had got held up because of his cuff-links and he arrived as the man beside me was making his brief speech, and so as not to interrupt he stood politely at the back. His cuff-links were beautiful, covered with diamonds, and they let me stay there for the program that followed.*

*And then it came. Disman's troupe marched onto the stage and up in front there was this kind of lanky lad and Mr. Disman said they were going to recite a poem composed especially in honour of Sir John by one of their members, Johnny Vrchcolab. And the kid bowed politely and they started reciting.*

*The poem was a voiceband thing. Churchill was in it, smoking a cigar, and it was about how the Brits landed in France during the Second World War. The whole thing was done in what they call heroic couplets, all rhyming, which is a purely British form, and Johnny combined them with this Burian-type voiceband technique. Only half the troupe recited the poem, and the rest of them hummed various melodies like It's a Lonk Vay to Tiperari or Lock Lomand and then, when the Brits began landing in France, the Beer Barrel Polka and at the end, when they landed successfully, Gott Safe de Kink.*

*Well, it was a tremendous success and the ladies in the short dresses (above) pawed and fawned over the talented lad and he took to it like a fish to water.*

*So you can understand my surprise when a year later – that year was the year of the February Victory of the People – I ran into the kid again, after the misunderstanding with a play of mine which I told you about in one of my earlier letters. As a punishment I was recruiting people for the mines in a pub in Cheb, and in the theatre next door there was a gala assembly of the Czechoslovak Union of Youth in honour of or to protest against or on the occasion of, I don't remember anymore. Our agit-prop unit got turfed out of the pub about eleven; it was a moonlit night in summer, and a column of blue-shirts was pouring out of the theatre. They sat down on the cobblestones and gaped longingly at a pedestal which was ready to receive an as yet unerected statue. And all of a sudden, up on the pedestal hops the kid himself in white trousers and a blue shirt, everyone falls silent and he raises his arms to the moon like the Great Gatsby, but instead of addressing the moon, he addresses Comrade Stalin. To this very day I remember it began more or less like this:*

> *Stalin the victor, Stalin the great,*
> *Stalin, the dream of our heart,*
> *Stalin, thou star, Stalin, our hope,*
> *Stalin, who all beauty art.*

*That was roughly how it was, more like Nezval, even though the echo of those heroic couplets was still there. And I tell you, my countryman, I was overcome more or less directly by a holy feeling, and it reminded me of one Italian film we saw during the war where Isa Miranda plays the white goddess of some African tribe deep in the jungle and she conducts a similar ritual by the light of the full moon, and her arms, as white as Vrchcolab's trousers, stretched up to the moon. But of course that ritual preceded a human sacrifice, while the one here did not; it was more like the aria from* Rusalka. *You know, countryman, I almost felt like breaking into song.... Stalin, thou on heaven high ... thine eyes see far and high ... thou wanderest far about the globe ... thou lookest into man's abode.... It was all I could do to keep from actually bursting into song.*

*I tell you it was breathtaking! The kid standing there in the pale light with his arms outstretched to the moon, and those youth union girls spread all about him picturesquely on the ground—countryman, I confess it gave me a hard-on, just like that time in the* Lidobio *when Isa Miranda played almost starkers for practically the whole film.*

*Unfortunately some rowdy disrupted the magic, but the young union types grabbed him and took him off to the local police station, and later they said he got fifteen years for it. It happened when Vrchcolab was just winding up; everyone including himself was in ecstasy and he was declaiming the final couplet, as I recall it went like this:*

> *Stalin, thou who knowest all we know not*
> *Stalin, Stalin, Stalin....*

*And right at this point the rowdy came stumbling out of the pub singing,*

> *Kolin, my lovely town*
> *My lovely hometown Kolin*
> *My darling here is serving beer,*
> *My love, my darling dear....*

*And when he heard Vrchcolab's last line, he stopped and then, into the silence that hung in the air after these great emotions, he sang in a drunken voice and to the melody of the incompleted verse he had just been singing,*

> *... to Stalin, little Stalin!*

*I've already told you how the youth unionists dealt with him.*

*Well, in short, I've been right lucky in my encounters with him, quite incredibly, really.*

*Whatever Vrchcolab put his hand to turned to gold. Now, according to my daughter Jana, he has turned to matters social and has made a genuinely interesting historical discovery, to wit, that there is not a single socialist state where anyone with a leading state function has ever quit his post simply because his term of office was up. Either – how should I put this to make it sound socialistic? Oh yes – either unpermissible methods of social justice and the like were used against him and he was physically annulled, or he was overthrown for reasons of health, or he was made to give up his function voluntarily, or he died, without the application of unpermissible methods, all by himself. So that such things won't happen anymore, Vrchcolab is putting together a think-piece to the effect that we ought to permit a loyal socialist state opposition, to revive Communism. I'm just as happy it's more or less in limbo right now. We're living better, more joyously, without it.*

*The only trouble is, whatever the kid turns his hand to always seems to work out, so I reckon he'll find support in the Party for his think-piece. When that happens, I will start looking round for the best place to emigrate to. Where would you go in a case like that? I'll take Honduras. I happen to know their honorary consul in Prague, on a purely social basis. He knows how to play betl so well that he can win even when he's got all four aces and the fifth up his sleeve!*

*Your fellow countryman,*
*Vratislavek*

*P.S. Jana's just brought me the manuscript of the anniversary play. There's a scene where all the girls in the dormitory are wearing only their underthings. I approved it on condition that they be woollen underthings, non-transparent and reaching at least half-way down their thighs, and that Jana have on her grandmother's petticoat that looks more like a ballroom dress. No daughter of mine is going to appear in public in her knickers! And most certainly not for nothing!*

*P.P.S. All that came to naught. Jana (the wife) censored it, and they're all going to have to wear dressing-gowns.*

*P.P.P.S. After mature reflection, I have decided that if Vrchcolab insists on seeing underwear on the stage, let him rewrite the scene to take place in a men's dormitory.*

*P.P.P.P.S. It's a nice play, very progressive. About how young people all pull together so they'll grow up to be upright men and women of character, the way actors traditionally are anyway.*

●

Percy recognized the voice. Barbara did not even have to introduce herself.

"Look," she said into the receiver, calmly, but there was no indifference beneath the surface of the calm, "Look, I could have made an anonymous phone call. But I want to play straight with you, even if Milan didn't play straight with me. Maybe it doesn't matter to you – a lot of people don't care these days. I'm only telling you this so you'll know, in all events."

"Aren't you just being jealous?"

"Of course I'm being jealous," she said. "I'm only the second person she's been leading around by the nose. Do you think I find it funny? I saw her clothes lying there in his room, after the party. Goodbye, Percy."

She hung up, and before he could organize his thoughts the phone rang again.

"It's me, Percy."

"Hi," he said coldly.

The voice was distant, lost in the telephone wires. Something in it called out to Percy, but did not reach him.

"Percy, I'm sorry about yesterday, but I – when I'm angry I – "

He interrupted her. "I already know what you do when you're angry."

The girl heard the coldness, despite the bad connection. He heard the weak voice, getting weaker all the time: "Are you very angry?"

"No, why should I be?"

"Well, I wasn't very nice to you."

"But on the other hand you were very nice to your compatriot, Veronika."

The small voice spoke gravely: "But Percy – Barb must have – look, it was a mistake."

"You're right. It *was* a mistake."

He didn't want to talk to her like that. It was like a bad movie. He surprised himself by what he was saying to her, but he said it anyway. She was silent for a long time.

"Can I see you tonight, Percy?"

He replied, against his own will, "I think not, Veronika."

"Ah," she said, "so you're dumping me." Now it was Percy's turn to be silent. Veronika sighed. "Well, it's not exactly a new experience for me."

"I'm sure it isn't. Goodbye."

He hung up.

The girl in the phone booth held the receiver in her hand a while longer. Then she lifted the corner of her mouth in a characteristic half-smile and sighed. "Ah well. Bye, Percy. I guess it just didn't work out."

She hung up and looked out of the booth at the towers of St. James' Town in the rain. She began to feel terribly homesick for something. It was a feeling she could not overcome. Tears fell from her eyes. Not just because of that Canadian.

●

"Yass, yass, I see," said Milan into the receiver. Veronika was sitting once more in his furnished bachelor apartment, the colour television staring like a bulging cataracted eyeball, a pile of nostalgic records in badly repaired sleeves under the stereo set, the blow-up of Suzi Kajetanova in its golden frame. Milan hung up and said:

"He's flown off to Guadeloupe and he'll be there at least a month."

She nodded; her long blonde hair fell across her face and she gathered it behind her ear. She was sitting on the couch, her legs in shiny pantyhose, dangling one of her shoes on the end of her toes.

"So it's Guadeloupe," she said. "Well, I guess that ends another chapter in the life of Veronika Prstova, adventuress."

Milan reached for his glass; the ice tinkled gratifyingly, and he took a drink. He was at the end of his tether, Veronika said, when she told me about it that afternoon. I knew it, she said, but so was I, and I can't stand it when two people become close simply because they both happened to get punched on the nose at the same time.

"Do you love him?" I asked.

"I guess so," she said. After a pause she went on, "Sometimes I have a kind of singer's nightmare. The band starts off in one key, I start singing and I'm completely off pitch. So the boys change key, and I'm off again. I can't seem to find the right key. I always wake up in a sweat."

She lowered her head. "That's the way it is with Percy. We never seem to be in tune. I can't be with him. In the end he'd drive me crazy." She looked at me. "It's like this country. It's beautiful, but in the end it would drive me out of my mind."

I didn't take what she said seriously. I didn't hear the threat implied by her syntax.

"Out of sight, out of mind," I said. "You're still young."

"That's what I say too," said Veronika. "Whisky, please, or I'll go out of my mind right here in your living room."

"... in the life of the washed-up adventuress Veronika Prstova," she said.

"Would you entertain the possibility," Milan said, "of starting a new chapter? With me, for instance?"

Veronika looked at the voluntary exile. Then she raised the corner of her mouth meaningfully and turned her grey eyes unmistakably towards the golden frame.

"I can take that down," said the voluntary exile. "No problem."

"Am I underneath her?"

"Sure. You want to have a look?"

She nodded, the corner of her mouth still curled ironically. Milan stepped briskly up to the frame and tore Suzi Kajetanova out, revealing Veronika's sad eyes enlarged to a diameter of three inches. Veronika got up, stood in front of her own mega-portrait and stared at it. The exile, already considerably under the influence of the Scotch, drank in with his eyes the slender legs in glossy pantyhose. She took off her other shoe and he could see her sweet little toes under the transparent material. She had painted her toenails a silver grey, the colour of her sadness. She was wearing a black silk midi and a white blouse with black orchids. He had never seen her looking so pretty. She brought back memories. He was overwhelmed by sadness.

She placed her arms in their long silk sleeves behind her back and stared at her portrait for a long time.

"You know, Milan," she said, "someone once said somewhere that it's better to be number one in Lovosice than number two in Prague."

"Sounds like something that bitch Kajetanova would have said." He took a drink, spilling whisky on his shirt. The girl turned to look at him and nodded reproachfully.

"Besides, you're bombed out of your mind, Milan. When was the last time I saw you sober?"

"Back home, probably," he said gruffly. "In Prague." He took his empty glass into the kitchen. She followed him. He had a new gadget there, a deep freezer with a special device on the door. You no longer had to open the fridge to get ice: you just held your glass under a chrome spout, pulled a lever, and the freezer would spit two cubes of ice into the glass, beautifully regular and as flawless as diamonds.

"Besides," said the exile, "how are you supposed to stay sober with this damned ice-shitter in the kitchen?"

"Simple," said Nika. "Don't add any whisky. Just suck the ice. That will straighten you out."

She went back and sat down on the couch. Milan grasped the bottle and drowned the ice-cubes in an amber Niagara. He heard Nika's dear and slightly desperate voice from the couch: "On second thought, I could use some of that stuff too. You've never seen me drunk anyway."

He picked up the gallon jug of Johnnie Walker and wobbled over to the couch. The girl held out a glass, the amber fluid flowed from the neck and splashed over her knee.

"Watch out!" she cried. "I'll end up smelling like a wino."

He turned around and clumsily set the bottle on the edge of the commode. The girl reached out and pushed it back from the edge. He watched this, then spoke to her urgently.

"Nika, maybe you'll despise me, but I've made up my mind. I'm going to do it. I'm not mixed up in politics, and I'm not a writer. All I want to do is live. And to live, I need Prague. I've found that much out, Nika. Give me Prague, and I'll – "

"Once – and you were bombed out of your mind then, too, remember? – you were shouting for them to give you something, but it wasn't Prague. Something about freedom – "

"Right!" said Milan, surprise in his drunken eyes. "But how d'you explain it, Nika? Here I am, free, and it's like – like it's not worth anything to me – I – I suppose you think I'm a bloody fool or something...."

Veronika took a deep drink and pressed the remote control button for the television. On the screen, one heavily made-up woman was just confessing to another that she suffered from constipation; from the expression on her face, her suffering must have been considerable. Veronika said, "I guess we need them both, Prague and freedom. But the way things are, we can't have both. It's either-or."

The voluntary exile swirled his drink, splashing whisky over himself again. He sat down on the couch beside the girl, who put her hand on his chest to hold him off, but she needn't have for his intentions no longer ran that way. He placed his hand beside hers, saying hoarsely, "But don't you think – or what I mean is – isn't Prague somewhere deeper – here ...?"

Nika raised the corner of her mouth in that characteristic way of hers. "If you're thinking of your heart, buddy, it's a little bit higher and on the other side. That's your gall-bladder you're holding on to."

She poked him in the stomach with her fingers and stood up. Offended, he grabbed the bottle, spilling whisky on the couch.

"Nika, you've turned into a – a – a cynic. I – I – mean it seriously."

"So – so – so do I, Milanek," said the girl.

"It's just that, well, everything is so – buggered up ...," she said to me. And I never saw Veronika again.

●

It is a damp, rainy Canadian spring. I am standing at the bus-stop outside the college because they are changing the gearbox in my Plymouth. A cold wind is blowing and it is drizzling. As always the cold wind and the touch of raindrops on my face make me feel good. I close my eyes, the cold foam of the South Pacific off the prow of the *Jane Guy* sprays into my face – and suddenly a horn sounds and I open my eyes. It's the Svenssons' Cadillac with Irene behind the wheel. As at the beginning of the winter, she says, "Want a lift?"

"That's very kind of you."

I slide into the front seat beside her. The seat is the size of a small double bed; there is at least a yard between myself and the girl. Irene steps on the gas and the automobile undulates gently over the asphalt. She has on a black sweater, a kilt and plaid knee-socks. Her knees are bare, the foot on the accelerator in a shoe with a large floppy tongue.

As soon as I get in I sense that something has happened, but Irene is silent. We drive onto the highway, and still not a word.

"What is it?" I ask her at last.

"Nothing."

Once again a long silence. Grey patches of fog are rolling over the ground. The landscape seems strange. Perhaps it is the fog.

"Blue mood?" She stares straight ahead, her hands, an elegant ring on one of the fingers, gripping the steering wheel – in them, the certainty of the children of this country, who seem to have been born behind the wheel. Without looking at me she asks, "How's Veronika getting along?"

"Veronika? I don't know."

"She hasn't been to lectures for a week."

"No?"

I suddenly realize that the sad girl has actually been cutting classes.

"Now that you mention it, you're right. I haven't seen her for a long time either."

"Except the day before yesterday."

I peer sharply at the northern girl. She is still staring straight ahead. It has become dark outside the car. The white knees are luminescent below the wheel.

"Who did the legwork for you?"

"Wendy. She was visiting a friend who lives in the same apartment building as you, on the same floor, as a matter of fact."

"So what?"

Silence again, then: "You just said you hadn't seen her for a long time."

"I meant at college. Yes, I've seen her privately. She came to see me a couple of days ago."

"Why?"

"Are you gathering intelligence for your brother?"

She does not reply, only stares ahead. She has not looked at me once.

"But he's gone to Guadeloupe, hasn't he? At least that's what I heard."

Once more, nothing. It really is getting dark. I look out the window and see that we are driving through woods. I turn to the girl from the north. "Where are you taking me?"

She is still silent. Then she lifts her chin slightly, with a touch of pride. "Are you sleeping with her?"

Oh my gosh! I cry in my mind, as I used to in those long-ago times. The Cadillac bounces softly up and down on the narrow road through the woods and I feel that I am being spirited away into the kingdom of absurdity, that in an odd way an old, old dream of mine is coming true – one, however, whose fulfilment I no longer care much about because I know that life is not a dream. *That Chicago girl has set my heart a-spinning ... When I look into her cool grey eyes, I'm grinning....* I hear lyrics I composed so long ago ... *like a drunken fool, her Yankee charm's so winning ...* the Cadillac pushes its way farther and farther into the darkness of the woods.

"No, I'm not," I say.

"Are you lying?"

"If your father has a Bible in that glove compartment, I'll swear on it for you."

"Then why did she break off with Percy?"

Can this interrogation be taking place at the request of her older brother after all? We would not then be in the woods of absurdity.

"Your brother did throw her out of the car. He told her she could go wherever she pleased."

"How do you know?"

"She told me."

"Why you?"

"Well, we be of one blood, she and I. We keep together. At least in a foreign country."

Silence once more, and she still hasn't favoured me with a glance. *I love her so 'cause she's got a white elevator ... goes to Paris every spring on her Daddy's private freighter ... and she swims in a pool with her own pet alligator....*

"I still think you're lying."

"All right, I'm lying. As you wish, Irene."

She raises her chin again. The road has started climbing. Fresh fog is pouring down it towards us like a mountain stream.

"Percy split up with her because she slept with someone else and then tried to deny it."

I feel that my doom is sealed. We are driving deeper and deeper into the woods of absurdity, and not even the final irony in a life already full of it will pass me by.

"And why should that somebody else be me?"

"It was a Czech."

"I'm not the only Czech in Toronto."

"But why did she go straight to you after she called him and he told her?"

"What did he tell her?"

"That he knew she'd slept with him. With that Czech."

Veronika had told me about it. "He must have heard it from Barbie," she had said. "Perhaps she came back to the house that night after the party, when we were both asleep. I had a feeling I heard someone open the door."

"Even if it were true," I said, "why is he taking it so seriously? After all, it's not very modern of him – "

"Percy loves her," says Irene. She stares ahead into the darkness. She adds, "And anyway, it's just a myth that people don't mind. Everybody minds."

"And why are *you* taking it so seriously?"

We reach the top of the hill and Irene turns into a narrow road that disappears into a woodlot. Beside it there is a sign burned into a pinewood board: PRIVATE ROAD.

"Because you love your brother?"

She lifts her chin, takes her foot off the gas and brakes. We are surrounded by a low pine forest, and tongues of fog creep among the trees like the multi-coloured currents in the delta of the Mississippi.

And all of a sudden, it happens. The girl collapses on the steering wheel and commences to sob bitterly. Heaving sobs. I can't really believe it's happening but it is. I have never been able to see into people's minds.

I put my hand on her shoulder. "Don't cry, you've no reason to."

She lifts a tearful face to me and looks at me at last. When she speaks, it might as well be from a suburb of Prague; it makes no difference that she is from Wiltshire Boulevard.

"You never pay any attention to me! ... You just ignore me! ... You don't! You don't ...!"

"I do notice you. You're beautiful. And I haven't slept with Veronika. Word of honour."

She flings herself on my chest, nearly knocking one of my teeth out with her forehead. She is neither modern nor typical. Or rather she is. I no longer say anything. I place my hand under her kilt. Over the tangle of blonde hair I see her reach blindly for something on the dashboard, and with the precision of a concert pianist she presses one of an array of buttons. For an instant I brace myself for a gag – the canvas roof of the Cadillac will fold back and it will start raining on us. But I forget – she was born in a car. The wide back of the front seat begins slowly, quietly to recline. A genuine

double bed. The milk-thick fog forms a muslin curtain around our matrimonial bed. Irene loses her virginity in high style, in a car.

•

"Uher?" said Lida Lewisova. "He disappeared. They say all the secret policemen who went over to Pavel in '68 were liquidated."

"They could hardly keep that a secret."

"I don't exactly mean physically liquidated. Maybe they only got sent
to the Soyuz, perhaps for re-indoctrination. All I know is he's not living in
our building any more. And after the invasion he advised some people to
emigrate."

I recalled the former theological student and our infrequent
encounters – so that's how the renegade priest ended up. God knows if he's
still alive. What could have happened to him? What could have happened
*inside* him? I have never been able to see into anyone. People have always
been other than what I thought they were. Lida was lingering over her pecan
ice cream and the Marika Café on Bloor Street was half empty.

"Why do you suppose he did it?"

"I guess he'd just had enough."

"Enough dirty work? He didn't look particularly thin-skinned."

"Appearances can be deceiving," Lida said. "I'll bet he knew a lot
about things that we only suspect, and it got to him in the end."

"That sounds more like it. More likely than a change of heart. I always
thought he was an absolute...."

"Scoundrel?"

"No, more a sort of perverted saint who never had the slightest doubt,
ever, that the ends justify the means. And perhaps they do, who knows?"

"If you ask me," said Lida, "you've already been infected by the
West."

"Haven't you?"

"Not me. Whenever I feel the infection getting to me, I go back to
Czechoslovakia. It's a great place to recuperate from progressivitis."

We laughed. I recalled how the renegade priest had refused to cloister
me that cold night when we met in the church, how he hadn't ratted on me
after I'd said too much that autumn day on the train, and the strange night
pilgrimage of Father Hunak.

"The poor fellow," said Lida. "Maybe it's all over for him now. And
what a career! D'you know that he was posted to the United Nations in the
1960s?"

Yes, I knew that. That was where I'd had my third encounter with this
elusive personage. In 1966 (they had invited me from Prague to a confer-

ence at Long Island University), on the observation deck of the Empire State Building, where I had tried to dream my old dream of America and found I couldn't do it anymore. There, for the third time, I came up against Uher.

What was he like then?

Neutral. He was standing by the railing talking to a man in Russian. He noticed me and pretended not to know me. When they had shaken hands and the Russian had left, Uher came over and greeted me as he had in the church so many years before.

"Ahoj," I replied. "Look, if you've defected, I refuse to talk to you."

He looked into my eyes. It was not exactly a friendly look. "Those regulations weren't made for the fun of it, you know. But I'm here officially."

"What are you doing here, representing the Revolutionary Trades Union Movement or something?"

He studied me with those eyes, neither friendly nor unfriendly: neutral. Cold eyes, as though he were examining a steer at a cattle auction. Eyes of power, almost the eyes of God.

"Don't tell me you don't know I haven't been with them for a long time."

"Oddly enough, I don't. I haven't taken much interest in you, Uher. I hope you haven't been taking an interest in me, either."

"Only in the course of my work," he said. I felt a chill in my spine. "It would seem you're clean. Perhaps you took my advice to heart. In the train, remember?"

It was understandable that I should remember. But was it understandable that he did too? I suppose it was. A good spook has to have a good memory.

"I did take it to heart," I said.

"Except for the odd moment of weakness here or there, eh? Like Allen, for example."

"It's tough, you know. I got mixed up in that without even – "

"I don't mean in Prague. I mean here."

That really startled me. Was their network so extensive that they could follow my every step, even here in New York? And if someone like me was worth the effort, what about.... During one of those cosy little interviews with the security police before my departure for the congress they had warned me against meeting Allen. On an official trip, I didn't particularly want to meet with him either. What for? His inclinations were different from mine, and we had nothing of burning importance to say to each other. If I had ever had any ambition to be the friend of Whitman's heir, the desire had been crushed when I was interrogated by the secret police after his *Majales* trouble in 1965, and he was expelled from Czechoslovakia. Despite all this, I bumped into him on my very first day in New York, in Grand Central Station. Murphy's Law again. He moistened me with enthusiastic kisses and invited me to his place. There was no polite way I could say no.

"That was pure coincidence," I said. "And anyway, how do you know about it?"

"Every city – " Uher said, and stopped, gesturing strangely to one side with his eyes. I looked, then realized that the conversation coming from that direction was in Czech. A woman of about fifty, primped up as if she were going to a cocktail party, was standing by the railing with an elderly man in a gaudy jacket and Stetson hat. I was about to witness one of the tried-and-true methods of a police spy in action.

"You don't say!" the woman was saying in astonished tones. "And they built this in such a short time? A huge building like this? Back home it would have taken them ten times longer and in the end it would fall down anyway. Or the bricks would start falling on people's heads. Did you know that last year three people in Prague alone got killed that way?"

"Oh!" said the old man and continued, "Is that why they have scaffolding all over Prague?" He spoke Czech with a strong American accent.

"Certainly. Everything there's in a mess. But what can you expect when all the Commies care about is getting their noses in the feed-trough...."

I felt awful. I thought of saying something very loud in Czech to warn the wretched woman, but Uher smiled coldly at me and put his finger to his lips. The compleat police spy. And anyway it was too late, he already had her in his claws. So we stood silently by the railing and tried to look as though we were meditating on the canyons of New York City. A helicopter throbbed past and landed on the roof of the Pan Am Building. The poor woman had obviously had to pick her way along miles of corridors and climb over mountains of red tape to get permission for her trip. Now she was promising the elderly man that, when he repaid her visit, she would take him around Prague. She was obviously a comrade who had been screened and found reliable. And here, on the observation deck of the Empire State Building, she had completely undone all that and compromised herself in the worst possible way.

They left at last.

"As I was about to say," continued Uher with that cold smile, "every large city is really just a village. They all have a few village squares where all the tourists go. That lady over there demonstrated perfectly what I mean, don't you agree?"

"Are you going to make trouble for her?"

Uher thought a moment, then said, "How would it be if I asked you to do that?"

My old friend fear touched me again, and again I was trapped.

"I'll find out what her name is, and I'll give you a telephone number to call in Prague. And anyway, the comrades in Prague told you to report on things like this, didn't they?"

What could I say? "But surely you can do it better."

"Oh no, no!" he said with a smile. That old familiar, hard-to-define smile. "Just think of it as returning a favour."

"Returning a favour?"

"Yes," he said slowly. "After all, you were very good friends with that ... and you were in Kostelec just at the time when...." He stopped. "Let's just call it a favour. I'm not going back to Prague till the year after next."

Any pleasure I might have had from my trip to America was gone and I felt once more the way I had in that room with a view of Cerna Hora on a winter Sunday afternoon.

"Nothing much will happen to her," said Uher. "She won't be going abroad again for a while, that's all. But you will."

I was overwhelmed by a sensation of having been through this same scene once before. Or that I had read about it. The Empire State Building began to seem like a high mountain.

"I'll think it over," I said.

"As you wish. In any case, I'll be giving you the name of that woman."

In the hotel I stopped answering my phone. But they took messages at the reception desk. The next day, the receptionist handed me a note along with my key. It was in the receptionist's hand. All it said was "Mary Squari-likova" followed by a telephone number. With five digits. A Prague number.

•

I'm afraid you will be, Hakim. Among the first. But of course it's all the same to me. It's your life. Perhaps it's your choice, perhaps your fate. No one can know that. Perhaps, too, the revolution has outgrown that sort of thing. Perhaps it was really just scientific terror, scientifically making terrified mice out of men and women, and next time round it can permit the mice gradually to become men and women again, and then –

That vicious cycle.

"The symbol of human heads, stuck on poles around Kurtz's palace, is one of Conrad's most perceptive prophecies," I say quietly. Dianne is writing it all down furiously, and I only hope that she will not be able to read it later. I am almost frightened to think of how it will come out in the papers she writes in the other courses given by my colleagues. "Mr. Kurtz, as the Russian harlequin sees him, is an incredibly precise prefiguration ...," I say. "'"Ah! I'll never, never meet such a man again,"'" laments the harlequin.

' "You ought to have heard him recite poetry – his own, too, it was, he told me. Poetry!" ' That scene," I say, "is related to the famous scene in Chaplin's *The Great Dictator* where the dictator Hinkel, immediately after the inventor's death, plays Beethoven on the piano. Or think of a poetry-writing head of state who pulled a thousand flowers out of the ground, roots and all...."

I pause and meet the eyes of my class. Some of them are staring emptily and quickly begin to feign interest. Am I saying anything to them at all? Am I not merely talking to myself?

"Marlow also mentions the splendid monologues of Mr. Kurtz that the harlequin used to listen to in wonder," I continue. " 'On love, justice, conduct of life.' Just imagine these uplifting homilies, given in a house surrounded by human heads on sticks. The harlequin also described how the African chiefs came to see Mr. Kurtz and crawled up to him on their bellies. But the one who crawled most willingly of all, he said, was he himself, the harlequin. More eagerly than the most savage of the savages." Does that remind my charges of something? Or of anyone? Or does it only mean something to me, who wish to see in it – "And now listen carefully!" And I read: " 'These heads were the heads of rebels. I shocked him excessively by laughing. Rebels! What would be the next definition I was to hear? There had been enemies, criminals, workers – and these were rebels.' "

Bellissimmo stands up with an apologetic smile. Vicky and he are leaving me. "Sorry, we have a class. It's been terrific, sir!" Hakim gathers his books together too but he stays, although I know that he also takes Psychology 218, that interesting course on the laws that govern human attitudes. Professor Medley belongs to the Marxist study group.

"These central passages of *Heart of Darkness* are teeming with evocative images. In places they become Boschean or surrealistic caricatures, not too far removed from the more recent evocations in Solzhenitsyn's *The First Circle:* 'I saw him open his mouth wide – it gave him a weirdly voracious aspect, as though he had wanted to swallow all the air, all the earth, all the men before him.' And finally, of course, the famous conclusion, his death-bed cry, a single word: ' "The horror!" ' Whole generations of my colleagues played beautiful games with that word. What did the writer intend to say? Was he talking about the horror of human subconsciousness? Imperialist colonialism? Madness? Or some other interesting horror? He meant something else, also interesting as long as fate permits you what it permitted Marlow, and what it did not permit Kurtz: 'he had stepped over the edge, while I had been permitted to draw back my hesitating foot.' It is the horror of Marx's discovery, fully accepted by Lenin and made fully concrete by the will of the Generalissimo: that the only road to the future leads through a gateway made of the same material as Kurtz's fence."

Hakim is still hesitating; something is holding him to his chair like a tin soldier to a magnet.

"Marlow defines this gateway to the future in the same passage: 'He had summed up – he had judged. "The horror!" He was a remarkable man. After all, this was the expression of some sort of belief; it had candour, it had conviction, it had a vibrating note of revolt in its whisper, it had the appalling face of a glimpsed truth – the strange commingling of desire and hate.'"

I look around. Dianne is still writing. Wendy's wide eyes are upon me.

"Do you really think, sir, that this may happen here?"

Perhaps she understands me after all. Irene sighs, Hakim overcomes his momentary weakness and scowls, and then says in a tone used by the brothers superior:

"Conrad's novel is so vague that it's open to almost any interpretation you want. This is a characteristic feature of many works of bourgeois literature. Idealistic, decadent vagueness."

"But what is the Russian doing there?" cries Wendy.

Hakim shrugs and bares his beautiful Semitic teeth. "A caricature. Conrad didn't like Russians. The harlequin is simply a jester. A comic figure."

Is he really? But of course he is. *Meister* Ballon was a figure of fun too. As long as he didn't rat on us –

And what of the truth glimpsed in the horror?

I think of Lida Lewisova, who belongs to the same generation as Hakim. From another world. From the world of the future.

●

*July 4, 1967*
*Israel*

*Daniel,*
*When was the last time I wrote? It seems like a century ago. I only know that you replied with a long letter full of detailed descriptions of your trials and tribulations with a certain Mrs. Liza Neumannova-Hartlova who it seemed – then at least – succumbed neither to your masculine charms nor to your worldly fame. But so much water has gone under so many bridges that Mrs. Neumannova-Hartlova must be a grandmother by now and younger things attract your precious interest, am I right?*

*And if you're wondering why I'm writing you after all these years, it's because I now have a chance to become a grandmother myself. Our David has got married.*

*I should add, of course, that it was a hurry-up affair, but not because there was any danger of a premature birth. On the contrary, the danger was premature death. You must have been following the events. David had to enlist and because here in Israel mobilization can and usually does mean war – not like in Prague, where once in a blue moon the military overlords decide to show the country that though they may be good for nothing, they are still good at pushing everyone around– David decided to marry the girl he's been seeing for more or less a year now. They married, and ten minutes later David was driving away in his ugly steel vehicle into the Sinai desert. He's in a tank division, just like you used to be, you Great Paper Hero!*

*The girl, my daughter-in-law, is from historical stock. She is of those Jews who never left the promised land, not even when the Romans tore Jerusalem up by the roots. It's a good thing you're not here – she's a very beautiful girl. Dark complexion, black eyes the shape of almonds, beautiful white teeth, and the things that the Song of Solomon describes as two young roes that are twins which feed among the lilies are exactly as described. She is slender, independent, proud – rassig, as my late grandfather (Terezin, 1942) used to say of my poor mother (Auschwitz, 1943), although she was red-haired and freckled. But Naomi is rassig, whatever that means in Czech: beautiful, healthy, suntanned, a daughter of the tribe of David. They will certainly have a beautiful child together. Children, I hope.*

*And so David went off to war. I certainly don't have to describe my fears to you in colourful terms. The thought that after All That (you know what I mean by All That) all it takes is a single anti-tank rocket set off by some Egyptian farmer who knows nothing about All That and knows nothing about anything, and nothing would be left of All That but a Great Nothing – but I don't have to write about that to you.*

*But David came back. As a hero, etc. He put about six T-56s out of commission with his old-fashioned Centurion – I don't know how it happened. Perhaps, once more, our unreliable Yahveh has blessed us, for a change.*

*David came back and he's at the university now, not studying medicine, as I had hoped, but history. I'm not happy about that change of subject, but he's alive, he has Naomi, and everything is all right once more.*

*I've been reading the things that are happening back in Czechoslovakia. Please be careful. You know, Daniel, I'm an optimist, it's in my blood. Subconsciously I feel the Jews will survive everything. But my God, what a trial surviving is. In the end everything will turn out well, but almost everything before that final happy ending turns out badly. When I think to myself what "turning out badly" means, I am horrified. Auschwitz horror, if you can imagine even remotely what that means. Perhaps you can, because I remember you told me once about some sabotage that nearly got found out, if you weren't just trying to impress me. I was only twenty at the time, and I don't think I was all that impossible, even though I was nothing like the girl in that cup....*

*Daniel, I only hope the peace lasts ten years at least. But our Slavonic brothers will certainly do their best to ensure that it won't last that long. So I'll hope for at least five years. At least five.*

*And you people at home, be very very wary. The light is at the end of a terribly long, pitch-black tunnel.*

*Yours in life and in death,*

*Rebecca, née Silbernaglova*

●

"That was stupid of me, I know," says Lida Lewisova. "People should have better memories, but they don't. The fact is that for girls just a little younger than me Marta isn't even a name anymore. Don't forget I was only thirteen when she kissed that man called Dubcek, Christian name Alex. Or was it Alfred?"

"Sometimes it's your memory that lets you down, sometimes it's something else," I say. "Did you ever know a man called Liberda?" I look at Mrs. Lewis in her utterly unnecessary five-hundred-dollar wig because underneath it she has honest red Czech hair. I drink a Rusty Nail to this twenty-year-old millionaire's wife. It's a good drink. Not for the liver. For the soul. That ought to be more important, at least if the venerable fathers are right. Liberda –

"He contributed to an anthology called *Ich klage an!* published in August 1968 by Hanser Verlag. It was a collection of articles condemning the Soviet invasion of Czechoslovakia or whatever they call it now. Liberda signed his piece Yehudi Fromme."

"Oh, come on!"

"A pseudonym has the great advantage of being useful no matter how things turn out. After the invasion, Liberda didn't know whether to be a 'sell-out' or part of the healthy nucleus. In the end he reckoned that being part of the healthy nucleus meant security, less work and more money. Now he writes articles about heroic struggles and bearded heroes – in other words, he's a foreign affairs correspondent. They pay his way, and he has no trouble getting a passport."

"Well," says Lida. "You teach English literature, so you should know. It's just like when the colonial empires were getting under way."

Of course, Lida, I know. The white man's burden. Christianity for the heathen. Civilization for the barbarians. Socialism for the Angolans. At the same time, it makes promising careers overseas. Young Englishmen formulate the slogan: My Country – Right or Wrong. Some things they see. Some things they don't. There are some things they don't believe, but taken as a whole, it seems plausible – so they take things as a whole. They don't exactly believe what comes out of their mouths. But the whole, wide, far-away world is waiting for them. Gin and tonic under the glowing moon of lovely Luanda.... *On the road to Mandalay ... where the flying fishes play....* So in the name of Christianity, in the name of civilization, in the name of the proletariat....

Some foolish Jonas Savimbi, some silly Alfred – was it Alfred? – Dubcek.

"And us, Lida?"

"What do you mean, 'us'?" replies the foxy girl. She has also long switched from ice cream to a Rusty Nail. "We've only got one life. Don't you belong to the cream of society again, professor? What's eating you so much? You're fifty. Capitalism will last for at least – I say at least – another ten years, with all its magnificent advantages."

"But what about you, Lida?"

"I hate them," she says. "I hate everything dull and clever. Everything that thinks it owns historical truth and therefore lies. But I'm just Lida Lewisova. I have only one life to live. And I've arranged that to suit myself. Everyone arranges it to suit themselves."

*Jenseits von Gut und Böse.* The Rusty Nail pounds its way pleasantly into my brain; Lida's eyes shine rustily. Lida, tell me, how did you arrange it?

"Fab!" said Lida Lewisova, just like the deathless girls of Kostelec used to. "For example, we've got a summer villa in Malta, you know? Seaview Lodge. Straight out of Chandler. You translated him, didn't you? Well, the villa is built on a rock. To the left there's an old fortress that once belonged to the Knights of Malta, with a beautiful harbour town around it, churches and little bars one on top of the other, and a magnificent, hundred percent genuine medieval theatre where they play Pinter, everything in orange stone. To the right there's a harbour and at four in the morning, at sunrise, a picturesque fleet of fishing-boats sails out to sea through the turquoise water and comes back at eight to take the catch to market. Technicolor sunrises and sunsets. We have a heated pool without sharks to swim in, a tennis court to keep trim in. We have the best-stocked bar in the world for happiness. You see all the nice things that can happen to one little Czech girl?"

"Everything," I say. "You know what?"

"Yes, I do," says the most gracious Mrs. Lewisova, and she turns her

Rusty Nail upside down. "All that's missing is for a little Czech girl to prostitute herself to someone in the Kremlin."

There is a discarnate rapport between us. I begin to believe what they say about national character.

"Couldn't your filthy rich husband establish a fellowship to encourage it?"

"He could," said Lida. They bring us two more Nails. "But even without it, I'm sure some little Czech girl will find herself a rich Soviet husband."

Lida and I dream about the bright future of mankind. Unfortunately it is quite far off. We dream about the fall of an empire, about that wonderful time when a new Comrade Czar will attend the performance of a new play by a new Comrade Gogol ... and after the performance of a new *Inspector General* ... the new Comrade Czar will say, You gave us a fine piece of your mind, Comrade ... Comrade Gogol expects to hear: To Siberia! ... but Comrade Czar says, Oh well, if your face is disfigured, don't look in the mirror ... *nu shto*. Just keep it up, Comrade Gogol ... just ... keep ... it ... up....

Rusty Nail! I got the Rusty Nail blues....

Lida Lewisova, in her eight-hundred-dollar dress, betakes herself to the Ladies.

It seems to me that life is beautiful after all.

•

"Do you want to hear it? Of course you do!" chuckles Bocar. "One comrade, a fellow called Slavek, wrote a television play about it, but they tossed him out on his ear and no surprise. He got the story from me, and I got it from a Gestapo fellow in the Rovnost camp. It's a kind of legend, in fact. A yarn. A piece of the unwritten history of our age. So do you want to hear it or not, damn it?"

We all nod enthusiastically. Dotty's charm-bracelet tinkles. Only Margitka does not nod; her lips are pursed and she lashes out at me with her eyes. That means: keep out of my sight. She already knows about Irene. *C'est la vie.*

"All right, so one of them survived," says Bocar. "I mean one of the men. All the rest were shot by the *Sicherheitspolizei* and some SS Kommandos, against the wall of the Lidice mill, including an informer the Gestapo had infiltrated among the townsfolk, who kept yelling out who he was till the last moment. Of course they knew very well who he was, which is why they gunned him down with the rest. You can't let a stoolie just walk away; in our enlightened age you have to shut his trap too. Fortunately somebody always survives, somebody whose trap has not been shut."

I see that Bocar has a firm grip on Margitka's thigh under the white satin of her evening gown. The folk ensemble on stage has been replaced by Mr. Mrkvicka's jazz band and they're playing "Sweet Sue." Mr. Mrkvicka swings beautifully on his Joe Venuti violin.

"While that was going on, the lone survivor was sitting in the Pankrac prison where he was just finishing up twenty years for second-degree murder. He'd killed his wife Jarmila, quite justifiably, because he was jealous of her. And that lousy Gestapo Rössler says to me, 'We read in the instructions that all the men from Lidice had to be arrested and shot, regardless of where they happened to be at the moment or where they were registered.' German thoroughness. All very well, except, says Rössler, we didn't have the heart for it. He was such a model prisoner, a veteran of the system, quiet, gentle, obedient, religious. So we didn't blow the whistle on him. On the other hand, just to be on the safe side, we didn't tell him either. And naturally no one read the daily newspapers in prison. So he had no idea what had happened. And when we let him out on Christmas Eve, because that was exactly when his twenty-year sentence was up, he still didn't suspect a thing, and off he went – "

– and he took the afternoon train to Kladno and from Kladno he set out on foot for Lidice. He hadn't been there for twenty years, but you never forget the way home. He walked along a district road in the dusk, with night rapidly descending, so that he was soon walking along in the dark beneath the winter constellations, the last hill ahead of him. When he got to the top, he would see....

What he saw was an empty valley. He was shocked. Then he thought: Well, it's been twenty years, after all – maybe it's over the next hill. He walked through the empty valley and up the hill on the other side. The white, snow-covered countryside, the winter stars, the empty plain sloping gently down towards Prague. The valley behind him. The valley of Lidice. But the village had vanished.

He thought he might have gone mad in prison. He walked back through the valley and returned to Kladno. Kladno was in its proper place, a wintry, blacked-out town, empty streets, everyone home by the Christmas tree. On the edge of town he found a pub where a couple of lonely old bachelors were drinking. "I've gone mad," he said. "Nonsense," said the innkeeper. "Come now, take a drink for your stomach's sake. It's Christmas Eve." He poured him a glass of the precious wartime house liquor. Even the Gestapo stay home on Christmas Eve, under the *Tannenbaum*. "I mean it. The village is gone." "What village? And you are talking nonsense." "I am not!"

"So he told them," says Bocar. "The old bachelors looked at each other and the publican tapped his forehead. 'What'd you do, rise from the dead?' he said, and the man replied, 'I'm Josef, the murderer of Jarmila, and it's been twenty years.' And at last they understood."

Slowly, carefully, they explained to the Last Living Man from Lidice what had happened. He stood up. "Where are you going?" He said nothing. He went out of the pub into the dark, asked no directions, and how he got there is a mystery. But at the Gestapo headquarters he said, "*Ich melde gehorsam,* a man to be shot." "What're you carrying on about?" asked the Gestapo officer, bored and annoyed that he had drawn duty on Christmas Eve. "A man reporting to be shot," he said. "*Auf Befehl des Herrn Staatsminister Karl Hermann Frank!*" "What are you bloody talking about?" asked the Gestapo man irritably. He told him.

"And the Gestapo fellow called in his colleague and they thought the whole thing was a riot," says Bocar. I notice that Mr. Zawynatch's eyebrows are oddly furrowed as he listens to this unwritten legend from an unreal time. The Mrkvicka boys are loosening up, the publisher on the floor dancing with Frank the Fascist. "Tiger Rag." "They refused to shoot him," Bocar goes on, "but they ordered him to report every Saturday morning. And he did. Every Saturday: '*Ich melde gehorsamst, ein Mann zum erschiessen.*' The Gestapo officers could have had kittens every time he did it. They thought it was hilarious. The fellow from Rovnost told us that."

"What happened to him in the end?" asks Dotty.

"First he got the rope," says Bocar.

"The Lidice murderer?"

"No. Our lousy Gestapo man. He said: When the judge read the verdict, I had a seizure and they had to carry me out of the courtroom. I thought I'd stay that way and they'd have to carry me stiff right to the gallows. Horrible! When the executioner breaks my neck! It'll be ghastly! Ghastly! Like all lice, stuff like that only bothered him when it involved him personally."

"Was he pardoned?"

"Yeah. Lice always are. His sentence was commuted to life. The same week they hanged Father Tiso. And the Lidice murderer? Well, they didn't shoot him. Pretty soon they had other things to worry about. He hit the booze and after the war he went back to his original profession, which was waitering. He just sozzled away and kept his mouth shut. But then the Lidice women started coming back from the concentration camps, and the government and foreign philanthropists built a New Lidice. It became a very good deal to marry a woman from Lidice with a nice new house in a nice little town near Prague – that was a real jackpot after the war. Still is today. A lot of sharp cookies married into the New Lidice. The murderer was just about to succumb to delirium tremens and one day he couldn't think of anything smarter to do than go to New Lidice and claim his right to one of those nice little new houses with the begonias. I mean, after all, he was a citizen of Lidice, wasn't he? But what do you suppose he got for his pains?"

"What?" says Mr. Zawynatch with those oddly bristling eyebrows.

"He didn't fit the legend," says Bocar. "They almost stung him to death. The female martyrs of Lidice, and even more their smart-ass husbands. So he went back to the pub where he worked slinging beer and drank a little longer until he began to see white mice, and they packed him off to the Bohnice nuthouse, where his life's journey came to an end." Bocar crosses himself ostentatiously.

"May God grant him eternal glory," says Father Hunak gravely.

"Of course he didn't fit the legend," says Mr. Zawynatch. "Lots of things don't fit. Do you remember, gentlemen, how Czech workers behaved during the war? The highest productivity in Europe. I told that – in defence of the middle classes, who bled – to Dr. Husak when we were in prison together. And you know what he said? He said, 'What did you expect? You bourgeoisie kept the workers in ignorance and poverty throughout Father Masaryk's first republic. Why should the working class have been interested in your war? No, no, dear friend. In the ranks of the working class there were only heroes, no collaborators. They didn't know what they were doing so it wasn't a sin.' Dr. Husak told me that, gentlemen."

"Perhaps he was right," I say. Fortunately most of the guests are out of it by this time.

"While Elias and the other heroes were laying down their lives for their nation – "

"For the bourgeois nation," I interject provocatively. Bocar looks at me strangely.

"Precisely," he says. "For an ideal. For a folly. Smartasses always win, and morons win even oftener. Heroes never win. It's a kind of law. Historical. Dialectical."

Then everything becomes Apollinaire's *Zone*. Somewhere in that fusion of events, Frank the Fascist tells me the Canadian courts have had Magister Maslo committed.

●

Uher's malice poisoned my stay in New York – at least until I finally thought of a way, a rather desperate way, to salvage something from the situation. I had to talk to Mary Squarilikova, and explain to her the nature of the quandary that she and I were in. Perhaps together we might think of a way out of it. If nothing else, at least she would know what to expect and could prepare a defence. But whatever happened, it would be difficult.

There were several Skvarils – the name had been neatly anglicized – in the New York telephone directory, but only one Skvarilik. I dialed the number. A man answered and I asked him in English if I might speak to Mrs. Skvarilikova.

"Just a sec," he said and then I could hear him shouting in Czech, "Mana! You're wanted on the phone!"

A few moments later a voice spoke into the receiver, filled with curiosity and a good deal of anxiety:

"Skvarilikova."

"I must speak with you," I said. "Can I come to see you at this address?"

"What ... what's it about?"

"I don't want to talk about it over the phone."

"And who are you?"

I could now hear the familiar fright in her voice.

"A friend." Mary Skvarilikova was no longer in any doubt that I was a secret agent. In New York.

"My God! What do you want of me?"

"This is in your own interest. I'll be at your place in half an hour." I hung up.

It occurred to me that Mary Skvarilikova had almost certainly been interviewed before her departure, as I had, and warned of her responsibilities. What if she were to try to neutralize my report in Prague with one of her own about my warning her?

There was still time to back out. But then, of course, I would have to do precisely what Uher wanted me to do. A bourgeois is incapable in practice of going beyond....

Half an hour later a black porter was announcing my presence over the house telephone to someone deep inside an elegant apartment on Riverside Drive. Two minutes later I was on the third floor being examined through a half-opened door by the same elderly gentleman who had been on the Empire State Building, this time without the Stetson.

"What do you want of Mana? She's having a nervous breakdown over this. Can't you talk to me about it?"

I thought it over. Why not?

"If you're trying to blackmail her, you've come to the wrong address. I'll have you picked up by the police."

This gave me an idea.

"I haven't come to blackmail Mrs. Skvarilikova at all, but to try and save her from potential blackmail."

"Is that so?"

"But I can settle it with you."

"Come on in."

He led me into a huge room with a view of the river. The room looked like a museum. There were hundreds of framed photographs of varying age on the wall. People and cities, mainly Prague. Also of Mrs. Skvarilikova. I explained to him briefly what had happened. He did not really comprehend. What did she say that was compromising? he wanted to know. I told him about those murderous bricks.

"Well, it's true, isn't it?"

"Yes, but at the same time it's thought of as slandering the state."

"Even if it's true?" He shook his head. Politically, he was an illiterate. I pointed out several more of Mana's indiscreet remarks, but in each case I had to admit that what she had said was true. He began to look at me with fresh suspicion in his eyes. So I mentioned her remark about the Commies with their noses in the feed-trough.

"Politicians are that way everywhere," he said. "Republicans, Democrats, why not Commies too?"

"If she'd made the remark about Republicans – "

"Are there any Republicans in Prague?"

"No, but – "

"Well then, how could she say that about the Republicans, if you haven't got any there? You've got Communists, so she had to say it about the Communists."

I scratched my head and gave up. He frowned at me warily, with faded eyes.

"I don't like it," he declared.

I wasn't quite sure what it was he didn't like.

"I don't like it one bit," he repeated. "I'm bringing Mana in."

He went out of the room and after a long time he came back with the woman I had seen the day before. She looked as though she had just suffered a serious heart attack.

"This gentleman here," said the elderly man sententiously, "claims that you're in trouble because yesterday, on the Empire State Building, you said that the Communists fight over the feed-trough and he says some police informer was standing beside us."

"Jesus Maria!" cried the woman, so loudly that the elderly man was startled. Then she sank to her knees, not because she was trying to make a dramatic impression but out of good, honest socialist fear – her knees had given out. "Comrade, I beg you! Don't turn me in! I didn't mean it that way … I – you heard me wrong. And you misunderstood."

She fainted. The old man and I carried her to the couch.

"I'll have the police on you," he growled at me. "But first I'll kick your teeth in." He did not carry out the threat straightaway, but hurried out of the room and came back with a bottle, from which he poured something into the woman's mouth. She began to cough, regained consciousness, opened her eyes, caught sight of me and shut them tightly again. I quickly explained the situation to her. She half-opened her eyes again.

"Comrade ... you're *really* not a comrade from ... the Interior?"

I assured her that I was not a comrade at all, let alone from the Interior.

"Then for God's sake, don't report me. I'll make it worth your while. Jerry here can pay you in dollars, can't you Jerry? He's rich – only please, I beg you, don't for God's sake – "

Very patiently I explained to her that if I did not report her both of us would be in hot water. But she was far too upset to think rationally. "Then don't go back!"

I explained to her that as a popular writer writing in Czech I had no intention of going into exile. She began to weep convulsively.

"Now do you understand?" I said to the old man.

"They'll throw me out of work!" wailed Mana. "They'll lock me up! Comrade! Jerry will make it worth your while. Couldn't you take the blame yourself?"

Once more, with extreme patience, I explained that I could not take the responsibility for the insulting remarks on myself, willing as I might be to do so for dollars, because the whole point was I did not hear them alone. As far as I was concerned, this whole affair was a test of my loyalty to the regime, whereas in her case the Ministry of the Interior would find out about her whether I reported her or not. I could do no more for her than what I was trying to do right now: forewarn her so that she might forearm herself.

"I'll deny I ever said it," she wailed. "But they've got their methods. Jesus Christ in heaven, what will I do?"

I really did not know. And it was clear that she and I were in a pretty mess, except for the fact that my bourgeois conscience could now rest easy. The old man glowered at me and at the woman, then took a drink from the bottle that had so recently revived her. I regretted greatly my Christian chivalry. Mana was literally writhing with fear on the couch and I found myself where I least wanted to be.

"And how did you wriggle out of that one?" asked Lida Lewisova, when I told her about it, all that time later.

"I was saved by the old gunslinger, Jerry Skvarilik."

"How?"

"Simple. Listening to us gave him a crash course in the political science of socialism. And when we had reached an utter impasse, he announced in an accent that brooked no argument that if that was the case Mana would not go back to Prague. And a week later – even before I returned to Prague myself – Mana had the same status as you do today."

"He married her!" cried Lida Lewisova, in that tone that always steals into women's voices when they hear that one of them has enjoyed good fortune. And Mana certainly had.

"Yes. I had the impression that he invited her to America with that in mind in the first place, but he'd been a widower for a long time and was therefore shy. Mana was his sister-in-law, the widow of his brother in Prague. So Uher was instrumental in helping another Czech girl find happiness."

"There, you see all the things that can happen to a Czech girl?" said Lida. "And what about Uher? Didn't he ever try to blackmail you later?"

"He couldn't. When I got back to Prague I delivered my report on Mrs. Skvarilik with great gusto. And Uher never bothered to look me up. I haven't seen him since then, I've merely heard stories about him."

"Nice stories, I'll bet."

"I don't know. Things like this are obviously relative," I said. "It's like you, when you told me over the phone that things were all right now back home. Did you know you made me so angry I hung up on you?"

●

In those dying days of the war the men's can was as crowded as a football match, and the smoke from home-grown tobacco was like a London fog. The humbled Eisler, who only came there to relieve himself, could barely squeeze his way through to the urinals, and then he was apologetic. The war was ending and its horrors were beginning to fade.

They were revived only in Vozenil's legends, which this particular day concerned love-life in the Reich.

"It was against the law for us to shaft German women," he told us, and in the gloomy London fog he looked like a huge tree-frog. "A deviolation of the race. But their husbands were at the front and the women were all horny. I tell you boys, you have no idea what them Brunhilds could get up to in bed. Trouble was you was risking life and limb. So we only shafted them for grub."

"What was the going rate?" asked the lad from the paint-shop.

"Mine was high. A week's meat coupons per," said the green man. "And they used to fight over me. But I had to be dead careful."

"I suppose you got shot for it, eh, you camel?" asked Malina.

"If that was all it wouldn't've been so bad. But they did lots worse."

"They torture you or something?" asked Kos.

"All depended on whether the little lady had a husband at the front or whether she was single. If she was single, they cut your balls off."

"Horseshit, you walrus. Show us."

"Did I say they cut my balls off? Not me. I covered my back every time. I gave one of the boys a third of the coupons to stand watch. But lots of my buddies was caught red-handed. Some of them was even married, poor bastards. But that wasn't so bad. If they caught you with a married woman, they cut your dick off."

"It's worse than having your balls cut off," said the lad from the paint-shop.

"No, it ain't," cried Kos. "If your balls are cut off, your worries are over, but without a dick, man...."

"Horrible," said Vozenil gloomily. "The fellows I've seen suffer, boys, and I mean suffer. You can't even wank off."

There was a horrified silence. Then a trembling voice piped up: "Did they put them to sleep at least before they did it?"

"That's a good one," said the green lad. "They did it when you was wide awake. But they was hygienic about it, so no one'd croak. Otherwise what's the point, eh?"

"I hear there's this operation and they can sew an artificial one on for you," said Filipec, a welder. "They did it to that woman Koubkova when they made her into a man."

"She already had one, but it was wizened up," the omniscient Vozenil corrected him. "All they did to her was they give her a shot to make it grow."

"That's not how I heard it. He's got an artificial one. He gave a talk about it."

"What's it made of, you elephant?" growled Malina.

"Rubber, I reckon."

"How could you get a rubber one up?"

"They make 'em that way to begin with."

"So how can you walk around with it sticking out like that, muttonhead?"

"Maybe you can take it off, like a wooden leg."

"It still wouldn't be worth a shit," said the green man. "You got the most important nerves right at the end of your dick so you can feel it. You can't make artificial nerves."

Once again we ruminated on the awful fate of over-sexed workers in the Reich.

"No, I tell you, boys," sighed Vozenil, "the only relief the poor buggers ever got was when they was so horny they shot off themselves."

"You're a fucking donkey," said Malina.

But Vozenil had not exhausted his catalogue of horrors. "In Hamburg," he said, "the Gestapo had an even worse method. They had this infected old whore there and every fellow who was caught had to get himself infected from her and then they tattooed a big S on his forehead, like he's got the syph, and not a single doctor in the Reich was allowed to treat him."

"You silly goddamn termite!" said Malina. "How would you like a kick in the fucking balls, if you got any left?"

"That's not so bad," said the lad from the paint-shop. "They can always get fixed up after the war. It's worse for them with their dicks –"

"You think so? And what about that big S on their foreheads?" asked Vozenil. "What girl is going to want to screw with any guy marked up like that?"

"You can get rid of tattoos," declared Kos.

"Not completely," said Vozenil. "And there's no cure for the syph. In the end you start falling apart. First your cock falls off, next your ears –"

"Why don't you go take a flying fuck, you tortoise," said Malina. "You're fucking hopeless."

"You can also pass it on to your kids," said the green man, unperturbed. "I knew a fellow in reform school, Olda Sadlo, and he didn't have no nose. And his dad was done in by the syph."

"And what did he have, if he didn't have no nose?"

"He only had nostrils. That is, he had one, right between his eyes. And that's what did him in, the poor bugger, when they put him in the water room."

"In the what?"

"That was a kind of punishment. It wasn't the worst one by a long shot," said Vozenil, and he began to describe an earlier period of his life, before the war. It turned out that even before the war, Vozenil's world had been full of horrors.

●

"It's a sure-fire thing," says Mr. Pohorsky. He seems to be wasting away, nervous, miserable. "You just take an ordinary picture postcard and write a message on it so it sounds kind of mysterious, suspicious. Like for instance: 'Message passed on to Lilac. M. will arrange. Await further instructions.' Something like that. Then you send the postcard to a big-shot Commie. Do that three or four times and it makes the secret police suspicious and they lay into him. And now get this. Every exile knows at least two big-shot Commies. If only half of them write...." Mr. Pohorsky applies the familiar geometrical progression and estimates that by the end of this calendar year about fifty thousand big-shots in the Republic will have had nervous breakdowns, and furthermore, the secret police apparatus will be so overworked that its employees will begin to collapse as well. But Dotty is skeptical.

"It's too far out," she says. "When they don't find anything behind any of those postcards, and when no sabotage takes place, they'll see it's a hoax."

"Quite the contrary!" An anxious, dwindling hope quavers in the former UN representative's voice, but he clings firmly to it. "It'll drive them all crazy. They'll live in fear and trembling of the mails, and in two years the Party will be on the point of collapse."

"It won't work," Dotty insists. "Wouldn't it make more sense to mail letterbombs?"

"What?"

"Letterbombs. They're kind of tiny, flat bombs that fit into envelopes. I haven't a clue how you make them, but they're always going on about them in the papers."

•

*The 25 July 1967*
*Dresden*

*Dear Dan,*
*I adres you with these few lines to let you know I am well and hope you are injoying the same blesing at present. Im writing you this leter from a cultural tour in the German demokratish republik. Our colective farm won the tour as a reward for being the best colective farm in the district. We get the tour for nothing and I am going to write an artical about it as soon as I get back home and theyre giving me eighty crowns for it. Its my 37th artical I've already wrote 36 and they printed all of them and paid me 70-100 crowns a peice acording to how long they was. All they have to do is correct my speling here and there because I went to a Czech school and now Im living in Slovakea, where they have speling too but diferent.*

*I like it a lot in the German demokratish republik they have diferent goods for sale here and they have private stores here where the owners are politer. We also went to Karl-Max Stad that used to be called Chemnits and there was a lot of memries there for me. Thats where I used to work for Meister Radac when Meister Akrman in Obersharau got killed by a bomb he was a very fine boss there was always enough to eat and he only had one arm so he didnt have to go in the army. He lost his arm fighting against the reaction airies as he often use to tell us. He also wore a uniform but I cant remember what his movemint was called but it wasnt the Nazies. Meistr Radac wasnt a Nazie but he was in an organization I cant remembr the name of with brown shirts and pants but it wasnt the NSDAP nor the SS. He lost his arm in battles at the beginning of the movement I think that Meister Radac was an anty Nazie because he was a decent fellow on the whole.*

*In Dresdin we was in the Pina Kotex where they have paintings by old masters and also an exibision called Terrorangrif an Dresdin about the Amerikan imperialist airaid on Dresdin where more than 200,000 inocent people died. We got took round by our German comrade who described the airaid in detale because he was in Dresdin at the time as a soldier with the Luftabver and his speech was translated for us by a comrade from the union of youth. But I didn't need to have it translated because I still understand German very good. This comrade spoke about how the people of Dresdin was longing for peace but the Amerikan war mungers sent huge squadrins of airplanes and flying fortresses and dropped more than 500,000 tons of fire and explosiv bombs on the city. It was a inhuman crime against the peace loving people of the German demokratish republik by the war mungers who started the second world war and other wars sinse then like Koria for example and Vietnam and against Egypd in Izrail. They are crimes against the people as the exibision Terrorangrif and Dresdin proves beyond a dout. Even so you can find people who suport them. When the German comrade spoke about the sufering of the people who only wanted peace which the Amerikan imperialists had no use for one man punched him in the face without no provokation. He was a tourist from Ostria and I guess he was a Kike he had this funny nose and bushy eyebrows and he shouted that the people of Dresdin had it comin to them and they had to hold him back and then take him away because he got real historical. Our comrade tour directer said he probly was mentaly ill because only people who are mentaly ill could posibly suport the Amerikan war mungers against the inocent people of the GDR.*

*We also visited the consantration camp at Buchenval and that was also very interesting especialy the torcher chamber were they hung the prisoners up on hooks. They dont use that camp in the German demokratish republik any more because the comrade said in the German demokratish republik there is hardly any more crime to speak of.*

*My daughter Suleika finished studying to be a hairdresser and she got a good job in Bratislava where she gets upwards of 3000 crowns a month, mostly in tips and all the importent customers in Bratislava come to her to get there hair done like the wife of the atterny general*

CONRAD

*and the daughter of the first secretary of the Slovak Comunist Party. Im real proud of her and Im only sory we never had more kids we wantid boys too. But you cant have everything.*

*As an old buff I went to the movies here and saw a film called Die Traktoristin but I was disapointed because it wasnt much good. They used to make better films in the German demokratish republik like Die Grose Fritz or Pandur Trenk with Hans Alberts that was an expensive film and there was something to look at. But Der Traktoristin was cheap only the actres was, well, okay, but she wasnt very well drest for almost the whole film.*

*The wife and I go to the movies regular at home twice a week. We seen Black Peter by M. Forman but it was boring and the main actres wasn't yet developed and they shouldnt hire actreses like her for movies. Daizies was even worse — one of the actreses was good-looking but the other was ugly I realy dont know why they put scar-crows like that on the screen. They also ought to bann films when workers can't understand them. The Big Country with G. Pek was a beautiful film, Amerikan. I also liked Loves of a Blond a lot even if the actris was no shakes either, except they showd her naked even if not all of her. She has a nice body but her face is a little pufy. I gess they couldn't get any pretty girls to strip for them. The movie Apartment was also real nice where they had meals all ready all you had to do was warm them up in the oven but that was in America.*

*To conclude my leter please except my warmest wishis and fondest memries.*

*Your friend,*
*Lojza*

•

My class has shrunk to the faithful Irene, the diligent Dianne, and Hakim, who is about to leave, but he has stayed so long already that he will miss his lecture on the mysteries of the human mind from the point of view of behaviourism and Marxism. His own mind has been touched by the dark forces that have played with my life too; so he is probably the only one who is genuinely interested in my biased psychoanalysis of *Heart of Darkness*. Dianne is a crammer, Irene is simply Irene. Hakim will almost certainly reject my fancy as easily controvertible nonsense, but God knows, perhaps the only thing we really are capable of doing in this world is dispensing drops of poison. Taken drop by drop, it may perhaps have a homeopathic effect.

"At the end of the novel," I say, "Conrad invests Mr. Kurtz with the final and quite unmistakable outlines of the concrete future. I'll be brief – I don't want to keep you from more scientifically grounded ways of spending your time in Edenvale College. But take Marlow's conversation with a representative of the Company after the captain's return from the Congo to Belgium. The representative asks Marlow to turn over all of Kurtz's documents to him because 'the Company had the right to every bit of information about its "territories."' And Marlow? 'I assured him Mr. Kurtz's knowledge, however extensive, did not bear upon the problems of commerce or administration. He then invoked the name of science.... I offered him the report on the "Suppression of Savage Customs," with the postscriptum torn off.' But what was that postscriptum? Come on now, think. Yes, what else could it have been but Kurtz's own savage command: 'Exterminate all the brutes!' – that remarkable conclusion of Kurtz's 'science.'"

Dianne writes all this down unquestioningly; the secretaries from the Humanities Department have finished their coffee break and are lazily making their way back to their typewriters. I read incomprehension in Irene's eyes. But it is not Kurtz she is trying to understand. Hakim is frowning, but he remains seated, his hand resting on a psychology text. I go on:

"Two pages later, a journalist who has come to dig out information on Kurtz claims that Mr. Kurtz had the faith. '"Don't you see – he had the faith."' Doesn't that strike you as interesting? The representative of the Company appeals to science, to the scientific value of Kurtz's documents. The journalist emphasizes his 'faith.' Kurtz had written a scientific work on the Suppression of Savage Customs and he had finished with a *declaration of faith:* '"Exterminate all the brutes!"' The title of the essay suggests nineteenth-century science – the outburst in the postscriptum is the voice of a barbarian demagogue from biblical times and the dark ages ... kill them all, women, children, and old people ... *ceterum autem censeo Carta-ginem....*"

Am I taking my own delirium seriously? Conrad's delirium? For such art is delirium. Such an author is merely a sounding board amplifying the dark pulsing powers of bloody experience. The powers of visions, intimations, the suprarational powers of art....

"Translated into the sober language of history: Marx subjected the problem of society to scientific investigation: his science is not without error in all its details, but no science is. Unlike the old socialists who based their theories on feelings of sociability and talked about reforming a society which was run unscientifically according to the laws of the jungle, Marx accepted those jungle laws as given and erected his notion of revolution on that basis. After him, Lenin and Stalin transformed his science into an ideology, that is into false consciousness, that is into a faith, and they both came to the same conclusions as Kurtz: '"Exterminate all the brutes!"' – get rid of everyone who cannot be enlightened. So let us evoke Mr. Kurtz in our minds and observe a minute's silence in his memory. Kurtz, the scientist with that gift of faith; Kurtz, the reformer who ended up advocating absolute reform: the extermination of the unreformable; Kurtz, like Lenin in his Testament, having in the last minutes of his life a vision whose name is horror. 'The Horror! The Horror!' The horror whose name is Terror."

Having convinced myself, I pause. On this sleepy afternoon, in this cafeteria, it all seems so distant. Dianne has already become faint and is looking merely vacant, hardly listening anymore. Irene is thinking her own thoughts. Hakim burns holes in me with the eyes of Nadia Jirouskova.

"This vision," I say, "is repeated at the end of the book about Master Kurtz, that terrible lord of the jungle, when Marlow rings the doorbell of Kurtz's fiancée. 'I had a vision of him on the stretcher, opening his mouth voraciously, as if to devour all the earth with all its mankind ... he seemed to stare at me out of the glassy panel – stare with that wide and immense stare embracing, condemning, loathing all the universe. I seemed to hear the whispered cry: The Horror! The Horror!' "

I fall silent.

"Is that all?" asks Hakim. Dianne screws the top onto her ballpoint pen with a deep sigh.

"Yes. Except perhaps that the journalist – so that there would be no doubts about the real significance of what Kurtz is meant to foreshadow – says that 'Kurtz's proper sphere ought to have been politics "on the popular side." ' ' "He drew men towards him by what was best in them," ' is how Kurtz's fiancée puts it. And the journalist says, ' "He would have been a splendid leader of an extreme party." ' " "What party?" " asks Marlow – and think why he does so. ' "Any party," ' replies the journalist. ' "He was an – an – extremist." ' "

Hakim is silent.

"I think that fits in very well with Conrad's description of genuine revolutionaries. Idealists. People who are drawn to violence by what is best in them."

"Because there is no other way to exterminate the savage customs of the old society than by violence," cries Hakim. "And that is a *scientific* observation. *Faith* is believing it can be done any other way."

Now I am silent. For a long time. Dianne would like to write something down but she does not know what.

"Customs cannot be exterminated at all," I say quietly. "They do not exist apart from people. Only people can be exterminated."

Hakim loses his self-control. "If they are brutes from the jungle, then I say: Go ahead!"

If, of course, they are brutes from the jungle.

I look at my Nicole. What can she be thinking of? She is different from us. As Fitzgerald knew. Just as the nonexistent Al Capone made her. I look around and remember that song, once, in the room right next door, that doubtful interpretation of one tiny murder, one insignificant extermination ... *why should I be the one....*

Beyond the panoramic windows a sad expanse of flat land, and on it, through a pre-spring mist, the Edenvale raven struts and frets towards Lake Ontario. *Voron. Havran.* Raven. Once upon a time Manitou stumbled here, held out his arm to break his fall and the palm of his hand made that vast watery plain, and the five fingers of his hand made those five long lakes with the lovely names: Canandaigua, Keuka, Seneca, Cayuga, Owasco....

# CHAPTER SEVEN

These were days when my heart was volcanic
 As the scoriac rivers that roll –
 As the lavas that restlessly roll
Their sulphurous currents down Yaanek
 In the ultimate climes of the pole – ...

Well I know, now, this dim lake of Auber –
 This misty mid region of Weir –
Well I know, now, this dank tarn of Auber....
... Ah, what demon has tempted me here?

EDGAR ALLAN POE, "Ulalume"


We are such stuff
As dreams are made on, and our little life
Is rounded with a sleep.

WILLIAM SHAKESPEARE, *The Tempest*

●

# Lovecraft

*Toronto
October 29, 1976*

**L**ida, *my darling, my little pussy!*
 *Why don't you write? Has something happened? I cannot sleep, I cannot eat, I cannot work. What is happening? I think of the moonlight, of the white, pliant hills on the horizon of the pillow.... Ah Lida, I can wait no longer! Write!*

*I can't think of anything but you. Only once in a while I am upset by some political outrage or other, like Sakharov, who claims that American workers are better off than Soviet workers. American workers may have higher wages – and the freedom to fight for them in continual struggles – but I know very well how workers in your country live in security, in peace, how they are cared for in every way by the state. When will men like Sakharov finally see that in this alone lies true freedom of the spirit?*

*Write, Lida, or I'll go crazy.*

*Yours,*
*Booker*

●

"May I?"

"You may." Nosek let me in. A few moments later Nadia had slipped into the ferroflux room after me. Nosek greeted her with a "How d'you do, milady," and Nadia blushed. Then Nosek slipped out and locked the room from the outside. I grasped Nadia and we kissed. Nadia said, "Where did he go?"

"To the can. They just had a roust-out. Now they'll have peace and quiet for at least an hour."

She giggled.

"What are you fellows up to in there all the time?"

"We shoot the bull."

"I know. You talk dirty talk."

"How do you know?"

"I just know. I'll bet the most else you ever talk about is football."

"Not even that. We talk more about life."

"What do you mean 'life'?"

"You know, sort of philosophical stuff." I didn't really want to pursue the matter, but Nadia thought about that. Nosek had deliberately scribbled mathematical formulae all over the little window of the ferroflux room so no one could see in. Beyond it I could see the moving shadows of people crammed into sweat-suits with blue coveralls over them. The heating system had broken down and it was almost freezing in the work hall. They were calling it "Siberia." Nadia too had come to work that morning in a sweat-suit, with her grey skirt on over it. To take her mind off what I'd just said, I teased her about it.

"Don't laugh," she said touchily. "I could easily get inflammation of the ovaries in this weather."

I was unprepared for her response. She had never talked about delicate matters, and ovaries seemed like a delicate matter to me, if not to her. I said, "Well, at least you could get off work. You could easily pretend you have that kind of trouble since you're a woman."

"But I want to have children. If your ovaries get inflamed then sometimes you can't have them any more."

"What do you want children for?"

She looked at me uncomprehendingly.

"Every woman wants children. That's the way the Lord meant it. Don't you?"

"I don't like kids," I said with a nightclub scowl. "When they're small they're always filling their pants, then they ask stupid questions, then they get on your nerves and finally – "

"No, they don't!" she almost shouted. "They're – sweet and nice and – and everything," she said firmly. "You don't really live until you have children."

She frowned at me. We had never argued like this before. Ballon's silhouette passssed by the ferroflux room. We ducked down behind a vat, Ballon jiggled the door-handle and then disappeared. I was possessed by the devil of temptation:

"Ballon was a kid once too, you know," I whispered.

She frowned, then turned accusatory, burning eyes on me. "Why do you say things like that? So were you!"

"Of course I was. I pooped my pants and asked stupid questions and got on people's nerves too."

"No, you didn't. When you were a child you didn't. But you do now."

Her burning eyes were moist. She was so different. Different from me, that is, the same as all girls. Irena also sang the praises of children. Marie? "It's a beautiful thing to give life," she had said to me once.

"Sure, but it's rotten that everyone has to die."

"Except that before they die, most people have children."

"And so on," I said.

"And so on," said Marie, but in a different tone of voice.

"What's the point?"

"What's the point if you don't have children?"

"At least then one of the more embarrassing causal nexuses gets broken." Shortly before that I had tried to tempt her to go to the theatre with me. She had refused, and then gone to the same play with Kocandrle. I was angry, and my nihilism was born of that anger. "It's pure selfishness. You want children because you like them. It's purely for your own private pleasure. You couldn't care less that they're going to die one day."

Marie made a face. We were standing in the corridor and down below, in the schoolyard, some fools were batting a volleyball back and forth. The bell rang to signal the end of the break.

"My God, you are the philosopher. What did you get in the Intro to Philosophy course? An F?"

"They haven't taught that for years. And why should I have – "

"Don't you enjoy playing the sax?"

"What's that got – "

"Well, maybe my kids will like playing the sax too. Maybe they'll always be trying to get someone to go out with them – "

"If it's with someone like you – "

"Or someone like you. And isn't it selfish not to give them the chance?"

"Now wait a minute, Molly. Who's trying to – "

"I have to fly! I'm in for a grilling in chem."

She turned and ran off after a group of pupils rapidly disappearing into the chemistry lab.

Me a philosopher!

"Dan," said Nadia after a few moments of frowning silence. "What's – philosophy?"

"Well, it's about the meaning of life and stuff like that." Nothing more erudite came to mind. I was, after all, a mere apprentice.

"Is it something like – religion?"

"Something like that."

"And you talk about *that* in the toilets?"

"Where else? There's no other place in the factory. Besides, what do you girls talk about in the can?"

Nadia blushed.

"I'll bet you talk about boys."

She lowered those eyes.

"Sometimes. But we also talk about – about how tough it is to get food and stuff – and about children."

"I'll bet you talk about dirty things."

"I don't," said Nadia. "You do, though."

"I don't either. At least, not much. I just listen."

"But you're educated. And decent."

"I don't know about educated – "

"You've been to grammar school."

Outside the room a salvo of reports from the pneumatic hammers rang out. Puffs of steam rose like cloudlets of breath from giant maws.

"I listen to them because I'm curious," I said. "I also copy out the dirty stuff written on the walls."

"I don't believe you," said Nadia.

The devil of temptation whispered in my ear again: "Are there filthy things written on the walls of the women's can?"

"I don't know."

"You're lying, Nadia," I said. "That's a sin."

"Don't tease me!"

"And you read them, don't you? You read them and pretend you don't."

"I'm not talking to you any more." She stood up and walked over to the door, but it was locked from the outside. She stood there with her back to me, her dark blue sweat-suit filling out her grey skirt so that she looked almost full-bodied. No, she wasn't the same as the other girls, not the ones I knew best. She was different. I couldn't understand her. I only knew there were certain things you couldn't talk to her about. You could talk about almost anything with most girls if you chose your words cleverly enough. With Nadia it wasn't the words that were most important.

"Are you angry, Nadia?"

"Yes."

And yet she would neck with me, and here she was engaged to her Franta. Where was the logic in it?

I was young and foolish. There is no logic, I said to myself.

"But not very."

"Yes, very."

"Why?"

"Because you're being ugly with me."

"Me? Ugly?"

"You think ugly things about me. Maybe you even say ugly things about me, in the toilets."

"Nadia! I don't! I swear I don't do that!"

I went over to her and took her by the shoulders, thin under the sweat-suit.

"D'you really mean that?" she asked.

"Really. I swear."

She wiped away the tears. I stroked her feverish cheeks, then kissed her large mouth.

"I never talk about stuff like that, Dan. Except with Kveta at home. She's my best friend. She never tattles to anyone."

"D'you talk to her about me?"

She lowered her eyes. "I have to, because I'm real fond of you. But only nice things. I could never say anything bad about you, Dan."

"And I couldn't about you either, Nadia. And I don't talk about you, not even with my very best friends." I was telling the truth. I was lying.

Outside the door, Nosek began rattling the handle. Nadia's hot cheeks flared up. We jumped apart, and Nosek entered the room.

"Begging your pardon," he said. "Eisler came in and we've got to go back into the cold. Sorry about this, miss...."

A blushing Nadia left the ferroflux room. Nosek and I sat there for a few minutes longer.

"She's skinny, but apart from that, man, she's a dish. Got a sensational mouth."

"She happens to be a wonderful girl."

"Salt of the earth," he said, with a leer. "So how is she, then – is she good?"

"Everything Nadia does is good," I said. "Compared to her I'm a real nebbish."

•

20.12.68
Kostelec
Czechoslovakia

Dear Danny,
It looks to me like we castled right past each other. I been in Kostelec for almost two months now and here you are in Canada! We couldn't of dreamed that one up if we'd of wanted to. I kept wondering should I or shouldn't I but by that time we were into the Atlantic Ocean sailing around Africa and I sold everything in Australia, my house and all the furniture, so I said what the hell, I'll give it a burl no matter what. Also I thought it would help being a British subject and anyways you wrote that the lawyer told you she'd checked it out and all the court records were lost, and besides they drop charges after twenty years, so on I went. Well, you can imagine how glad Mom was, of course she hadn't seen me for twenty years. The poor woman is pretty old now and all bent over and she cried because Dad never lived to see me again. I live with her now, they let her keep one room and the kitchen, there's a tenant in the other room. They had to give up my old room when I ran away, so they put a tenant in there too. He's still there, married with a kid. There's a terrible shortage of flats and houses so not all that much has changed. I got work right away in a foundry, but it's not in Kostelec. I have to take the train to Rounov every day. At first getting up early in the morning really got to me. In Australia the only people who start work at six in the morning are farmers, but I got used to it by now. I make pretty decent money by the standards here and doctors are free. The only thing was I thought I'd have a new set of dentures made up for me since it's free but then I found out that they aren't free here either, so I kept my old pair from Australia.

But I tell you after twenty years, drinking real Pilsner straight from the tap is something. Or watching TV and hearing them speak real Czech. When I told Benda that he said I ought to listen to what they're actually saying. Now I know what he was talking about. Benda still looks almost the same, except he's put on a lot of weight. He's still a bachelor, same as me, but with him it's because he's left-handed when it comes to women, not like me. In Australia all I had to choose from *were those bloody tea-swillers or Eyetalian women and that type of thing, the pits. I also talked to Vahar, he came to see me and he's a real bourgeois, weighs about a hundred kilos with a gut like that friend of yours used to have, you remember, his parents owned the pharmacy? They say he's an officer in the army now, with the military band. There's hardly anybody left in Kostelec from your old buddies in the band except that painter, Rosta. He's married and also got locked up for a time but he's out again and he's got a cute little wife, a sales clerk in a fancy-goods shop, and a son that's the spitting image of him. He worked for a while in the mines but then they let him join the Party so now he's teaching again. And he's still keen on girls! There was a great scandal in the school where he teaches drawing because some of the girls posed for him naked and their parents complained. But it got hushed up on account of he's in the Party. Also those girls you used to hang around with are mostly gone, except for Marie Dreslerova, who married Kocandrle from the municipal office. They have a daughter and she'll be nineteen this year and I must say, buddy, she'd be worth the sinning. Her name is Dana. I also talked with her mother, you know I hardly knew her when we were young, she being a student and all, but I said to myself what the heck, I'm an old man now so I spoke to her and she was real nice to me and we talked, mostly about you. So I got the feeling, old buddy, that love never grows rusty.... It was damn stupid of you not to marry her. Women like her are hard to come by, and you certainly won't find any of them in your tea-swilling countries. And what kind of a life can she have with an old fart like Kocandrle? He's always sitting in the Beranek drinking beer, playing cards and he's got a paunch on him about as big as Vahar. But she's still as pretty as they come so I bought her a kind of kerchief in Hradec with negroes on it, Eyetalian import. I found out she gave it to Dana, but it don't matter because it looks nice on her too.*

*I've been round to see all the places we used to go when we were kids. Went to look at Hycmans' factory where they make toys now. In Biloves I went to get some mineral water for Mother and I also visited that old cottage on Cerna Hora where you hid out. I went to Dad's grave too and while I was in the churchyard I took a look round to see who else had passed on in the meantime. Ponykl is dead now, died of cancer, maybe you already knew. And that fellow Nejezchleba, the one you rolled the barrels with in the Messerschmitt plant, he was locked up for a long time and came down with a heart disease in the clink. I also found the grave of that bird from Cerna Hora, the one you fell for, Nadia Melicharova, she's buried right next to the Monument to the Victims of Nazism. They say she wanted it that way because the*

Germans did her father in. So I started feeling like old Methuzela because so many of them were gone, and I went to the Beranek and that old beard-plucker Lenecek was sitting there, and we got so pissed I almost missed my train to work next morning.

Yes, old buddy, it's a real pity you aren't here. We'd have a lot more laughs. Except I wasn't born yesterday and my eyes are wide open. Workers are not so bad off here, but you wouldn't get very far with your job nowadays. What's it like in Canada? Would there be any work there? I might show up one day to visit you. I'm a British subject and I have a British passport, so I've got an advantage over the others.

I also talked to Zdena Pastalkova. Her name is Rykrova now, she married young Rykr from the sweetshop. Both of them work in the old Mautner place on the looms. She's my cousin and she told me how General Jablonkovsky was in Kostelec for the 20th anniversary of the liberation. You probably remember him, a short little guy with red hair, the one Kurt Schnobel shot at while he was giving a speech up there on the 9th of May. And you must remember how a little girl in a folk costume recited a poem for him, and the general lifted her up in his arms along with the bouquay and so you called her the portable kid. Anyway later they locked up my uncle, that is her father, because he was a secretary in the People's Party and they arrested her mother too, because they said she knew about it. My uncle died in prison and my aunt did fifteen years and when the 20th anniversary of the liberation came round she was still inside. When the general came to Kostelec he didn't remember anybody, which isn't too surprising because they locked up no end of people, like old mayor Prudivy, who also died in prison, and the only bigshot left was Pytlik and now he isn't there anymore either. They say that they shuffled him off to be an ambassador somewhere after last spring. So the only one the general remembered was the portable kid and he was bound he was going to see her and you can imagine how embarrassing it was for them since she never got to go to school because of her father being a political prisoner and she had to work in the dyeing plant. But the general stuck to his guns so they arranged it and the old goat went crackers over her and the whole two weeks he was in Kostelec he never let her out of his sight. They had to give her time off at the factory and she went to all the bashes with him, even the one at the Party Secretariat. But the general's wife fell for her too and when they heard she was an orphan they asked her if she wouldn't like them to adopt her, and go with them to Moscow. Because at the Secretariat they'd told her she had to tell the general she was an orphan because there'd have been a scandal if

*the truth ever got out. The general's wife said she was the spitting
image of their daughter Marusiya who was killed at the front in the last
war, and instead of being jealous she got so fond of her she wouldn't
take no for an answer and finally they adopted her officially at the
National Committee so Zdenka now has three living parents. And
they invited her to Moscow, but when she actually tried to go there
because she'd never been out of the country before, they fixed it at the
Secretariat so she didn't get a visa and she ended up going nowhere.
Then she got married. She's a real pretty girl with big wide eyes, and
anyways the general died and they let her mother out of prison but the
poor woman also died soon after because she took a stroke in prison.
Zdenka has two kids, both boys and she's happy.*

    *Well, buddy, I've kind of run off at the mouth here but you know,
there's always something going on here, not like in Australia where it's
big news when a dog dies. Write me what it's like in Canada. Maybe
I'll come over to see you some day, it's a real shame we crossed paths
like that and never met.*

    *All the best to you,*

> *Your old buddy*
> *Prema*

•

I lose my temper. I shouldn't, but I do. I see red. I see blood. Not my own.

    "Sugar!" I shout. "Sugar darling! Do you go along with this? With
*this*?" and I read her the bulletin of Camstarve, that organization which,
according to its own blurb, exists "to help eradicate hunger, poverty, injustice and inequality in the world."

    I read: "Angola brought Camstarve face to face with a new problem,
because there were several competing liberation movements there fighting
both against each other and against the Portuguese. After careful investigations, however, the directors of Camstarve have decided that we must support the MPLA, a movement which, although it is by far the smallest
numerically, is the only one with roots in a cross-section of the whole Angolan people and does not derive its support from any one of the tribal groupings. Events after the declaration of independence have confirmed this conviction."

    "And isn't it true?" Sugar asks stubbornly. "Savimbi only represents
his own tribe. And so does Holden Roberto."

    "And what percentage of the whole Angolan population do those two
tribes represent, Sugar?"

    Sugar is the founder of the college Marxist circle, but she has no answer. She is too simple-minded for Marxism. I turn to the chairman, for he, as *primus inter pares*, will certainly reply. He smiles the smile that the British of imperial times reserved for all foreigners.

"No doubt you'll also point out the presence of Cuban troops," he begins. I already know his speech by heart. It bears that stamp of unchanging wisdom which now, thanks to the well-armed Cuban soldiers, is already canonized wisdom. "But as society develops there are situations where a quantitatively insignificant minority may be in the right. In such cases, the great powers who are ideologically closest to them have not only the right but, more important, the responsibility, to intervene and aid that minority, because otherwise social truth would be defeated. And in any case, the old imperialist powers did it all the time – "

"And were they supporting social truth?"

"Don't try to trip me up on details. Of course they weren't. But those who today are in the right are simply using their own methods against them."

"In Angola today, as far as I know, there are only natives. The imperialists are staying clear of it."

Freddy Cohen, whose pipe creates an atmosphere of comfortable ease in the common room, says nervously, "It would appear, Bill, that the MPLA in fact represents only a small minority. I don't mean to say we should ignore the demands of minorities, but to force those demands on a majority, and on top of that, to invite a foreign army in to help you do it – well, we've just condemned the same thing in Vietnam...."

Poor Freddy. An incurable American. The Canadian Brit is one revolution ahead of him. I am two ahead. The Canadian Brit declares haughtily – for haughtiness is a tone appropriate to those who are one revolution up, if only theoretically – "The MPLA is the only group whose ideology is not tribal. Savimbi and Roberto are quite simply men of the past. Subjectively they may well be honourable men, but objectively they are attempting to preserve tribal customs that prevent the Angolans from creating a unified Angolan nation."

I look at this gentleman. Perhaps he is right. But even if he is right, his truth smells of a strange lie. I've come across it before. I know where, of course. If there actually exists anywhere a genuinely international fraternity standing above nations and classes, then it is the fraternity of these men. Perhaps they do possess a sort of objective truth. But before I would live under their truth, and be worked over by their menmashers and their re-educators, I would rather consort with the cannibal Savimbi.

The chairman of the study circle strokes his old-fashioned British moustache and gazes triumphantly at poor Freddy Cohen.

"May I read you something?" I ask acidly, and without waiting for the first among equals to give his assent, I read from the same issue of the *Camstarve Bulletin*. It is a petition that Camstarve is asking its supporters to sign:

"To his Excellency the Right Honourable Jules Léger, Governor General of the Dominion of Canada. Aware that it is the policy of the Canadian government to replace the traditional culture of the native peoples of Canada by the dominant culture of Canadian society, we demand that the Canadian government recognize the Déné nation (Indian and Métis) as the sole owners of the traditional land of the Déné, including its mineral resources, and to postpone the development of projects that require the use of the traditional lands of the Déné nation – including the Mackenzie Valley pipeline – until such time as those traditional rights are formally recognized."

The chairman sits unmoved.

"The traditional rights of the Déné nation ought to be recognized, I agree," I say. "It's hard to object to that. The tribe of Jonas Savimbi – you do call it a tribe, don't you? – which by the way is about a hundred times larger than the Déné nation – this tribe, then, should give up its traditional rights in the name of enlightenment imported from overseas, is that it?"

Bill Hogarth will not be moved. He knows everything, like all those who know so little.

"That is something qualitatively different," he says with the sangfroid of an Englishman. "Canadian society has already destroyed the traditional culture of the Déné nation through greed. The victory of the MPLA will be a guarantee that the tribes of both Savimbi and Roberto will be able to preserve their national, or if you like, their tribal, particularities. It will merely eliminate their chauvinistic animosities – it will be a culture with a national form, and international con – "

"Didn't the American government eliminate the traditional animosities of the Indian tribes?"

Were he not still British, he would perhaps begin to lose his temper.

"Yes. In bloody wars."

"I don't know. It doesn't seem to me that Katyushas and T-54s are qualitatively any different from the Winchesters of the Texas Rangers. They are just a hell of a lot more effective and a hundred years later."

"The participation of the Cubans, with their weapons, is merely proof that – "

"Before the Cubans and their weapons intervened, it looked as though Dr. Neto and his supra-tribal apostles of national unity would be wiped out!"

I am seeing red. Even the Brit is finally losing his manners.

"That is precisely why international assistance was necessary – "

I explode: "My dear friend, the Cuban soldiers are no more and no less than a repayment of debts to the Soviets. Mr. Castro is paying his debts in what is traditionally called cannon-fodder."

"That's an insult to the fighting men of the *territorio libre!*" roars the Brit.

"And what you say is an insult to Savimbi and the soldiers of free Angola!" I roar back.

We are screaming at each other like two old fools.

"Gentlemen, gentlemen!" cries Freddy Cohen. "Calm down. Personally I think Cuba should not have intervened. It only makes for bad blood – "

"That it does. Literally. A lot of blood," I say.

"Danny," says Sugar unhappily, "what if the Cubans hadn't intervened – why, a minority was being threatened with slaughter."

"Perhaps, Sugar," I say. "After all, they're just poor black barbarians. Five hundred years under a colonial government. Dr. Neto is more civilized. He can play the harp. In Russian gloves."

She does not understand. How could she? She has never taken a course in Soviet film, and no one has ever informed her of Sergei Eisenstein's classic error.

A weariness comes over me. What do I know about Angola? But what do Sugar and her chairman know about it either? I know something about my own country: about international assistance, supra-national justice, the class solutions to problems. Is it any different in Angola? Why? Ought I to be a racist? Am I to believe that there are some things that miserable coloured barbarians don't need to live full lives?

I look at the red British face. He too has lit a pipe. I feel as though I am lying beneath the juggernaut of history, on which he sits with his pipe, eternally. From the height of his comfort he breaks my bones, and grinds a black face into the ground, eternally.

"Okay, Sugar," I say. "Let's leave it to the horses."

"What's that?" asks Freddy curiously. "Why to the horses?"

"It's a Czech idiom translated literally," I say. "It means that they have bigger heads, so they're cleverer. Bigger is always cleverer, which translates into another idiom in German: *Macht geht vor Recht.* Might before right. So let's talk about women. Sugar, when are you planning to get married? And would you marry a black?"

●

March 7th, 1970
Prague

Dear Dan,

Are you sad too, in far-off Canada? I feel wretched, Dan, I've never felt worse. I read Holan:

> And never say that the poet hyperbolizes.

He does not hyperbolize. I look into the mirror:

> ... the scored and wrinkled face of one who knows
> that even God, and not long after, regretted making man.

Something has happened to people. No one gets together with anyone any more; people don't believe each other. There is only envy.... You must have read the recantations of those who wish to go on publishing. But those poor wretches are mistaken. They will save nothing that way. Their friends hate them, their enemies despise them. And that terribly short memory, God, that brief little memory! Yesterday they gave their word of honour, today – And after all that it's impossible to write anything at all, as long as what happened is not reflected in it, because it did happen, Dan. Whatever was to come, they flattened us with an iron fist, and that is never just. It cannot be. The iron glove transmits no feeling to the heart. Yes, twenty years ago they were right when they said that the spirit of February 1948 must permeate everything we write. And today? They insist that 1968 must never be mentioned. It is true that one is now allowed to poeticize – I use that word deliberately – about things that were forbidden after 1948: love, flowers, nature. But one may write about anything else only if one omits the annus mirabilis as it really was, that is, as it was for almost everyone, except for that almost microscopic, unobserved minority who were on the side of the iron fist.

I haven't the strength to go on. The familiar merry-go-round has started up again: the ascendent generation of compulsive young writers willing to make the required omissions if only they are allowed to see themselves in print. Every ascendent generation is like that, I suppose. We made our omissions too, so we have no right to hold it against them. I just don't have the strength to go on. And I condemn those in power for so cynically exploiting the hunger of those writers. Because, Dan, I have finally reached the conclusion that there are all kinds of risks involved in freedom – but the risks of unfreedom are unbearable.

*I can't bear those risks any longer. I don't write. What is more terrible, I no longer write even for myself, "for the desk drawer." I only read occasionally what they write – the young, and those eternal old swine. How easy it would be to write satires of their regurgitations. But I no longer have the strength.*

*My old nightmare is returning: that shop window at Rupa. Who really won the great war, Dan? Who really won that stupid, terrible war?*

*Today we feel only vanity,*
*the grave has become mere earth,*
*a pre-Christian wind whines through all,*
*through fatal interstices between the laths ...*
*and they grabble vainly after life*
*and polish the brass of their delights*
*and twist and convolute their spines*
*And still the dogs howl, and sniff the wind,*
*and prophesy....*

*Do you know who wrote that? Holan. But in 1939-40!*
*That window at Rupa. Ah, that window!*
*Write to me, Dan. Perhaps in Canada you will find at least a little light – something to light up the age for an instant –*
*Yours sincerely,*
*Jan*

●

"They had this sort of room in the cellar, made of concrete," said the green man in his expressionless voice, "where they'd lock the delinquents up and then fill it full of water. There was no windows and the water come almost up to the ceiling, except they'd always leave about a centimetre of air. You had to stand on your tiptoes and stick your nose out of the water so you could breathe. In total darkness, and sometimes they left you there for twelve hours. And that's where Olda Sadlo lost his life. He drowned cause he didn't have no nose, just this hole in his head, see, and the water got in and he drowned."

"You ass!" said Malina.

"What if someone was so small they couldn't even keep above water on their tiptoes?" asked Kos.

"They treaded water," I suggested.

Vozenil shook his head. "He wouldn't've lasted long. They could raise or lower the floor according to how tall you was."

"Did they put you in there too?" asked Nejezchleba.

"Of course. I was in there at least ten times."

"You centipede!" said Malina. "I'd of liked to've seen you."

"That was nothing," said the master of horrors. "The worst thing in that reform school was another room with the lights on. It was a long thin room, made out of concrete too, and they'd lock you in there bare naked. Two walls was made of iron and they could shift them closer together. There was these long, sharp-edged spikes sticking out all over the place just like bayonets, about half a metre long."

"You stupid sloth!" said Malina.

"They had big wheels on the other side of the walls so they could be slowly screwed together. There was just enough space between them knives so that if you was quick enough you could twist yourself round so that, when the points of the bayonets touched the other wall and the walls stopped moving, you could stay twisted up between all them knives and you'd be okay. Except for the odd cut or two. Only not too many was that quick. Mostly they came away with real ugly cuts, sometimes right to the bone."

"Bullshit, you turd," said Malina. I looked at him in astonishment. "Clumsy bugger," he added.

Without a word the green man unbuttoned his coveralls, lifted up his cotton shirt, and undid his filthy underwear to reveal a green stomach with a long red scar stretched across it. Everyone bent down to examine it more closely. The green man puffed out his stomach and said, "Sometimes you had to stand all twisted up between them blades for three or four hours at a time, sometimes only on one leg. Nobody could do that. Everybody cut themselves a little."

"And shat themselves a little," said Kos.

"And pissed themselves a little," said Malina. "You fucking mammoth."

A ray of pre-spring sunlight filtered through the fly-spattered windowpane and fell on the green stomach. It must have been an ugly appendectomy. The green fellow did himself up, while the smoke from the homegrown tobacco made fantastical shapes in that long-ago ray of hope.

"The walls had different patterns of holes," Vozenil went on, "and each time they put the knives in different holes so that even if you went through it two or three times, you was never prepared for it. They kept track of the patterns they set for each guy, and it was never the same twice in a row. Each time you had to twist yourself different."

"You goddamn buffalo!" said Malina. "How'd you like to give us a demonstration? We'll all piss at you and you can twist yourself into funny shapes so we don't hit you."

"Once," said the chlorophyll man, "I had to hold myself like this for four hours."

He stood on one foot, his knee slightly bent, and put his other foot straight out ahead of him as though he were doing a Cossack dance. He leaned far forward with one arm, bent at the elbow, over his head, and the second one he stretched forward and twisted around as though he had rheumatism. Kos was getting ready to piss at him, but when he saw the position he was in, he stuffed his penis back into his overalls.

"I was surrounded by knives from both sides," said Vozenil, holding the position like a yogi. "One of them was right here," and he pointed to his stomach. "That time I couldn't last the four hours, and I had to let my stomach out. That's where this scar comes from. I'd had the biscuit – I wanted to commit hara-kiri. My guts spilled out. But they watch you through this hole in the wall and when my guts spilled out they pulled back the walls, unwound my guts from the blades, stuffed them back in again and took me off to the hospital."

Malina had run out of zoological insults. We stood in amazement over the green yogi. He was still in that contorted position, the only sign of discomfort being a slight darkening of his green complexion.

"You really know your stuff," said Nejezchleba. "Did they hang you up by the balls too?"

"Not that," said Vozenil. "But by my big toes they did."

Then he straightened out and rolled himself a cigarette from newspaper.

"I've heard about that somewhere," I said. "Wasn't there some kind of pendulum that was as sharp as a razor on the bottom edge and it swung back and forth over a bench where they strapped you down? And then they gradually lowered the pendulum until it cut you up, either crosswise or lengthwise?"

The green man turned an expressionless gaze on me. The sunlight ignited rusty sparks in the greasy tufts of his hair.

"You heard right," he said. "Only they didn't let the pendulum down. That was fastened solid to the ceiling and you had to suck your stomach in so you wouldn't get cut. Sometimes they left you like that for eight hours. If you let go, the pendulum would slit your belly."

"And your guts would fall out?" asked the fellow from the paint-shop.

"No. They always adjusted it according to how big you were so it would just cut your skin. The fellows who were worst off were those with bellybuttons that stood out."

Kos shut his eyes and whistled.

"Dinosaur!" announced Malina.

The lad from the paint-shop turned around, rushed over to one of the toilets and began to vomit.

"Boy, you've got to have tough nerves to listen to you," said Nejezchleba. "You ought to be X-rated."

The green man didn't even crack a smile. "I tell you, boys," he said, "there's nothing can touch me. Before they shifted me to the Reich, I was a grave-digger, and I seen some things that'd *really* make you shiver."

"You anaconda!" said Malina. "It's a wonder they didn't fucking bury you alive."

"Not me," said Vozenil. "But there were cases...."

•

They have rented the entire Benes Inn for the occasion, and the entire Benes family, in tuxedos and black silk dresses, are diligently at work, though today their smiles are not merely professional. The guests, dressed to the nines, intoxicated and thoroughly Czech, give stormy encouragement to the newly-weds, who are combining their efforts to cut a giant cake shaped like Karlstejn Castle. Sartorially, the bridegroom has broken all previous records. His wedding suit is black, but when he embraces the bride it begins to turn pink, intensifying until it is completely red. He first demonstrated this marvel at St. Wenceslas Church when he kissed the bride after the ceremony, and Father Hunak groaned because he thought it was the onset of a stroke. Here at the Benes Inn, Mr. Zawynatch is constantly changing colour, from pink to red then back to black again – that is, as long as his guests allow him to, for his bride is being passed from hand to hand more frequently perhaps than any other bride in the history of the Toronto Czech community. But the new husband observes the demand for his bedewed flower with fondness, his face wearing a permanent smile and his goatee beard nesting in the golden lace on his shirt-front.

Dotty, on the contrary and to general amazement, showed up in church wearing the classic, chaste white uniform of demure brides, enveloped in a thick white veil and wearing a garland of myrrh almost as large as Christ's crown of thorns. Which merely confirms my suspicion that all those creations she used to deck herself out in were meant to serve a single purpose. And it was in a good cause. Dotty has given herself in wedlock with dignity. Now she has laid aside her veil and her sweet face, made up like an Easter egg, beams with simple happiness, Max Factor and mother-of-pearl teeth.

Everyone is here. The rotund man is just finishing his fifth helping of sauerbraten, and he roars at the couple cutting the cake with the voice of a royal stag: "Go to it! Keep it up! Drive it in up to the hilt!" Frank, the haggard fascist, is listening to Mr. Pohorsky, who has a new, visionary message. Mr. Pohorsky has cut himself while shaving, and he looks old and diminished. Dr. Toth is here with his fiancée, imported at last from England, and she has turned out to be a Chilean beauty, born by some accident of fate on the Kerguelen Islands. She fits in well amid this gathering of Czech beauties. Even Jirina O'Reilly looks happy. She is here alone, for her kept man and master has developed a grudge against the reactionary Czech nation – and in addition the wedding coincided with a protest march against sexual discrimination in Andorra. During the ceremony Jirina played Wagner's "Here Comes the Bride" straight from the heart. While listening to it Mr. Senka was almost overcome by a cramp in his eyelids, but now he is gulping down champagne, and instead of the tiny myrtle sprig on his lapel he has pinned on (upside down) a large Czechoslovak flag. Margitka is here in a new dress – white, naturally – with a positively heathen *décolletage* equalled only by the one worn by the scintillating blonde, blue and beige Georgiana Akoratova. Margitka has a new platinum rinse and I am back in her good graces. Her face too radiates happiness, the kind that possesses the huntress when she finally runs the rabbit to ground. Bocar, for fun, has wound the white ribbon from his myrtle sprig through the spokes of his chrome-plated wheelchair. Mrs. Santner, the publisher, is gulping down cigarettes, but she has a new wig, ginger, somewhat Afro in style, and there is a magnificent pendant around her neck – a piece of Czech folk-art, she claims, and undoubtedly smuggled duty-free into exile. Mr. Sestak with his band of tramps, and Mr. Mrkvicka, stand at the ready around Jingling Johnnys made of crutches. Everyone is here, everyone. Only Veronika is missing, of course....

Veronika. I cannot fit into this general feeling of happiness. Euphoria does not come. I am weary. Shouts of delight and applause resound through the room. "And he's done it! Up to the hilt!" rejoices the rotund man, his voice rising above the tumult. Not even Mr. Senka is offended.

"So to get back to Vachousek," says Bocar, "the long and short of it is, they laid a trap for him. Uher was the one who masterminded it. Pankorek, the double agent, arranged the meeting between The Priest and Vachousek in his own flat, and when Vachousek showed up the cops jumped out at him from another room. Vachousek pulled out his gun and there was some confused shooting, during which Pankorek got it in the head. It's debatable whether it was Vachousek who killed him or not. He claimed, at least, that he shot at the others. Probably a shoot-out like that suited their plans, and Pankorek wasn't any more use to them after that. Vachousek got hit in the leg, so they overpowered him, and all Uher got was a graze on the ass. Except, you know how it is, Vachousek shot once, and for that you get the gallows, whether you hit anybody or not."

I can see my old foreman now, transformed, as he was that night, into an unlikely zoot-suiter. I can see him as I've never seen him before. "He sat there on death row for more than four months. Almost five," says Bocar. "Bad luck that was. It was right at the time when the Communists were giving people the rope wholesale, and the hangman couldn't keep up. They said he had bad dreams from it all, started to go loony – an odd hangman," says Bocar. "Most of those characters weren't so tender-hearted. One of them, his name was Jarda Zruda – good name for him, eh? Jarda the Monster –"

I see my old foreman in the cell, waiting for death. The terror of the war comes back to me and I feel cold sweat on my back. That cold winter Sunday afternoon – and yet it was not I who had been in a trap at all. I merely thought I was. It was the foreman who was in it. A terrible, conclusive, air-tight trap. I see him, and against that background of martyrdom Mrs. Dotty Zawynatch is dancing with a blushing suit of clothes. Was he terrified too? Certainly he was; everyone is. I am not afraid of death anymore, but that is because I do not know when it will come. Not even the foreman knew that precisely. But he did know it would be soon, it would be ignominious, ghastly, with all his senses intact. Jarda Zruda would gloat over that unique execution. As long as he lived, Jarda Zruda would remember those wonderful times when the hangman had nightmares. "... Zruda had this old worn-out joke, worn out except for the fact that of course it never wore out on the condemned man. They did their hanging twice a week, and the prisoners had to shave themselves for the occasion. No pampering like in the old days. No last requests. And no last meal before the execution. No indeed. Shave! And do it proper! Don't leave any stubble there, boy!" Bocar rumbles on, obsessed by his gruesome memories. I've heard this story three times now, how through the slot in the door they watched the prisoners lathering themselves, shaving with trembling hands, so that every last one of them cut himself, and had to stop the blood with alum. "And when they finished shaving, Jarda Zruda would come in, run his hand over their chins and roar, 'You call that a close shave? Get back in there and do it again!' And they would do it again, like little boys, the blood trickling from their chins. And then Jarda Zruda would come again and say, 'Back to your cells, gentlemen. The execution is postponed till Friday!' That was his worn-out joke. And you could tell that the poor buggers actually felt relieved. It meant nothing at all. A reprieve of two days. In fact two more days of fear. And yet they were relieved."

While all of that was happening we were building socialism. Vrchcolab, the boy wonder on his pedestal in the moonlight like Isa Miranda, charming green youth into a love of Stalin. While the foreman went through all that; it seems to me as though he went through it for me. I feel ashamed, desperate. Where is he, the foreman? He doesn't even have a grave. They gave him to medical students for dissection in anatomy classes, students who disemboweled him inexpertly, frittered him away bit by bit, put a piece of him between two slices of bread and planted it in the lunch-bag of the prettiest medical student. The worn-out jokes they play every-where. Or they put him in a communal grave – laid them in vertical layers eight feet deep, according to Bocar. "Once," he says, "they rehabilitated someone called Pech. A clear case of judicial error, and besides that he had an influential uncle, an old Communist. So his mother wanted to re-bury him. At that time I was washing floors in the police station so I heard what Jarda Zruda told her in that swinish lingo of his: 'Sorry, Comrade,' he said to the mother, who had come dressed in black. 'He's sixth from the top and it's been three years and who's gonna go rooting around in all that guck? And anyways, they're all mushed in together so how you gonna tell them apart?' The woman in black fainted on the spot, and can you blame her?"

I can see Kostelec now, that beautiful countryside, Cerna Hora, autumn, the town in the valley, the smoke rising from it. Vachousek the foreman. Why? What for? Millions have ended up in the multi-tiered graves of history, some of them immortalized in pictures from a barbarian age when people had not yet learned to be ashamed of their barbarism – broken bodies woven among wheel-spokes in Gothic paintings, the terrible suffer-ing of the crucified, men sawn in two, from the crotch to the head, a little dog beside them gnawing at a severed hand. But we lived in an epoch of prescribed art, of national and socialist realism. One painted beautifully. Delightfully. One wrote in a charming Czech....

"What's the matter?" I hear Bocar say. "Don't let it get to you. It's all over for him. Long over. He was straight. They didn't break him."

And what good did it do him, my foreman? When all we have is life, and only this one?

Applause, the dance is over, Mr. Zawynatch pales to a shade of grey, then to black. "My dear woman!" comes the thunderous appeal, "and now a spin with me!" Dotty smiles radiantly, the fat man presses her to his bosom, his moon-like face reddens. Dotty bounces off him as though she were on a well-sprung trampoline, the rotund man grasps her by the hand and begins jumping up and down like a rubber elephant ... Jirina O'Reilly steps gaily around the floor, her legs flashing ... Mr. Senka also has a go ... Mr. Zawynatch dances with the publisher and his suit too begins to turn an embarrassing red ... Bosch ... Brueghel ... it is all we have ... there is nothing else.

●

"Your trouble, Hakim, is the same as Sutpen's trouble."

This is the first time he has sought me out in my office, the first time we have been together alone, and I try to interpret the message in his eyes. In his lapel he is wearing a large green button showing a variation of the hammer and sickle, with a star and the letters MPLA. So he is supporting aid to cannon-fodder in a country that is not his own – but Hakim does not have a country. He is an outcast. To call it by its proper name, he is a deserter.

But he has come to see me of his own accord. If the voice in his eyes spoke only orthodox contempt, he would have come at most to rail against me, not to sit down, look at me, and pose questions in a contemptuous voice.

"I don't understand," he says. "Sutpen's trouble was innocence. If I understood you correctly in class, Sutpen's innocence was lack of awareness of the class nature of society. So where's the connection between Sutpen and me?"

"Did your instructors ever instruct you about the theory of spiral development?"

Of course they did. Communism is a return to that happy, protogenetic, collective society, but one twist of the spiral higher. That catechism is international. We know as little about the state of mind of people under Communism as we do about the state of mind of people in protogenetic societies. As far as I know, they were afraid of evil spirits.

"Yes," I say. "Faulkner's description in the seventh chapter of *Absalom, Absalom!* is a pretty fair Marxist analysis of the origin of class hatred. In fact, it's an excellent account of racism in class antagonism. Remember?" And I read: "'They (the niggers) were not it, not what you wanted to hit ... you knew when you hit them you would just be hitting a child's toy balloon with a face painted on it.' And then of course that most archetypical of scenes, when young Sutpen is forced to go around to the back door by a black in fancy livery and he loses his innocence. Only a true artist can do that: express ideas through a story, make the point that class antagonism runs deeper than racism, that one of the functions of racial hatred is to distract attention from social wrongs. So far, I would say, it's pure Marxism. Yet Faulkner ends up putting Lenin in the same boat as Hitler – long before Solzhenitsyn ever did. And in the most anti-racist novel he ever wrote, *Intruder in the Dust*, he not only says some very unflattering things about the Soviet Union, but he also – and the critics claim he does so rather vaguely – he also rejects the notion of any Yankee intervention whatsoever in support of the Southern blacks."

"Faulkner could not overcome in ideology the limits that.... On the one hand he's a humanist, on the other he's a Southern aristocrat.... He couldn't stand the thought that his prejudices are no different from...."

Although it no longer ought to, the infallibility of the pigeonholes astonishes me yet again: the human personality neatly divisible into aspects which can complement each other or just as precisely limit each other. Everything that conflicts with this pigeonhole wisdom is a prejudice.

"Hakim," I say, "Southern aristocrats aren't the only ones who may not know how to overcome some things through philosophy. Perhaps Faulkner's prejudice was his wisdom. The wisdom of a writer is different from the wisdom of your instructors. One Czech poet – you don't know him, nobody knows him, because he is condemned to obscurity by the minority language he wrote in – wrote: '... the poet's fleeting heart beats strongest in small stories.... Knowledge of events is nothing to him, and science, that cow on stilts, is nothing' – "

"That's irrational."

"You have to take that into account. What we feel is obviously more important than what we know. That's what we live for. We may think we live for wisdom, but in fact we're living for the pleasure wisdom brings us. Perhaps our feelings do guide us to the most reasonable solution. Remember Hawthorne? We are Epicurean beings. Maybe our greatness lies in our irrationality. In the way we sometimes irrationally go against reason in order to achieve rationality. Who knows? I don't."

"You're talking like a preacher." Hakim frowns. "In paradoxes."

"So I'll make it dry and clear. If Faulkner rejects a Yankee solution – that is, an imported solution to the racial problem – he rejects it because it's an outrage to the intelligence of his compatriots. Every violent import – and I repeat: *violent* import – is such an outrage. Ideas can be imported without outrage only in the form of ideas, not with weapons. Every *conquistador* treats the population of the country he has conquered as inferior – he makes that plain to them through conquest. But if there is anything really inferior in all this, it is those ideas which can win out only through force of arms."

"But that would mean that every revolution...."

"Yes." I nod. "Every violent revolution ends with mass exodus back to the ideals that have been violated by the revolution itself."

"Examples! Give me examples!" cries Hakim, as Wendy once cried out for examples of a just war. I try again to read the dark Semitic eyes. Do I see in them a desperate and therefore hopeful flash of doubt? The Venerable Fathers of old used to claim that doubt was the beginning of faith. I think they were wrong. Doubt is the end of faith. But perhaps it is also how wisdom begins. The wisdom that ultimately leads us, in the realm of the Venerable Fathers, to Jesus Christ. Not because He allegedly died for us on the cross, since at the very most that was His own private illusion, but because He was such a kind person. He always stuck by those who had been humiliated. Always. And with all of them. Not, like Angela, only with some. He was a naive, socialist Christ, not like the Marxists who rule with tanks behind them in my country, the Angola of Europe –

"Hakim," I say. "I'm not going to give you any examples because you're innocent. Just like Sutpen in the mountains of West Virginia, when he had never imagined ... 'a land divided neatly up and actually owned by men who did nothing but ride over it on fine horses or sit in fine clothes on the galleries of big houses while other people worked for them' – "

"That's a picture of capitalism, not socialism," he interrupts me. "I know a country like that and I'm living in it. I'm not innocent just because I'm a socialist."

"You're an innocent socialist, Hakim." Now I can read the answer in those dark eyes. There is conflict in them. Is he on the road to action? A finger pressing a trigger is not the only form of action. "It would be a good idea if you lost your innocence before you come across that black in livery. Before he sends you round to the back door. If you lose it before that, what happened to Sutpen won't happen to you."

"The preacher again," he says with a wry smile. "More paradoxes."

"Then it won't happen to you, as it did to Sutpen, that you'll have to accept filth, even when it disgusted him, as it will you, because unlike him you won't believe there is no other way to reach the goal except through filth." And like a preacher with a Bible, I raise Faulkner and begin to read: "'All of a sudden he discovered, not what he wanted to do but what he just had to do, had to do it whether he wanted to or not.... And that at the very moment when he discovered what it was, he found out that this was the last thing in the world he was equipped to do because he not only had not known that he would have to do this, he did not even know that it existed to be wanted, to need to be done ...!'"

Hakim scowls. "Faulkner in his bourgeois-mystical phase."

"Faulkner in his Hemingway phase," I say. "Trying to understand what he really feels instead of feeling what he is supposed to feel ... trying to feel only what he really feels and not what he thinks he ought to feel. Struggling with the complexity that is the essence of our human world. Anti-aesthetic Faulkner. Faulkner concerned with analysis, not illustrating the ancient truths of the heart, which are in fact just as complex as atoms. Post-Democritean Faulkner – "

"A preacher, not a scientist."

"I only hope, Hakim, that you realize what that 'last thing in the world you are equipped to do' is. But I also hope that you won't give in to fatalism, that you'll decide in the end you don't have to do it, that you'll look for another – "

"But it has to be done!" cries Hakim, the black angel. "And I will do it! I will struggle! Because it is a just struggle!"

Even so, I sincerely hope that the Southern aristocrat has provided a counterbalance to the pamphlets.

"Struggle, Hakim, but don't be cruel. Don't accept the rules of the game. That's only innocence one twist of the spiral higher. A just cause can become terribly polluted by injustice – "

"The world is struggle! Irreconcilable antagonism, as long as – " The brochure's wisdom flies out of him – or their half-truths, their demi-wisdom.

"The only irreconcilable antagonism is the absence of antagonism, Hakim," I say. "Because that does not exist. There exists only the iron lid, and when that comes down...."

Am I right? Perhaps. I am speaking in paradoxes, and they are only partially true, I know, but they roust the intellect out of its winter's sleep of adaptation. But does not the same hold true for the brochures? Those shocking half-truths? Those half-educated simplifications, prodding the indifference of established scholars so that some of them join the great movements of simplification, which then radically shake the world? Leaving their intellect behind, they lend the movement only their names, and someday those same names will prod the children of those movements back to a time when scholars were still educated, scientific, indifferent to the ways of the trigger, but active in the search. When they helped with beaver-like teeth *de omnibus dubitare* – the only thing antagonistic to man is the absence of antagonism – of contradictions perhaps not antagonistic, but of contradictions –

I think of Veronika. How she loved it in Canada, yet as she listened to that record in Milan's flat, her nostalgic contradictions – the longing to possess everything – that immoderation – perhaps the most human of all characteristics –

Beneath the window of my office, across the plain towards the lake where once great Manitou, a great Raven. *Havran. Voron* –

•

3 Feb 1972
Munich

*My dear transoceanic Brimpaunch,*
*Heartfelt greetings from an old socialist, now languishing in the*
*bosom of capitulatism. The buggers have finally forced me to work!*
*Me, who am accustomed to lounging about while the money flows in,*
*tossing off a play now and again on the side. Now I'm expected to*
*write and write and write, one damn screenplay after the other, and it's*
*not that they don't like what I write, not at all, but after all it's their*
*own capitalist money they're putting into it. So they hum and haw and*
*research the market and the results are usually pretty pale because*
*there's no porn in my stuff. So they want me to slip in a little*

technicolour fornication. Not that I'm unwilling to prostitute myself. After all, I've done it often enough in politics, and in both art and politics you meet many the whore, though as you well know prostitution was the dues you had to pay back home for occasionally striking a live nerve, so they wouldn't decide to strike one of your live nerves. But now I'm trying in vain to explain to the Krauts that I have always lived a decent, monogamous married life, that we always did It with the lights out, that I've never even read any theoretical stuff about It. After all, I can't give them something I don't know first hand, because I've always written straight from experience, or at the very most from fear. They suggested I should at least go to the movies and see how it's done. But I look old for my age and I couldn't bear to have some pretty little usherette in one of those Schweinkinos think I'm a dirty old man. So I haven't been able to work myself up enough to go to a Schweinkino yet and as a result I just can't dish out the porn the capitalists desire; all I can produce are moral parables. They were great hits back home because they don't have any movie houses there for dirty old men. Here, of course, moral parables don't break any box-office records and it's practically impossible to find anyone crazy enough to invest money in morality. So I'm living on advances, and even though I always finish the works right on schedule, so far they always put them way to the back of the stove, so I have no assurance quousque tandem the advances will keep rolling in. Do you think there might be an opening for me in Canada as a card hustler? Or have you got any connections in Las Vegas? I can still play a pretty fair hand of poker, just need a little polishing up is all.

What a fool I was not to stay behind in our occupied homeland, brother. Look at that Kopidlno. A muttonhead, literally one of God's dumb little animals, an endearing but compulsive writer pious to the tune of ten painful rosaries a day and queer as boots into the bargain. And look how he's raking it in now! He's pulling one manuscript after another out of his desk drawer, stuff the revisionists wouldn't have touched with a barge-pole, all about the delicate problems sensitive souls have, basically homosexual. And now they print every word he writes. And he goes on gaily penning his reviews and his glosses and his feuilletons and everything, according to that wonderful axiom: Let the Commies slit each others' gullets, it's got nothing to do with me! I want to be published, and I will give out for anyone who will publish me. And so he puts out, does our little queen, for everyone, and they publish him and publish and publish, more and more and more. And of course that's all he cares about, not whether anybody actually reads the stuff. That is beside the point.

*But why didn't I stay home! On the other hand I always wanted to make people laugh, and to do that people have to be able to read the stuff you wrote, and such things the Commies would rather not print — and rightly so. Unless I were to shift over to writing straight crime stories, but unfortunately I don't know how to do it. To this day I don't know why the ostrich can't fly. It's a bird, isn't it?*

*And then, too, I was a Commie and now the Commies are getting their just desserts and the shit is coming down on their heads. I guess there's a certain historical justice in all this, and I've always been one for evading justice. First it was class justice, and to evade that I joined the Party. Today it's historical justice and so I defected to the Reich. But back then I was so thick-skulled a few people had to hang before it began to dawn on me, and even then it was a long slow dawn because I still figured it was best to stay in the Party and try to edify the comrades, having an unshakable faith in the edificability of people, even comrades. Finally I realized that some people are completely and utterly unedifiable, because they've already been so edified they can't be edified any more.*

*So I betrayed the whole works and fled from historical justice, and being still thick-skulled (though less so now) I came to the Reich instead of going to the Kerguelen Islands where they'll never get their tanks because there's no room. So now back home the Party is administering historical justice to those comrades who have not yet been sufficiently edified — I mean the ones who haven't been edified to the point where they can be edified no more. I hope that they are edified at last and that they throw their whole weight behind the status quo because, as Engels says, wisdom lies in the comprehension of stupidity. The very same historical justice has fated me to become a script-teaser and maker of pornographic films, which is like asking Solzhenitsyn to write a new Soviet national anthem. If I consider why I'm here, it's basically for a rather odd reason: when those Soviet war chariots rolled in, I shat myself for fear I'd shit myself all over again later on and let myself be edified to the point where I could be edified no longer. In fact, I defecated to the West so that I could act like Master Jan Hus from Husinec, and stand in the truth and defend the truth, except that I improved on his burning example by preserving myself for the nation, and instead of letting myself be dragged off to Konstanz I defected to Wycliffe and from here, under his protection, I bravely condemn the cardinals back home who, with cold and therefore physically harmless flames, burn the gullible faithful who remained in Konstanz because they think you can talk a cardinal out of it. You can't.*

*One of those gullible faithful, my dear Canadian bourjoy friend,* was here recently, none other than our mutual friend the kid, Vrchcolab, Jan. As in Hus. And I tell you, he is a real Hus. When he could still come here to see me I told him they wouldn't do him the pleasure of putting him in jail. And they didn't. You probably know that when they stopped letting him travel abroad he started issuing various highly treasonous declarations to the Western press – but they let him run around loose for a while, though for all the effort he put into getting himself arrested the poor goose didn't deserve such a fate. And now get this. I'm sitting in the lobby of the Hotel Graf Etlü, where I occasionally hie me to play tarok with a madman who has commissioned me to write a realistic screenplay based on Andersen's tale of The Nakid Emperor (he's an old queen and has a young boyfriend he wants to slip into the title role), when all at once who do I spy but the kid himself, in a rather threadbare confection from Carnaby Street, slinking across the lobby. I tell you, old cynic, I was so glad to see him after all these years that I stood up from my game of tarok and laid a double Khrushchev on him before he had a chance to recover from his astonishment, a rather unpleasant astonishment at that because he had two goons from the international assistance brigade glued to his heels and looking as though they were right at home in the Etlü. I first noticed them when they stopped, probably trying hard to remember mug shots of traitors to see if they could identify me. But I've changed a lot. I've grown a Kaiser moustache to compensate for the fact that my hair has all but given up the ghost from overwork, and I also wear capitalist spectacles made of genuine tortoiseshell, whereas back home I had rimless specs from the Eye Optics National Enterprise, the kind that give you eggzema. And then the poor kid says, "Ahoj! How are you? Well, I hope," then he lowered his voice, "but if you wouldn't mind letting go of me. They even follow me into the toilets." I realized that I'd made a foe paw, but I snapped to at once and played out a little étude on the theme of The Great Mistake. In my very best Bavarian German, straight out of a two-litre beer stein, I implored, "I beg your pardon, sir, but you did so remind me of my poor dead wife!" I did it all clearly and articulately, hoping that the goons from the international assistance brigade understood enough German to be taken in. And Kid Vrchcolab looked at me with an awful, and I mean awful, baleful look, a kind of hangdog look, you know, like when you take a dog's bone away from it, tie a tin can around its tail and then kick it out into the nut-freezing cold saying, "Go on, pussycat, git, git."

I'll never forget that look as long as I'm alive. It was like our whole country looking out at me, from the deep dark depths of some Russian Orthodox enlightenment, the kind of black light that the old whore

Vaclav Vonavka yclept Rezac once wrote a novel about in better times.

And the next day the tragedy peaked – a huge article in the Süddoitsher Kurieranzeiger (which, for your information, you uninformed Canadian, is an unabhängige Zeitung which, you Anglophony troglodyte, means a newspaper independent of the facts, dependent only on fraternal assistance channelled through the Deutsche Demagogische Republik). And it said there was always talk in the bourzhwa media about so-called dissident writers in the C.S.S.R. being under house arrest or police surveillance if not actually undergoing re-education, and yet only yesterday one of the leading figures of the so-called dissident movement, Jan Vrchcolab, attended the première of his new play, an adaptation of the reactionary czarist playwright Nureyev. Is this not proof enough, asked this independent journal, that all the stories about a cultural Biafra in the C.S.S.R. are a tissue of lies fabricated by the forces of international reaction? Herr Vrchcolab spent three days moving quite freely (they put that in italics, not me: they couldn't have been informed) around Munich and refused to give interviews. Clearly, the newspaper said, he knew very well it would be difficult to explain wie es möglich ist, that he can travel freely to West Germany, when people like him in Prague allegedly can't even fart without the police knowing about it. That is a free translation of the sentence: sich nicht einmal an die Toilette begeben zu künnen vermögen dürfen, or something like that.

I agree the kid would have a hard time explaining that one. It's even harder for him to explain in Prague than it is in Munich. I deliberately went to the WC of the Graf Etlü, locked myself in a compartment and poked a hole in the wall with my pocket corkscrew. I waited there for what seemed like hours until the kid finally came to relieve himself. And sure enough, the internationalists came right in there with him. They did not relieve themselves, but merely stood about three paces away and followed his every movement with eagle eyes lest he try sticking some secret message from Prague under the bowl with the chewing-gun.

So I mentally forgave him, not that I have a great deal to hold against him. He means well and he always did. But he makes me think terribly suspicious thoughts, and I wonder whether those who mean well shouldn't occasionally just be a smidgen more swinish, because this is a swinish world, and I don't see how you can establish decency any other way than through indecency.

From which, I conclude to my horror, it should be clear to you that I'm still a Leninist.

*Forgive me if you can. And anyway, you always passed for a Christian wherever you were. Maybe a little too clever by half, but all the same you ought to forgive me. Besides, I might also remind you that it's your Christian duty to do so.*

*But I ought to try to establish a more cheerful note to end on. My daughter Janka has learned to speak German so fantastically well that she can talk just like Ilse Seligerova, if you still remember her. She was a kind of pretty, fleshy blonde in a dirndl. Of course my daughter Janka doesn't wear a dirndl. Now she's going out with some Bavarian palaeontologist (they claim it's a legit science, a German science, but I can't see that it's good for anything at all; something like dialectic materialism), but she's forever nagging at him, often quite nastily (I wonder who the child takes after? Did you ever have something going with my wife Janka that I didn't know about and later attributed to myself, erroneously?). She calls him a thick-skulled Kraut, simply because once in a while the poor naive lad timidly suggests to her that if Janka wouldn't object, he'd kind of like to, you know, perhaps not vote for the Christian Democrats, but the Social Democrats instead. Or he whispers even more timidly in her ear that if it doesn't upset her too much, he would, with all due apologies, like to express the opinion, which is not final, you understand, that perhaps something somewhat more substantial might be done to meet the cultural needs of the Turkish and Yugoslavian Gastarbeiters, of course, he's willing to stand corrected on this, but something more, perhaps, than pornographic films might be provided. It's like pouring gas on a fire. What a delight to hear that girl swing the lingo. The only thing that mystifies me is why the palaeontologist hasn't long ago given Janka a swift boot up the – but how shall I say this politely yet unambiguously? – up the* Arsch, *when the sweetest thing I ever heard her say to him was,* Halt's Maul, du Trottel! Du bist aber ein Idiot, Harry! Das ist ganz unglaublich, dass es im zwanzigsten Jahrhundert solche Dinosaure noch immer gibt! *He's as tickled as a clam that she calls him Harry and not Horst, which is his real name, because he was born in 1942, but that, ideologically, is not his fault though he's still ashamed of it. Of course I'm not with them when they go off together to dig up dragons' teeth or whatever it is they do when they're alone, and what they do when they are alone I don't know and don't want to. I'm an old-fashioned father and I hope he behaves honourably. Although he'd be better off giving Janka a boot up the* Arsch *to defend his own honour.*

*Otherwise I'm quite satisfied with the palaeontologist. He's a* Dozent *in the university here, he's got tenure and he's just published an eight-hundred-page* Werk *called* Kurze Einleitung in die Theorie der

Stosszähne der Dinotheria von der Süddeutschen Ebene um München, *or since you've almost certainly forgotten your German, you Anglophile,* A Brief Introduction to the Theory of the Tusks of Dinotheria in the South German Plain around Munich. *It's about creatures I've never heard of in my life. If you ask me he fabricated the whole shebang in the interests of his career. But he claims that because of this fabrication he's in line for a full professorship, and he claims that he's only waiting for the appointment before he does the honourable thing by our Janka, the old whoremonger.*

*I'm going to have to finish. Janka (the wife) is after me to get to work. So on the basis of those advances I'm going to work on the* Nakid Emperor. *The producer doesn't expect me to come up with any fornication, so I'll be able to satisfy him. I've seen a naked fellow before, in the army, so I'll be able to remain faithful to the principles of authenticity.*

*Next time, my fellow countryman and Canadian, I hope I'll write you something more relevant and uncompromising, and not just a load of superficial pasquinades.*

> *Your*
> *Zurückheil Glücker*
>
> *(that's how I've translated my name now I'm a citizen of the Reich)*

●

Irene pulled her toys out of the suitcase with the breathless enthusiasm of youth. When we arrived at Yvette's Hotel on the Place Convention, and found ourselves alone in a beautiful Parisian *fille-de-joie* chamber with a wide double bed and a bidet hiding behind a folding screen, she produced a package she had smuggled into the land of love from the Lovecraft shop in Toronto. It contained twelve condoms. Now I stand looking at those apostles of natural vice, spread out on the non-connubial bed, and the disgusting rubber protuberances on them make me feel slightly ill.

"Ugh, Irene!" I say to the girl standing modestly beside this display in an elegant dress bought especially for Paris, entirely convinced that she has made me a gift of unconventional delight. "What are they?"

"Safes."

"I thought they were special educational models to demonstrate what malignant tumours look like."

"Are you kidding?"

"Well, what do you think?"

She is uncertain, but concludes that I must be kidding.

Gazing at the horrors, I ask, "But aren't you on the pill?"

"Of course I am!" She blushes unexpectedly.

"So what are these for? We might hurt ourselves or something."

"You know what they're for."

"Sure, to prevent pregnancy and disease. But you're on the pill and while we're here I take it you intend to make love exclusively with me. Or am I mistaken?"

"It's supposed to be better with them on."

"But, Svensson," I say. "Those things are for arousing bodies that are resistant to sensual delight. Look, you're making me feel like a corrupter of youth. Let's go to the movies instead. There are some beautiful European films on here, Resnais, Bresson, Visconti...."

Red to the ears, she gathers her horrors from the bed and stuffs them back into her suitcase.

"Or we can read. We've come here for reading week, after all."

For that, to be precise, is why we're here. At home – not that they were overly concerned – she announced that she was going to spend reading week in the family's hideaway in the Rocky Mountains. Instead, we met at the airport and skipped across the ocean in a jumbo. I am sampling the perks of the Western world in the last quarter of the twentieth century. There is something about Yvette's Hotel that reminds me of Rosta's cottage, the scene of many an unsuccessful attempt and the final resting-place of many an unused condom.

"Okay," says Irene. "Make fun of me if you like. But I still love you."

"How nice," I say. "So get washed, dressed and powdered and let's take in a Paris evening."

She retires obediently behind the folding screen. Her dress flies over the top, followed by smoke-coloured pantyhose and the other miniature parts of her *ensemble du fling*. The splashing of water. I listen to discover whether or not the bidet is in use. Irene will certainly be curious about a device like that, relatively unknown even in the finest Toronto households. But she does not dare use it. There is also the possibility that she does not know what it is. God knows whether she's read *Tropic of Cancer* or not. Her knowledge and the gaps in it are sometimes surprising.

She emerges naked, blushing again, but she walks confidently, aware of her firm pliability and her liberated estate. From her suitcase she plucks two other scanty accessories, slips into them and tosses over them a magnificent creation which she tells me is from Altman's of New York. She touches a little Spirit of Fifth Avenue behind her ears (now back to their normal colour) and is ready to imbibe the vices of Europe.

We are sitting in *Les Deux Magots*. I tell her that Hemingway sat here too. Irene says, "I wish Wendy could see us here. Or Dianne."

A girl from Kostelec on a secret rendezvous in Carlsbad. Life is international.

"Or Rosemary," I say.

"Well ...," she says uncertainly.

Sitting at the tables around us are American tourists and people who may be artists. We are drinking Pernod. In Paris it is inimitably spring. It overpowers Irene, and me as well. It is wonderful to sit here with this beautiful Scandinavian girl who despite her brave self-confidence is still full of the wonder of life. The air is redolent of Parisian exhaust fumes. Irene has never been here before. She has only been once in Kiruna. Kiruna is not Paris.

"Let's come here again, shall we?"

"But we've just got here."

"But we'll do it again. When...."

"When?"

"When we get married."

"What makes you so sure I'll marry you, Svensson?"

"It's obvious," says my Nicole, "because I'm going to marry you."

Her tone is formal. She is learning. Before she turns me out to pasture, perhaps I shall be able, after all, to teach her something of the ancient art of conversation.

"In that case it can't be helped."

She looks at me. Pernod on an empty stomach? Or are Marie Dreslerova, Irena, Lucie, really looking at me through those grey eyes? They say that returning in daydreams to an idealized youth is the first sign of old age. In that case I must be Methuselah. I am even idealizing this Swedish-Canadian girl. She gives me a droll look.

"The idea doesn't exactly seem to fill you with delight, sir."

"Oh, it does," I say. "But it's too good to be true."

"We'll make an interesting couple. Everyone will think I'm your daughter."

"Almost my grand-daughter."

"Maybe. They'll say, 'You have a delightful daughter, Professor.'"

"A pretty little Lolita."

The pearly teeth, well protected since childhood by fluoride, sparkle in the Paris evening.

"I'm already too old to be a Lolita."

"Poor old Svensson."

"Why can't you be younger?"

"Why can't *you* be younger?"

"Then you couldn't marry me."

The night is warm, the colourful capitalist crowd flows slowly down the boulevard. The Pernod is fragrant. A man in a top-hat walks by, out of an Evelyn Waugh story, and a couple of drunk Americans.

"We'll come here again, on our honeymoon," says Irene.

"Oh no. We're going somewhere else for our honeymoon."

"Where?"

"Do you know Lovecraft?"

She blushes. "Well," she hesitates, "I bought those – things – at Lovecraft."

I laugh, and a wrinkle appears on the Scandinavian brow. My Nicole is a little hurt once again, but not too much.

"What's so funny, wise guy?" she asks, piqued. "Well, I'll give you that. They *are* stupid. I'll throw them away – "

"Nicole," I say. "On our honeymoon, we will go to the Mountains of Madness."

"To the Mountains of Madness? Oh, I see." She relaxes, accepting the game of fantasy. I see that she is, after all, still not very well versed in American literature. "Okay. Where are the Mountains of Madness?"

"Much farther away than Paris."

"Where?"

"In the Antarctic."

This disappoints her.

"But there's nothing there," she says. "Kathleen Young went there with her family. It's all ice, snow and weather stations. And penguins. They are funny," she admits. "But apart from that, there's nothing. The only ones who go there are people who've been everywhere else, just so they can say they've been to the Antarctic too."

"Kathleen Young never made it to the Mountains of Madness."

"But where are the Mountains of Madness?"

"South of the South Pole."

Her disappointment disappears. She suddenly recalls how I have educated them.

"D'you mean Symzonia? That tunnel that runs along the axis of the earth? The one where the Atlantic flows into the Arctic Ocean?"

"You get an A, Svensson. Except that there's no tunnel there."

"But Mr. Pym saw it with his own eyes."

"But Mr. Verne, when he set out in the footsteps of Mr. Pym, did not."

"Maybe he was as observant as Kathleen Young. He only saw penguins." My Nicole is beautiful, young and – free. For no logical reason, I think of poor Nadia. The girls of Kostelec who stayed there. They were never in Symzonia. "And Kathleen never saw the Mountains of Madness either," she adds.

"She went there on a guided tour."

"And how will we go?"

*Les Deux Magots* is full to bursting. I order another round of Pernods. Alcohol and literature, two faithful, destructive friends. The ghosts walk by, poor Scott, vulnerable Hem, Bill just in for a brief spell, alien to the poetry of this city, mad Ezra, selfish Joyce, Gertrude the lesbian. They drink, the ghosts of Paris, risen from the dead. They sit here with us, and also poor Nadia ... astonished ... she gazes round with her glowing eyes, like Ligeia's.... "Oh, it's beautiful here!"

"Hawthorne wanted to go there. A pity he never did. He might well have made it to the Mountains of Madness."

"Shall we go with Hawthorne?" asks Irene breathlessly. "In spirit?"

I shake my head.

"No. With Lovecraft."

"Stop it!" she says in genuine anger. "Here we are having such a nice talk. I'll never go to Lovecraft again, if you don't want me to. And that's a promise."

"Svensson, Svensson," I shake my head sadly. "Here you got an A, and you don't even know that Lovecraft was an American writer."

"Really?" She stares at me with innocent eyes.

"You get an F."

"I'm going straight back to my hotel and I'm going to start to read and I won't budge an inch from the room and I'm just going to read and read. After all, this is reading week," she says. "Now tell me, please, Professor, who was Lovecraft?"

"A kind of hack writer," I say. "He imitated Poe. Wrote macabre stuff. In fact he wrote only a few brilliant pages in his life. Only one scene."

"What about?"

I notice that the artists, if that is what they are, at the tables around, have noticed my Scandinavian. Their artist girlfriends have noticed her New York fashions. And I never cease to notice her beauty, sad, as all beauty is, because it is not eternal. Unless it becomes so when Irene is transformed into literature. As she most certainly will be. Even in the literary wilderness of Canada there must be a writer who can see that Irene is the most important thing in that country. In any country. In the world.

"What about?" she presses breathlessly.

I see the purple mountains, even farther on, beyond the Mountains of Madness.

"Lovecraft was the only person to visit the land south of the South Pole and live to tell about it. He flew over the Mountains of Madness in an aeroplane. We shall fly there with him. That is the land that poor Poe was looking for, that poor Pym reached, that Captain Guy penetrated. Far to the south of the Kerguelen Islands. We shall go there, dear Irene – ”

"By plane?"

"Perhaps by plane – across the Oyster Sea...."

Three Pernods on an empty stomach have wrecked me quite handsomely.

"Shall we go?"

Shall we?

We shall....

●

Frank is sitting in the corner between the coat-rack and the steps leading down to the washroom. They too are decorated with myrtle sprigs. The publisher's gloomy husband is with him.

"Ahoj, Frank. How are things?"

"Not worth a kiss on the youknowwhat."

"Are you still with...."

It is as if he's never heard of the place in his life. It isn't so long ago, after all, that I gave him a lift. Three months? Life under capitalism moves quickly.

"I thought you said you had a job?"

"Oh that. I haven't been working there for a long time."

"What are you doing now?"

"For the moment, nothing."

I don't feel like enquiring any further.

"The comrades are trying to wipe him out," says the publisher's husband. "Like me. Except in my case it's the comrades in reverse."

"What did you do, insult Lenin in front of the liberals again, Frank?"

"He insulted somebody's wife," said the husband. "He called her, if you'll pardon my language, a cow."

"And isn't she?" retorts Frank almost angrily. "And she's got the brain of a chicken to boot."

Frank looks like a sad basset hound. The publisher's husband empties the bottle of champagne. There are bottles of it everywhere, as though Mr. Zawynatch were a wholesale wine merchant.

"In my case, they're out to get me because they think I'm a former Communist," says the publisher's husband. "So how am I supposed to prove I wasn't? D'you think they'd confirm it for me at the Czech embassy?"

"Who's out to get you, the liberals?"

"No, no. Some Czech immigrants right here in Toronto."

"The embassy would only get you deeper in trouble, Bert," says Frank.

"How can you prove you never were something?" the husband asks reflectively. Suddenly he jerks to attention. "That's him over there," and he nods his head towards the bar where a man about thirty-five in an obvious toupee is standing, talking English with an air of great self-confidence. "Seymour," mutters the husband.

"Seymour?"

"Actually his name is Pomajzl. Honza Pomajzl. He changed it. He wrote a nasty letter about me to the executive of the Czechoslovak Association of Canada but fortunately the secretary there is a decent fellow, a former political prisoner, so he let me read it. I tell you, Professor, it was like being back in Prague again."

"What did you do to deserve that?"

"It wasn't anything I did, but what my wife did. She once told Pomajzl that she gets along better with decent Communists than she does with democratic bastards like him. And he quoted that in the letter. He said that 'decent Communists' was an *ejaculatio in adiecto*, just to show off his university degree – and that, he claimed, threw a very clear light on my wife's political past."

"What is her political past?"

"She doesn't have one. She was a cabaret singer. But the local comrades – I mean, some of the local gentlemen here – cannot forgive her for running a successful publishing house in Canada, and so they claim she's infected by Communism. And I was a theatre director back home. Seymour claims that anyone who was a director had to be in the Party. He knows it for a fact, he says, because he can travel back and forth."

I look over at Seymour-Pomajzl. He is well repaired. A made-to-measure hairpiece, sutured to his skin, a luxurious set of dentures, a three-piece suit that is definitely not off the rack. I have seen comrades like him. In suits from the best tailor in Prague, quietly discussing the class struggle over free luncheons in the Writers' Club.

"At the same time he sucked up to Ancerl," Frank interjects gruffly. "And Ancerl not only was a Commie, he was a Hebe as well."

"But he was a world-famous conductor," says the husband. "My wife is not, and I, as you know, deliver parcels for Eaton's."

"The Party always draws fine distinctions," I say.

"And at the same time, Ancerl was exactly the kind of Communist my wife likes," says the husband. "He was a very nice chap, a lot of fun to be with. Seymour's about as much fun as Comrade Kral from the cultural department used to be."

He looks hatefully at the hairpiece conversing in fluent English with Mr. Benes, who in turn talks like Hyman Kaplan.

"Why don't you write to them? Tell them that when your wife made the statement, she had in mind the same Mr. Ancerl who was awarded the Order of Canada."

The husband waves his hand. "I wouldn't demean myself. Luckily there are more democrats on the executive of the Czechoslovak Association of Canada than there are comrades. It's my wife I'm worried about."

"But it's her readers keep her going, isn't it? And there aren't many comrades in her readership. Comrades don't read, they only poison wells. Is Seymour one of her customers?"

"Of course he isn't. It's just that my wife is such a neurotic. She takes everything too much to heart. I'm not worried about her publishing business – that will hang together. I only hope," the husband declares despondently, "the publisher hangs together too," and he submerges his nose in a cup of champagne. Then he turns his sad eyes on me once more.

"So you don't think I can count on the embassy to be of any help?"

"Isn't there someone around from your old theatre who was in the Party? Someone who could confirm you never were a Party member?"

"Well, there was one lighting technician. Now he's a location manager in Hollywood. But he" – and he nods his head sharply towards Seymour – "claims that Communists are not trustworthy witnesses, that even a solemn oath is just a scrap of paper for them."

Howard Seymour. His dentures are indeed a magnificent piece of work, but he's a little young for them. He escaped with his family when he was eight. If old Pomajzl had stayed in Czechoslovakia.... "Well, you're probably up the creek," I say to the husband. "It's always a lot harder to prove you never were something than to prove the contrary. And the fact is that you most certainly worked in Czechoslovakia, which is to say you collaborated, whereas Comrade Seymour-Pomajzl only travels there to spend hard currency. C'est la vie."

A pale Magister Maslo emerges from the crowd wearing a large boutonnière. Frank waves at him. They are still after him. Not long ago he was released from the hospital but immediately afterwards two men from the Royal Canadian Mounted Police found him tied up in a parked car. Czech agents were about to do him in when the Mounties interrupted them, so once more, by the grace of God, Maslo escaped with his life intact. We live in a dangerous world.

•

PRAGUE (Reuters) – Yet another Czech writer has been added to the list of those who committed suicide after the Soviet invasion of Czechoslovakia. The poet Jan Prouza was found dead in his flat on August 28, 1972. He had apparently hanged himself.

The literary career of this poet, who is little known to the public, was marked by a long series of conflicts with the administrators of official culture, beginning in 1955 when he published a collection of poems called *Oddities of Love*. The situation came to a head in 1970 when he was arrested and held in custody for a short time for signing a petition demanding the release of several imprisoned supporters of Alexander Dubcek.

The immediate reason for his suicide is not known. It appears that Mr. Prouza left no letter behind, though sources say it is not out of the question that the police may have removed it from the scene.

●

She came into my compartment in the train wearing a green Tyrolean hat and a white dirndl, plump, pretty, blonde, eyes like forget-me-nots set in red, highlander's cheeks.

"Ahoj, Ilse!" I shouted. I was glad to see her. Her highland face did not light up with a smile, as it usually did, revealing a healthy set of somewhat equine teeth.

"*Ach, du bist's....*"

"*Ja, ich bin's,*" I said.

"Is it *frei* here?" she asked, pointlessly, for the compartment was gapingly empty and smelling of the cigar that Prema had given me yesterday from one of his father's secret caches. Even so she looked around.

"So you're a real German now, Ilse," I said. "I say 'ahoj' to you and you — "

"I *am* a German," she said. She sat down, crossed her stout legs and ostentatiously pulled a brochure out of her handbag. The title was written in a Gothic script so orthodox I couldn't read it.

"What's that you're reading?"

Without a word she held the book close to my eyes. I deciphered the title like a rebus: "*Vom — Kaiser — hof — bis — zur — Reichs*. Is that what they make you read at the German grammar school?"

"I'm reading it because I want to know what it says," she replied self-righteously. "It's one of the fundamental works of National Socialism."

"Well, it must be — interesting."

"Very." She plunged back into her reading. I noticed, however, that the forget-me-nots were not moving.

"Look," I said, "why not forget the reading? You'll ruin your eyes. It's kind of smoky in here. Let's just talk instead. We haven't seen each other in donkey's years."

She would clearly rather have talked, but she fixed those forget-me-nots on the Gothic script for a while longer, before turning them on me. "Are you still in the B-form?"

"No. I'm in A now. I transferred because of English. In the B-form they start French in fifth."

She smiled at me with a suggestion of reproach. "An Anglophile."

"It's strictly because of jazz."

"Six of one, half a dozen of the other."

Ilse may have been a Brunhild, almost a Sudeten German, but she still talked like a native. Her command of the idiom made me feel good.

"Don't you like jazz?"

She shook her head.

"But you used to."

"I had bad taste. Now it hurts my ears. You can't hide the fact that it's basically just nigger music."

"Of course it is. Negroes are great musicians."

She shrugged her shoulders. "Is that Jew still playing with you?"

"D'you mean Benno?"

"That's the one."

"Sure. Best trumpet player in the district."

"And is he still going to the grammar school?"

"Sure he is. Almost got the boot, though. Last year he had to write three sups — "

"What I mean is, are they still *allowing* him to go to school?"

There was winter light in the forget-me-nots. It made me feel cold. What had happened to Ilse? She had been a sweet girl. She used to let me copy out her answers in math. What had happened to her?

That, of course, was a rhetorical question. I knew very well what had happened to her, but I had not known it had happened quite so completely.

"Ilse, come off it," I said.

"What do you mean?"

"I mean come off it. You're from Kostelec, after all."

"I have no idea what you're talking about." She lifted up her volume of Goebbels and fixed the forget-me-nots on a very pointed, sharp "S".

"You danced swing with the rest of us! And Benno the Jew even played for you."

She snapped the book shut. "We're not going to talk about it," she said. "Look, Smiricky. I'm a National Socialist. That changes a person.

I've understood things that weren't very clear before. I have grown up, ideologically."

"So have I," I said.

She looked at me sharply. "What do you mean by that?"

"At least a metre."

"Talk seriously, will you?"

The forget-me-nots were blue ice.

It had really happened.

The train stopped. Opocno.

"Hey, Ilse, you remember?"

She said nothing. But I remembered. How she was crazy about Jarka
Pila from Opocno. How she peroxided her hair because Jarka announced
that he preferred blondes. She was still blonde. I pointed to her hair. "Is that
still because of Jarka, or does it just suit the race better?"

She blushed.

"You're disgusting. And if you insist on provoking me, I'll...."

"You'll what?"

The stationmaster blew his whistle, the train jerked into motion.

"Just you watch out," said Ilse. "The Reich is at war, and there are
some things you don't joke about."

"Like Jarka Pila?"

She blushed an even deeper red.

"Oh, I know you broke off with him because he's a Czech," I lied. I
was beginning to feel afraid. The fact was that Jarka threw her over because
he had at least three girls who were prettier. "I was sorry about that. You
made a nice couple. You're such a *rassig* German and him with that turned-
up nose – "

"He did not have a turned-up nose!" she blurted out.

I knew that too. I looked straight into the forget-me-nots.

"Ilse, look, we're old friends, aren't we?"

Someone was making a shadow on the glass door of the compartment.
I looked up. It was an SS man, as large as life and twice as unnatural.

"*Fräulein Ilse!*" he said happily and entered the compartment.

"*Herr Scharführer!*"

Ilse stood up and gave the Heil Hitler salute. Oh my God! The SS man
sat down and a lively conversation ensued, during which I learned a great
deal about life in Paris, excluding, of course, the sexual side of things. I
listened, remembering her standing red-eyed by the girls' washroom with
Dadka Habrova who was trying to comfort her, and how Jarka Pila, to
charm a certain Icka from the third form, curled his lips over teeth that were
already slightly yellowed from too many cigarettes, though he was only a

fifth-former; and how Ilse's brand-new blonde hair glistened in the autumn sun and was utterly useless to her in her quest. I toyed with the idea of talking Czech to them to embarrass Ilse, but in the end I decided against it. It wasn't really Ilse. She was somehow artificial, and I was a little wary – with the SS man there too – wary of pushing things too far. The train stopped at Jaromer and I got out. "*Grüss Gott*, Ilse!" I said, causing the SS man to stare at me in astonishment. Ilse said nothing. But those forget-me-nots looked at me, and through them I felt the cold air of distant reaches, where I have never, ever been able to go.

•

*Darwin, Australia*
*7.9.70*

*Dear Danny,*
*Thought I might stop off to see you in Canada, but the money wouldn't stretch that far so I went straight home, though not to Sydney this time, because I didn't reckon I'd turn up any decent jobs there. I went to Darwin, it's a new city in the Northern Territory where there's construction going on, and I'm working on a construction site. I make a pile of money but I booze a lot of it away, it's as hot as a Chinese laundry here. Also since I been away the prices have shot way up and it's getting so I can only afford meat as a Sunday treat. I sounded off about it in the tavern and now the local Czeeks think I got infected with Communism when I was back home for so long, but hell, the Communists don't have a patent on stupidity. You probably read that Labour here won the elections and I'm sort of glad because they started to introduce some of that social security stuff we've had back home for fifty years but here they're just getting around to it. Now they ought to try and do something about this inflation. During the time I was away beer went from 25 to 35 cents a draught and for a room like the one you used to have for your maid I pay $15 a week. I almost forgot to mention, I guess I didn't write you from home that they expelled me, in fact told me to take my pick: either be a British subject or a Czechoslovak citizen. Somebody ratted on me when I criticized the way they were doing some things in the factory and the cops told me I was an undesirable element unless I decided to give up my British subjecthood and I wouldn't go along with that, because they could stick me straight into the cooler for shooting my mouth off. So they gave me 48 hours to clear out and I didn't even have time to say my farewells, except at Mom and Dad's grave. Mom died, I think I might have sent you the obituary, she had a heart attack so it was an easy death and at*

*the time it looked as though I'd be staying home. So I was almost glad, she was 75 and if she'd been alive to see how they threw me out I doubt she would of lived through it. I managed to go and see Marie and she sends her greetings to you. And then I just had time to catch the express to Chocen and then through Brno to Austria and then Trieste.*

*The weather is nice here except it's God-awful hot but after work I always get on my bike and go down to the beach. And to the taverns in the evening. There aren't too many Czeeks here and the ones that are suspect I'm a pinko so I don't hang about with anyone. It's best that way. When I was back home in Kostelec I hung around mostly with Lenecek, he's married but it hasn't worked out too happy so I don't really regret still being single. I reckon I'll work till about January and then take a holiday and pay another visit to Hawaii. I tell you, buddy, it's no place for us to be any more back home, we aren't used to hold-ing our tongue all the time and sitting tight in one spot, it's just not the place for us any more. But it would be nice if you could drop over here sometime, it shouldn't be too dear for you if you're a professor now. We could talk about old times. Seems like it was about a thousand years ago and here it is not even thirty. I can't hardly believe it. And if you can't make it, then write me a letter at least.*

> *Sincere greetings,*
> *Your old buddy,*
> *Prema*

•

The Colonial Tavern is bathed in the familiar North American semi-darkness. Erroll Garner is sitting at the piano making miracles. The piano rumbles like a power plant. Garner's enormous hands extract huge rhythmic block chords from the keyboard, the left hand pumping out a syn-copated back beat under the tantalizing ornamental phrases, sudden surprising harmonies and old-time tremolo blues chords executed by the right. I am slowly getting drunk at the bar, already quite blasé about sitting here while a living legend plays opposite me. I am a very happy man.

Then I see him out of the corner of my eye and an old memory galvan-izes me. The same surprise. A zoot-suiter in Harris tweed, hair carefully styled. If only Garner knew who he was playing for. "Ain't Misbehavin". Still seated on my bar-stool I lean over to Uher and say, "Boo!"

That startles him. Just as I was startled that time in the washroom, so startled that I almost pissed over my pants. A latter-day zoot-suiter. Zoot Uher.

"Hi," he says.

"You're supposed to be dead, you son-of-a-bitch."

He laughs acidly. "Nobody's told me about it yet."

"It's happened before – you're dead and you don't know it yet."

"That so? I guess that's me, then."

I look at him. There is a Florida tan on his cheeks, a genuine one, not the kind from a bottle.

"I heard you were on Dubcek's side in sixty-eight," I say meditatively. "Did you get that suntan in Siberia?"

He guesses the state I'm in.

"You've got a skull-full."

"Full of brains."

"And the brain's full of alcohol."

"And the alcohol's full of memories. Strange memories. What are you doing here and how come they haven't liquidated you?"

"If I were you I wouldn't give too much credence to émigré gossip."

"Aha," I say, "so the story that you were with Dubcek's boys is either just a lot of gossip or else you were just – "

He interrupts me. "Listen to the music, why don't you? That was always your thing, wasn't it?" and he turns and stares at the black man on the piano, who is sitting on a telephone book and looks like a black painted Jew out of an anti-Semitic caricature. If Comrade Jodas were in power in Canada –

"There's a time for everything," I say. "Or else you were just there to spy on Dubcek."

Once again he studies me, as he already has several times in his life, intently. The bar is lined with quaffing Canadians, a black man with a freckled girl, some drunken Babbitt in a Shriner's fez, and I am vividly aware of the simultaneity of the world: Irene feeding herself with Paris oysters, Uher in his Harris tweed – that cancer cell metastasizing here and now in the Colonial Tavern beside a spiffy little black man and his white girlfriend – this is our world, we who have been worn thin by the world. It is not a world of innocents.

"You're scammered," says Uher. "But if you'd rather talk about that than listen to this great jazz, then no, I wouldn't put it that way. Dubcek's boys just wanted power. And revenge. The people who were concerned about the cause had to intervene, that's all."

"Who'd he want revenge on, you?"

"He was out to settle some personal scores."

"Scores left over from the Spanish Civil War, is that it?"

He says nothing. Then: "And besides, what am I talking to you for? You chose exile, and we have nothing left to say to each other."

"That's where you're wrong, cop."

A muscle in his face twitches. He doesn't like that title, I suppose. But once again he says nothing, so I continue:

"Scores ... all those gallows! You don't just put scores like that out of your mind. That's human, isn't it?"

"It's human not to lose your perspective."

"No, that's inhuman. *Errare humanum est*, Venerable Father. Except that you've never erred."

He shrugs his shoulders. "Neither have you," he says. "We each have our own truth and, as I can see, we've each remained faithful to it."

"What the hell do you know about my truth?"

"You're here, aren't you? That says a lot about your truth."

"And do you know why I'm here?"

"You came in search of your own truth."

"A lot you know," I say, and Garner starts in on "Beale Street Blues." "I ran away from your truth because it can't stand to have any other truth on its own little pile of rubbish."

"There can only be one truth."

"You've just uttered a great truth," I say. "Only that one truth has to be a little more ample than yours."

He grins. "Truth by itself, without works, is dead."

It is my turn to grin. "You've forgotten almost everything you learned in the seminary, I see. It is not truth, it's *faith* without works. Works more often than not kill the truth."

He slips off the bar stool and stretches.

"Well, I'm off. So long."

"Don't go yet," I say. "Let me tell you what I know about you, stuff that could interest the RCMP."

He stops, but betrays no emotion. Then he slides back up on the bar stool. "More of the same?" the barman asks.

Uher nods.

"I don't know what it is you're after here," I say. "But I don't want you here. And there are people here who know you better than I do. Do you remember Vachousek, the foreman?"

How he lured him into the trap, those sweet nothings of his about perspectives and truths and movements, lured Vachousek into a deadly trap baited and set to spring and he knew very well that the only way out led to that yard with the hanging tree. And he knew very well that the double agent would die, whether Vachousek actually managed to shoot him or not.

And in the night he brought Father Hunak to minister unto him.

And in the train he warned me.

And on the roof of the Empire State Building he caught me in his snare. Without old Skvarilik –

"So forget about him," I say.

"What – exactly – do you mean by that?"

"Forget about Vachousek and clear out. Just get out of here. Your face makes me sick."

He hesitates, uncertain what to do. But here I am not under his jurisdiction. Not anymore. And he knows me well enough to know that I can't be bought. Not for money, not for those sweet nothings about socialism and the rest of it. He knows that I don't include him in that category. I suppose I'm a bourgeois. I cannot go any further in feeling than....

"Get out of here. And write a report about me and send it to Prague. Tell them I get drunk in the Colonial Tavern to the sounds of jazz. Tell them I do it out of despair. Not despair for my own fate. Because of people like you."

He gets up. "How would you like to get together?"

"Get together?"

"When you're sober. We could have a little chat about it."

"Clear out, cop!"

He shrugs his shoulders and leaves. The coloured lights slide over the sheen of his hair. Erroll Garner rams wedges of rhythm in between the chords.

I know I won't report him to the RCMP. I can't bring myself to do something like that. It won't help the poor foreman anyway. Even if Uher were put out of commission, there'd be someone else. I want to shout after him: Uher, you son-of-a-bitch! What kind of undercover cop are you anyway? Giving me fair warning! Taking priests to prisoners in the night! Why aren't you the way you should be? Why don't you fit the stereotype? So I'd know for sure –

And does it matter?

So what?

●

"There were cases," said the green man, "where people buried alive kept themselves going for half a year on worms. There was always water seeping through to them, so thirst was no problem. The main problem was food, and that was mostly worms. Once in a while they'd get a mole or something – "

"Where did they shit, man?" asked Kos aggressively.

"That was the awfullest part," said Vozenil. "Lots of times when we dug up cases like that, they was all covered in their own shit."

"You buffalo," said Malina.

"Every once in a while some of them was able to dig their way to other coffins. Then you had cases of cannibalism of corpses. Once we dug up this real well-fed fellow. He ate his own wife and grandfather, all of them died at once of mushroom poisoning, but he was immune to mushroom poison so he just seemed to be dead."

"You fucking rhododendron!"

Vozenil's horrors were clearly too much for mere zoology. Perhaps he realized this too, for he looked calmly at the enraged Malina and said, "You don't have to believe me if you don't want to."

He lit another newspaperette. The stench assailed our nostrils. Or perhaps it was someone relieving himself in one of the toilets in the back — or could it be that the home-grown tobacco had run out and Vozenil was smoking dried horse-dung? A distinct possibility, in his case.

"What happened to the cannibal?" asked the lad from the paint-shop.

"They hung him," replied the chlorophyll lad. "Cannibalism is a hanging crime."

"You doughnut," said Malina, his zoological vocabulary utterly exhausted. "If he had the strength to dig his way to other corpses why didn't he just dig himself straight out of the grave?"

"Because you lose your sense of direction underground. There was cases where we found people buried alive, of course they was dead by then, but they managed to dig themselves twenty metres farther down before they finally croaked. Under the ground you can't tell which way is up 'cause you can't feel gravity."

"You stupid wig!" shouted Malina angrily. "You're so fucking stupid you can smell it."

"You don't have to believe me," said the green man. "Next time they bury you alive I'd like to see you there, chewing away on the roots."

"If I find roots, you dink," said Malina, "then at least I'll know which way's up and I'll crawl out and punch your fucking teeth in."

"Some of them managed to do it," said Vozenil, unmoved. "But mostly they kicked off right away. From the horror of it all. If they ever bury you, dead or alive, that's the end. The best you can hope for is death."

●

"Hey, this should interest you, young fellow!" Bocar is reading *Rude Pravo*. "Pleasant greetings from your home town." And he reads:

"A POWERFUL BLOW TO TRAITORS. Joining ranks with the hundreds of enterprises which have already expressed their strong disagreement with the anti-socialist pamphlet Charter 77 is the Kovotechna National

Enterprise in Kostelec. At a mass meeting held in the large Klement Gottwald assembly hall the workers unanimously signed a resolution which, among other things, states, 'We soundly condemn those who try to undermine our republic! We demand strict adherence to the Helsinki Agreements.'"

Bocar looks up abruptly. "My God," he says, "isn't that resolution some kind of prevarication? Strict adherence to Helsinki – I'd say there was some kind of sabotage going on in your home town, by God."

*Ibis redibis non moriaris –*

"Did someone faint while they were signing it?" I ask.

"What?"

"I'm just wondering if anyone fainted while they were signing the resolution?"

"It doesn't say here," said Bocar. "And even if they did, it's not important. It would never go down in history. The important thing is they signed it, not whether some feeble son-of-a-bitch fainted."

*Ibis redibis.*

A tragedy that repeats itself is a farce.

A farce that repeats itself is –

●

For he was a jolly good fellow
For he was a jolly good fellow
For he was a jolly good fellow
And let him rest in peace!

The vocal ensemble of the Ontario Rangers Community finished the song and raised the chalices to the memory of Milan. Unlike almost everyone else, Milan had made his decision publicly. He had sold all his expensive household effects, including the ice-shitter, and thrown a party for his friends. He had even invited me, for I had, after all, been a witness to his abrupt debarkation in the land of freedom, and I was therefore to be a witness as well to his departure back to the land of the Prague Castle and Pilsener beer. He had tried to invite Veronika, but she was not answering her telephone.

The party at the Benes' is extravagant and quite atypical: those who return usually take their savings and their quadraphonic sound system and other precious appliances with them. Even as a returning migrant, however, Milan cared less about gadgets than he did about his friends. Perhaps he felt he was betraying them by going back. They, however, merely think he is being a fool.

The feast is winding down to its terrible conclusion, for Milan's charter flight is to take off in two hours and he is in a meditative mood. "What do you suppose can happen to me?"

"Nothing. Of course, they'll lock you up."

"No, they won't," says Marylin Postrihovska. "They'll stick you in a re-education camp for a few months."

"I can survive that."

"If all you care about is surviving, you can do that almost anywhere."

Of course, what he cares about is life. I can already see him in the airplane, suspended over the Atlantic, too late to turn back. The lid has come down. An exile's nightmare come true. Comrade Sedlacek or Prochazka or the like walking down the aisle handing out questionnaires ... which immigrants did you consort with ... which of them are active in anti-Czechoslovak organizations ... what offices do they hold ... which of them, in your opinion, would consider repatriation ... which of them would be open to discussions ... that little Instant Informer Course. And then the gentleman who makes jokes about Pilsener beer, that it has to come straight from the tap or it's just not the same thing – certainly not from bottles in the Benes Inn: from the tap! And that loud-mouth who is already going around deliberately calling everybody "comrade" at the top of his lungs.... That tearful woman ... that man of fear who is already composing in his mind his *apologia pro stupiditatem suam*: he left because he was afraid that war would break out in Europe ... he succumbed to enemy propaganda ... and to emotional –

I stop my reverie. I find it unbearable. I hear Sestak say, "No, they won't make fun of you. They'll say: It's obvious, a pompous non-entity like him would never find a niche for himself in capitalism. It's a tough world over there and it's only for tough customers. He did the right thing to come back. Bohemia is the only place for nebbishes like him, Bohemia is the only place...."

By this time they have had a lot to drink and are becoming less considerate. They begin a well-informed debate about the delights of waiting for years for flats, of living in public dormitories for unmarried men; the beauties of the collective life with children, parents and grandparents in two rooms, a bathroom on the balcony and a portable bathtub in the kitchen; about registering with the police, reporting to them; the endless requests; the endless demands; standing in line for cucumbers. Milan drinks himself into a stupor and they have to call a taxi for him. They give the driver twenty dollars to transport to the airport what is, practically speaking, a corpse. Perhaps he will come to by the time he reaches Prague. The worst thing about an execution is the long journey to the gallows.

He leaves a hundred dollars behind. The whisky is still flowing freely, the guests are singing at the top of their lungs and eating sandwiches. Mr. Sestak pounds the floor with his Jingling Johnny and Marilyn takes the soprano:

> And that's the story 'bout the birth of swing
> A drunken sailor on a fling
> turned a stagger
> into a.....

But I neither drink nor sing. I am wondering whether I would ever return, though only to give myself something to think about. I know that I could not. Every return is an illusion. No man can step into the same river twice. "You Can't Go Home Again." Because I know this, I don't suffer from nostalgia. I am only sad – quite pleasantly sad, usually.

Pleasantly? Why yes. I remember Paris in 1968. We were standing in front of *Les Deux Magots* like poor relations whose house had just burned down and Milan Kundera said, "I only hope I die soon. There's been too much of everything. How much longer do you think we can last?" I too had felt the longing for death. The Death Wish. The tanks had suddenly turned a theoretical Freudian concept into a real feeling. It soothed me.

I feel pleasantly sad, because I am tired. A platitude. Too much for a single generation. Also a platitude. In the end, nothing much ever happened to me.... All platitudes. Yet somehow everything lost its meaning – not because I left the country, but because everything was set back twenty years. But my life cannot be put back. Biology, unlike history, is not a reversible process. History that repeats itself is a farce. A wicked Feydeauesque farce. Thank God biology can't repeat itself.

Of course I do return, constantly. To Kostelec. But I can do that as easily in Canada as I can in Prague. Here in Canada, with all the creature comforts, in the safety of a decadently anti-police democracy. When I fall asleep I am aware of the validity of yet another cliché. How beautiful life is when everything loses its meaning and one begins to live simply for life itself:

Perhaps the great historical failure of a small episode in history, in the year 1968, has in fact helped me to arrive at this wisdom. I have not lost the meaning of life, merely the illusion that life has a meaning. If it had not all happened, biology would have run its usual course, in the grip of oppressive illusions and terrors in that tiny hothouse of an unfortunate and apathetic little nation –

Now that country interests me only as a subject of research, its language as a plaything suitable for puns and verbal games. I am no longer a part of it: I carry my native land in my heart. National in form, international in feeling. I am now a part of that non-nation which is a million people scattered over prairies and islands and continents, to whom nothing much happens any longer. The days pass, I live, I enjoy, I observe the relentless advance of biology, death appears to me as the beneficent end to magnificent but inconsequential days.... Whenever something passes out of the body, it brings one pleasure – that was how Milos Forman philosophically put it that time in Neuilly, and Sylva told him to keep his disgusting metaphysics to himself because she'd heard them already. He ignored her protestations: when your bladder is full and you urinate, it brings relief. When you need to move your bowels and you can't because you've eaten too much and you finally manage to shit, you experience pleasure. When you're in the army, added Pavelka, and there are no women and all you can do is go into the room for mass culture to masturbate (and Sylva said "Phooey! That's Pavelka for you! Known the world over as a man of sizeable parts") and then you go on leave and find yourself a girl and your seed flows from you, said Milos – delight of delights. When your spirit passes out of your body, it must be the greatest pleasure of all. Far greater than when you merely shit or come –

"You old goat!" said Sylva, though in Malina's time she had not yet been born. But Milos' theory was not just empty wit. He belongs, as I do, to those who seek after meaning and he had discovered that meaning was no more than a gilded statue, a seven-day wonder, and a rather tasteless statue at that. Before God a profound democracy rules. Meaning is a compulsive neurosis. It is only when the neurosis goes away, or when we are cured of it, that we can live.

And go on doing everything we did before. For the fun, the delight of it.

I feel pleasantly sad, and not even very sad at that. The Jingling Johnny crashes rhythmically up and down and Marilyn sings about a valley somewhere, an absurd song about going over Niagara Falls. I get up and go to the telephone.

"Irene?"

"Hi, buddy!"

"How are you?"

"Just wonderful."

"So am I."

"Do you love me?"

"I am allowing myself the luxury of that folly."

"What's that?"

"I'm thinking of a Cadillac. It has a lot of buttons on the dashboard. If

I had been the one to press the button, I would probably have switched on a siren and brought all the police-cars in earshot down on top of us. But fortunately a certain clever young lady pressed it...."

I hear laughter.

"Have you written your paper on Faulkner, Svensson?"

"I bought it."

"For how much?"

"Fifty dollars."

"Are you that much afraid of me, Svensson?"

"Yes, I am."

"A five-dollar paper would have been enough for you."

"Then you'd fail me."

"I'll fail you anyway."

"I don't mind, as long as you don't fail me in Daddy's Caddy."

"As long as you push the right buttons...."

Laughter again, and in it the sound of ... as Fitz said ... but nicely. My Nicole is from quite another era.

"Sweet dreams, Svensson."

"You too. About me."

Quiet laughter, the telephone gently hung up.

I hang up too.

"Come and have a drink, Doctor."

The singers are standing at attention, their glasses raised. I raise my glass. Mr. Sestak looks at his large waterproof skin-divers' wristwatch.

"By now they're closer to the shores of the Old World than they are to the New."

"To the eternal memory of Milan Fikejz, a good-natured fool!"

We raise our glasses and drink silently. The door of the restaurant flies open with a crash. Milan is standing there, as pale as death.

"Help!" shrieks Marilyn. "They've crashed! It's a ghost!"

●

"Come! Come and have a look!" Mr. Senka is tugging at my sleeve and trembling with excitement, as though he had discovered a corpse in the Zawynatch cellar. I get up from the living-room bar, which is framed by a plastic trellis with plastic grapevines weaving in and out of it; behind it a hired black bartender is mixing cocktails, and behind him on the wall, in an ornamental frame, there is a hand-painted oil, executed in a style dear to cheap art galleries, depicting a girl in a Moravian folk costume and high red leather boots. The folk costume, however, reaches only to her waist, above which she is topless right up to her golden hair. She is decked in a wreath that also has its provenance in folklore. Tanzanian, perhaps.

I follow an excited Mr. Senka across the spacious salon that serves simultaneously as a domestic tavern, a pool-room and a picture gallery. All three available walls are covered with paintings, and all the Czech and Slovak abstractionists who fled to Canada from European *Realpolitik* are represented. "Well, when they came, you know how it is," Mr. Zawynatch explained to us earlier, "they had no cash, and no work, so I bought whatever they painted to give them a little boost in their new homeland. I helped them out a little." I look at this private Hermitage, the frameless canvases crowded together on the walls from the floor to the ceiling, each one more fantastic than the next. It is clear that Mr. Zawynatch has lost nothing by his philanthropy. I recall an abstractionist with the surrealist name Arzen Veprovy cursing his stupidity over a beer at Benes'. In Prague in the early sixties they had confiscated an entire exhibition of his works. Later, in Canada, he discovered that a hundred bucks for an oil painting three feet by six, which he toiled over for three months, was not such a good price. Now that same oil painting is hanging on the wall directly opposite the half-dressed ethnic maiden. Mr. Senka drags me past it through a door into an alcove where Mr. Zawynatch has assembled the paintings that, to avoid the criticisms of good Christians and patriotic countrymen, he has not hung in his nightclub.

"Look at that!" Mr. Senka whispers. "Isn't that something?"

He stares wide-eyed at a diabolically black mons painted realistically on an otherwise stylized nude study of Veprovy's young wife. She is recognizable by her prominent ears. She modelled for him because one-hundred-dollar fees were scarcely enough to permit hiring a woman of professional immodesty.

"Have you ever seen anything like it?"

"I have," I say. "I'm not married, but I have seen it before."

Mr. Senka waggles a finger at me. "I'll bet you're quite the one. But that's not what I meant. I meant have you ever seen it in a picture before? Or on a statue?"

I look at the black, mysterious entity. "You'd have a hard time sculpting that," I offer.

"You're right." Mr. Senka thinks for a moment, then says, "But I imagine it's pretty easy to paint. Even so — just take all those Venuses and Aphrodites — they're all absolutely bare down there. But *these* — " and he looks around. Similar improprieties cover all four walls of the alcove. "Just take a look. My God! Look at the one she's got!" and his finger singles out a nude by a painter who otherwise abstracts landscapes into spheres and squares. I take a closer look. This one has a ginger mons. I look at it, and despite the stylization something familiar emerges from the forms of the face and body, reduced though they are to their fundamental elements. Of course. Dotty. This one probably cost Mr. Zawynatch more than a hundred. A commissioned painting. Dotty has beautiful ginger pubic hair – so ginger may well be the real colour of her hair, which is now a light chestnut brown with a verdigris wash.

"I don't believe it!" breathes Mr. Senka. "I don't believe it."

"What do you expect? We're living in a period of realism," I say. "The artists of earlier ages idealized their subjects. I doubt that Venus would have shaved herself."

Mr. Senka giggles and winks at me. "Have you seen *Deep Throat*?"

I shake my head. I have seen it, of course, but I am interested in how it impressed Mr. Senka.

"She shaves herself there. On the *screen*! And she uses a *razor blade*! It gives a body the shivers." He looks around. "That one there is the only one without it," and he points to a pink nude that appears to have come from the same brush as the one decorating Mr. Zawynatch's bar. "That one's not realistic," he says almost sadly.

"It's not. If it were, she would have to have a crack down below."

I say that deliberately. Mr. Senka is seized by a new fit of merriment.

"And listen – statues too! Venus, and all those like her – not one of them is" – he lowers his voice to a whisper – "cracked down below."

Choking, giggling laughter.

"A very interesting observation," I say. "The realists of antique times didn't carry their realism that far. Of course," I add in mock thoughtfulness, "they had to solve a far greater problem in the case of male statues. There, obviously, it was quite impossible to stylize."

Mr. Senka clings to me with his eyes, his little mouth opening and closing, swallowing: "D'you mean ...?"

"Do you know the statue of Doryphoros, for example? He's carrying a spear on his shoulder, and the spear is broken off." Imitating him, I lower my voice. "But – down in front" – I say, extending the euphemism – "it's not broken off."

Mr. Senka almost shouts, "Now I remember. Of course!" Then that stage whisper. "And you know what I could never figure out? Why he's got such a – how should I put it – so...."

I take refuge in the directness of slang. "You mean he's poorly hung."

But the upright, decent Mr. Senka is not familiar with the expression. "What?"

I whisper, scarcely audible, "He's got such a tiny little – thing."

This nets me a brotherly pat on the shoulder. The aroma of Mr. Senka's mouthwash wafts about me.

"That's exactly what I meant." Then he stops. "But wait – on that very same statue – there's also" – he is still reluctant to allow the proper word to escape his lips – "what there isn't on those Venuses, but what's on this one here." And he points his finger at the undergrowth in Dotty's little garden of delights.

"I say, you are observant," I marvel, and feign an intense interest in the nude study of our hostess. "That's a fact. Doryphoros does have pubic hair."

I continue to stare at Dotty.

"Mr. Senka, don't you find something rather striking about this nude?"

Brother Senka looks sharply at the picture. First he peers closely at the ginger triangle, then at the navel and then at the right breast.

"What did you have in mind?"

"Look at the face."

He does so, for a long time. Suddenly he almost jumps.

"Do you suppose ...?"

Wordlessly I point to the date under the painter's signature. It is very recent.

"Well I never!"

"The lady of the house," I say.

Mr. Senka covers his mouth with his hand. An excited pair of blue eyes stares at me over the fingers.

"Well I – well, knock me down with a feather! Have you ever seen the ...?"

"What do you think I am? I've never even seen the good lady in a bathing-suit, let alone – "

"That's not what I meant." He giggles. "But imagine someone having his own wife painted – without any clothes on – and then hanging it up for people to look at!"

"I suppose he loves her so much he wants to share his joy with others."

Once again he shakes his finger at me waggishly. "I can tell you're quite the one!" He submits the nude to another thorough examination. Then he actually jabs me with his elbow. "I just hope he didn't share it with the painter."

"The man of the house was certainly present just in case."

Mr. Senka bows deeply. He threatens me with a wavering finger. "Let's get out of here before I lose control."

We return to the larger and more public Hermitage. Bocar is sitting by the bar in his wheelchair, drinking with Dotty. The black bartender is wielding the silver shaker. Mr. Zawynatch is graciously showing his collection of rings to Margitka. He is wearing a creation of green and blue checks, with gold shoes to go with it. Dotty's sartorial simplicity has not lasted beyond the matrimonial celebration: she walks from guest to guest in a full-length skirt made of thin strips of multi-coloured brocade, and with each step her long legs are visible right up to her panties. The panties, however, are part of the ensemble. They are opaque, black, and sprinkled with star-dust. Mr. Senka stares at them intently, with eyes like tiny X-ray cameras.

●

## LETTER BOMB DEATH

TORONTO (CP) – A man died last night in an explosion that rocked a West Toronto rooming-house shortly after midnight.

The man has been identified as Jerry Pohorsky, age 61.

Tenants in the Parkdale rooming-house were awakened by the blast and broke down Pohorsky's door. They found him lying on the floor seriously wounded in his smoke-filled room.

According to police, Pohorsky, unemployed, had apparently been trying to manufacture a letter bomb when the explosion took place.

A pamphlet was found dealing with the construction of letter bombs, put out by the Urban Guerrilla Press of Milburn, New Jersey.

Police are also investigating a possible connection between the dead man and a group of supporters of the military junta recently overthrown in Greece.

Damage from the bomb was estimated at $700.

Pohorsky died shortly after his arrival at Toronto General Hospital.

●

"Someday that will have historical value," said Irena. Like a coddled lapdog, I sat on the couch between the two sisters, looking at Irena's scuffed knees, while Alena examined the snapshots of her sister which I had taken just before the warehouse exploded.

"Don't brag so, sister dear," said Alena.

"Don't try to be so witty, sister dear," retorted Irena. "Danny, take a picture of our baby here or she'll cry."

"All right!" cried Alena, and she bounced to her feet and pulled her short skirt up to reveal her straight suntanned legs, lithe from playing basketball. "You can take all of me, not just from the waist up like my dear sister."

"Be good enough to take my dear sister from the waist down," said

Irena. "It'll be far prettier. And don't be so shameless," she said, irritated because she could not bear comments about her legs. They were a little like hockey sticks.

"I can say what I want in front of dear Daniel," said Alena, and she pulled her skirt up so far my eyes popped. But she knew where to stop. "As a friend of the family, he's family."

Conspicuously I focused on Irena's knees. In those days girls wore short skirts, and when they sat on the couch, it couldn't be helped – so Irena's skirt had slipped above her knees and, try as she might, she could not tug it down to cover them.

"Don't stare!" she said. "But I mean it, Danny, they *are* historical pictures. Look!" Irena handed Alena a handful of photographs which had immortalized the greatest act of sabotage Kostelec had ever seen. The snapshots had more than lived up to my expectations, and I hadn't even planned them.

"My dear hero," said Alena, "I won't say another word."

The alderman walked into the room, and Alena immediately handed him the photographs. He set his pince-nez on his nose and gravely studied my creations.

"These will be historical pictures one day, Mr. Smiricky," he announced. "Frankly, though, I don't know whether it was worth it or not." He handed the pictures back to me. "They've already arrested thirty people and we haven't seen the end of it yet. I wouldn't show these pictures to anyone, Mr. Smiricky, if I were you. Not until the war's over."

"He should show these instead," said Alena, pointing to the pictures I had gathered up from the couch.

"May I see them?" asked the alderman.

"They're just sort of ... portraits...."

The alderman reached out and I handed him the photographs I had taken of his daughter, photographs brimming with love. He began examining them as closely as he had the historical photos. The sun, reflecting off the crowns of the oak trees on the opposite bank of the river, was beaming into the room. The sweet smell of hops from the nearby brewery drifted through the open window. The snapshots of his pretty daughter clearly made the alderman feel as good as they did me.

"What kind of camera do you have?" he asked, so that he would not have to praise his own photogenic offspring. "These shots turned out very well."

"A Voigtländer," I said and eagerly handed the alderman the camera. Again, he examined it with the same care as he had the pictures. Then he looked at us. We were sitting side by side on the couch, with me in the middle between his two daughters.

"Would you have any objections if I were to photograph you?" he asked. "Just as you are now – it would make a nice souvenir."

"Of course, sir!" I said quickly. I had no picture of me and Irena together. My camera did not have an automatic shutter. Now there was a chance to obtain such a rarity, and with the blessings of her father.

"My nose is shiny," grumbled Alena.

"So put your hand over it and pretend you're thinking, dear sister," said Irena.

"A good idea, dear sister." Alena took hold of her nose with one hand.

"Now," said the alderman, putting one eye to the viewfinder, "if you'd just shift together a little so I can get you all in."

Quite willingly I moved close to Irena. I could feel her hot thigh in the thin skirt through my pantleg.

"He said shift together," said Alena. "Why did you shift away from me, dear friend of the family?"

"I can't shift together in two directions at once," I replied.

"Then I'll shift closer to you, if my dear sister will permit," said Alena.

"Alena!" cried the alderman from behind the camera.

Alena sat on my lap. Her buttocks were firm. That was from basketball, too.

"Now Alenka!" The alderman was very disapproving.

"Oh, heck," said Alena in mock sadness. She slid off my lap but sat down firmly against my other leg. I sat there between them like a slice of bread in a toaster. My body reacted. I put both my hands in my lap to hide it.

"Nobody move!" said the alderman.

"I have to sneeze," muttered Alena.

But the alderman had already pressed the shutter.

Then I photographed the alderman between the two sisters and the alderman with each of his daughters respectively. He asked us to wait a moment and left the room. The minute he had gone, Alena jumped up on the couch and pulled up her skirt.

"Take a picture of my legs, Danny, so I'll have a souvenir when I have varicose veins from standing around waiting for my dates to show up."

Before Irena could say anything, I snapped her picture. As a photographer I had always been quite quick. As a photographer.

"Now take a picture of Irena's legs, so she won't be so stuck up."

"Don't you want him to photograph you in the nude, dear sister?" said Irena irately.

"Well, if he wants to.... But wouldn't you rather he took you that way, dear sister? I know *he* would, wouldn't you, Danny?"

"Girls, girls," I said.

The alderman returned with a carafe of blueberry wine and four small, elegant glasses on a tray. This had never before happened to me at the alderman's – and a good deal had happened to me there.

"I think we ought to celebrate, don't you agree? That bit of sabotage – I'm afraid it will cost us dear, but – *c'est la guerre.*"

Alena was silent now. The alderman poured us each half a glass and we touched glasses. The hops were fragrant, the wine smelled of blueberries, the river was murmuring. An armoured car clattered across the bridge.

"I used to be a keen photographer myself," the alderman was saying, "when I was young. In those days we used plates, the camera had to be on a tripod and you focused with a black rag over your head. But the quality of the picture was magnificent."

"Show us something, Daddy," said Irena. "Danny's never seen your pictures yet."

"Now we're not going to bore Mr. Smiricky with our family album."

Nothing concerning Irena and her family could ever bore me, and I hastened to assure the alderman of this. He needed no further encouragement and he left the room again. "Do you know what he's going to see, dear sister?" said Alena.

"Our mother at various seasons of the year," said Irena.

"That too. But also – "

Before she could finish, the alderman had returned, almost at a trot, with a missal in hard covers upholstered in red velvet. He sat next to me, between Irena and me – deliberately, I imagine, for he was not as unobservant as he looked. And then it began. The alderman's wife, whom he kept referring to as "my dear departed spouse," really had been taken at different seasons of the year, in comic hat, in ankle-length skirts, in a skiing outfit, her skis with dangerously curved tips, in a formal satin gown, and even in a Columbine costume from a fancy-dress ball, which permitted me to observe that the dear departed had legs like Alena. She was a pretty woman and the photographs were flawlessly in focus. Then followed a photograph of her in a bathing-suit. The suit was provided with a knee-length skirt with diagonal stripes. This confirmed my observation about her legs. She was beautifully slim and there were some palm trees behind her.

"That was taken in Ostend," said the alderman, and his voice caught. "We were there on our honeymoon."

"Really? Then why do the wedding pictures come afterwards?" Alena asked.

"They're a different size, Alenka," said the alderman curtly and turned the page, but not before I had caught a glimpse of his own picture, in a swimming suit with suspenders, and the same palm trees in the background. He had hockey-stick legs. "I put this album together partly chronologically, and partly according to format." The next page displayed a large wedding picture, an assembly of many gentlemen in black and ladies in white, the bridesmaids arranged in size from a three-year-old to one the same height as the bride, and in the centre the young alderman in a morning suit and the dear deceased bride all in white. The alderman took off his pince-nez and began to clean it.

"Those are really very beautiful photographs," I said quickly. "I mean yours. The wedding photos are nice too, but a professional did them. Yours are nicer."

The alderman coughed, put his pince-nez back on again and turned to the next page. On it was a salon portrait of the newlyweds with a painted backdrop intended to represent an old castle.

"It was the fashion in those days," said the alderman. "Today you probably find it laughable."

"Not at all. It's ... rather quaint."

The alderman snapped the missal shut. "Well, you've seen it. We'll have another drink and – " He pulled his watch out of his vest. "It's almost six...."

I understood. "It's time I was going," I said.

"Don't go yet." Alena grabbed the album. "You haven't seen it all yet."

"Alenka! Mr. Smiricky must be bored to death already." The alderman tried to take the missal away from Alena, but she already had it open and thrust it under my nose.

"That's our Irena," she said triumphantly.

The photograph showed a naked child on a sheepskin rug. A naked baby's bottom protruded from the furry rug and the child stared stupidly into the camera, its face slightly blurred.

Alena turned the page rapidly. "And this is me."

Another naked baby, just as silly.

"That's nice," I said.

"Well, that was a fashion in those days, too," said the alderman. "So – here's to your health!"

We drank. I took the book and looked at the naked babies.

"Which one of us was sexier then?" asked Alena.

"Alenka!" said the alderman. He flushed slightly. Not that he was ashamed. I had the distinct impression that he was suppressing laughter. Then he firmly took charge of the missal, and perhaps he meant it as a punishment for he showed me a long series of gradually maturing girls who eventually developed into Alena and Irena. There were no more pictures like the first two.

With a clink, the alderman dropped a glass stopper into the neck of the cut-glass carafe, although there was still quite a bit of wine left in it, and stood up. I took the hint and said my farewells. Irena was beautiful but she still looked tense. Alena was funny and her nose shone.

I walked through the early evening of a late summer's day, past the station and towards home, so overflowing with love that I almost walked right past Marie Dreslerova in front of the Hotel Granada without noticing her. She was with her aunt, so I couldn't have started a conversation with her anyway. There was barely enough time for me to yell, "Good evening, ladies," and Marie replied with a very neutral "Ahoj."

●

"Are you alive or dead?" asks Mr. Sestak.

"Gentlemen," says the ghost, "I arrived at the airport and walked through that tunnel, the one that takes you to the planes. And right there in the doorway was this ... this...."

"Comrade," I suggest.

"Yes, that's the word. Comrade. When I saw this comrade, my legs turned to wood. The comrade smiled at me, and it nearly froze me. It was like something took me by the shoulders and made me do an about-face – "

"Your guardian angel," interposes Marilyn.

"So here I am!" marvels Milan.

Mr. Sestak hits the floor with the Jingling Johnny and starts, in his magnificently cracked bass, "For he's a jolly good fellow!"

We all join in. Milan smiles sheepishly, reaches for a bottle and puts it to his lips. We all gather around him. Marilyn kisses him, Sestak and the democratic youth grab him and toss him up in the air. We catch him and toss him up and down for a while. Mrkvicka accompanies us with a few swing riffs on the violin.

Then Milan sinks down in a chair.

"But oh God, it's awful!"

"What? What's happened?"

"Veronika, I saw her looking out the window. She was inside the plane. For Czechoslovakia. She – she's gone crazy...."

●

*21 July, 1974*
*Munich*

*Brother,*
*Today I shall be brief, not that I don't enjoy writing to you, that would be against me own natural inklination for I'm an inkslinger – tho I am no longer a member of the Checkoslovak Union of tripewriters – but only of the ferreiner der doitchen socialistishen schriftsteller. Today*

*I'm stelling my schrift in a declining position, holding my pen in my mouth and writing on a piece of paper that a chubby little sister of mercy is holding over my head, and I can't understand her because she speaks* Plattdoitch. *And because it's a fountain pen and ink doesn't run up hill all by itelf, I made a hole in the bottom of the pen (which is relative: in normal circumstances the hole would be in the top) and when I'm stelling my schrift I blow out at the same time so that the ink will actually flow onto what would normally be the underside of the paper, if you follow me. Ferstanden?*

*The thing is I've had a coronary, or a hard attack as the popular expression has it, what they used to call in the old days a seizure, but I'm not seized up completely yet, as you can see – even though by the time you read this I will be, you never can tell, as Mrs. Skocdopole always used to say when I'd go over with Franta Kocandrle to play cards and partake of slivovice, purely for charitable reasons, because Mr. Skocdopole was a rank hamateur – at cards, not at the plum brandy – but in his declining days he couldn't walk so he was cut off from the Beranek. His legs swelled up and they said it was from all those long marches during the First World War and since he's only got one good hand his wife had to lay down his tricks for him.*

*During the long nights here in the crankenhouse* der heiligen Tereza vom Jesuskind *I mull over my life so far and medi(da?)tate on what it was could have brought on the seizure when I never did very much in my life, only stelled my schrift and otherwise my life was a quiet one, almost sleepy you might say, with a kind of lullaby rhythm that rocked me from scandal to scandal, and I managed to survive everything, so far. The only thing I discovered was a tendency for the scandals to get progressively larger, from the time I got caught smoking while sitting on the barrel of gas at Helebrants – or when Helebrant told my father I was drawing Alena the alderman's daughter naked and my father says to him: "If only that was all the little bugger was up to ..." with those three dots, very significant, only the way Helebrant interpreted their significants was not quite on, by which I mean it was completely off the mark, because unlike my father he had not secretly read the letters his daughter Janka sent me after what I did when she was in Prague to see* The Battered Bride, *and for which my father gave me the dickens and almost in the same breath told me what the sign Sheiks for Security!! on the door of Helebrant's drugstore meant, so when Helebrant came to him with that drawing problem he was so taken aback he didn't know if he ought to tell Helebrant what I done to his daughter in Prague when she was there allegedly to see* The Battered Bride, *and how (that is: how he was going to tell Helebrant, not how I did it.*

*Janka didn't go into the details in her letter because she didn't even know herself and neither did I, heck I'd never done it before and I was as surprised as all hell that I managed to pull it off at all), anyway he was so taken aback that he just said: "If only that was all the little bugger was up to ..." with those three dots, and he left it hanging there as a generality with no concrete reference to Janka Helebrantova, and where was I? Oh yes, that daisy chain of scandals stretching through my life from the sneaking of my first smoke on a barrel of gas, through all my theatrical plays, to the day I crapped out so I wouldn't crap out later on and betrayed the Party and the government by defecating to the Reich (I couldn't possibly have betrayed the Czech people or Czech literature in this case, since they have no executive power over me), right up to that date, not so long ago, when I had my coronary, and I read in* Der Spiegel *that our lad Honza Vrchcolab had a coronary as well, even though he didn't betray the Party, much less the government, and the people don't enter into it in his case at all. When I read that description of how the executive arm of the Party and the government dragged his pretty wife over the cobblestones by the hair and even dealt roughly with him, I suddenly went all out of kilter and felt that pain in the middle of my chest, clinically described, and Honza Vrchcolab, as they say in books, not only the kind I wrote, flashed like a rocket across the screen of my inner vision and all of a sudden I saw that he had a kind of philogenetive life, as my erudite near-son-in-law Horst would say, a kind of para-dime, as one university professor would say, also a Czech, who I play cards with here and who has done a switcheroo from Communist ideology to structuralist ideology because he's got ideology in his blood and everything has to belong in the proper pidgin hole. That lad, Vrchcolab, was such a gullible little fool in his childhood and youth that he fell for every flumdiddle and con game in the books. He could get excited about anything, about a stogie and a Georgian moustache, and all inside a single calendar year, until at last he slowly wisened up, purely from personal experience not from the books he might have read and got wise from straight away, but he didn't start to wisen up until he had already garnered some wisdom from personal experience. I tell you, isn't he the living prefiguration of each of our individual lives? It's enough to recall you, for example, the way you used to gabble and chatter away almost to death and all purely to entertain those birds, who were pretty, I'll grant you that, Irena the alderman's daughter and Molly D'Eussleur (I can't remember any more of their names but there were so many you must have gabbled away the equivalent of the compleat works — including them as were lost — of the Elizabethan dramaturdgists, plus*

*those by Zahradnik-Brodsky and his imitators), and because you gab-*
*bled so much, it probably never even crossed your mind that a fellow,*
*especially when he's young, has another physical organ at his disposal*
*besides his mouth for discourse with women. That's how bone-headed*
*you were.*

*All of us were, every Jack and Jill of us, except that some were politi-*
*cally on the proper side and they got locked up, and today it seems like*
*they were smart from the start. Poor old Vrchco, he was stupid at the*
*start and on the wrong side politically, so today it looks as though he*
*was born stupid, even though from the material point of view there*
*were no flies on him, though there are today. On the other hand, today*
*he is wise, though not so much from the material and career point of*
*view; there are other hustlerati around who are better at that today,*
*somebody like Los, for example, also a playright, or that mob of hacks*
*who make a living out of the moving pictures. I can't help feeling that*
*laughable as Vrchcolab seemed for most of his life, he doesn't seem as*
*ridiculous today, but maybe that's also because I have this kind of*
*Czech philogenetic inferiority complex — he didn't crap out whereas I*
*did. What the hell can he expect to get from it all besides so-called*
*immortality and a so-called clean conscience, when clearly neither is*
*worth the effort as proved by the example of the Czech people, the so-*
*called overwhelming majority of whom shit regally on both immortal-*
*ity and conscience and hang out their flags, drink their beer and talk*
*their talk but only when there's no one nearby to overhear them?*

*Ah well, life is one of the most difficult, as the Czech folk say, and*
*they're right. There's a certain apostle of the Holy Church, one Josef*
*Beran, who comes to the crankenhouse to visit me and so carry out his*
*duty to Minister to the Sick. About five and twenty years ago he was*
*stupid on the right side of things so he was locked away for twelve, but*
*because he's a Christian, and humble, he doesn't now try to pretend he*
*was always clever, he only tries to save my soul, if I have one, which is*
*far from certain. Anyway, to make him happy I let myself be*
*christened here on this my death bed and I'm now a Christian like you,*
*brother, and at the same time an old social democrat, which doesn't go*
*together, say the co-frères of my apostle, Josef Beran from the Rosary*
*Brotherhood of St. Tereza of the Christchild, but it seems to me that it*
*goes together just dandy. I guess I'm still just stupid. And believe it or*
*not, this Josef Beran had trouble with the Rosary brothers because of*
*me, defending my former activity (i.e., in dramatics) and the fact that I*
*once testified at a rehabilitational hearing in favour of some Catholic*
*men of letters saying that they were both good and innocent, which*
*they were, even more the former than the latter. After this apologia,*

the most faithful of the Rosary brothers lit into him quite sharply because they said I had been in the Party and once a Party member, always a criminal, is how they felt about it. This Brother Beran did not deny but said something about some other criminal on another Rosary brother's right hand, but I don't know anything about that, because I haven't got that far yet in my study of the catechism, I have to take it slowly because I'm terminally ill. But the brothers would not apply the analogy to my case and so Brother Beran got pissed off, or rather was moved to wrath, but it was the wrath of the just, and he told them they were just the same as the Communists only on the other side of the spectrum, and now as far as I can tell he's in the bad books of the Rosary brotherhood. He told me there are not one but three Holy Churches, the Suffering Church, the Fighting Church and the Victorious Church, but he forgot to tell me which is which. I reckon he is the Sufferer, and the Rosary brothers are the Fighters, except that would leave me Victorious and I don't know about that since I neither Suffered nor Fought for the Church, so I'm just collecting unearned, spiritual dividends from it now, and that's all. Which, come to think of it, you could interpret as a victory.

But for all this I'm not in very good shape, brother, I mean physically. It must be all that blowing into the pen that does it. I swallowed some ink and my mouth is aquamarine so when Janka (the wife) came to visit me with Janka (the daughter) a while ago they were startled because they thought I was blue and therefore a corpse, but I'm not one yet and perhaps the Lard will allow and I won't be one for a while yet (that is as long as He Himself is not like Rosary bros. and for the love of God I hope He isn't, because then He'd be something like Stalin, and Jesus Maria Josef he can't be like that, even though — as Beran, Josef, says — His ways are mysterious and we ought not to inquire after His counsels — I don't know what he means by counsels, it must be something intimate, so I didn't ask since I've always been discreet).

Meanwhile the girls have recovered and they're pretending it's nothing and that everything is ganz normal, except for the fact that the nuns are keeping me here because of this cold. Horst doesn't know how to hide his feelings so well, after all he's not a woman and he's never been to drammer school, so he goes around with a face like a dyplo dokus, that is a lunk-headed look even though he isn't a lunk-head at all. Why didn't we, brother, devote all our energies to exhuming prehistoric beasts? That sort of thing doesn't bother any regime because the creatures are safely dead, at least as long as you don't start drawing any philosophistic conclusions like Darwin, or Marks after *him, did. That would bother them, especially today when I get the impression old Marks is starting to bother his own Rosy Krishna Brotherhood, so they turned him into a catechism instead of following his example, because he was a thinker, not an obedient follower of the Party and the Government.*

*And so, fellow countryman, I say farewell to you today, maybe not for ever, but should it be so, so what? Whatever happens, we'll all meet in that great card-index in the sky. They never destroy your file, because the times are always changing and you never know what might come in handy to someone.*

*So I'll give one more toot into my pen and say:*

*All the best to you, and when you think of me at all, think well.*

> *Your*
> *Vratislav*

> *redeemed sinner, as our dear departed*
> *Nadia might have said of me today*

•

I managed to find a paperback edition of *At the Mountains of Madness* in an American-style drugstore on our way to the Savoie restaurant, where we are now banqueting on oysters. The cover displays a fur-covered skull with two yellowed, rodent-like teeth and from the hollow eye-sockets there burn two pairs of bright eyes belonging to formless Kafkaesque beasties. A furry worm is crawling in and out of the sockets.

"Is *that* where you want us to go?" Irene shudders. "It looks horrible."

"Even horror has its beauty, Svensson," I reply. "And anyway, what is beauty in art? The realization that this is exactly how it is in reality or in nightmares. But nightmare and reality often overlap, and reality is always less perfect, in both the positive and the negative sense. Art captures that essence which reality, sometimes more, sometimes less, spreads thin. In art, the essence presents itself as an undiluted, powerful possibility. And because art incarnates what is possible, it can mean anything under the sun."

Irene furrows her delicate brow. "I'm just an undergraduate; I haven't taken aesthetics yet."

"Your mistake. I'll give you another F. For failure."

We are sitting in the Savoie restaurant, above us the Van Gogh sky, the bells of Notre Dame are carolling and questionable-looking beauties are promenading up and down the embankment. I have ordered a triple portion of oysters. "This will make us sick," Svensson says. "We won't be up to making love." I reassure her that if the stomach can bear them, oysters act as an aphrodisiac.

I open Lovecraft and, above the Seine, beside Irene who does not suspect that the Mountains of Madness lie only a few miles from here and that in their defiles and passageways lurk terrible Shoggoths with land-mines and computerized records, beneath the safe Parisian skies, I begin to read:

" 'It was young Danforth who drew our notice to the curious regulari-ties of the higher mountain sky line – regularities like clinging fragments of perfect cubes, which Lake had mentioned in his messages, and which indeed justified his comparison with the dreamlike suggestions of primordial tem-ple ruins, on cloudy Asian mountaintops so subtly and strangely painted by Roerich.... I had felt it in October when we had first caught sight of Victoria Land, and I felt it afresh now. I felt, too, another wave of uneasy conscious-ness of Archaean mythical resemblances; of how disturbingly this lethal realm corresponded to the evilly famed plateau of Leng in the primal writ-ings. Mythologists have placed Leng in Central Asia; but the racial memory of man – or of his predecessors – is long, and it may well be that certain tales have come down from lands and mountains and temples of horror earlier than Asia and earlier than any human world we know. A few daring mystics have hinted at a pre-Pleistocene origin for the fragmentary Pnakotic Manuscripts, and have suggested that the devotees of Tsathoggua were as alien to mankind as Tsathoggua was itself. Leng, wherever in space or time it might brood, was not a region I would care to be in or near....' "

"Uff!" remarks Svensson. "And you want us to go there on our honey-moon?"

I silence her with a wave of my hand, for I do not wish to be distracted from the magic naivety of that very wise vision.

" 'At that moment I felt sorry that I had ever read the abhorred *Necro-nomicon*, or talked so much with that unpleasantly erudite folklorist Wil-marth –' "

"What was that? Necro...."

" –nomicon. A book written by the dead."

She shudders. It is a balmy evening in Paris.

"I'm not going there with you," she shakes her head. "If you insist on a literary honeymoon, let's go down to the Mississippi. There's a tourist agency that has put those old stern-wheelers back in commission – "

"You don't like dead folk?"

"What kind of question is that?"

She looks at me uncomprehendingly, she has beautiful faded eyes. I feel a great compassion for Nicole. God knows what's awaiting her. I have known girls like her. *Necronomicon.* A kind of joke for crazy friends.

"Nigger Jim," I say to her gently. "D'you remember? When Huck, who is supposed to be dead, frightens him on that island in the Mississippi?"

She claps her forehead in mock exasperation. "Of course, I wrote a paper about it."

"Then I guess you couldn't have read it, Svensson. And it was a good paper. Must have cost you at least thirty dollars."

"I wrote *some* of my papers myself, sir."

"They would be overpriced at five."

"You're sitting on me, sir."

"Sometimes you sit on me," I say cynically and she blushes. "And for our honeymoon we're going to the plateau of Leng. Whether you want to or not. Sooner or later, we will all go there."

"On our honeymoons?"

"Yes. Like witches used to. On their brooms. Then they kissed the devil's bare ass and fornicated with goats."

"Don't talk like that."

"I don't have such absolute faith in the power of words to believe that what we do not say does not exist. It was and will be, whether we talk about it or not. They kissed the devil's bare bum, and if he commanded, they would even dance the Cossack, to the Russian beat. The thin and the fat, the highly placed and the well-informed, they would all fornicate with a goat when he, the devil, commanded. And they will, when he commands. I see them everywhere around me. Even in the United States, and in Canada – "

"You haven't had that much to drink."

"It's not the alcohol that's talking. And listen, Svensson, so you'll be at least a little bit prepared. One day you'll see that land with your own eyes."

And I read:

" 'As we drew near the forbidding peaks, dark and sinister above the line of crevasse-riven snow and interstitial glaciers, we noticed more and more the curiously regular formations clinging to the slopes; and thought again of the strange Asian paintings of Nicholas Roerich.' "

"Who was Nicholas Roerich?"

"A Russian painter."

"What's a Russian doing there?"

I shrug. "He was simply there, Nicole," and I continue reading: " 'The ancient and wind-weathered rock strata fully verified all of Lake's bulletins, and proved that these pinnacles had been towering up in exactly the same way since a surprisingly early time in earth's history – perhaps over fifty million years.' "

The waiter brings us two small mountains of oysters.

"It's starting to get repetitive," says Irene. "You've already read me something about that Roerich. And about Lake."

"Lovecraft didn't have a great range of fantasy, but what he had was intense. It was more like an obsession than a fantasy. Like all prophets."

"What did he prophesy?" asks Irene incuriously. Her interest is focused now on those living animals in their ugly carapaces. With her gentle hand she grasps the oyster knife.

"The same as all prophets, Nicole. Doom."

She slips the creature between her pretty lips. "It's delicious!"

I'm silent. I remember too much. I am struck abruptly by the unjustly different fates in this world. I look at this child of the West who before me, under Eastern eyes, is cruelly slicing through the muscle and tissues of another dying creature and squeezing sharp lemon juice into its vital parts. "Mm!" the knife flashes again, as we stood with Sylva, I a dead man, Sylva scarcely twenty-five, in Neuilly, a short distance from here, and Sylva said,

"How many should I get?"

"I don't know. A dozen?"

"For each of us?"

"Maybe."

"I'll get two to make sure."

She bought eight dozen oysters. Not a muscle in the vendor's face moved. The huge bag of shells must have weighed ten kilos. We drank champagne with them. Pavelka was soon stiff, Milos Forman had to go to a business meeting, and Sylva and I were left alone. In that two-storey house in Neuilly. Martin and Martina were asleep upstairs in the children's room. We had already squeezed about a dozen lemons dry and we were still eating and drinking. After midnight Sylva collapsed in an armchair and said, "I feel *enceinte*."

"Maybe you are."

"Don't tempt the devil, for crying out loud. I've got a première coming up in a month."

"Are you going back?"

"Of course. I can't leave them in the lurch, can I?" she sighed. "Here it hurts, there it aches, and here I've got a shooting pain," and she laid her hand on her stomach. "We should've bought fewer."

"Or not eaten so many."

"Or drunk more with them," she said and took an intemperate gulp of champagne.

"Or put more lemon juice on them," I said. "I'm not going back."

"What are you going to do?"

"Die, of course. And be born again."

"Jeepers creepers!" she groaned a dated oath. "Can you have little ones from oysters?"

"Little oysters?"

"Little people, you dunce. Go back home. What would you do anywhere else?"

"What would I do back home?"

"What you always did," she grimaced.

"Does your tummy hurt?"

"That's another way of putting it," she said. She stood up, wavered, and rushed to the door.

I looked at the remaining oysters. We had opened them all up in advance and there were about fifteen of them left, dying, on the plate. I cut short their suffering. Next morning Sylva was sitting at the table like a dead man's wife, drinking Alka-Seltzer and chewing on charcoal from Prague.

"Did they give you the runs too?" asked her husband.

I shook my head. "They made me hungry. I got up in the night and cleaned out your icebox." Pavelka wasn't with us any longer. In the night he had added everything up in his mind and taken the morning express back to Prague.

I look at Nicole. "They seem to agree with you," I say. "You said I'd ordered too many and now you haven't left me one."

She shakes her head, her mouth stuffed with the last oyster. Her eyes laugh with the innocent malice of youth.

"You can't get them as good as this in Toronto. Not this fresh," she says with her mouth full.

We have another glass of champagne and I pick up Lovecraft.

"Are you going to read any more?" she asks, clearly bored.

"Just one more passage," I say. "Let the old man have his pleasure."

"And then we'll go back to the hotel?"

"Then we'll go back to the hotel."

"Or should we go to the Crazy Horse first?"

"Now surely we don't need to do that, Svensson. And listen – a reading from the epistle of H.P. Lovecraft, the twelfth chapter, God knows what verse: 'There now lay revealed on the ultimate white horizon behind the grotesque city a dim, elfin line of pinnacled violet whose needle-pointed heights loomed dreamlike against the beckoning rose colour of the western sky. Up toward this shimmering rim sloped the ancient tableland, the depressed course of the bygone river traversing it as an irregular ribbon of shadow. For a second we gasped in admiration of the scene's unearthly cosmic beauty, and then vague horror began to creep into our souls. For this far violet line could be nothing else than the terrible mountains of the forbidden land – highest of the earth's peaks and focus of earth's evil;

harbourers of nameless horrors and Archaean secrets; shunned and prayed to by those who feared to carve their meaning; untrodden by any living thing on earth, but visited by the sinister lightnings and sending strange beams across the plains in the polar night – beyond doubt the unknown archetype of that dreaded Kadath in the Cold Waste beyond abhorrent Leng, whereof primal legends hint evasively.' The Mountains of Madness."

"Brrr!" says Irene. "There is no way we're going there! We couldn't make love."

"We are going there," I say gloomily. "I've already been there. People do make love, even there – "

"How come you're still alive?" asks Nicole. "If everyone died?"

"I did die," I say. "But I was born again."

"You grew old pretty fast, then."

"I was born too late."

Suddenly Nicole makes up her mind. "Let's go back to the hotel!"

"And we'll read in bed. It's reading week, after all."

She jumps up and clutches her stomach. "Oh, my God." Her faded eyes are frantic.

"You're pregnant," I say. "You'll have young oysters."

"Where's the ladies' room?" she asks in confusion. The waiter rushes up. "*Où est – où est – *" the child asks in her Toronto French, her forehead bedewed with perspiration, "*la – la toilette?*"

The waiter whispers something discreetly in her ear. Nicole, in her eight-hundred-dollar dress, vanishes behind a curtain.

Ah child. Sweet child of the West. *Dominus tecum* – in those Mountains of Madness....

•

"Booker!" says Dotty in a domineering voice to the black barman. "How many drinks did Mr. Senka have?"

"Just one, ma'am," says the barman.

"Booker!" Dotty's voice cuts like ice. "Make Mr. Senka another screwdriver."

The barman shakes his shaker and his eyes shine behind the artificial grapevine. With great effort, Mr. Senka tears his eyes away from Dotty's star-spangled crotch. "That's it, my dear," he giggles, "a screwdriver. I like screwdrivers."

"That guide in Moscow," Dotty is saying, "just about flipped when I told her we were Czechs. She said we had wasted so many of their best young men. You know, exed them. Well, I told her she was off her rocker and if anyone did any killing it was more likely the other way around. But she gave us these dirty looks all during our honeymoon. She was convinced that Prague was a slaughterhouse!"

"The Soviet people will fall for anything. A nation of true believers," says Bocar, and he holds out an empty glass.

"Booker!" Dotty calls out sharply, as though she were on a plantation a century ago. "Can't you see our guest has an empty glass?"

"Yes, ma'am," replies the black bartender. As though he too were on a plantation. He shakes his shaker feverishly. Bocar holds out another empty glass. "And my wife is drinking Pink Ladies."

"Did you get that, Booker?" Dotty says in an irritating tone of voice. Could she have become such a shrew since getting married? Well, they have just come back from a honeymoon in the Soviet Union.

Booker takes a second shaker in his left hand and shakes.

"It looks very nice on you, madame," sighs Mr. Senka and he stares again at the sparkling panties. Dotty crosses her legs, registers Mr. Senka's stare, and begins to glance furtively at her attire to make sure something hasn't come undone somewhere.

Margitka leaves for the washroom. I watch her go so I don't have to look at Dotty, but Dotty also gets up and leaves the room. She is clearly going to ask Margitka to check her to see if she's decent.

"Young man," I hear Bocar say in a half-whisper. I don't know why he always addresses me in such an absurd fashion. Mr. Senka has turned towards the bar, and is filling a pipe from a metal box. "Young fellow," whispers Bocar.

"Yes?" I turn to him. The whisky has ignited his eyes.

"Let me thank you."

"What for?"

My heart jumps. In the whiskied eyes there is a hint of ridicule, a hint of desperation, but still friendship. Even so, I find myself short of breath.

"Don't pretend you don't know what I'm talking about."

I feel a rush of hot blood. I suppose I'm blushing like a little boy caught stealing plums.

"Don't take it so hard," says Bocar gruffly. "I'm not a monster. She deserves it."

I try to blurt out something, except that I don't know what to blurt. Such are the strange times we live in.

"She's a saint," says Bocar. "Any other woman would have shat on a cripple like me long ago. All the more so when ... for so many years before...."

Again I try to stammer something. But for even the most basic linguistic efforts one must have something to say.

Bocar has recovered from his sentimental recollections and looks at me roguishly. "What are you blushing like a schoolgirl for? The world is queer and that's normal. Come on. Let's drink to it."

For the last time I try to stammer something, but all I manage to say is "Cheers!"

"Cheers!" cries Bocar. "Long may it thrive."

We touch glasses, and in honour of the infidelity of Bocar's beloved wife we drink Mr. Zawynatch's Chivas Regal.

Mr. Senka, standing by the bar, is looking at his host and chortling with irrepressible laughter. Mr. Zawynatch bares an expensive set of dentures.

"What is it? Tell me!" he demands.

"I'd have to whisper it to you."

"So whisper it to me."

Mr. Zawynatch leans his ear towards Mr. Senka and his clothes sparkle kaleidoscopically. Booker is shaking away furiously. Against the background of the topless ethnic beauty's pink skin a first-class set of glint shines in his dark face.

•

*Darwin*
*May 7, 1977*

*Dear Mr. Smiricky,*
*It is with great regret that I must inform you that your letter addressed to Mr. Skocdopole cannot be delivered, because the addressee died tragically in the recent hurricane which struck our city.*
*Please accept my deepest condolences.*
*Yours sincerely,*
*Kevin W. McIntyre,*
*Chief Postmaster of the City of Darwin*

•

I went to the factory because I had nothing else to do. The *Werkschutz* Blühme was sitting at the game and he smiled amiably at me. I told him I'd been sick, but Blühme just brushed the remark off with a wave of his hand.

"Not to worry. Almost everybody's sick."

He was tamed, and had begun to speak Czech again, even though he had not yet changed his name back to its original Czech form Bluma. Also his sense of self-importance had radically diminished, and he had regained his sense of humour. It was gallows humour, of course, but perhaps there is no other kind. I walked across the yard to the hall where last winter Nadia and I had drilled the cross-brackets for the Messerschmitts. Nejezchleba was sitting on a green barrel in front of the welding section, shamelessly puffing on something that looked like a huge cigar rolled from newspapers. Before I reached him, Gerta Ceehova came out of the administrative building in a grey skirt and a brown shirt, her blonde hair tied up neatly in a bun. She was carrying files, and she walked past the smoking Nejezchleba as though she saw nothing at all. Nejezchleba jumped down from his seat and joined me.

"Are you going for your pay packet?"

It was Saturday.

"D'you mean they're still handing out pay?"

"Sure. Kleinenherr is looking after it. All the rest of the Krauts have cleared out. Except for Ceehova, of course," and he looked round after the austere National Socialist who was just disappearing into the payroll department.

We went into "Siberia." There were quite a few people there but that was because they had come for their wages. The place was also uncommonly quiet. Instead of the racket of the pneumatic hammers, which always reminded me of machine-gun fire, all that could be heard was the screeching of a saw coming from the head of the line and then a whistling sound as someone let compressed air into a drill. Hetflajs and Svestka were still working and old man Varecka was standing nearby. But when I came nearer, I saw that they were making a fancy doghouse out of the duralumin underwing mounting panel for the Bf 109's auxiliary wing cannon.

We went into the can. In the familiar London fog the old debating circle was debating. Today they had a guest. It was the *Werkschutz* Eisler, and he was shouting away like the old days except now he was falling all over his tongue. There was still a spark of life in him; he wasn't as wilted as Blühme in the porter's lodge, and he too was shouting in Czech. At least partly. But unlike the old times, the seminar members no longer bothered to sit with their trousers down on the latrines. They were pumping Eisler for information.

"And he *does* have a *Geheimwaffe*! *Der Führer* has it," screeched Eisler. "One *Geheimwaffe* like that and the enemy is *kaputt*."

"What is it, trained pinworms, you onionhead?" asked Malina.

"The *Geheimwaffe* is *fertig* already and you'll soon be laughing on the other side of your face! When things get really bad, the *Geheimwaffe* will force the army to throw up in the towel."

"So what's the secret weapon, peacock feathers?" said Nosek. "To tickle the army's throat with?"

"He means the knights of Blanik," said the lad from the paint-shop. "He did say, 'when things get really bad.'"

"The knights of Blanik aren't going to bloody help the Krauts, you peacock," said Malina.

"Why not? Good King Wenceslas is a collaborator now, isn't he?"

"How'd you like a biff on the biscuit," said the pious lad from the paint-shop.

"The *Geheimwaffe* is for breaking up atoms!" shouted Eisler and took a drink from a pocket flask.

"Give us a lick, Eisler," said Kos.

Eisler rocked back and forth gently in high boots no longer as carefully polished as in the old days. He tried to refocus his inebriated eyes on Kos and said, "I will, if you'll drink to the *Geheimwaffe*."

"Why not," said Kos. "Drink to the bloody Jap suicide pilots if you want."

"Drink to them too, *richtig*. But first to the *Geheimwaffe*."

He handed the pocket flask to Kos, Kos took a deep swig, and instead of returning it to Eisler he passed it over to Malina.

"Here's to the *Geheimwaffe*," said Malina, "you mouse." He drank and the bottle started making the rounds.

"Wait a minute. *Halt!*" shouted Eisler. "I want my schnapps back."

"Eisler!" said Vozenil. "Surely you can't have nothing against us drinking to the gehimewaffy!"

"Of course not," roared the *Werkschutz* and he pulled another flask out of his other pocket. It was full. Eisler was well prepared for the end of the war. "The atoms will blow everything to *Rattescheisse*. There's going to be a huge bang."

"That there will," said Kos.

"What do you mean 'atom'?" asked Malina. "What's this snail ranting about?"

"Atoms," said Eisler, taking a deep draught so that the bottle was immediately half empty. "They make up *die Masse*. And atoms are full of — *die Energie*. Boom!" he cried, so loudly that the little window of the can opened a crack. He leaned back vacantly against the wall.

"What's he on about 'massa'?" asked Kos.

"*Masse* is German for matter," said Nosek. "Matter is made of atoms with electrons spinning around their nucleus."

"Matter?" asked Malina. "You mean stuff like earth, you gorilla? They're making their gehimewaffie out of dirt?"

"Any kind of matter," said Nosek. "Like your saw, for instance."

There was a massive saw sticking out of Malina's blue coveralls. He too was probably trying to make some kind of doghouse.

"This? You trying to tell me there's something spinning around inside this, you chimpanzee?"

"Electrons," said Nosek. "The saw is made of steel, steel is made of iron atoms and every iron atom has a nucleus with some electrons, I don't know exactly how many, spinning around it. Just like the solar system. The planets spin around the sun."

"Isn't there something spinning round inside your head?" asked Kos. "How'd you like a sock in the snoot to make them spin faster?"

"You can read a book about it if you want," said Nosek. "I take it you can read?"

Malina looked intently at the saw. Then he held it in front of Nosek's face.

"There is fuck all spinning around in this. There would have to be some air bubbles in it, and then it would break, you dromedary."

"Atoms are invisible to the naked eye," said Nosek. "But if you look at them through an electron microscope, you can see them spinning about. That saw is just seething with life, you'd be amazed."

Malina raised the saw threateningly. "So you're trying to tell me this saw is crawling like a piece of wormy cheese, you limburger!"

"Maybe that's the gehimewaffie, boys," said the green veteran from the Reich. "They've got these supplies of wormy cheese and they're going to dump it from planes and the Red Army will be scared shitless by the stench."

Eisler emitted an ugly belching sound and along with it came a rush of ugly, greenish bile, soiling Malina's blue coveralls. Malina began to curse vehemently. Kos and Vozenil grabbed the *Werkschutz* by the arms and dragged him over to one of the bowls. Eisler retched helplessly and noisily passed wind.

"Long live the gehimebarf!" said the lad from the paint-shop. Malina stood by the filthy washbasins in vomit-covered coveralls, wiping the secret weapon from his trouser legs with a dirty rag.

•

*He that believeth in me, though*
*he were dead, yet shall he live.*
JOHN 11:25

*The Lord God Almighty has called unto Himself*
*the soul of my beloved wife*

*Nadezda Melicharova*
*née Jirouskova*

*She passed away after great suffering on the Day of the Feast*
*of the Betrothal of the Virgin Mary, January 23, 1946, at the*

*age of 21 years. Her last remains will be interred on January
27 in the Kostelec Municipal Cemetery, where she will await
the Resurrection in glory.
Mass for the soul of the deceased will be held on Sunday,
January 28 at 10 a.m. in the Cathedral Church of St. Lawrence.*

*In the name of family and relatives,
Frantisek Melichar, husband*

•

I pushed the receipt across the counter to Vrata Blazej and at that moment Irena and Alena came into the shop. I told them excitedly that the pictures were ready. Then we waited until Vrata came back from the office where Mr. Helebrant kept the developed pictures in little bags with the customers' names on them. Alena was afraid she would look awful. When Vrata came back, she snatched the bag from his hands and she and Irena eagerly pulled out the pictures. I watched over their shoulders. The first one showed Alena with the alderman. Alena was prettier in the picture than in reality.

"Your nose isn't shiny," I said.

"Hey, Vrata, do you think you could cut Daddy out and just have me enlarged?" asked Alena.

She meant it seriously. It was a very pretty picture of her. Meanwhile Irena had laid another snapshot aside on the counter, having hardly looked at it. Vrata picked it up.

"Whose are these, your dad's?" he asked.

"Let's see!" Alena took the picture out of his hand. "Are you blind, Vratislav? Those are my legs."

So they were. I had captured them precisely. The hem of her skirt was not in the picture at all — only those bare, suntanned, beautiful legs, run into shape playing the pivot position in basketball. "Why didn't you go any higher, you artist?" said Vrata.

"Any higher was her skirt," I said. "This way it at least unleashes your fantasy."

Vrata examined the photograph while Alena and Irena looked at the rest. Irena with the alderman, smiling like Deanna Durbin, though her face looked somewhat chubby. Strange — she was prettier in reality than in the photograph. She uncovered another photo, this one with the happy father between two dear sisters, Irena turned two-thirds profile and almost as beautiful as she was in reality, Alena with her hand over her mouth and her nose gleaming as brightly as the ring on her index finger.

"That's a good picture, Danny," said Irena.

"Could you cut me out of that one?" asked Alena, "and put me back from the first picture?"

"Nothing easier," I said. "A simple photomontage."

"Just put her legs there," said Irena. "That's what you like best about her anyway."

"You're quite bright, dear sister. By the way, where are my legs?" Alena looked around. "Vrata! What are you doing?"

She shrieked so loudly that Mr. Helebrant came into the front of the shop behind Vrata.

"I'm just making my imagination concrete," said Vrata. He had placed the photograph of Alena's legs on white wrapping paper and he was drawing in the rest of her body with a soft pencil, naturally with nothing on. Vrata knew how to draw. The naked body was almost as realistic as the picture of the legs. "I'll put a photograph of your head on top from the best picture, the one where your nose isn't shining," he said.

All at once a resounding slap spun him around.

"Blazej! What are you doing?"

"I'm just sketching, sir. I was intending to draw the clothes over the top, sir."

"Clothes, shmlothes! You clear out of here back into the stockroom and unwrap the ammonia." Then he resolutely tore off the piece of paper with the beautiful naked body, handed the photo of the legs back to Alena and got ready to crumple the sketch up.

"Give it to me, Mr. Helebrant!" begged Alena. Mr. Helebrant stopped.

"What d'you want with that, Alena?"

"I'll give it to Daddy. He'd never believe me that Vrata is that dirty. I'm going to ask him to tell Vrata's parents."

I knew she was lying. Alena was no tattle and Vrata's drawing had turned out very nicely. Perhaps she wanted to finish the montage herself, as a souvenir for her children.

"I can do that myself. But let me think it over first," said Mr. Helebrant, and like a barbarian he crumpled the lovely nude into a formless ball. "I'll make Vratislav work in the stockroom after closing hours as a punishment."

Alena made a sad face and waited to see where Mr. Helebrant would toss the paper. He stuck it into his pocket. I made up my mind to go to the Slovan wine room that evening where Mr. Helebrant went to drink secret supplies of wine with Mr. Skocdopole. The formless ball was not lost yet.

"Come on, sister, let's go," announced Irena suddenly. "A packet of alum, please, Mr. Helebrant." She handed me the pictures. "They really turned out very nicely, Dannykins," she said sweetly. Except that when Irena said something that sweetly, and when she called me Dannykins, it meant she was being venomous. She got the alum, paid for it and took Alena by the hand.

"We haven't seen them all yet," protested Alena.

"You saw yourself, and you have your legs. Let's go, dear sister."

And she energetically thrust Alena out of the shop ahead of her.

I didn't understand what was going on. I went back to looking at my snapshots, but this time Mr. Helebrant was looking over my shoulder. Alena with the alderman. Irena with the alderman. The alderman between Alena and Irena. Then, "A double exposure," said Mr. Helebrant knowledgeably.

What a fool! I had forgotten to advance the film. There I was, sitting on the couch at the alderman's house, Alena squeezed up to my left, prettier than in reality and her nose not shining, and to my right a ghost. But the identity of the ghost was unmistakable. It was Marie Dreslerova, sticking her tongue out at the camera – and it suited her enormously. I had met her, my camera freshly charged, the day before I had gone to the alderman's to show off in front of the dear sisters with my historical snapshots. But this snapshot turned out to be the most historical of them all.

•

*February 12, 1974*
*Tel Aviv*

*Dear Danny,*

*Please don't be surprised that I'm writing you after all these years and please forgive me for not answering your letter giving me your Canadian address. I didn't answer, dear Danny, because I'm practically speaking dead, and I'm writing you now because you're the only person I have left in the world. Does that seem ridiculous to you? But you are – the only one I have left.*

*I have to write it. David is no longer alive. Neither is his wife Naomi. A month after the war they were killed by a bomb in a café on Rabbi Leov Boulevard.*

*Danny, my last friend. When the soldiers came to tell me I didn't even cry. I couldn't cry, because I died at that moment. Once before that I had nearly died of fear, when David was called up again, though "called up" is not the right word for it. As soon as he heard on the radio how our Semitic cousins had defiled Yom Kippur, he rushed straight to his command headquarters. For three weeks I had no word from him, and it was a bloody war. I don't have to tell you what it was like, and anyway I couldn't possibly describe it. Naomi and I worked* in the hospital, although Naomi was already seven months pregnant, and so we saw with our own eyes what the war cost us. But David came back. He had several new medals and he was in the group that had crossed the Suez and surrounded an entire army of cousins.

I can't cry any more, Danny, but for the first time, I think, since that first war, the one I spent in Auschwitz, I feel hatred. I swear to you I never hated the cousins before. I don't know why. Perhaps the Germans took all the room I had for hate, and also they seemed like children to me, playing with fire, but children all the same. Now I hate them. May God forgive me. Ever since the soldiers came to tell me that David and Naomi were no longer alive, I've been reading and reading. Books about the Arabs and what they were doing when I was in Auschwitz during the war. Did you know they even had an SS division called the Muslim SS Handschar Division, led by some colonel Sauberzweig, and they were so good that Himmler held them up as an example to the rest of the German SS? And did you know too that there were no Arab units in the British Army at all because the British thought they were unreliable, but all during the war the Great Mufti of Jerusalem broadcast to the Arabs from Berlin?

I know. You couldn't tell your friends in Canada that. They would say that the Arabs were under the British thumb, and that every enemy of the British was automatically their friend, and that you have to understand them. But if you have to understand that, why can't people understand us? We've been living under the world's thumb for centuries and we had to wear the Star of David way back when the Arabs conquered Spain. Can't they understand that we want our own country at last and anyone who tries to deny it to us will be our enemy? No, I'll never be at home here, Danny. Till my dying day I'll always be from Kostelec. But our children – ah well, not mine. Now at last I'm crying, Danny. For the first time in my life I've said to myself what the women in Auschwitz would say when their husbands, their children, their families, everyone was killed: Why couldn't I have gone up that chimney too?

I'm trying to be cynical to stop the crying.

Write me, Danny, so I'll have something to read. Something that won't arouse hatred in me. Like how we used to go swimming at the Jericho pool in Kostelec with Benno when we were kids, or else write me how you're living in Canada. If you're alive. Write whatever you want. Danny, my dear friend, write and tell me what life really is.

Yours,<br>Rebecca

•

Dotty is behaving very nastily to the black bartender. It is not even in Deep South style anymore, but more like Nero's ancient Rome.

"What's going on, Mrs. Zawynatch?" I ask. "You shouldn't have gone to Moscow, it's made a racist out of you."

"It has not made a racist out of me," says Dotty with dignity. "But I can't stand idiots. Did you hear me, Booker? I can't stand idiots."

"Mrs. Zawynatch," says the barman imploringly, "I did my best. I studied the newspapers and pamphlets. I read – "

"Oh, shut up!"

"What did he do to you?" I ask in Czech.

"He bungled everything," she shoots back. "Not even the secret police could believe those letters he wrote were for real."

"What letters?"

"To my friend Lida, of course. I wanted to marry her off, marry her off to someone in the West so that she could get out."

Domineeringly she orders a White Lady. When Booker finally mixes the drink to her satisfaction, she stabs him with a look that could open an oyster and the poor fellow retreats behind the plastic grapevines.

"I told him the letters had to be sexy, amorous, passionate," she says angrily, as the tragedy slowly unfolds. "And I told him they should be politically with it. But the idiot made them *totally* political, so political that not even the hardest-line newspaper back home would print them! They'd think it was a piece of pure provocation!"

Booker gathers the courage to stick his head out from behind the grapevines. "Mrs. Zawynatch. I *read* the American *Worker*, editorials by Gus Hall! I borrowed Soviet novels from the library of Soviet-Canadian Friendship on Avenue Road! I tried to *imitate* that style – "

"Numbskull! Chickenheaded monster!" cries Dotty. "Do you really think *they* think people actually think that way?"

"I thought since they write like that in the papers – "

"But you were supposed to be writing private letters, you nincompoop!" wails Dotty.

"Well," I try to defend Booker. "Didn't *you* check those letters, Dotty?"

Dotty turns, and her fierce eyes now focus on me.

"I didn't know then what kind of crap he was writing her. He just showed me copies now. You'll see. I'll give them to you. But the secret police summoned her and told her not to try and kid them with that cheap trick, they knew all about that one, and just imagine, Danny," and she grasps at my hand, "they had the gall to tell her that she can make just as good a living walking the streets in Prague. My best friend! And she wants to work as an interpreter here. She told me herself."

Dotty scowls in righteous indignation. I steal a glance at Booker. He is huddled over behind the grapevine, beneath the left breast of the ethnic stripper.

"Booker's upset," I whisper to Dotty. She whips an angry glance in his direction.

"Well, and why shouldn't he be?" she says strangely. "Would you believe it, to top it all off, he fell for her."

"He fell in love with Lida?"

"You better believe it," says Dotty. "He had to show up first in Prague – like you always do. The trick wouldn't work otherwise – the police have to believe it's a love affair. So Brian and I paid for his way there, he met her, and now he's nuts about her. A real heart attack."

I look with sympathy at the black bartender.

"*And* she fell for him too. Oh shit! Now I'll have to hire somebody else and start the whole thing all over again. This time I'll pick an Italian. At least they've got experience with Communism."

"What if the Italian falls for Lida too?"

"Well, let them fight it out among themselves," says Dotty. All at once her eyes begin to brighten. "Look here, Danny. Couldn't we arrange for them to have a duel as soon as Lida gets out? One of them would knock the other off and get sent down for life or at least for ten years, or else he'll be forced to lie low, and then I'll marry Lida off to you. You're single. And she's my bosom friend, and she's so sexy she'll reduce you to a bag of skin on your wedding night."

●

*We send you heartfelt thanks for your expression of condolence on the occasion of the sudden death of our husband, father and father-in-law,*

*Vratislav Blazej*

*Jana Blazejova, wife*
*Jana von Kleinenschütz, daughter*
*Prof. Dr. Harry von Kleinenschütz, son-in-law*

*Munich, August 21, 1974*

●

●

*November 11, 1976*
*London*

Dear Mr. Smiricky,
You don't know me, but I understand you were acquainted with my
mother, Venus Paroubkova. I'm in England just now on a tour with
the group Jazz 1975, and I'm staying with Mr. Fonda Cemelik, who
gave me your Four Seasons to read, so naturally the conversation came
round to Benno Manes. The thing is, I was present when Benno died in
the Russian barracks in Bratislava, so Mr. Cemelik sat me down at the
table here so I could write to you.

No doubt you are aware that Benno Manes was the leader of the
Dance and Jazz Orchestra of the Army Artistic Troupe, an organization that helps musicians from outside Prague to get to Prague, in uniform, but it's better than nothing. Benno Manes turned my life around
when I was auditioning and he shouted out, in the middle of the fourth
chorus of Porter's "What is This Thing called Love," "That'll do!
We'll take him!" You see, I didn't want to go into the normal army
after university (history and Czech in Pilsen) so I tried out for the
AAT, and I have stayed with music ever since.

We toured about the army bases with the AAT orchestra, playing
music by local and other people's democratic composers, and naturally we smuggled other things into the program as well, under false
names, like "Tiger Rag," which we called "Red Flag," and that kind of
thing. Benno said you used to do the same thing during the war, but of
course I was still just a glint in my father's eye then so I don't
remember it. Unfortunately we also played in Russian barracks. The
last tour took us to Slovakia, I can't remember exactly when it began,
but I recall the last two days very well. The second-last day of Benno's
life we were in a village called Sofron. We weren't scheduled to play,
but there was a big wedding – the daughter of the head man on the
local farmers' co-operative was getting married. This guy claimed he
went to primary school with you, and since he obviously swings a lot
of influence he arranged it so we could play at his daughter's wedding.
Their co-op had just been given some pennant, so they combined the
two celebrations into one. It may have helped that his daughter was
marrying a Soviet officer, which doesn't happen very often these days.
I say Soviet deliberately, because this particular Russian was a Georgian, and the bride was in a state that could easily have provoked international unpleasantness.

*They produced a fantastic feed, with buckets of wine and barrels of vodka. Benno, unfortunately, got properly soaked. It was that evening that we first got on a first-name basis. He poured me a "killer," as they say, and himself as well, and named me chief of the "jazz section," as we called our small quartet inside the orchestra – piano, bass, drums and trumpet – that only played jazz. Benno got very drunk and unhappy. It really bothered him to be one of the first musicians who had to play for the Russians after the entry of the fraternalized armies into Prague. I tried to console him by pointing out that everyone understood, that nothing could be done about it, that he was under army discipline and had a wife and kids to support and music was the only thing he knew how to do. If they threw him out he'd have to do manual labour, and he was too overweight and too sick for that. But I wasn't able to make him feel much better.*

*Next day we went to Bratislava and Pepicek Syrovatko, who plays French horn in the Bratislava television orchestra and who apparently used to play baritone sax with you during the war, invited Benno home for lunch – he said afterwards that Benno enjoyed the meal a lot and talked for a long time about Kostelec and times past. That evening we played quite a way outside Bratislava, at the end of one of the bus lines, at an army base where there are only Russians now, in a kind of long hall that for some strange reason wasn't decorated in red. Maybe they had a little bust of Lenin there, but it must have been extremely. modest because I don't remember seeing it. The first half of the program went off smoothly, except that Benno was sweating a lot, I mean more than usual, and he unbuttoned his shirt down to his waist and was breathing heavily. There was a kind of small dressing-room backstage, and at the end of the break he called me over and explained to me at great length that Private Hemele, who was on loan to us from the Bratislava base instead of our regular master of ceremonies who was sick, refused to emcee the show in Russian, and the program was too short, so we had to add some jazz after the break. I said okay. When we came back out we played one number with the whole band, then Benno gave me a wink and sat down in the wings where he undid his shirt again and stuck his pot belly out at me and puffed away, wiping the sweat off his forehead. I was close by, because the keyboard of the piano was near the wings. It was a beautiful instrument, by the way. They probably used to have serious performers at those bases, because it was a Petroff. I winked back at him and we played Shoof's "Horn Sound," which has a 32-bar theme in G minor with a simple harmonic structure. The trombone carries the melody. Honza Stichl blew the* theme and we came in with the choruses. I recall that I played a part of the last chorus as free jazz, which didn't happen very often, but we always did it when we were playing for the Russians, just to put the wind up them a bit. Then the whole band played Benno's own composition "Memories of a Small Town," and Benno returned and Miluska Patejzlova sang the chorus. She's a blonde with a very large, beautiful bosom. Benno admired her a great deal, and her singing wasn't bad – we used to call her a baroque angel, blue eyes, curly blonde hair, behaviour a little naive, nineteen years old. As far as I know the only one who's had any luck with her is the guitarist Karel Kozel, a big handsome fellow with a green Gibson, and we call him Gorgonzola because he loves that kind of cheese – but the main thing was those breasts – I can still see them today. As she was singing his song, Benno stumbled a bit and the boys in the sax line told him to go off, that we'd finish it without him, because we never took Benno's conducting too seriously anyway. He could play the trumpet but in those last few years he didn't have the breath for it so he only conducted. There were five saxes in the front line, four trombones behind them and three trumpets up at the back. Benno was still trying to conduct, Miluska was singing, and all of a sudden Benno kind of lurched to the left, towards the piano, and fell down. Pavel Zamecnik, a trumpet player, was the first one to reach him and he pulled the left curtain closed while I took care of the right one and Miluska started screaming. Benno's face was the colour of a strawberry, completely red. So Private Hemele, who had refused to talk Russian, went out in front of the curtain and asked in Russian if there was a doctor in the house. A Russian doctor came up and apparently kept Benno in a state of clinical death for another thirty minutes. About an hour later, a Czech doctor arrived from a hospital that was just around the corner, and all he did was declare him officially dead. Benno was lying on his back, naked from the waist up. Everyone left. The last thing I remember, and I'll never forget it, was how he was lying there in that empty hall on an empty stage, with his huge belly completely purple, and dark grey trousers, and you couldn't see his head for the stomach, and all around there was yellow bunting, that awful yellow bunting. Yellow and purple, maybe the bust of some statesman behind it but all I could see when I looked into the hall for the last time was that ghastly purple stomach and the yellow bunting. Then we left for Prague.

   I thought you might be interested in how your friend died.

                                  Yours sincerely,
                                  Demosthenes Paroubek-Kubiska

CANADIAN TRANSATLANTIC CABLE
MR. D. SVIRICYI
217 ST. JAMES TOWN
TORONTO, ONT. M4X 2W5

IM A FOOL STOP VERONIKA

●

## NEW ARRESTS IN PRAGUE

PRAGUE April 4 (Reuters) – Dissident circles reported the arrest over the weekend of several writers, among them the prominent reformist and signatory of the Charter '77 human rights manifesto, Jan Vrchcolab.

In a parallel release, CTK, the Czechoslovak Press Agency, maintains that the arrests were in no way connected with the campaign directed against signatories of Charter '77, issued earlier this year. The agency claims that Mr. Vrchcolab, named only by initials, was filmed by a hidden camera in a Prague park last year while handing over "information of an espionage nature" to a member of the Canadian diplomatic corps. This is a reference to the Canadian cultural attaché Benjamin Harkins, who was subsequently expelled by the Czechoslovak government.

In a press conference in Ottawa, Mr. Harkins confirmed that he had received material from Mr. Vrchcolab, but denied that it was of an espionage nature. He said it was a manuscript of poems by a deceased Czech poet, Jan Prouza, who committed suicide five years ago in Prague.

Harkins said he turned the manuscript over to Mrs. Santner, who runs a small ethnic publishing house in Toronto.

●

Karlsbad
The 7 May 1975

Dear Dan,
I adres you with these few lines to tell you I am well and hope you are injoying the same blesing at present. I been at the Karlsbad spa for upwords of a week and Im doing fine. Im at the spa on account of a acute atack of gall stones not like 30 years back when I had shaddows on my lungs. I got this atack on my dauhgter Sulejka's weding day

that I sent you an invitation to and I wonder if you got it. I also sent you a pitcher of the bride and groom and all the gests.

It was the hapiest day of my life if only I didnt come down with acute gall stones. But you know, old freind, that when you marry off your only dauhgter you cant hold back. We killed two pig and we had upwords of 150 gests. Also our Peasants Coop won the red penant as the best in the distrikt, so we celabrated the penant along with the weding. The whole family came, including my brother Olda, who is directer of a textile coop. My brother Olda had a big tradgedy in his famly when his wife who is a engineer and a Lithuanean ran away right after the fraternal armys came and took her 2 kids with her and run to the United States of North America where she is staying with relativs. My brother Olda asked the International Red Cross to get his kids back for him since his wife run away ilegal and without permision but the Red Cross rote and told him that the kids is already over eihgteen and they desided to stay with there mother in the United States of North America. I was glad my brother could injoy himself at the weding of my dauhgter Sulejka he was hear with his second wife who is 30 and shes a Germen from the Germen Democratik Republik.

My dauhgter Sulejka maried a Rusian oficer Sulimann Akibidze who is a Gorgian. My dauhgter Sulejka has a Gorgian name too becaus when her mother was pregnint with her she injoyd singing a Gorgian song Who Are You Sulejka, and because the old prejudises dont exist any more like they use to, I can tell you right out that our dauhgter Sulejka was also pregnint so we had to hury with the weding. Right after the weding my son in law got transfured to the Germen Demokratik Republik because there is still some people who make life miserble for our girls who mary Russian solgers I gess there are stupid people even in socialism. Im looking forward to being a grandad soon.

I gess it woud interst you who playd at the weding. There was musishans from Prague and gess who was conducter? It was the milatary danse orchester under the batten of Benno Manes from Kosteletz. So we talked about old times when you used to blow on some musical insterment in Kosteletz. Benno liked the wine and the blood sausages agreed with him, since he ate a mountin of them, and I did too and there was to much fat in them and I had this gall stone atack so bad they had to take me straight from the table to the local hospital in a milatary jeep. And so here I am in the spa which is a grate thing for peasents not like in captialism when only the rich use to come here and now the peasents can come too. I gess in Kanada its only the rich that get to go to the spa because Kanada is still a capitalist state.

Now a lot of people are coming back after leaving without thinking when the fraternl armys came. Nothing hapens to them exsept they have to find a place in the work proces. I wanted to write you to tell you that you could come back too. We need writers and they get good mony. And the writers hav also become ingaged and now thay write good things about the workers not like befor with all that decadent kafka stuff. And you coud too, I remember during the war you worked in a factry and you know workers from your own experiens and you coud write the truth about them and maybe eavn get a state prize. I also have to say that people stil read your books eavn thouhg since you left ilegaly to Kanada they took your books out of the libarys. Of course theyll put them back as soon as you come back and join in the proces like the other writers.

I just had a article printed in the People's Fist, which is the district organ of our peasent coop that was juged the best in the district. It hapend to be my 150eth article. And they printed all of them with only a few changes. Who woud of thouhgt, my freind, 30 years ago that you and me both woud end up writers?

Were living beter and more cultural all the time. Just befor I came to the spa we was at a performns of the Soviet Circus it was very nice speshialy the trainors of the syberian tigers. And we go to the pictures regular twice a week, we seen a nice Soviet film about the liberation of the Ukrane I fergot the title and a Czech film a lot like it by O. Vavra, Sokolovo. There was nice seens in it with tanks and lots of exsiting batles. The polititians wasnt so ineresting exsept they pickt out komrade Godwalt nice (I mean the actor who playd him) but otherwise he din't look like Kom. Godwalt at all. But he playd good. We also seen a film by J. Wensel, who shot a film for you about them girls. This one was called Feet in the Mud and it was ineresting, about the working class and optimistik. But the actrises in the old days was pretier. Take Barova or Heide Marie Hatajer — they was real women.

To conclude my leter with plese exsept my warmist wishes and fondist memries.

Your old freind,
Lojza

## About the Author

Josef Skvorecky is Professor of English at Erindale College of the University of Toronto. He emigrated to Canada after the Soviet invasion of Czechoslovakia in 1968, and he and his wife, the novelist Zdena Salivarova, continue to keep Czech literature alive through their Czech-language publishing house, Sixty-Eight Publishers. Skvorecky's novels include *The Cowards*, *Miss Silver's Past* and *The Bass Saxophone* (also available from Washington Square Press). In addition, he has written many short stories and filmscripts, and is the winner of the 1980 Neustadt International Prize for Literature, and the 1984 Governor General's Award for Fiction.

## About the Translator

Paul Wilson moved to Czechoslovakia in 1967 and spent ten years working as a translator and English teacher and playing in an underground rock band, before he was expelled for his activities. His translations include many novels and essays by such writers as Vaclav Havel and Ladislav Klima. He now lives in Toronto.